FOUR G

HORACE WALPOLE (1717–97) was born in London, the youngest son of Sir Robert Walpole, and educated at Eton and King's College, Cambridge. Between 1739 and 1741 he toured France and Italy with the poet Thomas Gray. Soon after his return, he became a Member of Parliament and in 1747 he bought the villa at Twickenham which he renamed Strawberry Hill. Remodelled, extended, and embellished in the 'gothick' style over two decades, it became a popular tourist attraction. He established a printing-press there and published many of his own works as well as those of others. Apart from *The Castle of Otranto* (1764) his books include the *Catalogue of Royal and Noble Authors of England* (1758) and *Historic Doubts on Richard III* (1768).

WILLIAM BECKFORD was born, probably in London, in 1760. On the death of his father in 1770 he inherited an immense fortune. At nineteen he left for a tour of Holland, Germany, Italy, and France and over the next forty years he was often away from England, at times in order to escape scandal. In 1783 he married, and in the following year he became the Member of Parliament for Wells. He spent large sums in collecting works of art and curios and in the building and extravagant decoration of his mansion, Fonthill Abbey. He died in 1844 from a severe attack of influenza.

Beckford was eccentric, extravagant, and of undoubted intellectual ability. *Vathek*, first written in French at the age of twenty-one, was translated under his supervision and published in England in 1786. His other books include *Dreams, Waking Thoughts, and Incidents* (1783, revised 1834) and *Recollections of an Excursion to the Monasteries of Alcobaça and Batalka* (1835).

MATTHEW LEWIS was born in 1775 into a rich, influential family. His father was a politician, his mother attended court. He was educated at Westminster and Christ Church. In 1792 he went to Weimar, and in 1794 became attaché to the British embassy in the Hague where he wrote *The Monk*. The indecency of the tale provoked many protests and he was obliged to expunge many passages for the second edition. He sat in the House of Commons 1796–1802, during which time he wrote many plays and poems. Lewis wrote no more plays after his father's death in 1812, and from 1815 to 1818 he went twice to Jamaica to organize his estates there, and also visited Italy. On his return to England from his second visit to Jamaica he died of yellow fever and was buried at sea.

MARY WOLLSTONECRAFT SHELLEY was born in 1797, the only daughter of William Godwin and Mary Wollstonecraft. Her mother died a few days after Mary's birth.

Mary was courted by the poet Percy Bysshe Shelley, who was already married, in the summer of 1814. They eloped to the Continent in July. In 1816 they spent the summer with Lord Byron near Geneva, during which time *Frankenstein* was begun. That same year, Shelley's wife committed suicide and he married Mary. Their two small children died in 1818 and 1819, and in 1822 Shelley himself was drowned. Mary was heart-broken, as her diaries show, and in 1823 she returned to England with her younger son. She had little money, but, largely supporting herself by writing, she managed to send her son to Harrow and Cambridge. In 1844 Shelley's father died, leaving Mary in better circumstances. She died in 1851 and was buried in Bournemouth.

HORACE WALPOLE

The Castle of Otranto

WILLIAM BECKFORD

Vathek

MATTHEW LEWIS

The Monk

MARY SHELLEY

Frankenstein

OXFORD
UNIVERSITY PRESS

OXFORD
UNIVERSITY PRESS

Great Clarendon Street, Oxford OX2 6DP

Oxford University Press is a department of the University of Oxford.
It furthers the University's objective of excellence in research, scholarship,
and education by publishing worldwide in

Oxford New York

Athens Auckland Bangkok Bogotá Buenos Aires Calcutta
Cape Town Chennai Dar es Salaam Delhi Florence Hong Kong Istanbul
Karachi Kuala Lumpur Madrid Melbourne Mexico City Mumbai
Nairobi Paris São Paulo Singapore Taipei Tokyo Toronto Warsaw

with associated companies in Berlin Ibadan

Oxford is a registered trade mark of Oxford University Press
in the UK and in certain other countries

Published in the United States
by Oxford University Press Inc., New York

© Oxford University Press 1994

The moral rights of the author have been asserted

Database right Oxford University Press (maker)

First published in Oxford paperbacks 1994

British Library Cataloguing in Publication Data

Data available

Library of Congress Cataloging in Publication Data

Four gothic novels.
Contents: The Castle of Otranto / Horace Walpole—Vathek /
William Beckford—The monk / Matthew Lewis—Frankenstein / Mary
Shelley.   I. Horror tales, English.   2. Gothic revival (Literature)—Great Britain.
I. Walpole, Horace, 1717–1797.   II. Title: 4 gothic novels.
8239.0872908—dc20   PR1309.H6F68   1994   93–37471

ISBN–13: 978–0–19–282331–1
ISBN–10: 0–19–282331–0

10

Printed in Great Britain by
Clays Ltd, St Ives plc

CONTENTS

HORACE WALPOLE

The Castle of Otranto

A CHRONOLOGY OF HORACE WALPOLE

1717	24 September, born in Arlington Street, London, the third surviving son of Sir Robert Walpole and Catherine Shorter
1727–34	Eton
1735–9	King's College, Cambridge
1737	Lady Walpole dies; shortly afterwards Sir Robert marries his mistress, Maria Skerrett, who dies 1738
1739–41	Takes Thomas Gray, his intimate friend at Eton and Cambridge, on the Grand Tour to France and Italy
1741	Elected to Parliament for a family borough in Cornwall while still abroad. His places in the Exchequer, secured for him by his father, rise in time to as much as £5,000 a year
1742	Sir Robert resigns as Prime Minister and is created Earl of Orford; his last three years are spent chiefly at Houghton, his house in Norfolk
1747	Horace Walpole's first book, *Aedes Walpolianae*, an account of the pictures at Houghton, published
1747	Leases Strawberry Hill, Twickenham
1749	Buys Strawberry Hill and begins to remodel it in the Gothic manner
1751	Begins writing his *Memoirs*, which he continues to 1791
1755	First attack of gout, to which he became a martyr
1757	Erects a private printing press at Strawberry Hill, where he brings out books and ephemera until 1789. These include his own *Catalogue of Royal and Noble Authors*, 2 vols., 1758, *Anecdotes of Painting in England*, 5 vols., 1762–80, and *The Mysterious Mother* (a tragedy), 1768
1764	24 December, *The Castle of Otranto* published
1768	*Historic Doubts on the Life and Reign of King Richard the Third* published; retires from Parliament
1777	Unfairly charged with contributing to Chatterton's death
1791	5 December, succeeds his nephew as 4th Earl of Orford
1797	Dies, unmarried, at his home in Berkeley Square in his eightieth year

The Castle of Otranto,

A STORY.

Translated by William Marshal, Gent.
From the Original Italian of
Onuphrio Muralto,
Canon of the Church of St. Nicholas
at Otranto.

PREFACE TO THE FIRST EDITION

THE following work was found in the library of an ancient catholic family in the north of England. It was printed at Naples, in the black letter, in the year 1529. How much sooner it was written does not appear. The principal incidents are such as were believed in the darkest ages of christianity; but the language and conduct have nothing that favours of barbarism. The style is the purest Italian. If the story was written near the time when it is supposed to have happened, it must have been between 1095, the æra of the first crusade, and 1243, the date of the last, or not long afterwards. There is no other circumstance in the work that can lead us to guess at the period in which the scene is laid: the names of the actors are evidently fictitious, and probably disguised on purpose: yet the Spanish names of the domestics seem to indicate that this work was not composed until the establishment of the Arragonian kings in Naples had made Spanish appellations familiar in that country. The beauty of the diction, and the zeal of the author, [moderated however by singular judgment] concur to make me think that the date of the composition was little antecedent to that of the impression. Letters were then in their most flourishing state in Italy, and contributed to dispel the empire of superstition, at that time so forcibly attacked by the reformers. It is not unlikely that an artful priest might endeavour to turn their own arms on the innovators; and might avail himself of his abilities as an author to confirm the populace in their ancient errors and superstitions. If this was his view, he has certainly acted with signal address. Such a work as the following would enslave a hundred vulgar minds beyond half the books of controversy that have been written from the days of Luther to the present hour.

The solution of the author's motives is however offered as a mere conjecture. Whatever his views were, or whatever effects the execution of them might have, his work can only be laid before the public at present as a matter of entertainment. Even as such, some apology for it is necessary. Miracles, visions, necromancy, dreams, and other preternatural events, are exploded now even from romances. That was not the case when our author wrote; much less when the story itself is supposed to have happened. Belief in every kind of prodigy was so established in those dark ages, that an author would not be faithful to the *manners* of the times who should omit all mention of them. He is not bound to believe them himself, but he must represent his actors as believing them.

If this *air* of the *miraculous* is excused, the reader will find nothing else unworthy of his perusal. Allow the possibility of the facts, and all the actors comport themselves as persons would do in their situation. There is no bombast, no similes, flowers, digressions, or unnecessary descriptions. Every thing tends directly to the catastrophe. Never is the reader's attention relaxed. The rules of the drama are almost observed throughout the conduct of the piece. The characters are well drawn, and still better maintained. Terror, the author's principal engine, prevents the story from ever languishing; and it is so often contrasted by pity, that the mind is kept up in a constant vicissitude of interesting passions.

Some persons may perhaps think the characters of the domestics too little serious for the general cast of the story; but besides their opposition to the principal personages, the art of the author is very observable in his conduct of the subalterns. They discover many passages essential to the story, which could not well be brought to light but by their *naïveté* and simplicity: in particular, the womanish terror and foibles of Bianca, in the last chapter, conduce essentially towards advancing the catastrophe.

It is natural for a translator to be prejudiced in favour of his adopted work. More impartial readers may not be so much struck with the beauties of this piece as I was. Yet I am not blind to my author's defects. I could wish he had grounded his plan on a more useful moral than this; that *the sins of fathers are visited on their children to the third and fourth generation.* I doubt whether in his time, any more than at present, ambition curbed its appetite of dominion from the dread of so remote a punishment. And yet this moral is weakened by that less direct insinuation, that even such anathema may be diverted by devotion to saint Nicholas. Here the interest of the monk plainly gets the better of the judgment of the author. However, with all its faults, I have no doubt but the English reader will be pleased with a sight of this performance. The piety that reigns throughout, the lessons of virtue that are inculcated, and the rigid purity of the sentiments, exempt this work from the censure to which romances are but too liable. Should it meet with the success I hope for, I may be encouraged to re-print the original Italian, though it will tend to depreciate my own labour. Our language falls far short of the charms of the Italian, both for variety and harmony. The latter is peculiarly excellent for simple narrative. It is difficult in English *to relate* without falling too low or rising too high; a fault obviously occasioned by the little care taken to speak pure language in common conversation. Every Italian or Frenchman of any rank piques himself on speaking his own tongue correctly and with choice. I cannot flatter myself with having done justice to my author in this respect: his style is as elegant as his conduct of the passions is masterly. It is pity that he did not apply his talents to what they were evidently proper for, the theatre.

I will detain the reader no longer but to make one short remark. Though the machinery is invention, and the names of the actors imaginary, I cannot but believe that the groundwork of the story is founded on truth. The scene is undoubtedly laid in some real castle. The author seems frequently, without design, to describe particular parts. *The chamber*, says he, *on the right hand; the door on the left hand; the distance from the chapel to Conrad's apartment*: these and other passages are strong presumptions that the author had some certain building in his eye. Curious persons, who have leisure to employ in such researches, may possibly discover in the Italian writers the foundation on which our author has built. If a catastrophe, at all resembling that which he describes, is believed to have given rise to this work, it will contribute to interest the reader, and will make *The Castle of Otranto* a still more moving story.

PREFACE TO THE SECOND EDITION

THE favourable manner in which this little piece has been received by the public, calls upon the author to explain the grounds on which he composed it. But before he opens those motives, it is fit that he should ask pardon of his readers for having offered his work to them under the borrowed personage of a translator. As diffidence of his own abilities, and the novelty of the attempt, were his sole inducements to assume that disguise, he flatters himself he shall appear excusable. He resigned his performance to the impartial judgment of the public; determined to let it perish in obscurity, if disapproved; nor meaning to avow such a trifle, unless better judges should pronounce that he might own it without a blush.

It was an attempt to blend the two kinds of romance, the ancient and the modern. In the former all was imagination and improbability: in the latter, nature is always intended to be, and sometimes has been, copied with success. Invention has not been wanting; but the great resources of fancy have been dammed up, by a strict adherence to common life. But if in the latter species Nature has cramped imagination, she did but take her revenge, having been totally excluded from old romances. The actions, sentiments, conversations, of the heroes and heroines of ancient days were as unnatural as the machines employed to put them in motion.

The author of the following pages thought it possible to reconcile the two kinds. Desirous of leaving the powers of fancy at liberty to expatiate through the boundless realms of invention, and thence of creating more interesting situations, he wished to conduct the mortal agents in his drama according to the rules of probability; in short, to make them think, speak and act, as it might be supposed mere men and women would do in extraordinary positions. He had observed, that in all inspired writings, the personages under the dispensation of miracles, and witnesses to the most stupendous phenomena, never lose sight of their human character: whereas in the productions of romantic story, an improbable event never fails to be attended by an absurd dialogue. The actors seem to lose their senses the moment the laws of nature have lost their tone. As the public have applauded the attempt, the author must not say he was entirely unequal to the task he had und rtaken: yet if the new route he has struck out shall have paved a road for men of brighter talents, he shall own with pleasure and modesty, that he was sensible the plan was capable of receiving greater embellishments than his imagination or conduct of the passions could bestow on it.

With regard to the deportment of the domestics, on which I have touched in the former preface, I will beg leave to add a few words. The simplicity of their behaviour, almost tending to excite smiles, which at first seem not consonant to the serious cast of the work, appeared to me not only not improper, but was marked designedly in that manner. My rule was nature. However grave, important, or even melancholy, the sensations of princes and heroes may be, they do not stamp the same affections on their domestics: at least the latter do not, or should not be made to express their passions in the same dignified tone. In my humble opinion, the contrast between the sublime of the one, and the *naïveté* of the other, sets the pathetic of the former in a stronger light. The very impatience which a reader feels, while delayed by the coarse pleasantries of vulgar actors from arriving at the knowledge of the important catastrophe he expects, perhaps heightens, certainly proves that he has been artfully interested in, the depending event. But I had higher authority than my own opinion for this conduct. That great master of nature, Shakespeare, was the model I copied. Let me ask if his tragedies of Hamlet and Julius Caesar would not lose a considerable share of the spirit and wonderful beauties, if the humour of the grave-diggers, the fooleries of Polonius, and the clumsy jests of the Roman citizens were omitted, or vested in heroics? Is not the eloquence of Antony, the nobler and affectedly unaffected oration of Brutus, artificially exalted by the rude bursts of nature from the mouths of their auditors? These touches remind one of the Grecian sculptor, who, to convey the idea of a Colossus within the dimensions of a seal, inserted a little boy measuring his thumb.

No, says Voltaire in his edition of Corneille, this mixture of buffoonery and solemnity is intolerable—Voltaire is a genius[1]—but not of Shakespeare's magnitude. Without recurring to disputable authority, I appeal from Voltaire to himself. I shall not avail myself of his former encomiums on our mighty poet; though the French critic has twice translated the same speech in Hamlet, some years ago in admiration, latterly in derision; and I am sorry to find that his judgment grows weaker, when it ought to be farther matured. But I shall make use of his own words, delivered on the general

---

[1] The following remark is foreign to the present question, yet excusable in an Englishman, who is willing to think that the severe criticisms of so masterly a writer as Voltaire on our immortal countryman, may have been the effusions of wit and precipitation, rather than the result of judgment and attention. May not the critic's skill in the force and powers of our language have been as incorrect and incompetent as his knowledge of our history? Of the latter his own pen has dropped glaring evidence. In his preface to Thomas Corneille's Earl of Essex, monsieur de Voltaire allows that the truth of history has been grossly perverted in that piece. In excuse he pleads, that when Corneille wrote, the noblesse of France were much unread in English story; but now, says the commentator, that they study it, such misrepresentation would not be suffered——Yet forgetting that the period of ignorance is lapsed, and that it is not very necessary to instruct the knowing, he undertakes from the overflowing of his own reading to give the nobility of his own country a detail of queen Elizabeth's favourites—of whom, says he, Robert Dudley was the first, and the earl of Leicester the second.——Could one have believed that it could be necessary to inform monsieur de Voltaire himself, that Robert Dudley and the earl of Leicester were the same person?

topic of the theatre, when he was neither thinking to recommend or decry Shakespeare's practice; consequently at a moment when Voltaire was impartial. In the preface to his *Enfant prodigue*, that exquisite piece of which I declare my admiration, and which, should I live twenty years longer, I trust I should never attempt to ridicule, he has these words, speaking of comedy, [but equally applicable to tragedy, if tragedy is, as surely it ought to be, a picture of human life; nor can I conceive why occasional pleasantry ought more to be banished from the tragic scene, than pathetic seriousness from the comic] *On y voit un melange de serieux et de plaisanterie, de comique et de touchant*; souvent même une seule avanture *produit tous ces contrastes.* Rien *n'est si commun qu'une maison dans laquelle* un pere gronde, une fille occupée de sa passion pleure; *le fils se moque des deux, et quelques parens prennent part differemment à la scene, &c. Nous n'inferons pas de là que toute comedie doive avoir des scenes de bouffonnerie et des scenes attendrissantes: il y a beaucoup de tres bonnes pieces où il ne regne que de la gayeté; d'autres toutes serieuses; d'autres melangées: d'autres où l'attendrissement va jusques aux larmes:* il ne faut donner l'exclusion à aucun genre: *et si l'on me demandoit, quel genre est le meilleur, je repondrois, celui qui est le mieux traité.* Surely if a comedy may be *toute serieuse*, tragedy may now and then, soberly, be indulged in a smile. Who shall proscribe it? Shall the critic, who in self-defence declares that *no kind* ought to be excluded from comedy, give laws to Shakespeare?

I am aware that the preface from whence I have quoted these passages does not stand in monsieur de Voltaire's name, but in that of his editor; yet who doubts that the editor and author were the same person? Or where is the editor, who has so happily possessed himself of his author's style and brilliant ease of argument? These passages were indubitably the genuine sentiments of that great writer. In his epistle to Maffei, prefixed to his *Merope*, he delivers almost the same opinion, though I doubt with a little irony. I will repeat his words, and then give my reason for quoting them. After translating a passage in Maffei's *Merope*, monsieur de Voltaire adds, *Tous ces traits sont naïfs: tout y est convenable à ceux que vous introduisez sur la scene,* et aux mœurs que vous leur donnez. *Ces familiarités naturelles eussent été, à ce que je crois, bien reçues dans Athenes; mais Paris et notre parterre veulent une autre espece de simplicité.* I doubt, I say, whether there is not a grain of sneer in this and other passages of that epistle; yet the force of truth is not damaged by being tinged with ridicule. Maffei was to represent a Grecian story: surely the Athenians were as competent judges of Grecian manners, and of the propriety of introducing them, as the parterre of Paris. On the contrary, says Voltaire [and I cannot but admire his reasoning] there were but ten thousand citizens at Athens, and Paris has near eight hundred thousand inhabitants, among whom one may reckon thirty thousand judges of dramatic works.—Indeed!—But allowing so numerous a tribunal, I believe this is the only instance in which it was ever pretended that thirty thousand persons, living near two thousand years after the æra in question, were, upon the mere face of the poll, declared better judges than the Grecians themselves of what ought to be the manners of a tragedy written on a Grecian story.

I will not enter into a discussion of the *espece de simplicité*, which the *parterre* of Paris demands, nor of the shackles with which *the thirty thousand judges* have cramped their poetry, the chief merit of which, as I gather from repeated passages in The New Commentary on Corneille, consists in vaulting in spite of those fetters; a merit which, if true, would reduce poetry from the lofty effort of imagination, to a puerile and most contemptible labour—*difficiles nuga* with a witness! I cannot help however mentioning a couplet, which to my English ears always sounded as the flattest and most trifling instance of circumstantial propriety; but which Voltaire, who has dealt so severely with nine parts in ten of Corneille's works, has singled out to defend in Racine;

> *De son appartement cette porte est prochaine,*
> *Et cette autre conduit dans celui de la reine.*

In English,
> *To* Cæsar's *closet through this door you come,*
> *And t'other leads to the queen's drawing-room.*

Unhappy Shakespeare! hadst thou made Rosencrans inform his compeer Guildenstern of the ichnography of the palace of Copenhagen, instead of presenting us with a moral dialogue between the prince of Denmark and the grave-digger, the illuminated pit of Paris would have been instructed a *second time* to adore thy talents.

The result of all I have said is to shelter my own daring under the cannon of the brightest genius this country, at least, has produced. I might have pleaded, that having created a new species of romance, I was at liberty to lay down what rules I thought fit for the conduct of it: but I should be more proud of having imitated, however faintly, weakly, and at a distance, so masterly a pattern, than to enjoy the entire merit of invention, unless I could have marked my work with genius as well as with originality. Such as it is, the public have honoured it sufficiently, whatever rank their suffrages allot to it.

SONNET

TO THE RIGHT HONOURABLE
LADY MARY COKE

THE gentle maid, whose hapless tale
These melancholy pages speak;
Say, gracious lady, shall she fail
To draw the tear adown thy cheek?

No; never was thy pitying breast
Insensible to human woes;
Tender, though firm, it melts distrest
For weaknesses it never knows.

Oh! guard the marvels I relate
Of fell ambition scourg'd by fate,
  From reason's peevish blame:
Blest with thy smile, my dauntless sail
I dare expand to fancy's gale,
  For sure thy smiles are fame.

H. W.

THE CASTLE OF OTRANTO

A Gothic Story

━━━

CHAPTER I

MANFRED, prince of Otranto, had one son and one daughter: the latter, a most beautiful virgin, aged eighteen, was called Matilda. Conrad, the son, was three years younger, a homely youth, sickly, and of no promising disposition; yet he was the darling of his father, who never showed any symptoms of affection to Matilda. Manfred had contracted a marriage for his son with the marquis of Vicenza's daughter, Isabella; and she had already been delivered by her guardians into the hands of Manfred, that he might celebrate the wedding as soon as Conrad's infirm state of health would permit. Manfred's impatience for this ceremonial was remarked by his family and neighbours. The former, indeed, apprehending the severity of their prince's disposition, did not dare to utter their surmises on this precipitation. Hippolita, his wife, an amiable lady, did sometimes venture to represent the danger of marrying their only son so early, considering his great youth, and greater infirmities; but she never received any other answer than reflections on her own sterility, who had given him but one heir. His tenants and subjects were less cautious in their discourses: they attributed this hasty wedding to the prince's dread of seeing accomplished an ancient prophecy, which was said to have pronounced, *That the castle and lordship of Otranto should pass from the present family, whenever the real owner should be grown too large to inhabit it.* It was difficult to make any sense of this prophecy; and still less easy to conceive what it had to do with the marriage in question. Yet these mysteries, or contradictions, did not make the populace adhere the less to their opinion.

Young Conrad's birth-day was fixed for his espousals. The company was assembled in the chapel of the castle, and every thing ready for beginning the livine office, when Conrad himself was missing. Manfred, impatient of the least delay, and who had not observed his son retire, dispatched one of his attendants to summon the young prince. The servant, who had not staid long enough to have crossed the court to Conrad's apartment, came running back breathless, in a frantic manner, his eyes staring, and foaming at the mouth. He said nothing, but pointed to the court. The company were struck with terror and amazement. The princess Hippolita, without knowing what was the matter, but anxious for her son, swooned away. Manfred, less apprehensive than enraged at the procrastination of the nuptials, and at the folly of his domestic, asked imperiously, what was the matter? The fellow made no answer, but continued pointing towards the court-yard; and at last, after repeated questions put to him, cried out, Oh, the helmet! the helmet! In the mean time some of the company had run into the court, from whence was heard a confused noise of shrieks, horror, and surprise. Manfred, who began to be alarmed at not seeing his son, went himself to get information of what occasioned this strange confusion. Matilda remained endeavouring to assist her mother, and Isabella staid for the same purpose, and to avoid showing any impatience for the bridegroom, for whom, in truth, she had conceived little affection.

The first thing that struck Manfred's eyes was a group of his servants endeavouring to raise something that appeared to him a mountain of sable plumes. He gazed without believing his sight. What are ye doing? cried Manfred, wrathfully: Where is my son? A volley of voices replied, Oh, my lord! the prince! the prince! the helmet! the helmet! Shocked with these lamentable sounds, and dreading he knew not what, he advanced hastily— But what a sight for a father's eyes!—He beheld his child dashed to pieces, and almost buried under an enormous helmet, an hundred times more large than any casque ever made for human being, and shaded with a proportionable quantity of black feathers.

The horror of the spectacle, the ignorance of all around how this misfortune happened, and above all, the tremendous phænomenon before him, took away the prince's speech. Yet his silence lasted longer than even grief could occasion. He fixed his eyes on what he wished in vain to believe a vision; and seemed less attentive to his loss, than buried in meditation on the stupendous object that had occasioned it. He touched, he examined the fatal casque; nor could even the bleeding mangled remains of the young prince divert the eyes of Manfred from the portent before him. All who had known his partial fondness for young Conrad, were as much surprised at their prince's insensibility, as thunderstruck themselves at the miracle of the helmet. They conveyed the disfigured corpse into the hall, without receiving the least direction from Manfred. As little was he attentive to the ladies who remained in the chapel: on the contrary, without mentioning the unhappy princesses his wife and daughter, the first sounds that dropped from Manfred's lips were, Take care of the lady Isabella.

The domestics, without observing the singularity of this direction, were guided by their affection to their mistress to consider it as peculiarly addressed to her situation, and flew to her assistance. They conveyed her to her chamber more dead than alive, and indifferent to all the strange circumstances she heard, except the death of her son. Matilda, who doted on her mother, smothered her own grief and amazement, and thought of nothing but assisting and comforting her afflicted parent. Isabella, who had been treated by Hippolita like a daughter, and who returned that tenderness with equal duty and affection, was scarce less assiduous about the princess; at the same time endeavouring to partake and lessen the weight of sorrow which she saw Matilda strove to suppress, for whom she had conceived the warmest sympathy of friendship. Yet her own situation could not help finding its place in her thoughts. She felt no concern for the death of young Conrad, except commiseration; and she was not sorry to be delivered from a marriage which had promised her little felicity, either from her destined bridegroom, or from the severe temper of Manfred, who, though he had distinguished her by great indulgence, had imprinted her mind with terror, from his causeless rigour to such amiable princesses as Hippolita and Matilda.

While the ladies were conveying the wretched mother to her bed, Manfred remained in the court, gazing on the ominous casque, and regardless of the crowd which the strangeness of the event had now assembled round him. The few words he articulated tended solely to enquiries, whether any man knew from whence it could have come? Nobody could give him the least information. However, as it seemed to be the sole object of his curiosity, it soon became so to the rest of the spectators, whose conjectures were as absurd and improbable as the catastrophe itself was unprecedented. In the midst of their senseless guesses a young peasant, whom rumour had drawn thither from a neighbouring village, observed that the miraculous helmet was exactly like that on the figure in black marble of Alfonso the Good, one of their former princes, in the church of St Nicholas. Villain! What sayest thou? cried Manfred, starting from his trance in a tempest of rage, and seizing the young man by the collar: How darest thou utter such treason? Thy life shall pay for it. The spectators, who as little comprehended the cause of the prince's fury as all the rest they had seen, were at a loss to unravel this new circumstance. The young peasant himself was still more astonished, not conceiving how he had offended the prince: yet recollecting himself, with a mixture of grace and humility, he disengaged himself from Manfred's gripe, and then, with an obeisance which discovered more jealousy of innocence, than dismay, he asked with respect, of what he was guilty! Manfred, more enraged at the vigour, however decently exerted, with which the young man had shaken off his hold, than appeased by his submission, ordered his attendants to seize him, and, if he had not been withheld by his friends whom he had invited to the nuptials, would have poignarded the peasant in their arms.

During this altercation some of the vulgar spectators had run to the great church which stood near the castle, and came back open-mouthed, declaring the helmet was missing from Alfonso's statue. Manfred, at this news, grew perfectly frantic; and, as if he sought a subject on which to vent the tempest within him, he rushed again on the young peasant, crying, Villain! monster! sorcerer! 'tis thou hast slain my son! The mob, who wanted some object within the scope of their capacities on whom they might discharge their bewildered reasonings, caught the words from the mouth of their lord, and re-echoed, Ay, ay, 'tis he, 'tis he: he has stolen the helmet from good Alfonso's tomb, and dashed out the brains of our young prince with it:—never reflecting how enormous the disproportion was between the marble helmet that had been in the church, and that of steel before their eyes; nor how impossible it was for a youth, seemingly not twenty, to wield a piece of armour of so prodigious a weight.

The folly of these ejaculations brought Manfred to himself: yet whether provoked at the peasant having observed the resemblance between the two helmets, and thereby led to the farther discovery of the absence of that in the church; or wishing to bury any fresh rumour under so impertinent a supposition; he gravely pronounced that the young man was certainly a necromancer, and that till the church could take cognizance of the affair, he would have the magician, whom they had thus detected, kept prisoner under the helmet itself, which he ordered his attendants to raise, and place the young man under it; declaring he should be kept there without food, with which his own infernal art might furnish him.

It was in vain for the youth to represent against this preposterous sentence: in vain did Manfred's friends endeavour to divert him from this savage and ill-grounded resolution. The generality were charmed with their lord's decision, which to their apprehensions carried great appearance of justice, as the magician was to be punished by the very instrument with which he had offended: nor were they struck with the least compunction at the probability of the youth being starved, for they firmly believed that by his diabolical skill he could easily supply himself with nutriment.

Manfred thus saw his commands even cheerfully obeyed; and appointing a guard with strict orders to prevent any food being conveyed to the prisoner, he dismissed his friends and attendants, and retired to his own chamber, after locking the gates of the castle, in which he suffered none but his domestics to remain.

In the mean time, the care and zeal of the young ladies had brought the princess Hippolita to herself, who amidst the transports of her own sorrow frequently demanded news of her lord, would have dismissed her attendants to watch over him, and at last enjoined Matilda to leave her, and visit and comfort her father. Matilda, who wanted no affectionate duty to Manfred, though she trembled at his austerity, obeyed the orders of Hippolita, whom she tenderly recommended to Isabella; and enquiring of the domestics for her father, was informed that he was retired to his chamber, and had commanded that nobody should have admittance to him. Concluding that he was immersed in sorrow for the death of her brother, and fearing to renew his tears by the sight of his sole remaining child, she hesitated whether she should break in upon his affliction; yet solicitude for him, backed by the commands of her mother, encouraged her to venture disobeying the orders he had given; a fault she had never been guilty of before. The gentle timidity of her nature made her pause for some minutes at his door. She heard him traverse his chamber backwards and forwards with disordered steps; a mood which increased her apprehensions. She was however just going to beg admittance, when Manfred suddenly opened the door; and as it was now twilight, concurring with the disorder of his mind, he did not distinguish the person, but asked angrily who it was? Matilda replied trembling, My dearest father, it is I, your daughter. Manfred, stepping back hastily, cried, Begone, I do not want a daughter; and, flinging back abruptly, clapped the door against the terrified Matilda.

She was too well acquainted with her father's impetuosity to venture a second intrusion. When she had a little recovered the shock of so bitter a reception, she wiped away her tears, to prevent the additional stab that the knowledge of it would give to Hippolita, who questioned her in the most anxious terms on the health of Manfred, and how he bore his loss. Matilda assured her he was well, and supported his misfortune with manly fortitude. But will he not let me see him? said Hippolita mournfully: Will he not permit me to blend my tears with his, and shed a mother's sorrows in the bosom of her lord? Or do you deceive me, Matilda? I know how Manfred doted on his son: Is not the stroke too heavy for him? Has he not sunk under it?—You do not answer me—Alas, I dread the worst!—Raise me, my maidens: I will, I will see my lord. Bear me to him instantly; he is dearer to me even than my children. Matilda made signs to Isabella to prevent Hippolita's rising; and both these lovely young women were using their gentle violence to stop and calm the princess, when a servant on the part of Manfred arrived, and told Isabella that his lord demanded to speak with her.

With me! cried Isabella. Go, said Hippolita, relieved by a message from her lord: Manfred cannot support the sight of his own family. He thinks you less disordered than we are, and dreads the shock of my grief. Console him, dear Isabella, and tell him I will smother my own anguish rather than add to his.

It was now evening; the servant who conducted Isabella bore a torch before her. When they came to Manfred, who was walking impatiently about the gallery, he started and said hastily, Take away that light, and begone. Then shutting the door impetuously, he flung himself upon a bench against the wall, and bade Isabella sit by him. She obeyed trembling. I sent for you, lady, said he,—and then stopped under great appearance of confusion. My lord!—Yes, I sent for you on a matter of great moment, resumed he:—Dry your tears, young lady—you have lost your bridegroom:—yes, cruel fate, and I have lost the hopes of my race!—But Conrad was not worthy of your beauty.—How! my lord, said Isabella; sure you do not suspect me of not feeling the concern I ought? My duty and affection would have always— Think no more of him, interrupted Manfred; he was a sickly puny child, and heaven has perhaps taken him away that I might not trust the honours of my house on so frail a foundation. The line of Manfred calls for numerous supports. My foolish fondness for that boy blinded the eyes of my prudence— but it is better as it is. I hope in a few years to have reason to rejoice at the death of Conrad.

Words cannot paint the astonishment of Isabella. At first she apprehended that grief had disordered Manfred's understanding. Her next thought suggested that this strange discourse was designed to ensnare her: she feared that Manfred had perceived her indifference for his son: and in consequence of that idea she replied, Good my lord, do not doubt my tenderness; my heart would have accompanied my hand. Conrad would have engrossed all my care; and wherever fate shall dispose of me, I shall always cherish his memory, and regard your highness and the virtuous Hippolita as my parents. Curse on Hippolita! cried Manfred: forget her from this moment, as I do. In short, lady, you have missed a husband undeserving of your charms: they shall now be better disposed of. Instead of a sickly boy, you shall have a husband in the prime of his age, who will know how to value your beauties, and who may expect a numerous offspring. Alas, my lord, said Isabella, my mind is too sadly engrossed by the recent catastrophe in your family to think of another marriage. If ever my father returns, and it shall be his pleasure, I shall obey, as I did when I consented to give my hand to your son: but until his return permit me to remain under your hospitable roof, and employ the melancholy hours in assuaging yours, Hippolita's, and the fair Matilda's affliction.

I desired you once before, said Manfred angrily, not to name that woman; from this hour she must be a stranger to you, as she must be to me:—in short, Isabella, since I cannot give you my son, I offer you myself.—Heavens! cried Isabella, waking from her delusion, what do I hear! You, my lord! You! My father in law! the father of Conrad! the husband of the virtuous and tender Hippolita!—I tell you, said Manfred imperiously, Hippolita is no longer my wife; I divorce her from this hour. Too long has she cursed me by her unfruitfulness: my fate depends on having sons,—and this night I trust will give a new date to my hopes. At those words he seized the cold hand of Isabella, who was half-dead with fright and horror. She shrieked, and started from him. Manfred rose to pursue her; when the moon, which was now up, and gleamed in at the opposite casement, presented to his sight the plumes of the fatal helmet, which rose to the height of the windows, waving backwards and forwards in a tempestuous manner, and accompanied with a hollow and rustling sound. Isabella, who gathered courage from her situation, and who dreaded nothing so much as Manfred's pursuit of his declaration, cried, Look, my lord! see heaven itself declares against your impious intentions!—Heaven nor hell shall impede my designs, said Manfred, advancing again to seize the princess. At that instant the portrait of his grandfather, which hung over the bench where they had been sitting, uttered a deep sigh and heaved its breast. Isabella, whose back was turned to the picture, saw not the motion, nor knew whence the sound came, but started and said, Hark my lord! what sound was that? and at the same time made towards the door. Manfred, distracted between the flight of Isabella, who had now reached the stairs, and his inability to keep his eyes from the picture, which began to move, had however advanced some steps after her, still looking backwards on the portrait, when he saw it quit its pannel, and descend on the floor with a grave and melancholy air. Do I dream? cried Manfred returning, or are the devils themselves in league against me? Speak, infernal spectre! Or, if thou art my grandsire, why dost thou too conspire against thy wretched descendant, who too dearly pays for—Ere he could finish the sentence the vision sighed again, and made a sign to Manfred to follow him. Lead on! cried Manfred; I will follow thee to the gulph of perdition. The spectre marched sedately, but dejected, to the end of the gallery, and turned into a chamber on the right hand. Manfred accompanied him at a little distance, full of anxiety and horror, but resolved. As he would have entered the chamber, the door was clapped-to with violence by an invisible hand. The prince, collecting courage from this delay, would have forcibly burst open the door with his foot, but found that it resisted his utmost efforts. Since hell will not satisfy my curiosity, said Manfred, I will use the human means in my power for preserving my race; Isabella shall not escape me.

That lady, whose resolution had given way to terror the moment she had quitted Manfred, continued her flight to the bottom of the principal staircase. There she stopped, not knowing whither to direct her steps, nor how to escape from the impetuosity of the prince. The gates of the castle she knew were locked, and guards placed in the court. Should she, as her heart prompted her, go and prepare Hippolita for the cruel destiny that awaited her, she did not doubt but Manfred would seek her there, and that his violence would incite him to double the injury he meditated, without leaving room for them to avoid the impetuosity of his passions. Delay might give him time to reflect on the horrid measures he had conceived, or produce some circumstance in her favour, if she could for that night at least avoid his odious purpose.—Yet where conceal herself! How avoid the pursuit he would infallibly make throughout the castle! As these thoughts passed rapidly through her mind, she recollected a subterraneous passage which led from the vaults of the castle to the church of saint Nicholas. Could she reach the altar before she was overtaken, she knew even Manfred's violence would not dare to profane the sacredness of the place; and she determined, if no other means of deliverance offered, to shut herself up for ever among the holy virgins, whose convent was contiguous to the cathedral. In this resolution, she seized a lamp that burned at the foot of the staircase, and hurried towards the secret passage.

The lower part of the castle was hollowed into several intricate cloisters; and it was not easy for one under so much anxiety to find the door that opened into the cavern. An awful silence reigned throughout those subterraneous regions, except now and then some blasts of wind that shook the doors she had passed, and which grating on the rusty hinges were re-echoed through that long labyrinth of darkness. Every murmur struck her with new terror;—yet more she dreaded to hear the wrathful voice of Manfred urging his domestics to pursue her. She trod as softly as impatience would give her leave,—yet frequently stopped and listened to hear if she was followed. In one of those moments she thought she heard a sigh. She shuddered, and recoiled a few paces. In a moment she thought she heard the step of some person. Her blood curdled; she concluded it was Manfred. Every suggestion that horror could inspire rushed into her mind. She condemned her rash flight, which had thus exposed her to his rage in a place where her cries were not likely to draw any body to her assistance.—Yet the sound seemed not to come from behind;—if Manfred knew where she was, he must have followed her: she was still in one of the cloisters, and the steps she had heard were too distinct to proceed from the way she had come. Cheered with this reflection, and hoping to find a friend in whoever was not the prince; she was going to advance, when a door that stood a-jar, at some distance to the left, was opened gently; but ere her lamp, which she held up, could discover who opened it, the person retreated precipitately on seeing the light.

Isabella, whom every incident was sufficient to dismay, hesitated whether she should proceed. Her dread of Manfred soon outweighed every other terror. The very circumstance of the person avoiding her, gave her a sort of courage. It could only be, she thought, some domestic belonging to the castle. Her gentleness had never raised her an enemy, and conscious innocence made her hope that, unless sent by the prince's order to seek her, his servants would rather assist than prevent her flight. Fortifying herself with these reflections, and believing, by what she could observe, that she was near the mouth of the subterraneous cavern, she approached the door that had been opened; but a sudden gust of wind that met her at the door extinguished her lamp, and left her in total darkness.

Words cannot paint the horror of the princess's situation. Alone in so dismal a place, her mind imprinted with all the terrible events of the day, hopeless of escaping, expecting every moment the arrival of Manfred, and far from tranquil on knowing she was within reach of somebody, she knew not whom, who for some cause seemed concealed thereabouts, all these thoughts crowded on her distracted mind, and she was ready to sink under her apprehensions. She addressed herself to every saint in heaven, and inwardly implored their assistance. For a considerable time she remained in an agony of despair. At last, as softly as was possible, she felt for the door, and, having found it, entered trembling into the vault from whence she had heard the sigh and steps. It gave her a kind of momentary joy to perceive an imperfect ray of clouded moonshine gleam from the roof of the vault, which seemed to be fallen in, and from whence hung a fragment of earth or building, she could not distinguish which, that appeared to have been crushed inwards. She advanced eagerly towards this chasm, when she discerned a human form standing close against the wall.

She shrieked, believing it the ghost of her betrothed Conrad. The figure advancing, said in a submissive voice, Be not alarmed, lady; I will not injure you. Isabella, a little encouraged by the words and tone of voice of the stranger, and recollecting that this must be the person who had opened the door, recovered her spirits enough to reply, Sir, whoever you are, take pity on a wretched princess standing on the brink of destruction: assist me to escape from this fatal castle, or in a few moments I may be made miserable for ever. Alas! said the stranger, what can I do to assist you? I will die in your defence; but I am unacquainted with the castle, and want—Oh! said Isabella, hastily interrupting him, help me but to find a trap-door that must be hereabout, and it is the greatest service you can do me; for I have not a minute to lose. Saying these words she felt about on the pavement, and directed the stranger to search likewise for a smooth piece of brass inclosed in one of the stones. That, said she, is the lock, which opens with a spring, of which I know the secret. If I can find that, I may escape—if not, alas, courteous stranger, I fear I shall have involved you in my misfortunes: Manfred will suspect you for the accomplice of my flight, and you will fall a victim to his resentment. I value not my life, said the stranger; and it will be some comfort to lose it in trying to deliver you from his tyranny. Generous youth, said Isabella, how shall I ever requite—As she uttered those words, a ray of moonshine streaming through a cranny of the ruin above shone directly on the lock they sought—Oh, transport! said Isabella, here is the trap-door! and taking out a key, she touched the spring, which starting aside discovered an iron ring. Lift up the door, said the princess. The stranger obeyed; and beneath appeared some stone steps descending into a vault totally dark. We must go down here, said Isabella: follow me; dark and dismal as it is, we cannot miss our way; it leads directly to the church of saint Nicholas—But perhaps, added the princess modestly, you have no reason to leave the castle, nor have I farther occasion for your service; in a few minutes I shall be safe from Manfred's rage—only let me know to whom I am so much obliged. I will never quit you, said the stranger eagerly, till I have placed you in safety—nor think me, princess, more

generous than I am: though you are my principal care—The stranger was
interrupted by a sudden noise of voices that seemed approaching, and they
soon distinguished these words: Talk not to me of necromancers; I tell you
she must be in the castle; I will find her in spite of enchantment.—Oh,
heavens! cried Isabella, it is the voice of Manfred! Make haste, or we are
ruined! and shut the trap-door after you. Saying this, she descended the
steps precipitately; and as the stranger hastened to follow her, he let the door
slip out of his hands: it fell, and the spring closed over it. He tried in vain
to open it, not having observed Isabella's method of touching the spring, nor
had he many moments to make an essay. The noise of the falling door had
been heard by Manfred, who, directed by the sound, hastened thither,
attended by his servants with torches. It must be Isabella, cried Manfred
before he entered the vault; she is escaping by the subterraneous passage,
but she cannot have got far.—What was the astonishment of the prince,
when, instead of Isabella, the light of the torches discovered to him the
young peasant, whom he thought confined under the fatal helmet! Traitor!
said Manfred, how camest thou here! I thought thee in durance above in
the court. I am no traitor, replied the young man boldly, nor am I
answerable for your thoughts. Presumptuous villain! cried Manfred, dost
thou provoke my wrath? Tell me; how hast thou escaped from above? Thou
hast corrupted thy guards, and their lives shall answer it. My poverty, said
the peasant calmly, will disculpate them: though the ministers of a tyrant's
wrath, to thee they are faithful, and but too willing to execute the orders
which you unjustly imposed upon them. Art thou so hardy as to dare my
vengeance? said the prince—but tortures shall force the truth from thee.
Tell me, I will know thy accomplices. There was my accomplice! said the
youth smiling, and pointing to the roof. Manfred ordered the torches to be
held up, and perceived that one of the cheeks of the enchanted casque had
forced its way through the pavement of the court, as his servants had let it
fall over the peasant, and had broken through into the vault, leaving a gap
through which the peasant had pressed himself some minutes before he was
found by Isabella. Was that the way by which thou didst descend? said
Manfred. It was, said the youth. But what noise was that, said Manfred,
which I heard as I entered the cloister? A door clapped, said the peasant; I
heard it as well as you. What door? said Manfred hastily. I am not
acquainted with your castle, said the peasant; this is the first time I ever
entered it, and this vault the only part of it within which I ever was. But I
tell thee, said Manfred, [wishing to find out if the youth had discovered the
trap-door] it was this way I heard the noise: my servants heard it too.—My
lord, interrupted one of them officiously, to be sure it was the trap-door, and
he was going to make his escape. Peace! blockhead, said the prince angrily;
if he was going to escape, how should he come on this side? I will know from
his own mouth what noise it was I heard. Tell me truly; thy life depends on

thy veracity. My veracity is dearer to me than my life, said the peasant; nor would I purchase the one by forfeiting the other. Indeed! young philosopher! said Manfred contemptuously: tell me then, what was the noise I heard? Ask me what I can answer, said he, and put me to death instantly if I tell you a lie. Manfred, growing impatient at the steady valour and indifference of the youth, cried, Well then, thou man of truth! answer; was it the fall of the trap-door that I heard? It was, said the youth. It was! said the prince; and how didst thou come to know there was a trap-door here? I saw the plate of brass by a gleam of moonshine, replied he. But what told thee it was a lock? said Manfred: How didst thou discover the secret of opening it? Providence, that delivered me from the helmet, was able to direct me to the spring of a lock, said he. Providence should have gone a little farther, and have placed thee out of the reach of my resentment, said Manfred: when Providence had taught thee to open the lock, it abandoned thee for a fool, who did not know how to make use of its favours. Why didst thou not pursue the path pointed out for thy escape? Why didst thou shut the trap-door before thou hadst descended the steps? I might ask you, my lord, said the peasant, how I, totally unacquainted with your castle, was to know that those steps led to any outlet? but I scorn to evade your questions. Wherever those steps lead to, perhaps I should have explored the way—I could not have been in a worse situation than I was. But the truth is, I let the trap-door fall: your immediate arrival followed. I had given the alarm—what imported it to me whether I was seized a minute sooner or a minute later? Thou art a resolute villain for thy years, said Manfred—yet on reflection I suspect thou dost but trifle with me: thou hast not yet told me how thou didst open the lock. That I will show you, my lord, said the peasant; and taking up a fragment of stone that had fallen from above, he laid himself on the trap-door, and began to beat on the piece of brass that covered it; meaning to gain time for the escape of the princess. This presence of mind, joined to the frankness of the youth, staggered Manfred. He even felt a disposition towards pardoning one who had been guilty of no crime. Manfred was not one of those savage tyrants who wanton in cruelty unprovoked. The circumstances of his fortune had given an asperity to his temper, which was naturally humane; and his virtues were always ready to operate, when his passion did not obscure his reason.

While the prince was in this suspense, a confused noise of voices echoed through the distant vaults. As the sound approached, he distinguished the clamour of some of his domestics, whom he had dispersed through the castle in search of Isabella, calling out, Where is my lord? Where is the prince? Here I am, said Manfred, as they came nearer; have you found the princess? The first that arrived replied, Oh, my lord! I am glad we have found you.—Found me! said Manfred: have you found the princess? We thought we had, my lord, said the fellow looking terrified—but—But what? cried the prince: has she escaped?—Jaquez and I, my lord—Yes, I and Diego, interrupted the second, who came up in still greater consternation—Speak one of you at a time, said Manfred; I ask you, where is the princess? We do not know, said they both together: but we are frightened out of our wits.—So I think, blockheads, said Manfred: what is it has scared you thus?—Oh, my lord! said Jaquez, Diego has seen such a sight! your highness would not believe our eyes.—What new absurdity is this? cried Manfred— Give me a direct answer, or by heaven—Why, my lord, if it please your highness to hear me, said the poor fellow; Diego and I—Yes, I and Jaquez, cried his comrade—Did not I forbid you to speak both at a time? said the prince: You, Jaquez, answer; for the other fool seems more distracted than thou art; what is the matter? My gracious lord, said Jaquez, if it please your highness to hear me; Diego and I, according to your highness's orders, went to search for the young lady; but being comprehensive that we might meet the ghost of my young lord, your highness's son, God rest his soul, as he has not received christian burial—Sot! cried Manfred in a rage, is it only a ghost then that thou hast seen? Oh, worse! worse! my lord! cried Diego: I had rather have seen ten whole ghosts.—Grant me patience! said Manfred; these blockheads distract me—Out of my sight, Diego! And thou, Jaquez, tell me in one word, art thou sober? art thou raving? Thou wast wont to have some sense: has the other sot frightened himself and thee too? Speak; what is it he fancies he has seen? Why, my lord, replied Jaquez trembling, I was going to tell your highness, that since the calamitous misfortune of my young lord, God rest his soul! not one of us your highness's faithful servants, indeed we are, my lord, though poor men; I say, not one of us has dared to set a foot about the castle, but two together: so Diego and I, thinking that my young lady might be in the great gallery, went up there to look for her, and tell her your highness wanted something to impart to her.—O blundering fools! cried Manfred: and in the mean time she has made her escape, because you were afraid of goblins! Why, thou knave! she left me in the gallery; I came from thence myself.—For all that, she may be there still for aught I know, said Jaquez; but the devil shall have me before I seek her there again!—Poor Diego! I do not believe he will ever recover it! Recover what? said Manfred; am I never to learn what it is has terrified these rascals? But I lose my time; follow me, slave! I will see if she is in the gallery.—For heaven's sake, my dear good lord, cried Jaquez, do not go to the gallery! Satan himself I believe is in the great chamber next to the gallery.—Manfred, who hitherto had treated the terror of his servants as an idle panic, was struck at this new circumstance. He recollected the apparition of the portrait, and the sudden closing of the door at the end of the gallery—his voice faltered, and he asked with disorder, what is in the great chamber? My lord, said Jaquez, when Diego and I came into the gallery, he went first, for he said he had more courage than I. So when we came into the gallery, we found nobody. We looked under every bench and stool; and still we found nobody.—Were all the pictures in their places? said Manfred. Yes, my lord, answered Jaquez; but we did not think of looking behind them.—Well, well! said Manfred; proceed. When we came to the door of the great chamber, continued Jaquez, we found it shut.—And could not you open it? said Manfred. Oh! yes, my lord, would to heaven we had not! replied he—Nay, it was not I neither, it was Diego: he was grown foolhardy, and would go on, though I advised him not—If ever I open a door that is shut again—Trifle not, said Manfred shuddering, but tell me what you saw in the great chamber on opening the door.—I! my lord! said Jaquez, I saw nothing; I was behind Diego;—but I heard the noise.—Jaquez, said Manfred in a solemn tone of voice, tell me, I adjure thee by the souls of my ancestors, what it was thou sawest; what it was thou heardest? It was Diego saw it, my lord, it was not I, replied Jaquez; I only heard the noise. Diego had no sooner opened the door, than he cried out and ran back—I ran back too, and said, Is it the ghost? The ghost! No, no, said Diego, and his hair stood on end—it is a giant, I believe; he is all clad in armour, for I saw his foot and part of his leg, and they are as large as the helmet below in the court. As he said these words, my lord, we heard a violent motion and the rattling of armour, as if the giant was rising; for Diego has told me since, that he believes the giant was lying down, for the foot and leg were stretched at length on the floor. Before we could get to the end of the gallery, we heard the door of the great chamber clap behind us, but we did not dare turn back to see if the giant was following us—Yet now I think on it, we must have heard him if he had pursued us—But for heaven's sake, good my lord, send for the chaplain and have the castle exorcised, for, for certain, it is enchanted. Ay, pray do, my lord, cried all the servants at once, or we must leave your highness's service.—Peace, dotards! said Manfred, and follow me; I will know what all this means. We! my lord! cried they with one voice; we would not go up to the gallery for your highness's revenue. The young peasant, who had stood silent, now spoke. Will your highness, said he, permit me to try this adventure? My life is of consequence to nobody: I fear no bad angel, and have offended no good one. Your behaviour is above your seeming, said Manfred; viewing him with surprise and admiration—hereafter I will reward your bravery—but now, continued he with a sigh, I am so circumstanced, that I dare trust no eyes but my own—However, I give you leave to accompany me.

Manfred, when he first followed Isabella from the gallery, had gone directly to the apartment of his wife, concluding the princess had retired thither. Hippolita, who knew his step, rose with anxious fondness to meet her lord, whom she had not seen since the death of their son. She would have flown in a transport mixed of joy and grief to his bosom; but he pushed her rudely off, and said, Where is Isabella? Isabella! my lord! said the astonished Hippolita. Yes, Isabella; cried Manfred imperiously; I want Isabella. My lord, replied Matilda, who perceived how much his behaviour had shocked her mother, she has not been with us since your highness summoned her to your apartment. Tell me where she is, said the prince; I do not want to know where she has been. My good lord, said Hippolita, your daughter tells you the truth: Isabella left us by your command, and has not returned since:—but, my good lord, compose yourself: retire to your rest: this dismal day has disordered you. Isabella shall wait your orders in the morning. What, then you know where she is? cried Manfred: tell me directly, for I will not lose an instant—And you, woman, speaking to his wife, order your chaplain to attend me forthwith. Isabella, said Hippolita calmly, is retired I suppose to her chamber: she is not accustomed to watch at this late hour. Gracious my lord, continued she, let me know what has disturbed you: has Isabella offended you? Trouble me not with questions, said Manfred, but tell me where she is. Matilda shall call her, said the princess—sit down, my lord, and resume your wonted fortitude.—What, art thou jealous of Isabella, replied he, that you wish to be present at our interview? Good heavens! my lord, said Hippolita, what is it your highness means? Thou wilt know ere many minutes are passed, said the cruel prince. Send your chaplain to me, and wait my pleasure here. At these words he flung out of the room in search of Isabella; leaving the amazed ladies thunder-struck with his words and frantic deportment, and lost in vain conjectures on what he was meditating.

Manfred was now returning from the vault, attended by the peasant and a few of his servants whom he had obliged to accompany him. He ascended the stair-case without stopping till he arrived at the gallery, at the door of which he met Hippolita and her chaplain. When Diego had been dismissed by Manfred, he had gone directly to the princess's apartment with the alarm of what he had seen. That excellent lady, who no more than Manfred doubted of the reality of the vision, yet affected to treat it as a delirium of the servant. Willing, however, to save her lord from any additional shock, and prepared by a series of grief not to tremble at any accession to it; she determined to make herself the first sacrifice, if fate had marked the present hour for their destruction. Dismissing the reluctant Matilda to her rest, who in vain sued for leave to accompany her mother, and attended only by her chaplain, Hippolita had visited the gallery and great chamber: and now, with more serenity of soul than she had felt for many hours, she met her lord, and assured him that the vision of the gigantic leg and foot was all a fable; and no doubt an impression made by fear, and the dark and dismal hour of the night, on the minds of his servants: She and the chaplain had examined the chamber, and found every thing in the usual order.

Manfred, though persuaded, like his wife, that the vision had been no work of fancy, recovered a little from the tempest of mind into which so many strange events had thrown him. Ashamed too of his inhuman treatment of a princess, who returned every injury with new marks of tenderness and duty, he felt returning love forcing itself into his eyes—but not less ashamed of feeling remorse towards one, against whom he was inwardly meditating a yet more bitter outrage, he curbed the yearnings of his heart, and did not dare to lean even towards pity. The next transition of his soul was to exquisite villainy. Presuming on the unshaken submission of Hippolita, he flattered himself that she would not only acquiesce with patience to a divorce, but would obey, if it was his pleasure, in endeavouring to persuade Isabella to give him her hand—But ere he could indulge this horrid hope, he reflected that Isabella was not to be found. Coming to himself, he gave orders that every avenue to the castle should be strictly guarded, and charged his domestics on pain of their lives to suffer nobody to pass out. The young peasant, to whom he spoke favourably, he ordered to remain in a small chamber on the stairs, in which there was a pallet-bed, and the key of which he took away himself, telling the youth he would talk with him in the morning. Then dismissing his attendants, and bestowing a sullen kind of half-nod on Hippolita, he retired to his own chamber.

CHAPTER II

MATILDA, who by Hippolita's order had retired to her apartment, was ill-disposed to take any rest. The shocking fate of her brother had deeply affected her. She was surprised at not seeing Isabella: but the strange words which had fallen from her father, and his obscure menace to the princess his wife, accompanied by the most furious behaviour, had filled her gentle mind with terror and alarm. She waited anxiously for the return of Bianca, a young damsel that attended her, whom she had sent to learn what was become of Isabella. Bianca soon appeared, and informed her mistress of what she had gathered from the servants, that Isabella was no where to be found. She related the adventure of the young peasant, who had been discovered in the vault, though with many simple additions from the incoherent accounts of the domestics; and she dwelled principally on the gigantic leg and foot which had been seen in the gallery-chamber. This last circumstance had terrified Bianca so much, that she was rejoiced when Matilda told her that she would not go to rest, but would watch till the princess should rise.

The young princess wearied herself in conjectures on the flight of Isabella, and on the threats of Manfred to her mother. But what business could he have so urgent with the chaplain? said Matilda. Does he intend to have my brother's body interred privately in the chapel? Oh! madam, said Bianca, now I guess. As you are become his heiress, he is impatient to have you married: he has always been raving for more sons; I warrant he is now impatient for grandsons. As sure as I live, madam, I shall see you a bride at last. Good madam, you won't cast off your faithful Bianca: you won't put Donna Rosara over me, now you are a great princess? My poor Bianca, said Matilda, how fast your thoughts amble! I a great princess! What hast thou seen in Manfred's behaviour since my brother's death that bespeaks any increase of tenderness to me? No, Bianca, his heart was ever a stranger to me—but he is my father, and I must not complain. Nay, if heaven shuts my father's heart against me, it over-pays my little merit in the tenderness of my mother—O that dear mother! Yes, Bianca, 'tis there I feel the rugged temper of Manfred. I can support his harshness to me with patience; but it wounds my soul when I am witness to his causeless severity towards her. Oh, madam, said Bianca, all men use their wives so, when they are weary of them.—And yet you congratulated me but now, said Matilda, when you fancied my father intended to dispose of me. I would have you a great lady, replied Bianca, come what will. I do not wish to see you moped in a convent, as you would be if you had your will, and if my lady your mother, who knows that a bad husband is better than no husband at all, did not hinder you.—Bless me! what noise is that? Saint Nicholas forgive me! I was but in jest. It is the wind, said Matilda, whistling through the battlements in the tower above: you have heard it a thousand times. Nay, said Bianca, there was no harm neither in what I said: it is no sin to talk of matrimony— And so, madam, as I was saying; if my lord Manfred should offer you a handsome young prince for a bridegroom, you would drop him a curtsy, and tell him you would rather take the veil. Thank heaven! I am in no such danger, said Matilda: you know how many proposals for me he has rejected.—And you thank him, like a dutiful daughter, do you, madam?— But come, madam; suppose, to-morrow morning he was to send for you to the great council-chamber, and there you should find at his elbow a lovely young prince, with large black eyes, a smooth white forehead, and manly curling locks like jet; in short, madam, a young hero resembling the picture of the good Alfonso in the gallery, which you sit and gaze at for hours together.—Do not speak lightly of that picture, interrupted Matilda sighing: I know the adoration with which I look at that picture is uncommon—but I am not in love with a coloured pannel. The character of that virtuous prince, the veneration with which my mother has inspired me for his memory, the orisons which I know not why she has enjoined me to pour forth at his tomb, all have concurred to persuade me that somehow or other my destiny is linked with something relating to him.—Lord! madam, how should that be? said Bianca: I have always heard that your family was no way related to his: and I am sure I cannot conceive why my lady, the princess, sends you in a cold morning, or a damp evening, to pray at his tomb: he is no saint by the almanack. If you must pray, why does not she bid you address yourself to our great saint Nicholas? I am sure he is the saint I pray to for a husband. Perhaps my mind would be less affected, said Matilda, if my mother would explain her reasons to me: but it is the mystery she observes, that inspires me with this—I know not what to call it. As she never acts from caprice, I am sure there is some fatal secret at bottom—nay, I know there is: in her agony of grief for my brother's death she dropped some words that intimated as much.—Oh, dear madam, cried Bianca, what were they? No, said Matilda: if a parent lets fall a word, and wishes it recalled, it is not for a child to utter it. What! was she sorry for what she had said? asked Bianca—I am sure, madam, you may trust me.—With my own little secrets, when I have any, I may, said Matilda; but never with my mother's: a child ought to have no ears or eyes but as a parent directs. Well! to be sure, madam, you was born to be a saint, said Bianca, and there's no resisting one's vocation: you will end in a convent at last. But there is my lady Isabella would not be so reserved to me: she will let me talk to her of young men; and when a handsome cavalier has come to the castle, she has owned to me that she wished your brother Conrad resembled him. Bianca, said the princess, I do not allow you to mention my friend disrespectfully. Isabella is of a cheerful disposition, but her soul is pure as virtue itself. She knows your idle babbling humour, and perhaps has now and then encouraged it, to divert melancholy, and to enliven the solitude in which my father keeps us.—Blessed Mary! said Bianca starting, there it is again!—Dear madam, do you hear nothing?—This castle is certainly haunted!—Peace! said Matilda, and listen! I did think I heard a voice—but it must be fancy; your terrors I suppose have infected me. Indeed! indeed! madam, said Bianca, half-weeping with agony, I am sure I heard a voice. Does any body lie in the chamber beneath? said the princess. Nobody has dared to lie there, answered Bianca, since the great astrologer that was your brother's tutor drowned himself. For certain, madam, his ghost and the young prince's are now met in the chamber below—for heaven's sake let us fly to your mother's apartment! I charge you not to stir, said Matilda. If they are spirits in pain, we may ease their sufferings by questioning them. They can mean no hurt to us, for we have not injured them—and if they should, shall we be more safe in one chamber than in another? Reach me my beads; we will say a prayer, and then speak to them. Oh, dear lady, I would not speak to a ghost for the world, cried Bianca—As she said those words, they heard the casement of the little chamber below Matilda's open. They listened attentively, and in few minutes thought they heard a person sing, but could not distinguish the words. This can be no evil spirit, said the princess in a low voice: it is undoubtedly one of the family—open the window, and we shall know the voice. I dare not indeed, madam, said Bianca. Thou art a very fool, said Matilda, opening the window gently herself. The noise the princess made was however heard by the person beneath, who stopped, and, they concluded, had heard the casement open. Is any body below? said the princess: if there is, speak. Yes, said an unknown voice. Who is it? said Matilda. A stranger, replied the voice. What stranger? said she; and how didst thou come there at this unusual hour, when all the gates of the castle are locked? I am not here willingly, answered the voice—but pardon me, lady, if I have disturbed your rest: I knew not that I was overheard. Sleep had forsaken me: I left a restless couch, and came to waste the irksome hours with gazing on the fair approach of morning, impatient to be dismissed from this castle. Thy words and accents, said Matilda, are of a melancholy cast: if thou art unhappy, I pity thee. If poverty afflicts thee, let me know it; I will mention thee to the princess, whose beneficent soul ever melts for the distressed; and she will relieve thee. I am indeed unhappy, said the stranger; and I know not what wealth is: but I do not complain of the lot which heaven has cast for me: I am young and healthy, and am not ashamed of owing my support to myself—yet think me not proud, or that I disdain your generous offers. I will remember you in my orisons, and will pray for blessings on your gracious self and your noble mistress—If I sigh, lady, it is for others, not for myself. Now I have it, madam, said Bianca whispering the princess. This is certainly the young peasant; and by my conscience he is in love!—Well, this is a charming adventure!—Do, madam, let us sift him. He does not know you, but takes you for one of my lady Hippolita's women. Art thou not ashamed, Bianca? said the princess: what right have we to pry into the secrets of this young man's heart? He seems virtuous and frank, and tells us he is unhappy: are those circumstances that authorize us to make a property of him? How are we entitled to his confidence? Lord! madam, how little you know of love! replied Bianca: why, lovers have no pleasure equal to talking of their mistress. And would you have *me* become a peasant's confidante? said the princess. Well then, let me talk to him, said Bianca: though I have the honour of being your highness's maid of honour, I was not always so great: besides, if love levels ranks, it raises them too: I have a respect for any young man in love.—Peace, simpleton! said the princess. Though he said he was unhappy, it does not follow that he must be in love. Think of all that has happened today, and tell me if there are no misfortunes but what love causes. Stranger, resumed the princess, if thy misfortunes have not been occasioned by thy own fault, and are within the compass of the princess Hippolita's power to redress, I will take upon me to answer that she will be thy protectress. When thou art dismissed from this castle, repair to holy father Jerome at the convent adjoining the church of saint Nicholas, and make thy story known to him, as far as thou thinkest meet: he will not fail to inform the princess, who is the mother of all that want her assistance. Farewell: it is not seemly for me to hold farther converse with a man at this unwonted hour. May the saints guard thee, gracious lady! replied the peasant—but oh, if a poor and worthless stranger might presume to beg a minute's audience farther—am I so happy?—the casement is not shut—might I venture to ask—Speak quickly, said Matilda; the morning dawns apace: should the labourers come into the fields and perceive us—What wouldst thou ask—I know not how—I know not if I dare, said the young stranger faltering—yet the humanity with which you have spoken to me emboldens—Lady! dare I trust you?—Heavens! said Matilda, what dost thou mean? with what wouldst thou trust me? Speak boldly, if thy secret is fit to be entrusted to a virtuous breast.—I would ask, said the peasant, recollecting himself, whether what I have heard from the domestics is true, that the princess is missing from the castle? What imports it to thee to know? replied Matilda. Thy first words bespoke a prudent and becoming gravity. Dost thou come hither to pry into the secrets of Manfred? Adieu. I have been mistaken in thee.—Saying these words, she shut the casement hastily, without giving the young man time to reply. I had acted more wisely, said the princess to Bianca with some sharpness, if I had let thee converse with this peasant: his inquisitiveness seems of a piece with thy own. It is not fit for me to argue with your highness, replied Bianca; but perhaps the questions I should have put to him, would have been more to the purpose, than those you have been pleased to ask him. Oh, no doubt, said Matilda; you are a very discreet personage! May I know what you would have asked him? A by-stander often sees more of the game than those that play, answered Bianca. Does your highness think, madam, that his question about my lady Isabella was the result of mere curiosity? No, no, madam; there is more in it than you great folks are aware of. Lopez told me, that all the servants believe this young fellow contrived my lady Isabella's escape—Now, pray, madam, observe——You and I both know that my lady Isabella never much fancied the prince your brother.—Well! he is killed just in the critical minute—I accuse nobody. A helmet falls from the moon—so my lord your father says; but Lopez and all the servants say that this young spark is a magician, and stole it from Alfonso's tomb.—Have done with this rhapsody of impertinence, said Matilda. Nay, madam, as you please, cried Bianca—yet it is very particular though, that my lady Isabella should be missing the very same day, and that this young sorcerer should be found at the mouth of the trap-door—I accuse nobody—but if my young lord came honestly by his death—Dare not on thy duty, said Matilda, to breathe a suspicion on the purity of my dear Isabella's fame.—Purity, or not purity, said Bianca, gone she is: a stranger is found that nobody knows: you question him yourself: he tells you he is in love, or unhappy, it is the same thing—nay, he owned he was unhappy about others; and is any body unhappy about another, unless they are in love with them? And at the very next word he asks innocently, poor soul! if my lady Isabella is missing.—To be sure, said Matilda, thy observations are not totally without foundation—Isabella's

flight amazes me: the curiosity of this stranger is very particular—yet
Isabella never concealed a thought from me.—So she told you, said Bianca,
to fish out your secrets—but who knows, madam, but this stranger may be
some prince in disguise?—Do, madam, let me open the window, and ask
him a few questions. No, replied Matilda, I will ask him myself, if he knows
aught of Isabella: he is not worthy that I should converse farther with him.
She was going to open the casement, when they heard the bell ring at the
postern-gate of the castle, which is on the right hand of the tower, where
Matilda lay. This prevented the princess from renewing the conversation
with the stranger.

After continuing silent for some time; I am persuaded, said she to Bianca,
that whatever be the cause of Isabella's flight, it had no unworthy motive.
If this stranger was accessary to it, she must be satisfied of his fidelity and
worth. I observed, did not you, Bianca? that his words were tinctured with
an uncommon infusion of piety. It was no ruffian's speech: his phrases were
becoming a man of gentle birth. I told you, madam, said Bianca, that I was
sure he was some prince in disguise.—Yet, said Matilda, if he was privy to
her escape, how will you account for his not accompanying her in her flight?
Why expose himself unnecessarily and rashly to my father's resentment? As
for that, madam, replied she, if he could get from under the helmet, he will
find ways of eluding your father's anger. I do not doubt but he has some
talisman or other about him.—You resolve every thing into magic, said
Matilda—but a man who has any intercourse with infernal spirits does not
dare to make use of those tremendous and holy words which he uttered.
Didst thou not observe with what fervour he vowed to remember *me* to
heaven in his prayers? Yes, Isabella was undoubtedly convinced of his
piety.—Commend me to the piety of a young fellow and a damsel that
consult to elope! said Bianca. No, no, madam; my lady Isabella is of
another guess mould than you take her for. She used indeed to sigh and lift
up her eyes in your company, because she knows you are a saint—but when
your back was turned—You wrong her, said Matilda; Isabella is no
hypocrite: she has a due sense of devotion, but never affected a call she has
not. On the contrary, she always combated my inclination for the cloister:
and though I own the mystery she has made to me of her flight confounds
me; though it seems inconsistent with the friendship between us; I cannot
forget the disinterested warmth with which she always opposed my taking
the veil: she wished to see me married, though my dower would have been a
loss to her and my brother's children. For her sake I will believe well of this
young peasant. Then you do think there is some liking between them? said
Bianca.—While she was speaking, a servant came hastily into the chamber,
and told the princess that the lady Isabella was found. Where? said Matilda.
She has taken sanctuary in saint Nicholas's church, replied the servant:
father Jerome has brought the news himself: he is below with his highness.

Where is my mother? said Matilda. She is in her own chamber, madam, and has asked for you.

Manfred had risen at the first dawn of light, and gone to Hippolita's apartment, to enquire if she knew ought of Isabella. While he was questioning her, word was brought that Jerome demanded to speak with him. Manfred, little suspecting the cause of the friar's arrival, and knowing he was employed by Hippolita in her charities, ordered him to be admitted, intending to leave them together, while he pursued his search after Isabella. Is your business with me or the princess? said Manfred. With both, replied the holy man. The lady Isabella—What of her? interrupted Manfred eagerly—is at saint Nicholas's altar, replied Jerome. That is no business of Hippolita, said Manfred with confusion: let us retire to my chamber, father; and inform me how she came thither. No, my lord, replied the good man with an air of firmness and authority that daunted even the resolute Manfred, who could not help revering the saint-like virtues of Jerome: my commission is to both; and, with your highness's good-liking, in the presence of both I shall deliver it—But first, my lord, I must interrogate the princess, whether she is acquainted with the cause of the lady Isabella's retirement from your castle.—No, on my soul, said Hippolita; does Isabella charge me with being privy to it?—Father, interrupted Manfred, I pay due reverence to your holy profession; but I am sovereign here, and will allow no meddling priest to interfere in the affairs of my domestic. If you have aught to say, attend me to my chamber—I do not use to let my wife be acquainted with the secret affairs of my state; they are not within a woman's province. My lord, said the holy man, I am no intruder into the secrets of families. My office is to promote peace, to heal divisions, to preach repentance, and teach mankind to curb their headstrong passions. I forgive your highness's uncharitable apostrophe: I know my duty, and am the minister of a mightier prince than Manfred. Hearken to him who speaks through my organs. Manfred trembled with rage and shame. Hippolita's countenance declared her astonishment, and impatience to know where this would end: her silence more strongly spoke her observance of Manfred.

The lady Isabella, resumed Jerome, commends herself to both your highnesses; she thanks both for the kindness with which she has been treated in your castle: she deplores the loss of your son, and her own misfortune in not becoming the daughter of such wise and noble princes, whom she shall always respect as *parents*: she prays for uninterrupted union and felicity between you: [Manfred's colour changed] but as it is no longer possible for her to be allied to you, she entreats your consent to remain in sanctuary till she can learn news of her father; or, by the certainty of his death, be at liberty, with the approbation of her guardians, to dispose of herself in suitable marriage. I shall give no such consent, said the prince; but insist on her return to the castle without delay: I am answerable for her person to her guardians, and will not brook her being in any hands but my own. Your highness will recollect whether that can any longer be proper, replied the friar. I want no monitor, said Manfred colouring. Isabella's conduct leaves room for strange suspicions—and that young villain, who was at least the accomplice of her flight, if not the cause of it—The cause! interrupted Jerome: was a *young* man the cause? This is not to be borne! cried Manfred. Am I to be bearded in my own palace by an insolent monk? Thou art privy, I guess, to their amours. I would pray to heaven to clear up your uncharitable surmises, said Jerome, if your highness were not satisfied in your conscience how unjustly you accuse me. I do pray to heaven to pardon that uncharitableness: and I implore your highness to leave the princess at peace in that holy place, where she is not liable to be disturbed by such vain and worldly fantasies as discourses of love from any man. Cant not to me, said Manfred, but return, and bring the princess to her duty. It is my duty to prevent her return hither, said Jerome. She is where orphans and virgins are safest from the snares and wiles of this world; and nothing but a parent's authority shall take her thence. I am her parent, cried Manfred, and demand her. She wished to have you for her parent, said the friar; but heaven, that forbad that connexion, has for ever dissolved all ties betwixt you: and I announce to your highness—Stop! audacious man, said Manfred, and dread my displeasure. Holy father, said Hippolita, it is your office to be no respecter of persons: you must speak as your duty prescribes: but it is my duty to hear nothing that it pleases not my lord I should hear. I will retire to my oratory, and pray to the blessed Virgin to inspire you with her holy counsels, and to restore the heart of my gracious lord to its wonted peace and gentleness. Excellent woman! said the friar.—My lord, I attend your pleasure.

Manfred, accompanied by the friar, passed to his own apartment; where shutting the door, I perceive, father, said he, that Isabella has acquainted you with my purpose. Now hear my resolve, and obey. Reasons of state, most urgent reasons, my own and the safety of my people, demand that I should have a son. It is in vain to expect an heir from Hippolita. I have made choice of Isabella. You must bring her back; and you must do more. I know the influence you have with Hippolita: her conscience is in your hands. She is, I allow, a faultless woman: her soul is set on heaven, and scorns the little grandeur of this world: you can withdraw her from it entirely. Persuade her to consent to the dissolution of our marriage, and to retire into a monastery—she shall endow one if she will; and she shall have the means of being as liberal to your order as she or you can wish. Thus you will divert the calamities that are hanging over our heads, and have the merit of saving the principality of Otranto from destruction. You are a prudent man; and though the warmth of my temper betrayed me into some unbecoming expressions, I honour your virtue, and wish to be indebted to you for the repose of my life and the preservation of my family.

The will of heaven be done! said the friar. I am but its worthless instrument. It makes use of my tongue to tell thee, prince, of thy unwarrantable designs. The injuries of the virtuous Hippolita have mounted to the throne of pity. By me thou art reprimanded for thy adulterous intention of repudiating her: by me thou art warned not to pursue the incestuous design on thy contracted daughter. Heaven, that delivered her from thy fury, when the judgments so recently fallen on thy house ought to have inspired thee with other thoughts, will continue to watch over her. Even I, a poor and despised friar, am able to protect her from thy violence.—I, sinner as I am, and uncharitably reviled by your highness as an accomplice of I know not what amours, scorn the allurements with which it has pleased thee to tempt mine honesty. I love my order; I honour devout souls; I respect the piety of thy princess—but I will not betray the confidence she reposes in me, nor serve even the cause of religion by foul and sinful compliances—But forsooth! the welfare of the state depends on your highness having a son. Heaven mocks the short-sighted views of man. But yester-morn, whose house was so great, so flourishing as Manfred's?—Where is young Conrad now?—My lord, I respect your tears—but I mean not to check them—Let them flow, prince! they will weigh more with heaven towards the welfare of thy subjects, than a marriage, which, founded on lust or policy, could never prosper. The sceptre, which passed from the race of Alfonso to thine, cannot be preserved by a match which the church will never allow. If it is the will of the Most High that Manfred's name must perish, resign yourself, my lord, to its decrees; and thus deserve a crown that can never pass away.—Come, my lord, I like this sorrow—Let us return to the princess: she is not apprized of your cruel intentions; nor did I mean more than to alarm you. You saw with what gentle patience, with what efforts of love, she heard, she rejected hearing the extent of your guilt. I know she longs to fold you in her arms, and assure you of her unalterable affection. Father, said the prince, you mistake my compunction: true, I honour Hippolita's virtues; I think her a saint; and wish it were for my soul's health to tie faster the knot that has united us.—But alas! father, you know not the bitterest of my pangs! It is some time that I have had scruples on the legality of our union: Hippolita is related to me in the fourth degree—It is true, we had a dispensation; but I have been informed that she had also been contracted to another. This it is that sits heavy at my heart: to this state of unlawful wedlock I impute the visitation that has fallen on me in the death of Conrad!—Ease my conscience of this burden; dissolve our marriage, and accomplish the work of godliness which your divine exhortations have commenced in my soul.

How cutting was the anguish which the good man felt, when he perceived this turn in the wily prince! He trembled for Hippolita, whose ruin he saw was determined; and he feared, if Manfred had no hope of recovering Isabella, that his impatience for a son would direct him to some other object, who might not be equally proof against the temptation of Manfred's rank. For some time the holy man remained absorbed in thought. At length, conceiving some hope from delay, he thought the wisest conduct would be to prevent the prince from despairing of recovering Isabella. Her the friar knew he could dispose, from her affection to Hippolita, and from the aversion she had expressed to him for Manfred's addresses, to second his views, till the censures of the church could be fulminated against a divorce. With this intention, as if struck with the prince's scruples, he at length said, My lord, I have been pondering on what your highness has said; and if in truth it is delicacy of conscience that is the real motive of your repugnance to your virtuous lady, far be it from me to endeavour to harden your heart! The church is an indulgent mother; unfold your griefs to her: she alone can administer comfort to your soul, either by satisfying your conscience, or, upon examination of your scruples, by setting you at liberty, and indulging you in the lawful means of continuing your lineage. In the latter case, if the lady Isabella can be brought to consent——Manfred, who concluded that he had either over-reached the good man, or that his first warmth had been but a tribute paid to appearance, was overjoyed at this sudden turn, and repeated the most magnificent promises, if he should succeed by the friar's mediation. The well-meaning priest suffered him to deceive himself, fully determined to traverse his views, instead of seconding them.

Since we now understand one another, resumed the prince, I expect, father, that you satisfy me in one point. Who is the youth that we found in the vault? He must have been privy to Isabella's flight: tell me truly; is he her lover? or is he an agent for another's passion? I have often suspected Isabella's indifference to my son: a thousand circumstances crowd on my mind that confirm that suspicion. She herself was so conscious of it, that, while I discoursed her in the gallery, she outran my suspicions, and endeavoured to justify herself from coolness to Conrad. The friar, who knew nothing of the youth but what he had learnt occasionally from the princess, ignorant what was become of him, and not sufficiently reflecting on the impetuosity of Manfred's temper, conceived that it might not be amiss to sow the seeds of jealousy in his mind: they might be turned to some use hereafter, either by prejudicing the prince against Isabella, if he persisted in that union; or, by diverting his attention to a wrong scent, and employing his thoughts on a visionary intrigue, prevent his engaging in any new pursuit. With this unhappy policy, he answered in a manner to confirm Manfred in the belief of some connexion between Isabella and the youth. The prince, whose passions wanted little fuel to throw them into a blaze, fell into a rage at the idea of what the friar suggested. I will fathom to the bottom of this intrigue, cried he; and quitting Jerome abruptly, with a command to remain there till his return, he hastened to the great hall of the castle, and ordered the peasant to be brought before him.

Thou hardened young impostor! said the prince, as soon as he saw the youth; what becomes of thy boasted veracity now? It was Providence, was it, and the light of the moon, that discovered the lock of the trap-door to thee? Tell me, audacious boy, who thou art, and how long thou hast been acquainted with the princess—and take care to answer with less equivocation than thou didst last night, or tortures shall wring the truth from thee. The young man, perceiving that his share in the flight of the princess was discovered, and concluding that any thing he should say could no longer be of service or detriment to her, replied, I am no impostor, my lord; nor have I deserved opprobrious language. I answered to every question your highness put to me last night with the same veracity that I shall speak now: and that will not be from fear of your tortures, but because my soul abhors a falsehood. Please to repeat your questions, my lord; I am ready to give you all the satisfaction in my power. You know my questions, replied the prince, and only want time to prepare an evasion. Speak directly; who art thou? and how long hast thou been known to the princess? I am a labourer at the next village, said the peasant; my name is Theodore. The princess found me in the vault last night: before that hour I never was in her presence.—I may believe as much or as little as I please of this, said Manfred; but I will hear thy own story, before I examine into the truth of it. Tell me, what reason did the princess give thee for making her escape? Thy life depends on thy answer. She told me, replied Theodore, that she was on the brink of destruction; and that, if she could not escape from the castle, she was in danger in a few moments of being made miserable for ever. And on this slight foundation, on a silly girl's report, said Manfred, thou didst hazard my displeasure? I fear no man's displeasure, said Theodore, when a woman in distress puts herself under my protection.—During this examination, Matilda was going to the apartment of Hippolita. At the upper end of the hall, where Manfred sat, was a boarded gallery with latticed windows, through which Matilda and Bianca were to pass. Hearing her father's voice, and seeing the servants assembled round him, she stopped to learn the occasion. The prisoner soon drew her attention: the steady and composed manner in which he answered, and the gallantry of his last reply, which were the first words she heard distinctly, interested her in his favour. His person was noble, handsome and commanding, even in that situation: but his countenance soon engrossed her whole care. Heavens! Bianca, said the princess softly, do I dream! or is not that youth the exact resemblance of Alfonso's picture in the gallery? She could say no more, for her father's voice grew louder at every word. This bravado, said he, surpasses all thy former insolence. Thou shalt experience the wrath with which thou darest to trifle. Seize him, continued Manfred, and bind him—the first news the princess hears of her champion shall be, that he has lost his head for her sake. The injustice of which thou art guilty towards me, said Theodore, convinces me that I have done a good deed in delivering the princess from thy tyranny. May she be happy, whatever becomes of me!—This is a lover! cried Manfred in a rage: a peasant within sight of death is not animated by such sentiments. Tell me, tell me, rash boy, who thou art, or the rack shall force thy secret from thee. Thou hast threatened me with death already, said the youth, for the truth I have told thee: if that is all the encouragement I am to expect for sincerity, I am not tempted to indulge thy vain curiosity farther. Then thou wilt not speak? said Manfred. I will not, replied he. Bear him away into the court-yard, said Manfred; I will see his head this instant severed from his body.—Matilda fainted at hearing those words. Bianca shrieked, and cried, Help! help! the princess is dead! Manfred started at this ejaculation, and demanded what was the matter. The young peasant, who heard it too, was struck with horror, and asked eagerly the same question; but Manfred ordered him to be hurried into the court, and kept there for execution, till he had informed himself of the cause of Bianca's shrieks. When he learned the meaning, he treated it as a womanish panic; and ordering Matilda to be carried to her apartment, he rushed into the court, and, calling for one of his guards, bade Theodore kneel down and prepare to receive the fatal blow.

The undaunted youth received the bitter sentence with a resignation that touched every heart but Manfred's. He wished earnestly to know the meaning of the words he had heard relating to the princess; but, fearing to exasperate the tyrant more against her, he desisted. The only boon he deigned to ask was, that he might be permitted to have a confessor, and make his peace with heaven. Manfred, who hoped by the confessor's means to come at the youth's history, readily granted his request: and being convinced that father Jerome was now in his interest, he ordered him to be called and shrieve the prisoner. The holy man, who had little foreseen the catastrophe that his imprudence occasioned, fell on his knees to the prince, and adjured him in the most solemn manner not to shed innocent blood. He accused himself in the bitterest terms for his indiscretion, endeavoured to disculpate the youth, and left no method untried to soften the tyrant's rage. Manfred, more incensed than appeased by Jerome's intercession, whose retraction now made him suspect he had been imposed upon by both, commanded the friar to do his duty, telling him he would not allow the prisoner many minutes for confession. Nor do I ask many, my lord, said the unhappy young man. My sins, thank heaven! have not been numerous; nor exceed what might be expected at my years. Dry your tears, good father, and let us dispatch: this is a bad world; nor have I had cause to leave it with regret. Oh! wretched youth! said Jerome; how canst thou bear the sight of me with patience? I am thy murderer! It is I have brought this dismal hour upon thee!—I forgive thee from my soul, said the youth, as I hope heaven will pardon me. Hear my confession, father; and give me thy blessing. How can I prepare thee for thy passage, as I ought? said Jerome. Thou canst not be saved without pardoning thy foes—and canst thou forgive that impious man there? I can, said Theodore; I do.—And does not this touch thee, cruel prince? said the friar. I sent for thee to confess him, said Manfred sternly; not to plead for him. Thou didst first incense me against him—his blood be upon thy head!—It will! it will! said the good man in an agony of sorrow. Thou and I must never hope to go where this blessed youth is going.—Dispatch! said Manfred: I am no more to be moved by the whining of priests, than by the shrieks of women. What! said the youth, is it possible that my fate could have occasioned what I heard? Is the princess then again in thy power?—Thou dost but remember me of my wrath, said Manfred: prepare thee, for this moment is thy last. The youth, who felt his indignation rise, and who was touched with the sorrow which he saw he had infused into all the spectators, as well as into the friar, suppressed his emotions, and, putting off his doublet and unbuttoning his collar, knelt down to his prayers. As he stooped, his shirt flipped down below his shoulder, and discovered the mark of a bloody arrow. Gracious heaven! cried the holy man starting, what do I see? It is my child! my Theodore!

The passions that ensued must be conceived; they cannot be painted. The tears of the assistants were suspended by wonder, rather than stopped by joy. They seemed to enquire in the eyes of their lord what they ought to feel. Surprise, doubt, tenderness, respect, succeeded each other in the countenance of the youth. He received with modest submission the effusion of the old man's tears and embraces: yet afraid of giving a loose to hope, and suspecting from what had passed the inflexibility of Manfred's temper, he cast a glance towards the prince, as if to say, Canst thou be unmoved at such a scene as this?

Manfred's heart was capable of being touched. He forgot his anger in his astonishment; yet his pride forbad his owning himself affected. He even doubted whether this discovery was not a contrivance of the friar to save the youth. What may this mean! said he. How can he be thy son? Is it consistent with thy profession or reputed sanctity to avow a peasant's offspring for the fruit of thy irregular amours?—Oh God! said the holy man, dost thou question his being mine? Could I feel the anguish I do, if I were not his father? Spare him! good prince, spare him! and revile me as thou pleasest.—Spare him! spare him! cried the attendants, for this good man's sake!—Peace! said Manfred sternly: I must know more, ere I am disposed to pardon. A saint's bastard may be no saint himself—Injurious lord! said Theodore: add not insult to cruelty. If I am this venerable man's son, though no prince as thou art, know, the blood that flows in my veins—Yes, said the friar, interrupting him, his blood is noble: nor is he that abject thing, my lord, you speak him. He is my lawful son; and Sicily can boast of few houses more ancient than that of Falconara—But alas! my lord, what is blood? what is nobility? We are all reptiles, miserable sinful creatures. It is piety alone that can distinguish us from the dust whence we sprung, and whither we must return.—Truce to your sermon, said Manfred; you forget you are no longer friar Jerome, but the count of Falconara. Let me know your history; you will have time to moralize hereafter, if you should not happen to obtain the grace of that sturdy criminal there. Mother of God! said the friar, is it possible my lord can refuse a father the life of his only, his long lost child? Trample me, my lord, scorn, afflict me, accept my life for his, but spare my son!—Thou canst feel then, said Manfred, what it is to lose an only son? A little hour ago thou didst preach up resignation to me: *my* house, if fate so pleased, must perish—but the count of Falconara—Alas! my lord, said Jerome, I confess I have offended; but aggravate not an old man's sufferings. I boast not of my family, nor think of such vanities—it is nature that pleads for this boy; it is the memory of the dear woman that bore him—Is she, Theodore, is she dead?—Her soul has long been with the blessed, said Theodore. Oh how? cried Jerome, tell me—No—she is happy! Thou art all my care now!—Most dread lord! will you—will you grant me my poor boy's life? Return to thy convent, answered Manfred; conduct the princess hither; obey me in what else thou knowest; and I promise thee the life of thy son.——Oh! my lord, said Jerome, is honesty the price I must pay for this dear youth's safety?—For me! cried Theodore: let me die a thousand deaths, rather than stain thy conscience. What is it the tyrant would exact of thee? Is the princess safe from his power? Protect her, thou venerable old man! and let all his wrath fall on me. Jerome endeavoured to check the impetuosity of the youth; and ere Manfred could reply, the trampling of horses was heard, and a brazen trumpet, which hung without the gate of the castle, was suddenly sounded. At the same instant the sable plumes on the enchanted helmet, which still remained at the other end of the court, were tempestuously agitated, and nodded thrice, as if bowed by some invisible wearer.

CHAPTER III

MANFRED's heart misgave him when he beheld the plumage on the miraculous casque shaken in concert with the sounding of the brazen trumpet. Father! said he to Jerome, whom he now ceased to treat as count of Falconara, what mean these portents? If I have offended—[the plumes were shaken with greater violence than before] Unhappy prince that I am! cried Manfred—Holy Father! will you not assist me with your prayers?—My lord, replied Jerome, heaven is no doubt displeased with your mockery of its servants. Submit yourself to the church; and cease to persecute her ministers. Dismiss this innocent youth; and learn to respect the holy character I wear: heaven will not be trifled with: you see—[the trumpet sounded again] I acknowledge I have been too hasty, said Manfred. Father, do you go to the wicket, and demand who is at the gate. Do you grant me the life of Theodore? replied the friar. I do, said Manfred; but enquire who is without.

Jerome, falling on the neck of his son, discharged a flood of tears, that spoke the fulness of his soul. You promised to go to the gate, said Manfred. I thought, replied the friar, your highness would excuse my thanking you first in this tribute of my heart. Go, dearest sir, said Theodore, obey the prince; I do not deserve that you should delay his satisfaction for me.

Jerome, enquiring who was without, was answered, A herald. From whom? said he. From the knight of the gigantic sabre, said the herald: and I must speak with the usurper of Otranto. Jerome returned to the prince, and did not fail to repeat the message in the very words it had been uttered. The first sounds struck Manfred with terror; but when he heard himself styled usurper, his rage rekindled, and all his courage revived. Usurper!— Insolent villain! cried he, who dares to question my title? Retire, father; this is no business for monks: I will meet this presumptuous man myself. Go to your convent, and prepare the princess's return: your son shall be a hostage for your fidelity: his life depends on your obedience.—Good heaven! my lord, cried Jerome, your highness did but this instant freely pardon my child—have you so soon forgot the interposition of heaven?—Heaven, replied Manfred, does not send heralds to question the title of a lawful prince—I doubt whether it even notifies its will through friars—but that is your affair, not mine. At present you know my pleasure; and it is not a saucy herald that shall save your son, if you do not return with the princess.

It was in vain for the holy man to reply. Manfred commanded him to be conducted to the postern-gate, and shut out from the castle: and he ordered some of his attendants to carry Theodore to the top of the black tower, and guard him strictly; scarce permitting the father and son to exchange a hasty embrace at parting. He then withdrew to the hall, and, seating himself in princely state, ordered the herald to be admitted to his presence.

Well, thou insolent, said the prince, what wouldst thou with me? I come, replied he, to thee, Manfred, usurper of the principality of Otranto, from the renowned and invincible knight, the knight of the gigantic sabre: in the name of his lord, Frederic marquis of Vicenza, he demands the lady Isabella, daughter of that prince, whom thou hast basely and traitorously got into thy power, by bribing her false guardians during his absence: and he requires thee to resign the principality of Otranto, which thou hast usurped from the said lord Frederic, the nearest of blood to the last rightful lord Alfonso the Good. If thou dost not instantly comply with these just demands, he defies thee to single combat to the last extremity. And so saying, the herald cast down his warder.

And where is this braggart, who sends thee? said Manfred. At the distance of a league, said the herald: he comes to make good his lord's claim against thee, as he is a true knight, and thou an usurper and ravisher.

Injurious as this challenge was, Manfred reflected that it was not his interest to provoke the marquis. He knew how well-founded the claim of Frederic was; nor was this the first time he had heard of it. Frederic's ancestors had assumed the style of princes of Otranto, from the death of Alfonso the Good without issue: but Manfred, his father, and grandfather, had been too powerful for the house of Vicenza to dispossess them. Frederic, a martial and amorous young prince, had married a beautiful young lady, of whom he was enamoured, and who had died in childbed of Isabella. Her death affected him so much, that he had taken the cross and gone to the Holy Land, where he was wounded in an engagement against the infidels, made prisoner, and reported to be dead. When the news reached Manfred's ears, he bribed the guardians of the lady Isabella to deliver her up to him as a bride for his son Conrad; by which alliance he had purposed to unite the claims of the two houses. This motive, on Conrad's death, had co-operated to make him so suddenly resolve on espousing her himself; and the same reflection determined him now to endeavour at obtaining the consent of Frederic to this marriage. A like policy inspired him with the thought of inviting Frederic's champion into his castle, lest he should be informed of Isabella's flight, which he strictly enjoined his domestics not to disclose to any of the knight's retinue.

Herald, said Manfred, as soon as he had digested these reflections, return to thy master, and tell him, ere we liquidate our differences by the sword, Manfred would hold some converse with him. Bid him welcome to my castle, where, by my faith, as I am a true knight, he shall have courteous reception, and full security for himself and followers. If we cannot adjust our quarrel by amicable means, I swear he shall depart in safety, and shall have full satisfaction according to the law of arms: so help me God and his holy Trinity!—The herald made three obeisances, and retired.

During this interview Jerome's mind was agitated by a thousand contrary passions. He trembled for the life of his son, and his first idea was to persuade Isabella to return to the castle. Yet he was scarce less alarmed at the thought of her union with Manfred. He dreaded Hippolita's unbounded submission to the will of her lord: and though he did not doubt but he could alarm her piety not to consent to a divorce, if he could get access to her; yet should Manfred discover that the obstruction came from him, it might be equally fatal to Theodore. He was impatient to know whence came the herald, who with so little management had questioned the title of Manfred: yet he did not dare absent himself from the convent, lest Isabella should leave it, and her flight be imputed to him. He returned disconsolately to the monastery, uncertain on what conduct to resolve. A monk, who met him in the porch and observed his melancholy air, said, Alas! brother, is it then true that we have lost our excellent princess Hippolita? The holy man started, and cried, What meanest thou, brother? I come this instant from the castle, and left her in perfect health. Martelli, replied the other friar, passed by the convent but a quarter of an hour ago on his way from the castle, and reported that her highness was dead. All our brethren are gone to the chapel to pray for her happy transit to a better life, and willed me to wait thy arrival. They know thy holy attachment to that good lady, and are anxious for the affliction it will cause in thee—Indeed we have all reason to weep; she was a mother to our house—But this life is but a pilgrimage; we must not murmur—we shall all follow her; may our end be like hers!—Good brother, thou dreamest, said Jerome: I tell thee I come from the castle, and left the princess well—Where is the lady Isabella?—Poor gentlewoman! replied the friar; I told her the sad news, and offered her spiritual comfort; I reminded her of the transitory condition of mortality, and advised her to take the veil: I quoted the example of the holy princess Sanchia of Aragon.—Thy zeal was laudable, said Jerome impatiently; but at present it was unnecessary: Hippolita is well—at least I trust in the Lord she is; I heard nothing to the contrary—Yet methinks the prince's earnestness—Well, brother, but where is the lady Isabella?—I know not, said the friar: she wept much, and said she would retire to her chamber. Jerome left his comrade abruptly, and hasted to the princess, but she was not in her chamber. He enquired of the domestics of the convent, but could learn no news of her. He searched in vain throughout the monastery and the church, and dispatched messengers round the neighbourhood, to get intelligence if she had been seen; but to no purpose. Nothing could equal the good man's perplexity. He judged that Isabella, suspecting Manfred of having precipitated his wife's death, had taken the alarm, and withdrawn herself to some more secret place of concealment. This new flight would probably carry the prince's fury to the height. The report of Hippolita's death, though it seemed almost incredible, increased his consternation; and though Isabella's escape bespoke her aversion of Manfred for a husband, Jerome could feel no comfort from it, while it endangered the life of his son. He determined to return to the castle, and made several of his brethern accompany him, to attest his innocence to Manfred, and, if necessary, join their intercession with his for Theodore.

The prince, in the mean time, had passed into the court, and ordered the gates of the castle to be flung open for the reception of the stranger knight and his train. In a few minutes the cavalcade arrived. First came two harbingers with wands. Next a herald, followed by two pages and two trumpets. Then an hundred foot-guards. These were attended by as many horse. After them fifty footmen, clothed in scarlet and black, the colours of the knight. Then a led horse. Two heralds on each side of a gentleman on horseback bearing a banner with the arms of Vicenza and Otranto quarter-ly—a circumstance that much offended Manfred—but he stifled his resentment. Two more pages. The knight's confessor telling his beads. Fifty more footmen, clad as before. Two knights habited in complete armour, their beavers down, comrades to the principal knight. The 'squires of the two knights, carrying their shields and devices. The knight's own 'squire. An hundred gentlemen bearing an enormous sword, and seeming to faint under the weight of it. The knight himself on a chestnut steed, in complete armour, his lance in the rest, his face entirely concealed by his vizor, which was surmounted by a large plume of scarlet and black feathers. Fifty foot-guards with drums and trumpets closed the procession, which wheeled off to the right and left to make room for the principal knight.

As soon as he approached the gate, he stopped; and the herald advancing, read again the words of the challenge. Manfred's eyes were fixed on the gigantic sword, and he scarce seemed to attend to the cartel: but his attention was soon diverted by a tempest of wind that rose behind him. He turned, and beheld the plumes of the enchanted helmet agitated in the same extraordinary manner as before. It required intrepidity like Manfred's not to sink under a concurrence of circumstances that seemed to announce his fate. Yet scorning in the presence of strangers to betray the courage he had always manifested, he said boldly, Sir knight, whoever thou art, I bid thee welcome. If thou art of mortal mould, thy valour shall meet its equal: and if thou art a true knight, thou wilt scorn to employ sorcery to carry thy point. Be these omens from heaven or hell, Manfred trusts to the righteousness of his cause and to the aid of saint Nicholas, who has ever protected his house. Alight, sir knight, and repose thyself. To-morrow thou shalt have a fair field; and heaven befriend the juster side!

The knight made no reply, but, dismounting, was conducted by Manfred to the great hall of the castle. As they traversed the court, the knight stopped to gaze at the miraculous casque; and, kneeling down, seemed to pray inwardly for some minutes. Rising, he made a sign to the prince to lead on. As soon as they entered the hall, Manfred proposed to the stranger to disarm; but the knight shook his head in token of refusal. Sir knight, said Manfred, this is not courteous; but by my good faith I will not cross thee! nor shalt thou have cause to complain of the prince of Otranto. No treachery is designed on my part: I hope none is intended on thine. Here take my gage: [giving him his ring] your friends and you shall enjoy the laws of hospitality. Rest here until refreshments are brought: I will but give orders for the accommodation of your train, and return to you. The three knights bowed, as accepting his courtesy. Manfred directed the stranger's retinue to be conducted to an adjacent hospital, founded by the princess Hippolita for the reception of pilgrims. As they made the circuit of the court to return towards the gate, the gigantic sword burst from the supporters, and, falling to the ground opposite to the helmet, remained immoveable. Manfred, almost hardened to preternatural appearances, surmounted the shock of this new prodigy; and returning to the hall, where by this time the feast was ready, he invited his silent guests to take their places. Manfred, however ill his heart was at ease, endeavoured to inspire the company with mirth. He put several questions to them, but was answered only by signs. They raised their vizors but sufficiently to feed themselves, and that sparingly. Sirs, said the prince, ye are the first guests I ever treated within these walls, who scorned to hold any intercourse with me: nor has it oft been customary, I ween, for princes to hazard their state and dignity against strangers and mutes. You say you come in the name of Frederic of Vicenza: I have ever heard that he was a gallant and courteous knight; nor would he, I am bold to say, think it beneath him to mix in social converse with a prince that is his equal, and not unknown by deeds in arms.—Still ye are silent—Well! be it as it may—by the laws of hospitality and chivalry ye are masters under this roof: ye shall do your pleasure—but come, give me a goblet of wine; ye will not refuse to pledge me to the healths of your fair mistresses. The principal knight sighed and crossed himself, and was rising from the board—Sir knight, said Manfred, what I said was but in sport: I shall constrain you in nothing; use your good liking. Since mirth is not your mood, let us be sad. Business may hit your fancies better: let us withdraw; and hear if what I have to unfold may be better relished than the vain efforts I have made for your pastime.

Manfred, then, conducting the three knights into an inner chamber, shut the door, and, inviting them to be seated, began thus, addressing himself to the chief personage:

You come, sir knight, as I understand, in the name of the marquis of Vicenza, to re-demand the lady Isabella his daughter, who has been contracted in the face of holy church to my son, by the consent of her legal guardians; and to require me to resign my dominions to your lord, who gives himself for the nearest of blood to prince Alfonso, whose soul God rest! I shall speak to the latter article of your demands first. You must know, your lord knows, that I enjoy the principality of Otranto from my father Don Manuel, as he received it from his father Don Ricardo. Alfonso, their predecessor, dying childless in the Holy Land, bequeathed his estates to my grandfather Don Ricardo, in consideration of his faithful services—[The stranger shook his head]—Sir knight, said Manfred warmly, Ricardo was a valiant and upright man; he was a pious man; witness his munificent foundation of the adjoining church and two convents. He was peculiarly patronized by saint Nicholas—My grandfather was incapable—I say, sir, Don Ricardo was incapable—Excuse me, your interruption has disordered me—I venerate the memory of my grandfather—Well, sirs! he held this estate; he held it by his good sword, and by the favour of saint Nicholas—so did my father; and so, sirs, will I, come what will.—But Frederic, your lord, is nearest in blood—I have consented to put my title to the issue of the sword—does that imply a vitious title? I might have asked, where is Frederic, your lord? Report speaks him dead in captivity. You say, your actions say, he lives—I question it not—I might, sirs, I might—but I do not. Other princes would bid Frederic take his inheritance by force, if he can: they would not stake their dignity on a single combat: they would not submit it to the decision of unknown mutes! Pardon me, gentlemen, I am too warm: but suppose yourselves in my situation: as ye are stout knights, would it not move your choler to have your own and the honour of your ancestors called in question?—But to the point. Ye require me to deliver up the lady Isabella—Sirs, I must ask if ye are authorized to receive her? [The knight nodded.] Receive her—continued Manfred: Well! you are authorized to receive her—But, gentle knight, may I ask if you have full powers? [The knight nodded.] 'Tis well, said Manfred: then hear what I have to offer—Ye see, gentlemen, before you the most unhappy of men! [he began to weep] afford me your compassion; I am entitled to it; indeed I am. Know, I have lost my only hope, my joy, the support of my house—Conrad died yester-morning. [The knights discovered signs of surprise.] Yes, sirs, fate has disposed of my son. Isabella is at liberty.—Do you then restore her, cried the chief knight, breaking silence. Afford me your patience, said Manfred. I rejoice to find, by this testimony of your good-will, that this matter may be adjusted without blood. It is no interest of mine dictates what little I have farther to say. Ye behold in me a man disgusted with the world: the loss of my son has weaned me from earthly cares. Power and greatness have no longer any charms in my eyes. I wished to transmit the sceptre I had received from my ancestors with honour to my son—but that is over! Life itself is so indifferent to me, that I accepted your defiance with joy: a good knight cannot go to the grave with more satisfaction than when falling in his vocation. Whatever is the will of heaven, I submit; for, alas! sirs, I am a man of many sorrows. Manfred is no object of envy—but no doubt you are acquainted with my story. [The knight made signs of ignorance, and seemed curious to have Manfred proceed.] Is it possible, sirs, continued the prince, that my story should be a secret to you? Have you heard nothing relating to me and the princess Hippolita? [They shook their heads]—No! Thus then, sirs, it is. You think me ambitious: ambition, alas, is composed of more rugged materials. If I were ambitious, I should not for so many years have been a prey to the hell of conscientious scruples—But I weary your patience: I will be brief. Know then, that I have long been troubled in mind on my union with the princess Hippolita.—Oh! sirs, if ye were acquainted with that excellent woman! if ye knew that I adore her like a mistress, and cherish her as a friend—But man was not born for perfect happiness! She shares my scruples, and with her consent I have brought this matter before the church, for we are related within the forbidden degrees. I expect every hour the definitive sentence that must separate us forever. I am sure you feel for me—I see you do—Pardon these tears! [The knights gazed on each other, wondering where this would end.] Manfred continued: The death of my son betiding while my soul was under this anxiety, I thought of nothing but resigning my dominions, and retiring forever from the sight of mankind. My only difficulty was to fix on a successor, who would be tender of my people, and to dispose of the lady Isabella, who is dear to me as my own blood. I was willing to restore the line of Alfonso, even in his most distant kindred: and though, pardon me, I am satisfied it was his will that Ricardo's lineage should take place of his own relations; yet, where was I to search for those relations? I knew of none but Frederic, your lord: he was a captive to the infidels, or dead; and were he living, and at home, would he quit the flourishing state of Vicenza for the inconsiderable principality of Otranto? If he would not, could I bear the thought of seeing a hard unfeeling viceroy set over my poor faithful people?—for, sirs, I love my people, and thank heaven am beloved by them.—But ye will ask, Whither tends this long discourse? Briefly then, thus, sirs. Heaven in your arrival seems to point out a remedy for these difficulties and my misfortunes. The lady Isabella is at liberty: I shall soon be so. I would submit to any thing for the good of my people—Were it not the best, the only way to extinguish the feuds between our families, if I were to take the lady Isabella to wife?—You start—But though Hippolita's virtues will ever be dear to me, a prince must not consider himself; he is born for his people.—A servant at that instant entering the chamber, apprized Manfred that Jerome and several of his brethren demanded immediate access to him.

The prince, provoked at this interruption, and fearing that the friar would discover to the strangers that Isabella had taken sanctuary, was going to forbid Jerome's entrance. But recollecting that he was certainly arrived to notify the princess's return, Manfred began to excuse himself to the knights for leaving them for a few moments, but was prevented by the arrival of the friars. Manfred angrily reprimanded them for their intrusion, and would have forced them back from the chamber; but Jerome was too much agitated to be repulsed. He declared aloud the flight of Isabella, with protestations of his own innocence. Manfred, distracted at the news, and not less at its coming to the knowledge of the strangers, uttered nothing but incoherent sentences, now upbraiding the friar, now apologizing to the knights, earnest to know what was become of Isabella, yet equally afraid of their knowing, impatient to pursue her, yet dreading to have them join in the pursuit. He offered to dispatch messengers in quest of her:—but the chief knight, no longer keeping silence, reproached Manfred in bitter terms for his dark and ambiguous dealing, and demanded the cause of Isabella's first absence from the castle. Manfred, casting a stern look at Jerome, implying a command of silence, pretended that on Conrad's death he had placed her in sanctuary until he could determine how to dispose of her. Jerome, who trembled for his son's life, did not dare contradict this falsehood; but one of his brethren, not under the same anxiety, declared frankly that she had fled to their church in the preceding night. The prince in vain endeavoured to stop this discovery, which overwhelmed him with shame and confusion. The principal stranger, amazed at the contradictions he heard, and more than half persuaded that Manfred had secreted the princess, notwithstanding the concern he expressed at her flight, rushing to the door, said, Thou traitor-prince! Isabella shall be found. Manfred endeavoured to hold him; but the other knights assisting their comrade, he broke from the prince, and hastened into the court, demanding his attendants. Manfred, finding it in vain to divert him from the pursuit, offered to accompany him; and summoning his attendants, and taking Jerome and some of the friars to guide them, they issued from the castle; Manfred privately giving orders to have the knight's company secured, while to the knight he affected to dispatch a messenger to require their assistance.

The company had no sooner quitted the castle, than Matilda, who felt herself deeply interested for the young peasant, since she had seen him condemned to death in the hall, and whose thoughts had been taken up with concerting measures to save him, was informed by some of the female attendants that Manfred had dispatched all his men various ways in pursuit of Isabella. He had in his hurry given this order in general terms, not meaning to extend it to the guard he had set upon Theodore, but forgetting it. The domestics, officious to obey so peremptory a prince, and urged by their own curiosity and love of novelty to join in any precipitate chace, had to a man left the castle. Matilda disengaged herself from her women, stole up to the black tower, and, unbolting the door, presented herself to the astonished Theodore. Young man, said she, though filial duty and womanly modesty condemn the step I am taking, yet holy charity, surmounting all other ties, justifies this act. Fly; the doors of thy prison are open: my father and his domestics are absent; but they may soon return: begone in safety; and may the angels of heaven direct thy course!—Thou art surely one of those angels! said the enraptured Theodore: none but a blessed saint could speak, could act, could look like thee!—May I not know the name of my divine protectress? Methought thou namedst thy father: is it possible? can Manfred's blood feel holy pity?—Lovely lady, thou answerest not—But how art thou here thyself? Why dost thou neglect thy own safety, and waste a thought on a wretch like Theodore? Let us fly together: the life thou bestowest shall be dedicated to thy defence. Alas! thou mistakest, said Matilda sighing: I am Manfred's daughter, but no dangers await me. Amazement! said Theodore: but last night I blessed myself for yielding thee the service thy gracious compassion so charitably returns me now. Still thou art in an error, said the princess; but this is no time for explanation. Fly, virtuous youth, while it is in my power to save thee: should my father return, thou and I both should indeed have cause to tremble. How? said Theodore: thinkest thou, charming maid, that I will accept of life at the hazard of aught calamitous to thee? Better I endured a thousand deaths——I run no risk, said Matilda, but by thy delay. Depart: it cannot be known that I assisted thy flight. Swear by the saints above, said Theodore, that thou canst not be suspected; else here I vow to await whatever can befall me. Oh! thou art too generous, said Matilda; but rest assured that no suspicion can alight on me. Give me thy beauteous hand in token that thou dost not deceive me, said Theodore; and let me bathe it with the warm tears of gratitude.—Forbear, said the princess: this must not be.—Alas! said Theodore, I have never known but calamity until this hour—perhaps shall never know other fortune again: suffer the chaste raptures of holy gratitude: 'tis my soul would print its effusions on thy hand.—Forbear, and begone, said Matilda: how would Isabella approve of seeing thee at my feet? Who is Isabella? said the young man with surprise. Ah me! I fear, said the princess, I am serving a deceitful one! Hast thou forgot thy curiosity this morning?—Thy looks, thy actions, all thy beauteous self seems an emanation of divinity, said Theodore, but thy words are dark and mysterious——Speak, lady, speak to thy servant's comprehension.—Thou understandest but too well, said Matilda: but once more I command thee to be gone: thy blood, which I may preserve, will be on my head, if I waste the time in vain discourse. I go, lady, said Theodore, because it is thy will, and because I would not bring the grey hairs of my father with sorrow to the grave. Say but, adored lady, that I have thy gentle pity.—Stay, said Matilda; I will conduct thee to the subterraneous vault by which Isabella escaped; it will lead thee to the church of saint Nicholas, where thou mayst take sanctuary.—What! said Theodore, was it another, and not thy lovely self, that I assisted to find the subterraneous passage? It was, said Matilda: but ask no more; I tremble to see thee still abide here: fly to the sanctuary.—To sanctuary! said Theodore: No princess; sanctuaries are for helpless damsels, or for criminals. Theodore's soul is free from guilt, nor will wear the appearance of it. Give me a sword, lady, and thy father shall learn that Theodore scorns an ignominious flight. Rash youth! said Matilda, thou wouldst not dare to lift thy presumptuous arm against the prince of Otranto? Not against *thy* father; indeed I dare not, said Theodore: excuse me, lady; I had forgotten—but could I gaze on thee, and remember thou art sprung from the tyrant Manfred?—But he is thy father, and from this moment my injuries are buried in oblivion. A deep and hollow groan, which seemed to come from above, startled the princess and Theodore. Good heaven! we are overheard! said the princess. They listened; but perceiving no farther noise, they both concluded it the effect of pent-up vapours: and the princess, preceding Theodore softly, carried him to her father's armoury; where equipping him with a complete suit, he was conducted by Matilda to the postern-gate. Avoid the town, said the princess, and all the western side of the castle: 'tis there the search must be making by Manfred and the strangers: but hie thee to the opposite quarter. Yonder, behind that forest to the east is a chain of rocks, hollowed into a labyrinth of caverns that reach to the sea-coast. There thou mayst lie concealed, till thou canst make signs to some vessel to put on shore and take thee off. Go! heaven be thy guide!—and sometimes in thy prayers remember—Matilda!— Theodore flung himself at her feet, and seizing her lily hand, which with struggles she suffered him to kiss, he vowed on the earliest opportunity to get himself knighted, and fervently entreated her permission to swear himself eternally her knight.—Ere the princess could reply, a clap of thunder was suddenly heard, that shook the battlements. Theodore, regardless of the tempest, would have urged his suit; but the princess, dismayed, retreated hastily into the castle, and commanded the youth to be gone, with an air that would not be disobeyed. He sighed, and retired, but with eyes fixed on the gate, until Matilda closing it put an end to an interview, in which the hearts of both had drunk so deeply of a passion which both now tasted for the first time.

Theodore went pensively to the convent, to acquaint his father with his deliverance. There he learned the absence of Jerome, and the pursuit that was making after the lady Isabella, with some particulars of whose story he now first became acquainted. The generous gallantry of his nature prompted him to wish to assist her; but the monks could lend him no lights to guess at the route she had taken. He was not tempted to wander far in search of her; for the idea of Matilda had imprinted itself so strongly on his heart, that he could not bear to absent himself at much distance from her abode. The tenderness Jerome had expressed for him concurred to confirm this reluctance; and he even persuaded himself that filial affection was the chief cause of his hovering between the castle and monastery. Until Jerome should return at night, Theodore at length determined to repair to the forest that Matilda had pointed out to him. Arriving there, he sought the gloomiest shades, as best suited to the pleasing melancholy that reigned in his mind. In this mood he roved insensibly to the caves which had formerly served as a retreat to hermits, and were now reported round the country to be haunted by evil spirits. He recollected to have heard this tradition; and being of a brave and adventurous disposition, he willingly indulged his curiosity in exploring the secret recesses of this labyrinth. He had not penetrated far before he thought he heard the steps of some person who seemed to retreat before him. Theodore, though firmly grounded in all our holy faith enjoins to be believed, had no apprehension that good men were abandoned without cause to the malice of the powers of darkness. He thought the place more likely to be infested by robbers, than by those infernal agents who are reported to molest and bewilder travellers. He had long burned with impatience to approve his valour. Drawing his sabre, he marched sedately onwards, still directing his steps as the imperfect rustling sound before him led the way. The armour he wore was a like indication to the person who avoided him. Theodore, now convinced that he was not mistaken, redoubled his pace, and evidently gained on the person that fled; whose haste increasing, Theodore came up just as a woman fell breathless before him. He hasted to raise her; but her terror was so great, that he apprehended she would faint in his arms. He used every gentle word to dispel her alarms, and assured her that, far from injuring, he would defend her at the peril of his life. The lady recovering her spirits from his courteous demeanour, and gazing on her protector, said, Sure I have heard that voice before?—Not to my knowledge, replied Theodore, unless, as I conjecture, thou art the lady Isabella.—Merciful heaven! cried she, thou are not sent in quest of me, art thou? And saying those words she threw herself at his feet, and besought him not to deliver her up to Manfred. To Manfred! cried Theodore—No, lady: I have once already delivered thee from his tyranny, and it shall fare hard with me now, but I will place thee out of the reach of his daring. Is it possible, said she, that thou shouldst be the generous unknown I met last night in the vault of the castle? Sure thou art not a mortal, but my guardian angel: on my knees let me thank—Hold, gentle princess, said Theodore, nor demean thyself before a poor and friendless young man. If heaven has selected me for thy deliverer, it will accomplish its work, and strengthen my arm in thy cause. But come, lady, we are too near the mouth of the cavern; let us seek its inmost recesses: I can have no tranquillity till I have placed thee beyond the reach of danger.—Alas! what mean you, sir? said she. Though all your actions are noble, though your sentiments speak the purity of your soul, is it fitting that I should accompany you alone into these perplexed retreats? Should we be found together, what would a censorious world think of my conduct?—I respect your virtuous delicacy, said Theodore; nor do you harbour a suspicion that wounds my honour. I meant to conduct you into the most private cavity of these rocks; and then, at the hazard of my life, to guard their entrance against every living thing. Besides, lady, continued he, drawing a deep sigh, beauteous and all perfect as your form is, and though my wishes are not guiltless of aspiring, know, my soul is dedicated to another; and although——A sudden noise prevented Theodore from proceeding. They soon distinguished these sounds, Isabella! What ho! Isabella!— The trembling princess relapsed into her former agony of fear. Theodore endeavoured to encourage her, but in vain. He assured her he would die rather than suffer her to return under Manfred's power; and begging her to remain concealed, he went forth to prevent the person in search of her from approaching.

At the mouth of the cavern he found an armed knight discoursing with a peasant, who assured him he had seen a lady enter the passes of the rock. The knight was preparing to seek her, when Theodore, placing himself in his way, with his sword drawn, sternly forbad him at his peril to advance. And who are thou who darest to cross my way? said the knight haughtily. One who does not dare more than he will perform, said Theodore. I seek the lady Isabella, said the knight; and understand she has taken refuge among these rocks. Impede me not, or thou wilt repent having provoked my resentment.—Thy purpose is as odious as thy resentment is contemptible, said Theodore. Return whence thou camest, or we shall soon know whose resentment is most terrible.—The stranger, who was the principal knight that had arrived from the marquis of Vicenza, had galloped from Manfred as he was busied in getting information of the princess, and giving various orders to prevent her falling into the power of the three knights. Their chief had suspected Manfred of being privy to the princess's absconding; and this insult from a man who he concluded was stationed by that prince to secrete her, confirming his suspicions, he made no reply, but, discharging a blow with his sabre at Theodore, would soon have removed all obstruction, if Theodore, who took him for one of Manfred's captains, and who had no sooner given the provocation than prepared to support it, had not received the stroke on his shield. The valour that had so long been smothered in his breast, broke forth at once: he rushed impetuously on the knight, whose pride and wrath were not less powerful incentives to hardy deeds. The combat was furious, but not long. Theodore wounded the knight in three several places, and at last disarmed him as he fainted by the loss of blood. The peasant, who had fled on the first onset, had given the alarm to some of Manfred's domestics, who by his orders were dispersed through the forest in pursuit of Isabella. They came up as the knight fell, whom they soon discovered to be the noble stranger. Theodore, notwithstanding his hatred to Manfred, could not behold the victory he had gained without emotions of pity and generosity: but he was more touched, when he learned the quality of his adversary, and was informed that he was no retainer, but an enemy of Manfred. He assisted the servants of the latter in disarming the knight, and in endeavouring to staunch the blood that flowed from his wounds. The knight, recovering his speech, said in a faint and faltering voice, Generous foe, we have both been in an error: I took thee for an instrument of the tyrant; I perceive thou hast made the like mistake—It is too late for excuses—I faint.—If Isabella is at hand, call her—I have important secrets to—He is dying! said one of the attendants; has nobody a crucifix about them? Andrea, do thou pray over him.—Fetch some water, said Theodore, and pour it down his throat, while I hasten to the princess. Saying this, he flew to Isabella; and in a few words told her modestly, that he had been so unfortunate by mistake as to wound a gentleman from her father's court, who wished ere he died to impart something of consequence to her. The princess, who had been transported at hearing the voice of Theodore as he called her to come forth, was astonished at what she heard. Suffering herself to be conducted by Theodore, the new proof of whose valour recalled her dispersed spirits, she came where the bleeding knight lay speechless on the ground—but her fears returned when she beheld the domestics of Manfred. She would again have fled, if Theodore had not made her observe that they were unarmed, and had not threatened them with instant death, if they should dare to seize the princess. The stranger, opening his eyes, and beholding a woman, said, Art thou—pray tell me truly—art thou Isabella of Vicenza? I am, said she; good heaven restore thee!—Then thou—then thou—said the knight, struggling for utterance—seest—thy father!—Give me one——Oh! amazement! horror! what do I hear? what do I see? cried Isabella. My father! You my father! How come you here, sir? For heaven's sake speak!—Oh! run for help, or he will expire!—'Tis most true, said the wounded knight, exerting all his force; I am Frederic thy father—Yes, I came to deliver thee—It will not be—Give me a parting kiss, and take——Sir, said Theodore, do not exhaust yourself: suffer us to convey you to the castle.—To the castle! said Isabella: Is there no help nearer than the castle? Would you expose my father to the tyrant? If he goes thither, I dare not accompany him.—And yet, can I leave him?—My child, said Frederic, it matters not for me whither I am carried: a few minutes will place me beyond danger: but while I have eyes to dote on thee, forsake me not, dear Isabella! This brave knight—I know not who he is—will protect thy innocence. Sir, you will not abandon my child, will you?—Theodore, shedding tears over his victim, and vowing to guard the princess at the expence of his life, persuaded Frederic to suffer himself to be conducted to the castle. They placed him on a horse belonging to one of the domestics, after binding up his wounds as well as they were able. Theodore marched by his side; and the afflicted Isabella, who could not bear to quit him, followed mournfully behind.

CHAPTER IV

THE sorrowful troop no sooner arrived at the castle, than they were met by Hippolita and Matilda, whom Isabella had sent one of the domestics before to advertise of their approach. The ladies, causing Frederic to be conveyed into the nearest chamber, retired, while the surgeons examined his wounds. Matilda blushed at seeing Theodore and Isabella together; but endeavoured to conceal it by embracing the latter, and condoling with her on her father's mischance. The surgeons soon came to acquaint Hippolita that none of the marquis's wounds were dangerous; and that he was desirous of seeing his daughter and the princesses. Theodore, under pretence of expressing his joy at being freed from his apprehensions of the combat being fatal to Frederic, could not resist the impulse of following Matilda. Her eyes were so often cast down on meeting his, that Isabella, who regarded Theodore as attentively as he gazed on Matilda, soon divined who the object was that he had told her in the cave engaged his affections. While this mute scene passed, Hippolita demanded of Frederic the cause of his having taken that mysterious course for reclaiming his daughter; and threw in various apologies to excuse her lord for the match contracted between their children. Frederic, however incensed against Manfred, was not insensible to the courtesy and benevolence of Hippolita: but he was still more struck with the lovely form of Matilda. Wishing to detain them by his bedside, he informed Hippolita of his story. He told her, that, while prisoner to the infidels, he had dreamed that his daughter, of whom he had learned no news since his captivity, was detained in a castle, where she was in danger of the most dreadful misfortunes; and that if he obtained his liberty, and repaired to a wood near Joppa, he would learn more. Alarmed at this dream, and incapable of obeying the direction given by it, his chains became more grievous than ever. But while his thoughts were occupied on the means of obtaining his liberty, he received the agreeable news that the confederate princes, who were warring in Palestine, had paid his ransom. He instantly set out for the wood that had been marked in his dream. For three days he and his attendants had wandered in the forest without seeing a human form: but on the evening of the third they came to a cell, in which they found a venerable hermit in the agonies of death. Applying rich cordials, they brought the saint-like man to his speech. My sons, said he, I am bounden to your charity—but it is in vain—I am going to my eternal rest—yet I die with the satisfaction of performing the will of heaven. When first I repaired to this solitude, after seeing my country become a prey to unbelievers [it is, alas! above fifty years since I was witness to that dreadful scene!] saint Nicholas appeared to me, and revealed a secret, which he bade me never disclose to mortal man, but on my death-bed. This is that tremendous hour, and ye are no doubt the chosen warriors to whom I was ordered to reveal my trust. As soon as ye have done the last offices to this wretched corse, dig under the seventh tree on the left hand of this poor cave, and your pains will—Oh! good heaven receive my soul! With those words the devout man breathed his last. By break of day, continued Frederic, when we had committed the holy relics to earth, we dug according to direction—But what was our astonishment, when about the depth of six feet we discovered an enormous sabre—the very weapon yonder in the court? On the blade, which was then partly out of the scabbard, though since closed by our efforts in removing it, were written the following lines——No; excuse me, madam, added the marquis, turning to Hippolita, if I forbear to repeat them: I respect your sex and rank, and would not be guilty of offending your ear with sounds injurious to aught that is dear to you.—He paused. Hippolita trembled. She did not doubt but Frederic was destined by heaven to accomplish the fate that seemed to threaten her house. Looking with anxious fondness at Matilda, a silent tear stole down her cheek; but recollecting herself, she said, Proceed, my lord; heaven does nothing in vain: mortals must receive its divine behests with lowliness and submission. It is our part to deprecate its wrath, or bow to its decrees. Repeat the sentence, my lord: we listen resigned.—Frederic was grieved that he had proceeded so far. The dignity and patient firmness of Hippolita penetrated him with respect, and the tender silent affection, with which the princess and her daughter regarded each other, melted him almost to tears. Yet apprehensive that his forbearance to obey would be more alarming, he repeated in a faltering and low voice the following lines:

> Where'er a casque that suits this sword is found,
> With perils is thy daughter compass'd round:
> Alfonso's blood alone can save the maid,
> And quiet a long-restless prince's shade.

What is there in these lines, said Theodore impatiently, that affects these princesses? Why were they to be shocked by a mysterious delicacy, that has so little foundation? Your words are rude, young man, said the marquis; and though fortune has favoured you once—My honoured lord, said Isabella, who resented Theodore's warmth, which she perceived was dictated by his sentiments for Matilda, discompose not yourself for the glosing of a peasant's son: he forgets the reverence he owes you; but he is not accustomed—Hippolita, concerned at the heat that had arisen, checked Theodore for his boldness, but with an air acknowledging his zeal; and, changing the conversation, demanded of Frederic where he had left her lord? As the marquis was going to reply, they heard a noise without; and rising to enquire the cause, Manfred, Jerome, and part of the troop, who had met an imperfect rumour of what had happened, entered the chamber. Manfred advanced hastily towards Frederic's bed to condole with him on his misfortune, and to learn the circumstances of the combat; when starting in an agony of terror and amazement, he cried, Ha! what art thou, thou dreadful spectre! Is my hour come?—My dearest, gracious lord, cried Hippolita, clasping him in her arms, what is it you see? Why do you fix your eye-balls thus?—What! cried Manfred breathless—dost thou see nothing. Hippolita? Is this ghastly phantom sent to me alone—to me, who did not——For mercy's sweetest self, my lord, said Hippolita, resume your soul, command your reason. There is none here but we, your friends.—What, is not that Alfonso? cried Manfred: dost thou not see him? Can it be my brain's delirium?—This! my lord, said Hippolita: this is Theodore, the youth who has been so unfortunate—Theodore! said Manfred mournfully, and striking his forehead—Theodore, or a phantom, he has unhinged the soul of Manfred.—But how comes he here? and how comes he in armour? I believe he went in search of Isabella, said Hippolita. Of Isabella? said Manfred, relapsing into rage—Yes, yes, that is not doubtful—But how did he escape from durance in which I left him? Was it Isabella, or this hypocritical old friar, that procured his enlargement?—And would a parent be criminal, my lord, said Theodore, if he meditated the deliverance of his child? Jerome, amazed to hear himself in a manner accused by his son, and without foundation, knew not what to think. He could not comprehend how Theodore had escaped, how he came to be armed, and to encounter Frederic. Still he would not venture to ask any questions that might tend to inflame Manfred's wrath against his son. Jerome's silence convinced Manfred that he had contrived Theodore's release.—And is it thus, thou ungrateful old man, said the prince, addressing himself to the friar, that thou repayest mine and Hippolita's bounties? And not content with traversing my heart's nearest wishes, thou armest thy bastard, and bringest him into my own castle to insult me!—My lord, said Theodore, you wrong my father, nor he nor I is capable of harbouring a thought against your peace. Is it insolence thus to surrender myself to your highness's pleasure? added he, laying his sword respectfully at Manfred's feet. Behold my bosom; strike, my lord, if you suspect that a disloyal thought is lodged there. There is not a sentiment engraven on my heart, that does not venerate you and yours. The grace and fervour with which Theodore uttered these words, interested every person present in his favour. Even Manfred was touched—yet still possessed with his resemblance to Alfonso, his admiration was dashed with secret horror. Rise, said he; thy life is not my present purpose.—But tell me thy history, and how thou camest connected with this old traitor here. My lord! said Jerome eagerly.—Peace, impostor! said Manfred; I will not have him prompted. My lord, said Theodore, I want no assistance; my story is very brief. I was carried at five years of age to Algiers with my mother, who had been taken by corsairs from the coast of Sicily. She died of grief in less than a twelvemonth.—The tears gushed from Jerome's eyes, on whose countenance a thousand anxious passions stood expressed. Before she died, continued Theodore, she bound a writing about my arm under my garments, which told me I was the son of the count Falconara.—It is most true, said Jerome; I am that wretched father.—Again I enjoin thee silence, said Manfred: proceed. I remained in slavery, said Theodore, until within these two years, when attending on my master in his cruizes, I was delivered by a christian vessel, which overpowered the pirate; and discovering myself to the captain, he generously put me on shore in Sicily. But alas! instead of finding a father, I learned that his estate, which was situated on the coast, had during his absence been laid waste by the rover who had carried my mother and me into captivity: that his castle had been burnt to the ground: and that my father on his return had sold what remained, and was retired into religion in the kingdom of Naples, but where, no man could inform me. Destitute and friendless, hopeless almost of attaining the transport of a parent's embrace, I took the first opportunity of setting sail for Naples; from whence within these six days I wandered into this province, still supporting myself by the labour of my hands; nor till yester-morn did I believe that heaven had reserved any lot for me but peace of mind and contented poverty. This, my lord, is Theodore's story. I am blessed beyond my hope in finding a father; I am unfortunate beyond my desert in having incurred your highness's displeasure. He ceased. A murmur of approbation gently arose from the audience. This is not all, said Frederic; I am bound in honour to add what he suppresses. Though he is modest, I must be generous—he is one of the bravest youths on christian ground. He is warm too; and from the short knowledge I have of him, I will pledge myself for his veracity: if what he reports of himself were not true, he would not utter it—and for me, youth, I honour a frankness which becomes thy birth. But now, and thou didst offend me; yet the noble blood which flows in thy veins may well be allowed to boil out, when it has so recently traced itself to its source. Come, my lord, [turning to Manfred] if I can pardon him, surely you may: it is not the youth's fault, if you took him for a spectre. This bitter taunt galled the soul of Manfred. If beings from another world, replied he haughtily, have power to impress my mind with awe, it is more than living man can do; nor could a stripling's arm——My lord, interrupted Hippolita, your guest has occasion for repose; shall we not leave him to his rest? Saying this, and taking Manfred by the hand, she took leave of Frederic, and led the company forth. The prince, not sorry to quit a conversation which recalled to mind the discovery he had made of his most secret sensations, suffered himself to be conducted to his own apartment, after permitting Theodore, though under engagement to return to the castle on the morrow, [a condition the young man gladly accepted] to retire with his father to the convent. Matilda and Isabella were too much occupied with their own reflections, and too little content with each other, to wish for farther converse that night. They separated each to her chamber, with more expressions of ceremony, and fewer of affection, than had passed between them since their childhood.

If they parted with small cordiality, they did but meet with greater impatience as soon as the sun was risen. Their minds were in a situation that excluded sleep, and each recollected a thousand questions which she wished she had put to the other overnight. Matilda reflected that Isabella had been twice delivered by Theodore in very critical situations, which she could not believe accidental. His eyes, it was true, had been fixed on her in Frederic's chamber; but that might have been to disguise his passion for Isabella from the fathers of both. It were better to clear this up. She wished to know the truth, lest she should wrong her friend by entertaining a passion for Isabella's lover. Thus jealousy prompted, and at the same time borrowed an excuse from friendship to justify its curiosity.

Isabella, not less restless, had better foundation for her suspicions. Both Theodore's tongue and eyes had told her his heart was engaged, it was true—yet perhaps Matilda might not correspond to his passion—She had ever appeared insensible to love; all her thoughts were set on heaven—Why did I dissuade her? said Isabella to herself; I am punished for my generosity—But when did they meet? where?—It cannot be; I have deceived myself.—Perhaps last night was the first time they ever beheld each other—it must be some other object that has prepossessed his affections—If it is, I am not so unhappy as I thought; if it is not my friend Matilda—How! can I stoop to wish for the affection of a man, who rudely and unnecessarily acquainted me with his indifference? and that at the very moment in which common courtesy demanded at least expressions of civility. I will go to my dear Matilda, who will confirm me in this becoming pride—Man is false—I will advise with her on taking the veil: she will rejoice to find me in this disposition; and I will acquaint her that I no longer oppose her inclination for the cloister. In this frame of mind, and determined to open her heart entirely to Matilda, she went to that princess's chamber, whom she found already dressed, and leaning pensively on her arm. This attitude, so correspondent to what she felt herself, revived Isabella's suspicions, and destroyed the confidence she had purposed to place in her friend. They blushed at meeting, and were too much novices to disguise their sensations with address. After some unmeaning questions and replies, Matilda demanded of Isabella the cause of her flight. The latter, who had almost forgotten Manfred's passion, so entirely was she occupied by her own, concluding that Matilda referred to her last escape from the convent, which had occasioned the events of the preceding evening, replied, Martelli brought word to the convent that your mother was dead.—Oh! said Matilda interrupting her, Bianca has explained that mistake to me: on seeing me faint, she cried out, The princess is dead! and Martelli, who had come for the usual dole to the castle——And what made you faint? said Isabella, indifferent to the rest. Matilda blushed, and stammered—My father—he was sitting in judgment on a criminal.—What criminal? said Isabella eagerly.——A young man, said Matilda—I believe—I think it was that young man that—What, Theodore? said Isabella—Yes, answered she; I never saw him before; I do not know how he had offended my father—but, as he has been of service to you, I am glad my lord has pardoned him. Served me? replied Isabella: do you term it serving me, to wound my father, and almost occasion his death? Though it is but since yesterday that I am blessed with knowing a parent, I hope Matilda does not think I am such a stranger to filial tenderness as not to resent the boldness of that audacious youth, and that it is impossible for me ever to feel any affection for one who dared to lift his arm against the author of my being. No, Matilda, my heart abhors him; and if you still retain the friendship for me that you have vowed from your infancy, you will detest a man who has been on the point of making me miserable for ever. Matilda held down her head, and replied, I hope my dearest Isabella does not doubt her Matilda's friendship: I never beheld that youth until yesterday; he is almost a stranger to me: but as the surgeons have pronounced your father out of danger, you ought not to harbour uncharitable resentment against one who I am persuaded did not know the marquis was related to you. You plead his cause very pathetically, said Isabella, considering he is so much a stranger to you! I am mistaken, or he returns your charity. What mean you? said Matilda. Nothing, said Isabella; repenting that she had given Matilda a hint of Theodore's inclination for her. Then changing the discourse, she asked Matilda what occasioned Manfred to take Theodore for a spectre? Bless me, said Matilda, did not you observe his extreme resemblance to the portrait of Alfonso in the gallery? I took notice of it to Bianca even before I saw him in armour; but with the helmet on, he is the very image of that picture. I do not much observe pictures, said Isabella; much less have I examined this young man so attentively as you seem to have done.——Ah! Matilda, your heart is in danger——but let me warn you as a friend——He has owned to me that he is in love: it cannot be with you, for yesterday was the first time you ever met——was it not? Certainly, replied Matilda. But why does my dearest Isabella conclude from any thing I have said, that——She paused——then continuing, He saw you first, and I am far from having the vanity to think that my little portion of charms could engage a heart devoted to you. May you be happy, Isabella, whatever is the fate of Matilda!——My lovely friend, said Isabella, whose heart was too honest to resist a kind expression, it is you that Theodore admires; I saw it; I am persuaded of it; nor shall a thought of my own happiness suffer me to interfere with yours. This frankness drew tears from the gentle Matilda; and jealousy, that for a moment had raised a coolness between these amiable maidens, soon gave way to the natural sincerity and candour of their souls. Each confessed to the other the impression that Theodore had made on her; and this confidence was followed by a struggle of generosity, each insisting on yielding her claim to her friend. At length, the dignity of Isabella's virtue reminding her of the preference which Theodore had almost declared for her rival, made her determine to conquer her passion, and cede the beloved object to her friend.

During this contest of amity, Hippolita entered her daughter's chamber. Madam, said she to Isabella, you have so much tenderness for Matilda, and interest yourself so kindly in whatever affects our wretched house, that I can have no secrets with my child, which are not proper for you to hear. The princesses were all attention and anxiety. Know then, madam, continued Hippolita, and you, my dearest Matilda, that being convinced by all the events of these two last ominous days, that heaven purposes the sceptre of Otranto should pass from Manfred's hands into those of the marquis Frederic, I have been perhaps inspired with the thought of averting our total destruction by the union of our rival houses. With this view I have been proposing to Manfred my lord to tender this dear dear child to Frederic your father—Me to lord Frederic! cried Matilda—Good heavens! my gracious mother—and have you named it to my father? I have, said Hippolita: he listened benignly to my proposal, and is gone to break it to the marquis. Ah! wretched princess! cried Isabella, what hast thou done? What ruin has thy inadvertent goodness been preparing for thyself, for me, and for Matilda! Ruin from me to you and to my child! said Hippolita: What can this mean? Alas! said Isabella, the purity of your own heart prevents your seeing the depravity of others. Manfred, your lord, that impious man——Hold, said Hippolita; you must not in my presence, young lady, mention Manfred with disrespect: he is my lord and husband, and—Will not be long so, said Isabella, if his wicked purposes can be carried into execution. This language amazes me, said Hippolita. Your feeling, Isabella, is warm; but until this hour I never knew it betray you into intemperance. What deed of Manfred authorizes you to treat him as a murderer, an assassin? Thou virtuous and too credulous princess! replied Isabella; it is not thy life he aims at—it is to separate himself from thee! to divorce thee! To—to divorce me! To divorce my mother! cried Hippolita and Matilda at once.—Yes, said Isabella; and to complete his crime, he meditates—I cannot speak it! What can surpass what thou hast already uttered? said Matilda. Hippolita was silent. Grief choked her speech: and the recollection of Manfred's late ambiguous discourses confirmed what she heard. Excellent, dear lady! madam! mother! cried Isabella, flinging herself at Hippolita's feet in a transport of passion; trust me, believe me, I will die a thousand deaths sooner than consent to injure you, than yield to so odious—oh!—This is too much! cried Hippolita: what crimes does one crime suggest! Rise, dear Isabella; I do not doubt your virtue. Oh! Matilda, this stroke is too heavy for thee! Weep not, my child; and not a murmur, I charge thee. Remember, he is *thy* father still.—But you are my mother too, said Matilda fervently; and *you* are virtuous, *you* are guiltless!—Oh! must not I, must not I complain? You must not, said Hippolita—Come, all will yet be well. Manfred, in the agony for the loss of thy brother, knew not what he said: perhaps Isabella misunderstood him: his heart is good—and, my child, thou knowest not all. There is a destiny hangs over us; the hand of Providence is stretched out—Oh! could I but save thee from the wreck!—Yes, continued she in a firmer tone, perhaps the sacrifice of myself may atone for all——I will go and offer myself to this divorce—it boots not what becomes of me. I will withdraw into the neighbouring monastery, and waste the remainder of life in prayers and tears for my child and—the prince! Thou art as much too good for this world, said Isabella, as Manfred is execrable—But think not, lady, that thy weakness shall determine for me. I swear—hear me, all ye angels——Stop, I adjure thee, cried Hippolita; remember, thou dost not depend on thyself; thou hast a father.—My father is too pious, too noble, interrupted Isabella, to command an impious deed. But should he command it, can a father enjoin a cursed act? I was contracted to the son; can I wed the father?—No, madam, no; force should not drag me to Manfred's hated bed. I loathe him, I abhor him: divine and human laws forbid.—And my friend, my dearest Matilda! would I wound her tender soul by injuring her adored mother? my own mother—I never have known another.——Oh! she is the mother of both! cried Matilda. Can we, can we, Isabella, adore her too much? My lovely children, said the touched Hippolita, your tenderness overpowers me—but I must not give way to it. It is not ours to make election for ourselves; heaven, our fathers, and our husbands, must decide for us. Have patience until you hear what Manfred and Frederic have determined. If the marquis accepts Matilda's hand, I know she will readily obey. Heaven may interpose and prevent the rest. What means my child? continued she, seeing Matilda fall at her feet with a flood of speechless tears—But no; answer me not, my daughter; I must not hear a word against the pleasure of thy father. Oh! doubt not my obedience, my dreadful obedience to him and to you! said Matilda. But can I, most respected of women, can I experience all this tenderness, this world of goodness, and conceal a thought from the best of mothers? What art thou going to utter? said Isabella trembling. Recollect thyself, Matilda. No, Isabella, said the princess, I should not deserve this incomparable parent, if the inmost recesses of my soul harboured a thought without her permission—Nay, I have offended her; I have suffered a passion to enter my heart without her avowal—But here I disclaim it; here I vow to heaven and her——My child! my child! said Hippolita, what words are these? What new calamities has fate in store for us? Thou, a passion! thou, in this hour of destruction——Oh! I see all my guilt! said Matilda. I abhor myself, if I cost my mother a pang. She is the dearest thing I have on earth—Oh! I will never, never behold him more! Isabella, said Hippolita, thou art conscious to this unhappy secret, whatever it is. Speak—What! cried Matilda, have I so forfeited my mother's love that she will not permit me even to speak my own guilt? Oh! wretched, wretched Matilda!—Thou art too cruel, said Isabella to Hippolita: canst thou behold this anguish of a virtuous mind, and not commiserate it? Not pity my child! said Hippolita, catching Matilda in her arms—Oh! I know she is good, she is all virtue, all tenderness, and duty. I do forgive thee, my excellent, my only hope! The princesses then revealed to Hippolita their mutual inclination for Theodore, and the purpose of Isabella to resign him to Matilda. Hippolita blamed their imprudence, and shewed them the improbability that either father would consent to bestow his heiress on so poor a man, though nobly born. Some comfort it gave her to find their passion of so recent a date, and that Theodore had but little cause to suspect it in either. She strictly enjoined them to avoid all correspondence with him. This Matilda fervently promised: but Isabella, who flattered herself that she meant no more than to promote his union with her friend, could not determine to avoid him; and made no reply. I will go to the convent, said Hippolita, and order new masses to be said for a deliverance from these calamities.—Oh! my mother, said Matilda, you mean to quit us: you mean to take sanctuary, and to give my father an opportunity of pursuing his fatal intention. Alas! on my knees I supplicate you to forbear—Will you leave me a prey to Frederic? I will follow you to the convent.—Be at peace, my child, said Hippolita: I will return instantly. I will never abandon thee, until I know it is the will of heaven, and for thy benefit. Do not deceive me, said Matilda. I will not marry Frederic until thou commandest it. Alas! what will become of me!—Why that exclamation! said Hippolita. I have promised thee to return.—Ah! my mother, replied Matilda, stay and save me from myself. A frown from thee can do more than all my father's severity. I have given away my heart, and you alone can make me recall it. No more, said Hippolita: thou must not relapse, Matilda. I can quit Theodore, said she, but must I wed another? Let me attend thee to the altar, and shut myself from the world forever. Thy fate depends on thy father, said Hippolita: I have ill bestowed my tenderness, if it has taught thee to revere aught beyond him. Adieu, my child! I go to pray for thee.

Hippolita's real purpose was to demand of Jerome, whether in conscience she might not consent to the divorce. She had oft urged Manfred to resign the principality, which the delicacy of her conscience rendered an hourly burthen to her. These scruples concurred to make the separation from her husband appear less dreadful to her than it would have seemed in any other situation.

Jerome, at quitting the castle overnight, had questioned Theodore severely why he had accused him to Manfred of being privy to his escape. Theodore owned it had been with design to prevent Manfred's suspicion from alighting on Matilda; and added, the holiness of Jerome's life and character secured him from the tyrant's wrath. Jerome was heartily grieved to discover his son's inclination for that princess; and, leaving him to his rest, promised in the morning to acquaint him with important reasons for conquering his passion. Theodore, like Isabella, was too recently acquainted with parental authority to submit to its decisions against the impulse of his heart. He had little curiosity to learn the friar's reasons, and less disposition to obey them. The lovely Matilda had made stronger impressions on him than filial affection. All night he pleased himself with visions of love; and it was not till late after the morning-office, that he recollected the friar's commands to attend him at Alfonso's tomb.

Young man, said Jerome, when he saw him, this tardiness does not please me. Have a father's commands already so little weight? Theodore made awkward excuses, and attributed his delay to having overslept himself. And on whom were thy dreams employed? said the friar sternly. His son blushed. Come, come, resumed the friar, inconsiderate youth, this must not be; eradicate this guilty passion from thy breast.—Guilty passion! cried Theodore: can guilt dwell with innocent beauty and virtuous modesty? It is sinful, replied the friar, to cherish those whom heaven has doomed to destruction. A tyrant's race must be swept from the earth to the third and fourth generation. Will heaven visit the innocent for the crimes of the guilty? said Theodore. The fair Matilda has virtues enough—To undo thee, interrupted Jerome. Hast thou so soon forgotten that twice the savage Manfred has pronounced thy sentence? Nor have I forgotten, sir, said Theodore, that the charity of his daughter delivered me from his power. I can forget injuries, but never benefits. The injuries thou hast received from Manfred's race, said the friar, are beyond what thou canst conceive.—Reply not, but view this holy image! Beneath this marble monument rest the ashes of the good Alfonso; a prince adorned with every virtue: the father of his people! the delight of mankind! Kneel, headstrong boy, and list, while a father unfolds a tale of horror, that will expel every sentiment from thy soul, but sensations of sacred vengeance.—Alfonso! much-injured prince! let thy unsatisfied shade sit awful on the troubled air, while these trembling lips—Ha! who comes there?—The most wretched of women, said Hippolita, entering the choir. Good father, art thou at leisure?—But why this kneeling youth? what means the horror imprinted on each countenance? why at this venerable tomb—Alas! hast thou seen aught? We were pouring forth our orisons to heaven, replied the friar with some confusion, to put an end to the woes of this deplorable province. Join with us, lady! thy spotless soul may obtain an exemption from the judgments which the portents of these days but too speakingly denounce against thy house. I pray fervently to heaven to divert them, said the pious princess. Thou knowest it has been the occupation of my life to wrest a blessing for my lord and my harmless children—One, alas! is taken from me! Would heaven but hear me for my poor Matilda! Father, intercede for her!—Every heart will bless her, cried Theodore with rapture.—Be dumb, rash youth! said Jerome. And thou, fond princess, contend not with the powers above! The Lord giveth, and the Lord taketh away: bless his holy name, and submit to his decrees. I do most devoutly, said Hippolita: but will he not spare my only comfort? must Matilda perish too?—Ah! father, I came—But dismiss thy son. No ear but thine must hear what I have to utter. May heaven grant thy every wish, most excellent princess! said Theodore retiring. Jerome frowned.

Hippolita then acquainted the friar with the proposal she had suggested to Manfred, his approbation of it, and the tender of Matilda that he was gone to make to Frederic. Jerome could not conceal his dislike of the motion, which he covered under pretence of the improbability that Frederic, the nearest of blood to Alfonso, and who was come to claim his succession, would yield to an alliance with the usurper of his right. But nothing could equal the perplexity of the friar, when Hippolita confessed her readiness not to oppose the separation, and demanded his opinion on the legality of her acquiescence. The friar catched eagerly at her request of his advice; and without explaining his aversion to the proposed marriage of Manfred and Isabella, he painted to Hippolita in the most alarming colours the sinfulness of her consent, denounced judgments against her if she complied, and enjoined her in the severest terms to treat any such proposition with every mark of indignation and refusal.

Manfred, in the mean time, had broken his purpose to Frederic, and proposed the double marriage. That weak prince, who had been struck with the charms of Matilda, listened but too eagerly to the offer. He forgot his enmity to Manfred, whom he saw but little hope of dispossessing by force; and flattering himself that no issue might succeed from the union of his daughter with the tyrant, he looked upon his own succession to the principality as facilitated by wedding Matilda. He made faint opposition to the proposal; affecting, for form only, not to acquiesce unless Hippolita should consent to the divorce. Manfred took that upon himself. Transported with his success, and impatient to see himself in a situation to expect sons, he hastened to his wife's apartment, determined to extort her compliance. He learned with indignation that she was absent at the convent. His guilt suggested to him that she had probably been informed by Isabella of his purpose. He doubted whether her retirement to the convent did not import an intention of remaining there, until she could raise obstacles to their divorce; and the suspicions he had already entertained of Jerome, made him apprehend that the friar would not only traverse his views, but might have inspired Hippolita with the resolution of taking sanctuary. Impatient to unravel this clue, and to defeat its success, Manfred hastened to the convent, and arrived there as the friar was earnestly exhorting the princess never to yield to the divorce.

Madam, said Manfred, what business drew you hither? Why did not you await my return from the marquis? I came to implore a blessing on your councils, replied Hippolita. My councils do not need a friar's intervention, said Manfred—and of all men living is that hoary traitor the only one whom you delight to confer with? Profane prince! said Jerome: is it at the altar that thou choosest to insult the servants of the altar?—But, Manfred, thy impious schemes are known. Heaven and this virtuous lady know them. Nay, frown not, prince. The church despises thy menaces. Her thunders will be heard above thy wrath. Dare to proceed in thy curst purpose of a divorce, until her sentence be known, and here I lance her anathema at thy head. Audacious rebel! said Manfred, endeavouring to conceal the awe with which the friar's words inspired him; dost thou presume to threaten thy lawful prince? Thou art no lawful prince, said Jerome; thou art no prince—Go, discuss thy claim with Frederic, and when that is done—It is done, replied Manfred: Frederic accepts Matilda's hand, and is content to wave his claim, unless I have no male issue.—As he spoke those words three drops of blood fell from the nose of Alfonso's statue. Manfred turned pale, and the princess sunk on her knees. Behold! said the friar: mark this miraculous indication that the blood of Alfonso will never mix with that of Manfred! My gracious lord, said Hippolita, let us submit ourselves to heaven. Think not thy ever obedient wife rebels against thy authority. I have no will but that of my lord and the church. To that revered tribunal let us appeal. It does not depend on us to burst the bonds that unite us. If the church shall approve the dissolution of our marriage, be it so—I have but few years, and those of sorrow, to pass. Where can they be worn away so well as at the foot of this altar, in prayers for thine and Matilda's safety?—But thou shalt not remain here until then, said Manfred. Repair with me to the castle, and there I will advise on the proper measures for a divorce.—But this meddling friar comes not thither; my hospitable roof shall never more harbour a traitor—and for thy reverence's offspring, continued he, I banish him from my dominions. He, I ween, is no sacred personage, nor under the protection of the church. Whoever weds Isabella, it shall not be father Falconara's started-up son. They start up, said the friar, who are suddenly beheld in the seat of lawful princes; but they wither away like the grass, and their place knows them no more. Manfred, casting a look of scorn at the friar, led Hippolita forth; but at the door of the church whispered one of his attendants to remain concealed about the convent, and bring him instant notice, if any one from the castle should repair thither.

CHAPTER V

EVERY reflection which Manfred made on the friar's behaviour, conspired to persuade him that Jerome was privy to an amour between Isabella and Theodore. But Jerome's new presumption, so dissonant from his former meekness, suggested still deeper apprehensions. The prince even suspected that the friar depended on some secret support from Frederic, whose arrival coinciding with the novel appearance of Theodore seemed to bespeak a correspondence. Still more was he troubled with the resemblance of Theodore to Alfonso's portrait. The latter he knew had unquestionably died without issue. Frederic had consented to bestow Isabella on him. These contradictions agitated his mind with numberless pangs. He saw but two methods of extricating himself from his difficulties. The one was to resign his dominions to the marquis.—Pride, ambition, and his reliance on ancient prophecies, which had pointed out a possibility of his preserving them to his posterity, combated that thought. The other was to press his marriage with Isabella. After long ruminating on these anxious thoughts, as he marched silently with Hippolita to the castle, he at last discoursed with that princess on the subject of his disquiet, and used every insinuating and plausible argument to extract her consent to, even her promise of promoting, the divorce. Hippolita needed little persuasion to bend her to his pleasure. She endeavoured to win him over to the measure of resigning his dominions; but finding her exhortations fruitless, she assured him, that as far as her conscience would allow, she would raise no opposition to a separation, though, without better founded scruples than what he yet alleged, she would not engage to be active in demanding it.

This compliance, though inadequate, was sufficient to raise Manfred's hopes. He trusted that his power and wealth would easily advance his suit at the court of Rome, whither he resolved to engage Frederic to take a journey on purpose. That prince had discovered so much passion for Matilda, that Manfred hoped to obtain all he wished by holding out or withdrawing his daughter's charms, according as the marquis should appear more or less disposed to co-operate in his views. Even the absence of Frederic would be a material point gained, until he could take farther measures for his security.

Dismissing Hippolita to her apartment, he repaired to that of the marquis; but crossing the great hall through which he was to pass, he met Bianca. That damsel he knew was in the confidence of both the young ladies. It immediately occurred to him to sift her on the subject of Isabella and Theodore. Calling her aside into the recess of the oriel window of the hall, and soothing her with many fair words and promises, he demanded of her whether she knew aught of the state of Isabella's affections. I! my lord? No, my lord—Yes, my lord—Poor lady! she is wonderfully alarmed about her father's wounds; but I tell her he will do well; don't your highness think so? I do not ask you, replied Manfred, what she thinks about her father: but you are in her secrets: come, be a good girl and tell me, is there any young man—ha?—you understand me. Lord bless me! understand your highness? No, not I: I told her a few vulnerary herbs and repose——I am not talking, replied the prince impatiently, about her father: I know he will do well. Bless me, I rejoice to hear your highness say so; for though I thought it right not to let my young lady despond, methought his greatness had a wan look, and a something—I remember when young Ferdinand was wounded by the Venetian. Thou answerest from the point, interrupted Manfred; but here, take this jewel, perhaps that may fix thy attention—Nay, no reverences; my favour shall not stop here—Come, tell me truly; how stands Isabella's heart? Well, your highness has such a way, said Bianca—to be sure—but can your highness keep a secret? If it should ever come out of your lips——It shall not, it shall not, cried Manfred. Nay, but swear, your highness—by my halidame, if it should ever be known that I said it—Why, truth is truth, I do not think my lady Isabella ever much affectioned my young lord, your son: yet he was a sweet youth as one should see. I am sure if I had been a princess—But bless me! I must attend my lady Matilda; she will marvel what is become of me.—Stay, cried Manfred, thou hast not satisfied my question. Hast thou ever carried any message, any letter?—I! Good gracious! cried Bianca: I carry a letter? I would not to be a queen. I hope your highness thinks, though I am poor, I am honest. Did your highness never hear what count Marsigli offered me, when he came a-wooing to my lady Matilda?—I have not leisure, said Manfred, to listen to thy tales. I do not question thy honesty; but it is thy duty to conceal nothing from me. How long has Isabella been acquainted with Theodore?—Nay, there is nothing can escape your highness, said Bianca—not that I know any thing of the matter. Theodore, to be sure, is a proper young man, and, as my lady Matilda says, the very image of good Alfonso: Has not your highness remarked it? Yes, yes—No—thou torturest me, said Manfred: Where did they meet? when?— Who, my lady Matilda? said Bianca. No, no, not Matilda; Isabella: When did Isabella first become acquainted with this Theodore?—Virgin Mary! said Bianca, how should I know? Thou dost know, said Manfred; and I must know; I will.—Lord! your highness is not jealous of young Theodore? said Bianca.—Jealous! No, no: why should I be jealous?—Perhaps I mean to unite them—if I was sure Isabella would have no repugnance.—Repugnance! No, I'll warrant her, said Bianca: he is as comely a youth as ever trod on christian ground: we are all in love with him: there is not a soul in the castle but would be rejoiced to have him for our prince—I mean, when it shall please heaven to call your highness to itself.—Indeed! said Manfred: has it gone so far? Oh! this cursed friar!—But I must not lose time—Go, Bianca, attend Isabella; but I charge thee, not a word of what has passed. Find out how she is affected towards Theodore; bring me good news, and that ring has a companion. Wait at the foot of the winding staircase: I am going to visit the marquis, and will talk farther with thee at my return.

Manfred, after some general conversation, desired Frederic to dismiss the two knights his companions, having to talk with him on urgent affairs. As soon as they were alone, he began in artful guise to sound the marquis on the subject of Matilda; and finding him disposed to his wish, he let drop hints on the difficulties that would attend the celebration of their marriage, unless——At that instant Bianca burst into the room, with a wildness in her look and gestures that spoke the utmost terror. Oh! my lord, my lord! cried she, we are all undone! It is come again! it is come again!—What is come again? cried Manfred amazed.—Oh! the hand! the giant! the hand!—Support me! I am terrified out of my senses, cried Bianca: I will not sleep in the castle to-night. Where shall I go? My things may come after me to-morrow.—Would I had been content to wed Francesco! This comes of ambition!—What has terrified thee thus, young woman? said the marquis: thou art safe here; be not alarmed. Oh! your greatness is wonderfully good, said Bianca, but I dare not—No, pray let me go—I had rather leave every thing behind me, than stay another hour under this roof. Go to, thou hast lost thy senses, said Manfred. Interrupt us not; we were communing on important matters.—My lord, this wench is subject to fits—Come with me, Bianca.— Oh! the saints! No, said Bianca—for certain it comes to warn your highness; why should it appear to me else! I say my prayers morning and evening— Oh! if your highness had believed Diego! 'Tis the same hand that he saw the foot to in the gallery-chamber—Father Jerome has often told us the prophecy would be out one of these days—Bianca, said he, mark my words.—Thou ravest, said Manfred in a rage: Begone, and keep these fooleries to frighten thy companions.—What! my lord, cried Bianca, do you think I have seen nothing? Go to the foot of the great stairs yourself—As I live I saw it. Saw what? Tell us fair maid, what thou hast seen, said Frederic. Can your highness listen, said Manfred, to the delirium of a silly wench, who has heard stories of apparitions until she believes them? This is more than fancy, said the marquis; her terror is too natural and too strongly impressed to be the work of imagination. Tell us, fair maiden, what it is has moved thee thus. Yes, my lord, thank your greatness, said Bianca—I believe I look very pale; I shall be better when I have recovered myself.—I was going to my lady Isabella's chamber by his highness's order—We do not want the circumstances, interrupted Manfred: since his highness will have it so, proceed; but be brief.—Lord, your highness thwarts one so! replied Bianca—I fear my hair—I am sure I never in my life—Well! as I was telling your greatness, I was going by his highness's order to my lady Isabella's chamber: she lies in the watchet-coloured chamber, on the right hand, one pair of stairs: so when I came to the great stairs—I was looking on his highness's present here. Grant me patience! said Manfred, will this wench never come to the point? What imports it to the marquis, that I gave thee a bawble for thy faithful attendance on my daughter? We want to know what thou sawest. I was going to tell your highness, said Bianca, if you would permit me.—So, as I was rubbing the ring—I am sure I had not gone up three steps, but I heard the rattling of armour; for all the world such a clatter, as Diego says he heard when the giant turned him about in the gallery-chamber.—What does she mean, my lord? said the marquis. Is your castle haunted by giants and goblins?—Lord, what, has not your greatness heard the story of the giant in the gallery-chamber? cried Bianca. I marvel his highness has not told you—mayhap you do not know there is a prophecy—This trifling is intolerable, interrupted Manfred. Let us dismiss this silly wench, my lord: we have more important affairs to discuss. By your favour, said Frederic, these are no trifles: the enormous sabre I was directed to in the wood; yon casque, its fellow—are these visions of this poor maiden's brain?—So Jaquez thinks, may it please your greatness, said Bianca. He says this moon will not be out without our seeing some strange revolution. For my part, I should not be surprised if it was to happen to-morrow; for, as I was saying, when I heard the clattering of armour, I was all in a cold sweat—I looked up, and, if your greatness will believe me, I saw upon the uppermost banister of the great stairs a hand in armour as big, as big—I thought I should have swooned—I never stopped until I came hither—Would I were well out of this castle! My lady Matilda told me but yester-morning that her highness Hippolita knows something—Thou art an insolent! cried Manfred—Lord marquis, it much misgives me that this scene is concerted to affront me. Are my own domestics suborned to spread tales injurious to my honour? Pursue your claim by manly daring; or let us bury our feuds, as was proposed, by the intermarriage of our children: but trust me, it ill becomes a prince of your bearing to practise on mercenary wenches.—I scorn your imputation, said Frederic; until this hour I never set eyes on this damsel: I have given her no jewel!—My lord, my lord, your conscience, your guilt accuses you, and would throw the suspicion on me—But keep your daughter, and think no more of Isabella: the judgments already fallen on your house forbid me matching into it.

Manfred, alarmed at the resolute tone in which Frederic delivered these words, endeavoured to pacify him. Dismissing Bianca, he made such submissions to the marquis, and threw in such artful encomiums on Matilda, that Frederic was once more staggered. However, as his passion was of so recent a date, it could not at once surmount the scruples he had conceived. He had gathered enough from Bianca's discourse to persuade him that heaven declared itself against Manfred. The proposed marriages too removed his claim to a distance: and the principality of Otranto was a stronger temptation, than the contingent reversion of it with Matilda. Still he would not absolutely recede from his engagements; but purposing to gain time, he demanded of Manfred if it was true in fact that Hippolita consented to the divorce. The prince, transported to find no other obstacle, and depending on his influence over his wife, assured the marquis it was so, and that he might satisfy himself of the truth from her own mouth.

As they were thus discoursing, word was brought that the banquet was prepared. Manfred conducted Frederic to the great hall, where they were received by Hippolita and the young princesses. Manfred placed the marquis next to Matilda, and seated himself between his wife and Isabella. Hippolita comported herself with an easy gravity; but the young ladies were silent and melancholy. Manfred, who was determined to pursue his point with the marquis in the remainder of the evening, pushed on the feast until it waxed late; affecting unrestrained gaiety, and plying Frederic with repeated goblets of wine. The latter, more upon his guard than Manfred wished, declined his frequent challenges, on pretence of his late loss of blood; while the prince, to raise his own disordered spirits, and to counterfeit unconcern, indulged himself in plentiful draughts, though not to the intoxication of his senses.

The evening being far advanced, the banquet concluded. Manfred would have withdrawn with Frederic; but the latter, pleading weakness and want of repose, retired to his chamber, gallantly telling the prince, that his daughter should amuse his highness until himself could attend him. Manfred accepted the party; and, to the no small grief of Isabella, accompanied her to her apartment. Matilda waited on her mother, to enjoy the freshness of the evening on the ramparts of the castle.

Soon as the company was dispersed their several ways, Frederic, quitting his chamber, enquired if Hippolita was alone; and was told by one of her attendants, who had not noticed her going forth, that at that hour she generally withdrew to her oratory, where he probably would find her. The marquis during the repast had beheld Matilda with increase of passion. He now wished to find Hippolita in the disposition her lord had promised. The portents that had alarmed him were forgotten in his desires. Stealing softly and unobserved to the apartment of Hippolita, he entered it with a resolution to encourage her acquiescence to the divorce, having perceived that Manfred was resolved to make the possession of Isabella an unalterable condition, before he would grant Matilda to his wishes.

The marquis was not surprised at the silence that reigned in the princess's apartment. Concluding her, as he had been advertised, in her oratory, he passed on. The door was a-jar; the evening gloomy and overcast. Pushing open the door gently, he saw a person kneeling before the altar. As he approached nearer, it seemed not a woman, but one in a long woollen weed, whose back was towards him. The person seemed absorbed in prayer. The marquis was about to return, when the figure rising, stood some moments fixed in meditation, without regarding him. The marquis, expecting the holy person to come forth, and meaning to excuse his uncivil interruption, said, Reverend father, I sought the lady Hippolita.—Hippolita! replied a hollow voice: camest thou to this castle to seek Hippolita?—And then the figure, turning slowly round, discovered to Frederic the fleshless jaws and empty sockets of a skeleton, wrapt in a hermit's cowl. Angels of grace, protect me! cried Frederic recoiling. Deserve their protection, said the spectre. Frederic, falling on his knees, adjured the phantom to take pity on him. Dost thou not remember me? said the apparition. Remember the wood of Joppa! Art thou that holy hermit? cried Frederic trembling—can I do aught for thy eternal peace?—Wast thou delivered from bondage, said the spectre, to pursue carnal delights? Hast thou forgotten the buried sabre, and the behest of heaven engraven on it?—I have not, I have not, said Frederic—But say, blest spirit, what is thy errand to me? what remains to be done? To forget Matilda! said the apparition—and vanished.

Frederic's blood froze in his veins. For some minutes he remained motionless. Then falling prostrate on his face before the altar, he besought the intercession of every saint for pardon. A flood of tears succeeded to this transport; and the image of the beauteous Matilda rushing in spite of him on his thoughts, he lay on the ground in a conflict of penitence and passion. Ere he could recover from this agony of his spirits, the princess Hippolita, with a taper in her hand, entered the oratory alone. Seeing a man without motion on the floor, she gave a shriek, concluding him dead. Her fright brought Frederic to himself. Rising suddenly, his face bedewed with tears, he would have rushed from her presence; but Hippolita, stopping him, conjured him in the most plaintive accents to explain the cause of his disorder, and by what strange chance she had found him there in that posture. Ah! virtuous princess! said the marquis, penetrated with grief—and stopped. For the love of heaven, my lord, said Hippolita, disclose the cause of this transport! What mean these doleful sounds, this alarming exclamation on my name? What woes has heaven still in store for the wretched Hippolita?—Yet silent?—By every pitying angel, I adjure thee, noble prince, continued she, falling at his feet, to disclose the purport of what lies at thy heart—I see thou feelest for me; thou feelest the sharp pangs that thou inflictest—Speak, for pity!—Does aught thou knowest concern my child?—I cannot speak, cried Frederic, bursting from her—Oh! Matilda!

Quitting the princess thus abruptly, he hastened to his own apartment. At the door of it he was accosted by Manfred, who, flushed by wine and love, had come to seek him, and to propose to waste some hours of the night in music and revelling. Frederic, offended at an invitation so dissonant from the mood of his soul, pushed him rudely aside, and, entering his chamber, flung the door intemperately against Manfred, and bolted it inwards. The haughty prince, enraged at this unaccountable behaviour, withdrew in a frame of mind capable of the most fatal excesses. As he crossed the court, he was met by the domestic whom he had planted at the convent as a spy on Jerome and Theodore. This man, almost breathless with the haste he had made, informed his lord, that Theodore and some lady from the castle were at that instant in private conference at the tomb of Alfonso in St Nicholas's church. He had dogged Theodore thither, but the gloominess of the night had prevented his discovering who the woman was.

Manfred, whose spirits were inflamed, and whom Isabella had driven from her on his urging his passion with too little reserve, did not doubt but the inquietude she had expressed had been occasioned by her impatience to meet Theodore. Provoked by this conjecture, and enraged at her father, he hastened secretly to the great church. Gliding softly between the aisles, and guided by an imperfect gleam of moonshine that shone faintly through the illuminated windows, he stole towards the tomb of Alfonso, to which he was directed by indistinct whispers of the persons he sought. The first sounds he could distinguish were—Does it, alas, depend on me? Manfred will never permit our union.—No, this shall prevent it! cried the tyrant, drawing his dagger, and plunging it over her shoulder into the bosom of the person that spoke—Ah me, I am slain! cried Matilda sinking: Good heaven, receive my soul!—Savage, inhuman monster! what hast thou done? cried Theodore, rushing on him, and wrenching his dagger from him.—Stop, stop thy impious hand, cried Matilda; it is my father!—Manfred, waking as from a trance, beat his breast, twisted his hands in his locks, and endeavoured to recover his dagger from Theodore to dispatch himself. Theodore, scarce less distracted, and only mastering the transports of his grief to assist Matilda, had now by his cries drawn some of the monks to his aid. While part of them endeavoured in concert with the afflicted Theodore to stop the blood of the dying princess, the rest prevented Manfred from laying violent hands on himself.

Matilda, resigning herself patiently to her fate, acknowledged with looks of grateful love the zeal of Theodore. Yet oft as her faintness would permit her speech its way, she begged the assistants to comfort her father. Jerome by this time had learnt the fatal news, and reached the church. His looks seemed to reproach Theodore; but turning to Manfred, he said, Now, tyrant! behold the completion of woe fulfilled on thy impious and devoted head! The blood of Alfonso cried to heaven for vengeance; and heaven has permitted its altar to be polluted by assassination, that thou mightest shed thy own blood at the foot of that prince's sepulchre!—Cruel man! cried Matilda, to aggravate the woes of a parent! May heaven bless my father, and forgive him as I do! My lord, my gracious sire, dost thou forgive thy child? Indeed I came not hither to meet Theodore! I found him praying at this tomb, whither my mother sent me to intercede for thee, for her—Dearest father, bless your child, and say you forgive her.—Forgive thee! Murderous monster! cried Manfred—can assassins forgive? I took thee for Isabella; but heaven directed my bloody hand to the heart of my child!—Oh! Matilda—I cannot utter it—canst thou forgive the blindness of my rage?—I can, I do, and may heaven confirm it! said Matilda—But while I have life to ask it—oh, my mother! what will she feel!—Will you comfort her, my lord? Will you not put her away? Indeed she loves you—Oh, I am faint! bear me to the castle—can I live to have her close my eyes?

Theodore and the monks besought her earnestly to suffer herself to be borne into the convent; but her instances were so pressing to be carried to the castle, that, placing her on a litter, they conveyed her thither as she requested. Theodore supporting her head with his arm, and hanging over her in an agony of despairing love, still endeavoured to inspire her with hopes of life. Jerome on the other side comforted her with discourses of heaven, and holding a crucifix before her, which she bathed with innocent tears, prepared her for her passage to immortality. Manfred, plunged in the deepest affliction, followed the litter in despair.

Ere they reached the castle, Hippolita, informed of the dreadful catastrophe, had flown to meet her murdered child; but when she saw the afflicted procession, the mightiness of her grief deprived her of her senses, and she fell lifeless to the earth in a swoon. Isabella and Frederic, who attended her, were overwhelmed in almost equal sorrow. Matilda alone seemed insensible to her own situation: every thought was lost in tenderness for her mother. Ordering the litter to stop, as soon as Hippolita was brought to herself, she asked for her father. He approached, unable to speak. Matilda, seizing his hand and her mother's, locked them in her own, and then clasped them to her heart. Manfred could not support this act of pathetic piety. He dashed himself on the ground, and cursed the day he was born. Isabella, apprehensive that these struggles of passion were more than Matilda could support, took upon herself to order Manfred to be borne to his apartment, while she caused Matilda to be conveyed to the nearest chamber. Hippolita, scarce more alive than her daughter, was regardless of every thing but her: but when the tender Isabella's care would have likewise removed her, while the surgeons examined Matilda's wound, she cried, Remove me? Never! never! I lived but in her, and will expire with her. Matilda raised her eyes at her mother's voice, but closed them again without speaking. Her sinking pulse, and the damp coldness of her hand, soon dispelled all hopes of recovery. Theodore followed the surgeons into the outer chamber, and heard them pronounce the fatal sentence with a transport equal to phrensy—Since she cannot live mine, cried he, at least she shall be mine in death!—Father! Jerome! will you not join our hands? cried he to the friar, who with the marquis had accompanied the surgeons. What means thy distracted rashness? said Jerome: is this an hour for marriage? It is, it is, cried Theodore: alas, there is no other! Young man, thou art too unadvised, said Frederic: dost thou think we are to listen to thy fond transports in this hour of fate? What pretensions hast thou to the princess? Those of a prince, said Theodore; of the sovereign of Otranto. This reverend man, my father, has informed me who I am. Thou ravest, said the marquis: there is no prince of Otranto but myself now Manfred by murder, by sacrilegious murder, has forfeited all pretensions. My lord, said Jerome, assuming an air of command, he tells you true. It was not my purpose the secret should have been divulged so soon; but fate presses onward to its work. What his hot-headed passion has revealed, my tongue confirms. Know, prince, that when Alfonso set sail for the Holy Land—Is this a season for explanations? cried Theodore. Father, come and unite me to the princess: she shall be mine—in every other thing I will dutifully obey you. My life! my adored Matilda! continued Theodore, rushing back into the inner chamber, will you not be mine? will you not bless your——Isabella made signs to him to be silent, apprehending the princess was near her end. What, is she dead? cried Theodore: is it possible? The violence of his exclamations brought Matilda to herself. Lifting up her eyes she looked round for her mother—Life of my soul! I am here, cried Hippolita: think not I will quit thee!—Oh! you are too good, said Matilda—but weep not for me, my mother! I am going where sorrow never dwells.—Isabella, thou hast loved me; wot thou not supply my fondness to this dear, dear woman? Indeed I am faint!—Oh! my child! my child! said Hippolita in a flood of tears, can I not withhold thee a moment?—It will not be, said Matilda— Commend me to heaven—Where is my father? Forgive him, dearest mother—forgive him my death; it was an error—Oh! I had forgotten—Dear- est mother, I vowed never to see Theodore more—Perhaps that has drawn down this calamity—but it was not intentional—can you pardon me?—Oh! wound not my agonizing soul! said Hippolita; thou never couldst offend me.—Alas, she faints! Help! help!—I would say something more, said Matilda struggling, but it wonnot be—Isabella—Theodore—for my sake— oh!—She expired. Isabella and her women tore Hippolita from the corse; but Theodore threatened destruction to all who attempted to remove him from it. He printed a thousand kisses on her clay-cold hands, and uttered every expression that despairing love could dictate.

Isabella, in the mean time, was accompanying the afflicted Hippolita to her apartment; but in the middle of the court they were met by Manfred, who, distracted with his own thoughts, and anxious once more to behold his daughter, was advancing to the chamber where she lay. As the moon was now at its height, he read in the countenances of this unhappy company the event he dreaded. What! is she dead? cried he in wild confusion—A clap of thunder at that instant shook the castle to its foundations; the earth rocked, and the clank of more than mortal armour was heard behind. Frederic and Jerome thought the last day was at hand. The latter, forcing Theodore along with them, rushed into the court. The moment Theodore appeared, the walls of the castle behind Manfred were thrown down with a mighty force, and the form of Alfonso, dilated to an immense magnitude, appeared in the centre of the ruins. Behold in Theodore, the true heir of Alfonso! said the vision: and having pronounced those words, accompanied by a clap of thunder, it ascended solemnly towards heaven, where the clouds parting asunder, the form of saint

Nicholas was seen; and receiving Alfonso's shade, they were soon wrapt from mortal eyes in a blaze of glory.

The beholders fell prostrate on their faces, acknowledging the divine will. The first that broke silence was Hippolita. My lord, said she to the desponding Manfred, behold the vanity of human greatness! Conrad is gone! Matilda is no more! in Theodore we view the true prince of Otranto. By what miracle he is so, I know not—suffice it to us, our doom is pronounced! Shall we not, can we but dedicate the few deplorable hours we have to live, in deprecating the farther wrath of heaven? Heaven ejects us—whither can we fly, but to you holy cells that yet offer us a retreat?—Thou guiltless but unhappy woman! unhappy by my crimes! replied Manfred, my heart at last is open to thy devout admonitions. Oh! could—but it cannot be—ye are lost in wonder—let me at last do justice on myself! To heap shame on my own head is all the satisfaction I have left to offer to offended heaven. My story has drawn down these judgments: let my confession atone—But ah! what can atone for usurpation and a murdered child? a child murdered in a consecrated place!——List, sirs, and may this bloody record be a warning to future tyrants!

Alfonso, ye all know, died in the Holy Land—Ye would interrupt me; ye would say he came not fairly to his end—It is most true—why else this bitter cup which Manfred must drink to the dregs? Ricardo, my grandfather, was his chamberlain—I would draw a veil over my ancestor's crimes—but it is in vain: Alfonso died by poison. A fictitious will declared Ricardo his heir. His crimes pursued him—yet he lost no Conrad, no Matilda! I pay the price of usurpation for all! A storm overtook him. Haunted by his guilt, he vowed to saint Nicholas to found a church and two convents if he lived to reach Otranto. The sacrifice was accepted: the saint appeared to him in a dream, and promised that Ricardo's posterity should reign in Otranto until the rightful owner should be grown too large to inhabit the castle, and as long as issue-male from Ricardo's loins should remain to enjoy it.—Alas! alas! nor male nor female, except myself, remains of all his wretched race!—I have done—the woes of these three days speak the rest. How this young man can be Alfonso's heir I know not—yet I do not doubt it. His are these dominions; I resign them—yet I knew not Alfonso had an heir—I question not the will of heaven—poverty and prayer must fill up the woeful space, until Manfred shall be summoned to Ricardo.

What remains is my part to declare, said Jerome. When Alfonso set sail for the Holy Land, he was driven by a storm on the coast of Sicily. The other vessel, which bore Ricardo and his train, as your *lordship* must have heard, was separated from him. It is most true, said Manfred; and the title you give me is more than an out-cast can claim—Well, be it so—proceed. Jerome blushed, and continued. For three months lord Alfonso was wind-bound in Sicily. There he became enamoured of a fair virgin named

Victoria. He was too pious to tempt her to forbidden pleasures. They were married. Yet deeming this amour incongruous with the holy vow of arms by which he was bound, he was determined to conceal their nuptials until his return from the crusado, when he purposed to seek and acknowledge her for his lawful wife. He left her pregnant. During his absence she was delivered of a daughter: but scarce had she felt a mother's pangs, ere she heard the fatal rumour of her lord's death, and the succession of Ricardo. What could a friendless, helpless woman do? would her testimony avail?—Yet, my lord, I have an authentic writing.—It needs not, said Manfred; the horrors of these days, the vision we have but now seen, all corroborate thy evidence beyond a thousand parchments. Matilda's death and my expulsion—Be composed, my lord, said Hippolita; this holy man did not mean to recall your griefs. Jerome proceeded.

I shall not dwell on what is needless. The daughter of which Victoria was delivered, was at her maturity bestowed in marriage on me. Victoria died; and the secret remained locked in my breast. Theodore's narrative has told the rest.

The friar ceased. The disconsolate company retired to the remaining part of the castle. In the morning Manfred signed his abdication of the principality, with the approbation of Hippolita, and each took on them the habit of religion in the neighbouring convents. Frederic offered his daughter to the new prince, which Hippolita's tenderness for Isabella concurred to promote: but Theodore's grief was too fresh to admit the thought of another love; and it was not till after frequent discourses with Isabella, of his dear Matilda, that he was persuaded he could know no happiness but in the society of one with whom he could forever indulge the melancholy that had taken possession of his soul.

WILLIAM BECKFORD

Vathek

൹

A CHRONOLOGY OF WILLIAM BECKFORD

1760   (29 September) Born, probably in London

1770   (21 June) Death of his father

1777   (autumn) Sent under his tutor, John Lettice, to Geneva. Writes *The Long Story*
        and *Hylas*

1778   (November) Brought home by Mrs. Beckford

1779   (summer) Meets William Courtenay (aged 11) at Powderham Castle, near
        Exeter

1780–3 Works spasmodically on translation of the Wortley Montagu Arabian MSS.

1780   (early) *Biographical Memoirs of Extraordinary Painters* published (written 1777);
        (19 June) leaves on Grand Tour with Lettice, visiting Holland, Germany,
        Italy, and France

1781   (14 April) Returns to England; (September) Coming-of-age festivities at
        Fonthill; (Christmas) House party at Fonthill

1782   (January–May) In London; writes *Vathek*; (15 May) leaves for Germany and
        Italy with Lettice, partly due to scandal over his relations with Louisa B., his
        cousin's wife; (9 November) returns to England

1783   (15 April) Under family pressure, suppresses *Dreams, Waking Thoughts, and
        Incidents*, 500 copies of which had been printed in March (printed as vol. i of
        Italy (1834)); (5 May) marries Lady Margaret Gordon, daughter of the Earl
        of Aboyne. Leaves for Switzerland and Paris

1784   (c. 18 March) Returns to England; (April) enters Parliament as M.P. for Wells;
        (September) stays at Powderham; scandal over accusation of misconduct with
        William Courtenay followed by press campaign against him

1785   (February–April) Corresponding with Henley over translation of *Vathek*;
        (9 April) birth of daughter, Maria Margaret Elizabeth; (23 July) under family
        pressure leaves for Switzerland

1786   (9 February) Forbids Henley to publish *Vathek* before the *Episodes*; (14 May)
        birth of daughter, Susan Euphemia; (26 May) death of his wife; (7 June)
        English translation of *Vathek* published by Henley in London; (?December)
        French text of *Vathek* published at Lausanne

1787   (January) Returns from Paris to Fonthill; (3 March) abandons plan of going
        to Jamaica; (15 March) sails for Portugal, living in Lisbon and Cintra; (late
        June) Paris edition of *Vathek* published; (12 December) moves to Madrid

1788   (12 June) Leaves for Paris; (autumn) in Switzerland

1789   (October) Returns to Fonthill, planning building improvements

1790   (October) In Paris

1791   *Popular Tales of the Germans*, translated from J. C. A. Musaeus, published;
        (June) returns to Fonthill; (November) leaves for Paris

1792   (July) Leaves for Savoy; (November) returns to Paris

1793   (1 February) France declares war on England; (May) returns to Fonthill;
        receives plans for a new building from Wyatt; (November) leaves for Lisbon

1794   (June) Tour of monasteries of Alcobaça and Batalha

1796   (June) Returns to England; *Modern Novel Writing, or the Elegant Enthusiast* published

1797   *Azemia: A Descriptive and Sentimental Novel* published

1797-8   Offers to negotiate peace with France rejected by Pitt

1798   (July) Death of his mother; (15 October) leaves for Portugal

1799   (*c.* 10 July) Returns to England; *The Story of Al Raoui*, attributed to Beckford, published

1800-3   Unsuccessful attempts to obtain a peerage

1800   (23 December) Entertains Sir William and Lady Hamilton and Lord Nelson at Fonthill

1801 (May)-1803 (May)   In France and Switzerland, until renewal of hostilities with France

1807   (summer) Moves into the South Wing of the new Fonthill Abbey

1808-9   Tower and Octagon of Fonthill Abbey completed

1810   (26 April) Marriage of Susan Euphemia B. to Marquess of Douglas, later Duke of Hamilton

1811   (16 May) Elopement of Maria Margaret B. with Col. James Orde

1814   Visits Paris

1817   (autumn) Visited at Fonthill by Samuel Rogers

1819   *Repertorium Bibliographicum* (to which he may have contributed) and *A Dialogue in the Shades* published; short visit to Paris

1822   (5 October) Fonthill Abbey sold to John Farquhar for £300,000. Beckford moves to Lansdown Tower, Bath

1825   (December) Collapse of the main tower of Fonthill

1834   *Italy; with Sketches of Spain and Portugal* published

1835   *Recollections of an Excursion to the Monasteries of Alcobaça and Batalha* published

1844   (2 May) Dies at Bath from a severe attack of influenza

VATHEK

VATHEK, ninth Caliph of the race of the Abassides, was the son of
Motassem, and the grandson of Haroun al Raschid. From an early accession
to the throne, and the talents he possessed to adorn it, his subjects were
induced to expect that his reign would be long and happy. His figure was
pleasing and majestic; but when he was angry, one of his eyes became so
terrible, that no person could bear to behold it; and the wretch upon whom
it was fixed, instantly fell backward, and sometimes expired. For fear,
however, of depopulating his dominions and making his palace desolate, he
but rarely gave way to his anger.

Being much addicted to women and the pleasures of the table, he sought
by his affability, to produce agreeable companions; and he succeeded the
better as his generosity was unbounded and his indulgencies unrestrained:
for he did not think, with the Caliph Omar Ben Abdalaziz that it was
necessary to make a hell of this world to enjoy paradise in the next.

He surpassed in magnificence all his predecessors. The palace of Alkoremi,
which his father, Motassem, had erected on the hill of Pied Horses, and
which commanded the whole city of Samarah, was, in his idea far too
scanty: he added, therefore, five wings, or rather other palaces, which he
destined for the particular gratification of each of the senses.

In the first of these were tables continually covered with the most exquisite
dainties; which were supplied both by night and by day, according to their
constant consumption; whilst the most delicious wines and the choicest
cordials flowed forth from a hundred fountains that were never exhausted.
This palace was called *The Eternal or unsatiating Banquet.*

The second was styled, *The Temple of Melody,* or *The Nectar of the Soul.* It was
inhabited by the most skilful musicians and admired poets of the time; who
not only displayed their talents within, but dispersing in bands without,
caused every surrounding scene to reverberate their songs; which were
continually varied in the most delightful succession.

The palace named *The Delight of the Eyes,* or *The Support of Memory,* was one
entire enchantment. Rarities, collected from every corner of the earth were
there found in such profusion as to dazzle and confound, but for the order
in which they were arranged. One gallery exhibited the pictures of the
celebrated Mani, and statues, that seemed to be alive. Here a well-managed
perspective attracted the sight; there the magic of optics agreeably deceived

it: whilst the naturalist on his part, exhibited in their several classes the various gifts that Heaven had bestowed on our globe. In a word, Vathek omitted nothing in this palace, that might gratify the curiosity of those who resorted to it, although he was not able to satisfy his own; for, of all men, he was the most curious.

The Palace of Perfumes, which was termed likewise *The Incentive to Pleasure*, consisted of various halls, where the different perfumes which the earth produces were kept perpetually burning in censers of gold. Flambeaux and aromatic lamps were here lighted in open day. But the too powerful effects of this agreeable delirium might be alleviated by descending into an immense garden, where an assemblage of every fragrant flower diffused through the air the purest odours.

The fifth palace, denominated *The Retreat of Mirth, or the Dangerous*, was frequented by troops of young females beautiful as the Houris, and not less seducing; who never failed to receive with caresses, all whom the Caliph allowed to approach them, and enjoy a few hours of their company.

Notwithstanding the sensuality in which Vathek indulged, he experienced no abatement in the love of his people, who thought that a sovereign giving himself up to pleasure, was as able to govern, as one who declared himself an enemy to it. But the unquiet and impetuous disposition of the Caliph would not allow him to rest there. He had studied so much for his amusement in the life-time of his father, as to acquire a great deal of knowledge, though not a sufficiency to satisfy himself; for he wished to know every thing; even sciences that did not exist. He was fond of engaging in disputes with the learned, but did not allow them to push their opposition with warmth. He stopped with presents the mouths of those whose mouths could be stopped; whilst others, whom his liberality was unable to subdue, he sent to prison to cool their blood; a remedy that often succeeded.

Vathek discovered also a predilection for theological controversy; but it was not with the orthodox that he usually held. By this means he induced the zealots to oppose him, and then persecuted them in return; for he resolved, at any rate, to have reason on his side.

The great prophet, Mahomet, whose vicars the caliphs are, beheld with indignation from his abode in the seventh heaven, the irreligious conduct of such a vicegerent. 'Let us leave him to himself,' said he to the Genii, who are always ready to receive his commands: 'let us see to what lengths his folly and impiety will carry him: if he run into excess, we shall know how to chastise him. Assist him, therefore, to complete the tower, which, in imitation of Nimrod, he hath begun; not, like that great warrior, to escape being drowned, but from the insolent curiosity of penetrating the secrets of heaven:—he will not divine the fate that awaits him.'

The Genii obeyed; and, when the workmen had raised their structure a cubit in the day time, two cubits more were added in the night. The expedition, with which the fabric arose, was not a little flattering to the vanity of Vathek: he fancied, that even insensible matter shewed a forwardness to subserve his designs; not considering, that the successes of the foolish and wicked form the first rod of their chastisement.

His pride arrived at its height, when having ascended, for the first time, the fifteen hundred stairs of his tower, he cast his eyes below, and beheld men not larger than pismires; mountains, than shells; and cities, than bee-hives. The idea, which such an elevation inspired of his own grandeur, completely bewildered him: he was almost ready to adore himself; till, lifting his eyes upward, he saw the stars as high above him as they appeared when he stood on the surface of the earth. He consoled himself, however, for this intruding and unwelcome perception of his littleness, with the thought of being great in the eyes of others; and flattered himself that the light of his mind would extend beyond the reach of his sight, and extort from the stars the decrees of his destiny.

With this view, the inquisitive Prince passed most of his nights on the summit of his tower, till becoming an adept in the mysteries of astrology, he imagined that the planets had disclosed to him the most marvellous adventures, which were to be accomplished by an extraordinary personage, from a country altogether unknown. Prompted by motives of curiosity, he had always been courteous to strangers; but, from this instant, he redoubled his attention, and ordered it to be announced, by sound of trumpet through all the streets of Samarah, that no one of his subjects, on peril of his displeasure, should either lodge or detain a traveller, but forthwith bring him to the palace.

Not long after this proclamation, arrived in his metropolis a man so abominably hideous that the very guards, who arrested him, were forced to shut their eyes, as they led him along: the Caliph himself appeared startled at so horrible a visage; but joy succeeded to this emotion of terror, when the stranger displayed to his view such rarities as he had never before seen, and of which he had no conception.

In reality, nothing was ever so extraordinary as the merchandize this stranger produced: most of his curiosities, which were not less admirable for their workmanship than splendour, had, besides, their several virtues described on a parchment fastened to each. There were slippers, which, by spontaneous springs, enabled the feet to walk; knives, that cut without motion of the hand; sabres, that dealt the blow at the person they were wished to strike; and the whole enriched with gems, that were hitherto unknown.

The sabres, especially, the blades of which, emitted a dazzling radiance, fixed, more than all the rest, the Caliph's attention; who promised himself to decipher, at his leisure, the uncouth characters engraven on their sides. Without, therefore, demanding their price, he ordered all the coined gold to be brought from his treasury, and commanded the merchant to take what he pleased. The stranger obeyed, took little, and remained silent.

Vathek, imagining that the merchant's taciturnity was occasioned by the awe which his presence inspired, encouraged him to advance; and asked him, with an air of condescension, who he was? whence he came? and where he obtained such beautiful commodities? The man, or rather monster, instead of making a reply, thrice rubbed his forehead, which, as well as his body, was blacker than ebony; four times clapped his paunch, the projection of which was enormous; opened wide his huge eyes, which glowed like firebrands; began to laugh with a hideous noise, and discovered his long amber-coloured teeth, bestreaked with green.

The Caliph, though a little startled, renewed his inquiries, but without being able to procure a reply. At which, beginning to be ruffled, he exclaimed:—'Knowest thou, wretch, who I am, and at whom thou art aiming thy gibes?'—Then, addressing his guards,—'Have ye heard him speak?—is he dumb?'—'He hath spoken,' they replied, 'but to no purpose.' 'Let him speak then again,' said Vathek, 'and tell me who he is, from whence he came, and where he procured these singular curiosities; or I swear, by the ass of Balaam, that I will make him rue his pertinacity.'

This menace was accompanied by one of the Caliph's angry and perilous glances, which the stranger sustained without the slightest emotion; although his eyes were fixed on the terrible eye of the Prince.

No words can describe the amazement of the courtiers, when they beheld this rude merchant withstand the encounter unshocked. They all fell prostrate with their faces on the ground, to avoid the risk of their lives; and would have continued in the same abject posture, had not the Caliph exclaimed in a furious tone—'Up, cowards! seize the miscreant! see that he be committed to prison, and guarded by the best of my soldiers! Let him, however, retain the money I gave him; it is not my intent to take from him his property; I only want him to speak.'

No sooner had he uttered these words, than the stranger was surrounded, pinioned and bound with strong fetters, and hurried away to the prison of the great tower; which was encompassed by seven empalements of iron bars, and armed with spikes in every direction, longer and sharper than spits. The Caliph, nevertheless, remained in the most violent agitation. He sat down indeed to eat; but, of the three hundred dishes that were daily placed before him, he could taste of no more than thirty-two.

A diet, to which he had been so little accustomed, was sufficient of itself to prevent him from sleeping; what then must be its effect when joined to the anxiety that preyed upon his spirits? At the first glimpse of dawn he hastened to the prison, again to importune this intractable stranger; but the rage of Vathek exceeded all bounds on finding the prison empty; the grates burst asunder, and his guards lying lifeless around him. In the paroxysm of his passion he fell furiously on the poor carcases, and kicked them till evening without intermission. His courtiers and vizirs exerted their efforts to soothe his extravagance; but, finding every expedient ineffectual, they all united in one vociferation—'The Caliph is gone mad! the Caliph is out of his senses!'

This outcry, which soon resounded through the streets of Samarah, at length reached the ears of Carathis, his mother, who flew in the utmost consternation to try her ascendancy on the mind of her son. Her tears and caresses called off his attention; and he was prevailed upon, by her intreaties, to be brought back to the palace.

Carathis, apprehensive of leaving Vathek to himself, had him put to bed; and, seating herself by him, endeavoured by her conversation to appease and compose him. Nor could any one have attempted it with better success; for the Caliph not only loved her as a mother, but respected her as a person of superior genius. It was she who had induced him, being a Greek herself, to adopt the sciences and systems of her country which all good Mussulmans hold in such thorough abhorrence.

Judiciary astrology was one of those sciences, in which Carathis was a perfect adept. She began, therefore, with reminding her son of the promise which the stars had made him; and intimated an intention of consulting them again. 'Alas!' said the Caliph as soon as he could speak, 'what a fool I have been! not for having bestowed forty thousand kicks on my guards, who so tamely submitted to death; but for never considering that this extraordinary man was the same that the planets had foretold; whom, instead of ill-treating, I should have conciliated by all the arts of persuasion.'

'The past,' said Carathis, 'cannot be recalled; but it behoves us to think of the future: perhaps, you may again see the object you so much regret: it is possible the inscriptions on the sabres will afford information. Eat, therefore, and take thy repose, my dear son. We will consider, tomorrow, in what manner to act.'

Vathek yielded to her counsel as well as he could, and arose in the morning with a mind more at ease. The sabres he commanded to be instantly brought; and, poring upon them, through a coloured glass, that their glittering might not dazzle, he set himself in earnest to decipher the inscriptions; but his reiterated attempts were all of them nugatory: in vain did he beat his head, and bite his nails; not a letter of the whole was he able to ascertain. So unlucky a disappointment would have undone him again, had not Carathis, by good fortune, entered the apartment.

'Have patience, my son!' said she:—'you certainly are possessed of every important science; but the knowledge of languages is a trifle at best; and the accomplishment of none but a pedant. Issue a proclamation, that you will confer such rewards as become your greatness, upon any one that shall interpret what you do not understand, and what is beneath you to learn; you will soon find your curiosity gratified.'

'That may be,' said the Caliph; 'but, in the mean time, I shall be horribly disgusted by a crowd of smatterers, who will come to the trial as much for the pleasure of retailing their jargon, as from the hope of gaining the reward. To avoid this evil, it will be proper to add, that I will put every candidate to death, who shall fail to give satisfaction: for, thank Heaven! I have skill enough to distinguish, whether one translates or invents.'

'Of that I have no doubt,' replied Carathis; 'but, to put the ignorant to death is somewhat severe, and may be productive of dangerous effects. Content yourself with commanding their beards to be burnt:—beards in a state are not quite so essential as men.'

The Caliph submitted to the reasons of his mother; and, sending for Morakanabad, his prime vizir, said,—'Let the common criers proclaim, not only in Samarah, but throughout every city in my empire, that whosoever will repair hither and decipher certain characters which appear to be inexplicable, shall experience that liberality for which I am renowned; but, that all who fail upon trial shall have their beards burnt off to the last hair. Let them add, also, that I will bestow fifty beautiful slaves, and as many jars of apricots from the Isle of Kirmith, upon any man that shall bring me intelligence of the stranger.'

The subjects of the Caliph, like their sovereign, being great admirers of women and apricots from Kirmith, felt their mouths water at these promises, but were totally unable to gratify their hankering; for no one knew what had become of the stranger.

As to the Caliph's other requisition, the result was different. The learned, the half learned, and those who were neither, but fancied themselves equal to both, came boldly to hazard their beards, and all shamefully lost them. The exaction of these forfeitures, which found sufficient employment for the eunuchs, gave them such a smell of singed hair, as greatly to disgust the ladies of the seraglio, and to make it necessary that this new occupation of their guardians should be transferred to other hands.

At length, however, an old man presented himself, whose beard was a cubit and a half longer than any that had appeared before him. The officers of the palace whispered to each other, as they ushered him in—'What a pity, oh! what a great pity that such a beard should be burnt!' Even the Caliph, when he saw it, concurred with them in opinion; but his concern was entirely needless. This venerable personage read the characters with facility, and explained them verbatim as follows: 'We were made where every thing is well made: we are the least of the wonders of a place where all is wonderful and deserving, the sight of the first potentate on earth.'

'You translate admirably!' cried Vathek; 'I know to what these marvellous characters allude. Let him receive as many robes of honour and thousands of sequins of gold as he hath spoken words. I am in some measure relieved from the perplexity that embarrassed me!' Vathek invited the old man to dine, and even to remain some days in the palace.

Unluckily for him, he accepted the offer; for the Caliph having ordered him next morning to be called, said—'Read again to me what you have read already; I cannot hear too often the promise that is made me—the completion of which I languish to obtain.' The old man forthwith put on his green spectacles, but they instantly dropped from his nose, on perceiving that the characters he had read the day preceding, had given place to others of different import. 'What ails you?' asked the Caliph; 'and why these symptoms of wonder?'—'Sovereign of the world!' replied the old man, 'these sabres hold another language to-day from that they yesterday held.'—'How say you?' returned Vathek:—'but it matters not; tell me, if you can, what they mean.'—'It is this, my lord,' rejoined the old man: 'Woe to the rash mortal who seeks to know that of which he should remain ignorant; and to undertake that which surpasseth his power!'—'And woe to thee!' cried the Caliph, in a burst of indignation, 'to-day thou art void of understanding: begone from my presence, they shall burn but the half of thy beard, because thou wert yesterday fortunate in guessing:—my gifts I never resume.' The old man, wise enough to perceive he had luckily escaped, considering the folly of disclosing so disgusting a truth, immediately withdrew and appeared not again.

But it was not long before Vathek discovered abundant reason to regret his precipitation; for, though he could not decipher the characters himself, yet, by constantly poring upon them, he plainly perceived that they every day changed; and, unfortunately, no other candidate offered to explain them. This perplexing occupation inflamed his blood, dazzled his sight, and brought on such a giddiness and debility that he could hardly support himself. He failed not, however, though in so reduced a condition, to be often carried to his tower, as he flattered himself that he might there read in the stars, which he went to consult, something more congruous to his wishes; but in this his hopes were deluded: for his eyes, dimmed by the vapours of his head, began to subserve his curiosity so ill, that he beheld nothing but a thick, dun cloud, which he took for the most direful of omens.

Agitated with so much anxiety, Vathek entirely lost all firmness; a fever seized him, and his appetite failed. Instead of being one of the greatest eaters, he became as distinguished for drinking. So insatiable was the thirst which tormented him, that his mouth, like a funnel, was always open to receive the various liquors that might be poured into it, and especially cold water, which calmed him more than any other.

This unhappy prince, being thus incapacitated for the enjoyment of any pleasure, commanded the palaces of the five senses to be shut up; forebore to appear in public, either to display his magnificence, or administer justice, and retired to the inmost apartment of his harem. As he had ever been an excellent husband, his wives, overwhelmed with grief at his deplorable situation, incessantly supplied him with prayers for his health, and water for his thirst.

In the mean time the Princess Carathis, whose affliction no words can describe, instead of confining herself to sobbing and tears, was closetted daily with the vizir Morakanabad, to find out some cure, or mitigation, of the Caliph's disease. Under the persuasion that it was caused by enchantment, they turned over together, leaf by leaf, all the books of magic that might point out a remedy; and caused the horrible stranger, whom they accused as the enchanter, to be every where sought for, with the strictest diligence.

At the distance of a few miles from Samarah stood a high mountain, whose sides were swarded with wild thyme and basil, and its summit overspread with so delightful a plain, that it might have been taken for the Paradise destined for the faithful. Upon it grew a hundred thickets of eglantine and other fragrant shrubs; a hundred arbours of roses, entwined with jessamine and honey-suckle; as many clumps of orange trees, cedar, and citron; whose branches, interwoven with the palm, the pomegranate, and the vine, presented every luxury that could regale the eye or the taste. The ground was strewed with violets, hare-bells, and pansies; in the midst of which numerous tufts of jonquils, hyacinths, and carnations perfumed the air. Four fountains, not less clear than deep, and so abundant as to slake the thirst of ten armies, seemed purposely placed here, to make the scene more resemble the garden of Eden watered by four sacred rivers. Here, the nightingale sang the birth of the rose, her well-beloved, and, at the same time, lamented its short-lived beauty; whilst the dove deplored the loss of more substantial pleasures; and the wakeful lark hailed the rising light that re-animates the whole creation. Here, more than any where, the mingled melodies of birds expressed the various passions which inspired them; and the exquisite fruits, which they pecked at pleasure, seemed to have given them a double energy.

To this mountain Vathek was sometimes brought, for the sake of breathing a purer air; and, especially, to drink at will of the four fountains. His attendants were his mother, his wives, and some eunuchs, who assiduously employed themselves in filling capacious bowls of rock crystal, and emulously presenting them to him. But it frequently happened, that his avidity exceeded their zeal, insomuch, that he would prostrate himself upon the ground to lap the water, of which he could never have enough.

One day, when this unhappy Prince had been long lying in so debasing a posture, a voice, hoarse but strong, thus addressed him: 'Why dost thou assimilate thyself to a dog, O Caliph, proud as thou art of thy dignity and power?' At this apostrophe, he raised up his head, and beheld the stranger that had caused him so much affliction. Inflamed with anger at the sight, he exclaimed:—'Accursed Giaour! what comest thou hither to do?—is it not enough to have transformed a prince, remarkable for his agility, into a water budget? Perceivest thou not, that I may perish by drinking to excess, as well as by thirst?'

'Drink then this draught,' said the stranger, as he presented to him a phial of a red and yellow mixture: 'and, to satiate the thirst of thy soul, as well as of thy body, know, that I am an Indian; but, from a region of India, which is wholly unknown.'

The Caliph, delighted to see his desires accomplished in part, and flattering himself with the hope of obtaining their entire fulfilment, without a moment's hesitation swallowed the potion, and instantaneously found his health restored, his thirst appeased, and his limbs as agile as ever. In the transports of his joy, Vathek leaped upon the neck of the frightful Indian, and kissed his horrid mouth and hollow cheeks, as though they had been the coral lips and the lilies and roses of his most beautiful wives.

Nor would these transports have ceased, had not the eloquence of Carathis repressed them. Having prevailed upon him to return to Samarah, she caused a herald to proclaim as loudly as possible—'The wonderful stranger hath appeared again; he hath healed the Caliph;—he hath spoken! he hath spoken!'

Forthwith, all the inhabitants of this vast city quitted their habitations, and ran together in crowds to see the procession of Vathek and the Indian, whom they now blessed as much as they had before execrated, incessantly shouting—'He hath healed our sovereign;—he hath spoken! he hath spoken!' Nor were these words forgotten in the public festivals, which were celebrated the same evening, to testify the general joy; for the poets applied them as a chorus to all the songs they composed on this interesting subject.

The Caliph, in the meanwhile, caused the palaces of the senses to be again set open; and, as he found himself naturally prompted to visit that of Taste in preference to the rest, immediately ordered a splendid entertainment, to which his great officers and favourite courtiers were all invited. The Indian, who was placed near the Prince, seemed to think that, as a proper acknowledgment of so distinguished a privilege, he could neither eat, drink, nor talk too much. The various dainties were no sooner served up than they vanished, to the great mortification of Vathek, who piqued himself on being the greatest eater alive; and, at this time in particular, was blessed with an excellent appetite.

The rest of the company looked round at each other in amazement; but the Indian, without appearing to observe it, quaffed large bumpers to the health of each of them; sung in a style altogether extravagant; related stories, at which he laughed immoderately; and poured forth extemporaneous verses, which would not have been thought bad, but for the strange grimaces with which they were uttered. In a word, his loquacity was equal to that of a hundred astrologers; he ate as much as a hundred porters, and caroused in proportion.

The Caliph, notwithstanding the table had been thirty-two times covered, found himself incommoded by the voraciousness of his guest, who was now considerably declined in the Prince's esteem. Vathek, however, being unwilling to betray the chagrin he could hardly disguise, said in a whisper to Bababalouk, the chief of his eunuchs, 'You see how enormous his performances are in every way; what would be the consequence should he get at my wives!—Go! redouble your vigilance, and be sure look well to my Circassians, who would be more to his taste than all of the rest.'

The bird of the morning had thrice renewed his song, when the hour of the Divan was announced. Vathek, in gratitude to his subjects, having promised to attend, immediately arose from table, and repaired thither, leaning upon his vizir who could scarcely support him: so disordered was the poor Prince by the wine he had drunk, and still more by the extravagant vagaries of his boisterous guest.

The vizirs, the officers of the crown and of the law, arranged themselves in a semicircle about their sovereign, and preserved a respectful silence; whilst the Indian, who looked as cool as if he had been fasting, sat down without ceremony on one of the steps of the throne, laughing in his sleeve at the indignation with which his temerity had filled the spectators.

The Caliph, however, whose ideas were confused, and whose head was embarrassed, went on administering justice at haphazard; till at length the prime vizir, perceiving his situation, hit upon a sudden expedient to interrupt the audience and rescue the honour of his master, to whom he said in a whisper:—'My lord, the Princess Carathis, who hath passed the night in consulting the planets, informs you, that they portend you evil, and the danger is urgent. Beware, lest this stranger, whom you have so lavishly recompensed for his magical gewgaws, should make some attempt on your life: his liquor, which at first had the appearance of effecting your cure, may be no more than a poison, the operation of which will be sudden.—Slight not this surmise: ask him, at least, of what it was compounded, whence he procured it; and mention the sabres, which you seem to have forgotten.'

Vathek, to whom the insolent airs of the stranger became every moment less supportable, intimated to his vizir, by a wink of acquiescence, that he would adopt his advice; and, at once turning towards the Indian, said—'Get up, and declare in full Divan of what drugs was compounded the liquor you enjoined me to take, for it is suspected to be poison: give also, that explanation I have so earnestly desired, concerning the sabres you sold me, and thus shew your gratitude for the favours heaped on you.'

Having pronounced these words, in as moderate a tone as he well could, he waited in silent expectation for an answer. But the Indian, still keeping his seat, began to renew his loud shouts of laughter, and exhibit the same horrid grimaces he had shewn them before, without vouchsafing a word in reply. Vathek, no longer able to brook such insolence, immediately kicked him from the steps; instantly descending, repeated his blow; and persisted, with such assiduity, as incited all who were present to follow his example. Every foot was up and aimed at the Indian, and no sooner had any one given him a kick, than he felt himself constrained to reiterate the stroke.

The stranger afforded them no small entertainment: for, being both short and plump, he collected himself into a ball, and rolled round on all sides, at the blows of his assailants, who pressed after him, wherever he turned, with an eagerness beyond conception, whilst their numbers were every moment increasing. The ball indeed, in passing from one apartment to another, drew every person after it that came in its way; insomuch, that the whole palace was thrown into confusion and resounded with a tremendous clamour. The women of the harem, amazed at the uproar, flew to their blinds to discover the cause; but, no sooner did they catch a glimpse of the ball, than, feeling themselves unable to refrain, they broke from the clutches of their eunuchs, who, to stop their flight, pinched them till they bled; but, in vain: whilst themselves, though trembling with terror at the escape of their charge, were as incapable of resisting the attraction.

After having traversed the halls, galleries, chambers, kitchens, gardens, and stables of the palace, the Indian at last took his course through the courts; whilst the Caliph, pursuing him closer than the rest, bestowed as many kicks as he possibly could; yet, not without receiving now and then a few which his competitors, in their eagerness, designed for the ball.

Carathis, Morakanabad, and two or three old vizirs, whose wisdom had hitherto withstood the attraction, wishing to prevent Vathek from exposing himself in the presence of his subjects, fell down on his way to impede the pursuit: but he, regardless of their obstruction, leaped over their heads, and went on as before. They then ordered the Muezins to call the people to prayers; both for the sake of getting them out of the way, and of endeavouring, by their petitions, to avert the calamity; but neither of these expedients was a whit more successful. The sight of this fatal ball was alone sufficient to draw after it every beholder. The Muezins themselves, though they saw it but at a distance, hastened down from their minarets, and mixed with the crowd; which continued to increase in so surprising a manner, that scarce an inhabitant was left in Samarah, except the aged; the sick, confined to their beds; and infants at the breast, whose nurses could run more nimbly without them. Even Carathis, Morakanabad, and the rest, were all become of the party. The shrill screams of the females, who had broken from their apartments, and were unable to extricate themselves from the pressure of the crowd, together with those of the eunuchs jostling after them, and terrified lest their charge should escape from their sight; the execrations of husbands, urging forward and menacing each other; kicks given and received; stumblings and overthrows at every step; in a word, the confusion that universally prevailed, rendered Samarah like a city taken by storm, and devoted to absolute plunder. At last, the cursed Indian, who still preserved his rotundity of figure, after passing through all the streets and public places, and leaving them empty, rolled onwards to the plain of Catoul, and entered the valley at the foot of the mountain of the four fountains.

As a continual fall of water had excavated an immense gulph in the valley whose opposite side was closed in by a steep acclivity, the Caliph and his attendants were apprehensive, lest the ball should bound into the chasm, and, to prevent it, redoubled their efforts, but in vain. The Indian persevered in his onward direction; and, as had been apprehended, glancing from the precipice with the rapidity of lightning, was lost in the gulph below.

Vathek would have followed the perfidious Giaour, had not an invisible agency arrested his progress. The multitude that pressed after him were at once checked in the same manner, and a calm instantaneously ensued. They all gazed at each other with an air of astonishment, and notwithstanding that the loss of veils and turbans, together with torn habits, and dust blended with sweat, presented a most laughable spectacle, yet there was not one smile to be seen. On the contrary, all with looks of confusion and sadness returned in silence to Samarah, and retired to their inmost apartments, without ever reflecting, that they had been impelled by an invisible power into the extravagance, for which they reproached themselves: for it is but just that men, who so often arrogate to their own merit the good of which they are but instruments, should also attribute to themselves absurdities which they could not prevent.

The Caliph was the only person who refused to leave the valley. He commanded his tents to be pitched there, and stationed himself on the very edge of the precipice, in spite of the representations of Carathis and Morakanabad, who pointed out the hazard of its brink giving way, and the vicinity to the magician, that had so cruelly tormented him. Vathek derided all their remonstrances; and, having ordered a thousand flambeaux to be lighted, and directed his attendants to proceed in lighting more, lay down on the slippery margin, and attempted, by the help of this artificial splendour, to look through that gloom, which all the fires of the empyrean had been insufficient to pervade. One while he fancied to himself voices arising from the depth of the gulph; at another, he seemed to distinguish the accents of the Indian; but all was no more than the hollow murmur of waters, and the din of the cataracts that rushed from steep to steep down the sides of the mountain.

Having passed the night in this cruel perturbation, the Caliph, at day-break, retired to his tent; where, without taking the least sustenance, he continued to doze till the dusk of evening began again to come on. He then resumed his vigils as before, and persevered in observing them for many nights together. At length, fatigued with so fruitless an employment, he sought relief from change. To this end, he sometimes paced with hasty strides across the plain; and, as he wildly gazed at the stars, reproached them with having deceived him; but, lo! on a sudden, the clear blue sky appeared streaked over with streams of blood, which reached from the valley even to the city of Samarah. As this awful phenomenon seemed to touch his tower, Vathek at first thought of repairing thither to view it more distinctly; but, feeling himself unable to advance, and being overcome with apprehension, he muffled up his face in the folds of his robe.

Terrifying as these prodigies were, this impression upon him was no more than momentary, and served only to stimulate his love of the marvellous. Instead, therefore, of returning to his palace, he persisted in the resolution of abiding where the Indian had vanished from his view. One night, however, while he was walking as usual on the plain, the moon and stars were eclipsed at once, and a total darkness ensued. The earth trembled beneath him, and a voice came forth, the voice of the Giaour, who, in accents more sonorous than thunder, thus addressed him: 'Wouldest thou devote thyself to me? adore the terrestrial influences, and abjure Mahomet? On these conditions I will bring thee to the Palace of Subterranean Fire. There shalt thou behold, in immense depositories, the treasures which the stars have promised thee; and which will be conferred by those intelligences, whom thou shalt thus render propitious. It was from thence I brought my sabres, and it is there that Soliman Ben Daoud reposes, surrounded by the talismans that control the world.'

The astonished Caliph trembled as he answered, yet he answered in a style that shewed him to be no novice in preternatural adventures: 'Where art thou? be present to my eyes; dissipate the gloom that perplexes me, and of which I deem thee the cause. After the many flambeaux I have burnt to discover thee, thou mayest, at least, grant a glimpse of thy horrible visage.'—'Abjure then Mahomet!' replied the Indian, 'and promise me full proofs of thy sincerity: otherwise, thou shalt never behold me again.'

The unhappy Caliph, instigated by insatiable curiosity, lavished his promises in the utmost profusion. The sky immediately brightened; and, by the light of the planets, which seemed almost to blaze, Vathek beheld the earth open; and, at the extremity of a vast black chasm, a portal of ebony, before which stood the Indian, holding in his hand a golden key, which he sounded against the lock.

'How,' cried Vathek, 'can I descend to thee;—Come, take me, and instantly open the portal.'—'Not so fast,' replied the Indian, 'impatient Caliph!—Know that I am parched with thirst, and cannot open this door, till my thirst be thoroughly appeased; I require the blood of fifty children. Take them from among the most beautiful sons of thy vizirs and great men; or, neither can my thirst nor thy curiosity be satisfied. Return to Samarah;

procure for me this necessary libation; come back hither; throw it thyself into this chasm, and then shalt thou see!'

Having thus spoken, the Indian turned his back on the Caliph, who, incited by the suggestions of demons, resolved on the direful sacrifice.—He now pretended to have regained his tranquillity, and set out for Samarah amidst the acclamations of a people who still loved him, and forbore not to rejoice, when they believed him to have recovered his reason. So successfully did he conceal the emotion of his heart, that even Carathis and Morakanabad were equally deceived with the rest. Nothing was heard of but festivals and rejoicings. The fatal ball, which no tongue had hitherto ventured to mention, was brought on the tapis. A general laugh went round, though many, still smarting under the hands of the surgeon, from the hurts received in that memorable adventure, had no great reason for mirth.

The prevalence of this gay humour was not a little grateful to Vathek, who perceived how much it conduced to his project. He put on the appearance of affability to every one; but especially to his vizirs, and the grandees of his court, whom he failed not to regale with a sumptuous banquet; during which, he insensibly directed the conversation to the children of his guests. Having asked, with a good-natured air, which of them were blessed with the handsomest boys, every father at once asserted the pretensions of his own; and the contest imperceptibly grew so warm, that nothing could have withholden them from coming to blows, but their profound reverence for the person of the Caliph. Under the pretence, therefore, of reconciling the disputants, Vathek took upon him to decide; and, with this view, commanded the boys to be brought.

It was not long before a troop of these poor children made their appearance, all equipped by their fond mothers with such ornaments, as might give the greatest relief to their beauty, or most advantageously display the graces of their age. But, whilst this brilliant assemblage attracted the eyes and hearts of every one besides, the Caliph scrutinized each, in his turn, with a malignant avidity that passed for attention, and selected from their number the fifty whom he judged the Giaour would prefer.

With an equal shew of kindness as before, he proposed to celebrate a festival on the plain, for the entertainment of his young favourites, who, he said, ought to rejoice still more than all, at the restoration of his health, on account of the favours he intended for them.

The Caliph's proposal was received with the greatest delight, and soon published through Samarah. Litters, camels, and horses were prepared. Women and children, old men and young, every one placed himself as he chose. The cavalcade set forward, attended by all the confectioners in the city and its precincts; the populace, following on foot, composed an amazing crowd, and occasioned no little noise. All was joy; nor did any one call to mind, what most of them had suffered, when they lately travelled the road they were now passing so gaily.

The evening was serene, the air refreshing, the sky clear, and the flowers exhaled their fragrance. The beams of the declining sun, whose mild splendour reposed on the summit of the mountain, shed a glow of ruddy light over its green declivity, and the white flocks sporting upon it. No sounds were heard, save the murmurs of the four fountains; and the reeds and voices of shepherds calling to each other from different eminences.

The lovely innocents destined for the sacrifice, added not a little to the hilarity of the scene. They approached the plain full of sportiveness, some coursing butterflies, others culling flowers, or picking up the shining little pebbles that attracted their notice. At intervals they nimbly started from each other for the sake of being caught again, and mutually imparting a thousand caresses.

The dreadful chasm, at whose bottom the portal of ebony was placed, began to appear at a distance. It looked like a black streak that divided the plain. Morakanabad and his companions, took it for some work which the Caliph had ordered. Unhappy men! little did they surmise for what it was destined. Vathek unwilling that they should examine it too nearly, stopped the procession, and ordered a spacious circle to be formed on this side, at some distance from the accursed chasm. The body-guard of eunuchs was detached, to measure out the lists intended for the games; and prepare the rings for the arrows of the young archers. The fifty competitors were soon stripped, and presented to the admiration of the spectators the suppleness and grace of their delicate limbs. Their eyes sparkled with a joy, which those of their fond parents reflected. Every one offered wishes for the little candidate nearest his heart, and doubted not of his being victorious. A breathless suspence awaited the contest of these amiable and innocent victims.

The Caliph, availing himself of the first moment to retire from the crowd, advanced towards the chasm; and there heard, yet not without shuddering, the voice of the Indian; who, gnashing his teeth, eagerly demanded: 'Where are they?—Where are they?—perceivest thou not how my mouth waters?'—'Relentless Giaour!' answered Vathek, with emotion; 'can nothing content thee but the massacre of these lovely victims? Ah! wert thou to behold their beauty, it must certainly move thy compassion.'—'Perdition on thy compassion, babbler!' cried the Indian: 'give them me; instantly give them me, or, my portal shall be closed against thee for ever!'—'Not so loudly,' replied the Caliph, blushing.—'I understand thee,' returned the Giaour with the grin of an Ogre; 'thou wantest no presence of mind: I will, for a moment, forbear.'

During this exquisite dialogue, the games went forward with all alacrity, and at length concluded, just as the twilight began to overcast the mountains. Vathek, who was still standing on the edge of the chasm, called out, with all his might:—'Let my fifty little favourites approach me, separately; and let them come in the order of their success. To the first, I will give my diamond bracelet; to the second, my collar of emeralds; to the third, my aigret of rubies; to the fourth, my girdle of topazes; and to the rest, each a part of my dress, even down to my slippers.'

This declaration was received was reiterated acclamations; and all extolled the liberality of a prince, who would thus strip himself, for the amusement of his subjects, and the encouragement of the rising generation. The Caliph, in the meanwhile, undressed himself by degrees; and, raising his arm as high as he was able, made each of the prizes glitter in the air; but, whilst he delivered it, with one hand, to the child, who sprung forward to receive it; he, with the other, pushed the poor innocent into the gulph; where the Giaour, with a sullen muttering, incessantly repeated; 'more! more!'

This dreadful device was executed with so much dexterity, that the boy who was approaching him, remained unconscious of the fate of his forerunner; and, as to the spectators, the shades of evening, together with their distance, precluded them from perceiving any object distinctly. Vathek, having in this manner thrown in the last of the fifty; and, expecting that the Giaour, on receiving him, would have presented the key; already fancied himself, as great as Soliman, and, consequently, above being amenable for what he had done:—when, to his utter amazement, the chasm closed, and the ground became as entire as the rest of the plain.

No language could express his rage and despair. He execrated the perfidy of the Indian; loaded him with the most infamous invectives; and stamped with his foot, as resolving to be heard. He persisted in this till his strength failed him; and, then, fell on the earth like one void of sense. His vizirs and grandees, who were nearer than the rest, supposed him, at first, to be sitting on the grass, at play with their amiable children; but, at length, prompted by doubt, they advanced towards the spot, and found the Caliph alone, who wildly demanded what they wanted? 'Our children! our children!' cried they. 'It is, assuredly, pleasant,' said he, 'to make me accountable for accidents. Your children, while at play, fell from the precipice, and I should have experienced their fate, had I not suddenly started back.'

At these words, the fathers of the fifty boys cried out aloud; the mothers repeated their exclamations an octave higher; whilst the rest, without knowing the cause, soon drowned the voices of both, with still louder lamentations of their own. 'Our Caliph,' said they, and the report soon circulated, 'our Caliph has played us this trick, to gratify his accursed Giaour. Let us punish him for perfidy! let us avenge ourselves! let us avenge the blood of the innocent! let us throw this cruel prince into the gulph that is near, and let his name be mentioned no more!'

At this rumour and these menaces, Carathis, full of consternation, hastened to Morakanabad, and said: 'Vizir, you have lost two beautiful boys, and must necessarily be the most afflicted of fathers; but you are virtuous; save your master.'—'I will brave every hazard,' replied the vizir, 'to rescue him from his present danger; but, afterwards, will abandon him to his fate. Bababalouk,' continued he, 'put yourself at the head of your eunuchs: disperse the mob, and, if possible, bring back this unhappy prince to his palace.' Bababalouk and his fraternity, felicitating each other in a low voice on their having been spared the cares as well as the honour of paternity, obeyed the mandate of the vizir; who, seconding their exertions, to the utmost of his power, at length, accomplished his generous enterprize; and retired, as he resolved, to lament at his leisure.

No sooner had the Caliph re-entered his palace, than Carathis commanded the doors to be fastened; but, perceiving the tumult to be still violent, and hearing the imprecations which resounded from all quarters, she said to her son: 'Whether the populace be right or wrong, it behoves you to provide for your safety; let us retire to your own apartment, and, from thence, through the subterranean passage, known only to ourselves, into your tower: there, with the assistance of the mutes who never leave it, we may be able to make a powerful resistance. Bababalouk, supposing us to be still in the palace, will guard its avenues, for his own sake; and we shall soon find, without the counsels of that blubberer Morakanabad, what expedient may be the best to adopt.'

Vathek, without making the least reply, acquiesced in his mother's proposal, and repeated as he went: 'Nefarious Giaour! where art thou? hast thou not yet devoured those poor children? where are thy sabres? thy golden key? thy talismans?'—Carathis, who guessed from these interrogations a part of the truth, had no difficulty to apprehend, in getting at the whole as soon as he should be a little composed in his tower. This Princess was so far from being influenced by scruples, that she was as wicked, as woman could be; which is not saying a little; for the sex pique themselves on their superiority, in every competition. The recital of the Caliph, therefore, occasioned neither terror nor surprize to his mother: she felt no emotion but from the promises of the Giaour, and said to her son: 'This Giaour, it must be confessed, is somewhat sanguinary in his taste; but, the terrestrial powers are always terrible; nevertheless, what the one hath promised, and the others can confer, will prove a sufficient indemnification. No crimes should be thought too dear for such a reward: forbear, then, to revile the Indian; you have not fulfilled the conditions to which his services are annexed: for instance; is not a sacrifice to the subterranean Genii required? and should we not be prepared to offer it as soon as the tumult is subsided? This charge I will take on myself, and have no doubt of succeeding, by means of your treasures, which as there are now so many others in store, may, without fear, be exhausted.' Accordingly, the Princess, who possessed the most consummate skill in the art of persuasion, went immediately back through the subterranean passage; and, presenting herself to the populace, from a window of the palace, began to harangue them with all the address of which she was mistress; whilst Bababalouk, showered money from both hands amongst the crowd, who by these united means were soon appeased. Every person retired to his home, and Carathis returned to the tower.

Prayer at break of day was announced, when Carathis and Vathek ascended the steps, which led to the summit of the tower; where they remained for some time though the weather was lowering and wet. This impending gloom corresponded with their malignant dispositions; but when the sun began to break through the clouds, they ordered a pavilion to be raised, as a screen against the intrusion of his beams. The Caliph, overcome with fatigue, sought refreshment from repose; at the same time, hoping that significant dreams might attend on his slumbers; whilst the indefatigable Carathis, followed by a party of her mutes, descended to prepare whatever she judged proper, for the oblation of the approaching night.

By secret stairs, contrived within the thickness of the wall, and known only to herself and her son, she first repaired to the mysterious recesses in which were deposited the mummies that had been wrested from the catacombs of the ancient Pharaohs. Of these she ordered several to be taken. From thence, she resorted to a gallery; where, under the guard of fifty female negroes mute and blind of the right eye, were preserved the oil of the most venomous serpents; rhinoceros' horns; and woods of a subtile and penetrating odour, procured from the interior of the Indies, together with a thousand other horrible rarities. This collection had been formed for a purpose like the present, by Carathis herself; from a presentiment, that she might one day, enjoy some intercourse with the infernal powers: to whom she had ever been passionately attached, and to whose taste she was no stranger.

To familiarize herself the better with the horrors in view, the Princess remained in the company of her negresses, who squinted in the most amiable manner from the only eye they had; and leered with exquisite delight, at the sculls and skeletons which Carathis had drawn forth from her cabinets; all of them making the most frightful contortions and uttering such shrill chatterings, that the Princess stunned by them and suffocated by the potency of the exhalations, was forced to quit the gallery, after stripping it of a part of its abominable treasures.

Whilst she was thus occupied, the Caliph, who instead of the visions he expected, had acquired in these unsubstantial regions a voracious appetite, was greatly provoked at the mutes. For having totally forgotten their deafness, he had impatiently asked them for food; and seeing them regardless of his demand, he began to cuff, pinch, and bite them, till Carathis arrived to terminate a scene so indecent, to the great content of these miserable creatures: 'Son! what means all this?' said she, panting for breath. 'I thought I heard as I came up, the shrieks of a thousand bats, torn from their crannies in the recesses of a cavern; and it was the outcry only of these poor mutes, whom you were so unmercifully abusing. In truth, you but ill deserve the admirable provision I have brought you.'—'Give it me instantly,' exclaimed the Caliph; 'I am perishing for hunger!'—'As to that,' answered she, 'you must have an excellent stomach if it can digest what I have brought.'—'Be quick,' replied the Caliph;—'but, oh heavens! what horrors! what do you intend?' 'Come; come;' returned Carathis, 'be not so squeamish; but help me to arrange every thing properly; and you shall see that, what you reject with such symptoms of disgust, will soon complete your felicity. Let us get ready the pile, for the sacrifice of to-night; and think not of eating, till that is performed: know you not, that all solemn rites ought to be preceded by a rigorous abstinence?'

The Caliph, not daring to object, abandoned himself to grief and the wind that ravaged his entrails, whilst his mother went forward with the requisite operations. Phials of serpents' oil, mummies, and bones, were soon set in order on the balustrade of the tower. The pile began to rise; and in three hours was twenty cubits high. At length darkness approached, and Carathis, having stripped herself to her inmost garment, clapped her hands in an impulse of ecstacy; the mutes followed her example; but Vathek, extenuated with hunger and impatience, was unable to support himself, and fell down in a swoon. The sparks had already kindled the dry wood; the venomous oil burst into a thousand blue flames; the mummies, dissolving, emitted a thick dun vapour; and the rhinoceros' horns, beginning to consume; all together diffused such a stench, that the Caliph, recovering, started from his trance, and gazed wildly on the scene in full blaze around him. The oil gushed forth in a plenitude of streams; and the negresses, who supplied it without intermission, united their cries to those of the Princess. At last, the fire became so violent, and the flames reflected from the polished marble so dazzling, that the Caliph, unable to withstand the heat and the blaze, effected his escape; and took shelter under the imperial standard.

In the mean time, the inhabitants of Samarah, scared at the light which shone over the city, arose in haste; ascended their roofs; beheld the tower on fire, and hurried, half naked to the square. Their love for their sovereign immediately awoke; and, apprehending him in danger of perishing in his tower, their whole thoughts were occupied with the means of his safety. Morakanabad flew from his retirement, wiped away his tears, and cried out for water like the rest. Bababalouk, whose olfactory nerves were more familiarized to magical odours, readily conjecturing, that Carathis was engaged in her favourite amusements, strenuously exhorted them not to be alarmed. Him, however, they treated as an old poltroon, and styled him a rascally traitor. The camels and dromedaries were advancing with water; but, no one knew by which way to enter the tower. Whilst the populace was obstinate in forcing the doors, a violent north-east wind drove an immense volume of flame against them. At first, they recoiled, but soon came back with redoubled zeal. At the same time, the stench of the horns and mummies increasing, most of the crowd fell backward in a state of suffocation. Those that kept their feet, mutually wondered at the cause of the smell; and admonished each other to retire. Morakanabad, more sick than the rest, remained in a piteous condition. Holding his nose with one hand, every one persisted in his efforts with the other to burst open the doors and obtain admission. A hundred and forty of the strongest and most resolute, at length accomplished their purpose. Having gained the stair-case, by their violent exertions, they attained a great height in a quarter of an hour.

Carathis, alarmed at the signs of her mutes, advanced to the stair-case; went down a few steps, and heard several voices calling out from below: 'You shall, in a moment have water!' Being rather alert, considering her age, she presently regained the top of the tower; and bade her son suspend the sacrifice for some minutes; adding,—'We shall soon be enabled to render it more grateful. Certain dolts of your subjects, imagining no doubt that we were on fire, have been rash enough to break through those doors, which had hitherto remained inviolate; for the sake of bringing up water. They are very kind, you must allow, so soon to forget the wrongs you have done them; but that is of little moment. Let us offer them to the Giaour,—let them come up; our mutes, who neither want strength nor experience, will soon dispatch them; exhausted as they are, with fatigue.'—'Be it so,' answered the Caliph, 'provided we finish, and I dine.' In fact, these good people, out of breath from ascending fifteen hundred stairs in such haste; and chagrined, at having spilt by the way, the water they had taken, were no sooner arrived at the top, than the blaze of the flames, and the fumes of the mummies, at once overpowered their senses. It was a pity! for they beheld not the agreeable smile, with which the mutes and negresses adjusted the cord to their necks: these amiable personages rejoiced, however, no less at the scene. Never before had the ceremony of strangling been performed with so much facility. They all fell, without the least resistance or struggle: so that Vathek, in the space of a few moments, found himself surrounded by the dead bodies of the most faithful of his subjects; all which were thrown on the top of the pile. Carathis, whose presence of mind never forsook her, perceiving that she had carcasses sufficient to complete her oblation, commanded the chains to be stretched across the stair-case, and the iron doors barricadoed, that no more might come up.

No sooner were these orders obeyed, than the tower shook; the dead bodies vanished in the flames; which, at once, changed from a swarthy crimson, to a bright rose colour: an ambient vapour emitted the most exquisite fragrance; the marble columns rang with harmonious sounds, and the liquified horns diffused a delicious perfume. Carathis, in transports, anticipated the success of her enterprize; whilst her mutes and negresses, to whom these sweets had given the cholic, retired grumbling to their cells.

Scarcely were they gone, when, instead of the pile, horns, mummies and ashes, the Caliph both saw and felt, with a degree of pleasure which he could not express, a table, covered with the most magnificent repast: flaggons of wine, and vases of exquisite sherbet reposing on snow. He availed himself, without scruple, of such an entertainment; and had already laid hands on a lamb stuffed with pistachios, whilst Carathis was privately drawing from a fillagreen urn, a parchment that seemed to be endless; and which had escaped the notice of her son. Totally occupied in gratifying an importunate appetite, he left her to peruse it without interruption; which having finished, she said to him, in an authoritative tone, 'Put an end to your gluttony, and hear the splendid promises with which you are favoured!' She then read, as follows: 'Vathek, my well-beloved, thou hast surpassed my hopes: my nostrils have been regaled by the savour of thy mummies, thy horns; and, still more by the lives, devoted on the pile. At the full of the moon, cause the bands of thy musicians, and thy tymbals, to be heard; depart from thy palace, surrounded by all the pageants of majesty; thy most faithful slaves, thy best beloved wives; thy most magnificent litters; thy richest loaden camels; and set forward on thy way to Istakhar. There, I await thy coming: that is the region of wonders: there shalt thou receive the diadem of Gian Ben Gian; the talismans of Soliman; and the treasures of the pre-adamite sultans: there shalt thou be solaced with all kinds of delight.—But, beware how thou enterest any dwelling on thy route; or thou shalt feel the effects of my anger.'

The Caliph, notwithstanding his habitual luxury, had never before dined with so much satisfaction. He gave full scope to the joy of these golden tidings; and betook himself to drinking anew. Carathis, whose antipathy to wine was by no means insuperable, failed not to pledge him at every bumper he ironically quaffed to the health of Mahomet. This infernal liquor completed their impious temerity, and prompted them to utter a profusion of blasphemies. They gave a loose to their wit, at the expense of the ass of Balaam, the dog of the seven sleepers, and the other animals admitted into the paradise of Mahomet. In this sprightly humour, they descended the fifteen hundred stairs, diverting themselves as they went, at the anxious faces they saw on the square, through the barbacans and loop-holes of the tower; and, at length, arrived at the royal apartments, by the subterranean passage. Bababalouk was parading to and fro, and issuing his mandates, with great pomp to the eunuchs; who were snuffing the lights and painting the eyes of the Circassians. No sooner did he catch sight of the Caliph and his mother, than he exclaimed, 'Hah! you have, than, I perceive, escaped from the flames: I was not, however, altogether out of doubt.'—'Of what moment is it to us what you thought, or think?' cried Carathis: 'go; speed; tell

Morakanabad that we immediately want him: and take care, not to stop by the way, to make your insipid reflections.'

Morakanabad delayed not to obey the summons; and was received by Vathek and his mother, with great solemnity. They told him, with an air of composure and commiseration, that the fire at the top of the tower was extinguished; but that it had cost the lives of the brave people who sought to assist them.

'Still more misfortunes!' cried Morakanabad, with a sigh. 'Ah, commander of the faithful, our holy prophet is certainly irritated against us! it behoves you to appease him.'—'We will appease him, hereafter!' replied the Caliph, with a smile, that augured nothing of good. 'You will have leisure sufficient for your supplications, during my absence: for this country is the bane of my health. I am disgusted with the mountain of the four fountains, and am resolved to go and drink of the stream of Rocnabad. I long to refresh myself, in the delightful vallies which it waters. Do you, with the advice of my mother, govern my dominions, and take care to supply whatever her experiments may demand: for, you well know, that our tower abounds in materials for the advancement of science.'

The tower but ill suited Morakanabad's taste. Immense treasures had been lavished upon it; and nothing had he ever seen carried thither but female negroes, mutes and abominable drugs. Nor did he know well what to think of Carathis, who, like a cameleon, could assume all possible colours. Her cursed eloquence had often driven the poor mussulman to his last shifts. He considered, however, that if she possessed but few good qualities, her son had still fewer; and that the alternative, on the whole, would be in her favour. Consoled, therefore, with this reflection; he went, in good spirits, to soothe the populace, and make the proper arrangements for his master's journey.

Vathek, to conciliate the Spirits of the subterranean palace, resolved that his expedition should be uncommonly splendid. With this view, he confiscated, on all sides, the property of his subjects; whilst his worthy mother stripped the seraglios she visited, of the gems they contained. She collected all the sempstresses and embroiderers of Samarah and other cities, to the distance of sixty leagues; to prepare pavilions, palanquins; sofas, canopies, and litters for the train of the monarch. There was not left, in Masulipatan, a single piece of chintz; and so much muslin had been brought up to dress out Bababalouk and the other black eunuchs, that there remained not an ell of it in the whole Irak of Babylon.

During these preparations, Carathis, who never lost sight of her great object, which was to obtain favour with the powers of darkness, made select parties of the fairest and most delicate ladies of the city: but in the midst of their gaiety, she contrived to introduce vipers amongst them, and to break pots of scorpions under the table. They all bit to a wonder, and Carathis would have left her friends to die, were it not that, to fill up the time, she now and then amused herself in curing their wounds, with an excellent anodyne of her own invention: for this good Princess abhorred being indolent.

Vathek, who was not altogether so active as his mother, devoted his time to the sole gratification of his senses, in the palaces which were severally dedicated to them. He disgusted himself no more with the divan, or the mosque. One half of Samarah followed his example, whilst the other lamented the progress of corruption.

In the midst of these transactions, the embassy returned, which had been sent, in pious times, to Mecca. It consisted of the most reverend Moullahs who had fulfilled their commission, and brought back one of those precious besoms which are used to sweep the sacred Cahaba: a present truly worthy of the greatest potentate on earth!

The Caliph happened at this instant to be engaged in an apartment by no means adapted to the reception of embassies. He heard the voice of Bababalouk, calling out from between the door and the tapestry that hung before it: 'Here are the excellent Edris al Shafei, and the seraphic Al Mouhateddin, who have brought the besom from Mecca, and, with tears of joy, entreat they may present it to your majesty in person.'—'Let them bring the besom hither, it may be of use,' said Vathek. 'How!' answered Bababalouk, half aloud and amazed. 'Obey,' replied the Caliph, 'for it is my sovereign will; go instantly, vanish! for here will I receive the good folk who have thus filled thee with joy.'

The eunuch departed muttering, and bade the venerable train attend him. A sacred rapture was diffused amongst these reverend old men. Though fatigued with the length of their expedition, they followed Bababalouk with an alertness almost miraculous, and felt themselves highly flattered, as they swept along the stately porticos, that the Caliph would not receive them like ambassadors in ordinary in his hall of audience. Soon reaching the interior of the harem (where, through blinds of Persian, they perceived large soft eyes, dark and blue, that came and went like lightning) penetrated with respect and wonder, and full of their celestial mission, they advanced in procession towards the small corridors that appeared to terminate in nothing, but, nevertheless, led to the cell where the Caliph expected their coming.

'What! is the commander of the faithful sick?' said Edris al Shafei, in a low voice to his companion—'I rather think he is in his oratory,' answered Al Mouhateddin. Vathek, who heard the dialogue, cried out:—'What imports it you, how I am employed? approach without delay.' They advanced, whilst the Caliph, without shewing himself, put forth his hand from behind the tapestry that hung before the door, and demanded of them the besom. Having prostrated themselves as well as the corridor would permit, and, even in a tolerable semicircle, the venerable Al Shafei, drawing forth the besom from the embroidered and perfumed scarves, in which it had been enveloped, and secured from the profane gaze of vulgar eyes, arose from his associates, and advanced, with an air of the most awful solemnity towards the supposed oratory; but, with what astonishment! with what horror was he seized!——Vathek, bursting out into a villainous laugh, snatched the besom from his trembling hand, and, fixing upon some cobwebs, that hung from the ceiling, gravely brushed them away till not a single one remained. The old men, overpowered with amazement, were unable to lift their beards from the ground: for, as Vathek had carelessly left the tapestry between them half drawn, they were witnesses of the whole transaction. Their tears bedewed the marble. Al Mouhateddin swooned through mortification and fatigue, whilst the Caliph, throwing himself backward on his seat, shouted, and clapped his hands without mercy. At last, addressing himself to Bababalouk!—'My dear black,' said he, 'go, regale these pious poor souls, with my good wine from Shiraz, since they can boast of having seen more of my palace than any one besides.' Having said this, he threw the besom in their face, and went to enjoy the laugh with Carathis. Bababalouk did all in his power to console the ambassadors; but the two most infirm expired on the spot: the rest were carried to their beds, from whence, being heart-broken with sorrow and shame, they never arose.

The succeeding night, Vathek, attended by his mother, ascended the tower to see if every thing were ready for his journey: for, he had great faith in the influence of the stars. The planets appeared in their most favourable aspects. The Caliph, to enjoy so flattering a sight, supped gaily on the roof; and fancied that he heard, during his repast, loud shouts of laughter resound through the sky, in a manner, that inspired the fullest assurance.

All was in motion at the palace; lights were kept burning through the whole of the night: the sound of implements, and of artizans finishing their work; the voices of women, and their guardians, who sung at their embroidery: all conspired to interrupt the stillness of nature, and infinitely delighted the heart of Vathek who imagined himself going in triumph to sit upon the throne of Soliman. The people were not less satisfied than himself: all assisted to accelerate the moment, which should rescue them from the wayward caprices of so extravagant a master.

The day preceding the departure of this infatuated Prince, was employed by Carathis, in repeating to him the decrees of the mysterious parchment; which she had thoroughly gotten by heart; and, in recommending him, not to enter the habitation of any one by the way: 'for, well thou knowest,' added she, 'how liquorish thy taste is after good dishes and young damsels; let me, therefore, enjoin thee, to be content with thy old cooks, who are the best in the world: and not to forget that, in thy ambulatory seraglio, there are at least three dozen of pretty faces which Bababalouk hath not yet unveiled. I myself have a great desire to watch over thy conduct, and visit the subterranean palace, which, no doubt, contains whatever can interest persons, like us. There is nothing so pleasing as retiring to caverns: my taste for dead bodies, and every thing like mummy is decided: and, I am confident, thou wilt see the most exquisite of their kind. Forget me not then, but the moment thou art in possession of the talismans which are to open the way to the mineral kingdoms and the centre of the earth itself, fail not to dispatch some trusty genius to take me and my cabinet: for the oil of the serpents I have pinched to death will be a pretty present to the Giaour who cannot but be charmed with such dainties.'

Scarcely had Carathis ended this edifying discourse, when the sun, setting behind the mountain of the four fountains, gave place to the rising moon. This planet, being that evening at full, appeared of unusual beauty and magnitude, in the eyes of the women, the eunuchs and the pages who were all impatient to set forward. The city re-echoed with shouts of joy, and flourishing of trumpets. Nothing was visible, but plumes, nodding on pavilions, and aigrets shining in the mild lustre of the moon. The spacious square resembled an immense parterre variegated with the most stately tulips of the east.

Arrayed in the robes which were only worn at the most distinguished ceremonials, and supported by his vizir and Bababalouk, the Caliph descended the great staircase of the tower in the sight of all his people. He could not forbear pausing, at intervals, to admire the superb appearance which every where courted his view: whilst the whole multitude, even to the camels with their sumptuous burthens, knelt down before him. For some time a general stillness prevailed, which nothing happened to disturb, but the shrill screams of some eunuchs in the rear. These vigilant guards, having remarked certain cages of the ladies swagging somewhat awry, and discovered that a few adventurous gallants had contrived to get in, soon dislodged the enraptured culprits and consigned them, with good commendations, to the surgeons of the serail. The majesty of so magnificent a spectacle, was not, however, violated by incidents like these. Vathek, meanwhile, saluted the moon with an idolatrous air, that neither pleased Morakanabad, nor the doctors of the law, any more than the vizirs and grandees of his court, who were all assembled to enjoy the last view of their sovereign.

At length, the clarions and trumpets from the top of the tower, announced the prelude of departure. Though the instruments were in unison with each other, yet a singular dissonance was blended with their sounds. This proceeded from Carathis who was singing her direful orisons to the Giaour, whilst the negresses and mutes supplied thorough base, without articulating a word. The good Mussulmans fancied that they heard the sullen hum of those nocturnal insects, which presage evil; and importuned Vathek to beware how he ventured his sacred person.

On a given signal, the great standard of the Califat was displayed; twenty thousand lances shone around it; and the Caliph, treading royally on the cloth of gold, which had been spread for his feet, ascended his litter, amidst the general acclamations of his subjects.

The expedition commenced with the utmost order and so entire a silence, that, even the locusts were heard from the thickets on the plain of Catoul. Gaiety and good humour prevailing, they made full six leagues before the dawn; and the morning star was still glittering in the firmament, when the whole of this numerous train had halted on the banks of the Tigris, where they encamped to repose for the rest of the day.

The three days that followed were spent in the same manner; but, on the fourth, the heavens looked angry; lightnings broke forth, in frequent flashes; re-echoing peals of thunder succeeded; and the trembling Circassians clung with all their might, to their ugly guardians. The Caliph himself, was greatly inclined to take shelter in the large town of Ghulchissar, the governor of which, came forth to meet him, and tendered every kind of refreshment the place could supply. But, having examined his tablets, he suffered the rain to soak him, almost to the bone, notwithstanding the importunity of his first favourites. Though he began to regret the palace of the senses; yet, he lost not sight of his enterprize, and his sanguine expectation confirmed his resolution. His geographers were ordered to attend him; but, the weather proved so terrible that these poor people exhibited a lamentable appearance: and their maps of the different countries spoiled by the rain, were in a still worse plight than themselves. As no long journey had been undertaken since the time of Haroun al Raschid, every one was ignorant which way to turn; and Vathek, though well versed in the course of the heavens, no longer knew his situation on earth. He thundered even louder than the elements; and muttered forth certain hints of the bow-string which were not very soothing to literary ears. Disgusted at the toilsome weariness of the way, he determined to cross over the craggy heights and follow the guidance of a peasant, who undertook to bring him, in four days, to Rocnabad. Remonstrances were all to no purpose; his resolution was fixed.

The females and eunuchs uttered shrill wailings at the sight of the precipices below them, and the dreary prospects that opened, in the vast gorges of the mountains. Before they could reach the ascent of the steepest rock, night overtook them, and a boisterous tempest arose, which, having rent the awnings of the palanquins and cages, exposed to the raw gusts the poor ladies within, who had never before felt so piercing a cold. The dark clouds that overcast the face of the sky deepened the horrors of this disastrous night, insomuch that nothing could be heard distinctly, but the mewling of pages and lamentations of sultanas.

To increase the general misfortune, the frightful uproar of wild beasts resounded at a distance; and there were soon perceived in the forest they were skirting, the glaring of eyes, which could belong only to devils or tigers. The pioneers, who, as well as they could, had marked out a track; and a part of the advanced guard, were devoured, before they had been in the least apprized of their danger. The confusion that prevailed was extreme. Wolves, tigers, and other carnivorous animals, invited by the howling of their companions, flocked together from every quarter. The crashing of bones was heard on all sides, and a fearful rush of wings over head; for now vultures also began to be of the party.

The terror at length reached the main body of the troops which surrounded the monarch and his harem at the distance of two leagues from the scene. Vathek (voluptuously reposed in his capacious litter upon cushions of silk, with two little pages beside him of complexions more fair than the enamel of Franguistan, who were occupied in keeping off flies) was soundly asleep, and contemplating in his dreams the treasures of Soliman. The shrieks however of his wives, awoke him with a start; and, instead of the Giaour with his key of gold, he beheld Bababalouk full of consternation. 'Sire,' exclaimed this good servant of the most potent of monarchs, 'misfortune is arrived at its height, wild beasts, who entertain no more reverence for your sacred person, than for a dead ass, have beset your camels and their drivers; thirty of the most richly laden are already become their prey, as well as your confectioners, your cooks, and purveyors: and, unless our holy Prophet should protect us, we shall have all eaten our last meal.' At the mention of eating, the Caliph lost all patience. He began to bellow, and even beat himself (for there was no seeing in the dark). The rumour every instant increased; and Bababalouk, finding no good could be done with his master, stopped both his ears against the hurlyburly of the harem, and called out aloud: 'Come, ladies, and brothers! all hands to work: strike light in a moment! never shall it be said, that the commander of the faithful served to regale these infidel brutes.' Though there wanted not in this bevy of beauties, a sufficient number of capricious and wayward; yet, on the present occasion, they were all compliance. Fires were visible, in a twinkling, in all their cages. Ten thousand torches were lighted at once. The Caliph, himself, seized a large one of wax: every person followed his example; and, by kindling ropes ends, dipped in oil and fastened on poles, an amazing blaze was spread. The rocks were covered with the splendour of sun-shine. The trails of sparks, wafted by the wind, communicated to the dry fern, of which there was plenty. Serpents were observed to crawl forth from their retreats, with amazement and hissings; whilst the horses snorted, stamped the ground, tossed their noses in the air, and plunged about, without mercy.

One of the forests of cedar that bordered their way, took fire; and the branches that overhung the path, extending their flames to the muslins and chintzes, which covered the cages of the ladies obliged them to jump out, at the peril of their necks. Vathek, who vented on the occasion a thousand blasphemies, was himself compelled to touch, with his sacred feet, the naked earth.

Never had such an incident happened before. Full of mortification, shame, and despondence, and not knowing how to walk, the ladies fell into the dirt. 'Must I go on foot!' said one: 'Must I wet my feet!' cried another: 'Must I soil my dress!' asked a third. 'Execrable Bababalouk!' exclaimed all: 'Outcast of hell! what hast thou to do with torches! Better were it to be eaten by tigers, than to fall into our present condition! we are for ever undone! Not a porter is there in the army nor a currier of camels; but hath seen some part of our bodies; and, what is worse, our very faces!' On saying this, the most bashful amongst them hid their foreheads on the ground, whilst such as had more boldness flew at Bababalouk; but he, well apprized of their humour and not wanting in shrewdness, betook himself to his heels along with his comrades, all dropping their torches and striking their tymbals.

It was not less light than in the brightest of the dog-days, and the weather was hot in proportion; but how degrading was the spectacle, to behold the Caliph bespattered, like an ordinary mortal! As the exercise of his faculties seemed to be suspended, one of his Ethiopian wives (for he delighted in variety) clasped him in her arms; threw him upon her shoulder, like a sack of dates, and, finding that the fire was hemming them in, set off, with no small expedition, considering the weight of her burden. The other ladies, who had just learnt the use of their feet, followed her; their guards galloped after; and the camel-drivers brought up the rear, as fast as their charge would permit.

They soon reached the spot, where the wild beasts had commenced the carnage, but which they had too much good sense not to leave at the approaching of the tumult, having made besides a most luxurious supper. Bababalouk, nevertheless, seized on a few of the plumpest, which were unable to budge from the place, and began to flea them with admirable adroitness. The cavalcade having proceeded so far from the conflagration, that the heat felt rather grateful than violent, it was, immediately, resolved on to halt. The tattered chintzes were picked up; the scraps, left by the wolves and tigers, interred; and vengeance was taken on some dozens of vultures, that were too much glutted to rise on the wing. The camels, which had been left unmolested to make sal ammoniac, being numbered; and the ladies once more inclosed in their cages; the imperial tent was pitched on the levellest ground they could find.

Vathek, reposing upon a mattress of down, and tolerably recovered from the jolting of the Ethiopian, who, to his feelings, seemed the roughest trotting jade he had hitherto mounted, called out for something to eat. But, alas! those delicate cakes, which had been baked in silver ovens, for his royal mouth; those rich manchets; amber comfits; flaggons of Schiraz wine; porcelain vases of snow; and grapes from the banks of the Tigris; were all irremediably lost!—And nothing had Bababalouk to present in their stead, but a roasted wolf; vultures à la daube; aromatic herbs of the most acrid poignancy; rotten truffles; boiled thistles: and such other wild plants, as must ulcerate the throat and parch up the tongue. Nor was he better provided, in the article of drink: for he could procure nothing to accompany these irritating viands, but a few phials of abominable brandy which had been secreted by the scullions in their slippers. Vathek made wry faces at so savage a repast; and Bababalouk answered them, with shrugs and contortions. The Caliph, however, eat with tolerable appetite; and fell into a nap, that lasted six hours.

The splendour of the sun, reflected from the white cliffs of the mountains, in spite of the curtains that inclosed Vathek, at length disturbed his repose. He awoke, terrified; and stung to the quick by wormwood-colour flies, which emitted from their wings a suffocating stench. The miserable monarch was perplexed how to act; though his wits were not idle, in seeking expedients, whilst Bababalouk lay snoring, amidst a swarm of those insects that busily thronged, to pay court to his nose. The little pages, famished with hunger, had dropped their fans on the ground; and exerted their dying voices, in bitter reproaches on the Caliph; who now, for the first time, heard the language of truth.

Thus stimulated, he renewed his imprecations against the Giaour; and bestowed upon Mahomet some soothing expressions. 'Where am I?' cried he: 'What are these dreadful rocks? these valleys of darkness! are we arrived at the horrible Kaf! is the Simurgh coming to pluck out my eyes, as a punishment for undertaking this impious enterprize!' Having said this he turned himself towards an outlet in the side of his pavilion, but, alas! what objects occurred to his view? on one side, a plain of black sand that appeared to be unbounded; and, on the other, perpendicular crags, bristled over with those abominable thistles, which had, so severely, lacerated his tongue. He fancied, however, that he perceived, amongst the brambles and briars, some gigantic flowers but was mistaken: for, these were only the dangling palampores and variegated tatters of his gay retinue. As there were several clefts in the rock from whence water seemed to have flowed, Vathek applied his ear with the hope of catching the sound of some latent torrent; but could only distinguish the low murmurs of his people who were repining at their journey, and complaining for the want of water. 'To what purpose,' asked they, 'have we been brought hither? hath our Caliph another tower to build? or have the relentless afrits, whom Carathis so much loves, fixed their abode in this place?'

At the name of Carathis, Vathek recollected the tablets he had received from his mother; who assured him, they were fraught with preternatural qualities, and advised him to consult them, as emergencies might require. Whilst he was engaged in turning them over, he heard a shout of joy, and a loud clapping of hands. The curtains of his pavilion were soon drawn back and he beheld Bababalouk, followed by a troop of his favourites, conducting two dwarfs each a cubit high; who brought between them a large basket of melons, oranges, and pomegranates. They were singing in the sweetest tones the words that follow: 'We dwell on the top of these rocks, in a cabin of rushes and canes; the eagles envy us our nest: a small spring supplies us with water for the Abdest, and we daily repeat prayers, which the Prophet approves. We love you, O commander of the faithful! our master, the good Emir Fakreddin, loves you also: he reveres, in your person, the vicegerent of Mahomet. Little as we are, in us he confides: he knows our hearts to be as good, as our bodies are contemptible; and hath placed us here to aid those who are bewildered on these dreary mountains. Last night, whilst we were occupied within our cell in reading the holy Koran, a sudden hurricane blew out our lights, and rocked our habitation. For two whole hours, a palpable darkness prevailed; but we heard sounds at a distance, which we conjectured to proceed from the bells of a Cafila, passing over the rocks. Our ears were soon filled with deplorable shrieks, frightful roarings, and the sound of tymbals. Chilled with terror, we concluded that the Deggial, with his exterminating angels, had sent forth his plagues on the earth. In the midst of these melancholy reflections, we perceived flames of the deepest red, glow in the horizon; and found ourselves, in a few moments, covered with flakes of fire. Amazed at so strange an appearance, we took up the volume dictated by the blessed intelligence, and, kneeling, by the light of the fire that surrounded us, we recited the verse which says: 'Put no trust in any thing but the mercy of Heaven: there is no help, save in the holy Prophet: the mountain of Kaf, itself, may tremble; it is the power of Alla only, that cannot be moved.' After having pronounced these words, we felt consolation, and our minds were hushed into a sacred repose. Silence ensued, and our ears clearly distinguished a voice in the air, saying: 'Servants of my faithful servant! go down to the happy valley of Fakreddin: tell him that an illustrious opportunity now offers to satiate the thirst of his hospitable heart. The commander of true believers is, this day, bewildered amongst these mountains and stands in need of thy aid.'—We obeyed, with joy, the angelic mission; and our master, filled with pious zeal, hath culled, with his own hands, these melons, oranges, and pomegranates. He is following us, with a hundred dromedaries, laden with the purest waters of his fountains; and is coming to kiss the fringe of your consecrated robe, and implore you to enter his humble habitation which, placed amidst these barren wilds, resembles an emerald set in lead.' The dwarfs, having ended their address, remained still standing, and, with hands crossed upon their bosoms, preserved a respectful silence.

Vathek, in the midst of this curious harangue, seized the basket; and, long before it was finished, the fruits had dissolved in his mouth. As he continued to eat, his piety increased; and, in the same breath, he recited his prayers and called for the Koran and sugar.

Such was the state of his mind, when the tablets, which were thrown by, at the approach of the dwarfs, again attracted his eye. He took them up; but was ready to drop on the ground, when he beheld in large red characters inscribed by Carathis, these words; which were, indeed, enough to make him tremble; 'Beware of old doctors and their puny messengers of but one cubit high: distrust their pious frauds; and, instead of eating their melons, empale on a spit the bearers of them. Shouldest thou be such a fool as to visit them, the portal of the subterranean palace will shut in thy face with such force, as shall shake thee asunder: thy body shall be spit upon, and bats will nestle in thy belly.'

'To what tends this ominous rhapsody?' cries the Caliph: 'and must I then perish in these deserts, with thirst; whilst I may refresh myself in the delicious valley of melons and cucumbers?—Accursed be the Giaour with his portal of ebony! he hath made me dance attendance, too long already. Besides, who shall prescribe laws to me?—I, forsooth, must not enter any one's habitation! Be it so: but, what one can I enter, that is not my own!' Bababalouk, who lost not a syllable of this soliloquy, applauded it with all his heart; and the ladies, for the first time, agreed with him in opinion.

The dwarfs were entertained, caressed, and seated, with great ceremony, on little cushions of satin. The symmetry of their persons was a subject of admiration; not an inch of them was suffered to pass unexamined. Knick-nacks and dainties were offered in profusion; but all were declined, with respectful gravity. They climbed up the sides of the Caliph's seat; and, placing themselves each on one of his shoulders, began to whisper prayers in his ears. Their tongues quivered, like aspen leaves; and the patience of Vathek was almost exhausted, when the acclamations of the troops announced the approach of Fakreddin, who was come with a hundred old grey-beards, and as many Korans and dromedaries. They instantly set about their ablutions, and began to repeat the Bismillah. Vathek, to get rid of these officious monitors, followed their example; for his hands were burning.

The good emir, who was punctiliously religious, and likewise a great dealer in compliments, made an harangue five times more prolix and insipid than his little harbingers had already delivered. The Caliph, unable any longer to refrain, exclaimed: 'For the love of Mahomet, my dear Fakreddin, have done! let us proceed to your valley, and enjoy the fruits that Heaven hath vouchsafed you.' The hint of proceeding, put all into motion. The venerable attendants of the emir set forward, somewhat slowly; but Vathek, having ordered his little pages, in private, to goad on the dromedaries, loud fits of laughter broke forth from the cages; for, the unwieldy curvetting of these poor beasts, and the ridiculous distress of their superannuated riders, afforded the ladies no small entertainment.

They descended, however, unhurt into the valley, by the easy slopes which the emir had ordered to be cut in the rock; and already, the murmuring of streams and the rustling of leaves began to catch their attention. The cavalcade soon entered a path, which was skirted by flowering shrubs, and extended to a vast wood of palm trees, whose branches overspread a vast building of free stone. This edifice was crowned with nine domes, and adorned with as many portals of bronze, on which was engraven the following inscription: 'This is the asylum of pilgrims, the refuge of travellers, and the depositary of secrets from all parts of the world.'

Nine pages, beautiful as the day, and decently clothed in robes of Egyptian linen, were standing at each door. They received the whole retinue with an easy and inviting air. Four of the most amiable placed the Caliph on a magnificent tecthtrevan: four others, somewhat less graceful, took charge of Bababalouk, who capered for joy at the snug little cabin that fell to his share; the pages that remained waited on the rest of the train.

Every man being gone out of sight, the gate of a large inclosure, on the right, turned on its harmonious hinges; and a young female, of a slender form, came forth. Her light brown hair floated in the hazy breeze of the twilight. A troop of young maidens, like the Pleiades, attended her on tip-toe. They hastened to the pavilions that contained the sultanas: and the young lady, gracefully bending, said to them: 'Charming princesses, every thing is ready: we have prepared beds for your repose, and strewed your apartments with jasmine: no insects will keep off slumber from visiting your eye-lids; we will dispel them with a thousand plumes. Come then, amiable ladies, refresh your delicate feet, and your ivory limbs, in baths of rose water; and, by the light of perfumed lamps, your servants will amuse you with tales.' The sultanas accepted, with pleasure, these obliging offers; and followed the young lady to the emir's harem; where we must, for a moment, leave them, and return to the Caliph.

Vathek found himself beneath a vast dome, illuminated by a thousand lamps of rock crystal: as many vases of the same material, filled with excellent sherbet, sparkled on a large table, where a profusion of viands were spread. Amongst others, were rice boiled in milk of almonds, saffron soups, and lamb à la crême; of all which the Caliph was amazingly fond. He took of each, as much as he was able, testified his sense of the emir's friendship, by the gaiety of his heart; and made the dwarfs dance, against their will: for these little devotees durst not refuse the commander of the faithful. At last, he spread himself on the sopha, and slept sounder than he ever had before.

Beneath this dome, a general silence prevailed; for there was nothing to disturb it but the jaws of Bababalouk, who had untrussed himself to eat with greater advantage; being anxious to make amends for his fast, in the mountains. As his spirits were too high to admit of his sleeping; and hating to be idle, he proposed with himself to visit the harem and repair to his charge of the ladies: to examine if they had been properly lubricated with the balm of Mecca; if their eye-brows, and tresses, were in order; and, in a word, to perform all the little offices they might need. He sought for a long time together but without being able to find out the door. He durst not speak aloud for fear of disturbing the Caliph; and not a soul was stirring in the precincts of the palace. He almost despaired of effecting his purpose, when a low whispering just reached his ear. It came from the dwarfs, who were returned to their old occupation, and, for the nine hundred and ninety-ninth time in their lives, were reading over the Koran. They very politely invited Bababalouk to be of their party; but his head was full of other concerns. The dwarfs, though not a little scandalized at his dissolute morals, directed him to the apartments he wanted to find. His way thither lay through a hundred dark corridors, along which he groped as he went; and at last, began to catch, from the extremity of a passage, the charming gossiping of the women which not a little delighted his heart. 'Ah, ha! what not yet asleep?' cried he; and, taking long strides as he spoke, 'did you not suspect me of abjuring my charge?' Two of the black eunuchs, on hearing a voice so loud, left their party in haste, sabre in hand, to discover the cause: but, presently, was repeated on all sides: "Tis only Bababalouk! no one but Bababalouk!' This circumspect guardian, having gone up to a thin veil of carnation-colour silk that hung before the door-way, distinguished, by means of the softened splendor that shone through it, an oval bath of dark porphyry surrounded by curtains, festooned in large folds. Through the apertures between them, as they were not drawn close, groups of young slaves were visible; amongst whom, Bababalouk perceived his pupils, indulgingly expanding their arms, as if to embrace the perfumed water, and refresh themselves after their fatigues. The looks of tender languor; their confidential whispers; and the enchanting smiles with which they were imparted; the exquisite fragrance of the roses: all combined to inspire a voluptuousness, which even Bababalouk himself was scarce able to withstand.

He summoned up, however, his usual solemnity, and in the peremptory tone of authority, commanded the ladies, instantly, to leave the bath. Whilst he was issuing these mandates, the young Nouronihar, daughter of the emir, who was as sprightly as an antelope, and full of wanton gaiety, beckoned one of her slaves to let down the great swing which was suspended to the ceiling by cords of silk; and whilst this was doing, winked to her companions in the bath: who, chagrined to be forced from so soothing a state of indolence, began to twist and entangle their hair to plague and detain Bababalouk; and teased him besides with a thousand vagaries.

Nouronihar perceiving that he was nearly out of patience accosted him, with an arch air of respectful concern, and said: 'My lord! it is not, by any means decent, that the chief eunuch of the Caliph our sovereign should thus continue standing: deign but to recline your graceful person upon this sofa

which will burst with vexation, if it have not the honour to receive you.'
Caught by these flattering accents, Bababalouk gallantly replied: 'Delight of
the apple of my eye! I accept the invitation of your honied lips; and, to say
truth, my senses are dazzled with the radiance that beams from your
charms.'—'Repose, then, at your ease,' replied the beauty; as she placed
him on the pretended sofa which, quicker than lightning, flew up all at once.
The rest of the women, having aptly conceived her design, sprang naked
from the bath, and plied the swing, with such unmerciful jerks, that it swept
through the whole compass of a very lofty dome, and took from the poor
victim all power of respiration. Sometimes, his feet rased the surface of the
water; and, at others, the skylight almost flattened his nose. In vain did he
fill the air with the cries of a voice that resembled the ringing of a cracked
jar; their peals of laughter were still predominant.

Nouronihar, in the inebriety of youthful spirits, being used only to
eunuchs of ordinary harems; and having never seen any thing so eminently
disgusting, was far more diverted than all of the rest. She began to parody
some Persian verses and sang with an accent most demurely piquant: 'Oh
gentle white dove, as thou soar'st through the air, vouchsafe one kind glance
on the mate of thy love: melodious Philomel, I am thy rose; warble some
couplet to ravish my heart!'

The sultanas and their slaves, stimulated by these pleasantries, persevered
at the swing, with such unremitted assiduity, that at length, the cord which
had secured it, snapt suddenly asunder; and Bababalouk fell, floundering
like a turtle, to the bottom of the bath. This accident occasioned an
universal shout. Twelve little doors, till now unobserved, flew open at once;
and the ladies, in an instant, made their escape; but not before having
heaped all the towels on his head and put out the lights that remained.

The deplorable animal, in water to the chin, overwhelmed with darkness,
and unable to extricate himself from the wrappers that embarrassed him,
was still doomed to hear, for his further consolation, the fresh bursts of
merriment his disaster occasioned. He bustled, but in vain, to get from the
bath; for, the margin was become so slippery, with the oil spilt in breaking
the lamps, that, at every effort, he slid back with a plunge which resounded
aloud through the hollow of the dome. These cursed peals of laughter, were
redoubled at every relapse, and he, who thought the place infested rather
by devils than women, resolved to cease groping, and abide in the bath;
where he amused himself with soliloquies, interspersed with imprecations, of
which his malicious neighbours, reclining on down, suffered not an accent
to escape. In this delectable plight, the morning surprised him. The Caliph,
wondering at his absence, had caused him to be sought for every where. At
last, he was drawn forth almost smothered from under the wisp of linen, and
wet even to the marrow. Limping, and his teeth chattering with cold, he
approached his master; who inquired what was the matter, and how he

came soused in so strange a pickle?—'And why did you enter this cursed lodge?' answered Bababalouk, gruffly.—'Ought a monarch like you to visit with his harem, the abode of a grey-bearded emir, who knows nothing of life?—And, with what gracious damsels doth the place too abound! Fancy to yourself how they have soaked me like a burnt crust; and made me dance like a jack-pudding, the live-long night through, on their damnable swing. What an excellent lesson for your sultanas, into whom I had instilled such reserve and decorum!' Vathek, comprehending not a syllable of all this invective, obliged him to relate minutely the transaction: but, instead of sympathizing with the miserable sufferer, he laughed immoderately at the device of the swing and the figure of Bababalouk, mounted upon it. The stung eunuch could scarcely preserve the semblance of respect. 'Aye, laugh, my lord! laugh,' said he; 'but I wish this Nouronihar would play some trick on you; she is too wicked to spare even majesty itself.' These words made, for the present, but a slight impression on the Caliph; but they, not long after, recurred to his mind.

This conversation was cut short by Fakreddin, who came to request that Vathek would join in the prayers and ablutions, to be solemnized on a spacious meadow watered by innumerable streams. The Caliph found the waters refreshing, but the prayers abominably irksome. He diverted himself, however, with the multitude of calenders, santons, and derviches, who were continually coming and going; but especially with the bramins, faquirs, and other enthusiasts, who had travelled from the heart of India, and halted on their way with the emir. These latter had each of them some mummery peculiar to himself. One dragged a huge chain wherever he went; another an ouran-outang; whilst a third, was furnished with scourges; and all performed to a charm. Some would climb up trees, holding one foot in the air; others poise themselves over a fire, and, without mercy, fillip their noses. There were some amongst them that cherished vermin, which were not ungrateful in requiting their caresses. These rambling fanatics revolted the hearts of the derviches, the calenders, and santons; however, the vehemence of their aversion soon subsided, under the hope that the presence of the Caliph would cure their folly, and convert them to the mussulman faith. But, alas! how great was their disappointment! for Vathek, instead of preaching to them, treated them as buffoons, bade them present his compliments to Visnow and Ixhora, and discovered a predilection for a squat old man from the Isle of Serendib, who was more ridiculous than any of the rest. 'Come!' said he, 'for the love of your gods, bestow a few slaps on your chops to amuse me.' The old fellow, offended at such an address, began loudly to weep; but, as he betrayed a villainous drivelling in shedding tears, the Caliph turned his back and listened to Bababalouk, who whispered, whilst he held the umbrella over him: 'Your majesty should be cautious of this odd assembly; which hath been collected, I know not for what. Is it necessary to exhibit such spectacles to a mighty potentate, with interludes of talapoins more mangy than dogs? Were I you, I would command a fire to be kindled, and at once rid the estates of the emir, of his harem, and all his menagerie.'—'Tush, dolt,' answered Vathek; 'and know, that all this infinitely charms me. Nor shall I leave the meadow, till I have visited every hive of these pious mendicants.'

Wherever the Caliph directed his course, objects of pity were sure to swarm round him; the blind, the purblind, smarts without noses, damsels without ears, each to extol the munificence of Fakreddin, who, as well as his attendant grey-beards, dealt about, gratis, plasters and cataplasms to all that applied. At noon, a superb corps of cripples made its appearance; and soon after advanced, by platoons, on the plain, the completest association of invalids that had ever been embodied till then. The blind went groping with the blind, the lame limped on together, and the maimed made gestures to each other with the only arm that remained. The sides of a considerable water-fall were crowded by the deaf; amongst whom were some from Pegû, with ears uncommonly handsome and large, but who were still less able to hear than the rest. Nor were there wanting others in abundance with hump-backs; wenny necks; and even horns of an exquisite polish.

The emir, to aggrandize the solemnity of the festival, in honour of his illustrious visitant, ordered the turf to be spread, on all sides, with skins and table-cloths; upon which were served up for the good Mussulmans, pilaus of every hue, with other orthodox dishes; and, by the express order of Vathek, who was shamefully tolerant, small plates of abominations were prepared, to the great scandal of the faithful. The holy assembly began to fall to. The Caliph, in spite of every remonstrance from the chief of his eunuchs, resolved to have a dinner dressed on the spot. The complaisant emir immediately gave orders for a table to be placed in the shade of the willows. The first service consisted of fish, which they drew from a river, flowing over sands of gold at the foot of a lofty hill. These were broiled as fast as taken, and served up with a sauce of vinegar, and small herbs that grew on mount Sinai: for every thing with the emir was excellent and pious.

The desert was not quite set on, when the sound of lutes, from the hill, was repeated by the echoes of the neighbouring mountains. The Caliph, with an emotion of pleasure and surprize, had no sooner raised up his head, than a handful of jasmine dropped on his face. An abundance of tittering succeeded the frolic, and instantly appeared, through the bushes, the elegant forms of several young females, skipping and bounding like roes. The fragrance diffused from their hair, struck the sense of Vathek, who, in an ecstacy, suspending his repast, said to Bababalouk: 'Are the peries come down from their spheres? Note her, in particular, whose form is so perfect; venturously running on the brink of the precipice, and turning back her head, as regardless of nothing but the graceful flow of her robe. With what captivating impatience doth she contend with the bushes for her veil? could it be her who threw the jasmine at me!'—'Aye! she it was; and you too would she throw, from the top of the rock,' answered Bababalouk; 'for that is my good friend Nouronihar, who so kindly lent me her swing. My dear lord and master,' added he, wresting a twig from a willow, 'let me correct her for her want of respect: the emir will have no reason to complain; since (bating what I owe to his piety) he is much to be blamed for keeping a troop of girls on the mountains, where the sharpness of the air gives their blood too brisk a circulation.'

'Peace! blasphemer,' said the Caliph; 'speak not thus of her, who, over these mountains, leads my heart a willing captive. Contrive, rather, that my eyes may be fixed upon hers: that I may respire her sweet breath as she bounds panting along these delightful wilds!' On saying these words, Vathek extended his arms towards the hill, and directing his eyes, with an anxiety unknown to him before, endeavoured to keep within view the object that enthralled his soul: but her course was as difficult to follow, as the flight of one of those beautiful blue butterflies of Cachemire, which are, at once, so volatile and rare.

The Caliph, not satisfied with seeing, wished also to hear Nouronihar, and eagerly turned to catch the sound of her voice. At last, he distinguished her whispering to one of her companions behind the thicket from whence she had thrown the jasmine: 'A Caliph, it must be owned, is a fine thing to see; but my little Gulchenrouz is much more amiable: one lock of his hair is of more value to me than the richest embroidery of the Indies. I had rather that his teeth should mischievously press my finger, than the richest ring of the imperial treasure. Where have you left him, Sutlememe? and why is he not here?'

The agitated Caliph still wished to hear more; but she immediately retired with all her attendants. The fond monarch pursued her with his eyes till she was gone out of sight; and then continued like a bewildered and benighted traveller, from whom the clouds had obscured the constellation that guided his way. The curtain of night seemed dropped before him: every thing appeared discoloured. The falling waters filled his soul with dejection, and his tears trickled down the jasmines he had caught from Nouronihar, and placed in his inflamed bosom. He snatched up a few shining pebbles, to remind him of the scene where he felt the first tumults of love. Two hours were elapsed, and evening drew on, before he could resolve to depart from the place. He often, but in vain, attempted to go: a soft languor enervated the powers of his mind. Extending himself on the brink of the stream, he turned his eyes towards the blue summits of the mountain, and exclaimed, 'What concealest thou behind thee, pitiless rock? what is passing in thy solitudes? Whither is she gone? O heaven! perhaps she is now wandering in thy grottoes with her happy Gulchenrouz!'

In the mean time, the damps began to descend; and the emir, solicitous for the health of the Caliph, ordered the imperial litter to be brought. Vathek, absorbed in his reveries, was imperceptibly removed and conveyed back to the saloon, that received him the evening before. But, let us leave the Caliph immersed in his new passion: and attend Nouronihar beyond the rocks where she had again joined her beloved Gulchenrouz.

This Gulchenrouz was the son of Ali Hassan, brother to the emir: and the most delicate and lovely creature in the world. Ali Hassan, who had been absent ten years, on a voyage to the unknown seas, committed, at his departure, this child, the only survivor of many, to the care and protection of his brother. Gulchenrouz could write in various characters with precision, and paint upon vellum the most elegant arabesques that fancy could devise. His sweet voice accompanied the lute in the most enchanting manner; and, when he sang the loves of Megnoun and Leilah, or some unfortunate lovers of ancient days, tears insensibly overflowed the cheeks of his auditors. The verses he composed (for, like Megnoun, he, too, was a poet) inspired that unresisting languor, so frequently fatal to the female heart. The women all doated upon him; and, though he had passed his thirteenth year, they still detained him in the harem. His dancing was light as the gossamer waved by the zephyrs of spring; but his arms, which twined so gracefully with those of the young girls in the dance, could neither dart the lance in the chace, nor curb the steeds that pastured in his uncle's domains. The bow, however, he drew with a certain aim, and would have excelled his competitors in the race, could he have broken the ties that bound him to Nouronihar.

The two brothers had mutually engaged their children to each other; and Nouronihar loved her cousin, more than her own beautiful eyes. Both had the same tastes and amusements; the same long, languishing looks; the same tresses; the same fair complexions; and, when Gulchenrouz appeared in the dress of his cousin, he seemed to be more feminine than even herself. If, at any time, he left the harem, to visit Fakreddin; it was with all the bashfulness of a fawn, that consciously ventures from the lair of its dam: he was, however, wanton enough to mock the solemn old grey-beards, though sure to be rated without mercy in return. Whenever this happened, he would hastily plunge into the recesses of the harem; and, sobbing, take refuge in the fond arms of Nouronihar who loved even his faults beyond the virtues of others.

It fell out this evening, that, after leaving the Caliph in the meadow, she ran with Gulchenrouz over the green sward of the mountain, that sheltered the vale where Fakreddin had chosen to reside. The sun was dilated on the edge of the horizon; and the young people, whose fancies were lively and inventive, imagined they beheld, in the gorgeous clouds of the west, the domes of Shaddukian and Ambreabad, where the Peries have fixed their abode. Nouronihar, sitting on the slope of the hill, supported on her knees the perfumed head of Gulchenrouz. The unexpected arrival of the Caliph and the splendour that marked his appearance, had already filled with emotion the ardent soul of Nouronihar. Her vanity irresistibly prompted her to pique the prince's attention; and this, she before took good care to effect, whilst he picked up the jasmine she had thrown upon him. But, when Gulchenrouz asked after the flowers he had culled for her bosom, Nouronihar was all in confusion. She hastily kissed his forehead; arose in a flutter; and walked, with unequal steps, on the border of the precipice. Night advanced, and the pure gold of the setting sun had yielded to a sanguine red; the glow of which, like the reflection of a burning furnace, flushed Nouronihar's animated countenance. Gulchenrouz, alarmed at the agitation of his cousin, said to her, with a supplicating accent—'Let us begone; the sky looks portentous; the tamarisks tremble more than common; and the raw wind chills my very heart. Come! let us begone; 'tis a melancholy night!' Then, taking hold of her hand, he drew it towards the path he besought her to go. Nouronihar, unconsciously followed the attraction; for, a thousand strange imaginations occupied her spirits. She passed the large round of honey-suckles, her favourite resort, without ever vouchasfing it a glance; yet Gulchenrouz could not help snatching off a few shoots in his way, though he ran as if a wild beast were behind.

The young females seeing them approach in such haste, and, according to custom, expecting a dance, instantly assembled in a circle and took each other by the hand: but, Gulchenrouz coming up out of breath, fell down at once on the grass. This accident struck with consternation the whole of this frolicsome party; whilst Nouronihar, half distracted and overcome, both by the violence of her exercise, and the tumult of her thoughts, sunk feebly down at his side; cherished his cold hands in her bosom, and chafed his temples with a fragrant perfume. At length, he came to himself; and, wrapping up his head in the robe of his cousin, intreated that she would not return to the harem. He was afraid of being snapped at by Shaban his tutor; a wrinkled old eunuch of a surly disposition; for, having interrupted the wonted walk of Nouronihar, he dreaded lest the churl should take it amiss. The whole of this sprightly group, sitting round upon a mossy knoll, began to entertain themselves with various pastimes; whilst their superintendants, the eunuchs, were gravely conversing at a distance. The nurse of the emir's daughter, observing her pupil sit ruminating with her eyes on the ground, endeavoured to amuse her with diverting tales; to which Gulchenrouz, who had already forgotten his inquietudes, listened with a breathless attention. He laughed; he clapped his hands; and passed a hundred little tricks on the whole of the company, without omitting the eunuchs whom he provoked to run after him, in spite of their age and decrepitude.

During these occurrences, the moon arose, the wind subsided, and the evening became so serene and inviting, that a resolution was taken to sup on the spot. One of the eunuchs ran to fetch melons whilst others were employed in showering down almonds from the branches that overhung this amiable party. Sutlememe, who excelled in dressing a salad, having filled large bowls of porcelain with eggs of small birds, curds turned with citron juice, slices of cucumber, and the inmost leaves of delicate herbs, handed it round from one to another and gave each their shares with a large spoon of cocknos. Gulchenrouz, nestling, as usual, in the bosom of Nouronihar, pouted out his vermillion little lips against the offer of Sutlememe; and would take it, only, from the hand of his cousin, on whose mouth he hung, like a bee inebriated with the nectar of flowers.

In the midst of this festive scene, there appeared a light on the top of the highest mountain, which attracted the notice of every eye. This light was not less bright than the moon when at full, and might have been taken for her, had not the moon already risen. The phenomenon occasioned a general surprize and no one could conjecture the cause. It could not be a fire, for the light was clear and bluish: nor had meteors ever been seen of that magnitude or splendour. This strange light faded, for a moment; and immediately renewed its brightness. It first appeared motionless, at the foot of the rock; whence it darted in an instant, to sparkle in a thicket of palm-trees: from thence it glided along the torrent; and at last fixed in a glen that was narrow and dark. The moment it had taken its direction, Gulchen-rouz, whose heart always trembled at any thing sudden or rare, drew Nouronihar by the robe and anxiously requested her to return to the harem. The women were importunate in seconding the intreaty; but the curiosity of the emir's daughter prevailed. She not only refused to go back, but resolved, at all hazards, to pursue the appearance.

Whilst they were debating what was best to be done, the light shot forth so dazzling a blaze that they all fled away shrieking. Nouronihar followed them a few steps; but, coming to the turn of a little bye path, stopped, and went back alone. As she ran with an alertness peculiar to herself. it was not long before she came to the place, where they had just been supping. The globe of fire now appeared stationary in the glen, and burned in majestic stillness. Nouronihar, pressing her hands upon her bosom, hesitated, for some moments, to advance. The solitude of her situation was new; the silence of the night, awful; and every object inspired sensations, which, till then, she never had felt. The affright of Gulchenrouz recurred to her mind, and she, a thousand times turned to go back; but this luminous appearance was always before her. Urged on by an irresistible impulse, she continued to approach it, in defiance of every obstacle that opposed her progress.

At length she arrived at the opening of the glen; but, instead of coming up to the light, she found herself surrounded by darkness; excepting that, at a considerable distance, a faint spark glimmered by fits. She stopped, a second time: the sound of water-falls mingling their murmurs; the hollow rustlings among the palm-branches; and the funereal screams of the birds from their rifted trunks: all conspired to fill her soul with terror. She imagined, every moment, that she trod on some venomous reptile. All the stories of malignant Dives and dismal Goules thronged into her memory: but, her curiosity was, notwithstanding, more predominant than her fears. She, therefore, firmly entered a winding track that led towards the spark; but, being a stranger to the path, she had not gone far, till she began to repent of her rashness. 'Alas!' said she, 'that I were but in those secure and illuminated apartments, where my evenings glided on with Gulchenrouz! Dear child! how would thy heart flutter with terror, wert thou wandering in these wild solitudes, like me!' Thus speaking, she advanced, and, coming up to steps hewn in the rock, ascended them undismayed. The light, which was now gradually enlarging, appeared above her on the summit of the mountain, and as if proceeding from a cavern. At length, she distinguished a plaintive and melodious union of voices, that resembled the dirges which are sung over tombs. A sound, like that which arises from the filling of baths, struck her ear at the same time. She continued ascending, and discovered large wax torches in full blaze, planted here and there in the fissures of the rock. This appearance filled her with fear, whilst the subtle and potent odour, which the torches exhaled, caused her to sink, almost lifeless, at the entrance of the grot.

Casting her eyes within, in this kind of trance, she beheld a large cistern of gold, filled with a water, the vapour of which distilled on her face a dew of the essence of roses. A soft symphony resounded through the grot. On the sides of the cistern, she noticed appendages of royalty, diadems and feathers of the heron, all sparkling with carbuncles. Whilst her attention was fixed on this display of magnificence, the music ceased, and a voice instantly demanded: 'For what monarch are these torches kindled, this bath prepared, and these habiliments which belong, not only to the sovereigns of the earth, but even to the talismanick powers!' To which a second voice answered: 'They are for the charming daughter of the emir Fakreddin.'—'What,' replied the first, 'for that trifler, who consumes her time with a giddy child, immersed in softness, and who, at best, can make but a pitiful husband?'— 'And can she,' rejoined the other voice, 'be amused with such empty toys, whilst the Caliph, the sovereign of the world, he who is destined to enjoy the treasures of the pre-adamite sultans; a prince six feet high; and whose eyes pervade the inmost soul of a female, is inflamed with love for her. No! she will be wise enough to answer that passion alone, that can aggrandize her glory. No doubt she will; and despise the puppet of her fancy. Then all the riches this place contains, as well as the carbuncle of Giamschid, shall be hers.'—'You judge right,' returned the first voice; 'and I haste to Istakhar, to prepare the palace of subterranean fire for the reception of the bridal pair.'

The voices ceased; the torches were extinguished, the most entire darkness succeeded; and Nouronihar recovering, with a start, found herself reclined on a sofa, in the harem of her father. She clapped her hands, and immediately came together, Gulchenrouz and her women; who, in despair at having lost her, had dispatched eunuchs to seek her, in every direction. Shaban appeared with the rest, and began to reprimand her, with an air of consequence: 'Little impertinent,' said he, 'have you false keys, or are you beloved of some genius, that hath given you a picklock? I will try the extent of your power: come to the dark chamber, and expect not the company of Gulchenrouz:—be expeditious! I will shut you up, and turn the key twice upon you!' At these menaces, Nouronihar indignantly raised her head, opened on Shaban her black eyes, which, since the important dialogue of the enchanted grot, were considerably enlarged, and said: 'Go, speak thus to slaves; but learn to reverence her who is born to give laws and subject all to her power.'

Proceeding in the same style, she was interrupted by a sudden exclamation of, 'The Caliph! the Caliph!' All the curtains were thrown open, the slaves prostrated themselves in double rows, and poor little Gulchenrouz went to hide beneath the couch of a sofa. At first appeared a file of black eunuchs trailing after them long trains of muslin embroidered with gold, and holding in their hands censers, which dispensed, as they passed, the grateful perfume of the wood of aloes. Next marched Bababalouk with a solemn strut, and tossing his head, as not overpleased at the visit. Vathek came close after, superbly robed: his gait was unembarrassed and noble; and his presence would have engaged admiration, though he had not been the sovereign of the world. He approached Nouronihar with a throbbing heart, and seemed enraptured at the full effulgence of her radiant eyes, of which he had before caught but a few glimpses: but she instantly depressed them, and her confusion augmented her beauty.

Bababalouk, who was a thorough adept in coincidences of this nature, and knew that the worst game should be played with the best face, immediately made a signal for all to retire; and no sooner did he perceive beneath the sofa the little one's feet, than he drew him forth without ceremony, set him upon his shoulders, and lavished on him, as he went off, a thousand unwelcome caresses. Gulchenrouz cried out, and resisted till his cheeks became the colour of the blossom of pomegranates, and his tearful eyes sparkled with indignation. He cast a significant glance at Nouronihar, which the Caliph noticing, asked, 'Is that, then, your Gulchenrouz?'—'Sovereign of the world!' answered she, 'spare my cousin, whose innocence and gentleness deserve not your anger!'—'Take comfort,' said Vathek, with a smile; 'he is in good hands. Bababalouk is fond of children; and never goes without sweetmeats and comfits.' The daughter of Fakreddin was abashed, and suffered Gulchenrouz to be borne away without adding a word. The tumult of her bosom betrayed her confusion, and Vathek becoming still more impassioned, gave a loose to his frenzy; which had only not subdued the last faint strugglings of reluctance, when the emir suddenly bursting in, threw his face upon the ground, at the feet of the Caliph, and said: 'Commander of the faithful! abase not yourself to the meanness of your slave.'—'No, emir,' replied Vathek, 'I raise her to an equality with myself: I declare her my wife; and the glory of your race shall extend from one generation to another.'—'Alas! my lord,' said Fakreddin, as he plucked off a few grey hairs of his beard; 'cut short the days of your faithful servant, rather than force him to depart from his word. Nouronihar is solemnly promised to Gulchenrouz, the son of my brother Ali Hassan: they are united, also, in heart; their faith is mutually plighted; and affiances, so sacred, cannot be broken.'—'What then!' replied the Caliph, bluntly, 'would you surrender this divine beauty to a husband more womanish than herself; and can you imagine, that I will suffer her charms to decay in hands so inefficient and nerveless? No! she is destined to live out her life within my embraces: such is my will: retire; and disturb not the night I devote to the worship of her charms.'

The irritated emir drew forth his sabre, presented it to Vathek, and, stretching out his neck, said, in a firm tone of voice: 'Strike your unhappy host, my lord! he has lived long enough, since he hath seen the prophet's vicegerent violate the rights of hospitality.' At his uttering these words, Nouronihar, unable to support any longer the conflict of her passions, sunk down in a swoon. Vathek, both terrified for her life, and furious at an opposition to his will, bade Fakreddin assist his daughter, and withdrew; darting his terrible look at the unfortunate emir, who suddenly fell backward, bathed in a sweat as cold as the damp of death.

Gulchenrouz, who had escaped from the hands of Bababalouk and was, that instant, returned, called out for help, as loudly as he could, not having strength to afford it himself. Pale and panting, the poor child a.tempted to revive Nouronihar by caresses; and it happened, that the thrilling warmth of his lips restored her to life. Fakreddin beginning also to recover from the look of the Caliph, with difficulty tottered to a seat; and, after warily casting round his eye, to see if this dangerous Prince were gone, sent for Shaban and Sutlememe; and said to them apart: 'My friends! violent evils require violent remedies: the Caliph has brought desolation and horror into my family; and, how shall we resist his power? Another of his looks will send me to the grave. Fetch, then, that narcotick powder which a dervish brought me from Aracan. A dose of it, the effect of which will continue three days, must be administered to each of these children. The Caliph will believe them to be dead; for, they will have all the appearance of death. We shall go, as if to inter them in the cave of Meimoune, at the entrance of the great desert of sand and near the bower of my dwarfs. When all the spectators shall be withdrawn, you, Shaban, and four select eunuchs, shall convey them to the lake; where provision shall be ready to support them a month: for, one day allotted to the surprize this event will occasion; five, to the tears; a fortnight to reflection; and the rest, to prepare for renewing his progress; will, according to my calculation, fill up the whole time that Vathek will tarry; and I shall, then, be freed from his intrusion.'

'Your plan is good,' said Sutlememe, 'if it can but be effected. I have remarked, that Nouronihar is well able to support the glances of the Caliph: and, that he is far from being sparing of them to her: be assured, therefore, that notwithstanding her fondness for Gulchenrouz, she will never remain quiet, while she knows him to be here. Let us persuade her, that both herself and Gulchenrouz are really dead; and, that they were conveyed to those rocks, for a limited season, to expiate the little faults, of which their love was the cause. We will add, that we killed ourselves in despair; and that your dwarfs, whom they never yet saw, will preach to them delectable sermons. I will engage that every thing shall succeed to the bent of your wishes.'—'Be it so!' said Fakreddin, 'I approve your proposal: let us lose not a moment to give it effect.'

They hastened to seek for the powder which, being mixed in a sherbet, was immediately administered to Gulchenrouz and Nouronihar. Within the space of an hour, both were seized with violent palpitations; and a general numbness gradually ensued. They arose from the floor where they had remained ever since the Caliph's departure; and, ascending to the sofa, reclined themselves upon it, clasped in each other's embraces. 'Cherish me, my dear Nouronihar!' said Gulchenrouz: 'put thy hand upon my heart; it feels as if it were frozen. Alas! thou art as cold as myself! hath the Caliph murdered us both, with his terrible look?'—'I am dying!' cried she, in a faultering voice: 'Press me closer; I am ready to expire!'—'Let us die then, together,' answered the little Gulchenrouz; whilst his breast laboured with a convulsive sigh: 'let me, at least, breathe forth my soul on thy lips!' They spoke no more, and became as dead.

Immediately, the most piercing cries were heard through the harem; whilst Shaban and Sutlememe personated with great adroitness, the parts of persons in despair. The emir, who was sufficiently mortified, to be forced into such untoward expedients; and had now, for the first time, made a trial of his powder, was under no necessity of counter-feiting grief. The slaves, who had flocked together from all quarters, stood motionless, at the spectacle before them. All lights were extinguished, save two lamps; which shed a wan glimmering over the faces of these lovely flowers that seemed to be faded in the spring-time of life. Funeral vestments were prepared; their bodies were washed, with rose-water; their beautiful tresses were braided and incensed; and they were wrapped in symars whiter than alabaster.

At the moment, that their attendants were placing two wreaths of their favourite jasmines, on their brows, the Caliph, who had just heard the tragical catastrophe, arrived. He looked not less pale and haggard than the goules that wander, at night, among the graves. Forgetful of himself and every one else, he broke through the midst of the slaves; fell prostrate at the foot of the sofa; beat his bosom; called himself 'atrocious murderer!' and invoked upon his head, a thousand imprecations. With a trembling hand he raised the veil that covered the countenance of Nouronihar, and uttering a loud shriek, fell lifeless on the floor. The chief of the eunuchs dragged him off, with horrible grimaces, and repeated as he went, 'Aye, I foresaw she would play you some ungracious turn!'

No sooner was the Caliph gone, than the emir commanded biers to be brought, and forbad that any one should enter the harem. Every window was fastened; all instruments of music were broken; and the Imans began to recite their prayers. Towards the close of this melancholy day, Vathek sobbed in silence; for they had been forced to compose, with anodynes, his convulsions of rage and desperation.

At the dawn of the succeeding morning, the wide folding doors of the palace were set open, and the funeral procession moved forward for the mountain. The wailful cries of 'La Ilah illa Alla!' reached the Caliph, who was eager to cicatrize himself, and attend the ceremonial: nor could he have been dissuaded, had not his excessive weakness disabled him from walking. At the few first steps he fell on the ground, and his people were obliged to lay him on a bed, where he remained many days in such a state of insensibility as excited compassion in the emir himself.

When the procession was arrived at the grot of Meimoune, Shaban and Sutlememe dismissed the whole of the train, excepting the four confidential eunuchs who were appointed to remain. After resting some moments near the biers, which had been left in the open air; they caused them to be carried to the brink of a small lake, whose banks were overgrown with a hoary moss. This was the great resort of herons and storks which preyed continually on little blue fishes. The dwarfs, instructed by the emir, soon repaired thither; and, with the help of the eunuchs, began to construct cabins of rushes and reeds, a work in which they had admirable skill. A magazine also was contrived for provisions, with a small oratory for themselves, and a pyramid of wood, neatly piled to furnish the necessary fuel: for the air was bleak in the hollows of the mountains.

At evening two fires were kindled on the brink of the lake, and the two lovely bodies, taken from their biers, were carefully deposited upon a bed of dried leaves, within the same cabin. The dwarfs began to recite the Koran, with their clear, shrill voices; and Shaban and Sutlememe stood at some distance, anxiously waiting the effects of the powder. At length Nouronihar and Gulchenrouz faintly stretched out their arms; and, gradually opening their eyes, began to survey, with looks of increasing amazement, every object around them. They even attempted to rise; but, for want of strength, fell back again. Sutlememe, on this, administered a cordial, which the emir had taken care to provide.

Gulchenrouz, thoroughly aroused, sneezed out aloud: and, raising himself with an effort that expressed his surprize, left the cabin and inhaled the fresh air, with the greatest avidity. 'Yes,' said he, 'I breathe again! again do I exist! I hear sounds! I behold a firmament, spangled over with stars!'—Nouronihar, catching these beloved accents, extricated herself from the leaves and ran to clasp Gulchenrouz to her bosom. The first objects she remarked, were their long simars, their garlands of flowers, and their naked feet: she hid her face in her hands to reflect. The vision of the enchanted bath, the despair of her father, and, more vividly than both, the majestic figure of Vathek, recurred to her memory. She recollected also, that herself and Gulchenrouz had been sick and dying; but all these images bewildered her mind. Not knowing where she was, she turned her eyes on all sides, as if to recognize the surrounding scene. This singular lake, those flames reflected from its glassy surface, the pale hues of its banks, the romantic cabins, the bullrushes, that sadly waved their drooping heads; the storks, whose melancholy cries blended with the shrill voices of the dwarfs, every thing conspired to persuade her, that the angel of death had opened the portal of some other world.

Gulchenrouz, on his part, lost in wonder, clung to the neck of his cousin. He believed himself in the region of phantoms; and was terrified at the silence she preserved. At length addressing her; 'Speak,' said he, 'where are we? do you not see those spectres that are stirring the burning coals? Are they Monker and Nekir who are come to throw us into them? Does the fatal bridge cross this lake, whose solemn stillness, perhaps, conceals from us an abyss, in which, for whole ages, we shall be doomed incessantly to sink.'

'No, my children,' said Sutlememe, going towards them, 'take comfort! the exterminating angel, who conducted our souls hither after yours, hath assured us, that the chastisement of your indolent and voluptuous life, shall be restricted to a certain series of years, which you must pass in this dreary abode; where the sun is scarcely visible, and where the soil yields neither fruits nor flowers. These,' continued she, pointing to the dwarfs, 'will provide for our wants; for souls, so mundane as ours, retain too strong a tincture of their earthly extraction. Instead of meats, your food will be nothing but rice; and your bread shall be moistened in the fogs that brood over the surface of the lake.'

At this desolating prospect, the poor children burst into tears, and prostrated themselves before the dwarfs; who perfectly supported their characters, and delivered an excellent discourse, of a customary length, upon the sacred camel; which, after a thousand years, was to convey them to the paradise of the faithful.

The sermon being ended, and ablutions performed, they praised Alla and the Prophet; supped very indifferently; and retired to their withered leaves. Nouronihar and her little cousin, consoled themselves on finding that the dead might lay in one cabin. Having slept well before, the remainder of the night was spent in conversation on what had befallen them; and both, from a dread of apparitions, betook themselves for protection to one another's arms.

In the morning, which was lowering and rainy, the dwarfs mounted high poles, like minarets, and called them to prayers. The whole congregation, which consisted of Sutlememe, Shaban, the four eunuchs, and a few storks that were tired of fishing, was already assembled. The two children came forth from their cabin with a slow and dejected pace. As their minds were in a tender and melancholy mood, their devotions were performed with fervour. No sooner were they finished than Gulchenrouz demanded of Sutlememe, and the rest, 'how they happened to die so opportunely for his cousin and himself?'—'We killed ourselves,' returned Sutlememe, 'in despair at your death.' On this, Nouronihar who, notwithstanding what had past, had not yet forgotten her vision said—'And the Caliph! is he also dead of his grief? and will he likewise come hither?' The dwarfs, who were prepared with an answer, most demurely replied: 'Vathek is damned beyond all redemption!'—'I readily believe so,' said Gulchenrouz; 'and am glad, from my heart, to hear it; for I am convinced it was his horrible look that sent us hither, to listen to sermons, and mess upon rice.' One week passed away, on the side of the lake, unmarked by any variety: Nouronihar ruminating on the grandeur of which death had deprived her; and Gulchenrouz applying to prayers and basket-making with the dwarfs, who infinitely pleased him.

Whilst this scene of innocence was exhibiting in the mountains, the Caliph presented himself to the emir in a new light. The instant he recovered the use of his senses, with a voice that made Bababalouk quake, he thundered out: 'Perfidious Giaour! I renounce thee for ever! it is thou who hast slain my beloved Nouronihar! and I supplicate the pardon of Mahomet; who would have preserved her to me, had I been more wise. Let water be brought, to perform my ablutions, and let the pious Fakreddin be called to offer up his prayers with mine, and reconcile me to him. Afterwards, we will go together and visit the sepulchre of the unfortunate Nouronihar. I am resolved to become a hermit, and consume the residue of my days on this mountain, in hope of expiating my crimes.'—'And what do you intend to live upon there?' inquired Bababalouk: 'I hardly know,' replied Vathek, 'but I will tell you when I feel hungry—which, I believe, will not soon be the case.'

The arrival of Fakreddin put a stop to this conversation. As soon as Vathek saw him, he threw his arms around his neck, bedewed his face with a torrent of tears, and uttered things so affecting, so pious, that the emir, crying for joy, congratulated himself, in his heart upon having performed so admirable and unexpected a conversion. As for the pilgrimage to the mountain, Fakreddin had his reasons not to oppose it; therefore, each ascending his own litter, they started.

Notwithstanding the vigilance with which his attendants watched the Caliph, they could not prevent his harrowing his cheeks with a few scratches, when on the place where he was told Nouronihar had been buried; they were even obliged to drag him away, by force of hands, from the melancholy spot. However he swore, with a solemn oath, that he would return thither every day. This resolution did not exactly please the emir— yet he flattered himself that the Caliph might not proceed farther, and would merely perform his devotions in the cavern of Meimouné. Besides, the lake was so completely concealed within the solitary bosom of those tremendous rocks, that he thought it utterly impossible any one could ever find it. This security of Fakreddin was also considerably strengthened by the conduct of Vathek, who performed his vow most scrupulously, and returned daily from the hill so devout, and so contrite, that all the grey-beards were in a state of ecstasy on account of it.

Nouronihar was not altogether so content; for though she felt a fondness for Gulchenrouz, who, to augment the attachment, had been left at full liberty with her, yet she still regarded him as but a bauble that bore no competition with the carbuncle of Giamschid. At times, she indulged doubts on the mode of her being; and scarcely could believe that the dead had all the wants and the whims of the living. To gain satisfaction, however, on so perplexing a topic; one morning, whilst all were asleep, she arose with a breathless caution from the side of Gulchenrouz: and, after having given him a soft kiss, began to follow the windings of the lake, till it terminated with a rock, the top of which was accessible, though lofty. This she climbed with considerable toil; and, having reached the summit, set forward in a run, like a doe before the hunter. Though she skipped with the alertness of an antelope, yet, at intervals, she was forced to desist, and rest beneath the tamarisks to recover her breath. Whilst she, thus reclined, was occupied with her little reflections on the apprehension that she had some knowledge of the place; Vathek, who, finding himself that morning but ill at ease, had gone forth before the dawn, presented himself, on a sudden, to her view. Motionless with surprise, he durst not approach the figure before him trembling and pale, but yet lovely to behold. At length, Nouronihar, with a mixture of pleasure and affliction, raising her fine eyes to him, said: 'My lord! are you then come hither to eat rice and hear sermons with me?'— 'Beloved phantom!' cried Vathek, 'thou dost speak; thou hast the same graceful form; the same radiant features: art thou palpable likewise?' and, eagerly embracing her, added: 'Here are limbs and a bosom, animated with a gentle warmth!—What can such a prodigy mean?'

Nouronihar, with indifference answered: 'You know, my lord, that I died on the very night you honoured me with your visit. My cousin maintains it was from one of your glances; but I cannot believe him: for, to me, they seem not so dreadful. Gulchenrouz died with me, and we were both brought into a region of desolation, where we are fed with a wretched diet. If you be dead also, and are come hither to join us, I pity your lot: for, you will be stunned with the clang of the dwarfs and the storks. Besides, it is mortifying in the extreme, that you, as well as myself, should have lost the treasures of the subterranean palace.'

At the mention of the subterranean palace, the Caliph suspended his caresses, (which indeed had proceeded pretty far) to seek from Nouronihar an explanation of her meaning. She then recapitulated her vision; what immediately followed; and the history of her pretended death; adding, also, a description of the place of expiation, from whence she had fled; and all, in a manner, that would have extorted his laughter, had not the thoughts of Vathek been too deeply engaged. No sooner, however, had she ended, than he again clasped her to his bosom and said: 'Light of my eyes! the mystery is unravelled; we both are alive! Your father is a cheat, who, for the sake of dividing us, hath deluded us both: and the Giaour, whose design, as far as I can discover, is, that we shall proceed together, seems scarce a whit better. It shall be some time, at least, before he finds us in his palace of fire. Your lovely little person, in my estimation, is far more precious than all the treasures of the pre-adamite sultans; and I wish to possess it at pleasure, and, in open day, for many a moon, before I go to burrow under ground, like a mole. Forget this little trifler, Gulchenrouz; and'—'Ah! my lord!' interposed Nouronihar, 'let me intreat that you do him no evil.'—'No, no!' replied Vathek, 'I have already bid you forbear to alarm yourself for him. He has been brought up too much on milk and sugar to stimulate my jealousy. We will leave him with the dwarfs; who, by the bye, are my old acquaintances: their company will suit him far better than yours. As to other matters; I will return no more to your father's. I want not to have my ears dinned by him and his dotards with the violation of the rights of hospitality: as if it were less an honour for you to espouse the sovereign of the world, than a girl dressed up like a boy!'

Nouronihar could find nothing to oppose, in a discourse so eloquent. She only wished the amorous monarch had discovered more ardour for the carbuncle of Giamschid: but flattered herself it would gradually increase; and, therefore, yielded to his will, with the most bewitching submission.

When the Caliph judged it proper, he called for Bababalouk, who was asleep in the cave of Meimouné, and dreaming that the phantom of Nouronihar, having mounted him once more on her swing, had just given him such a jerk, that he, one moment, soared above the mountains, and the next, sunk into the abyss. Starting from his sleep at the sound of his master, he ran, gasping for breath, and had nearly fallen backward at the sight, as he believed, of the spectre, by whom he had, so lately, been haunted in his dream. 'Ah, my lord!' cried he, recoiling ten steps, and covering his eyes with both hands, 'do you then perform the office of a goul! have you dug up the dead? yet hope not to make her your prey: for, after all she hath caused me to suffer, she is wicked enough to prey even upon you.'

'Cease to play the fool,' said Vathek, 'and thou shalt soon be convinced that it is Nouronihar herself, alive and well, whom I clasp to my breast. Go and pitch my tents in the neighbouring valley. There will I fix my abode, with this beautiful tulip, whose colours I soon shall restore. There exert thy best endeavours to procure whatever can augment the enjoyments of life, till I shall disclose to thee more of my will.'

The news of so unlucky an event soon reached the ears of the emir, who abandoned himself to grief and despair, and began, as did his old greybeards, to begrime his visage with ashes. A total supineness ensued; travellers were no longer entertained; no more plasters were spread; and, instead of the charitable activity that had distinguished this asylum, the whole of its inhabitants exhibited only faces of half a cubit long, and uttered groans that accorded with their forlorn situation.

Though Fakreddin bewailed his daughter, as lost to him for ever, yet Gulchenrouz was not forgotten. He dispatched immediate instruction to Sutlememe, Shaban, and the dwarfs, enjoining them not to undeceive the child, in respect to his state; but, under some pretence, to convey him far from the lofty rock, at the extremity of the lake, to a place which he should appoint, as safer from danger, for he suspected that Vathek intended him evil.

Gulchenrouz, in the meanwhile, was filled with amazement, at not finding his cousin; nor were the dwarfs less surprised; but Sutlememe, who had more penetration, immediately guessed what had happened. Gulchenrouz was amused with the delusive hope of once more embracing Nouronihar, in the interior recesses of the mountains, where the ground, strewed over with orange blossoms and jasmines, offered beds much more inviting than the withered leaves in their cabin; where they might accompany, with their voices, the sounds of their lutes, and chase butterflies. Sutlememe was far gone in this sort of description, when one of the four eunuchs beckoned her aside, to apprize her of the arrival of a messenger from their fraternity, who had explained the secret of the flight of Nouronihar, and brought the commands of the emir. A council with Shaban and the dwarfs was immediately held. Their baggage being stowed in consequence of it, they embarked in a shallop, and quietly sailed with the little one, who acquiesced in all their proposals. Their voyage proceeded in the same manner, till they came to the place where the lake sinks beneath the hollow of a rock; but, as soon as the bark had entered it and Gulchenrouz found himself surrounded with darkness, he was seized with a dreadful consternation, and incessantly uttered the most piercing outcries; for he now was persuaded he should actually be damned for having taken too many little freedoms, in his life-time, with his cousin.

But let us return to the Caliph, and her who ruled over his heart. Bababalouk had pitched the tents, and closed up the extremities of the valley, with magnificent screens of India cloth, which were guarded by Ethiopian slaves with their drawn sabres. To preserve the verdure of this beautiful inclosure in its natural freshness, white eunuchs went continually round it with gilt water vessels. The waving of fans was heard near the imperial pavilion; where, by the voluptuous light that glowed through the muslins, the Caliph enjoyed, at full view, all the attractions of Nouronihar. Inebriated with delight, he was all ear to her charming voice, which accompanied the lute: while she was not less captivated with his descriptions of Samarah, and the tower full of wonders; but especially with his relation of the adventure of the ball, and the chasm of the Giaour, with its ebony portal.

In this manner they conversed the whole day, and at night they bathed together, in a basin of black marble, which admirably set off the fairness of Nouronihar. Bababalouk, whose good graces this beauty had regained, spared no attention, that their repasts might be served up with the minutest exactness: some exquisite rarity was ever placed before them; and he sent even to Schiraz, for that fragrant and delicious wine, which had been hoarded up in bottles, prior to the birth of Mahomet. He had excavated little ovens in the rock, to bake the nice manchets which were prepared by the hands of Nouronihar, from whence they had derived a flavour so grateful to Vathek, that he regarded the ragouts of his other wives as entirely maukish: whilst they would have died of chagrin at the emir's, at finding themselves so neglected, if Fakreddin, notwithstanding his resentment, had not taken pity upon them.

The sultana Dilara, who, till then, had been the favourite, took this dereliction of the Caliph to heart, with a vehemence natural to her character: for, during her continuance in favour, she had imbibed from Vathek many of his extravagant fancies, and was fired with impatience to behold the superb tombs of Istakar, and the palace of forty columns; besides, having been brought up amongst the magi, she had fondly cherished the idea of the Caliph's devoting himself to the worship of fire: thus, his voluptuous and desultory life with her rival, was to her a double source of affliction. The transient piety of Vathek had occasioned her some serious alarms; but the present was an evil of far greater magnitude. She resolved, therefore, without hesitation, to write to Carathis, and acquaint her that all things went ill; that they had eaten, slept, and revelled at an old emir's, whose sanctity was very formidable; and that, after all, the prospect of possessing the treasures of the pre-adamite sultans, was no less remote than before. This letter was entrusted to the care of two woodmen, who were at work in one of the great forests of the mountains; and who, being acquainted with the shortest cuts, arrived in ten days at Samarah.

The Princess Carathis was engaged at chess with Morakanabad, when the arrival of these wood-fellers was announced. She, after some weeks of Vathek's absence, had forsaken the upper regions of her tower, because every thing appeared in confusion among the stars, which she consulted, relative to the fate of her son. In vain did she renew her fumigations, and extend herself on the roof, to obtain mystic visions; nothing more could she see in her dreams, than pieces of brocade, nosegays of flowers, and other unmeaning gew-gaws. These disappointments had thrown her into a state of dejection, which no drug in her power was sufficient to remove. Her only resource was in Morakanabad, who was a good man, and endowed with a decent share of confidence; yet, whilst in her company, he never thought himself on roses.

No person knew aught of Vathek, and, of course, a thousand ridiculous stories were propagated at his expense. The eagerness of Carathis may be easily guessed at receiving the letter, as well as her rage at reading the dissolute conduct of her son. 'Is it so!' said she: 'either I will perish, or Vathek shall enter the palace of fire. Let me expire in flames, provided he may reign on the throne of Soliman!' Having said this, and whirled herself round in a magical manner, which struck Morakanabad with such terror as caused him to recoil, she ordered her great camel Alboufaki to be brought, and the hideous Nerkes, with the unrelenting Cafour, to attend. 'I require no other retinue,' said she to Morakanabad: 'I am going on affairs of emergency; a truce, therefore, to parade! Take you care of the people; fleece them well in my absence, for we shall expend large sums, and one knows not what may betide.'

The night was uncommonly dark, and a pestilential blast blew from the plain of Catoul, that would have deterred any other traveller however urgent the call: but Carathis enjoyed most whatever filled others with dread. Nerkes concurred in opinion with her; and Cafour had a particular predilection for a pestilence. In the morning this accomplished caravan, with the woodfellers, who directed their route, halted on the edge of an extensive marsh, from whence so noxious a vapour arose, as would have destroyed any animal but Alboufaki, who naturally inhaled these malignant fogs with delight. The peasants entreated their convoy not to sleep in this place. 'To sleep,' cried Carathis, 'what an excellent thought! I never sleep, but for visions; and, as to my attendants, their occupations are too many, to close the only eye they have.' The poor peasants, who were not over-pleased with their party, remained open-mouthed with surprise.

Carathis alighted, as well as her negresses; and, severally stripping off their outer garments, they all ran to cull from those spots, where the sun shone fiercest, the venomous plants that grew on the marsh. This provision was made for the family of the emir; and whoever might retard the expedition to Istakar. The woodmen were overcome with fear, when they beheld these three horrible phantoms run; and, not much relishing the company of Alboufaki, stood aghast at the command of Carathis to set forward; notwithstanding it was noon, and the heat fierce enough to calcine even rocks. In spite however, of every remonstrance, they were forced implicitly to submit.

Alboufaki, who delighted in solitude, constantly snorted whenever he perceived himself near a habitation; and Carathis, who was apt to spoil him with indulgence, as constantly turned him aside: so that the peasants were precluded from procuring subsistence; for, the milch goats and ewes, which Providence had sent towards the district they traversed to refresh travellers with their milk, all fled at the sight of the hideous animal and his strange riders. As to Carathis, she needed no common aliment; for, her invention had previously furnished her with an opiate, to stay her stomach; some of which she imparted to her mutes.

At dusk, Alboufaki making a sudden stop, stampt with his foot; which, to Carathis, who knew his ways, was a certain indication that she was near the confines of some cemetery. The moon shed a bright light on the spot, which served to discover a long wall with a large door in it, standing a-jar; and so high that Alboufaki might easily enter. The miserable guides, who perceived their end approaching, humbly implored Carathis, as she had now so good an opportunity, to inter them; and immediately gave up the ghost. Nerkes and Cafour, whose wit was of a style peculiar to themselves, were by no means parsimonious of it on the folly of these poor people; nor could any thing have been found more suited to their taste, than the site of the burying ground, and the sepulchres which its precincts contained. There were, at least, two thousand of them on the declivity of a hill. Carathis was too eager to execute her plan, to stop at the view, charming as it appeared in her eyes. Pondering the advantages that might accrue from her present situation, she said to herself, 'So beautiful a cemetery must be haunted by gouls! they never want for intelligence: having heedlessly suffered my stupid guides to expire, I will apply for directions to them; and, as an inducement, will invite them to regale on these fresh corpses.' After this wise soliloquy, she beckoned to Nerkes and Cafour, and made signs with her fingers, as much as to say: 'Go; knock against the sides of the tombs and strike up your delightful warblings.'

The negresses, full of joy at the behests of their mistress; and promising themselves much pleasure from the society of the gouls, went, with an air of conquest, and began their knockings at the tombs. As their strokes were repeated, a hollow noise was heard in the earth; the surface hove up into heaps; and the gouls, on all sides, protruded their noses to inhale the effluvia, which the carcases of the woodmen began to emit. They assembled before a sarcophagus of white marble, where Carathis was seated between the bodies of her miserable guides. The Princess received her visitants with distinguished politeness; and, supper being ended, they talked of business. Carathis soon learnt from them every thing she wanted to discover; and, without loss of time, prepared to set forward on her journey. Her negresses, who were forming tender connexions with the gouls, importuned her, with all their fingers, to wait at least till the dawn. But Carathis, being chastity in the abstract, and an implacable enemy to love intrigues and sloth, at once rejected their prayer; mounted Alboufaki, and commanded them to take their seats instantly. Four days and four nights, she continued her route without interruption. On the fifth, she traversed craggy mountains, and half-burnt forests; and arrived on the sixth, before the beautiful screens which concealed from all eyes the voluptuous wanderings of her son.

It was day-break, and the guards were snoring on their posts in careless security, when the rough trot of Alboufaki awoke them in consternation. Imagining that a group of spectres, ascended from the abyss, was approaching, they all, without ceremony, took to their heels. Vathek was, at that instant, with Nouronihar in the bath; hearing tales, and laughing at Bababalouk, who related them: but, no sooner did the outcry of his guards reach him, than he flounced from the water like a carp; and as soon threw himself back at the sight of Carathis; who, advancing with her negresses, upon Alboufaki, broke through the muslin awnings and veils of the pavilion. At this sudden apparition, Nouronihar (for she was not, at all times, free from remorse) fancied, that the moment of celestial vengeance was come; and clung about the Caliph, in amorous despondence.

Carathis, still seated on her camel, foamed with indignation, at the spectacle which obtruded itself on her chaste view. She thundered forth without check or mercy: 'Thou double-headed and four-legged monster! what means all this winding and writhing? art thou not ashamed to be seen grasping this limber sapling; in preference to the sceptre of the pre-adamite sultans? Is it then, for this paltry doxy, that thou hast violated the conditions in the parchment of our Giaour! Is it on her, thou hast lavished thy precious moments! Is this the fruit of the knowledge I have taught thee! Is this the end of thy journey? Tear thyself from the arms of this little simpleton; drown her, in the water before me; and, instantly follow my guidance.'

In the first ebullition of his fury, Vathek had resolved to rip open the body of Alboufaki and to stuff it with those of the negresses and of Carathis herself, but the remembrance of the Giaour, the palace of Istakar, the sabres, and the talismans, flashing before his imagination, with the simultaneousness of lightning, he became more moderate, and said to his mother, in a civil, but decisive tone; 'Dread lady! you shall be obeyed; but I will not drown Nouronihar. She is sweeter to me than a Myrabolan comfit; and is enamoured of carbuncles; especially that, of Giamschid; which hath also been promised to be conferred upon her: she, therefore, shall go along with us; for, I intend to repose with her upon the sofas of Soliman: I can sleep no more without her.'—'Be it so!' replied Carathis, alighting; and, at the same time, committing Alboufaki to the charge of her black women.

Nouronihar, who had not yet quitted her hold, began to take courage; and said, with an accent of fondness, to the Caliph: 'Dear sovereign of my soul! I will follow thee, if it be thy will, beyond the Kaf, in the land of the afrits. I will not hesitate to climb, for thee, the nest of the Simurgh; who, this lady excepted, is the most awful of created beings.'—'We have here then,' subjoined Carathis, 'a girl, both of courage and science!' Nouronihar had certainly both; but, notwithstanding all her firmness, she could not help casting back a thought of regret upon the graces of her little Gulchenrouz; and the days of tender endearments she had participated with him. She, even, dropped a few tears; which, the Caliph observed; and inadvertently breathed out with a sigh: 'Alas! my gentle cousin! what will become of thee!'—Vathek, at this apostrophe, knitted up his brows; and Carathis inquired what it could mean? 'She is preposterously sighing after a stripling with languishing eyes and soft hair, who loves her,' said the Caliph. 'Where is he?' asked Carathis. 'I must be acquainted with this pretty child: for,' added she, lowering her voice, 'I design, before I depart, to regain the favour of the Giaour. There is nothing so delicious, in his estimation, as the heart of a delicate boy palpitating with the first tumults of love.'

Vathek, as he came from the bath, commanded Bababalouk to collect the women, and other moveables of his harem; embody his troops; and hold himself in readiness to march within three days: whilst Carathis, retired alone to a tent, where the Giaour solaced her with encouraging visions: but, at length, waking, she found at her feet, Nerkes and Cafour, who informed her, by their signs, that having led Alboufaki to the borders of a lake; to browse on some grey moss, that looked tolerably venomous; they had discovered certain blue fishes, of the same kind with those in the reservoir on the top of the tower. 'Ah! ha!' said she, 'I will go thither to them. These fish are past doubt of a species that, by a small operation, I can render oracular. They may tell me, where this little Gulchenrouz is; whom I am bent upon sacrificing.' Having thus spoken, she immediately set out, with her swarthy retinue.

It being but seldom that time is lost, in the accomplishment of a wicked enterprize, Carathis and her negresses soon arrived at the lake; where, after burning the magical drugs, with which they were always provided; they stripped themselves naked, and waded to their chins; Nerkes and Cafour waving torches around them, and Carathis pronouncing her barbarous incantations. The fishes, with one accord, thrust forth their heads from the water; which was violently rippled by the flutter of their fins: and, at length, finding themselves constrained, by the potency of the charm, they opened their piteous mouths, and said: 'From gills to tail, we are yours; what seek ye to know?'—'Fishes,' answered she, 'I conjure you, by your glittering scales; tell me where now is Gulchenrouz?'—'Beyond the rock,' replied the shoal, in full chorus: 'will this content you? for we do not delight in expanding our mouths.'—'It will,' returned the Princess: 'I am not to learn, that you are not used to long conversations: I will leave you therefore to repose, though I had other questions to propound.' The instant she had spoken, the water became smooth; and the fishes, at once, disappeared.

Carathis, inflated with the venom of her projects, strode hastily over the rock; and found the amiable Gulchenrouz, asleep, in an arbour; whilst the two dwarfs were watching at his side, and ruminating their accustomed prayers. These diminutive personages possessed the gift of divining, whenever an enemy to good Mussulmans approached: thus, they anticipated the arrival of Carathis; who, stopping short, said to herself: 'How placidly doth he recline his lovely little head! how pale, and languishing, are his looks! it is just the very child of my wishes!' The dwarfs interrupted this delectable soliloquy, by leaping, instantly, upon her; and scratching her face, with their utmost zeal. But Nerkes and Cafour, betaking themselves to the succour of their mistress, pinched the dwarfs so severely, in return, that they both gave up the ghost; imploring Mahomet to inflict his sorest vengeance upon this wicked woman, and all her household.

At the noise which this strange conflict occasioned in the valley, Gulchenrouz awoke; and, bewildered with terror, sprung impetuously and climbed an old fig-tree that rose against the acclivity of the rocks; from thence he gained their summits, and ran for two hours without once looking back. At last, exhausted with fatigue, he fell senseless into the arms of a good old genius, whose fondness for the company of children, had made it his sole occupation to protect them. Whilst performing his wonted rounds through the air, he had pounced on the cruel Giaour, at the instant of his growling in the horrible chasm, and had rescued the fifty little victims which the impiety of Vathek had devoted to his voracity. These the genius brought up in nests still higher than the clouds, and himself fixed his abode, in a nest more capacious than the rest, from which he had expelled the Rocs that had built it.

These inviolable asylums were defended against the dives and the afrits, by waving streamers; on which were inscribed in characters of gold, that flashed like lightning, the names of Alla and the Prophet. It was there that Gulchenrouz, who, as yet remained undeceived with respect to his pretended death, thought himself in the mansions of eternal peace. He admitted without fear the congratulations of his little friends, who were all assembled in the nest of the venerable genius, and vied with each other in kissing his serene forehead and beautiful eye-lids.—Remote from the inquietudes of the world; the impertinence of harems, the brutality of eunuchs, and the inconstancy of women; there he found a place truly congenial to the delights of his soul. In this peaceable society his days, months, and years glided on; nor was he less happy than the rest of his companions: for the genius, instead of burthening his pupils with perishable riches and vain sciences, conferred upon them the boon of perpetual childhood.

Carathis, unaccustomed to the loss of her prey, vented a thousand execrations on her negresses, for not seizing the child, instead of amusing themselves with pinching to death two insignificant dwarfs from which they could gain no advantage. She returned into the valley murmuring; and, finding that her son was not risen from the arms of Nouronihar, discharged her ill-humour upon both. The idea, however, of departing next day for Istakar, and of cultivating, through the good offices of the Giaour, an intimacy with Eblis himself, at length consoled her chagrin. But fate had ordained it otherwise.

In the evening as Carathis was conversing with Dilara, who, through her contrivance had become of the party, and whose taste resembled her own, Bababalouk came to acquaint her that the sky towards Samarah looked of a fiery red, and seemed to portend some alarming disaster. Immediately recurring to her astrolabes and instruments of magic, she took the altitude of the planets, and discovered, by her calculations, to her great mortification, that a formidable revolt had taken place at Samarah, that Motavakel, availing himself of the disgust, which was inveterate against his brother, had incited commotions amongst the populace, made himself master of the palace, and actually invested the great tower, to which Morakanabad had retired, with a handful of the few that still remained faithful to Vathek.

'What!' exclaimed she; 'must I lose, then, my tower! my mutes! my negresses! my mummies! and, worse than all, the laboratory, the favourite resort of my nightly lucubrations, without knowing, at least, if my hair-brained son will complete his adventure? No! I will not be the dupe! immediately will I speed to support Morakanabad. By my formidable art, the clouds shall pour grape-shot in the faces of the assailants and shafts of red-hot iron on their heads. I will let loose my stores of hungry serpents and torpedos, from beneath them; and we shall soon see the stand they will make against such an explosion!'

Having thus spoken, Carathis hasted to her son who was tranquilly banqueting with Nouronihar, in his superb carnation-coloured tent. 'Glutton, that thou art!' cried she, 'were it not for me, thou wouldst soon find thyself the mere commander of savoury pies. Thy faithful subjects have abjured the faith they swore to thee. Motavakel, thy brother, now reigns on the hill of Pied Horses: and, had I not some slight resources in the tower, would not be easily persuaded to abdicate. But, that time may not be lost,

I shall only add a few words:—Strike tent to-night; set forward; and beware how thou loiterest again by the way. Though, thou hast forfeited the conditions of the parchment, I am not yet without hope: for, it cannot be denied, that thou hast violated, to admiration, the laws of hospitality by seducing the daughter of the emir, after having partaken of his bread and his salt. Such a conduct cannot but be delightful to the Giaour; and if, on thy march, thou canst signalize thyself, by an additional crime; all will still go well, and thou shalt enter the palace of Soliman, in triumph. Adieu! Alboufaki and my negresses are waiting at the door.'

The Caliph had nothing to offer in reply: he wished his mother a prosperous journey, and ate on till he had finished his supper. At midnight, the camp broke up, amidst the flourishing of trumpets and other martial instruments; but loud indeed must have been the sound of the tymbals, to overpower the blubbering of the emir, and his grey-beards; who, by an excessive profusion of tears, had so far exhausted the radical moisture, that their eyes shrivelled up in their sockets, and their hairs dropped off by the roots. Nouronihar, to whom such a symphony was painful, did not grieve to get out of hearing. She accompanied the Caliph in the imperial litter; where they amused themselves, with imagining the splendour which was soon to surround them. The other women, overcome with dejection were dolefully rocked in their cages; whilst Dilara consoled herself, with anticipating the joy of celebrating the rites of fire, on the stately terraces of Istakar.

In four days, they reached the spacious valley of Rocnabad. The season of spring was in all its vigour, and the grotesque branches of the almond trees, in full blossom, fantastically chequered with hyacinths and jonquils, breathed forth a delightful fragrance. Myriads of bees, and scarce fewer of santons, had there taken up their abode. On the banks of the stream, hives and oratories were alternately ranged; and their neatness and whiteness were set off, by the deep green of the cypresses, that spired up amongst them. These pious personages amused themselves, with cultivating little gardens, that abounded with flowers and fruits; especially, musk-melons, of the best flavour that Persia could boast. Sometimes dispersed over the meadow, they entertained themselves with feeding peacocks, whiter than snow; and turtles, more blue than the sapphire. In this manner were they occupied, when the harbingers of the imperial procession began to proclaim: 'Inhabitants of Rocnabad! prostrate yourselves on the brink of your pure waters; and tender your thanksgivings to heaven, that vouchsafeth to shew you a ray of its glory: for, lo! the commander of the faithful draws near.'

The poor santons, filled with holy energy, having bustled to light up wax torches in their oratories, and expand the Koran on their ebony desks, went forth to meet the Caliph with baskets of honeycomb, dates, and melons. But, whilst they were advancing in solemn procession and with measured steps, the horses, camels, and guards, wantoned over their tulips and other flowers, and made a terrible havoc amongst them. The santons could not help casting from one eye a look of pity on the ravages committing around them; whilst, the other was fixed upon the Caliph and heaven. Nouronihar, enraptured with the scenery of a place which brought back to her remembrance the pleasing solitudes where her infancy had passed, intreated Vathek to stop: but he, suspecting that these oratories might be deemed, by the Giaour, an habitation, commanded his pioneers to level them all. The santons stood motionless with horror, at the barbarous mandate; and, at last, broke out into lamentations; but these were uttered with so ill a grace, that Vathek bade his eunuchs to kick them from his presence. He then descended from the litter, with Nouronihar. They sauntered together in the meadow; and amused themselves with culling flowers, and passing a thousand pleasantries on each other. But the bees, who were staunch Mussulmans, thinking it their duty to revenge the insult offered to their dear masters, the santons, assembled so zealously to do it with good effect, that the Caliph and Nouronihar were glad to find their tents prepared to receive them.

Bababalouk, who, in capacity of purveyor, had acquitted himself with applause, as to peacocks and turtles; lost no time in consigning some dozens to the spit; and as many more to be fricasseed. Whilst they were feasting, laughing, carousing, and blaspheming at pleasure, on the banquet so liberally furnished; the moullahs, the sheiks, the cadis, and imans of Schiraz (who seemed not to have met the santons) arrived; leading by bridles of riband, inscribed from the Koran, a train of asses which were loaded with the choicest fruits the country could boast. Having presented their offerings to the Caliph; they petitioned him, to honour their city and mosques, with his presence. 'Fancy not,' said Vathek, 'that you can detain me. Your presents I condescend to accept; but beg you will let me be quiet; for, I am not over-fond of resisting temptation. Retire then:—Yet, as it is not decent, for personages so reverend, to return on foot; and, as you have not the appearance of expert riders, my eunuchs shall tie you on your asses with the precaution that your backs be not turned towards me: for, they understand etiquette.'—In this deputation, were some high-stomached sheiks who, taking Vathek for a fool, scrupled not to speak their opinion. These, Bababalouk girded with double cords; and having well disciplined their asses with nettles behind, they all started, with a preternatural alertness; plunging, kicking, and running foul of one another, in the most ludicrous manner imaginable.

Nouronihar and the Caliph mutually contended who should most enjoy so degrading a sight. They burst out in peals of laughter, to see the old men and their asses fall into the stream. The leg of one was fractured; the shoulder of another, dislocated; the teeth of a third, dashed out; and the rest suffered still worse.

Two days more, undistrubed by fresh embassies, having been devoted to the pleasures of Rocnabad, the expedition proceeded; leaving Schiraz on the right, and verging towards a large plain; from whence were discernible, on the edge of the horizon, the dark summits of the mountains of Istakar.

At this prospect, the Caliph and Nouronihar were unable to repress their transports. They bounded from their litter to the ground; and broke forth into such wild exclamations, as amazed all within hearing. Interrogating each other, they shouted, 'Are we not approaching the radiant palace of light? or gardens, more delightful than those of Sheddad?'—Infatuated mortals! they thus indulged delusive conjecture, unable to fathom the decrees of the Most High!

The good Genii, who had not totally relinquished the superintendence of Vathek; repairing to Mahomet, in the seventh heaven; said: 'Merciful Prophet! stretch forth thy propitious arms, towards thy vicegerent; who is ready to fall, irretrievably, into the snare, which his enemies, the dives, have prepared to destroy him. The Giaour is awaiting his arrival, in the abominable palace of fire; where, if he once set his foot, his perdition will be inevitable.' Mahomet answered, with an air of indignation: 'He hath too well deserved to be resigned to himself; but I permit you to try if one effort more will be effectual to divert him from pursuing his ruin.'

One of these beneficent Genii, assuming, without delay, the exterior of a shepherd, more renowned for his piety than all the derviches and santons of the region, took his station near a flock of white sheep, on the slope of a hill; and began to pour forth, from his flute, such airs of pathetic melody, as subdued the very soul; and, wakening remorse, drove, far from it, every frivolous fancy. At these energetic sounds, the sun hid himself beneath a gloomy cloud; and the waters of two little lakes, that were naturally clearer than crystal, became of a colour like blood. The whole of this superb assembly was involuntarily drawn towards the declivity of the hill. With downcast eyes, they all stood abashed; each upbraiding himself with the evil he had done. The heart of Dilara palpitated; and the chief of the eunuchs, with a sigh of contrition, implored pardon of the women, whom, for his own satisfaction, he had so often tormented.

Vathek and Nouronihar turned pale in their litter; and, regarding each other with haggard looks, reproached themselves—the one with a thousand of the blackest crimes; a thousand projects of impious ambition;—the other, with the desolation of her family; and the perdition of the amiable Gulchenrouz. Nouronihar persuaded herself that she heard, in the fatal music, the groans of her dying father; and Vathek, the sobs of the fifty children he had sacrificed to the Giaour. Amidst these complicated pangs of anguish, they perceived themselves impelled towards the shepherd, whose countenance was so commanding that Vathek, for the first time, felt overawed; whilst Nouronihar concealed her face with her hands. The music paused; and the Genius, addressing the Caliph, said: 'Deluded prince! to whom Providence hath confided the care of innumerable subjects; is it thus that thou fulfillest thy mission? Thy crimes are already completed; and, art thou now hastening towards thy punishment? Thou knowest that, beyond these mountains, Eblis and his accursed dives hold their infernal empire; and seduced by a malignant phantom, thou art proceeding to surrender thyself to them! This moment is the last of grace allowed thee: abandon thy atrocious purpose: return: give back Nouronihar to her father, who still retains a few sparks of life: destroy thy tower, with all its abominations: drive Carathis from thy councils: be just to thy subjects: respect the ministers of the Prophet; compensate for thy impieties, by an exemplary life: and, instead of squandering thy days in voluptuous indulgence, lament thy crimes on the sepulchres of thy ancestors. Thou beholdest the clouds that obscure the sun: at the instant he recovers his splendour, if thy heart be not changed, the time of mercy assigned thee will be past for ever.'

Vathek, depressed with fear, was on the point of prostrating himself at the feet of the shepherd; whom he perceived to be of a nature superior to man: but, his pride prevailing, he audaciously lifted his head, and, glancing at him one of his terrible looks, said: 'Whoever thou art, withhold thy useless admonitions: thou wouldst either delude me, or art thyself deceived. If what I have done be so criminal, as thou pretendest, there remains not for me a moment of grace. I have traversed a sea of blood, to acquire a power, which will make thy equals tremble: deem not that I shall retire, when in view of the port; or, that I will relinquish her, who is dearer to me than either my life, or thy mercy. Let the sun appear! let him illume my career! it matters not where it may end.' On uttering these words, which made even the Genius shudder, Vathek threw himself into the arms of Nouronihar; and commanded that his horses should be forced back to the road.

There was no difficulty in obeying these orders: for, the attraction had ceased: the sun shone forth in all his glory, and the shepherd vanished with a lamentable scream.

The fatal impression of the music of the Genius, remained, notwithstanding, in the heart of Vathek's attendants. They viewed each other with looks of consternation. At the approach of night, almost all of them escaped; and, of this numerous assemblage, there only remained the chief of the eunuchs, some idolatrous slaves, Dilara, and a few other women; who, like herself, were votaries of the religion of the Magi.

The Caliph, fired with the ambition of prescribing laws to the powers of darkness, was but little embarrassed at this dereliction. The impetuosity of his blood prevented him from sleeping; nor did he encamp any more, as before. Nouronihar, whose impatience, if possible exceeded his own, importuned him to hasten his march, and lavished on him a thousand caresses, to beguile all reflection. She fancied herself already more potent than Balkis, and pictured to her imagination the Genii falling prostrate at the foot of her throne. In this manner they advanced by moon-light, till they came within view of the two towering rocks that form a kind of portal to the valley, at the extremity of which, rose the vast ruins of Istakar. Aloft, on the mountain, glimmered the fronts of various royal mausoleums, the horror of which was deepened by the shadows of night. They passed through two villages, almost deserted; the only inhabitants remaining being a few feeble old men: who, at the sight of horses and litters, fell upon their knees, and cried out: 'O Heaven! is it then by these phantoms that we have been, for six months tormented! Alas! it was from the terror of these spectres and the noise beneath the mountains, that our people have fled, and left us at the mercy of the malificent spirits!' The Caliph, to whom these complaints were but unpromising auguries, drove over the bodies of these wretched old men; and, at length, arrived at the foot of the terrace of black marble. There he descended from his litter, handing down Nouronihar; both with beating hearts, stared wildly around them, and expected, with an apprehensive shudder, the approach of the Giaour. But nothing as yet announced his appearance.

A death-like stillness reigned over the mountain and through the air. The moon dilated on a vast platform, the shades of the lofty columns which reached from the terrace almost to the clouds. The gloomy watch-towers, whose number could not be counted, were covered by no roof; and their capitals, of an architecture unknown in the records of the earth, served as an asylum for the birds of night, which, alarmed at the approach of such visitants, fled away croaking.

The chief of the eunuchs, trembling with fear, besought Vathek that a fire might be kindled. 'No!' replied he, 'there is no time left to think of such trifles; abide where thou art, and expect my commands.' Having thus spoken, he presented his hand to Nouronihar; and, ascending the steps of a vast staircase, reached the terrace, which was flagged with squares of marble, and resembled a smooth expanse of water, upon whose surface not a blade of grass ever dared to vegetate. On the right rose the watch-towers, ranged before the ruins of an immense palace, whose walls were embossed with various figures. In front stood forth the colossal forms of four creatures, composed of the leopard and the griffin, and though but of stone, inspired emotions of terror. Near these were distinguished by the splendour of the moon, which streamed full on the place, characters like those on the sabres of the Giaour, and which possessed the same virtue of changing every moment. These, after vacillating for some time, fixed at last in Arabic letters, and prescribed to the Caliph the following words:—'Vathek! thou hast violated the conditions of my parchment, and deservest to be sent back, but in favour to thy companion, and, as the meed for what thou hast done to obtain it; Eblis permitteth that the portal of his palace shall be opened; and the subterranean fire will receive thee into the number of its adorers.'

He scarcely had read these words, before the mountain, against which the terrace was reared, trembled; and the watch-towers were ready to topple headlong upon them. The rock yawned, and disclosed within it a staircase of polished marble, that seemed to approach the abyss. Upon each stair were planted two large torches, like those Nouronihar had seen in her vision; the camphorated vapour of which ascended and gathered itself into a cloud under the hollow of the vault.

This appearance, instead of terrifying, gave new courage to the daughter of Fakreddin. Scarcely deigning to bid adieu to the moon, and the firmament; she abandoned, without hesitation, the pure atmosphere, to plunge into these infernal exhalations. The gait of those impious personages was haughty, and determined. As they descended, by the effulgence of the torches, they gazed on each other with mutual admiration; and both appeared so resplendent, that they already esteemed themselves spiritual intelligences. The only circumstance that perplexed them, was their not arriving at the bottom of the stairs. On hastening their descent, with an ardent impetuosity, they felt their steps accelerated to such a degree, that they seemed not walking but falling from a precipice. Their progress, however, was at length impeded, by a vast portal of ebony which the Caliph, without difficulty, recognized. Here, the Giaour awaited them, with the key in his hand. 'Ye are welcome!' said he to them, with a ghastly smile, 'in spite of Mahomet, and all his dependents. I will now usher you into that palace, where you have so highly merited a place.' Whilst he was uttering these words, he touched the enameled lock with his key; and the doors, at once, flew open with a noise still louder than the thunder of the dog days, and as suddenly recoiled, the moment they had entered.

The Caliph and Nouronihar beheld each other with amazement, at finding themselves in a place, which, though roofed with a vaulted ceiling, was so spacious and lofty, that, at first, they took it for an immeasurable plain. But their eyes, at length, growing familiar to the grandeur of the surrounding objects, they extended their view to those at a distance; and discovered rows of columns and arcades, which gradually diminished, till they terminated in a point radiant as the sun, when he darts his last beams athwart the ocean. The pavement, strewed over with gold dust and saffron, exhaled so subtile an odour, as almost overpowered them. They, however, went on; and observed an infinity of censers, in which, ambergrise and the wood of aloes, were continually burning. Between the several columns, were placed tables; each, spread with a profusion of viands; and wines, of every species, sparkling in vases of crystal. A throng of Genii, and other fantastic spirits, of either sex, danced lasciviously, at the sound of music, which issued from beneath.

In the midst of this immense hall, a vast multitude was incessantly passing; who severally kept their right hands on their hearts; without once regarding any thing around them. They had all, the livid paleness of death. Their eyes, deep sunk in their sockets, resembled those phosphoric meteors, that glimmer by night, in places of interment. Some stalked slowly on; absorbed in profound reverie: some shrieking with agony, ran furiously about like tigers, wounded with poisoned arrows; whilst others, grinding their teeth in rage, foamed along more frantic than the wildest maniac. They all avoided each other; and, though surrounded by a multitude that no one could number, each wandered at random, unheedful of the rest, as if alone on a desert where no foot had trodden.

Vathek and Nouronihar, frozen with terror, at a sight so baleful, demanded of the Giaour what these appearances might mean; and, why these ambulating spectres never withdrew their hands from their hearts? 'Perplex not yourselves, with so much at once,' replied he bluntly; 'you will soon be acquainted with all: let us haste, and present you to Eblis.' They continued their way, through the multitude; but, notwithstanding their confidence at first, they were not sufficiently composed to examine, with attention, the various perspectives of halls and of galleries, that opened on the right hand and left; which were all illuminated by torches and braziers, whose flames rose in pyramids to the centre of the vault. At length they came to a place, where long curtains brocaded with crimson and gold, fell from all parts in solemn confusion. Here, the choirs and dances were heard no longer. The light which glimmered, came from afar.

After some time, Vathek and Nouronihar perceived a gleam brightening through the drapery, and entered a vast tabernacle hung around with the skins of leopards. An infinity of elders with streaming beards, and afrits in complete armour, had prostrated themselves before the ascent of a lofty eminence; on the top of which, upon a globe of fire, sat the formidable Eblis. His person was that of a young man, whose noble and regular features seemed to have been tarnished by malignant vapours. In his large eyes appeared both pride and despair: his flowing hair retained some resemblance to that of an angel of light. In his hand, which thunder had blasted, he swayed the iron sceptre, that causes the monster Ouranbad, the afrits, and all the powers of the abyss to tremble. At his presence, the heart of the Caliph sunk within him; and he fell prostrate on his face. Nouronihar, however, though greatly dismayed, could not help admiring the person of Eblis: for, she expected to have seen some stupendous giant. Eblis, with a voice more mild than might be imagined, but such as penetrated the soul and filled it with the deepest melancholy, said: 'Creatures of clay, I receive you into mine empire: ye are numbered amongst my adorers: enjoy whatever this palace affords: the treasures of the pre-adamite sultans; their fulminating sabres; and those talismans, that compel the dives to open the subterranean expanses of the mountain of Kaf, which communicate with these. There, insatiable as your curiosity may be, shall you find sufficient objects to gratify it. You shall possess the exclusive privilege of entering the fortresses of Aherman, and the halls of Argenk, where are pourtrayed all creatures endowed with intelligence; and the various animals that inhabited the earth prior to the creation of that contemptible being whom ye denominate the father of mankind.'

Vathek and Nouronihar feeling themselves revived and encouraged by this harangue, eagerly said to the Giaour; 'Bring us instantly to the place which contains these precious talismans.'—'Come,' answered this wicked dive, with his malignant grin, 'come and possess all that my sovereign hath promised; and more.' He then conducted them into a long aisle adjoining the tabernacle; preceding them with hasty steps, and followed by his disciples with the utmost alacrity. They reached, at length, a hall of great extent, and covered with a lofty dome; around which appeared fifty portals of bronze, secured with as many fastenings of iron. A funereal gloom prevailed over the whole scene. Here, upon two beds of incorruptible cedar, lay recumbent the fleshless forms of the pre-adamite kings, who had been monarchs of the whole earth. They still possessed enough of life to be conscious of their deplorable condition. Their eyes retained a melancholy motion: they regarded one another with looks of the deepest dejection; each holding his right hand, motionless, on his heart. At their feet were inscribed the events of their several reigns, their power, their pride, and their crimes; Soliman Daki; and Soliman, called Gian Ben Gian, who, after having chained up the dives in the dark caverns of Kaf, became so presumptuous as to doubt of the Supreme Power. All these maintained great state; though not to be compared with the eminence of Soliman Ben Daoud.

This king, so renowned for his wisdom, was on the loftiest elevation; and placed immediately under the dome. He appeared to possess more animation than the rest. Though, from time to time, he laboured with profound sighs; and, like his companions, kept his right hand on his heart; yet his countenance was more composed, and he seemed to be listening to the sullen roar of a cataract visible in part through one of the grated portals. This was the only sound that intruded on the silence of these doleful mansions. A range of brazen vases surrounded the elevation. 'Remove the covers from these cabalistic depositaries,' said the Giaour to Vathek; 'and avail thyself of the talismans which will break asunder all these gates of bronze; and not only render thee master of the treasures contained within them, but also of the spirits by which they are guarded.'

The Caliph, whom this ominous preliminary had entirely disconcerted, approached the vases with faltering footsteps; and was ready to sink with terror when he heard the groans of Soliman. As he proceeded, a voice from the livid lips of the prophet articulated these words: 'In my lifetime, I filled a magnificent throne; having, on my right hand, twelve thousand seats of gold, where the patriarchs and the prophets heard my doctrines; on my left,

the sages and doctors, upon as many thrones of silver, were present at all
my decisions. Whilst I thus administered justice to innumerable multitudes,
the birds of the air, hovering over me, served as a canopy against the rays
of the sun. My people flourished; and my palace rose to the clouds. I erected
a temple to the Most High, which was the wonder of the universe: but, I
basely suffered myself to be seduced by the love of women, and a curiosity
that could not be restrained by sublunary things. I listened to the counsels
of Aherman, and the daughter of Pharaoh; and adored fire, and the hosts
of heaven. I forsook the holy city, and commanded the Genii to rear the
stupendous palace of Istakar, and the terrace of the watch towers; each of
which was consecrated to a star. There, for a while, I enjoyed myself in the
zenith of glory and pleasure. Not only men, but supernatural beings were
subject also to my will. I began to think, as these unhappy monarchs around
had already thought, that the vengeance of Heaven was asleep; when, at
once, the thunder burst my structures asunder, and precipitated me hither:
where, however, I do not remain, like the other inhabitants, totally destitute
of hope; for, an angel of light hath revealed that in consideration of the piety
of my early youth, my woes shall come to an end, when this cataract shall
for ever cease to flow. Till then I am in torments, ineffable torments! an
unrelenting fire preys on my heart.'

Having uttered this exclamation, Soliman raised his hands towards
heaven, in token of supplication; and the Caliph discerned through his
bosom, which was transparent as crystal, his heart enveloped in flames. At
a sight so full of horror, Nouronihar fell back, like one petrified, into the
arms of Vathek, who cried out with a convulsive sob; 'O Giaour! whither
hast thou brought us! Allow us to depart, and I will relinquish all thou hast
promised. O Mahomet! remains there no more mercy!'—'None! none!'
replied the malicious dive. 'Know, miserable prince! thou art now in the
abode of vengeance and despair. Thy heart, also, will be kindled like those
of the other votaries of Eblis. A few days are allotted thee previous to this
fatal period: employ them as thou wilt; recline on these heaps of gold;
command the infernal potentates; range, at thy pleasure, through these
immense subterranean domains: no barrier shall be shut against thee. As for
me, I have fulfilled my mission: I now leave thee to thyself.' At these words
he vanished.

The Caliph and Nouronihar remained in the most abject affliction. Their
tears were unable to flow, and scarcely could they support themselves. At
length, taking each other, despondingly, by the hand, they went faltering
from this fatal hall; indifferent which way they turned their steps. Every
portal opened at their approach. The dives fell prostrate before them. Every
reservoir of riches was disclosed to their view: but they no longer felt the
incentives of curiosity, of pride, or avarice. With like apathy they heard the
chorus of Genii, and saw the stately banquets prepared to regale them. They

went wandering on, from chamber to chamber; hall to hall; and gallery to gallery; all without bounds or limit; all distinguishable by the same louring gloom; all adorned with the same awful grandeur; all traversed by persons in search of repose and consolation; but, who sought them in vain; for every one carried within him a heart tormented in flames. Shunned by these various sufferers, who seemed by their looks to be upbraiding the partners of their guilt, they withdrew from them to wait, in direful suspense, the moment which should render them to each other the like objects of terror.

'What!' exclaimed Nouronihar; 'will the time come when I shall snatch my hand from thine!'—'Ah!' said Vathek, 'and shall my eyes ever cease to drink from thine long draughts of enjoyment! Shall the moments of our reciprocal ecstasies be reflected on with horror! It was not thou that broughtest me hither; the principles by which Carathis perverted my youth, have been the sole cause of my perdition! it is but right she should have her share of it.' Having given vent to these painful expressions, he called to an afrit, who was stirring up one of the braziers, and bade him fetch the Princess Carathis from the palace of Samarah.

After issuing these orders, the Caliph and Nouronihar continued walking amidst the silent croud, till they heard voices at the end of the gallery. Presuming them to proceed from some unhappy beings, who, like themselves, were awaiting their final doom; they followed the sound, and found it to come from a small square chamber, where they discovered, sitting on sofas, four young men, of goodly figure, and a lovely female, who were holding a melancholy conversation by the glimmering of a lonely lamp. Each had a gloomy and forlorn air; and two of them were embracing each other with great tenderness. On seeing the Caliph and the daughter of Fakreddin enter, they arose, saluted, and made room for them. Then he who appeared the most considerable of the group, addressed himself thus to Vathek:—'Strangers! who doubtless are in the same state of suspense with ourselves, as you do not yet bear your hand on your heart, if you are come hither to pass the interval allotted, previous to the infliction of our common punishment, condescend to relate the adventures that have brought you to this fatal place; and we, in return, will acquaint you with ours, which deserve but too well to be heard. To trace back our crimes to their source, though we are not permitted to repent, is the only employment suited to wretches like us!'

The Caliph and Nouronihar assented to the proposal; and Vathek began, not without tears and lamentations, a sincere recital of every circumstance that had passed. When the afflicting narrative was closed, the young man entered on his own. Each person proceeded in order; and, when the third prince had reached the midst of his adventures, a sudden noise interrupted him, which caused the vault to tremble and to open.

Immediately a cloud descended, which gradually dissipating, discovered Carathis on the back of an afrit, who grievously complained of his burden. She, instantly springing to the ground, advanced towards her son, and said, 'What dost thou here, in this little square chamber? As the dives are become subject to thy beck, I expected to have found thee on the throne of the pre-adamite kings.'

'Execrable woman!' answered the Caliph; 'cursed be the day thou gavest me birth! Go, follow this afrit; let him conduct thee to the hall of the Prophet Soliman: there thou wilt learn to what these palaces are destined, and how much I ought to abhor the impious knowledge thou hast taught me.'

'Has the height of power, to which thou art arrived, turned thy brain?' answered Carathis: 'but I ask no more than permission to shew my respect for Soliman the prophet. It is, however, proper thou shouldest know that (as the afrit has informed me neither of us shall return to Samarah) I requested his permission to arrange my affairs; and he politely consented. Availing myself, therefore, of the few moments allowed me, I set fire to the tower, and consumed in it the mutes, negresses, and serpents, which have rendered me so much good service: nor should I have been less kind to Morakanabad, had he not prevented me, by deserting at last to thy brother. As for Bababalouk, who had the folly to return to Samarah, to provide husbands for thy wives, I undoubtedly would have put him to the torture; but being in a hurry, I only hung him, after having decoyed him in a snare, with thy wives: whom I buried alive by the help of my negresses; who thus spent their last moments greatly to their satisfaction. With respect to Dilara, who ever stood high in my favour, she hath evinced the greatness of her mind, by fixing herself near, in the service of one of the magi; and, I think, will soon be one of our society.'

Vathek, too much cast down to express the indignation excited by such a discourse, ordered the afrit to remove Carathis from his presence, and continued immersed in thoughts which his companions durst not disturb.

Carathis, however, eagerly entered the dome of Soliman, and, without regarding in the least the groans of the prophet, undauntedly removed the covers of the vases, and violently seized on the talismans. Then, with a voice more loud than had hitherto been heard within these mansions, she compelled the dives to disclose to her the most secret treasures, the most profound stores, which the afrit himself had not seen. She passed, by rapid descents, known only to Eblis and his most favoured potentates; and thus penetrated the very entrails of the earth, where breathes the sansar, or the icy wind of death. Nothing appalled her dauntless soul. She perceived, however, in all the inmates who bore their hands on their heart, a little singularity, not much to her taste.

As she was emerging from one of the abysses, Eblis stood forth to her view; but, notwithstanding he displayed the full effulgence of his infernal majesty, she preserved her countenance unaltered; and even paid her compliments with considerable firmness.

This superb monarch thus answered: 'Princess, whose knowledge, and whose crimes, have merited a conspicuous rank in my empire; thou dost well to avail thyself of the leisure that remains: for, the flames and torments, which are ready to seize on thy heart, will not fail to provide thee soon with full employment.' He said, and was lost in the curtains of his tabernacle.

Carathis paused for a moment with surprise; but resolved to follow the advice of Eblis, she assembled all the choirs of genii, and all the dives, to pay her homage. Thus marched she, in triumph, through a vapour of perfumes, amidst the acclamations of all the malignant spirits; with most of whom she had formed a previous acquaintance. She even attempted to dethrone one of the Solimans, for the purpose of usurping his place; when a voice, proceeding from the abyss of death, proclaimed: 'All is accomplished!' Instantaneously, the haughty forehead of the intrepid princess became corrugated with agony: she uttered a tremendous yell; and fixed, no more to be withdrawn, her right hand upon her heart, which was become a receptacle of eternal fire.

In this delirium, forgetting all ambitious projects, and her thirst for that knowledge which should ever be hidden from mortals, she overturned the offerings of the genii; and, having execrated the hour she was begotten and the womb that had borne her, glanced off in a rapid whirl that rendered her invisible, and continued to revolve without intermission.

Almost at the same instant, the same voice announced to the Caliph, Nouronihar, the four princes, and the princess, the awful, and irrevocable decree. Their hearts immediately took fire, and they, at once, lost the most precious gift of heaven:—HOPE. These unhappy beings recoiled, with looks of the most furious distraction. Vathek beheld in the eyes of Nouronihar nothing but rage and vengeance; nor could she discern aught in his, but aversion and despair. The two princes who were friends, and, till that moment, had preserved their attachment, shrunk back, gnashing their teeth with mutual and unchangeable hatred. Kalilah and his sister made reciprocal gestures of imprecation; all testified their horror for each other by the most ghastly convulsions, and screams that could not be smothered. All severally plunged themselves into the accursed multitude, there to wander in an eternity of unabating anguish.

Such was, and such should be, the punishment of unrestrained passions and atrocious deeds! Such shall be, the chastisement of that blind curiosity, which would transgress those bounds the wisdom of the Creator has prescribed to human knowledge; and such the dreadful disappointment of that restless ambition, which, aiming at discoveries reserved for beings of a supernatural order, perceives not, through its infatuated pride, that the condition of man upon earth is to be—humble and ignorant.

Thus the Caliph Vathek, who, for the sake of empty pomp and forbidden power, had sullied himself with a thousand crimes, became a prey to grief without end, and remorse without mitigation: whilst the humble, the despised Gulchenrouz passed whole ages in undisturbed tranquillity, and in the pure happiness of childhood.

MATTHEW LEWIS

The Monk

A CHRONOLOGY OF MATTHEW LEWIS

1775   9 July, born in London, first-born of Matthew and Frances Maria Lewis

1792   Last half of year spent in Weimar, meets Goethe and Weiland

1794   Receives bachelor's degree, Christ Church, Oxford. 15 May, arrives at The Hague to take a position in the British Embassy to Holland. *The Monk* completed by 23 September at The Hague

1796   *The Monk: A Romance* (12 March). *Village Virtues: A Dramatic Satire*. Obtains seat in Parliament

1797   Receives master's degree, Oxford. Coleridge's review of *The Monk* leads the way for future attacks. *The Minister: A Tragedy, in Five Acts*

1798   *The Castle Spectre: A Drama in Five Acts* (Drury Lane, 14 December 1797). Meets Walter Scott

1799   *The Love of Gain: A Poem. The Twins; or, Is It He, or His Brother? A Farce in Two Acts*, unpublished (Drury Lane, 8 April 1799). *Rolla; or, The Peruvian Hero. A Tragedy in Five Acts*

1800   *The East Indian: A Comedy, in Five Acts* (Drury Lane, 22 April 1799)

1801   *Tales of Wonder. Adelmorn, the Outlaw: A Romantic Drama, in Three Acts* (Drury Lane, 4 May 1801). *Alfonso, King of Castile: A Tragedy in Five Acts* (Covent Garden, 15 January 1802)

1803   *The Captive: A Scene in a Private Mad-House*, not separately published (Covent Garden, 22 March 1803). *The Harper's Daughter; or, Love and Ambition. A Tragedy in Five Acts* (Covent Garden, 4 May 1803)

1805   *The Bravo of Venice: A Romance. Rugantino; or, The Bravo of Venice. A Grand Romantic Melodrama, in Two Acts* (Covent Garden, 18 October 1805)

1806   *Adelgitha; or, The Fruit of a Single Error. A Tragedy, in Five Acts* (Drury Lane, 30 April 1807). *Feudal Tyrants; or, The Counts of Carlsheim and Sargans, A Romance*

1807   *The Wood Daemon; or, The Clock has Struck. A Grand Romantic Melo-Drama, in Two Acts*, unpublished (Drury Lane, 1 April 1807)

1808   *He Loves and He Rides Away: A Favourite Ballad. Twelve Ballads, the Words and Music by M. G. Lewis. Romantic Tales*

1809   *Venoni; or, The Novice of St Mark's. A Drama in Three Acts* (Drury Lane, 1 December 1808). *Monody on the Death of Sir John Moore* (recited at Drury Lane 14 February 1809). *[Temper, or] The Domestic Tyrant: A Farce, in Two Acts* (Lyceum by Drury Lane Company, 1 May 1809)

1811   *Timour the Tartar: A Grand Romantic Melo-Drama, in Two Acts* (Covent Garden, 29 April 1811). *One O'Clock! or, The Knight and the Wood Daemon, A Grand Musical Romance, in Three Acts* (Lyceum, 1 August 1811)

1812   *Rich and Poor: A Comic Opera, in Three Acts* (Lyceum, 22 July 1812). *Poems*. Inherits a sizeable fortune when his father dies (17 May)

1813   Meets Byron

1815   Journeys to Jamaica, institutes humanitarian reforms in slave treatment. Departs for England on 1 April 1816

1816   Begins year and a half tour of the Continent, meets Shelley; gives Byron a spoken translation of *Faust*

1817   Returns to England for a brief stay, begins second journey to Jamaica on 5 November, more slave reforms

1818   4 May, departs for England; dies on 16 May; buried at sea

1834   *Journal of a West India Proprietor*

The Monk

A ROMANCE

Somnia, terrores magicos, miracula, fagas,
Nocturnos lemures, portentaque.
HORAT.

Dreams, magic terrors, spells of mighty power,
Witches, and ghosts who rove at midnight hour.

PREFACE

IMITATION OF HORACE
Ep. 20.—B. 1.

METHINKS, Oh! vain ill-judging Book,
I see thee cast a wishful look,
Where reputations won and lost are
In famous row called Paternoster.
Incensed to find your precious olio
Buried in unexplored port-folio,
You scorn the prudent lock and key,
And pant well bound and gilt to see
Your Volume in the window set
Of Stockdale, Hookham, or Debrett.

Go then, and pass that dangerous bourn
Whence never Book can back return:
And when you find, condemned, despised,
Neglected, blamed, and criticised,
Abuse from All who read you fall,
(If haply you be read at all)
Sorely will you your folly sigh at,
And wish for me, and home, and quiet.

Assuming now a conjuror's office, I
Thus on your future Fortune prophesy:—
Soon as your novelty is o'er,
And you are young and new no more,
In some dark dirty corner thrown,
Mouldy with damps, with cobwebs strown,
Your leaves shall be the Book-worm's prey;
Or sent to Chandler-Shop away,
And doomed to suffer public scandal,
Shall line the trunk, or wrap the candle!

But should you meet with approbation,
And some one find an inclination
To ask, by natural transition,
Respecting me and my condition;
That I am one, the enquirer teach,
Nor very poor, nor very rich;

Of passions strong, of hasty nature,
Of graceless form and dwarfish stature;
By few approved, and few approving;
Extreme in hating and in loving;

Abhorring all whom I dislike,
Adoring who my fancy strike;
In forming judgements never long,
And for the most part judging wrong;
In friendship firm, but still believing
Others are treacherous and deceiving,
And thinking in the present æra
That Friendship is a pure chimæra:
More passionate no creature living,
Proud, obstinate, and unforgiving,
But yet for those who kindness show,
Ready through fire and smoke to go.

Again, should it be asked your page,
'Pray, what may be the author's age?'
Your faults, no doubt, will make it clear,
I scarce have seen my twentieth year,
Which passed, kind Reader, on my word,
While England's Throne held George the Third.

Now then your venturous course pursue:
Go, my delight! Dear Book, adieu!

Hague,
Oct. 28, 1794.   M. G. L.

TABLE OF THE POETRY

ADVERTISEMENT

THE first idea of this Romance was suggested by the story of the *Santon Barsisa*, related in The Guardian.—The *Bleeding Nun* is a tradition still credited in many parts of Germany; and I have been told, that the ruins of the Castle of *Lauenstein*, which She is supposed to haunt, may yet be seen upon the borders of *Thuringia*.—The *Water-King*, from the third to the twelfth stanza, is the fragment of an original Danish Ballad—And *Belerma and Durandarte* is translated from some stanzas to be found in a collection of old Spanish poetry, which contains also the popular song of *Gayferos and Melesindra*, mentioned in Don Quixote.—I have now made a full avowal of all the plagiarisms of which I am aware myself; but I doubt not, many more may be found, of which I am at present totally unconscious.

VOLUME I

CHAPTER I

Lord Angelo is precise;
Stands at a guard with envy; Scarce confesses
That his blood flows, or that his appetite
Is more to bread than stone
Measure for Measure.

SCARCELY had the Abbey-Bell tolled for five minutes, and already was the Church of the Capuchins thronged with Auditors. Do not encourage the idea that the Crowd was assembled either from motives of piety or thirst of information. But very few were influenced by those reasons; and in a city where superstition reigns with such despotic sway as in Madrid, to seek for true devotion would be a fruitless attempt. The Audience now assembled in the Capuchin Church was collected by various causes, but all of them were foreign to the ostensible motive. The Women came to show themselves, the Men to see the Women: Some were attracted by curiosity to hear an Orator so celebrated; Some came because they had no better means of employing their time till the play began; Some, from being assured that it would be impossible to find places in the Church; and one half of Madrid was brought thither by expecting to meet the other half. The only persons truly anxious to hear the Preacher were a few antiquated devotees, and half a dozen rival Orators, determined to find fault with and ridicule the discourse. As to the remainder of the Audience, the Sermon might have been omitted altogether, certainly without their being disappointed, and very probably without their perceiving the omission.

Whatever was the occasion, it is at least certain that the Capuchin Church had never witnessed a more numerous assembly. Every corner was filled, every seat was occupied. The very Statues which ornamented the long aisles were pressed into the service. Boys suspended themselves upon the wings of Cherubims; St Francis and St Mark bore each a spectator on his shoulders; and St Agatha found herself under the necessity of carrying double. The consequence was, that in spite of all their hurry and expedition, our two newcomers, on entering the Church, looked round in vain for places.

However, the old Woman continued to move forwards. In vain were exclamations of displeasure vented against her from all sides: In vain was She addressed with—'I assure you, Segnora, there are no places here.'—'I beg, Segnora, that you will not crowd me so intolerably!'—'Segnora, you cannot pass this way. Bless me! How can people be so troublesome!'—The old Woman was obstinate, and on She went. By dint of perseverance and two brawny arms She made a passage through the Crowd, and managed to bustle herself into the very body of the Church, at no great distance from the Pulpit. Her companion had followed her with timidity and in silence, profiting by the exertions of her conductress.

'Holy Virgin!' exclaimed the old Woman in a tone of disappointment, while She threw a glance of enquiry round her; 'Holy Virgin! What heat! What a Crowd! I wonder what can be the meaning of all this. I believe we must return: There is no such thing as a seat to be had, and nobody seems kind enough to accommodate us with theirs.'

This broad hint attracted the notice of two Cavaliers, who occupied stools on the right hand, and were leaning their backs against the seventh column from the Pulpit. Both were young, and richly habited. Hearing this appeal to their politeness pronounced in a female voice, they interrupted their conversation to look at the speaker. She had thrown up her veil in order to take a clearer look round the Cathedral. Her hair was red, and She squinted. The Cavaliers turned round, and renewed their conversation.

'By all means,' replied the old Woman's companion; 'By all means, Leonella, let us return home immediately; The heat is excessive, and I am terrified at such a crowd.'

These words were pronounced in a tone of unexampled sweetness. The Cavaliers again broke off their discourse, but for this time they were not contented with looking up: Both started involuntarily from their seats, and turned themselves towards the Speaker.

The voice came from a female, the delicacy and elegance of whose figure inspired the Youths with the most lively curiosity to view the face to which it belonged. This satisfaction was denied them. Her features were hidden by a thick veil; But struggling through the crowd had deranged it sufficiently to discover a neck which for symmetry and beauty might have vied with the Medicean Venus. It was of the most dazzling whiteness, and received additional charms from being shaded by the tresses of her long fair hair, which descended in ringlets to her waist. Her figure was rather below than above the middle size: It was light and airy as that of an Hamadryad. Her bosom was carefully veiled. Her dress was white; it was fastened by a blue sash, and just permitted to peep out from under it a little foot of the most delicate proportions. A chaplet of large grains hung upon her arm, and her face was covered with a veil of thick black gauze. Such was the female, to whom the youngest of the Cavaliers now offered his seat, while the other thought it necessary to pay the same attention to her companion.

The old Lady with many expressions of gratitude, but without much difficulty, accepted the offer, and seated herself: The young one followed her example, but made no other compliment than a simple and graceful reverence. Don Lorenzo (such was the Cavalier's name, whose seat She had accepted) placed himself near her; But first He whispered a few words in his Friend's ear, who immediately took the hint, and endeavoured to draw off the old Woman's attention from her lovely charge.

'You are doubtless lately arrived at Madrid,' said Lorenzo to his fair Neighbour; 'It is impossible that such charms should have long remained unobserved; and had not this been your first public appearance, the envy of the Women and adoration of the Men would have rendered you already sufficiently remarkable.'

He paused, in expectation of an answer. As his speech did not absolutely require one, the Lady did not open her lips: After a few moments He resumed his discourse:

'Am I wrong in supposing you to be a Stranger to Madrid?'

The Lady hesitated; and at last, in so low a voice as to be scarcely intelligible, She made shift to answer,—'No, Segnor.'

'Do you intend making a stay of any length?'

'Yes, Segnor.'

'I should esteem myself fortunate, were it in my power to contribute to making your abode agreeable. I am well known at Madrid, and my Family has some interest at Court. If I can be of any service, you cannot honour or oblige me more than by permitting me to be of use to you.'—'Surely,' said He to himself, 'She cannot answer that by a monosyllable; now She must say something to me.'

Lorenzo was deceived, for the Lady answered only by a bow.

By this time He had discovered that his Neighbour was not very conversible; But whether her silence proceeded from pride, discretion, timidity, or idiotism, He was still unable to decide.

After a pause of some minutes—'It is certainly from your being a Stranger,' said He, 'and as yet unacquainted with our customs, that you continue to wear your veil. Permit me to remove it.'

At the same time He advanced his hand towards the Gauze: The Lady raised hers to prevent him.

'I never unveil in public, Segnor.'

'And where is the harm, I pray you?' interrupted her Companion somewhat sharply; 'Do not you see, that the other Ladies have all laid their veils aside, to do honour no doubt to the holy place in which we are? I have taken off mine already; and surely if I expose my features to general observation, you have no cause to put yourself in such a wonderful alarm!

Blessed Maria! Here is a fuss and a bustle about a chit's face! Come, come, Child! Uncover it; I warrant you that nobody will run away with it from you—'

'Dear aunt, it is not the custom in Murcia.'

'Murcia, indeed! Holy St Barbara, what does that signify? You are always putting me in mind of that villainous Province. If it is the custom in Madrid, that is all that we ought to mind, and therefore I desire you to take off your veil immediately. Obey me this moment Antonia, for you know that I cannot bear contradiction—'

Her niece was silent, but made no further opposition to Don Lorenzo's efforts, who armed with the Aunt's sanction hastened to remove the Gauze. What a Seraph's head presented itself to his admiration! Yet it was rather bewitching than beautiful; It was not so lovely from regularity of features, as from sweetness and sensibility of Countenance. The several parts of her face considered separately, many of them were far from handsome; but when examined together, the whole was adorable. Her skin though fair was not entirely without freckles; Her eyes were not very large, nor their lashes particularly long. But then her lips were of the most rosy freshness; Her fair and undulating hair, confined by a simple ribband, poured itself below her waist in a profusion of ringlets; Her throat was full and beautiful in the extreme; Her hand and arm were formed with the most perfect symmetry; Her mild blue eyes seemed an heaven of sweetness, and the crystal in which they moved, sparkled with all the brilliance of Diamonds: She appeared to be scarcely fifteen; An arch smile, playing round her mouth, declared her to be possessed of liveliness, which excess of timidity at present represt; She looked round her with a bashful glance; and whenever her eyes accidentally met Lorenzo's, She dropt them hastily upon her Rosary; Her cheek was immediately suffused with blushes, and She began to tell her beads; though her manner evidently showed that She knew not what She was about.

Lorenzo gazed upon her with mingled surprise and admiration; but the Aunt thought it necessary to apologize for Antonia's *mauvaise honte*.

' 'Tis a young Creature,' said She, 'who is totally ignorant of the world. She has been brought up in an old Castle in Murcia; with no other Society than her Mother's, who, God help her! has no more sense, good Soul, than is necessary to carry her Soup to her mouth. Yet She is my own Sister, both by Father and Mother.'

'And has so little sense?' said Don Christoval with feigned astonishment; 'How very Extraordinary!'

'Very true, Segnor; Is it not strange? However, such is the fact; and yet only to see the luck of some people! A young Nobleman, of the very first quality, took it into his head that Elvira had some pretensions to Beauty—As to pretensions, in truth, She had always enough of *them*; But as to Beauty. . . . ! If I had only taken half the pains to set myself off which She did. . . . ! But this is neither here nor there. As I was saying, Segnor, a young Nobleman fell in love with her, and married her unknown to his Father. Their union remained a secret near three years, But at last it came to the ears of the old Marquis, who, as you may well suppose, was not much pleased with the intelligence. Away He posted in all haste to Cordova, determined to seize Elvira, and send her away to some place or other, where She would never be heard of more. Holy St Paul! How He stormed on finding that She had escaped him, had joined her Husband, and that they had embarked together for the Indies. He swore at us all, as if the Evil Spirit had possessed him; He threw my Father into prison, as honest a pains-taking Shoe-maker as any in Cordova; and when He went away, He had the cruelty to take from us my Sister's little Boy, then scarcely two years old, and whom in the abruptness of her flight, She had been obliged to leave behind her. I suppose, that the poor little Wretch met with bitter bad treatment from him, for in a few months after, we received intelligence of his death.'

'Why, this was a most terrible old Fellow, Segnora!'

'Oh! shocking! and a Man so totally devoid of taste! Why, would you believe it, Segnor? When I attempted to pacify him, He cursed me for a Witch, and wished that to punish the Count, my Sister might become as ugly as myself! Ugly indeed! I like him for that.'

'Ridiculous', cried Don Christoval; 'Doubtless the Count would have thought himself fortunate, had he been permitted to exchange the one Sister for the other.'

'Oh! Christ! Segnor, you are really too polite. However, I am heartily glad that the Condé was of a different way of thinking. A mighty pretty piece of business, to be sure, Elvira has made of it! After broiling and stewing in the Indies for thirteen long years, her Husband dies, and She returns to Spain, without an House to hide her head, or money to procure her one! This Antonia was then but an Infant, and her only remaining Child. She found that her Father-in-Law had married again, that he was irreconcileable to the Condé, and that his second Wife had produced him a Son, who is reported to be a very fine young Man. The old Marquis refused to see my Sister or her Child; But sent her word that on condition of never hearing any more of her, He would assign her a small pension, and She might live in an old Castle which He possessed in Murcia; This had been the favourite habita-tion of his eldest Son; But since his flight from Spain, the old Marquis could not bear the place, but let it fall to ruin and confusion—My Sister accepted the proposal; She retired to Murcia, and has remained there till within the last Month.'

'And what brings her now to Madrid?' enquired Don Lorenzo, whom admiration of the young Antonia compelled to take a lively interest in the talkative old Woman's narration.

'Alas! Segnor, her Father-in-Law being lately dead, the Steward of his Murcian Estates has refused to pay her pension any longer. With the design of supplicating his Son to renew it, She is now come to Madrid; But I doubt, that She might have saved herself the trouble! You young Noblemen have always enough to do with your money, and are not very often disposed to throw it away upon old Women. I advised my Sister to send Antonia with her petition; But She would not hear of such a thing. She is so obstinate! Well! She will find herself the worse for not following my counsels: the Girl has a good pretty face, and possibly might have done much.'

'Ah! Segnora,' interrupted Don Christoval, counterfeiting a passionate air; 'If a pretty face will do the business, why has not your Sister recourse to you?'

'Oh! Jesus! my Lord, I swear you quite over-power me with your gallantry! But I promise you that I am too well aware of the danger of such Expeditions to trust myself in a young Nobleman's power! No, no; I have as yet preserved my reputation without blemish or reproach, and I always knew how to keep the Men at a proper distance.'

'Of that, Segnora, I have not the least doubt. But permit me to ask you; Have you then any aversion to Matrimony?'

'That is an home question. I cannot but confess, that if an amiable Cavalier was to present himself. . . .'

Here She intended to throw a tender and significant look upon Don Christoval; But, as She unluckily happened to squint most abominably, the glance fell directly upon his Companion: Lorenzo took the compliment to himself, and answered it by a profound bow.

'May I enquire,' said He, 'the name of the Marquis?'

'The Marquis de las Cisternas.'

'I know him intimately well. He is not at present in Madrid, but is expected here daily. He is one of the best of Men; and if the lovely Antonia will permit me to be her Advocate with him, I doubt not my being able to make a favourable report of her cause.'

Antonia raised her blue eyes, and silently thanked him for the offer by a smile of inexpressible sweetness. Leonella's satisfaction was much more loud and audible: Indeed, as her Niece was generally silent in her company, She thought it incumbent upon her to talk enough for both: This She managed without difficulty, for She very seldom found herself deficient in words.

'Oh! Segnor!' She cried; 'You will lay our whole family under the most signal obligations! I accept your offer with all possible gratitude, and return you a thousand thanks for the generosity of your proposal. Antonia, why do not you speak, Child? While the Cavalier says all sorts of civil things to you, you sit like a Statue, and never utter a syllable of thanks, either bad, good, or indifferent!'

'My dear Aunt, I am very sensible that. . . .'

'Fye, Niece! How often have I told you, that you never should interrupt a Person who is speaking!? When did you ever know me do such a thing? Are these your Murcian manners? Mercy on me! I shall never be able to make this Girl any thing like a Person of good-breeding. But pray, Segnor,' She continued, addressing herself to Don Christoval, 'inform me, why such a Crowd is assembled to-day in this Cathedral?'

'Can you possibly be ignorant, that Ambrosio, Abbot of this Monastery, pronounces a Sermon in this Church every Thursday? All Madrid rings with his praises. As yet He has preached but thrice; But all who have heard him are so delighted with his eloquence, that it is as difficult to obtain a place at Church, as at the first representation of a new Comedy. His fame certainly must have reached your ears—'

'Alas! Segnor, till yesterday I never had the good fortune to see Madrid; and at Cordova we are so little informed of what is passing in the rest of the world, that the name of Ambrosio has never been mentioned in its precincts.'

'You will find it in every one's mouth at Madrid. He seems to have fascinated the Inhabitants; and not having attended his Sermons myself, I am astonished at the Enthusiasm which He has excited. The adoration paid him both by Young and Old, by Man and Woman is unexampled. The Grandees load him with presents; Their Wives refuse to have any other Confessor, and he is known through all the city by the name of the "Man of Holiness".'

'Undoubtedly, Segnor, He is of noble origin—'

'That point still remains undecided. The late Superior of the Capuchins found him while yet an Infant at the Abbey-door. All attempts to discover who had left him there were vain, and the Child himself could give no account of his Parents. He was educated in the Monastery, where He has remained ever since. He early showed a strong inclination for study and retirement, and as soon as He was of a proper age, He pronounced his vows. No one has ever appeared to claim him, or clear up the mystery which conceals his birth; and the Monks, who find their account in the favour which is shewn to thier establishment from respect to him, have not hesitated to publish, that He is a present to them from the Virgin. In truth the singular austerity of his life gives some countenance to the report. He is now thirty years old, every hour of which period has been passed in study, total seclusion from the world, and mortification of the flesh. Till these last three weeks, when He was chosen superior of the Society to which He belongs, He had never been on the outside of the Abbey-walls: Even now He never quits them except on Thursdays, when He delivers a discourse in this Cathedral which all Madrid assembles to hear. His knowledge is said to be the most profound, his eloquence the most persuasive. In the whole course of his life He has never been known to transgress a single rule of his order;

The smallest stain is not to be discovered upon his character; and He is reported to be so strict an observer of Chastity, that He knows not in what consists the difference of Man and Woman. The common People therefore esteem him to be a Saint.'

'Does that make a Saint?' enquired Antonia; 'Bless me! Then am I one?'

'Holy St Barbara!' exclaimed Leonella; 'What a question! Fye, Child, Fye! These are not fit subjects for young Women to handle. You should not seem to remember, that there is such a thing as a Man in the world, and you ought to imagine every body to be of the same sex with yourself. I should like to see you give people to understand, that you know that a Man has no breasts, and no hips, and no. . .'.

Luckily for Antonia's ignorance which her Aunt's lecture would soon have dispelled, an universal murmur through the Church announced the Preacher's arrival. Donna Leonella rose from her seat to take a better view of him, and Antonia followed her example.

He was a Man of noble port and commanding presence. His stature was lofty, and his features uncommonly handsome. His Nose was aquiline, his eyes large black and sparkling, and his dark brows almost joined together. His complexion was of a deep but clear Brown; Study and watching had entirely deprived his cheek of colour. Tranquillity reigned upon his smooth unwrinkled forehead; and Content, expressed upon every feature, seemed to announce the Man equally unacquainted with cares and crimes. He bowed himself with humility to the audience: Still there was a certain severity in his look and manner that inspired universal awe, and few could sustain the glance of his eye at once fiery and penetrating. Such was Ambrosio, Abbot of the Capuchins, and surnamed, 'The Man of Holiness'.

Antonia, while She gazed upon him eagerly, felt a pleasure fluttering in her bosom which till then had been unknown to her, and for which She in vain endeavoured to account. She waited with impatience till the Sermon should begin; and when at length the Friar spoke, the sound of his voice seemed to penetrate into her very soul. Though no other of the Spectators felt such violent sensations as did the young Antonia, yet every one listened with interest and emotion. They who were insensible to Religion's merits, were still enchanted with Ambrosio's oratory. All found their attention irresistibly attracted while He spoke, and the most profound silence reigned through the crowded Aisles. Even Lorenzo could not resist the charm: He forgot that Antonia was seated near him, and listened to the Preacher with undivided attention.

In language nervous, clear, and simple, the Monk expatiated on the beauties of Religion. He explained some abstruse parts of the sacred writings in a style that carried with it universal conviction. His voice at once distinct and deep was fraught with all the terrors of the Tempest, while He inveighed against the vices of humanity, and described the punishments reserved for them in a future state. Every Hearer looked back upon his past offences, and trembled: The Thunder seemed to roll, whose bolt was destined to crush him, and the abyss of eternal destruction to open before his feet. But when Ambrosio changing his theme spoke of the excellence of an unsullied conscience, of the glorious prospect which Eternity presented to the Soul untainted with reproach, and of the recompense which awaited it in the regions of everlasting glory, His Auditors felt their scattered spirits insensibly return. They threw themselves with confidence upon the mercy of their Judge; They hung with delight upon the consoling words of the Preacher; and while his full voice swelled into melody, They were transported to those happy regions which He painted to their imaginations in colours so brilliant and glowing.

The discourse was of considerable length; Yet when it concluded, the Audience grieved that it had not lasted longer. Though the Monk had ceased to speak, enthusiastic silence still prevailed through the Church: At length the charm gradually dissolving, the general admiration was expressed in audible terms. As Ambrosio descended from the Pulpit, His Auditors crowded round him, loaded him with blessings, threw themselves at his feet, and kissed the hem of his Garment. He passed on slowly with his hands crossed devoutly upon his bosom, to the door opening into the Abbey-Chapel, at which his Monks waited to receive him. He ascended the Steps, and then turning towards his Followers, addressed to them a few words of gratitude, and exhortation. While He spoke, his Rosary, composed of large grains of amber, fell from his hand, and dropped among the surrounding multitude. It was seized eagerly, and immediately divided amidst the Spectators. Whoever became possessor of a Bead, preserved it as a sacred relique; and had it been the Chaplet of thrice-blessed St Francis himself, it could not have been disputed with greater vivacity. The Abbot, smiling at their eagerness, pronounced his benediction, and quitted the Church, while humility dwelt upon every feature. Dwelt She also in his heart?

Antonia's eyes followed him with anxiety. As the Door closed after him, it seemed to her as if she had lost some one essential to her happiness. A tear stole in silence down her cheek.

'He is separated from the world!' said She to herself; 'Perhaps, I shall never see him more!'

As she wiped away the tear, Lorenzo observed her action.

'Are you satisfied with our Orator?' said He; 'Or do you think that Madrid over-rates his talents?'

Antonia's heart was so filled with admiration for the Monk, that She eagerly seized the opportunity of speaking of him: Besides, as She now no longer considered Lorenzo as an absolute Stranger, She was less embarrassed by her excessive timidity.

'Oh! He far exceeds all my expectations,' answered She; 'Till this moment I had no idea of the powers of eloquence. But when He spoke, his voice inspired me with such interest, such esteem, I might almost say such affection for him, that I am myself astonished at the acuteness of my feelings.'

Lorenzo smiled at the strength of her expressions.

'You are young and just entering into life,' said He; 'Your heart new to the world, and full of warmth and sensibility, receives its first impressions with eagerness. Artless yourself, you suspect not others of deceit; and viewing the world through the medium of your own truth and innocence, you fancy all who surround you to deserve your confidence and esteem. What pity, that these gay visions must soon be dissipated! What pity, that you must soon discover the baseness of mankind, and guard against your fellow-creatures, as against your Foes!'

'Alas! Segnor,' replied Antonia; 'The misfortunes of my Parents have already placed before me but too many sad examples of the perfidy of the world! Yet surely in the present instance the warmth of sympathy cannot have deceived me.'

'In the present instance, I allow that it has not. Ambrosio's character is perfectly without reproach; and a Man who has passed the whole of his life within the walls of a Convent, cannot have found the opportunity to be guilty, even were He possessed of the inclination. But now, when, obliged by the duties of his situation, He must enter occasionally into the world, and be thrown into the way of temptation, it is now that it behoves him to show the brilliance of his virtue. The trial is dangerous; He is just at that period of life when the passions are most vigorous, unbridled, and despotic; His established reputation will mark him out to Seduction as an illustrious Victim; Novelty will give additional charms to the allurements of pleasure; and even the Talents with which Nature has endowed him will contribute to his ruin, by facilitating the means of obtaining his object. Very few would return victorious from a contest so severe.'

'Ah! surely Ambrosio will be one of those few.'

'Of that I have myself no doubt: By all accounts He is an exception to mankind in general, and Envy would seek in vain for a blot upon his character.'

'Segnor, you delight me by this assurance! It encourages me to indulge my prepossession in his favour; and you know not with what pain I should have repressed the sentiment! Ah! dearest Aunt, entreat my Mother to choose him for our Confessor.'

'I entreat her?' replied Leonella; 'I promise you that I shall do no such thing. I do not like this same Ambrosio in the least; He has a look of severity about him that made me tremble from head to foot: Were He my Confessor, I should never have the courage to avow one half of my peccadilloes, and then I should be in a rare condition! I never saw such a stern-looking

Mortal, and hope that I never shall see such another. His description of the Devil, God bless us! almost terrified me out of my wits, and when He spoke about Sinners He seemed as if He was ready to eat them.'

'You are right, Segnora,' answered Don Christoval; 'Too great severity is said to be Ambrosio's only fault. Exempted himself from human failings, He is not sufficiently indulgent to those of others; and though strictly just and disinterested in his decisions, his government of the Monks has already shown some proofs of his inflexibility. But the crowd is nearly dissipated: Will you permit us to attend you home?'

'Oh! Christ! Segnor,' exclaimed Leonella affecting to blush; 'I would not suffer such a thing for the Universe! If I came home attended by so gallant a Cavalier, My Sister is so scrupulous that She would read me an hour's lecture, and I should never hear the last of it. Besides, I rather wish you not to make your proposals just at present.'

'My proposals? I assure you, Segnora. . . .'

'Oh! Segnor, I believe that your assurances of impatience are all very true; But really I must desire a little respite. It would not be quite so delicate in me to accept your hand at first sight.'

'Accept my hand? As I hope to live and breathe. . . .'

'Oh! dear Segnor, press me no further, if you love me! I shall consider your obedience as a proof of your affection; You shall hear from me to-morrow, and so farewell. But pray, Cavaliers, may I not enquire your names?'

'My Friend's,' replied Lorenzo, 'is the Condé d'Ossorio, and mine Lorenzo de Medina.'

' 'Tis sufficient. Well, Don Lorenzo, I shall acquaint my Sister with your obliging offer, and let you know the result with all expedition. Where may I send to you?'

'I am always to be found at the Medina Palace.'

'You may depend upon hearing from me. Farewell, Cavaliers. Segnor Condé, let me entreat you to moderate the excessive ardour of your passion: However, to prove to you that I am not displeased with you, and prevent your abandoning yourself to despair, receive this mark of my affection, and sometimes bestow a thought upon the absent Leonella.'

As She said this, She extended a lean and wrinkled hand; which her supposed Admirer kissed with such sorry grace and constraint so evident, that Lorenzo with difficulty repressed his inclination to laugh. Leonella then hastened to quit the Church; The lovely Antonia followed her in silence; but when She reached the Porch, She turned involuntarily, and cast back her eyes towards Lorenzo. He bowed to her, as bidding her farewell; She returned the compliment, and hastily with-drew.

'So, Lorenzo!' said Don Christoval as soon as they were alone, 'You have procured me an agreeable Intrigue! To favour your designs upon Antonia, I obligingly make a few civil speeches which mean nothing, to the Aunt, and at the end of an hour I find myself upon the brink of Matrimony! How will you reward me for having suffered so grievously for your sake? What can repay me for having kissed the leathern paw of that confounded old Witch? Diavolo! She has left such a scent upon my lips, that I shall smell of garlick for this month to come! As I pass along the Prado, I shall be taken for a walking Omelet, or some large Onion running to seed!'

'I confess, my poor Count,' replied Lorenzo, 'that your service has been attended with danger; Yet am I so far from supposing it be past all endurance, that I shall probably solicit you to carry on your amours still further.'

'From that petition I conclude, that the little Antonia has made some impression upon you.'

'I cannot express to you how much I am charmed with her. Since my Father's death, My Uncle the Duke de Medina, has signified to me his wishes to see me married; I have till now eluded his hints, and refused to understand them; But what I have seen this Evening. . . .'

'Well? What have you seen this Evening? Why surely, Don Lorenzo, You cannot be mad enough to think of making a Wife out of this Grand-daughter of "as honest a pains-taking Shoe-maker as any in Cordova"?'

'You forget, that She is also the Grand-daughter of the late Marquis de las Cisternas; But without disputing about birth and titles, I must assure you, that I never beheld a Woman so interesting as Antonia.'

'Very possibly; But you cannot mean to marry her?'

'Why not, my dear Condé? I shall have wealth enough for both of us, and you know that my Uncle thinks liberally upon the subject. From what I have seen of Raymond de las Cisternas, I am certain that he will readily acknowledge Antonia for his Niece. Her birth therefore will be no objection to my offering her my hand. I should be a Villain, could I think of her on any other terms than marriage; and in truth She seems possessed of every quality requisite to make me happy in a Wife. Young, lovely, gentle, sensible. . . .'

'Sensible? Why, She said nothing but "Yes," and "No".'

'She did not say much more, I must confess—But then She always said "Yes," or "No," in the right place.'

'Did She so? Oh! your most obedient! That is using a right Lover's argument, and I dare dispute no longer with so profound a Casuist. Suppose we adjourn to the Comedy?'

'It is out of my power. I only arrived last night at Madrid, and have not yet had an opportunity of seeing my Sister; You know that her Convent is in this Street, and I was going thither, when the Crowd which I saw thronging into this Church excited my curiosity to know what was the matter. I shall now pursue my first intention, and probably pass the Evening with my Sister at the Parlour-grate.'

'Your Sister in a Convent, say you? Oh! very true, I had forgotten. And how does Donna Agnes? I am amazed, Don Lorenzo, how you could possibly think of immuring so charming a Girl within the walls of a Cloister!'

'I think of it, Don Christoval? How can you suspect me of such barbarity? You are conscious that She took the veil by her own desire, and that particular circumstances made her wish for a seclusion from the World. I used every means in my power to induce her to change her resolution; The endeavour was fruitless, and I lost a Sister!'

'The luckier fellow you; I think, Lorenzo, you were a considerable gainer by that loss: If I remember right, Donna Agnes had a portion of ten thousand pistoles, half of which reverted to your Lordship. By St Jago! I wish that I had fifty Sisters in the same predicament. I should consent to losing them every soul without much heart-burning—'

'How, Condé?' said Lorenzo in an angry voice; 'Do you suppose me base enough to have influenced my Sister's retirement? Do you suppose that the despicable wish to make myself Master of her fortune could. . . .'

'Admirable! Courage, Don Lorenzo! Now the Man is all in a blaze. God grant, that Antonia may soften that fiery temper, or we shall certainly cut each other's throat before the Month is over! However, to prevent such a tragical Catastrophe for the present, I shall make a retreat, and leave you Master of the field. Farewell, my Knight of Mount Ætna! Moderate that inflammable disposition, and remember that whenever it is necessary to make love to yonder Harridan, you may reckon upon my services.'

He said, and darted out of the Cathedral.

'How wild-brained!' said Lorenzo; 'With so excellent an heart, what pity that He possesses so little solidity of judgment!'

The night was now fast advancing. The Lamps were not yet lighted. The faint beams of the rising Moon scarcely could pierce through the gothic obscurity of the Church. Lorenzo found himself unable to quit the Spot. The void left in his bosom by Antonia's absence, and his Sister's sacrifice which Don Christoval had just recalled to his imagination, created that melancholy of mind, which accorded but too well with the religious gloom surrounding him. He was still leaning against the seventh column from the Pulpit. A soft and cooling air breathed along the solitary Aisles: The Moon-beams darting into the Church through painted windows, tinged the fretted roofs and massy pillars with a thousand various tints of light and colours: Universal silence prevailed around, only interrupted by the occasional closing of Doors in the adjoining Abbey.

The calm of the hour and solitude of the place contributed to nourish Lorenzo's disposition to melancholy. He threw himself upon a seat which stood near him, and abandoned himself to the delusions of his fancy. He thought of his union with Antonia; He thought of the obstacles which might oppose his wishes; and a thousand changing visions floated before his fancy, sad 'tis true, but not unpleasing. Sleep insensibly stole over him, and the tranquil solemnity of his mind when awake, for a while continued to influence his slumbers.

He still fancied himself to be in the Church of the Capuchins; but it was no longer dark and solitary. Multitudes of silver Lamps shed splendour from the vaulted Roof; Accompanied by the captivating chaunt of distant choristers, the Organ's melody swelled through the Church; The Altar seemed decorated as for some distinguished feast; It was surrounded by a brilliant Company; and near it stood Antonia arrayed in bridal white, and blushing with all the charms of Virgin Modesty.

Half hoping, half fearing, Lorenzo gazed upon the scene before him. Sudden the door leading to the Abbey unclosed, and He saw, attended by a long train of Monks, the Preacher advance to whom He had just listened with so much admiration. He drew near Antonia.

'And where is the Bridegroom?' said the imaginary Friar.

Antonia seemed to look round the Church with anxiety. Involuntarily the Youth advanced a few steps from his concealment. She saw him; The blush of pleasure glowed upon her cheek; With a graceful motion of her hand She beckoned to him to advance. He disobeyed not the command; He flew towards her, and threw himself at her feet.

She retreated for a moment; Then gazing upon him with unutterable delight;—'Yes!' She exclaimed, 'My Bridegroom! My destined Bridegroom!'

She said, and hastened to throw herself into his arms; But before He had time to receive her, an Unknown rushed between them. His form was gigantic; His complexion was swarthy, His eyes fierce and terrible; his Mouth breathed out volumes of fire; and on his forehead was written in legible characters—'Pride! Lust! Inhumanity!'

Antonia shrieked. The Monster clasped her in his arms, and springing with her upon the Altar, tortured her with his odious caresses. She endeavoured in vain to escape from his embrace. Lorenzo flew to her succour, but ere He had time to reach her, a loud burst of thunder was heard. Instantly the Cathedral seemed crumbling into pieces; The Monks betook themselves to flight, shrieking fearfully; The Lamps were extinguished, the Altar sank down, and in its place appeared an abyss vomiting forth clouds of flame. Uttering a loud and terrible cry the Monster plunged into the Gulph, and in his fall attempted to drag Antonia with him. He strove in vain. Animated by supernatural powers She disengaged herself from his embrace; But her white Robe was left in his possession. Instantly a wing of brilliant splendour spread itself from either of Antonia's arms. She darted upwards, and while ascending cried to Lorenzo,

'Friend! we shall meet above!'

At the same moment the Roof of the Cathedral opened; Harmonious voices pealed along the Vaults; and the glory into which Antonia was received, was composed of rays of such dazzling brightness, that Lorenzo was unable to sustain the gaze. His sight failed, and He sank upon the ground.

When He woke, He found himself extended upon the pavement of the Church: It was Illuminated, and the chaunt of Hymns sounded from a distance. For a while Lorenzo could not persuade himself that what He had just witnessed had been a dream, so strong an impression had it made upon his fancy. A little recollection convinced him of its fallacy: The Lamps had been lighted during his sleep, and the music which he heard, was occasioned by the Monks, who were celebrating their Vespers in the Abbey-Chapel.

Lorenzo rose, and prepared to bend his steps towards his Sister's Convent. His mind fully occupied by the singularity of his dream, He already drew near the Porch, when his attention was attracted by perceiving a Shadow moving upon the opposite wall. He looked curiously round, and soon descried a Man wrapped up in his Cloak, who seemed carefully examining whether his actions were observed. Very few people are exempt from the influence of curiosity. The Unknown seemed anxious to conceal his business in the Cathedral, and it was this very circumstance, which made Lorenzo wish to discover what He was about.

Our Hero was conscious that He had no right to pry into the secrets of this unknown Cavalier.

'I will go,' said Lorenzo. And Lorenzo stayed, where He was.

The shadow thrown by the Column, effectually concealed him from the Stranger, who continued to advance with caution. At length He drew a letter from beneath his cloak, and hastily placed it beneath a Colossal Statue of St Francis. Then retiring with precipitation, He concealed himself in a part of the Church at a considerable distance from that in which the Image stood.

'So!' said Lorenzo to himself; 'This is only some foolish love affair. I believe, I may as well be gone, for I can do no good in it.'

In truth till that moment it never came into his head, that He could do any good in it; But He thought it necessary to make some little excuse to himself for having indulged his curiosity. He now made a second attempt to retire from the Church: For this time He gained the Porch without meeting with any impediment; But it was destined that He should pay it another visit that night. As He descended the steps leading into the Street, a Cavalier rushed against him with such violence, that Both were nearly overturned by the concussion. Lorenzo put his hand to his sword.

'How now, Segnor?' said He; 'What mean you by this rudeness?'

'Ha! Is it you, Medina?' replied the New-comer, whom Lorenzo by his voice now recognized for Don Christoval; 'You are the luckiest Fellow in the Universe, not to have left the Church before my return. In, in my dear Lad! They will be here immediately!'

'Who will be here?'

'The old Hen and all her pretty little Chickens! In, I say, and then you shall know the whole History.'

Lorenzo followed him into the Cathedral, and they concealed themselves behind the Statue of St Francis.

'And now,' said our Hero, 'may I take the liberty of asking, what is the meaning of all this haste and rapture?'

'Oh! Lorenzo, we shall see such a glorious sight! The Prioress of St Clare and her whole train of Nuns are coming hither. You are to know, that the pious Father Ambrosio [The Lord reward him for it!] will upon no account move out of his own precincts: It being absolutely necessary for every fashionable Convent to have him for its Confessor, the Nuns are in consequence obliged to visit him at the Abbey; since when the Mountain will not come to Mahomet, Mahomet must needs go to the Mountain. Now the Prioress of St Clare, the better to escape the gaze of such impure eyes as belong to yourself and your humble Servant, thinks proper to bring her holy flock to confession in the Dusk: She is to be admitted into the Abbey-Chapel by you private door. The Porteress of St Clare, who is a worthy old Soul and a particular Friend of mine, has just assured me of their being here in a few moments. There is news for you, you Rogue! We shall see some of the prettiest faces in Madrid!'

'In truth, Christoval, we shall do no such thing. The Nuns are always veiled.'

'No! No! I know better. On entering a place of worship, they ever take off their veils from respect to the Saint to whom 'tis dedicated. But Hark! They are coming! Silence, silence! Observe, and be convinced.'

'Good!' said Lorenzo to himself; 'I may possibly discover to whom the vows are addressed of this mysterious Stranger.'

Scarcely had Don Christoval ceased to speak, when the Domina of St Clare appeared, followed by a long procession of Nuns. Each upon entering the Church took off her veil. The Prioress crossed her hands upon her bosom, and made a profound reverence as She passed the Statue of St Francis, the Patron of this Cathedral. The Nuns followed her example, and several moved onwards without having satisfied Lorenzo's curiosity. He almost began to despair of seeing the mystery cleared up, when in paying her respects to St Francis, one of the Nuns happened to drop her Rosary. As She stooped to pick it up, the light flashed full upon her face. At the same moment She dexterously removed the letter from beneath the Image, placed it in her bosom, and hastened to resume her rank in the procession.

'Ha!' said Christoval in a low voice; 'Here we have some little Intrigue, no doubt.'

'Agnes, by heaven!' cried Lorenzo.

'What, your Sister? Diavolo! Then somebody, I suppose, will have to pay for our peeping.'

'And shall pay for it without delay,' replied the incensed Brother.

The pious procession had now entered the Abbey; The Door was already closed upon it. The Unknown immediately quitted his concealment, and hastened to leave the Church: Ere He could effect his intention, He descried Medina stationed in his passage. The Stranger hastily retreated, and drew his Hat over his eyes.

'Attempt not to fly me!' exclaimed Lorenzo; 'I will know who you are, and what were the contents of that Letter.'

'Of that Letter?' repeated the Unknown. 'And by what title do you ask the question?'

'By a title of which I am now ashamed; But it becomes not you to question me. Either reply circumstantially to my demands, or answer me with your Sword.'

'The latter method will be the shortest,' rejoined the Other, drawing his Rapier; 'Come on, Segnor Bravo! I am ready!'

Burning with rage, Lorenzo hastened to the attack: The Antagonists had already exchanged several passes, before Christoval, who at that moment had more sense than either of them, could throw himself between their weapons.

'Hold! Hold! Medina!' He exclaimed; 'Remember the consequences of shedding blood on consecrated ground!'

The Stranger immediately dropped his Sword.

'Medina?' He cried; 'Great God, is it possible! Lorenzo, have you quite forgotten Raymond de las Cisternas?'

Lorenzo's astonishment increased with every succeeding moment. Raymond advanced towards him; but with a look of suspicion he drew back his hand, which the Other was preparing to take.

'You here, Marquis? What is the meaning of all this? You engaged in a clandestine correspondence with my Sister, whose affections. . . .'

'Have ever been, and still are mine. But this is no fit place for an explanation. Accompany me to my Hotel, and you shall know every thing. Who is that with you?'

'One whom I believe you to have seen before,' replied Don Christoval, 'though probably not at Church.'

'The Condé d'Ossorio?'

'Exactly so, Marquis.'

'I have no objection to entrusting you with my secret, for I am sure, that I may depend upon your silence.'

'Then your opinion of me is better than my own, and therefore I must beg leave to decline your confidence. Do you go your own way, and I shall go mine. Marquis, where are you to be found?'

'As usual, at the Hotel de las Cisternas; But remember, that I am incognito, and that if you wish to see me, you must ask for Alphonso d'Alvarada.'

'Good! Good! Farewell, Cavaliers!' said Don Christoval, and instantly departed.

'You, Marquis,' said Lorenzo in the accent of surprise; 'You, Alphonso d'Alvarada?'

'Even so, Lorenzo: But unless you have already heard my story from your Sister, I have much to relate that will astonish you. Follow me, therefore, to my Hotel without delay.'

At this moment the Porter of the Capuchins entered the Cathedral to lock up the doors for the night. The two Noblemen instantly withdrew, and hastened with all speed to the Palace de las Cisternas.

'Well, Antonia!' said the Aunt, as soon as She had quitted the Church; 'What think you of our Gallants? Don Lorenzo really seems a very obliging good sort of young Man: He paid you some attention, and nobody knows what may come of it. But as to Don Christoval, I protest to you, He is the very Phœnix of politeness. So gallant! so well-bred! So sensible, and so pathetic! Well! If ever Man can prevail upon me to break my vow never to marry, it will be that Don Christoval. You see, Niece, that every thing turns out exactly as I told you: The very moment that I produced myself in Madrid, I knew that I should be surrounded by Admirers. When I took off my veil, did you see, Antonia, what an effect the action had upon the Condé? And when I presented him my hand, did you observe the air of passion with which He kissed it? If ever I witnessed real love, I then saw it impressed upon Don Christoval's countenance!'

Now Antonia had observed the air, with which Don Christoval had kissed this same hand; But as She drew conclusions from it somewhat different from her Aunt's, She was wise enough to hold her tongue. As this is the only instance known of a Woman's ever having done so, it was judged worthy to be recorded here.

The old Lady continued her discourse to Antonia in the same strain, till they gained the Street in which was their Lodging. Here a Crowd collected before their door permitted them not to approach it; and placing themselves on the opposite side of the Street, they endeavoured to make out, what had drawn all these people together. After some minutes the Crowd formed itself into a Circle; And now Antonia perceived in the midst of it a Woman of extraordinary height, who whirled herself repeatedly round and round, using all sorts of extravagant gestures. Her dress was composed of shreds of various-coloured silks and Linens fantastically arranged, yet not entirely without taste. Her head was covered with a kind of Turban, ornamented with vine-leaves and wild flowers. She seemed much sun-burnt, and her complexion was of a deep olive: Her eyes looked fiery and strange; and in her hand She bore a long black Rod, with which She at intervals traced a variety of singular figures upon the ground, round about which She danced in all the eccentric attitudes of folly and delirium. Suddenly She broke off her dance, whirled herself round thrice with rapidity, and after a moment's pause She sang the following Ballad.

THE GYPSY'S SONG

Come, cross my hand! My art surpasses
   All that did ever Mortal know;
Come, Maidens, come! My magic glasses
   Your future Husband's form can show:

For 'tis to me the power is given
   Unclosed the book of Fate to see;
To read the fixed resolves of heaven,
   And dive into futurity.

I guide the pale Moon's silver waggon;
   The winds in magic bonds I hold;
I charm to sleep the crimson Dragon,
   Who loves to watch o'er buried gold:

Fenced round with spells, unhurt I venture
   Their sabbath strange where Witches keep;
Fearless the Sorcerer's circle enter,
   And woundless tread on snakes asleep.

Lo! Here are charms of mighty power!
   This makes secure an Husband's truth;
And this composed at midnight hour
   Will force to love the coldest Youth:

If any Maid too much has granted,
   Her loss this Philtre will repair;
This blooms a cheek where red is wanted,
   And this will make a brown girl fair!

Then silent hear, while I discover
   What I in Fortune's mirror view;
And each, when many a year is over,
   Shall own the Gypsy's sayings true.

'Dear Aunt!' said Antonia when the Stranger had finished, 'Is She not mad?'

'Mad? Not She, Child; She is only wicked. She is a Gypsy, a sort of Vagabond, whose sole occupation is to run about the country telling lyes, and pilfering from those who come by their money honestly. Out upon such Vermin! If I were King of Spain, every one of them should be burnt alive, who was found in my dominions after the next three weeks.'

These words were pronounced so audibly, that they reached the Gypsy's ears. She immediately pierced through the Crowd, and made towards the Ladies. She saluted them thrice in the Eastern fashion, and then addressed herself to Antonia.

THE GYPSY

> 'Lady! gentle Lady! Know,
> I your future fate can show;
> Give your hand, and do not fear;
> Lady! gentle Lady! hear!'

'Dearest Aunt!' said Antonia, 'Indulge me this once! Let me have my fortune told me!'

'Nonsense, Child! She will tell you nothing but falsehoods.'

'No matter; Let me at least hear what She has to say. Do, my dear Aunt! Oblige me, I beseech you!'

'Well, well! Antonia, since you are so bent upon the thing, . . . Here, good Woman, you shall see the hands of both of us. There is money for you, and now let me hear my fortune.'

As She said this, She drew off her glove, and presented her hand; The Gypsy looked at it for a moment, and then made this reply.

THE GYPSY

> 'Your fortune? You are now so old,
> Good Dame, that 'tis already told:
> Yet for your money, in a trice
> I will repay you in advice.
> Astonished at your childish vanity,
> Your Friends all tax you with insanity,
> And grieve to see you use your art
> To catch some youthful Lover's heart.
> Believe me, Dame, when all is done,
> Your age will still be fifty one;
> And Men will rarely take an hint
> Of love, from two grey eyes that squint.
> Take then my counsels; Lay aside
> Your paint and patches, lust and pride,
> And on the Poor those sums bestow,
> Which now are spent on useless show.
> Think on your Maker, not a Suitor;
> Think on your past faults, not on future;

And think Time's Scythe will quickly mow
The few red hairs, which deck your brow.'

The audience rang with laughter during the Gypsy's address; and—'fifty
one,'—'squinting eyes,'—'red hair,'—'paint and patches,'—&c. were ban-
died from mouth to mouth. Leonella was almost choaked with passion, and
loaded her malicious Adviser with the bitterest reproaches. The swarthy
Prophetess for some time listened to her with a contemptuous smile: at
length She made her a short answer, and then turned to Antonia.

THE GYPSY

'Peace, Lady! What I said was true;
And now, my lovely Maid
Give me your hand, and let me see
Your future doom, and heaven's decree.'

In imitation of Leonella, Antonia drew off her glove, and presented her
white hand to the Gypsy, who having gazed upon it for some time with a
mingled expression of pity and astonishment, pronounced her Oracle in the
following words.

THE GYPSY

'Jesus! what a palm is there!
Chaste, and gentle, young and fair,
Perfect mind and form possessing,
You would be some good Man's blessing:
But Alas! This line discovers,
That destruction o'er you hovers;
Lustful Man and crafty Devil
Will combine to work your evil;
And from earth by sorrows driven,
Soon your Soul must speed to heaven.
Yet your sufferings to delay,
Well remember what I say.
When you One more virtuous see
Than belongs to Man to be,
One, whose self no crimes assailing,
Pities not his Neighbour's Failing,
Call the Gypsy's words to mind:
Though He seem so good and kind,
Fair Exteriors oft will hide
Hearts, that swell with lust and pride!

> Lovely Maid, with tears I leave you!
> Let not my prediction grieve you;
> Rather with submission bending
> Calmly wait distress impending,
> And expect eternal bliss
> In a better world than this.'

Having said this, the Gypsy again whirled herself round thrice, and then hastened out of the Street with frantic gesture. The Crowd followed her; and Elvira's door being now unembarrassed Leonella entered the House out of honour with the Gypsy, with her Niece, and with the People; In short with every body, but herself and her charming Cavalier. The Gypsy's predictions had also considerably affected Antonia; But the impression soon wore off, and in a few hours She had forgotten the adventure, as totally as had it never taken place.

CHAPTER II

> Fòrse sé tu gustassi una sòl volta
> La millésima parte délle giòje,
> Ché gusta un còr amato riamando,
> Diresti ripentita sospirando,
> Perduto è tutto il tempo
> Ché in amar non si spènde.
>
> > Tasso.

> Hadst Thou but tasted once the thousandth part
> Of joys, which bless the loved and loving heart,
> Your words repentant and your sighs would prove,
> Lost is the time which is not past in love.

THE monks having attended their Abbot to the door of his Cell, He dismissed them with an air of conscious superiority, in which Humility's semblance combated with the reality of pride.

He was no sooner alone, than He gave free loose to the indulgence of his vanity. When He remembered the Enthusiasm which his discourse had excited, his heart swelled with rapture, and his imagination presented him with splendid visions of aggrandizement. He looked round him with exultation, and Pride told him loudly, that He was superior to the rest of his fellow-Creatures.

'Who,' thought He; 'Who but myself has passed the ordeal of Youth, yet sees no single stain upon his conscience? Who else has subdued the violence of strong passions and an impetuous temperament, and submitted even from the dawn of life to voluntary retirement? I seek for such a Man in vain. I see no one but myself possessed of such resolution. Religion cannot boast Ambrosio's equal! How powerful an effect did my discourse produce upon its Auditors! How they crowded round me! How they loaded me with benedictions, and pronounced me the sole uncorrupted Pillar of the Church! What then now is left for me to do? Nothing, but to watch as carefully over the conduct of my Brothers, as I have hitherto watched over my own. Yet hold! May I not be tempted from those paths, which till now I have pursued without one moment's wandering? Am I not a Man, whose nature is frail, and prone to error? I must now abandon the solitude of my retreat; The fairest and noblest Dames of Madrid continually present themselves at the Abbey, and will use no other Confessor. I must accustom my eyes to Objects of temptation, and expose myself to the seduction of luxury and desire. Should I meet in that world which I am constrained to enter some lovely Female, lovely . . . as you Madona. . . . !'

As He said this, He fixed his eyes upon a picture of the Virgin, which was suspended opposite to him: This for two years had been the Object of his increasing wonder and adoration. He paused, and gazed upon it with delight.

'What Beauty in that countenance!' He continued after a silence of some minutes; 'How graceful is the turn of that head! What sweetness, yet what majesty in her divine eyes! How softly her cheek reclines upon her hand! Can the Rose vie with the blush of that cheek? Can the Lily rival the whiteness of that hand? Oh! is such a Creature existed, and existed but for me! Were I permitted to twine round my fingers those golden ringlets, and press with my lips the treasures of that snowy bosom! Gracious God, should I then resist the temptation? Should I not barter for a single embrace the reward of my sufferings for thirty years? Should I not abandon. . . . Fool that I am! Whither do I suffer my admiration of this picture to hurry me? Away, impure ideas! Let me remember, that Woman is for ever lost to me. Never was Mortal formed so perfect as this picture. But even did such exist, the trial might be too mighty for a common virtue, but Ambrosio's is proof against temptation. Temptation, did I say? To me it would be none. What charms me, when ideal and considered as a superior Being, would disgust me, become Woman and tainted with all the failings of Mortality. It is not the Woman's beauty that fills me with such enthusiasm; It is the Painter's skill that I admire, it is the Divinity that I adore! Are not the passions dead in my bosom? Have I not freed myself from the frailty of Mankind? Fear not, Ambrosio! Take confidence in the strength of your virtue. Enter boldly into a world, to whose failings you are superior; Reflect that you are now exempted from Humanity's defects, and defy all the arts of the Spirits of Darkness. They shall know you for what you are!'

Here his Reverie was interrupted by three soft knocks at the door of his Cell. With difficulty did the Abbot awake from his delirium. The knocking was repeated.

'Who is there?' said Ambrosio at length.

'It is only Rosario,' replied a gentle voice.

'Enter! Enter, my Son!'

The Door was immediately opened, and Rosario appeared with a small basket in his hand.

Rosario was a young Novice belonging to the Monastery, who in three Months intended to make his profession. A sort of mystery enveloped this Youth which rendered him at once an object of interest and curiosity. His hatred of society, his profound melancholy, his rigid observation of the duties of his order, and his voluntary seclusion from the world at his age so unusual, attracted the notice of the whole fraternity. He seemed fearful of being recognised, and no one had ever seen his face. His head was continually muffled up in his Cowl; Yet such of his features as accident discovered, appeared the most beautiful and noble. Rosario was the only name by which He was known in the Monastery. No one knew from whence He came, and when questioned in the subject He preserved a profound silence. A Stranger, whose rich habit and magnificent equipage declared him to be of distinguished rank, had engaged the Monks to receive a Novice, and had deposited the necessary sums. The next day He returned with Rosario, and from that time no more had been heard of him.

The Youth had carefully avoided the company of the Monks: He answered their civilities with sweetness, but reserve, and evidently showed that his inclination led him to solitude. To this general rule the Superior was the only exception. To him He looked up with a respect approaching idolatry: He sought his company with the most attentive assiduity, and eagerly seized every means to ingratiate himself in his favour. In the Abbot's society his Heart seemed to be at ease, and an air of gaiety pervaded his whole manners and discourse. Ambrosio on his side did not feel less attracted towards the Youth; With him alone did He lay aside his habitual severity. When He spoke to him, He insensibly assumed a tone milder than was usual to him; and no voice sounded so sweet to him as did Rosario's. He repayed the Youth's attentions by instructing him in various sciences; The Novice received his lessons with docility; Ambrosio was every day more charmed with the vivacity of his Genius, the simplicity of his manners, and the rectitude of his heart: In short He loved him will all the affection of a Father. He could not help sometimes indulging a desire secretly to see the face of his Pupil; But his rule of self-denial extended even to curiosity, and prevented him from communicating his wishes to the Youth.

'Pardon my intrusion, Father,' said Rosario, while He placed his basket upon the Table; 'I come to you a Suppliant. Hearing that a dear Friend is dangerously ill, I entreat your prayers for his recovery. If supplications can prevail upon heaven to spare him, surely yours must be efficacious.'

'Whatever depends upon me, my Son, you know that you may command. What is your Friend's name?'

'Vincentio della Ronda.'

''Tis sufficient. I will not forget him in my prayers, and may our thrice-blessed St Francis deign to listen to my intercession!—What have you in your basket, Rosario?'

'A few of those flowers, reverend Father, which I have observed to be most acceptable to you. Will you permit my arranging them in your chamber?'

'Your attentions charm me, my Son.'

While Rosario dispersed the contents of his Basket in small Vases, placed for that purpose in various parts of the room, the Abbot thus continued the conversation.

'I saw you not in the Church this evening, Rosario.'

'Yet I was present, Father. I am too grateful for your protection to lose an opportunity of witnessing your Triumph.'

'Alas! Rosario, I have but little cause to triumph: The Saint spoke by my mouth; To him belongs all the merit. It seems then you were contented with my discourse?'

'Contented, say you? Oh! you surpassed yourself! Never did I hear such eloquence . . . save once!'

Here the Novice heaved an involuntary sigh.

'When was that once?' demanded the Abbot.

'When you preached upon the sudden indisposition of our late Superior.'

'I remember it: That is more than two years ago. And were you present? I knew you not at that time, Rosario.'

''Tis true, Father; and would to God! I had expired, ere I beheld that day! What sufferings, what sorrows should I have escaped!'

'Sufferings at your age, Rosario?'

'Aye, Father; Sufferings, which if known to you, would equally raise your anger and compassion! Sufferings, which form at once the torment and pleasure of my existence! Yet in this retreat my bosom would feel tranquil, were it not for the tortures of apprehension. Oh God! Oh God! how cruel is a life of fear!—Father! I have given up all; I have abandoned the world and its delights for ever: Nothing now remains, Nothing now has charms for me, but your friendship, but your affection. If I lose that, Father! Oh! if I lose that, tremble at the effects of my despair!'

'You apprehend the loss of my friendship? How has my conduct justified this fear? Know me better, Rosario, and think me worthy of your confidence. What are your sufferings? Reveal them to me, and believe that if 'tis in my power to relieve them. . . .'

'Ah! 'tis in no one's power but yours. Yet I must not let you know them. You would hate me for my avowal! You would drive me from your presence with scorn and ignominy!'

'My Son, I conjure you! I entreat you!'

'For pity's sake, enquire no further! I must not . . . I dare not . . . Hark! The Bell rings for Vespers! Father, your benediction, and I leave you!'

As He said this, He threw himself upon his knees, and received the blessing which He demanded. Then pressing the Abbot's hand to his lips, He started from the ground, and hastily quitted the apartment. Soon after Ambrosio descended to Vespers, [which were celebrated in a small chapel belonging to the Abbey] filled with surprise at the singularity of the Youth's behaviour.

Vespers being over, the Monks retired to their respective Cells. The Abbot alone remained in the Chapel to receive the Nuns of St Clare. He had not been long seated in the confessional chair, before the Prioress made her appearance. Each of the Nuns was heard in her turn, while the Others waited with the Domina in the adjoining Vestry. Ambrosio listened to the confessions with attention, made many exhortations, enjoined penance proportioned to each offence, and for some time every thing went on as usual: till at last one of the Nuns, conspicuous from the nobleness of her air and elegance of her figure carelessly permitted a letter to fall from her bosom. She was retiring, unconscious of her loss. Ambrosio supposed it to have been written by some one of her Relations, and picked it up intending to restore it to her.

'Stay, Daughter,' said He; 'You have let fall. . . .'

At this moment, the paper being already open, his eye involuntarily read the first words. He started back with surprise! The Nun had turned round on hearing his voice: She perceived her letter in his hand, and uttering a shriek of terror, flew hastily to regain it.

'Hold!' said the Friar in a tone of severity; 'Daughter, I must read this letter.'

'Then I am lost!' She exclaimed clasping her hands together wildly.

All colour instantly faded from her face; she trembled with agitation, and was obliged to fold her arms round a Pillar of the Chapel to save herself from sinking upon the floor. In the mean while the Abbot read the following lines.

'All is ready for your escape, my dearest Agnes. At twelve tomorrow night I shall expect to find you at the Garden-door: I have obtained the Key, and a few hours will suffice to place you in a secure asylum. Let no mistaken scruples induce you to reject the certain means of preserving yourself and the innocent Creature whom you nourish in your bosom. Remember that you had promised to be mine, long ere you engaged yourself to the church; that your situation will soon be evident to the prying eyes of your

Companions; and that flight is the only means of avoiding the effects of their malevolent resentment. Farewell, my Agnes! my dear and destined Wife! Fail not to be at the Garden-door at twelve!'

As soon as He had finished, Ambrosio bent an eye stern and angry upon the imprudent Nun.

'This letter must to the Prioress!' said He, and passed her.

His words sounded like thunder to her ears: She awoke from her torpidity only to be sensible of the dangers of her situation. She followed him hastily, and detained him by his garment.

'Stay! Oh! stay!' She cried in the accents of despair, while She threw herself at the Friar's feet, and bathed them with her tears. 'Father, compassionate my youth! Look with indulgence on a Woman's weakness, and deign to conceal my frailty! The remainder of my life shall be employed in expiating this single fault, and your lenity will bring back a soul to heaven!'

'Amazing confidence! What! Shall St Clare's Convent become the retreat of Prostitutes? Shall I suffer the Church of Christ to cherish in its bosom debauchery and shame? Unworthy Wretch! such lenity would make me your accomplice. Mercy would here be criminal. You have abandoned yourself to a Seducer's lust; You have defiled the sacred habit by your impurity; and still dare you think yourself deserving my compassion? Hence, nor detain me longer! Where is the Lady Prioress?' He added, raising his voice.

'Hold! Father, Hold! Hear me but for one moment! Tax me not with impurity, nor think that I have erred from the warmth of temperament. Long before I took the veil, Raymond was Master of my heart: He inspired me with the purest, the most irreproachable passion, and was on the point of becoming my lawful husband. An horrible adventure, and the treachery of a Relation, separated us from each other: I believed him for ever lost to me, and threw myself into a Convent from motives of despair. Accident again united us; I could not refuse myself the melancholy pleasure of mingling my tears with his: We met nightly in the Gardens of St Clare, and in an unguarded moment I violated my vows of Chastity. I shall soon become a Mother: Reverend Ambrosio, take compassion on me; take compassion on the innocent Being, whose existence is attached to mine. If you discover my imprudence to the Domina, both of us are lost: The punishment, which the laws of St Clare assign to Unfortunates like myself, is most severe and cruel. Worthy, worthy Father! Let not your own untainted conscience render you unfeeling towards those less able to withstand temptation! Let not mercy be the only virtue of which your heart is unsusceptible! Pity me, most reverend! Restore my letter, nor doom me to inevitable destruction!'

'Your boldness confounds me! Shall I conceal your crime, I whom you have deceived by your feigned confession? No, Daughter, no! I will render you a more essential service. I will rescue you from perdition in spite of yourself; Penance and mortification shall expiate your offence, and Severity force you back to the paths of holiness. What; Ho! Mother St Agatha!'

'Father! By all that is sacred, by all that is most dear to you, I supplicate, I entreat. . . .'

'Release me! I will not hear you. Where is the Domina? Mother St Agatha, where are you?'

The door of the Vestry opened, and the Prioress entered the Chapel, followed by her Nuns.

'Cruel! Cruel!' exclaimed Agnes, relinquishing her hold.

Wild and desperate, She threw herself upon the ground, beating her bosom, and rending her veil in all the delirium of despair. The Nuns gazed with astonishment upon the scene before them. The Friar now presented the fatal paper to the Prioress, informed her of the manner in which he had found it, and added, that it was her business to decide, what penance the delinquent merited.

While She perused the letter, the Domina's countenance grew inflamed with passion. What! Such a crime committed in her Convent, and made known to Ambrosio, to the Idol of Madrid, to the Man whom She was most anxious to impress with the opinion of the strictness and regularity of her House! Words were inadequate to express her fury. She was silent, and darted upon the prostrate Nun looks of menace and malignity.

'Away with her to the Convent!' said She at length to some of her Attendants.

Two of the oldest Nuns now approaching Agnes, raised her forcibly from the ground, and prepared to conduct her from the Chapel.

'What!' She exclaimed suddenly shaking off their hold with distracted gestures; 'Is all hope then lost? Already do you drag me to punishment? Where are you, Raymond? Oh! save me! save me!' Then casting upon the Abbot a frantic look, 'Hear me!' She continued; 'Man of an hard heart! Hear me, Proud, Stern, and Cruel! You could have saved me; you could have restored me to happiness and virtue, but would not! You are the destroyer of my Soul; You are my Murderer, and on you fall the curse of my death and my unborn Infant's! Insolent in your yet-unshaken virtue, you disdained the prayers of a Penitent; But God will show mercy, though you show none. And where is the merit of your boasted virtue? What temptations have you vanquished? Coward! you have fled from it, not opposed seduction. But the day of Trial will arrive! Oh! then when you yield to impetuous passions! when you feel that Man is weak, and born to err; When shuddering you look back upon your crimes, and solicit with terror the mercy of your God, Oh! in that fearful moment think upon me! Think upon your Cruelty! Think upon Agnes, and despair of pardon!'

As She uttered these last words, her strength was exhausted, and She sank inanimate upon the bosom of a Nun who stood near her. She was immediately conveyed from the Chapel, and her Companions followed her.

Ambrosio had not listened to her reproaches without emotion. A secret pang at his heart made him feel, that He had treated this Unfortunate with too great severity. He therefore detained the Prioress, and ventured to pronounce some words in favour of the Delinquent.

'The violence of her despair,' said He, 'proves, that at least Vice is not become familiar to her. Perhaps by treating her with somewhat less rigour than is generally practised, and mitigating in some degree the accustomed penance. . . .'

'Mitigate it, Father?' interrupted the Lady Prioress; 'Not I, believe me. The laws of our order are strict and severe; they have fallen into disuse of late, But the crime of Agnes shows me the necessity of their revival. I go to signify my intention to the Convent, and Agnes shall be the first to feel the rigour of those laws, which shall be obeyed to the very letter. Father, Farewell.'

Thus saying, She hastened out of the Chapel.

'I have done my duty,' said Ambrosio to himself.

Still did He not feel perfectly satisfied by this reflection. To dissipate the unpleasant ideas which this scene had excited in him, upon quitting the Chapel He descended into the Abbey-Garden. In all Madrid there was no spot more beautiful or better regulated. It was laid out with the most exquisite taste; The choicest flowers adorned it in the height of luxuriance, and though artfully arranged, seemed only planted by the hand of Nature: Fountains, springing from basons of white Marble, cooled the air with perpetual showers; and the Walls were entirely covered by Jessamine, vines, and Honeysuckles. The hour now added to the beauty of the scene. The full Moon ranging through a blue and cloudless sky, shed upon the trees a trembling lustre, and the waters of the fountains sparkled in the silver beam: A gentle breeze breathed the fragrance of Orange-blossoms along the Alleys; and the Nightingale poured forth her melodious murmur from the shelter of an artificial wilderness. Thither the Abbot bent his steps.

In the bosom of this little Grove stood a rustic Grotto, formed in imitation of an Hermitage. The walls were constructed of roots of trees, and the interstices filled up with Moss and Ivy. Seats of Turf were placed on either side, and a natural Cascade fell from the Rock above. Buried in himself the Monk approached the spot. The universal calm had communicated itself to his bosom, and a voluptuous tranquillity spread languor through his soul.

He reached the Hermitage, and was entering to repose himself, when He stopped on perceiving it to be already occupied. Extended upon one of the Banks lay a man in a melancholy posture. His head was supported upon his arm, and He seemed lost in meditation. The Monk drew nearer, and recognised Rosario: He watched him in silence, and entered not the

Hermitage. After some minutes the Youth raised his eyes, and fixed them mournfully upon the opposite Wall.

'Yes!' said He with a deep and plaintive sigh; 'I feel all the happiness of thy situation, all the misery of my own! Happy were I, could I think like Thee! Could I look like Thee with disgust upon Mankind, could bury myself for ever in some impenetrable solitude, and forget that the world holds Beings deserving to be loved! Oh God! What a blessing would Misanthropy be to me!'

'That is a singular thought, Rosario,' said the Abbot, entering the Grotto.

'You here, reverend Father?' cried the Novice.

At the same time starting from his place in confusion, He drew his Cowl hastily over his face. Ambrosio seated himself upon the Bank, and obliged the Youth to place himself by him.

'You must not indulge this disposition to melancholy,' said He; 'What can possibly have made you view in so desirable a light, Misanthropy, of all sentiments the most hateful?'

'The perusal of these Verses, Father, which till now had escaped my observation. The Brightness of the Moon-beams permitted my reading them; and Oh! how I envy the feelings of the Writer!'

As He said this, He pointed to a marble Tablet fixed against the opposite Wall: On it were engraved the following lines.

INSCRIPTION IN AN HERMITAGE

Who-e'er Thou art these lines now reading,
Think not, though from the world receding
I joy my lonely days to lead in
    This Desart drear,
That with remorse a conscience bleeding
    Hath led me here.

No thought of guilt my bosom sowrs:
Free-willed I fled from courtly bowers;
For well I saw in Halls and Towers
    That Lust and Pride,
The Arch-Fiend's dearest darkest Powers,
    In state preside.

I saw Mankind with vice incrusted;
I saw that Honour's sword was rusted;
That few for aught but folly lusted;
That He was still deceiv'd, who trusted
    In Love or Friend;
And hither came with Men disgusted
    My life to end.

In this lone Cave, in garments lowly,
Alike a Foe to noisy folly,
And brow-bent gloomy melancholy
          I wear away
My life, and in my office holy
          Consume the day.

Content and comfort bless me more in
This Grot, than e'er I felt before in
A Palace; and with thoughts still soaring
          To God on high,
Each night and morn with voice imploring
          This wish I sigh.

'Let me, Oh! Lord! from life retire,
Unknown each guilty worldly fire,
Remorseful throb, or loose desire;
          And when I die,
Let me in this belief expire,
          "To God I fly"!'

Stranger, if full of youth and riot
As yet no grief has marred thy quiet,
Thou haply throw'st a scornful eye at
          The Hermit's prayer:
But if Thou hast a cause to sigh at
          Thy fault, or care;

If Thou hast known false Love's vexation,
Or hast been exil'd from thy Nation,
Or guilt affrights thy contemplation,
          And makes thee pine,
Oh! how must Thou lament *thy* station,
          And envy mine!

'Were it possible' said the Friar, 'for Man to be so totally wrapped up in himself as to live in absolute seclusion from human nature, and could yet feel the contented tranquillity which these lines express, I allow that the situation would be more desirable, than to live in a world so pregnant with every vice and every folly. But this never can be the case. This inscription was merely placed here for the ornament of the Grotto, and the sentiments and the Hermit are equally imaginary. Man was born for society. However little He may be attached to the World, He never can wholly forget it, or bear to be wholly forgotten by it. Disgusted at the guilt or absurdity of Mankind, the Misanthrope flies from it: He resolves to become an Hermit,

and buries himself in the Cavern of some gloomy Rock. While Hate inflames
his bosom, possibly He may feel contented with his situation: But when his
passions begin to cool; when Time has mellowed his sorrows, and healed
those wounds which He bore with him to his solitude, think you that
Content becomes his Companion? Ah! no, Rosario. No longer sustained by
the violence of his passions, He feels all the monotony of his way of living,
and his heart becomes the prey of Ennui and weariness. He looks round,
and finds himself alone in the Universe: The love of society revives in his
bosom, and He pants to return to that world which He has abandoned.
Nature loses all her charms in his eyes: No one is near him to point out her
beauties, or share in his admiration of her excellence and variety. Propped
upon the fragment of some Rock, He gazes upon the tumbling water-fall
with a vacant eye, He views without emotion the glory of the setting Sun.
Slowly He returns to his Cell at Evening, for no one there is anxious for his
arrival; He has no comfort in his solitary unsavoury meal: He throws himself
upon his couch of Moss despondent and dissatisfied, and wakes only to pass
a day as joyless, as monotonous as the former.'

'You amaze me, Father! Suppose that circumstances condemned you to
solitude; Would not the duties of Religion and the consciousness of a life
well spent communicate to your heart that calm which. . . .'

'I should deceive myself, did I fancy that they could. I am convinced of
the contrary, and that all my fortitude would not prevent me from yielding
to melancholy and disgust. After consuming the day in study, if you knew
my pleasure at meeting my Brethren in the Evening! After passing many a
long hour in solitude, if I could express to you the joy which I feel at once
more beholding a fellow-Creature! 'Tis in this particular that I place the
principal merit of a Monastic Institution. It secludes Man from the temptations of Vice; It procures that leisure necessary for the proper service of
the Supreme; It spares him the mortification of witnessing the crimes of the
worldly, and yet permits him to enjoy the blessings of society. And do you,
Rosario, do *You* envy an Hermit's life? Can you be thus blind to the
happiness of your situation? Reflect upon it for a moment. This Abbey
is become your Asylum: Your regularity, your gentleness, your talents
have rendered you the object of universal esteem: You are secluded from
the world which you profess to hate; yet you remain in possession of the
benefits of society, and that a society composed of the most estimable of
Mankind.'

'Father! Father! 'tis that which causes my Torment! Happy had it been for
me, had my life been passed among the vicious and abandoned! Had I never
heard pronounced the name of Virtue! 'Tis my unbounded adoration of
religion; 'Tis my soul's exquisite sensibility of the beauty of fair and good,
that loads me with shame! that hurries me to perdition! Oh! that I had never
seen these Abbey-walls!'

'How, Rosario? When we last conversed, you spoke in a different tone. Is my friendship then become of such little consequence? Had you never seen these Abbey-walls, you never had seen me: Can that really be your wish?'

'Had never seen you?' repeated the Novice, starting from the Bank, and grasping the Friar's hand with a frantic air; 'You? You? Would to God, that lightning had blasted them, before you ever met my eyes! Would to God! that I were never to see you more, and could forget that I had ever seen you!'

With these words He flew hastily from the Grotto. Ambrosio remained in his former attitude, reflecting on the Youth's unaccountable behaviour. He was inclined to suspect the derangement of his senses: yet the general tenor of his conduct, the connexion of his ideas, and calmness of his demeanour till the moment of his quitting the Grotto, seemed to discountenance this conjecture. After a few minutes Rosario returned. He again seated himself upon the Bank: He reclined his cheek upon one hand, and with the other wiped away the tears which trickled from his eyes at intervals.

The Monk looked upon him with compassion, and forbore to interrupt his meditations. Both observed for some time a profound silence. The Nightingale had now taken her station upon an Orange Tree fronting the Hermitage, and poured forth a strain the most melancholy and melodious. Rosario raised his head, and listened to her with attention.

'It was thus,' said He, with a deep-drawn sigh; 'It was thus, that during the last month of her unhappy life, my Sister used to sit listening to the Nightingale. Poor Matilda! She sleeps in the Grave, and her broken heart throbs no more with passion.'

'You had a Sister?'

'You say right, that I *had*; Alas! I have one no longer. She sunk beneath the weight of her sorrows in the very spring of life.'

'What were those sorrows?'

'They will not excite *your* pity: *You* know not the power of those irresistible, those fatal sentiments, to which her Heart was a prey. Father, She loved unfortunately. A passion for One endowed with every virtue, for a Man, Oh! rather let me say, for a divinity, proved the bane of her existence. His noble form, his spotless character, his various talents, his wisdom solid, wonderful, and glorious, might have warmed the bosom of the most insensible. My Sister saw him, and dared to love though She never dared to hope.'

'If her love was so well bestowed, what forbad her to hope the obtaining of its object?'

'Father, before He knew her, Julian had already plighted his vows to a Bride most fair, most heavenly! Yet still my Sister loved, and for the Husband's sake She doted upon the Wife. One morning She found means to escape from our Father's House: Arrayed in humble weeds She offered herself as a Domestic to the Consort of her Beloved, and was accepted. She was now continually in his presence: She strove to ingratiate herself into his favour: She succeeded. Her attentions attracted Julian's notice; The virtuous are ever grateful, and He distinguished Matilda above the rest of her Companions.'

'And did not your Parents seek for her? Did they submit tamely to their loss, nor attempt to recover their wandering Daughter?'

'Ere they could find her, She discovered herself. Her love grew too violent for concealment; Yet She wished not for Julian's person, She ambitioned but a share of his heart. In an unguarded moment She confessed her affection. What was the return? Doting upon his Wife, and believing that a look of pity bestowed upon another, was a theft from what He owed to her, He drove Matilda from his presence. He forbad her ever again appearing before him. His severity broke her heart: She returned to her Father's, and in a few Months after was carried to her Grave.'

'Unhappy Girl! Surely her fate was too severe, and Julian was too cruel.'

'Do you think so, Father?' cried the Novice with vivacity; 'Do you think that He was cruel?'

'Doubtless I do, and pity her most sincerely.'

'You pity her? You pity her? Oh! Father! Father! Then pity me!'

The Friar started; when after a moment's pause Rosario added with a faltering voice,—'for my sufferings are still greater. My Sister had a Friend, a real Friend, who pitied the acuteness of her feelings, nor reproached her with her inability to repress them. I . . . ! I have no Friend! The whole wide world cannot furnish an heart, that is willing to participate in the sorrows of mine!'

As He uttered these words, He sobbed audibly. The Friar was affected. He took Rosario's hand, and pressed it with tenderness.

'You have no Friend, say you? What then am I? Why will you not confide in me, and what can you fear? My severity? Have I ever used it with you? The dignity of my habit? Rosario, I lay aside the Monk, and bid you consider me as no other than your Friend, your Father. Well may I assume that title, for never did Parent watch over a Child more fondly than I have watched over you. From the moment in which I first beheld you, I perceived sensations in my bosom, till then unknown to me; I found a delight in your society which no one's else could afford; and when I witnessed the extent of your genius and information, I rejoiced as does a Father in the perfections of his Son. Then lay aside your fears; Speak to me with openness: Speak to me, Rosario, and say that you will confide in me. If my aid or my pity can alleviate your distress. . . .'

'Yours can! Yours only can! Ah! Father, how willingly would I unveil to you my heart! How willingly would I declare the secret, which bows me down with its weight! But Oh! I fear! I fear!'

'What, my Son?'

'That you should abhor me for my weakness; That the reward of my confidence should be the loss of your esteem.'

'How shall I reassure you? Reflect upon the whole of my past conduct, upon the paternal tenderness which I have ever shown you. Abhor you, Rosario? It is no longer in my power. To give up your society would be to deprive myself of the greatest pleasure of my life. Then reveal to me what afflicts you, and believe me while I solemnly swear. . . .'

'Hold!' interrupted the Novice; 'Swear, that whatever be my secret, you will not oblige me to quit the Monastery till my Noviciate shall expire.'

'I promise it faithfully, and as I keep my vows to you, may Christ keep his to Mankind. Now then explain this mystery, and rely upon my indulgence.'

'I obey you. Know then . . . Oh! how I tremble to name the word! Listen to me with pity, revered Ambrosio! Call up every latent spark of human weakness that may teach you compassion for mine! Father!' continued He throwing himself at the Friar's feet, and pressing his hand to his lips with eagerness, while agitation for a moment choaked his voice; 'Father!' continued He in faltering accents, 'I am a Woman!'

The Abbot started at this unexpected avowal. Prostrated on the ground lay the feigned Rosario, as if waiting in silence the decision of his Judge. Astonishment on the one part, apprehension on the other, for some minutes chained them in the same attitudes, as had they been touched by the Rod of some Magician. At length recovering from his confusion, the Monk quitted the Grotto, and sped with precipitation towards the Abbey. His action did not escape the Suppliant. She sprang from the ground; She hastened to follow him, over-took him, threw herself in his passage, and embraced his knees. Ambrosio strove in vain to disengage himself from her grasp.

'Do not fly me!' She cried; 'Leave me not abandoned to the impulse of despair! Listen, while I excuse my imprudence; while I acknowledge my Sister's story to be my own! I am Matilda; You are her Beloved.'

If Ambrosio's surprise was great at her first avowal, upon hearing her second it exceeded all bounds. Amazed, embarrassed, and irresolute He found himself incapable of pronouncing a syllable, and remained in silence gazing upon Matilda: This gave her opportunity to continue her explanation as follows.

'Think not, Ambrosio, that I come to rob your Bride of your affections. No, believe me: Religion alone deserves you; and far is it from Matilda's wish to draw you from the paths of virtue. What I feel for you is love, not licentiousness; I sigh to be possessor of your heart, not lust for the enjoyment of your person. Deign to listen to my vindication: A few moments will convince you, that this holy retreat is not polluted by my presence, and that you may grant me your compassion without trespassing against your vows.'—She seated herself: Ambrosio, scarcely conscious of what He did, followed her example, and She proceeded in her discourse.

'I spring from a distinguished family: My Father was Chief of the noble House of Villanegas. He died, while I was still an Infant, and left me sole Heiress of his immense possessions. Young and wealthy, I was sought in marriage by the noblest Youths of Madrid; But no one succeeded in gaining my affections. I had been brought up under the care of an Uncle, possessed of the most solid judgment and extensive erudition. He took pleasure in communicating to me some portion of his knowledge. Under his instructions my understanding acquired more strength and justness, than generally falls to the lot of my sex: The ability of my Preceptor being aided by natural curiosity, I not only made a considerable progress in sciences universally studied, but in others, revealed but to few, and lying under censure from the blindness of superstition. But while my Guardian laboured to enlarge the sphere of my knowledge, He carefully inculcated every moral precept: He relieved me from the shackles of vulgar prejudice; He pointed out the beauty of Religion; He taught me to look with adoration upon the pure and virtuous, and, woe is me! I have obeyed him but too well!

'With such dispositions, Judge whether I could observe with any other sentiment than disgust the vice, dissipation, and ignorance, which disgrace our Spanish Youth. I rejected every offer with disdain. My heart remained without a Master, till chance conducted me to the Cathedral of the Capuchins. Oh! surely on that day my Guardian-Angel slumbered neglectful of his charge! Then was it that I first beheld you: You supplied the Superior's place, absent from illness. You cannot but remember the lively enthusiasm which your discourse created. Oh! how I drank your words! How your eloquence seemed to steal me from myself! I scarcely dared to breathe, fearing to lose a syllable; and while you spoke, Methought a radiant glory beamed round your head, and your countenance shone with the majesty of a God. I retired from the Church, glowing with admiration. From that moment you became the idol of my heart, the never-changing object of my Meditations. I enquired respecting you. The reports which were made me of your mode of life, of your knowledge, piety, and self-denial riveted the chains imposed on me by your eloquence. I was conscious that there was no longer a void in my heart; That I had found the Man whom I had sought till then in vain. In expectation of hearing you again every day I visited your Cathedral: You remained secluded within the Abbey-walls, and I always withdrew, wretched and disappointed. The Night was more propitious to me, for then you stood before me in my dreams; You vowed to me eternal friendship; You led me through the paths of virtue, and assisted me to support the vexations of life. The Morning dispelled these pleasing visions; I woke, and found myself separated from you by Barriers, which appeared insurmountable. Time seemed only to increase the strength of my passion: I grew melancholy and despondent; I fled from society, and my health declined daily. At length no longer able to exist in this state of torture, I resolved to assume the disguise in which you see me. My artifice was fortunate: I was received into the Monastery, and succeeded in gaining your esteem.

'Now then I should have felt compleatly happy, had not my quiet been disturbed by the fear of detection. The pleasure, which I received from your society, was embittered by the idea, that perhaps I should soon be deprived of it: and my heart throbbed so rapturously at obtaining the marks of your friendship, as to convince me that I never should survive its loss. I resolved, therefore, not to leave the discovery of my sex to chance, to confess the whole to you, and throw myself entirely on your mercy and indulgence. Ah! Ambrosio, can I have been deceived? Can you be less generous than I thought you? I will not suspect it. You will not drive a Wretch to despair; I shall still be permitted to see you, to converse with you, to adore you! Your virtues shall be my example through life; and when we expire, our bodies shall rest in the same Grave.'

She ceased. While She spoke, a thousand opposing sentiments combated in Ambrosio's bosom. Surprise at the singularity of this adventure, Confusion at her abrupt declaration, Resentment at her boldness in entering the Monastery, and Consciousness of the austerity with which it behoved him to reply, such were the sentiments of which He was aware; But there were others also which did not obtain his notice. He perceived not, that his vanity was flattered by the praises bestowed upon his eloquence and virtue; that He felt a secret pleasure in reflecting that a young and seemingly lovely Woman had for his sake abandoned the world, and sacrificed every other passion to that which He had inspired: Still less did He perceive that his heart throbbed with desire, while his hand was pressed gently by Matilda's ivory fingers.

By degrees He recovered from his confusion. His ideas became less bewildered: He was immediately sensible of the extreme impropriety, should Matilda be permitted to remain in the Abbey, after this avowal of her sex. He assumed an air of severity, and drew away his hand.

'How, Lady!' said He; 'Can you really hope for my permission to remain amongst us? Even were I to grant your request, what good could you derive from it? Think you, that I ever can reply to an affection which . . .'.

'No, Father, No! I expect not to inspire you with a love like mine. I only wish for the liberty to be near you, to pass some hours of the day in your society; to obtain your compassion, your friendship and esteem. Surely my request is not unreasonable.'

'But reflect, Lady! Reflect only for a moment on the impropriety of my harbouring a Woman in the Abbey; and that too a Woman, who confesses that She loves me. It must not be. The risque of your being discovered is too great, and I will not expose myself to so dangerous a temptation.'

'Temptation, say you? Forget, that I am a Woman, and it no longer exists: Consider me only as a Friend, as an Unfortunate, whose happiness, whose life depends upon your protection. Fear not, lest I should ever call to your remembrance, that love the most impetuous, the most unbounded, has induced me to disguise my sex; or that instigated by desires, offensive to *your* vows and my own honour, I should endeavour to seduce you from the path of rectitude. No, Ambrosio, learn to know me better. I love you for your virtues: Lose them, and with them you lose my affections. I look upon you as a Saint; Prove to me that you are no more than Man, and I quit you with disgust. Is it then from me that you fear temptation? From me, in whom the world's dazzling pleasures created no other sentiment than contempt? From me, whose attachment is grounded on your exemption from human frailty? Oh! dismiss such injurious apprehensions! Think nobler of me, think nobler of yourself. I am incapable of seducing you to error; and surely your Virtue is established on a basis too firm to be shaken by unwarranted desires. Ambrosio, dearest Ambrosio! drive me not from your presence; Remember your promise, and authorize my stay!'

'Impossible, Matilda; *Your* interest commands me to refuse your prayer, since I tremble for you, not for myself. After vanquishing the impetuous ebullitions of Youth; After passing thirty years in mortification and penance, I might safely permit your stay, nor fear your inspiring me with warmer sentiments than pity. But to yourself, remaining in the Abbey can produce none but fatal consequences. You will misconstrue my every word and action; You will seize every circumstance with avidity, which encourages you to hope the return of your affection; Insensibly your passions will gain a superiority over your reason; and far from these being repressed by my presence, every moment which we pass together, will only serve to irritate and excite them. Believe me, unhappy Woman! you possess my sincere compassion. I am convinced that you have hitherto acted upon the purest motives; But though you are blind to the imprudence of your conduct, in me it would be culpable not to open your eyes. I feel that Duty obliges my treating you with harshness: I must reject your prayer, and remove every shadow of hope, which may aid to nourish sentiments so pernicious to your repose. Matilda, you must from hence to-morrow.'

'To-morrow, Ambrosio? To-morrow? Oh! surely you cannot mean it! You cannot resolve on driving me to despair! You cannot have the cruelty....'

'You have heard my decision, and it must be obeyed. The Laws of our Order forbid your stay: It would be perjury to conceal that a Woman is within these Walls, and my vows will oblige me to declare your story to the Community. You must from hence!—I pity you, but can do no more!'

He pronounced these words in a faint and trembling voice: Then rising from his seat, He would have hastened towards the Monastery. Uttering a loud shriek, Matilda followed, and detained him.

'Stay yet one moment, Ambrosio! Hear me yet speak one word!'

'I dare not listen! Release me! You know my resolution!'

'But one word! But one last word, and I have done!'

'Leave me! Your entreaties are in vain! You must from hence to-morrow!'

'Go then, Barbarian! But this resource is still left me.'

As She said this, She suddenly drew a poignard: She rent open her garment, and placed the weapon's point against her bosom.

'Father, I will never quit these Walls alive!'

'Hold! Hold, Matilda! What would you do?'

'You are determined, so am I: The Moment that you leave me, I plunge this Steel in my heart.'

'Holy St Francis! Matilda, have you your senses? Do you know the consequences of your action? That Suicide is the greatest of crimes? That you destroy your Soul? That you lose your claim to salvation? That you prepare for yourself everlasting torments?'

'I care not! I care not!' She replied passionately; 'Either your hand guides me to Paradise, or my own dooms me to perdition! Speak to me, Ambrosio! Tell me that you will conceal my story, that I shall remain your Friend and your Companion, or this poignard drinks my blood!'

As She uttered these last words, She lifted her arm, and made a motion as if to stab herself. The Friar's eyes followed with dread the course of the dagger. She had torn open her habit, and her bosom was half exposed. The weapon's point rested upon her left breast: And Oh! that was such a breast! The Moon-beams darting full upon it, enabled the Monk to observe its dazzling whiteness. His eye dwelt with insatiable avidity upon the beauteous Orb. A sensation till then unknown filled his heart with a mixture of anxiety and delight: A raging fire shot through every limb; The blood boiled in his veins, and a thousand wild wishes bewildered his imagination.

'Hold!' He cried in an hurried faultering voice; 'I can resist no longer! Stay, then, Enchantress; Stay for my destruction!'

He said, and rushing from the place, hastened towards the Monastery: He regained his Cell, and threw himself upon his Couch, distracted irresolute and confused.

He found it impossible for some time to arrange his ideas. The scene in which He had been engaged, had excited such a variety of sentiments in his bosom, that He was incapable of deciding which was predominant. He was irresolute, what conduct He ought to hold with the disturber of his repose, He was conscious that prudence, religion, and propriety necessitated his obliging her to quit the Abbey: But on the other hand such powerful reasons authorized her stay, that He was but too much inclined to consent to her remaining. He could not avoid being flattered by Matilda's declaration, and at reflecting that He had unconsciously vanquished an heart, which had resisted the attacks of Spain's noblest Cavaliers: The manner in which He had gained her affections was also the most satisfactory to his vanity: He remembered, the many happy hours which He had passed in Rosario's society, and dreaded that void in his heart which parting with him would occasion. Besides all this, He considered, that as Matilda was wealthy, her favour might be of essential benefit to the Abbey.

'And what do I risque,' said He to himself, 'by authorizing her stay? May I not safely credit her assertions? Will it not be easy for me to forget her sex, and still consider her as my Friend and my disciple? Surely her love is as pure as She describes. Had it been the offspring of mere licentiousness, would She so long have concealed it in her own bosom? Would She not have employed some means to procure its gratification? She has done quite the contrary: She strove to keep me in ignorance of her sex; and nothing but the fear of detection, and my instances, would have compelled her to reveal the secret. She has observed the duties of religion not less strictly than myself. She has made no attempts to rouze my slumbering passions, nor has She ever conversed with me till this night on the subject of Love. Had She been desirous to gain my affections, not my esteem, She would not have concealed from me her charms so carefully: At this very moment I have never seen her face: Yet certainly that face must be lovely, and her person beautiful, to judge by her ... by what I have seen.'

As this last idea passed through his imagination, a blush spread itself over his cheek. Alarmed at the sentiments which He was indulging, He betook himself to prayer; He started from his Couch, knelt before the beautiful Madona, and entreated her assistance in stifling such culpable emotions. He then returned to his Bed, and resigned himself to slumber.

He awoke, heated and unrefreshed. During his sleep his inflamed imagination had presented him with none but the most voluptuous objects. Matilda stood before him in his dreams, and his eyes again dwelt upon her naked breast. She repeated her protestations of eternal love, threw her arms round his neck, and loaded him with kisses: He returned them; He clasped her passionately to his bosom, and ... the vision was dissolved. Sometimes his dreams presented the image of his favourite Madona, and He fancied that He was kneeling before her: As He offered up his vows to her, the eyes of the Figure seemed to beam on him with inexpressible sweetness. He pressed his lips to hers, and found them warm: The animated form started from the Canvas, embraced him affectionately, and his senses were unable to support delight so exquisite. Such were the scenes, on which his thoughts were employed while sleeping: His unsatisfied Desires placed before him the most lustful and provoking Images, and he rioted in joys till then unknown to him.

He started from his Couch, filled with confusion at the remembrance of his dreams. Scarcely was He less ashamed, when He reflected on his reasons of the former night, which induced him to authorize Matilda's stay. The cloud was now dissipated which had obscured his judgment: He shuddered, when He beheld his arguments blazoned in their proper colours, and found that He had been a slave to flattery, to avarice, and self-love. If in one hour's conversation Matilda had produced a change so remarkable in his sentiments, what had He not to dread from her remaining in the Abbey? Become sensible of his danger, awakened from his dream of confidence, He resolved to insist on her departing without delay. He began to feel that He was not proof against temptation; and that however Matilda might restrain herself within the bounds of modesty, He was unable to contend with those passions, from which He falsely thought himself exempted.

'Agnes! Agnes!' He exclaimed, while reflecting on his embarrassments, 'I already feel thy curse!'

He quitted his Cell, determined upon dismissing the feigned Rosario. He appeared at Matins; But his thoughts were absent, and He paid them but little attention. His heart and brain were both of them filled with worldly objects, and He prayed without devotion. The service over, He descended into the Garden. He bent his steps towards the same spot, where on the preceding night He had made this embarrassing discovery. He doubted not but that Matilda would seek him there: He was not deceived. She soon entered the Hermitage, and approached the Monk with a timid air. After a few minutes during which both were silent, She appeared as if on the point of speaking; But the Abbot, who during this time had been summoning up all his resolution, hastily interrupted her. Though still unconscious how extensive was its influence, He dreaded the melodious seduction of her voice.

'Seat yourself by my side, Matilda,' said He, assuming a look of firmness, though carefully avoiding the least mixture of severity; 'Listen to me patiently, and believe, that in what I shall say, I am not more influenced by my own interest, than by yours: Believe, that I feel for you the warmest friendship, the truest compassion, and that you cannot feel more grieved than I do, when I declare to you that we must never meet again.'

'Ambrosio!' She cried, in a voice at once expressive of surprise and sorrow.

'Be calm, my Friend! My Rosario! Still let me call you by that name so dear to me! Our separation is unavoidable; I blush to own, how sensibly it affects me.—But yet it must be so. I feel myself incapable of treating you with indifference, and that very conviction obliges me to insist upon your departure. Matilda, you must stay here no longer.'

'Oh! where shall I now seek for probity? Disgusted with a perfidious world, in what happy region does Truth conceal herself? Father, I hoped that She resided here; I thought that your bosom had been her favourite shrine. And you too prove false? Oh God! And you too can betray me?'

'Matilda!'

'Yes, Father, Yes! 'Tis with justice that I reproach you. Oh! where are your promises? My Noviciate is not expired, and yet will you compell me to quit the Monastery? Can you have the heart to drive me from you? And have I not received your solemn oath to the contrary?'

'I will not compell you to quit the Monastery: You have received my solemn oath to the contrary. But yet when I throw myself upon your generosity, when I declare to you the embarrassments in which your presence involves me, will you not release me from that oath? Reflect upon the danger of a discovery, upon the opprobrium in which such an event would plunge me: Reflect, that my honour and reputation are at stake, and that my peace of mind depends on your compliance. As yet my heart is free; I shall separate from you with regret, but not with despair. Stay here, and a few weeks will sacrifice my happiness on the altar of your charms. You are but too interesting, too amiable! I should love you, I should doat on you! My bosom would become the prey of desires, which Honour and my profession forbid me to gratify. If I resisted them, the impetuosity of my wishes unsatisfied would drive me to madness: If I yielded to the temptation, I should sacrifice to one moment of guilty pleasure my reputation in this world, my salvation in the next. To you then I fly for defence against myself. Preserve me from losing the reward of thirty years of sufferings! Preserve me from becoming the Victim of Remorse! *Your* heart has already felt the anguish of hopeless love; Oh! then if you really value me, spare mine that anguish! Give me back my promise; Fly from these walls. Go, and you bear with you my warmest prayers for your happiness, my friendship, my esteem and admiration: Stay, and you become to me the source of danger, of sufferings, of despair! Answer me, Matilda; What is your resolve?'—She was silent—'Will you not speak, Matilda? Will you not name your choice?'

'Cruel! Cruel!' She exclaimed, wringing her hands in agony; 'You know too well that you offer me no choice! You know too well that I can have no will but yours!'

'I was not then deceived! Matilda's generosity equals my expectations.'

'Yes; I will prove the truth of my affection by submitting to a decree which cuts me to the very heart. Take back your promise. I will quit the Monastery this very day. I have a Relation, Abbess of a Covent in Estramadura: To her will I bend my steps, and shut myself from the world for ever. Yet tell me, Father; Shall I bear your good wishes with me to my solitude? Will you sometimes abstract your attention from heavenly objects to bestow a thought upon me?'

'Ah! Matilda, I fear that I shall think on you but too often for my repose!'

'Then I have nothing more to wish for, save that we may meet in heaven. Farewell, my Friend! my Ambrosio!—And yet methinks, I would fain bear with me some token of your regard!'

'What shall I give you?'

'Something.—Any thing.—One of those flowers will be sufficient.' [Here She pointed to a bush of Roses, planted at the door of the Grotto.] 'I will hide it in my bosom, and when I am dead, the Nuns shall find it withered upon my heart.'

The Friar was unable to reply: With slow steps, and a soul heavy with affliction, He quitted the Hermitage. He approached the Bush, and stooped to pluck one of the Roses. Suddenly He uttered a piercing cry, started back hastily, and let the flower, which He already held, fall from his hand. Matilda heard the shriek, and flew anxiously towards him.

'What is the matter?' She cried; 'Answer me, for God's sake! What has happened?'

'I have received my death!' He replied in a faint voice; 'Concealed among the Roses . . . A Serpent . . .'

Here the pain of his wound became so exquisite, that Nature was unable to bear it: His senses abandoned him, and He sank inanimate into Matilda's arms.

Her distress was beyond the power of description. She rent her hair, beat her bosom, and not daring to quit Ambrosio, endeavoured by loud cries to summon the Monks to her assistance. She at length succeeded. Alarmed by her shrieks Several of the Brothers hastened to the spot, and the Superior was conveyed back to the Abbey. He was immediately put to bed, and the Monk, who officiated as Surgeon to the Fraternity, prepared to examine the wound. By this time Ambrosio's hand had swelled to an extraordinary size; The remedies which had been administered to him, 'tis true, restored him to life, but not to his senses; He raved in all the horrors of delirium, foamed at the mouth, and four of the strongest Monks were scarcely able to hold him in his bed.

Father Pablos, such was the Surgeon's name, hastened to examine the wounded hand. The Monks surrounded the Bed, anxiously waiting for the decision: Among these the feigned Rosario appeared not the most insensible to the Friar's calamity. He gazed upon the Sufferer with inexpressible anguish; and the groans, which every moment escaped from his bosom, sufficiently betrayed the violence of his affliction.

Father Pablos probed the wound. As He drew out his Lancet, its point was tinged with a greenish hue. He shook his head mournfully, and quitted the bed-side.

' 'Tis as I feared!' said He; 'There is no hope.'

'No hope?' exclaimed the Monks with one voice; 'Say you, no hope?'

'From the sudden effects, I suspected that the Abbot was stung by a Cientipedoro:[1] The venom which you see upon my Lancet confirms my idea: He cannot live three days.'

---

[1] The Cientipedoro is supposed to be a Native of Cuba, and to have been brought into Spain from that Island in the Vessels of Columbus.

'And can no possible remedy be found?' enquired Rosario.

'Without extracting the poison, He cannot recover; and how to extract it is to me still a secret. All that I can do is to apply such herbs to the wound, as will relieve the anguish: The Patient will be restored to his senses; But the venom will corrupt the whole mass of his blood, and in three days He will exist no longer.'

Excessive was the universal grief, at hearing this decision. Pablos, as He had promised, dressed the wound, and then retired, followed by his Companions: Rosario alone remained in the Cell, the Abbot at his urgent entreaty having been committed to his care. Ambrosio's strength worn out by the violence of his exertions, He had by this time fallen into a profound sleep. So totally was He overcome by weariness, that He scarcely gave any signs of life; He was still in this situation, when the Monks returned to enquire, whether any change had taken place. Pablos loosened the bandage which concealed the wound, more from a principle of curiosity, than from indulging the hope of discovering any favourable symptoms. What was his astonishment at finding, that the inflammation had totally subsided! He probed the hand; His Lancet came out pure and unsullied; No traces of the venom were perceptible; and had not the orifice still been visible, Pablos might have doubted that there had ever been a wound.

He communicated this intelligence to his Brethren; their delight was only equalled by their surprize. From the latter sentiment, however, they were soon released by explaining the circumstance according to their own ideas: They were perfectly convinced that their Superior was a Saint, and thought, that nothing could be more natural than for St Francis to have operated a miracle in his favour. This opinion was adopted unanimously: They declared it so loudly, and vociferated,—'A miracle! a miracle!'—with such fervour, that they soon interrupted Ambrosio's slumbers.

The Monks immediately crowded round his Bed, and expressed their satisfaction at his wonderful recovery. He was perfectly in his senses, and free from every complaint except feeling weak and languid. Pablos gave him a strengthening medicine, and advised his keeping his bed for the two succeeding days: He then retired, having desired his Patient not to exhaust himself by conversation, but rather to endeavour at taking some repose. The other Monks followed his example, and the Abbot and Rosario were left without Observers.

For some minutes Ambrosio regarded his Attendant with a look of mingled pleasure and apprehension. She was seated upon the side of the Bed, her head bending down, and as usual enveloped in the Cowl of her Habit.

'And you are still here, Matilda?' said the Friar at length. 'Are you not satisfied with having so nearly effected my destruction, that nothing but a miracle could have saved me from the Grave? Ah! surely Heaven sent that Serpent to punish. . . .'

Matilda interrupted him by putting her hand before his lips with an air of gaiety.

'Hush! Father, Hush! You must not talk!'

'He who imposed that order, knew not how interesting are the subjects on which I wish to speak.'

'But I know it, and yet issue the same positive command. I am appointed your Nurse, and you must not disobey my orders.'

'You are in spirits, Matilda!'

'Well may I be so: I have just received a pleasure unexampled through my whole life.'

'What was that pleasure?'

'What I must conceal from all, but most from you.'

'But most from me? Nay then, I entreat you, Matilda. . . .'

'Hush, Father! Hush! You must not talk. But as you do not seem inclined to sleep, shall I endeavour to amuse you with my Harp?'

'How? I knew not that you understood Music.'

'Oh! I am a sorry Performer! Yet as silence is prescribed you for eight and forty hours, I may possibly entertain you, when wearied of your own reflections. I go to fetch my Harp.'

She soon returned with it.

'Now, Father; What shall I sing? Will you hear the Ballad which treats of the gallant Durandarte, who died in the famous battle of Roncevalles?'

'What you please, Matilda.'

'Oh! call me not Matilda! Call me Rosario, call me your Friend! Those are the names, which I love to hear from your lips. Now listen!'

She then tuned her harp, and afterwards preluded for some moments with such exquisite taste, as to prove her a perfect Mistress of the Instrument. The air which She played was soft and plaintive: Ambrosio, while He listened, felt his uneasiness subside, and a pleasing melancholy spread itself into his bosom. Suddenly Matilda changed the strain: With an hand bold and rapid She struck a few loud martial chords, and then chaunted the following Ballad to an air at once simple and melodious.

DURANDARTE AND BELERMA

Sad and fearful is the story
Of the Roncevalles fight;
On those fatal plains of glory
Perished many a gallant Knight.

There fell Durandarte; Never
Verse a nobler Chieftain named:
He, before his lips for ever
Closed in silence thus exclaimed.

'Oh! Belerma! Oh! my dear-one!
For my pain and pleasure born!
Seven long years I served thee, fair-one,
Seven long years my fee was scorn:

'And when now thy heart replying
To my wishes, burns like mine,
Cruel Fate my bliss denying
Bids me every hope resign.

'Ah! Though young I fall, believe me,
Death would never claim a sigh;
'Tis to lose thee, 'tis to leave thee,
Makes me think it hard to die!

'Oh! my Cousin Montesinos,
By that friendship firm and dear
Which from Youth has lived between us,
Now my last petition hear!

'When my Soul these limbs forsaking
Eager seeks a purer air,
From my breast the cold heart taking,
Give it to Belerma's care.

'Say, I of my lands Possessor
Named her with my dying breath:
Say, my lips I op'd to bless her,
Ere they closed for aye in death:

'Twice a week too how sincerely
I adored her, Cousin, say;
Twice a week for one who dearly
Loved her, Cousin, bid her pray.

'Montesinos, now the hour
Marked by fate is near at hand:
Lo! my arm has lost its power!
Lo! I drop my trusty brand!

'Eyes, which forth beheld me going,
Homewards ne'er shall see me hie!
Cousin, stop those tears o'er-flowing,
Let me on thy bosom die!

'Thy kind hand my eye-lids closing,
Yet one favour I implore:

Pray Thou for my Soul's reposing,
When my heart shall throb no more;

'So shall Jesus, still attending
Gracious to a Christian's vow,
Pleased accept my Ghost ascending,
And a seat in heaven allow.'

Thus spoke gallant Durandarte;
Soon his brave heart broke in twain.
Greatly joyed the Moorish party,
That the gallant Knight was slain.

Bitter weeping Montesinos
Took from him his helm and glaive;
Bitter weeping Montesinos
Dug his gallant Cousin's grave.

To perform his promise made, He
Cut the heart from out the breast,
That Belerma, wretched Lady!
Might receive the last bequest.

Sad was Montesinos' heart, He
Felt distress his bosom rend.
'Oh! my Cousin Durandarte,
Woe is me to view thy end!

'Sweet in manners, fair in favour,
Mild in temper, fierce in fight,
Warrior, nobler, gentler, braver,
Never shall behold the light!

'Cousin, Lo! my tears bedew thee!
How shall I thy loss survive!
Durandarte, He who slew thee,
Wherefore left He me alive!'

While She sung, Ambrosio listened with delight: Never had He heard a
voice more harmonious; and He wondered, how such heavenly sounds could
be produced by any but Angels. But though He indulged the sense of
hearing; a single look convinced him, that He must not trust to that of sight.
The Songstress sat at a little distance from his Bed. The attitude in which
She bent over her harp, was easy and graceful: Her Cowl had fallen
backwarder than usual: Two coral lips were visible, ripe, fresh, and melting,
and a Chin in whose dimples seemed to lurk a thousand Cupids. Her

Habit's long sleeve would have swept along the Chords of the Instrument: To prevent this inconvenience She had drawn it above her elbow, and by this means an arm was discovered formed in the most perfect symmetry, the delicacy of whose skin might have contended with snow in whiteness. Ambrosio dared to look on her but once: That glance sufficed to convince him, how dangerous was the presence of this seducing Object. He closed his eyes, but strove in vain to banish her from his thoughts. There She still moved before him, adorned with all those charms which his heated imagination could supply: Every beauty which He had seen, appeared embellished, and those still concealed Fancy represented to him in glowing colours. Still, however, his vows and the necessity of keeping to them were present to his memory. He struggled with desire, and shuddered when He beheld, how deep was the precipice before him.

Matilda ceased to sing. Dreading the influence of her charms, Ambrosio remained with his eyes closed, and offered up his prayers to St Francis to assist him in this dangerous trial! Matilda believed that He was sleeping. She rose from her seat, approached the Bed softly, and for some minutes gazed upon him attentively.

'He sleeps!' said She at length in a low voice, but whose accents the Abbot distinguished perfectly; 'Now then I may gaze upon him without offence! I may mix my breath with his; I may doat upon his features, and He cannot suspect me of impurity and deceit!—He fears my seducing him to the violation of his vows! Oh! the Unjust! Were it my wish to excite desire, should I conceal my features from him so carefully? Those features, of which I daily hear him. . . .'

She stopped, and was lost in her reflections.

'It was but yesterday!' She continued; 'But a few short hours have past, since I was dear to him! He esteemed me, and my heart was satisfied! Now! . . . Oh! now how cruelly is my situation changed! He looks on me with suspicion! He bids me leave him, leave him for ever! Oh! You, my Saint! my Idol! You, holding the next place to God in my breast! Yet two days, and my heart will be unveiled to you.—Could you know my feelings, when I beheld your agony! Could you know, how much your sufferings have endeared you to me! But the time will come, when you will be convinced that my passion is pure and disinterested. Then you will pity me, and feel the whole weight of these sorrows!'

As She said this, her voice was choaked by weeping. While She bent over Ambrosio, a tear fell upon his cheek.

'Ah! I have disturbed him!' cried Matilda, and retreated hastily.

Her alarm was ungrounded. None sleep so profoundly, as those who are determined not to wake. The Friar was in this predicament: He still seemed buried in a repose, which every succeeding minute rendered him less capable of enjoying. The burning tear had communicated its warmth to his heart.

'What affection! What purity!' said He internally; 'Ah! since my bosom is thus sensible of pity, what would it be if agitated by love?'

Matilda again quitted her seat, and retired to some distance from the Bed. Ambrosio ventured to open his eyes, and to cast them upon her fearfully. Her face was turned from him. She rested her head in a melancholy posture upon her Harp, and gazed on the picture which hung opposite to the Bed.

'Happy, happy Image!' Thus did She address the beautiful Madona; ' 'Tis to you that He offers his prayers! 'Tis on you that He gazes with admiration! I thought, you would have lightened my sorrows; You have only served to increase their weight: You have made me feel that had I known him ere his vows were pronounced, Ambrosio and happiness might have been mine. With what pleasure He views this picture! With what fervour He addresses his prayers to the insensible Image! Ah! may not his sentiments be inspired by some kind and secret Genius, Friend to my affection? May it not be Man's natural instinct which informs him ... Be silent, idle hopes! Let me not encourage an idea, which takes from the brilliance of Ambrosio's virtue. 'Tis Religion, not Beauty which attracts his admiration; 'Tis not to the Woman, but the Divinity that He kneels. Would He but address to me the least tender expression, which He pours forth to this Madona! Would He but say, that were He not already affianced to the Church, He would not have despised Matilda! Oh! let me nourish that fond idea! Perhaps, He may yet acknowledge that He feels for me more than pity, and that affection like mine might well have deserved a return; Perhaps, He may own thus much when I lye on my death-bed! He then need not fear to infringe his vows, and the confession of his regard will soften the pangs of dying. Would I were sure of this! Oh! how earnestly should I sigh for the moment of dissolution!'

Of this discourse the Abbot lost not a syllable; and the tone in which She pronounced these last words pierced to his heart. Involuntarily He raised himself from his pillow.

'Matilda!' He said in a troubled voice; 'Oh! my Matilda!'

She started at the sound, and turned towards him hastily. The suddenness of her movement made her Cowl fall back from her head; Her features became visible to the Monk's enquiring eye. What was his amazement at beholding the exact resemblance of his admired Madona? The same exquisite proportion of features, the same profusion of golden hair, the same rosy lips, heavenly eyes, and majesty of countenance adorned Matilda! Uttering an exclamation of surprize, Ambrosio sank back upon his pillow, and doubted whether the Object before him was mortal or divine.

Matilda seemed penetrated with confusion. She remained motionless in her place, and supported herself upon her Instrument. Her eyes were bent upon the earth, and her fair cheeks over-spread with blushes. On recovering herself, her first action was to conceal her features. She then in an unsteady and troubled voice ventured to address these words to the Friar.

'Accident has made you Master of a secret, which I never would have revealed but on the Bed of death. Yes, Ambrosio; In Matilda de Villanegas you see the original of your beloved Madona. Soon after I conceived my unfortunate passion, I formed the project of conveying to you my Picture: Crowds of Admirers had persuaded me that I possessed some beauty, and I was anxious to know, what effect it would produce upon you. I caused my Portrait to be drawn by Martin Galuppi, a celebrated Venetian at that time resident in Madrid. The resemblance was striking: I sent it to the Capuchin-Abbey as if for sale, and the Jew from whom you bought it, was one of my Emissaries. You purchased it. Judge of my rapture, when informed, that you had gazed upon it with delight, or rather with adoration; that you had suspended it in your Cell, and that you addressed your supplications to no other Saint. Will this discovery make me still more regarded as an object of suspicion? Rather should it convince you how pure is my affection, and engage you to suffer me in your society and esteem. I heard you daily extol the praises of my Portrait: I was an eye-witness of the transports, which its beauty excited in you: Yet I forbore to use against your virtue those arms, with which yourself had furnished me. I concealed those features from your sight, which you loved unconsciously. I strove not to excite desire by displaying my charms, or to make myself Mistress of your heart through the medium of your senses. To attract your notice by studiously attending to religious duties, to endear myself to you by convincing you that my mind was virtuous and my attachment sincere, such was my only aim. I succeeded; I became your companion and your Friend. I concealed my sex from your knowledge; and had you not pressed me to reveal my secret, had I not been tormented by the fear of a discovery, never had you known me for any other than Rosario. And still are you resolved to drive me from you? The few hours of life which yet remain for me, may I not pass them in your presence? Oh! speak, Ambrosio, and tell me that I may stay!'

This speech gave the Abbot an opportunity of recollecting himself. He was conscious that in the present disposition of his mind, avoiding her society was his only refuge from the power of this enchanting Woman.

'Your declaration has so much astonished me,' said He, 'that I am at present incapable of answering you. Do not insist upon a reply, Matilda; Leave me to myself; I have need to be alone.'

'I obey you—But before I go, promise not to insist upon my quitting the Abbey immediately.'

'Matilda, reflect upon your situation; Reflect upon the consequences of your stay. Our separation is indispensable, and we must part.'

'But not to-day, Father! Oh! in pity not to-day!'

'You press me too hard, but I cannot resist that tone of supplication. Since you insist upon it, I yield to your prayer: I consent to your remaining here a sufficient time to prepare in some measure the Brethren for your departure. Stay yet two days; But on the third,' . . . [He sighed involuntarily.]—'Remember, that on the third we must part for ever!'

She caught his hand eagerly, and pressed it to her lips.

'On the third?' She exclaimed with an air of wild solemnity; 'You are right, Father! You are right! On the third we must part for ever!'

There was a dreadful expression in her eye as She uttered these words, which penetrated the Friar's soul with horror: Again She kissed his hand, and then fled with rapidity from the chamber.

Anxious to authorise the presence of his dangerous Guest, yet conscious that her stay was infringing the laws of his order, Ambrosio's bosom became the Theatre of a thousand contending passions. At length his attachment to the feigned Rosario, aided by the natural warmth of his temperament, seemed likely to obtain the victory: The success was assured, when that presumption which formed the ground-work of his character, came to Matilda's assistance. The Monk reflected, that to vanquish temptation was an infinitely greater merit than to avoid it: He thought, that He ought rather to rejoice in the opportunity given him of proving the firmness of his virtue. St Anthony had withstood all seductions to lust; Then why should not He? Besides, St Anthony was tempted by the Devil, who put every art into practice to excite his passions: Whereas, Ambrosio's danger proceeded from a mere mortal Woman, fearful and modest, whose apprehensions of his yielding were not less violent than his own.

'Yes,' said He; 'The Unfortunate shall stay; I have nothing to fear from her presence. Even should my own prove too weak to resist the temptation, I am secured from danger by the innocence of Matilda.'

Ambrosio was yet to learn, that to an heart unacquainted with her, Vice is ever most dangerous when lurking behind the Mask of Virtue.

He found himself so perfectly recovered, that when Father Pablos visited him again at night, He entreated permission to quit his chamber on the day following. His request was granted. Matilda appeared no more that evening, except in company with the Monks when they came in a body to enquire after the Abbot's health. She seemed fearful of conversing with him in private, and stayed but a few minutes in his room. The Friar slept well; But the dreams of the former night were repeated, and his sensations of voluptuousness were yet more keen and exquisite. The same lust-exciting visions floated before his eyes: Matilda, in all the pomp of beauty, warm, tender, and luxurious, clasped him to her bosom, and lavished upon him the most ardent caresses. He returned them as eagerly, and already was on the point of satisfying his desires, when the faithless form disappeared, and left him to all the horrors of shame and disappointment.

The Morning dawned. Fatigued, harassed, and exhausted by his provoking dreams, He was not disposed to quit his Bed. He excused himself from appearing at Matins: It was the first morning in his life that He had ever missed them. He rose late. During the whole of the day He had no opportunity of speaking to Matilda without witnesses. His Cell was thronged by the Monks, anxious to express their concern at his illness; And He was still occupied in receiving their compliments on his recovery, when the Bell summoned them to the Refectory.

After dinner the Monks separated, and dispersed themselves in various parts of the Garden, where the shade of trees or retirement of some Grotto presented the most agreeable means of enjoying the Siesta. The Abbot bent his steps towards the Hermitage: A glance of his eye invited Matilda to accompany him. She obeyed, and followed him thither in silence. They entered the Grotto, and seated themselves. Both seemed unwilling to begin the conversation, and to labour under the influence of mutual embarrassment. At length the Abbot spoke: He conversed only on indifferent topics, and Matilda answered him in the same tone. She seemed anxious to make him forget, that the Person who sat by him was any other than Rosario. Neither of them dared, or indeed wished to make an allusion, to the subject which was most at the hearts of both.

Matilda's efforts to appear gay were evidently forced: Her spirits were oppressed by the weight of anxiety, and when She spoke her voice was low and feeble. She seemed desirous of finishing a conversation which embarrassed her; and complaining that She was unwell, She requested Ambrosio's permission to return to the Abbey. He accompanied her to the door of her cell; and when arrived there, He stopped her to declare his consent to her continuing the Partner of his solitude so long as should be agreeable to herself.

She discovered no marks of pleasure at receiving this intelligence, though on the preceding day She had been so anxious to obtain the permission.

'Alas! Father,' She said, waving her head mournfully; 'Your kindness comes too late! My doom is fixed. We must separate for ever. Yet believe, that I am grateful for your generosity, for your compassion of an Unfortunate who is but too little deserving of it!'

She put her hand-kerchief to her eyes. Her Cowl was only half drawn over her face. Ambrosio observed that She was pale, and her eyes sunk and heavy.

'Good God!' He cried; 'You are very ill, Matilda! I shall send Father Pablos to you instantly.'

'No; Do not. I am ill, 'tis true; But He cannot cure my malady. Farewell, Father! Remember me in your prayers to-morrow, while I shall remember you in heaven!'

She entered her cell, and closed the door.

The Abbot dispatched to her the Physician without losing a moment, and waited his report impatiently. But Father Pablos soon returned, and declared that his errand had been fruitless. Rosario refused to admit him, and had positively rejected his offers of assistance. The uneasiness, which this account gave Ambrosio was not trifling: Yet He determined that Matilda should have her own way for that night: But that if her situation did not mend by the morning, he would insist upon her taking the advice of Father Pablos.

He did not find himself inclined to sleep. He opened his casement, and gazed upon the moon-beams as they played upon the small stream whose waters bathed the walls of the Monastery. The coolness of the night-breeze and tranquillity of the hour inspired the Friar's mind with sadness. He thought upon Matilda's beauty and affection; Upon the pleasures which He might have shared with her; had He not been restrained by monastic fetters. He reflected, that unsustained by hope her love for him could not long exist; That doubtless She would succeed in extinguishing her passion, and seek for happiness in the arms of One more fortunate. He shuddered at the void which her absence would leave in his bosom. He looked with disgust on the monotony of a Convent, and breathed a sigh towards that world, from which He was for ever separated. Such were the reflections, which a loud knocking at his door interrupted. The Bell of the Church had already struck Two. The Abbot hastened to enquire the cause of this disturbance. He opened the door of his Cell, and a Lay-Brother entered, whose looks declared his hurry and confusion.

'Hasten, reverend Father!' said He; 'Hasten to the young Rosario. He earnestly requests to see you; He lies at the point of death.'

'Gracious God! Where is Father Pablos? Why is He not with him? Oh! I fear! I fear!'

'Father Pablos has seen him, but his art can do nothing. He says, that He suspects the Youth to be poisoned.'

'Poisoned? Oh! The Unfortunate! It is then as I suspected! But let me not lose a moment; Perhaps it may yet be time to save her!'

He said, and flew towards the Cell of the Novice. Several Monks were already in the chamber. Father Pablos was one of them, and held a medicine in his hand, which He was endeavouring to persuade Rosario to swallow. The Others were employed in admiring the Patient's divine countenance, which They now saw for the first time. She looked lovelier than ever. She was no longer pale or languid; A bright glow had spread itself over her cheeks; her eyes sparkled with a serene delight, and her countenance was expressive of confidence and resignation.

'Oh! torment me no more!' was She saying to Pablos, when the terrified Abbot rushed hastily into the Cell; 'My disease is far beyond the reach of your skill, and I wish not to be cured of it'—Then perceiving Ambrosio,— 'Ah! 'tis He!' She cried; 'I see him once again, before we part for ever! Leave me, my Brethren; Much have I to tell this holy Man in private.'

The Monks retired immediately, and Matilda and the Abbot remained together.

'What have you done, imprudent Woman!' exclaimed the Latter, as soon as they were left alone; 'Tell me; Are my suspicions just? Am I indeed to lose you? Has your own hand been the instrument of your destruction?'

She smiled, and grasped his hand.

'In what have I been imprudent, Father? I have sacrificed a pebble, and saved a diamond: My death preserves a life valuable to the world, and more dear to me than my own. Yes, Father; I am poisoned; But know, that the poison once circulated in your veins.'

'Matilda!'

'What I tell you I resolved never to discover to you, but on the bed of death: That moment is now arrived. You cannot have forgotten the day already, when your life was endangered by the bite of a Cientipedoro. The Physician gave you over, declaring himself ignorant how to extract the venom: I knew but of one means, and hesitated not a moment to employ it. I was left alone with you: You slept; I loosened the bandage from your hand; I kissed the wound, and drew out the poison with my lips. The effect has been more sudden than I expected. I feel death at my heart; Yet an hour, and I shall be in a better world.'

'Almighty God!' exclaimed the Abbot, and sank almost lifeless upon the Bed.

After a few minutes He again raised himself up suddenly, and gazed upon Matilda with all the wildness of despair.

'And you have sacrificed yourself for me! You die, and die to preserve Ambrosio! And is there indeed no remedy, Matilda? And is there indeed no hope? Speak to me, Oh! speak to me! Tell me, that you have still the means of life!'

'Be comforted, my only Friend! Yes, I have still the means of life in my power: But 'tis a means which I dare not employ. It is dangerous! It is dreadful! Life would be purchased at too dear a rate, . . . unless it were permitted me to live for you.'

'Then live for me, Matilda, for me and gratitude!'—[He caught her hand, and pressed it rapturously to his lips.]—'Remember our late conversations; I now consent to every thing: Remember in what lively colours you described the union of souls; Be it ours to realize those ideas. Let us forget the distinctions of sex, despise the world's prejudices, and only consider each other as Brother and Friend. Live then, Matilda! Oh! live for me!'

'Ambrosio, it must not be. When I thought thus, I deceived both you and myself. Either I must die at present, or expire by the lingering torments of unsatisfied desire. Oh! since we last conversed together, a dreadful veil has been rent from before my eyes. I love you no longer with the devotion which is paid to a Saint: I prize you no more for the virtues of your soul; I lust for the enjoyment of your person. The Woman reigns in my bosom, and I am become a prey to the wildest of passions. Away with friendship! 'tis a cold unfeeling word. My bosom burns with love, with utterable love, and love must be its return. Tremble then, Ambrosio, tremble to succeed in your prayers. If I live, your truth, your reputation, your reward of a life past in sufferings, all that you value is irretrievably lost. I shall no longer be able to combat my passions, shall seize every opportunity to excite your desires, and labour to effect your dishonour and my own. No, no, Ambrosio; I must not live! I am convinced with every moment, that I have but one alternative; I feel with every heart-throb, that I must enjoy you, or die.'

'Amazement!—Matilda!—Can it be you who speak to me?'

He made a movement as if to quit his seat. She uttered a loud shriek, and raising herself half out of the Bed, threw her arms round the Friar to detain him.

'Oh! do not leave me! Listen to my errors with compassion! In a few hours I shall be no more; Yet a little, and I am free from this disgraceful passion.'

'Wretched Woman, what can I say to you! I cannot . . . I must not . . . But live, Matilda! Oh! live!'

'You do not reflect on what you ask. What? Live to plunge myself in infamy? To become the Agent of Hell? To work the destruction both of you and of Myself? Feel this heart, Father!'

She took his hand: Confused, embarrassed, and fascinated, He withdrew it not, and felt her heart throb under it.

'Feel this heart, Father! It is yet the seat of honour, truth, and chastity; If it beats to-morrow, it must fall a prey to the blackest crimes. Oh! let me then die to-day! Let me die, while I yet deserve the tears of the virtuous! Thus will I expire!'—[She reclined her head upon his shoulder; Her golden Hair poured itself over his Chest.]—'Folded in your arms, I shall sink to sleep; Your hand shall close my eyes for ever, and your lips receive my dying breath. And will you not sometimes think of me? Will you not sometimes shed a tear upon my Tomb? Oh! Yes! Yes! Yes! That kiss is my assurance!'

The hour was night. All was silence around. The faint beams of solitary Lamp darted upon Matilda's figure, and shed through the chamber a dim mysterious light. No prying eye, or curious ear was near the Lovers: Nothing was heard but Matilda's melodious accents. Ambrosio was in the full vigour of Manhood. He saw before him a young and beautiful Woman, the preserver of his life, the Adorer of his person, and whom affection for him had reduced to the brink of the Grave. He sat upon her Bed; His hand rested upon her bosom; Her head reclined voluptuously upon his breast. Who then can wonder, if He yielded to the temptation? Drunk with desire, He pressed his lips to those which sought them: His kisses vied with Matilda's in warmth and passion. He clasped her rapturously in his arms: He forgot his vows, his sanctity, and his fame: He remembered nothing but the pleasure and opportunity.

'Ambrosio! Oh! my Ambrosio!' sighed Matilda.

'Thine, ever thine!' murmured the Friar, and sank upon her bosom.

CHAPTER III

——These are the Villains
Whom all the Travellers do fear so much.
——Some of them are Gentlemen,
Such as the fury of ungoverned Youth
Thrust from the company of awful Men.
                        Two Gentlemen of Verona.

THE Marquis and Lorenzo proceeded to the Hotel in silence. The Former employed himself in calling every circumstance to his mind, which related might give Lorenzo's the most favourable idea of his connexion with Agnes. The Latter, justly alarmed for the honour of his family, felt embarrassed by the presence of the Marquis: The adventure which He had just witnessed, forbad his treating him as a Friend; and Antonia's interests being entrusted to his mediation, He saw the impolicy of treating him as a Foe. He concluded from these reflections, that profound silence would be the wisest plan, and waited with impatience for Don Raymond's explanation.

They arrived at the Hotel de las Cisternas. The Marquis immediately conducted him to his apartment, and began to express his satisfaction at finding him at Madrid. Lorenzo interrupted him.

'Excuse me, my Lord,' said He with a distant air, 'if I reply somewhat coldly to your expressions of regard. A Sister's honour is involved in this affair: Till that is established, and the purport of your correspondence with Agnes cleared up, I cannot consider you as my Friend. I am anxious to hear the meaning of your conduct, and hope, that you will not delay the promised explanation.'

'First give me your word, that you will listen with patience and indulgence.'

'I love my Sister too well to judge her harshly; and till this moment I possessed no Friend so dear to me as yourself. I will also confess, that your having it in your power to oblige me in a business which I have much at heart, makes me very anxious to find you still deserving my esteem.'

'Lorenzo, you transport me! No greater pleasure can be given me, than an opportunity of serving the Brother of Agnes.'

'Convince me that I can accept your favours without dishonour, and there is no Man in the world, to whom I am more willing to be obliged.'

'Probably, you have already heard your Sister mention the name of Alphonso d'Alvarada?'

'Never. Though I feel for Agnes an affection truly fraternal, circumstances have prevented us from being much together. While yet a Child She was consigned to the care of her Aunt, who had married a German Nobleman. At his Castle She remained till two years since, when She returned to Spain, determined upon secluding herself from the world.'

'Good God! Lorenzo, you knew of her intention, and yet strove not to make her change it?'

'Marquis, you wrong me. The intelligence, which I received at Naples, shocked me extremely, and I hastened my return to Madrid for the express purpose of preventing the sacrifice. The moment that I arrived, I flew to the Convent of St Clare, in which Agnes had chosen to perform her Noviciate. I requested to see my Sister. Conceive my surprise, when She sent me a refusal; She declared positively, that apprehending my influence over her mind, She would not trust herself in my society, till the day before that on which She was to receive the Veil. I supplicated the Nuns; I insisted upon seeing Agnes, and hesitated not to avow my suspicions, that her being kept from me was against her own inclinations. To free herself from the imputation of violence, the Prioress brought me a few lines written in my Sister's well-known hand, repeating the message already delivered. All future attempts to obtain a moment's conversation with her were as fruitless as the first. She was inflexible, and I was not permitted to see her till the day preceding that on which She entered the Cloister never to quit it more. This interview took place in the presence of our principal Relations. It was for the first time since her childhood that I saw her, and the scene was most affecting. She threw herself upon my bosom, kissed me, and wept bitterly. By every possible argument, by tears, by prayers, by kneeling, I strove to make her abandon her intention. I represented to her all the hardships of a religious life; I painted to her imagination all the pleasures which She was going to quit, and besought her to disclose to me, what occasioned her disgust to the world. At this last question She turned pale, and her tears flowed yet faster. She entreated me not to press her on that subject; That it sufficed me to know that her resolution was taken, and that a Convent was the only place where She could now hope for tranquillity. She persevered in her design, and made her profession. I visited her frequently at the Grate, and every moment that I passed with her, made me feel more affliction at her loss. I was shortly after obliged to quit Madrid; I returned but yesterday evening, and since then have not had time to call to St Clare's Convent.'

'Then till I mentioned it, you never heard the name of Alphonso d'Alvarada?'

'Pardon me: my Aunt wrote me word, that an Adventurer so called had found means to get introduced into the Castle of Lindenberg; That He had insinuated himself into my Sister's good graces, and that She had even consented to elope with him. However, before the plan could be executed, the Cavalier discovered, that the estates which He believed Agnes to possess in Hispaniola, in reality belonged to me. This intelligence made him change his intention; He disappeared on the day that the elopement was to have taken place, and Agnes in despair at his perfidy and meanness had resolved upon seclusion in a Convent. She added, that as this adventurer had given himself out to be a Friend of mine, She wished to know whether I had any knowledge of him. I replied in the negative. I had then very little idea, that Alphonso d'Alvarada and the Marquis de las Cisternas were one and the same person: The description given me of the first by no means tallied with what I knew of the latter.'

'In this I easily recognize Donna Rodolpha's perfidious character. Every word of this account is stamped with marks of her malice, of her falsehood, of her talents for misrepresenting those whom She wishes to injure. Forgive me, Medina, for speaking so freely of your Relation. The mischief which She has done me, authorises my resentment, and when you have heard my story, you will be convinced that my expressions have not been too severe.'

He then began his narrative in the following manner.

HISTORY OF DON RAYMOND,
MARQUIS DE LAS CISTERNAS

Long experience, my dear Lorenzo, has convinced me, how generous is your nature: I waited not for your declaration of ignorance respecting your Sister's adventures, to suppose that they had been purposely concealed from you. Had they reached your knowledge, from what misfortunes should both Agnes and myself have escaped! Fate had ordained it otherwise! You were on your Travels, when I first became acquainted with your Sister; and as our Enemies took care to conceal from her your direction, it was impossible for her to implore by letter your protection and advice.

On leaving Salamanca, at which University as I have since heard, you remained a year after I quitted it, I immediately set out upon my Travels. My Father supplied me liberally with money; But He insisted upon my concealing my rank, and presenting myself as no more than a private Gentleman. This command was issued by the counsels of his Friend, the Duke of Villa Hermosa, a Nobleman for whose abilities and knowledge of the world I have ever entertained the most profound veneration.

'Believe me,' said He, 'my dear Raymond, you will hereafter feel the benefits of this temporary degradation. 'Tis true, that as the Condé de las Cisternas you would have been received with open arms; and your youthful vanity might have felt gratified by the attentions showered upon you from all sides. At present, much will depend upon yourself: You have excellent recommendations, but it must be your own business to make them of use to you. You must lay yourself out to please; You must labour to gain the approbation of those, to whom you are presented: They who would have courted the friendship of the Condé de las Cisternas, will have no interest in finding out the merits, or bearing patiently with the faults of Alphonso d'Alvarada. Consequently, when you find yourself really liked, you may safely ascribe it to your good qualities, not your rank, and the distinction shown you will be infinitely more flattering. Besides, your exalted birth would not permit your mixing with the lower classes of society, which will now be in your power, and from which, in my opinion, you will derive considerable benefit. Do not confine yourself to the Illustrious of those Countries through which you pass. Examine the manners and customs of the multitude: Enter into the Cottages; and by observing how the Vassals of Foreigners are treated, learn to diminish the burthens, and augment the comforts of your own. According to my ideas, of those advantages, which a Youth destined to the possession of power and wealth may reap from travel, He should not consider as the least essential, the opportunity of mixing with the classes below him, and becoming an eye-witness of the sufferings of the People.'

Forgive me, Lorenzo, if I seem tedious in my narration. The close connexion which now exists between us, makes me anxious that you should know every particular respecting me; and in my fear of omitting the least circumstance which may induce you to think favourably of your Sister and myself, I may possibly relate many which you may think uninteresting.

I followed the Duke's advice; I was soon convinced of its wisdom. I quitted Spain, calling myself by the assumed title of Don Alphonso d'Alvarada, and attended by a single Domestic of approved fidelity. Paris was my first station. For some time I was enchanted with it, as indeed must be every Man, who is young, rich, and fond of pleasure. Yet among all its gaieties, I felt that something was wanting to my heart. I grew sick of dissipation: I discovered, that the People among whom I lived, and whose exterior was so polished and seducing, were at bottom frivolous, unfeeling and insincere. I turned from the Inhabitants of Paris with disgust, and quitted that Theatre of Luxury without heaving one sigh of regret.

I now bent my course towards Germany, intending to visit most of the principal courts: Prior to this expedition, I meant to make some little stay at Strasbourg. On quitting my Chaise at Luneville to take some refreshment, I observed a splendid Equipage, attended by four Domestics in rich liveries, waiting at the door of the Silver Lion. Soon after as I looked out of the window, I saw a Lady of noble presence, followed by two female Attendants, step into the Carriage, which drove off immediately.

I enquired of the Host, who the Lady was, that had just departed.

'A German Baroness, Monsieur, of great rank and fortune. She has been upon a visit to the Duchess of Longueville, as her Servants informed me;

She is going to Strasbourg, where She will find her Husband, and then both return to their Castle in Germany.'

I resumed my journey, intending to reach Strasbourg that night. My hopes, however were frustrated by the breaking down of my Chaise. The accident happened in the middle of a thick Forest, and I was not a little embarrassed as to the means of proceeding. It was the depth of winter: The night was already closing round us; and Strasbourg, which was the nearest Town, was still distant from us several leagues. It seemed to me, that my only alternative to passing the night in the Forest, was to take my Servant's Horse, and ride on to Strasbourg, an undertaking at that season very far from agreeable. However, seeing no other resource, I was obliged to make up my mind to it. Accordingly I communicated my design to the Postillion, telling him that I would send People to assist him as soon as I reached Strasbourg. I had not much confidence in his honesty; But Stephano being well-armed, and the Driver to all appearance considerably advanced in years, I believed I ran no danger of losing my Baggage.

Luckily, as I then thought, an opportunity presented itself of passing the night more agreeably than I expected. On mentioning my design of proceeding by myself to Strasbourg, the Postillion shook his head in disapprobation.

'It is a long way,' said He; 'You will find it a difficult matter to arrive there without a Guide. Besides, Monsieur seems unaccustomed to the season's severity, and 'tis possible that unable to sustain the excessive cold. . . .'

'What use is there to present me with all these objections?' said I, impatiently interrupting him; 'I have no other resource: I run still greater risque of perishing with cold by passing the night in the Forest.'

'Passing the night in the Forest?' He replied; 'Oh! by St Denis! We are not in quite so bad a plight as that comes to yet. If I am not mistaken, we are scarcely five minutes walk from the Cottage of my old Friend, Baptiste. He is a Wood-cutter, and a very honest Fellow. I doubt not, but He will shelter you for the night with pleasure. In the mean time I can take the saddle-Horse, ride to Strasbourg, and be back with proper people to mend your Carriage by break of day.'

'And in the name of God,' said I, 'How could you leave me so long in suspense? Why did you not tell me of this Cottage sooner? What excessive stupidity!'

'I thought, that perhaps Monsieur would not deign to accept. . . .'

'Absurd! Come, come! Say no more, but conduct us without delay to the Wood-man's Cottage.'

He obeyed, and we moved onwards: The Horses contrived with some difficulty to drag the shattered vehicle after us. My Servant was become almost speechless, and I began to feel the effects of the cold myself, before we reached the wished-for Cottage. It was a small but neat Building: As we drew near it, I rejoiced at observing through the window the blaze of a comfortable fire. Our Conductor knocked at the door: It was some time before any one answered; The People within seemed in doubt whether we should be admitted.

'Come! Come, Friend Baptiste!' cried the Driver with impatience; 'What are you about? Are you asleep? Or will you refuse a night's lodging to a Gentleman, whose Chaise has just broken down in the Forest?'

'Ah! is it you, honest Claude?' replied a Man's voice from within; 'Wait a moment, and the door shall be opened.'

Soon after the bolts were drawn back. The door was unclosed, and a Man presented himself to us with a Lamp in his hand. He gave the Guide an hearty reception, and then addressed himself to me.

'Walk in, Monsieur; Walk in, and welcome! Excuse me for not admitting you at first: But there are so many Rogues about this place, that saving your presence, I suspected you to be one.'

Thus saying, He ushered me into the room, where I had observed the fire: I was immediately placed in an Easy Chair, which stood close to the Hearth. A Female, whom I supposed to be the Wife of my Host, rose from her seat upon my entrance, and received me with a slight and distant reverence. She made no answer to my compliment, but immediately re-seating herself, continued the work on which She had been employed. Her Husband's manners were as friendly, as hers were harsh and repulsive.

'I wish, I could lodge you more conveniently, Monsieur,' said He; 'But we cannot boast of much spare room in this hovel. However, a chamber for yourself, and another for your Servant, I think, we can make shift to supply. You must content yourself with sorry fare; But to what we have, believe me, you are heartily welcome.'——Then turning to his wife—'Why, how you sit there, Marguerite, with as much tranquillity as if you had nothing better to do! Stir about, Dame! Stir about! Get some supper; Look out some sheets; Here, here; throw some logs upon the fire, for the Gentleman seems perished with cold.'

The Wife threw her work hastily upon the Table, and proceeded to execute his commands with every mark of unwillingness. Her countenance had displeased me on the first moment of my examining it. Yet upon the whole her features were handsome unquestionably; But her skin was sallow, and her person thin and meagre; A louring gloom over-spread her countenance; and it bore such visible marks of rancour and ill-will, as could not escape being noticed by the most inattentive Observer. Her every look and action expressed discontent and impatience, and the answers which She gave Baptiste, when He reproached her good-humouredly for her dissatisfied air, were tart, short, and cutting. In fine, I conceived at first sight equal disgust for her, and prepossession in favour of her Husband, whose appearance was calculated to inspire esteem and confidence. His countenance was open, sincere, and friendly; his manners had all the Peasant's honesty unaccompanied by his rudeness; His cheeks were broad, full, and ruddy; and in the solidity of his person He seemed to offer an ample apology for the leanness of his Wife's. From the wrinkles on his brow I judged him to be turned of sixty; But He bore his years well, and seemed still hearty and strong: The Wife could not be more than thirty, but in spirits and vivacity She was infinitely older than the Husband.

However, in spite of her unwillingness, Marguerite began to prepare the supper, while the Wood-man conversed gaily on different subjects. The Postillion who had been furnished with a bottle of spirits, was now ready to set out for Strasbourg, and enquired, whether I had any further commands.

'For Strasbourg?' interrupted Baptiste; 'You are not going thither to-night?'

'I beg your pardon: If I do not fetch Workmen to mend the Chaise, How is Monsieur to proceed tomorrow?'

'That is true, as you say; I had forgotten the Chaise. Well but Claude; You may at least eat your supper here? That can make you lose very little time, and Monsieur looks too kind-hearted to send you out with an empty stomach on such a bitter cold night as this is.'

To this I readily assented, telling the Postillion, that my reaching Strasbourg the next day an hour or two later would be perfectly immaterial. He thanked me, and then leaving the Cottage with Stephano, put up his Horses in the Wood-man's Stable. Baptiste followed them to the door, and looked out with anxiety.

' 'Tis a sharp biting wind!' said He; 'I wonder, what detains my Boys so long! Monsieur, I shall show you two of the finest Lads, that ever stept in shoe of leather. The eldest is three and twenty, the second a year younger: Their Equals for sense, courage, and activity, are not to be found within fifty miles of Strasbourg. Would They were back again! I begin to feel uneasy about them.'

Marguerite was at this time employed in laying the cloth.

'And are you equally anxious for the return of your Sons?' said I to her.

'Not I!' She replied peevishly; 'They are no children of mine.'

'Come! Come, Marguerite!' said the Husband; 'Do not be out of humour with the Gentleman for asking a simple question. Had you not looked so cross, He would never have thought you old enough to have a Son of three and twenty: But you see how many years ill-temper adds to you!—Excuse my Wife's rudeness, Monsieur. A little thing puts her out, and She is somewhat displeased, at your not thinking her to be under thirty. That is the truth, is it not, Marguerite? You know, Monsieur, that Age is always a ticklish subject with a Woman. Come! come! Marguerite, clear up a little. If you have not Sons as old, you will some twenty years hence, and I hope, that we shall live to see them just such Lads as Jacques and Robert.'

Marguerite clasped her hands together passionately.

'God forbid!' said She; 'God forbid! If I thought it, I would strangle them with my own hands!'

She quitted the room hastily, and went up stairs.

I could not help expressing to the Wood-man, how much I pitied him for being chained for life to a Partner of such ill-humour.

'Ah! Lord! Monsieur, Every one has his share of grievances, and Marguerite has fallen to mine. Besides, after all She is only cross, and not malicious. The worst is, that her affection for two children by a former Husband makes her play the Step-mother with my two Sons. She cannot bear the sight of them, and by her good-will they would never set a foot within my door. But on this point I always stand firm, and never will consent to abandon the poor Lads to the world's mercy, as She has often solicited me to do. In every thing else I let her have her own way; and truly She manages a family rarely, that I must say for her.'

We were conversing in this manner, when our discourse was interrupted by a loud halloo, which rang through the Forest.

'My Sons, I hope!' exclaimed the Wood-man, and ran to open the door.

The halloo was repeated: We now distinguished the trampling of Horses, and soon after a Carriage, attended by several Cavaliers stopped at the Cottage door. One of the Horse-men enquired how far they were still from Strasbourg. As He addressed himself to me, I answered in the number of miles which Claude had told me; Upon which a volley of curses was vented against the Drivers for having lost their way. The Persons in the Coach were now informed of the distance of Strasbourg, and also that the Horses were so fatigued as to be incapable of proceeding further. A Lady, who appeared to be the principal, expressed much chagrin at this intelligence; But as there was no remedy, one of the Attendants asked the Wood-man, whether He could furnish them with lodging for the night.

He seemed much embarrassed, and replied in the negative; Adding that a Spanish Gentleman and his Servant were already in possession of the only spare apartments in his House. On hearing this, the gallantry of my nation would not permit me to retain those accommodations, of which a Female was in want. I instantly signified to the Wood-man, that I transferred my right to the Lady; He made some objections; But I over-ruled them, and hastening to the Carriage, opened the door, and assisted the Lady to descend. I immediately recognized her for the same person, whom I had seen at the Inn at Luneville. I took an opportunity of asking one of her Attendants, what was her name?

'The Baroness Lindenberg,' was the answer.

I could not but remark how different a reception our Host had given these new-comers and myself. His reluctance to admit them was visibly expressed on his countenance, and He prevailed on himself with difficulty to tell the

Lady, that She was welcome. I conducted her into the House, and placed her in the armed-chair, which I had just quitted. She thanked me very graciously; and made a thousand apologies for putting me to an inconvenience. Suddenly the Wood-man's countenance cleared up.

'At last I have arranged it!' said He, interrupting her excuses; 'I can lodge you and your suite, Madam, and you will not be under the necessity of making this Gentleman suffer for his politeness. We have two spare chambers, one for the Lady, the other, Monsieur, for you: My Wife shall give up hers to the two Waiting-women; As for the Men-servants, they must content themselves with passing the night in a large Barn, which stands at a few yards distance from the House. There they shall have a blazing fire, and as good a supper as we can make shift to give them.'

After several expressions of gratitude on the Lady's part, and opposition on mine to Marguerite's giving up her bed, this arrangement was agreed to. As the Room was small, the Baroness immediately dismissed her Male Domestics: Baptiste was on the point of conducting them to the Barn which He had mentioned, when two young Men appeared at the door of the Cottage.

'Hell and Furies!' exclaimed the first starting back; 'Robert, the House is filled with Strangers!'

'Ha! There are my Sons!' cried our Host. 'Why, Jacques! Robert! whither are you running, Boys? There is room enough still for you.'

Upon this assurance the Youths returned. The Father presented them to the Baroness and myself: After which He withdrew with our Domestics, while at the request of the two Waiting-women, Marguerite conducted them to the room designed for their Mistress.

The two new-comers were tall, stout, well-made young Men, hard-featured, and very much sun-burnt. They paid their compliments to us in few words, and acknowledged Claude, who now entered the room, as an old acquaintance. They then threw aside their cloaks in which they were wrapped up, took off a leathern belt to which a large Cutlass was suspended, and each drawing a brace of pistols from his girdle laid them upon a shelf.

'You travel well-armed,' said I.

'True, Monsieur;' replied Robert. 'We left Strasbourg late this Evening, and 'tis necessary to take precautions at passing through this Forest after dark. It does not bear a good repute, I promise you.'

'How?' said the Baroness; 'Are there Robbers hereabout?'

'So it is said, Madame; For my own part, I have travelled through the wood at all hours, and never met with one of them.'

Here Marguerite returned. Her Step-sons drew her to the other end of the room, and whispered to her for some minutes. By the looks which they cast towards us at intervals, I conjectured them to be enquiring our business in the Cottage.

In the mean while the Baroness expressed her apprehensions, that her Husband would be suffering much anxiety upon her account. She had intended to send on one of her Servants to inform the Baron of her delay; But the account which the young Men gave of the Forest, rendered this plan impracticable. Claude relieved her from her embarrassment. He informed her, that He was under the necessity of reaching Strasbourg that night, and that would She trust him with a letter, She might depend upon its being safely delivered.

'And how comes it,' said I, 'that you are under no apprehension of meeting these Robbers?'

'Alas! Monsieur, a poor Man with a large family must not lose certain profit, because 'tis attended with a little danger, and perhaps my Lord the Baron may give me a trifle for my pains. Besides, I have nothing to lose except my life, and that will not be worth the Robbers taking.'

I thought his arguments bad, and advised his waiting till the Morning; But as the Baroness did not second me, I was obliged to give up the point. The Baroness Lindenberg, as I found afterwards, had long been accustomed to sacrifice the interests of others to her own, and her wish to send Claude to Strasbourg blinded her to the danger of the undertaking. Accordingly, it was resolved, that He should set out without delay. The Baroness wrote her letter to her Husband, and I sent a few lines to my Banker, apprising him that I should not be at Strasbourg till the next day. Claude took our letters, and left the Cottage.

The Lady declared herself much fatigued by her journey: Besides having come from some distance, the Drivers had contrived to lose their way in the Forest. She now addressed herself to Marguerite, desiring to be shown to her chamber, and permitted to take half an hour's repose. One of the Waiting-women was immediately summoned; She appeared with a light, and the Baroness followed her up stairs. The cloth was spreading in the chamber where I was, and Marguerite soon gave me to understand, that I was in her way. Her hints were too broad to be easily mistaken; I therefore desired one of the young Men to conduct me to the chamber where I was to sleep, and where I could remain till supper was ready.

'Which chamber is it, Mother?' said Robert.

'The One with green hangings,' She replied; 'I have just been at the trouble of getting it ready, and have put fresh sheets upon the Bed; If the Gentleman chooses to lollop and lounge upon it, He may make it again himself for me.'

'You are out of humour, Mother, but that is no novelty. Have the goodness to follow me, Monsieur.'

He opened the door, and advanced towards a narrow stair-case.

'You have got no light!' said Marguerite; 'Is it your own neck or the Gentleman's that you have a mind to break?'

She crossed by me, and put a candle into Robert's hand, having received which, He began to ascend the stair-case. Jacques was employed in laying the cloth, and his back was turned towards me. Marguerite seized the moment, when we were unobserved. She caught my hand, and pressed it strongly.

'Look at the Sheets!' said She as She passed me, and immediately resumed her former occupation.

Startled by the abruptness of her action, I remained as if petrified. Robert's voice, desiring me to follow him, recalled me to myself. I ascended the stair-case. My conductor ushered me into a chamber, where an excellent wood-fire was blazing upon the hearth. He placed the light upon the Table, enquired whether I had any further commands, and on my replying in the negative, He left me to myself. You may be certain, that the moment when I found myself alone, was that on which I complied with Marguerite's injunction. I took the candle, hastily approached the Bed, and turned down the Coverture. What was my astonishment, my horror, at finding the sheets crimsoned with blood!

At that moment a thousand confused ideas passed before my imagination. The Robbers who infested the Wood, Marguerite's exclamation respecting her Children, the arms and appearance of the two young Men, and the various Anecdotes which I had heard related, respecting the secret correspondence which frequently exists between Banditti and Postillions, all these circumstances flashed upon my mind, and inspired me with doubt and apprehension. I ruminated on the most probable means of ascertaining the truth of my conjectures. Suddenly I was aware of Some-one below pacing hastily backwards and forwards. Every thing now appeared to me an object of suspicion. With precaution I drew near the window, which, as the room had been long shut up, was left open in spite of the cold. I ventured to look out. The beams of the Moon permitted me to distinguish a Man, whom I had no difficulty to recognize for my Host. I watched his movements. He walked swiftly, then stopped, and seemed to listen: He stamped upon the ground, and beat his stomach with his arms as if to guard himself from the inclemency of the season. At the least noise, if a voice was heard in the lower part of the House, if a Bat flitted past him, or the wind rattled amidst the leafless boughs, He started, and looked round with anxiety.

'Plague take him!' said He at length with impatience; 'What can He be about!'

He spoke in a low voice; but as He was just below my window, I had no difficulty to distinguish his words.

I now heard the steps of one approaching. Baptiste went towards the sound; He joined a man, whom his low stature and the Horn suspended from his neck, declared to be no other than my faithful Claude, whom I had supposed to be already on his way to Strasbourg. Expecting their discourse to throw some light upon my situation, I hastened to put myself in a condition to hear it with safety. For this purpose I extinguished the candle, which stood upon a table near the Bed: The flame of the fire was not strong enough to betray me, and I immediately resumed my place at the window.

The objects of my curiosity had stationed themselves directly under it. I suppose, that during my momentary absence the Wood-man had been blaming Claude for tardiness, since when I returned to the window, the latter was endeavouring to excuse his fault.

'However,' added He, 'my diligence at present shall make up for my past delay.'

'On that condition,' answered Baptiste, 'I shall readily forgive you. But in truth as you share equally with us in our prizes, your own interest will make you use all possible diligence. 'Twould be a shame to let such a noble booty escape us! You say, that this Spaniard is rich?'

'His Servant boasted at the Inn, that the effects in his Chaise were worth above two thousand Pistoles.'

Oh! how I cursed Stephano's imprudent vanity!

'And I have been told,' continued the Postillion, 'that this Baroness carries about her a casket of jewels of immense value.'

'May be so, but I had rather She had stayed away. The Spaniard was a secure prey. The Boys and myself could easily have mastered him and his Servant, and then the two thousand Pistoles would have been shared between us four. Now we must let in the Band for a share, and perhaps the whole Covey may escape us. Should our Friends have betaken themselves to their different posts before you reach the Cavern, all will be lost. The Lady's Attendants are too numerous for us to over-power them: Unless our Associates arrive in time, we must needs let these Travellers set out to-morrow without damage or hurt.'

' 'Tis plaguy unlucky, that my Comrades, who drove the Coach, should be those unacquainted with out Confederacy! But never fear, Friend Baptiste. An hour will bring me to the Cavern; It is now but ten o'clock, and by twelve you may expect the arrival of the Band. By the bye, take care of your Wife: You know how strong is her repugnance to our mode of life, and She may find means to give information to the Lady's Servants of our design.'

'Oh! I am secure of her silence; She is too much afraid of me, and fond of her children, to dare to betray my secret. Besides, Jacques and Robert keep a strict eye over her, and She is not permitted to set a foot out of the Cottage. The Servants are safely lodged in the Barn; I shall endeavour to keep all quiet till the arrival of our Friends. Were I assured of your finding them, the Strangers should be dispatched this instant; But as it is possible for you to miss the Banditti, I am fearful of being summoned to produce them by their Domestics in the Morning.'

'And suppose either of the Travellers should discover your design?'

'Then we must poignard those in our power, and take our chance about mastering the rest. However, to avoid running such a risque, hasten to the Cavern: The Banditti never leave it before eleven, and if you use diligence, you may reach it in time to stop them.'

'Tell Robert, that I have taken his Horse: My own has broken his bridle, and escaped into the Wood. What is the watch-word?'

'The reward of Courage.'

' 'Tis sufficient. I hasten to the Cavern.'

'And I to rejoin my Guests, lest my absence should create suspicion. Farewell, and be diligent.'

These worthy Associates now separated: The One bent his course towards the Stable, while the Other returned to the House.

You may judge, what must have been my feelings during this conversation, of which I lost not a single syllable. I dared not trust myself to my reflections, nor did any means present itself to escape the dangers which threatened me. Resistance, I knew to be vain; I was unarmed, and a single Man against Three: However, I resolved at least to sell my life as dearly as I could. Dreading lest Baptiste should perceive my absence, and suspect me to have overheard the message with which Claude was dispatched, I hastily relighted my candle and quitted the chamber. On descending, I found the Table spread for six Persons. The Baroness sat by the fire-side: Marguerite was employed in dressing a sallad, and her Step-sons were whispering together at the further end of the room. Baptiste having the round of the Garden to make, ere He could reach the Cottage-door, was not yet arrived. I seated myself quietly opposite to the Baroness.

A glance upon Marguerite told her, that her hint had not been thrown away upon me. How different did She now appear to me! What before seemed gloom and sullenness, I now found to be disgust at her Associates, and compassion for my danger. I looked up to her as to my only resource; Yet knowing her to be watched by her Husband with a suspicious eye, I could place but little reliance on the exertions of her good-will.

In spite of all my endeavours to conceal it, my agitation was but too visibly expressed upon my countenance. I was pale, and both my words and actions were disordered and embarrassed. The young Men observed this, and enquired the cause. I attributed it to excess of fatigue, and the violent effect produced on me by the severity of the season. Whether they believed me or not, I will not pretend to say: They at least ceased to embarrass me with their questions. I strove to divert my attention from the perils which surrounded me, by conversing on different subjects with the Baroness. I talked of Germany, declaring my intention of visiting it immediately: God knows, that I little thought at that moment of ever seeing it! She replied to me with great ease and politeness, professed that the pleasure of making my acquaintance amply compensated for the delay in her journey, and gave me a pressing invitation to make some stay at the Castle of Lindenberg. As She spoke thus; the Youths exchanged a malicious smile, which declared that She would be fortunate if She ever reached that Castle herself. This action did not escape me; But I concealed the emotion which it excited in my breast. I continued to converse with the Lady; But my discourse was so frequently incoherent, that as She has since informed me, She began to doubt whether I was in my right senses. The fact was, that while my conversation turned upon one subject, my thoughts were entirely occupied by another. I meditated upon the means of quitting the Cottage, finding my way to the Barn, and giving the Domestics information of our Host's designs. I was soon convinced, how impracticable was the attempt. Jacques and Robert watched my every movement with an attentive eye, and I was obliged to abandon the idea. All my hopes now rested upon Claude's not finding the Banditti: In that case, according to what I had over-heard, we should be permitted to depart unhurt.

I shuddered involuntarily, as Baptiste entered the room. He made many apologies for his long absence, but 'He had been detained by affairs impossible to be delayed.' He then entreated permission for his family to sup at the same table with us, without which, respect would not authorize his taking such a liberty. Oh! how in my heart I cursed the Hypocrite! How I loathed his presence, who was on the point of depriving me of an existence, at that time infinitely dear! I had every reason to be satisfied with life; I had youth, wealth, rank, and education; and the fairest prospects presented themselves before me. I saw those prospects on the point of closing in the most horrible manner: Yet was I obliged to dissimulate, and to receive with a semblance of gratitude the false civilities of him, who held the dagger to my bosom.

The permission which our Host demanded, was easily obtained. We seated ourselves at the Table. The Baroness and myself occupied one side: The Sons were opposite to us with their backs to the door. Baptiste took his seat by the Baroness at the upper end, and the place next to him was left for his Wife. She soon entered the room, and placed before us a plain but comfortable Peasant's repast. Our Host thought it necessary to apologize for the poorness of the supper: 'He had not been apprized of our coming; He could only offer us such fare as had been intended for his own family:'

'But,' added He, 'should any accident detain my noble Guests longer than they at present intend, I hope to give them a better treatment.'

The Villain! I well knew the accident to which He alluded; I shuddered at the treatment which He taught us to expect!

My Companion in danger seemed entirely to have got rid of her chagrin at being delayed. She laughed, and conversed with the family with infinite gaiety. I strove but in vain to follow her example. My spirits were evidently forced, and the constraint which I put upon myself, escaped not Baptiste's observation.

'Come, come, Monsieur, cheer up!' said He; 'You seem not quite recovered from your fatigue. To raise your spirits, what say you to a glass of excellent old wine which was left me by my Father? God rest his soul, He is in a better world! I seldom produce this wine; But as I am not honoured with such Guests every day, this is an occasion which deserves a Bottle.'

He then gave his Wife a Key, and instructed her where to find the wine of which He spoke. She seemed by no means pleased with the commission; She took the Key with an embarrassed air, and hesitated to quit the Table.

'Did you hear me?' said Baptiste in an angry tone.

Marguerite darted upon him a look of mingled anger and fear, and left the chamber. His eyes followed her suspiciously, till She had closed the door.

She soon returned with a bottle sealed with yellow wax. She placed it upon the table, and gave the Key back to her Husband. I suspected that this liquor was not presented to us without design, and I watched Marguerite's movements with inquietude. She was employed in rinsing some small horn Goblets. As She placed them before Baptiste, She saw that my eye was fixed upon her; and at the moment when She thought herself unobserved by the Banditti, She motioned to me with her head not to taste the liquor. She then resumed her place.

In the mean while our Host had drawn the Cork, and filling two of the Goblets offered them to the Lady and myself. She at first made some objections, but the instances of Baptiste were so urgent, that She was obliged to comply. Fearing to excite suspicion, I hesitated not to take the Goblet presented to me. By its smell and colour I guessed it to be Champagne; But some grains of powder floating upon the top, convinced me that it was not unadulterated. However, I dared not to express my repugnance to drinking it; I lifted it to my lips, and seemed to be swallowing it: Suddenly starting from my chair, I made the best of my way towards a Vase of water at some distance, in which Marguerite had been rinsing the Goblets. I pretended to spit out the wine with disgust, and took an opportunity unperceived of emptying the liquor into the Vase.

The Banditti seemed alarmed at my action. Jacques half rose from his chair, put his hand into his bosom, and I discovered the haft of a dagger. I returned to my seat with tranquillity, and affected not to have observed their confusion.

'You have not suited my taste, honest Friend,' said I, addressing myself to Baptiste. 'I never can drink Champagne without its producing a violent illness. I swallowed a few mouthfuls ere I was aware of its quality, and fear that I shall suffer for my imprudence.'

Baptiste and Jacques exchanged looks of distrust.

'Perhaps,' said Robert, 'the smell may be disagreeable to you.'

He quitted his chair, and removed the Goblet. I observed, that He examined, whether it was nearly empty.

'He must have drank sufficient,' said He to his Brother in a low voice, while He reseated himself.

Marguerite looked apprehensive, that I had tasted the liquor: A glance from my eye re-assured her.

I waited with anxiety for the effects which the Beverage would produce upon the Lady. I doubted not but the grains which I had observed, were poisonous, and lamented, that it had been impossible for me to warn her of the danger. But a few minutes had elapsed, before I perceived her eyes grow heavy; Her head sank upon her shoulder, and She fell into a deep sleep. I affected not to attend to this circumstance, and continued my conversation with Baptiste, with all the outward gaiety in my power to assume. But He no longer answered me without constraint. He eyed me with distrust and astonishment, and I saw that the Banditti were frequently whispering among themselves. My situation became every moment more painful; I sustained the character of confidence with a worse grace than ever. Equally afraid of the arrival of their Accomplices, and of their suspecting my knowledge of their designs, I knew not how to dissipate the distrust, which the Banditti evidently entertained for me. In this new dilemma the friendly Marguerite again assisted me. She passed behind the Chairs of her Step-sons, stopped for a moment opposite to me, closed her eyes, and reclined her head upon her shoulder. This hint immediately dispelled my incertitude. It told me, that I ought to imitate the Baroness, and pretend that the liquor had taken its full effect upon me. I did so, and in a few minutes seemed perfectly overcome with slumber.

'So!' cried Baptiste, as I fell back in my chair; 'At last He sleeps! I began to think that He had scented our design, and that we should have been forced to dispatch him at all events.'

'And why not dispatch him at all events?' enquired the ferocious Jacques. 'Why leave him the possibility of betraying our secret? Marguerite, give me one of my Pistols: A single touch of the trigger will finish him at once.'

'And supposing,' rejoined the Father, 'Supposing that our Friends should not arrive to-night, a pretty figure we should make when the Servants enquire for him in the Morning! No, no, Jacques; We must wait for our Associates. If they join us, we are strong enough to dispatch the Domestics as well as their Masters, and the booty is our own; If Claude does not find the Troop, we must take patience, and suffer the prey to slip through our fingers. Ah! Boys, Boys, had you arrived but five minutes sooner, the Spaniard would have been done for, and two thousand Pistoles our own. But you are always out of the way when you are most wanted. You are the most unlucky Rogues!'

'Well, well, Father!' answered Jacques; 'Had you been of my mind, all would have been over by this time. You, Robert, Claude, and myself, why the Strangers were but double the number, and I warrant you we might have mastered them. However, Claude is gone; 'Tis too late to think of it now. We must wait patiently for the arrival of the Gang; and if the Travellers escape us to-night, we must take care to way-lay them to-morrow.'

'True! True!' said Baptiste; 'Marguerite, have you given the sleeping-draught to the Waiting-women?'

She replied in the affirmative.

'All then is safe. Come, come, Boys; Whatever falls out, we have no reason to complain of this adventure. We run no danger, may gain much, and can lose nothing.'

At this moment I heard a trampling of Horses. Oh! how dreadful was the sound to my ears. A cold sweat flowed down my forehead, and I felt all the terrors of impending death. I was by no means re-assured by hearing the compassionate Marguerite exclaim in the accents of despair.

'Almighty God! They are lost!'

Luckily the Wood-man and his Sons were too much occupied by the arrival of their Associates to attend to me, or the violence of my agitation would have convinced them, that my sleep was feigned.

'Open! Open!' exclaimed several voices on the outside of the Cottage.

'Yes! Yes!' cried Baptiste joyfully; 'They are our Friends sure enough! Now then our booty is certain. Away! Lads, Away! Lead them to the Barn; You know, what is to be done there.'

Robert hastened to open the door of the Cottage.

'But first,' said Jacques, taking up his arms; 'first let me dispatch these Sleepers.'

'No, no, no!' replied his Father; 'Go you to the Barn, where your presence is wanted. Leave me to take care of these and the Women above.'

Jacques obeyed, and followed his Brother. They seemed to converse with the New-Comers for a few minutes: After which I heard the Robbers dismount, and as I conjectured, bend their course towards the Barn.

'So! That is wisely done!' muttered Baptiste; 'They have quitted their Horses, that They may fall upon the Strangers by surprise. Good! Good! and now to business.'

I heard him approach a small Cup-board which was fixed up in a distant part of the room, and unlock it. At this moment I felt myself shaken gently.

'Now! Now!' whispered Marguerite.

I opened my eyes. Baptiste stood with his back towards me. No one else was in the room save Marguerite and the sleeping Lady. The Villain had taken a dagger from the Cup-board, and seemed examining whether it was sufficiently sharp. I had neglected to furnish myself with arms; But I perceived this to be my only chance of escaping, and resolved not to lose the opportunity. I sprang from my seat, darted suddenly upon Baptiste, and clasping my hands round his throat, pressed it so forcibly as to prevent his uttering a single cry. You may remember, that I was remarkable at Salamanca for the power of my arm: It now rendered me an essential service. Surprised, terrified, and breathless, the Villain was by no means an equal Antagonist. I threw him upon the ground; I grasped him still tighter; and while I fixed him without motion upon the floor, Marguerite wresting the dagger from his hand, plunged it repeatedly in his heart till He expired.

No sooner was this horrible but necessary act perpetrated, than Marguerite called on me to follow her.

'Flight is our only refuge!' said She; 'Quick! Quick! Away!'

I hesitated not to obey her: but unwilling to leave the Baroness a victim to the vengeance of the Robbers, I raised her in my arms still sleeping, and hastened after Marguerite. The Horses of the Banditti were fastened near the door: My Conductress sprang upon one of them. I followed her example, placed the Baroness before me, and spurred on my Horse. Our only hope was to reach Strasbourg, which was much nearer than the perfidious Claude had assured me. Marguerite was well acquainted with the road, and galloped on before me. We were obliged to pass by the Barn, where the Robbers were slaughtering our Domestics. The door was open: We distinguished the shrieks of the dying and imprecations of the Murderers! What I felt at that moment language is unable to describe!

Jacques heard the trampling of our Horses, as we rushed by the Barn. He flew to the Door with a burning Torch in his hand, and easily recognised the Fugitives.

'Betrayed! Betrayed!' He shouted to his Companions.

Instantly they left their bloody work, and hastened to regain their Horses. We heard no more. I buried my spurs in the sides of my Courser, and Marguerite goaded on hers with the poignard, which had already rendered us such good service. We flew like lightning, and gained the open plains. Already was Strasbourg's Steeple in sight, when we heard the Robbers pursuing us. Marguerite looked back, and distinguished our followers descending a small Hill at no great distance. It was in vain that we urged on our Horses; The noise approached nearer with every moment.

'We are lost!' She exclaimed; 'The Villains gain upon us!'

'On! On!' replied I; 'I hear the trampling of Horses coming from the Town.'

We redoubled our exertions, and were soon aware of a numerous band of Cavaliers, who came towards us at full speed. They were on the point of passing us.

'Stay! Stay!' shrieked Marguerite; 'Save us! For God's sake, save us!'

The Foremost, who seemed to act as Guide, immediately reined in his Steed.

' 'Tis She! 'Tis She!' exclaimed He, springing upon the ground; 'Stop, my Lord, stop! They are safe! 'Tis my Mother!'

At the same moment Marguerite threw herself from her Horse, clasped him in her arms, and covered him with Kisses. The other Cavaliers stopped at the exclamation.

'The Baroness Lindenberg?' cried another of the Strangers eagerly; 'Where is She? Is She not with you?'

He stopped on beholding her lying senseless in my arms. Hastily He caught her from me. The profound sleep in which She was plunged, made him at first tremble for her life; but the beating of her heart soon re-assured him.

'God be thanked!' said He; 'She has escaped unhurt.'

I interrupted his joy by pointing out the Brigands, who continued to approach. No sooner had I mentioned them, than the greatest part of the Company, which appeared to be chiefly composed of soldiers, hastened forward to meet them. The Villains stayed not to receive their attack: Perceiving their danger they turned the heads of their Horses, and fled into the wood, whither they were followed by our Preservers. In the mean while the Stranger, whom I guessed to be the Baron Lindenberg, after thanking me for my care of his Lady, proposed our returning with all speed to the Town. The Baroness, on whom the effects of the opiate had not ceased to operate, was placed before him; Marguerite and her Son remounted their Horses; the Baron's Domestics followed, and we soon arrived at the Inn, where He had taken his apartments.

This was at the Austrian Eagle, where my Banker, whom before my quitting Paris I had apprised of my intention to visit Strasbourg, had prepared Lodgings for me. I rejoiced at this circumstance. It gave me an opportunity of cultivating the Baron's acquaintance, which I foresaw would be of use to me in Germany. Immediately upon our arrival the Lady was conveyed to bed; A Physician was sent for, who prescribed a medicine likely to counteract the effects of the sleepy potion, and after it had been poured down her throat, She was committed to the care of the Hostess. The Baron then addressed himself to me, and entreated me to recount the particulars of this adventure. I complied with his request instantaneously; for in pain respecting Stephano's fate, whom I had been compelled to abandon to the cruelty of the Banditti, I found it impossible for me to repose, till I had some news of him. I received but too soon the intelligence, that my trusty Servant had perished. The Soldiers who had pursued the Brigands, returned while I was employed in relating my adventure to the Baron. By their account I found, that the Robbers had been overtaken: Guilt and true courage are incompatible; They had thrown themselves at the feet of their Pursuers, had surrendered themselves without striking a blow, had discovered their secret retreat, made known their signals by which the rest of the Gang might be seized, and in short had betrayed ever mark of cowardice and baseness. By this means the whole of the Band, consisting of near sixty persons, had been made Prisoners, bound, and conducted to Strasbourg. Some of the Soldiers hastened to the Cottage, One of the Banditti serving them as Guide. Their first visit was to the fatal Barn, where they were fortunate enough to find two of the Baron's Servants still alive, though desperately wounded. The rest had expired beneath the swords of the Robbers, and of these my unhappy Stephano was one.

Alarmed at our escape, the Robbers in their haste to over-take us, had neglected to visit the Cottage. In consequence, the Soldiers found the two Waiting-women unhurt, and buried in the same death-like slumber which had overpowered their Mistress. There was nobody else found in the Cottage, except a child not above four years old, which the Soldiers brought away with them. We were busying ourselves with conjectures respecting the birth of this little unfortunate, when Marguerite rushed into the room with the Baby in her arms. She fell at the feet of the Officer who was making us this report, and blessed him a thousand times for the preservation of her Child.

When the first burst of maternal tenderness was over, I besought her to declare, by what means She had been united to a Man whose principles seemed so totally discordant with her own. She bent her eyes down-wards, and wiped a few tears from her cheek.

'Gentlemen,' said She after a silence of some minutes, 'I would request a favour of you: You have a right to know, on whom you confer an obligation. I will not therefore stifle a confession which covers me with shame; But permit me to comprise it in as few words as possible.

'I was born in Strasbourg of respectable Parents; Their names I must at present conceal: My Father still lives, and deserves not to be involved in my infamy; If you grant my request, you shall be informed of my family name. A Villain made himself Master of my affections, and to follow him I quitted my Father's House. Yet though my passions over-powered my virtue, I sank not into that degeneracy of vice, but too commonly the lot of Women who make the first false step. I loved my Seducer; dearly loved him! I was true to his Bed; this Baby, and the Youth who warned you, my Lord Baron, of your Lady's danger, are the pledges of our affection. Even at this moment I lament his loss, though 'tis to him that I owe all the miseries of my existence.

'He was of noble birth, but He had squandered away his paternal inheritance. His Relations considered him as a disgrace to their name, and utterly discarded him. His excesses drew upon him the indignation of the Police. He was obliged to fly from Strasbourg, and saw no other resource from beggary, than an union with the Banditti, who infested the neighbour-ing Forest, and whose Troop was chiefly composed of Young Men of family in the same predicament with himself. I was determined not to forsake him. I followed him to the Cavern of the Brigands, and shared with him the misery inseparable from a life of pillage. But though I was aware that our existence was supported by plunder, I knew not all the horrible circumstances attached to my Lover's profession. These He concealed from me with the utmost care; He was conscious, that my sentiments were not sufficiently depraved to look without horror upon assassination: He supposed, and with justice, that I should fly with detestation from the embraces of a Murderer. Eight years of possession had not abated his love for me; and He cautiously removed from my knowledge every circumstance, which might lead me to suspect the crimes in which He but too often participated. He succeeded perfectly: It was not till after my Seducer's death, that I discovered his hands to have been stained with the blood of innocence.

'One fatal night He was brought back to the Cavern, covered with wounds: He received them in attacking an English Traveller, whom his Companions immediately sacrificed to their resentment. He had only time to entreat my pardon for all the sorrows which He had caused me: He pressed my hand to his lips, and expired. My grief was inexpressible. As soon as its violence abated, I resolved to return to Strasbourg, to throw myself with my two Children at my Father's feet, and implore his forgiveness, though I little hoped to obtain it. What was my consternation when informed, that no one entrusted with the secret of their retreat, was ever permitted to quit the troop of the Banditti; That I must give up all hopes of ever rejoining society, and consent instantly to accepting one of their Band for my Husband! My prayers and remonstrances were vain. They cast lots to decide to whose possession I should fall; I became the property of the infamous Baptiste. A Robber, who had once been a Monk, pronounced over us a burlesque rather than a religious Ceremony: I and my Children were delivered into the hands of my new Husband, and He conveyed us immediately to his home.

'He assured me that He had long entertained for me the most ardent regard; But that Friendship for my deceased Lover had obliged him to stifle his desires. He endeavoured to reconcile me to my fate, and for some time treated me with respect and gentleness: At length finding that my aversion rather increased than diminished, He obtained those favours by violence, which I persisted to refuse him. No resource remained for me but to bear my sorrows with patience; I was conscious, that I deserved them but too well. Flight was forbidden: My Children were in the power of Baptiste, and He had sworn that if I attempted to escape, their lives should pay for it. I had had too many opportunities of witnessing the barbarity of his nature, to doubt his fulfilling his oath to the very letter. Sad experience had convinced me of the horrors of my situation: My first Lover had carefully concealed them from me; Baptiste rather rejoiced in opening my eyes to the cruelties of his profession, and strove to familiarise me with blood and slaughter.

'My nature was licentious and warm, but not cruel: My conduct had been imprudent, but my heart was not unprincipled. Judge then what I must have felt at being a continual witness of crimes the most horrible and revolting! Judge how I must have grieved at being united to a Man, who received the unsuspecting Guest with an air of openness and hospitality, at the very moment that He meditated his destruction. Chagrin and discontent preyed upon my constitution: The few charms bestowed on me by nature withered away, and the dejection of my countenance denoted the sufferings of my heart. I was tempted a thousand times to put an end to my existence; But the remembrance of my Children held my hand. I trembled to leave my dear Boys in my Tyrant's power, and trembled yet more for their virtue than their lives. The Second was still too young to benefit by my instructions; But in the heart of my Eldest I laboured unceasingly to plant those principles, which might enable him to avoid the crimes of his Parents. He listened to me with docility, or rather with eagerness. Even at his early age, He showed that He was not calculated for the society of Villains; and the only comfort which I enjoyed among my sorrows, was to witness the dawning virtues of my Theodore.

'Such was my situation, when the perfidy of Don Alphonso's postillion conducted him to the Cottage. His youth, air, and manners interested me most forcibly in his behalf. The absence of my Husband's Sons gave me an opportunity which I had long wished to find, and I resolved to risque every thing to preserve the Stranger. The vigilance of Baptiste prevented me from warning Don Alphonso of his danger: I knew that my betraying the secret would be immediately punished with death; and however embittered was my life by calamities, I wanted courage to sacrifice it for the sake of preserving that of another Person. My only hope rested upon procuring succour from Strasbourg: At this I resolved to try; and should an opportunity offer of warning Don Alphonso of his danger unobserved, I was determined to seize it with avidity. By Baptiste's orders I went up stairs to make the Stranger's Bed: I spread upon it Sheets in which a Traveller had been murdered but a few nights before, and which still were stained with blood. I hoped that these marks would not escape the vigilance of our Guest, and that He would collect from them the designs of my perfidious Husband. Neither was this the only step, which I took to preserve the Stranger. Theodore was confined to his bed by illness. I stole into his room unobserved by my Tyrant, communicated to him my project, and He entered into it with eagerness. He rose in spite of his malady, and dressed himself with all speed. I fastened one of the Sheets round his arms, and lowered him from the Window. He flew to the Stable, took Claude's Horse, and hastened to Strasbourg. Had He been accosted by the Banditti, He was to have declared himself sent upon a message by Baptiste, but fortunately He reached the Town without meeting any obstacle. Immediately upon his arrival at Strasbourg, He entreated assistance from the Magistrature: His Story passed from mouth to mouth, and at length came to the knowledge of my Lord the Baron. Anxious for the safety of his Lady, whom He knew would be upon the road that Evening, it struck him that She might have fallen into the power of the Robbers. He accompanied Theodore who guided the Soldiers towards the Cottage, and arrived just in time to save us from falling once more into the hands of our Enemies.'

Here I interrupted Marguerite to enquire, why the sleepy potion had been presented to me. She said, that Baptiste supposed me to have arms about me, and wished to incapacitate me from making resistance: It was a precaution which He always took, since as the Travellers had no hopes of escaping, Despair would have incited them to sell their lives dearly.

The Baron then desired Marguerite to inform him, what were her present plans. I joined him in declaring my readiness to show my gratitude to her for the preservation of my life.

'Disgusted with a world,' She replied, 'in which I have met with nothing but misfortunes, my only wish is to retire into a Convent. But first I must provide for my Children. I find that my Mother is no more, probably driven to an untimely grave by my desertion! My Father is still living; He is not an hard Man; Perhaps, Gentlemen, in spite of my ingratitude and imprudence, your intercessions may induce him to forgive me, and to take charge of his unfortunate Grand-sons. If you obtain this boon for me, you will repay my services a thousand-fold!'

Both the Baron and myself assured Marguerite, that we would spare no pains to obtain her pardon: and that even should her Father be inflexible, She need be under no apprehensions respecting the fate of her Children. I engaged myself to provide for Theodore, and the Baron promised to take the youngest under his protection. The grateful Mother thanked us with tears for what She called generosity, but which in fact was no more than a proper sense of our obligations to her. She then left the room to put her little Boy to bed, whom fatigue and sleep had compleatly overpowered.

The Baroness, on recovering and being informed from what dangers I had rescued her, set no bounds to the expressions of her gratitude. She was joined so warmly by her Husband in pressing me to accompany them to their Castle in Bavaria, that I found it impossible to resist their entreaties. During a week which we passed at Strasbourg, the interests of Marguerite were not forgotten: In our application to her Father we succeeded as amply as we could wish. The good old Man had lost his Wife: He had no Children but this unfortunate Daughter, of whom He had received no news for almost fourteen years. He was surrounded by distant Relations, who waited with impatience for his decease in order to get possession of his money. When therefore Marguerite appeared again so unexpectedly, He considered her as a gift from heaven: He received her and her Children with open arms, and insisted upon their establishing themselves in his House without delay. The disappointed Cousins were obliged to give place. The old Man would not hear of his Daughter's retiring into a Convent: He said, that She was too necessary to his happiness, and She was easily persuaded to relinquish her design. But no persuasions could induce Theodore to give up the plan, which I had at first marked out for him. He had attached himself to me most sincerely, during my stay at Strasbourg; and when I was on the point of leaving it, He besought me with tears to take him into my service: He set forth all his little talents in the most favourable colours, and tried to convince me that I should find him of infinite use to me upon the road. I was unwilling to charge myself with a Lad but scarcely turned of thirteen, whom I knew, could only be a burthen to me: However, I could not resist the entreaties of this affectionate Youth, who in fact possessed a thousand estimable qualities. With some difficulty He persuaded his relations to let him follow me, and that permission once obtained, He was dubbed with the title of my Page. Having passed a week at Strasbourg, Theodore and myself set out for Bavaria in company with the Baron and his Lady. These Latter as well as myself had forced Marguerite to accept several presents of value, both for herself, and her youngest Son: On leaving her, I promised his Mother faithfully, that I would restore Theodore to her within the year.

I have related this adventure at length, Lorenzo, that you might understand the means, by which 'The Adventurer, Alphonso d'Alvarada got introduced into the Castle of Lindenberg.' Judge from this specimen, how much faith should be given to your Aunt's assertions!

END OF THE FIRST VOLUME

VOLUME II

CHAPTER I

Avaunt! and quit my sight! Let the Earth hide thee!
Thy bones are marrowless; thy blood is cold;
Thou hast no speculation in those eyes
Which Thou dost glare with! Hence, horrible shadow!
Unreal mockery hence!

Macbeth.

Continuation of the History of Don Raymond.

MY journey was uncommonly agreeable: I found the Baron a Man of some
sense, but little knowledge of the world. He had past a great part of his life
without stirring beyond the precincts of his own domains, and consequently
his manners were far from being the most polished: But He was hearty,
good-humoured, and friendly. His attention to me was all that I could wish,
and I had every reason to be satisfied with his behaviour. His ruling passion
was Hunting, which He had brought himself to consider as a serious
occupation; and when talking over some remarkable chace, He treated the
subject with as much gravity, as it had been a Battle on which the fate of
two kingdoms was depending. I happened to be a tolerable Sportsman: Soon
after my arrival at Lindenberg I gave some proofs of my dexterity. The
Baron immediately marked me down for a Man of Genius, and vowed to
me an eternal friendship.

   That friendship was become to me by no means indifferent. At the Castle
of Lindenberg I beheld for the first time your Sister, the lovely Agnes. For
me whose heart was unoccupied, and who grieved at the void, to see her
and to love her were the same. I found in Agnes all that was requisite to
secure my affection. She was then scarcely sixteen; Her person light and
elegant was already formed; She possessed several talents in perfection,
particularly those of Music and drawing: Her character was gay, open, and
good-humoured; and the graceful simplicity of her dress and manners
formed an advantageous contrast to the art and studied Coquetry of the
Parisian Dames, whom I had just quitted. From the moment that I beheld
her, I felt the most lively interest in her fate. I made many enquiries
respecting her of the Baroness.

'She is my Niece,' replied that Lady; 'You are still ignorant, Don Alphonso, that I am your Country-woman. I am Sister to the Duke of Medina Celi: Agnes is the Daughter of my second Brother, Don Gaston: She has been destined to the Convent from her cradle, and will soon make her profession at Madrid.'

[Here Lorenzo interrupted the Marquis by an exclamation of surprise.

'Intended for the Convent from her cradle?' said He; 'By heaven, this is the first word that I ever heard of such a design!'

'I believe it, my dear Lorenzo,' answered Don Raymond; 'But you must listen to me with patience. You will not be less surprised, when I relate some particulars of your family still unknown to you, and which I have learnt from the mouth of Agnes herself.'

He then resumed his narrative as follows.]

You cannot but be aware, that your Parents were unfortunately Slaves to the grossest superstition: When this foible was called into play, their every other sentiment, their every other passion yielded to its irresistible strength. While She was big with Agnes, your Mother was seized by a dangerous illness, and given over by her Physicians. In this situation, Donna Inesilla vowed, that if She recovered from her malady, the Child then living in her bosom if a Girl should be dedicated to St Clare, if a Boy to St Benedict. Her prayers were heard; She got rid of her complaint; Agnes entered the world alive, and was immediately destined to the service of St Clare.

Don Gaston readily chimed in with his Lady's wishes: But knowing the sentiments of the Duke, his Brother, respecting a Monastic life, it was determined that your Sister's destination should be carefully concealed from him. The better to guard the secret, it was resolved that Agnes should accompany her Aunt, Donna Rodolpha into Germany, whither that Lady was on the point of following her new-married Husband, Baron Lindenberg. On her arrival at that Estate, the young Agnes was put into a Convent, situated but a few miles from the Castle. The Nuns, to whom her education was confided, performed their charge with exactitude: They made her a perfect Mistress of many talents, and strove to infuse into her mind a taste for the retirement and tranquil pleasures of a Convent. But a secret instinct made the young Recluse sensible that She was not born for solitude: In all the freedom of youth and gaiety She scrupled not to treat as ridiculous many ceremonies, which the Nuns regarded with awe; and She was never more happy than when her lively imagination inspired her with some scheme to plague the stiff Lady Abbess, or the ugly ill-tempered old Porteress. She looked with disgust upon the prospect before her: However no alternative was offered to her, and She submitted to the decree of her Parents, though not without secret repining.

That repugnance She had not art enough to conceal long: Don Gaston was informed of it. Alarmed, Lorenzo, lest your affection for her should oppose itself to his projects, and lest you should positively object to your Sister's misery, He resolved to keep the whole affair from *your* knowledge as well as the Duke's, till the sacrifice should be consummated. The season of her taking the veil was fixed for the time when you should be upon your travels: In the mean while no hint was dropped of Donna Inesilla's fatal vow. Your Sister was never permitted to know your direction. All your letters were read before She received them, and those parts effaced, which were likely to nourish her inclination for the world: Her answers were dictated either by her Aunt, or by Dame Cunegonda, her Governess. These particulars I learnt partly from Agnes, partly from the Baroness herself.

I immediately determined upon rescuing this lovely Girl from a fate so contrary to her inclinations, and ill-suited to her merit. I endeavoured to ingratiate myself into her favour: I boasted of my friendship and intimacy with you. She listened to me with avidity; She seemed to devour my words while I spoke in your praise, and her eyes thanked me for my affection to her Brother. My constant and unremitted attention at length gained me her heart, and with difficulty I obliged her to confess that She loved me. When however, I proposed her quitting the Castle of Lindenberg, She rejected the idea in positive terms.

'Be generous, Alphonso,' She said; 'You possess my heart, but use not the gift ignobly. Employ not your ascendancy over me in persuading me to take a step, at which I should here-after have to blush. I am young and deserted: My Brother, my only Friend, is separated from me, and my other Relations act with me as my Enemies. Take pity on my unprotected situation. Instead of seducing me to an action which would cover me with shame, strive rather to gain the affections of those who govern me. The Baron esteems you. My Aunt, to others ever harsh proud and contemptuous, remembers that you rescued her from the hands of Murderers, and wears with you alone the appearance of kindness and benignity. Try then your influence over my Guardians. If they consent to our union my hand is yours: From your account of my Brother, I cannot doubt your obtaining his approbation: And when they find the impossibility of executing their design, I trust that my Parents will excuse my disobedience, and expiate by some other sacrifice my Mother's fatal vow.'

From the first moment that I beheld Agnes, I had endeavoured to conciliate the favour of her Relations. Authorised by the confession of her regard, I redoubled my exertions. My principal Battery was directed against the Baroness; It was easy to discover, that her word was law in the Castle: Her Husband paid her the most absolute submission, and considered her as a superior Being. She was about forty: In her youth She had been a Beauty; But her charms had been upon that large scale which can but ill sustain the shock of years: However She still possessed some remains of them. Her understanding was strong and excellent when not obscured by prejudice, which unluckily was but seldom the case. Her passions were violent: She spared no pains to gratify them, and pursued with unremitting vengeance those who opposed themselves to her wishes. The warmest of Friends, the most inveterate of Enemies, such was the Baroness Lindenberg.

I laboured incessantly to please her: Unluckily I succeeded but too well. She seemed gratified by my attention, and treated me with a distinction accorded by her to no one else. One of my daily occupations was reading to her for several hours: Those hours I should much rather have past with Agnes; But as I was conscious, that complaisance for her Aunt would advance our union, I submitted with a good grace to the penance imposed upon me. Donna Rodolpha's Library was principally composed of old Spanish Romances: These were her favourite studies, and once a day one of these unmerciful Volumes was put regularly into my hands. I read the wearisome adventures of *'Perceforest,' 'Tirante the White,' 'Palmerin of England,'* and *'the Knight of the Sun,'* till the Book was on the point of falling from my hands through Ennui. However, the increasing pleasure which the Baroness seemed to take in my society, encouraged me to persevere; and latterly She showed for me a partiality so marked, that Agnes advised me to seize the first opportunity of declaring our mutual passion to her Aunt.

One Evening, I was alone with Donna Rodolpha in her own apartment. As our readings generally treated of love, Agnes was never permitted to assist at them. I was just congratulating myself on having finished *'the Loves of Tristan and the Queen Iseult——'*

'Ah! The Unfortunates!' cried the Baroness; 'How say you, Segnor? Do you think it possible for Man to feel an attachment so disinterested and sincere?'

'I cannot doubt it,' replied I; 'My own heart furnishes me with the certainty. Ah! Donna Rodolpha, might I but hope for your approbation of my love! Might I but confess the name of my Mistress without incurring your resentment!'

She interrupted me.

'Suppose, I were to spare you that confession? Suppose, I were to acknowledge, that the object of your desires is not unknown to me? Suppose, I were to say that She returns your affection, and laments not less sincerely than yourself, the unhappy vows which separate her from you?'

'Ah! Donna Rodolpha!' I exclaimed, throwing myself upon my knees before her, and pressing her hand to my lips, 'You have discovered my secret! What is your decision? Must I despair, or may I reckon upon your favour?'

She withdrew not the hand which I held; But She turned from me, and covered her face with the other.

'How can I refuse it you?' She replied; 'Ah! Don Alphonso, I have long perceived to whom your attentions were directed, but till now I perceived not the impression which they made upon my heart. At length I can no longer

hide my weakness either from myself or from you. I yield to the violence of
my passion, and own, that I adore you! For three long months I stifled my
desires; But grown stronger by resistance, I submit to their impetuosity.
Pride, fear, and honour, respect for myself, and my engagements to the
Baron, all are vanquished. I sacrifice them to my love for you, and it still
seems to me that I pay too mean a price for your possession.'

She paused for an answer.—Judge, my Lorenzo, what must have been my
confusion at this discovery. I at once saw all the magnitude of this obstacle,
which I had raised myself to my happiness. The Baroness had placed those
attentions to her own account, which I had merely paid her for the sake of
Agnes: And the strength of her expressions, the looks which accompanied
them, and my knowledge of her revengeful disposition made me tremble for
myself and my Beloved. I was silent for some minutes. I knew not how to
reply to her declaration: I could only resolve to clear up the mistake without
delay, and for the present to conceal from her knowledge the name of my
Mistress. No sooner had She avowed her passion, than the transports which
before were evident in my features, gave place to consternation and
constraint. I dropped her hand, and rose from my knees. The change in my
countenance did not escape her observation.

'What means this silence?' said She in a trembling voice; 'Where is that
joy which you led me to expect?'

'Forgive me, Segnora,' I answered, 'if what necessity forces from me
should seem harsh and ungrateful: To encourage you in an error, which,
however it may flatter myself, must prove to you the source of disappointment, would make me appear criminal in every eye. Honour obliges me to
inform you, that you have mistaken for the solicitude of Love what was only
the attention of Friendship. The latter sentiment is that which I wished to
excite in your bosom: To entertain a warmer, respect for you forbids me,
and gratitude for the Baron's generous treatment. Perhaps these reasons
would not be sufficient to shield me from your attractions, were it not that
my affections are already bestowed upon another. You have charms,
Segnora, which might captivate the most insensible; No heart unoccupied
could resist them. Happy is it for me that mine is no longer in my possession;
or I should have to reproach myself for ever with having violated the Laws
of Hospitality. Recollect yourself, noble Lady; Recollect what is owed by
you to honour, by me to the Baron, and replace by esteem and friendship
those sentiments which I never can return.'

The Baroness turned pale at this unexpected and positive declaration: She
doubted whether She slept or woke. At length recovering from her surprise,
consternation gave place to rage, and the blood rushed back into her cheeks
with violence.

'Villain!' She cried; 'Monster of deceit! Thus is the avowal of my love
received? Is it thus that. . . . But no, no! It cannot, it shall not be! Alphonso,

behold me at your feet! Be witness of my despair! Look with pity on a Woman who loves you with sincere affection! She who possesses your heart, how has She merited such a treasure? What sacrifice has She made to you? What raises her above Rodolpha?'

I endeavoured to lift her from her Knees.

'For God's sake, Segnora, restrain these transports: They disgrace yourself and me. Your exclamations may be heard, and your secret divulged to your Attendants. I see, that my presence only irritates you: permit me to retire.'

I prepared to quit the apartment: The Baroness caught me suddenly by the arm.

'And who is this happy Rival?' said She in a menacing tone; 'I will know her name, and *when* I know it. . . .! She is some one in my power; You entreated my favour, my protection! Let me but find her, let me but know who dares to rob me of your heart, and She shall suffer every torment, which jealousy and disappointment can inflict! Who is She? Answer me this moment. Hope not to conceal her from my vengeance! Spies shall be set over you; every step, every look shall be watched; Your eyes will discover my Rival; I shall know her, and when She is found, tremble, Alphonso for her and for yourself!'

As She uttered these last words her fury mounted to such a pitch as to stop her powers of respiration. She panted, groaned, and at length fainted away. As She was falling I caught her in my arms, and placed her upon a Sopha. Then hastening to the door, I summoned her Women to her assistance; I committed her to their care, and seized the opportunity of escaping.

Agitated and confused beyond expression I bent my steps towards the Garden. The benignity with which the Baroness had listened to me at first raised my hopes to the highest pitch: I imagined her to have perceived my attachment for her Niece, and to approve of it. Extreme was my disappointment at understanding the true purport of her discourse. I knew not what course to take: The superstition of the Parents of Agnes, aided by her Aunt's unfortunate passion, seemed to oppose such obstacles to our union as were almost insurmountable.

As I past by a low parlour, whose windows looked into the Garden, through the door which stood half open I observed Agnes seated at a Table. She was occupied in drawing, and several unfinished sketches were scattered round her. I entered, still undetermined whether I should acquaint her with the declaration of the Baroness.

'Oh! is it only you?' said She, raising her head; 'You are no Stranger, and I shall continue my occupation without ceremony. Take a Chair, and seat yourself by me.'

I obeyed, and placed myself near the Table. Unconscious what I was doing, and totally occupied by the scene which had just passed, I took up some of the drawings, and cast my eye over them. One of the subjects struck me from its singularity. It represented the great Hall of the Castle of Lindenberg. A door conducting to a narrow stair-case stood half open. In the fore-ground appeared a Groupe of figures, placed in the most grotesque attitudes; Terror was expressed upon every countenance. Here was One upon his knees with his eyes cast up to heaven, and praying most devoutly; There Another was creeping away upon all fours. Some hid their faces in their cloaks or the laps of their Companions; Some had concealed themselves beneath a Table, on which the remnants of a feast were visible; While Others with gaping mouths and eyes wide-stretched pointed to a Figure, supposed to have created this disturbance. It represented a Female of more than human stature, clothed in the habit of some religious order. Her face was veiled; On her arm hung a chaplet of beads; Her dress was in several places stained with the blood which trickled from a wound upon her bosom. In one hand She held a Lamp, in the other a large Knife, and She seemed advancing towards the iron gates of the Hall.

'What does this mean, Agnes?' said I. 'Is this some invention of your own?' She cast her eye upon the drawing.

'Oh! no' She replied; ' 'Tis the invention of much wiser heads than mine. But can you possibly have lived at Lindenberg for three whole Months without hearing of the Bleeding Nun?'

'You are the first, who ever mentioned the name to me. Pray, who may the Lady be?'

'That is more than I can pretend to tell you. All my knowledge of her History comes from an old tradition in this family, which has been handed down from Father to Son, and is firmly credited throughout the Baron's domains. Nay, the Baron believes it himself; and as for my Aunt who has a natural turn for the marvellous, She would sooner doubt the veracity of the Bible, than of the Bleeding Nun. Shall I tell you this History?'

I answered that She would oblige me much by relating it: She resumed her drawing, and then proceeded as follows in a tone of burlesqued gravity.

'It is surprising that in all the Chronicles of past times, this remarkable Personage is never once mentioned. Fain would I recount to you her life; But unluckily till after her death She was never known to have existed. Then first did She think it necessary to make some noise in the world, and with that intention She made bold to seize upon the Castle of Lindenberg. Having a good taste, She took up her abode in the best room of the House: and once established there, She began to amuse herself by knocking about the tables and chairs in the middle of the night. Perhaps, She was a bad Sleeper, but this I have never been able to ascertain. According to the tradition, this entertainment commenced about a Century ago. It was accompanied with shrieking, howling, groaning, swearing, and many other agreeable noises of the same kind. But though one particular room was more especially honoured with her visits, She did not entirely confine herself to it. She occasionally ventured into the old Galleries, paced up and down the spacious Halls, or sometimes stopping at the doors of the Chambers, She wept and wailed there to the universal terror of the Inhabitants. In these nocturnal excursions She was seen by different People, who all describe her appearance as you behold it here, traced by the hand of her unworthy Historian.'

The singularity of this account insensibly engaged my attention.

'Did She never speak to those who met her?' said I.

'Not She. The specimens indeed which She gave nightly of her talents for conversation, were by no means inviting. Sometimes the Castle rung with oaths and execrations: A Moment after She repeated her Paternoster: Now She howled out the most horrible blasphemies, and then chaunted De Profundis, as orderly as if still in the Choir. In short She seemed a mighty capricious Being: But whether She prayed or cursed, whether She was impious or devout, She always contrived to terrify her Auditors out of their senses. The Castle became scarcely habitable; and its Lord was so frightened by these midnight Revels, that one fine morning He was found dead in his bed. This success seemed to please the Nun mightily, for now She made more noise than ever. But the next Baron proved too cunning for her. He made his appearance with a celebrated Exorciser in his hand, who feared not to shut himself up for a night in the haunted Chamber. There it seems, that He had an hard battle with the Ghost, before She would promise to be quiet. She was obstinate, but He was more so, and at length She consented to let the Inhabitants of the Castle take a good night's rest. For some time after no news was heard of her. But at the end of five years the Exorciser died, and then the Nun ventured to peep abroad again. However, She was now grown much more tractable and well-behaved. She walked about in silence, and never made her appearance above once in five years. This custom, if you will believe the Baron, She still continues. He is fully persuaded, that on the fifth of May of every fifth year, as soon as the Clock strikes One the Door of the haunted Chamber opens. [Observe, that this room has been shut up for near a Century.] Then out walks the Ghostly Nun with her Lamp and dagger: She descends the stair-case of the Eastern Tower; and crosses the great Hall! On that night the Porter always leaves the Gates of the Castle open, out of respect to the Apparition: Not that this is thought by any means necessary, since She could easily whip through the Key-hole if She chose it; But merely out of politeness, and to prevent her from making her exit in a way so derogatory to the dignity of her Ghost-ship.'

'And whither does She go on quitting the Castle?'

'To Heaven, I hope; But if She does, the place certainly is not to her taste, for She always returns after an hour's absence. The Lady then retires to her chamber, and is quiet for another five years.'

'And you believe this, Agnes?'

'How can you ask such a question? No, no, Alphonso! I have too much reason to lament superstition's influence to be its Victim myself. However I must not avow my incredulity to the Baroness: She entertains not a doubt of the truth of this History. As to Dame Cunegonda, my Governess, She protests that fifteen years ago She saw the Spectre with her own eyes. She related to me one evening, how She and several other Domestics had been terrified while at Supper by the appearance of the Bleeding Nun, as the Ghost is called in the Castle: 'Tis from her account that I drew this sketch, and you may be certain that Cunegonda was not omitted. There She is! I shall never forget what a passion She was in, and how ugly She looked while She scolded me for having made her picture so like herself!'

Here She pointed to a burlesque figure of an old Woman in an attitude of terror.

In spite of the melancholy which oppressed me, I could not help smiling at the playful imagination of Agnes: She had perfectly preserved Dame Cunegonda's resemblance, but had so much exaggerated every fault, and rendered every feature so irresistibly laughable, that I could easily conceive the Duenna's anger.

'The figure is admirable, my dear Agnes! I knew not that you possessed such talents for the ridiculous.'

'Stay a moment,' She replied; 'I will show you a figure still more ridiculous than Dame Cunegonda's. If it pleases you, you may dispose of it as seems best to yourself.'

She rose, and went to a Cabinet at some little distance. Unlocking a drawer, She took out a small case, which She opened, and presented to me.

'Do you know the resemblance?' said She smiling.

It was her own.

Transported at the gift, I pressed the portrait to my lips with passion: I threw myself at her feet, and declared my gratitude in the warmest and most affectionate terms. She listened to me with complaisance, and assured me that She shared my sentiments: When suddenly She uttered a loud shriek, disengaged the hand which I held, and flew from the room by a door which opened to the Garden. Amazed at this abrupt departure, I rose hastily from my knees. I beheld with confusion the Baroness standing near me glowing with jealousy, and almost choaked with rage. On recovering from her swoon, She had tortured her imagination to discover her concealed Rival. No one appeared to deserve her suspicions more than Agnes. She immediately hastened to find her Niece, tax her with encouraging my addresses, and assure herself whether her conjectures were well-grounded. Unfortunately She had already seen enough to need no other confirmation. She arrived at the door of the room at the precise moment, when Agnes gave me her Portrait. She heard me profess an everlasting attachment to her

Rival, and saw me kneeling at her feet. She advanced to separate us; We were too much occupied by each other to perceive her approach, and were not aware of it, till Agnes beheld her standing by my side.

Rage on the part of Donna Rodolpha, embarrassment on mine, for some time kept us both silent. The Lady recovered herself first.

'My suspicions then were just,' said She; 'The Coquetry of my Niece has triumphed, and 'tis to her that I am sacrificed. In one respect however I am fortunate: I shall not be the only one who laments a disappointed passion. You too shall know, what it is to love without hope! I daily expect orders for restoring Agnes to her Parents. Immediately upon her arrival in Spain, She will take the veil, and place an insuperable barrier to your union. You may spare your supplications.' She continued, perceiving me on the point of speaking; 'My resolution is fixed and immoveable. Your Mistress shall remain a close Prisoner in her chamber, till She exchanges this Castle for the Cloister. Solitude will perhaps recall her to a sense of her duty: But to prevent your opposing that wished event, I must inform you, Don Alphonso, that your presence here is no longer agreeable either to the Baron or Myself. It was not to talk nonsense to my Niece, that your Relations sent you to Germany: Your business was to travel, and I should be sorry to impede any longer so excellent a design. Farewell, Segnor; Remember, that to-morrow morning we meet for the last time.'

Having said this, She darted upon me a look of pride, contempt, and malice, and quitted the apartment. I also retired to mine, and consumed the night in planning the means of rescuing Agnes from the power of her tyrannical Aunt.

After the positive declaration of its Mistress, it was impossible for me to make a longer stay at the Castle of Lindenberg. Accordingly I the next day announced my immediate departure. The Baron declared that it gave him sincere pain; and He expressed himself in my favour so warmly, that I endeavoured to win him over to my interest. Scarcely had I mentioned the name of Agnes when He stopped me short, and said, that it was totally out of his power to interfere in the business. I saw that it was in vain to argue; The Baroness governed her Husband with despotic sway, and I easily perceived, that She had prejudiced him against the match. Agnes did not appear: I entreated permission to take leave of her, but my prayer was rejected. I was obliged to depart without seeing her.

At quitting him the Baron shook my hand affectionately, and assured me that as soon as his Niece was gone, I might consider his House as my own.

'Farewell, Don Alphonso!' said the Baroness, and stretched out her hand to me.

I took it, and offered to carry it to my lips. She prevented me. Her Husband was at the other end of the room, and out of hearing.

'Take care of yourself,' She continued; 'My love is become hatred, and my wounded pride shall not be un-atoned. Go where you will, my vengeance shall follow you!'

She accompanied these words with a look sufficient to make me tremble. I answered not, but hastened to quit the Castle.

As my Chaise drove out of the Court, I looked up to the windows of your Sister's chamber. Nobody was to be seen there: I threw myself back despondent in my Carriage. I was attended by no other servants than a French-man whom I had hired at Strasbourg in Stephano's room, and my little Page whom I before mentioned to you. The fidelity, intelligence, and good temper of Theodore had already made him dear to me; But He now prepared to lay an obligation on me, which made me look upon him as a Guardian Genius. Scarcely had we proceeded half a mile from the Castle, when He rode up to the Chaise-door.

'Take courage, Segnor!' said He in Spanish, which He had already learnt to speak with fluency and correctness. 'While you were with the Baron, I watched the moment when Dame Cunegonda was below stairs, and mounted into the chamber over that of Donna Agnes. I sang as loud as I could a little German air well-known to her, hoping that She would recollect my voice. I was not disappointed, for I soon heard her window open. I hastened to let down a string with which I had provided myself: Upon hearing the casement closed again, I drew up the string, and fastened to it I found this scrap of paper.'

He then presented me with a small note addressed to me. I opened it with impatience: It contained the following words written in pencil:

Conceal yourself for the next fortnight in some neighbouring Village. My Aunt will believe you to have quitted Lindenberg, and I shall be restored to liberty. I will be in the West Pavilion at twelve on the night of the thirtieth. Fail not to be there, and we shall have an opportunity of concerting our future plans. Adieu.

Agnes.

At perusing these lines my transports exceeded all bounds; Neither did I set any to the expressions of gratitude which I heaped upon Theodore. In fact his address and attention merited my warmest praise. You will readily believe, that I had not entrusted him with my passion for Agnes; But the arch Youth had too much discernment not to discover my secret, and too much discretion not to conceal his knowledge of it. He observed in silence what was going on, nor strove to make himself an Agent in the business till my interests required his interference. I equally admired his judgment, his penetration, his address, and his fidelity. This was not the first occasion in which I had found him of infinite use, and I was every day more convinced of his quickness and capacity. During my short stay at Strasbourg, He had applied himself diligently to learning the rudiments of Spanish: He continued to study it, and with so much success that He spoke it with the same facility as his native language. He past the greatest part of his time in reading; He had acquired much information for his Age; and united the advantages of a lively countenance and prepossessing figure to an excellent understanding, and the very best of hearts. He is now fifteen; He is still in my service, and when you see him, I am sure that He will please you. But excuse this digression: I return to the subject which I quitted.

I obeyed the instructions of Agnes. I proceeded to Munich. There I left my Chaise under the care of Lucas my French Servant, and then returned on Horse-back to a small Village about four miles distant from the Castle of Lindenberg. Upon arriving there a story was related to the Host at whose Inn I descended, which prevented his wondering at my making so long a stay in his House. The old Man fortunately was credulous and incurious: He believed all I said, and sought to know no more than what I thought proper to tell him. Nobody was with me but Theodore; Both were disguised, and as we kept ourselves close, we were not suspected to be other than what we seemed. In this manner the fortnight passed away. During that time I had the pleasing conviction that Agnes was once more at liberty. She past through the Village with Dame Cunegonda: She seemed in health and spirits, and talked to her Companion without any appearance of constraint.

'Who are those Ladies?' said I to my Host, as the Carriage past.

'Baron Lindenberg's Niece with her Governess,' He replied; 'She goes regularly every Friday to the Convent of St Catharine, in which She was brought up, and which is situated about a mile from hence.'

You may be certain that I waited with impatience for the ensuing Friday. I again beheld my lovely Mistress. She cast her eyes upon me, as She passed the Inn-door. A blush which overspread her cheek, told me that in spite of my disguise I had been recognised. I bowed profoundly. She returned the compliment by a slight inclination of the head as if made to one inferior, and looked another way till the Carriage was out of sight.

The long-expected, long-wished for night arrived. It was calm, and the Moon was at the full. As soon as the Clock struck eleven I hastened to my appointment, determined not to be too late. Theodore had provided a Ladder; I ascended the Garden-wall without difficulty; The Page followed me, and drew the Ladder after us. I posted myself in the West Pavilion, and waited impatiently for the approach of Agnes. Every breeze that whispered, every leaf that fell, I believed to be her footstep, and hastened to meet her. Thus was I obliged to pass a full hour, every minute of which appeared to me an age. The Castle-Bell at length tolled twelve, and scarcely could I believe the night to be no further advanced. Another quarter of an hour elapsed, and I heard the light foot of my Mistress approaching the Pavilion with precaution. I flew to receive her, and conducted her to a seat. I threw myself at her feet, and was expressing my joy at seeing her, when She thus interrupted me.

'We have no time to lose, Alphonso: The moments are precious, for though no more a Prisoner, Cunegonda watches my every step. An express is arrived from my Father; I must depart immediately for Madrid, and 'tis with difficulty that I have obtained a week's delay. The superstition of my Parents, supported by the representations of my cruel Aunt, leaves me no hope of softening them to compassion. In this dilemma I have resolved to commit myself to your honour: God grant, that you may never give me cause to repent my resolution! Flight is my only resource from the horrors of a Convent, and my imprudence must be excused by the urgency of the danger. Now listen to the plan, by which I hope to effect my escape.

'We are now at the thirtieth of April. On the fifth day from this the Visionary Nun is expected to appear. In my last visit to the Convent I provided myself with a dress proper for the character: A Friend, whom I have left there and to whom I made no scruple to confide my secret, readily consented to supply me with a religious habit. Provide a carriage, and be with it at a little distance from the great Gate of the Castle. As soon as the Clock strikes 'one,' I shall quit my chamber, drest in the same apparel as the Ghost is supposed to wear. Whoever meets me will be too much terrified to oppose my escape. I shall easily reach the door, and throw myself under your protection. Thus far success is certain: But Oh! Alphonso, should you deceive me! Should you despise my imprudence and reward it with ingratitude, the World will not hold a Being more wretched than myself! I feel all the dangers to which I shall be exposed. I feel, that I am giving you a right to treat me with levity: But I rely upon your love, upon your honour! The step, which I am on the point of taking, will incense my Relations against me: Should you desert me, should you betray the trust reposed in you, I shall have no friend to punish your insult, or support my cause. On yourself alone rests all my hope, and if your own heart does not plead in my behalf, I am undone for ever!'

The tone in which She pronounced these words was so touching, that in spite of my joy at receiving her promise to follow me, I could not help being affected. I also repined in secret, at not having taken the precaution to provide a Carriage at the Village, in which case I might have carried off Agnes that very night. Such an attempt was now impracticable: Neither Carriage or Horses were to be procured nearer than Munich, which was distant from Lindenberg two good days journey. I was therefore obliged to chime in with her plan, which in truth seemed well arranged: Her disguise would secure her from being stopped in quitting the Castle, and would enable her to step into the Carriage at the very Gate without difficulty or losing time.

Agnes reclined her head mournfully upon my shoulder, and by the light of the Moon I saw tears flowing down her cheek. I strove to dissipate her melancholy, and encouraged her to look forward to the prospect of happiness. I protested in the most solemn terms that her virtue and innocence would be safe in my keeping, and that till the church had made her my lawful Wife, her honour should be held by me as sacred as a Sister's. I told her, that my first care should be to find you out, Lorenzo, and reconcile you to our union; and I was continuing to speak in the same strain, when a noise without alarmed me. Suddenly the door of the Pavilion was thrown open, and Cunegonda stood before us. She had heard Agnes steal out of her chamber, followed her into the Garden, and perceived her entering the Pavilion. Favoured by the Trees, which shaded it, and unperceived by Theodore who waited at a little distance, She had approached in silence, and over-heard our whole conversation.

'Admirable!' cried Cunegonda in a voice shrill with passion, while Agnes uttered a loud shriek; 'By St Barbara, young Lady, you have an excellent invention! You must personate the Bleeding Nun, truly? What impiety! What incredulity! Marry, I have a good mind to let you pursue your plan: When the real Ghost met you, I warrant, you would be in a pretty condition! Don Alphonso, you ought to be ashamed of yourself for seducing a young ignorant Creature to leave her family and Friends: However, for this time at least I shall mar your wicked designs. The noble Lady shall be informed of the whole affair, and Agnes must defer playing the Spectre till a better opportunity. Farewell, Segnor—Donna Agnes, let me have the honour of conducting your Ghost-ship back to your apartment.'

She approached the Sopha on which her trembling Pupil was seated, took her by the hand, and prepared to lead her from the Pavilion.

I detained her, and strove by entreaties, soothing, promises, and flattery to win her to my party: But finding all that I could say of no avail, I abandoned the vain attempt.

'Your obstinacy must be its own punishment,' said I; 'But one resource remains to save Agnes and myself, and I shall not hesitate to employ it.'

Terrified at this menace, She again endeavoured to quit the Pavilion; But I seized her by the wrist, and detained her forcibly. At the same moment Theodore, who had followed her into the room, closed the door, and prevented her escape. I took the veil of Agnes: I threw it round the Duenna's head, who uttered such piercing shrieks that in spite of our distance from the Castle, I dreaded their being heard. At length I succeeded in gagging her so compleatly, that She could not produce a single sound. Theodore and myself with some difficulty next contrived to bind her hands and feet with our hand-kerchiefs; And I advised Agnes to regain her chamber with all diligence. I promised that no harm should happen to Cunegonda, bad her remember that on the fifth of May I should be in waiting at the Great Gate of the Castle, and took of her an affectionate farewell. Trembling and uneasy She had scarce power enough to signify her consent to my plans, and fled back to her apartment in disorder and confusion.

In the mean-while Theodore assisted me in carrying off my antiquated Prize. She was hoisted over the wall, placed before me upon my Horse like a Portmanteau, and I galloped away with her from the Castle of Lindenberg. The unlucky Duenna never had made a more disagreeable journey in her life: She was jolted and shaken till She was become little more than an animated Mummy; not to mention her fright, when we waded through a small River, through which it was necessary to pass in order to regain the Village. Before we reached the Inn, I had already determined how to dispose of the troublesome Cunegonda. We entered the Street in which the Inn stood, and while the page knocked, I waited at a little distance. The Landlord opened the door with a Lamp in his hand.

'Give me the light!' said Theodore; 'My Master is coming.'

He snatched the Lamp hastily, and purposely let it fall upon the ground: The Landlord returned to the Kitchen to re-light the Lamp, leaving the door open. I profited by the obscurity, sprang from my Horse with Cunegonda in my arms, darted up stairs, reached my chamber unperceived, and unlocking the door of a spacious Closet, stowed her within it, and then turned the Key. The Landlord and Theodore soon after appeared with lights: The Former expressed himself a little surprised at my returning so late, but asked no impertinent questions. He soon quitted the room, and left me to exult in the success of my undertaking.

I immediately paid a visit to my Prisoner. I strove to persuade her submitting with patience to her temporary confinement. My attempt was unsuccessful. Unable to speak or move, She expressed her fury by her looks, and except at meals I never dared to unbind her, or release her from the Gag. At such times I stood over her with a drawn sword, and protested, that if She uttered a single cry, I would plunge it in her bosom. As soon as She had done eating, the Gag was replaced. I was conscious, that this proceeding was cruel, and could only be justified by the urgency of circumstances: As to Theodore, He had no scruples upon the subject. Cunegonda's captivity entertained him beyond measure. During his abode in the Castle, a continual warfare had been carried on between him and the Duenna; and now that He found his Enemy so absolutely in his power, He triumphed without mercy. He seemed to think of nothing but how to find out new means of plaguing her: Sometimes He affected to pity her misfortune, then laughed at, abused, and mimicked her; He played her a thousand tricks, each more provoking than the other, and amused himself by telling her, that her elopement must have occasioned much surprise at the Baron's. This was in fact the case. No one except Agnes could imagine what was become of Dame Cunegonda: Every hole and corner was searched for her; The Ponds were dragged, and the Woods underwent a thorough examination. Still no Dame Cunegonda made her appearance. Agnes kept the secret, and I kept the Duenna: The Baroness, therefore, remained in total ignorance respecting the old Woman's fate, but suspected her to have perished by suicide. Thus past away five days, during which I had prepared every thing necessary for my enterprise. On quitting Agnes, I had made it my first business to dispatch a Peasant with a letter to Lucas at Munich, ordering him to take care that a Coach and four should arrive about ten o'clock on the fifth of May at the Village of Rosenwald. He obeyed my instructions punctually: The Equipage arrived at the time appointed. As the period of her Lady's elopement drew nearer, Cunegonda's rage increased. I verily believe that spight and passion would have killed her, had I not luckily discovered her prepossession in favour of Cherry-Brandy. With this favourite liquor She was plentifully supplied, and Theodore always remaining to guard her, the Gag was occasionally removed. The liquor seemed to have a wonderful effect in softening the acrimony of her nature; and her confinement not admitting of any other amusement, She got drunk regularly once a day just by way of passing the time.

The fifth of May arrived, a period by me never to be forgotten! Before the Clock struck twelve, I betook myself to the scene of action. Theodore followed me on horse-back. I concealed the Carriage in a spacious Cavern of the Hill, on whose brow the Castle was situated: This Cavern was of considerable depth, and among the peasants was known by the name of Lindenberg Hole. The night was calm and beautiful: The Moonbeams fell upon the antient Towers of the Castle, and shed upon their summits a silver light. All was still around me: Nothing was to be heard except the night-breeze sighing among the leaves, the distant barking of Village Dogs, or the Owl who had established herself in a nook of the deserted Eastern Turret. I heard her melancholy shriek, and looked upwards. She sat upon the ride of a window, which I recognized to be that of the haunted Room. This brought to my remembrance the story of the Bleeding Nun, and I sighed while I reflected on the influence of superstition and weakness of human reason. Suddenly I heard a faint chorus steal upon the silence of the night.

'What can occasion that noise, Theodore?'

'A Stranger of distinction,' replied He, 'passed through the Village to-day in his way to the Castle: He is reported to be the Father of Donna Agnes. Doubtless, the Baron has given an entertainment to celebrate his arrival.'

The Castle-Bell announced the hour of midnight: This was the usual signal for the family to retire to Bed. Soon after I perceived lights in the Castle moving backwards and forwards in different directions. I conjectured the company to be separating. I could hear the heavy doors grate as they opened with difficulty, and as they closed again the rotten Casements rattled in their frames. The chamber of Agnes was on the other side of the Castle. I trembled, lest She should have failed in obtaining the Key of the haunted Room: Through this it was necessary for her to pass, in order to reach the narrow Stair-case by which the Ghost was supposed to descend into the great Hall. Agitated by this apprehension, I kept my eyes constantly fixed upon the window, where I hoped to perceive the friendly glare of a Lamp borne by Agnes. I now heard the massy Gates unbarred. By the candle in his hand I distinguished old Conrad, the Porter. He set the Portal-doors wide open, and retired. The lights in the Castle gradually disappeared, and at length the whole Building was wrapt in darkness.

While I sat upon a broken ridge of the Hill, the stillness of the scene inspired me with melancholy ideas not altogether unpleasing. The Castle which stood full in my sight, formed an object equally awful and picturesque. Its ponderous Walls tinged by the moon with solemn brightness, its old and partly-ruined Towers lifting themselves into the clouds and seeming to frown on the plains around them, its lofty battlements oër-grown with ivy, and folding Gates expanding in honour of the Visionary Inhabitant, made me sensible of a sad and reverential horror. Yet did not these sensations occupy me so fully, as to prevent me from witnessing with impatience the slow progress of time. I approached the Castle, and ventured to walk round it. A few rays of light still glimmered in the chamber of Agnes. I observed them with joy. I was still gazing upon them, when I perceived a figure draw near the window, and the Curtain was carefully closed to conceal the Lamp which burned there. Convinced by this observation that Agnes had not abandoned our plan, I returned with a light heart to my former station.

The half-hour struck! The three-quarters struck! My bosom beat high with hope and expectation. At length the wished-for sound was heard. The Bell tolled 'One,' and the Mansion echoed with the noise loud and solemn. I looked up to the Casement of the haunted Chamber. Scarcely had five minutes elapsed, when the expected light appeared. I was now close to the Tower. The window was not so far from the Ground, but that I fancied I perceived a female figure with a Lamp in her hand moving slowly along the Apartment. The light soon faded away, and all was again dark and gloomy.

Occasional gleams of brightness darted from the Staircase windows, as the lovely Ghost past by them. I traced the light through the Hall: It reached the Portal, and at length I beheld Agnes pass through the folding-gates. She was habited exactly as She had described the Spectre. A chaplet of Beads hung upon her arm; her head was enveloped in a long white veil; Her Nun's dress was stained with blood, and She had taken care to provide herself with a Lamp and dagger. She advanced towards the spot where I stood. I flew to meet her, and clasped her in my arms.

'Agnes!' said I while I pressed her to my bosom,

Agnes! Agnes! Thou art mine!
Agnes! Agnes! I am thine!
In my veins while blood shall roll,
Thou art mine!
I am thine!
Thine my body! Thine my soul!

Terrified and breathless She was unable to speak: She dropt her Lamp and dagger, and sank upon my bosom in silence. I raised her in my arms, and conveyed her to the Carriage. Theodore remained behind in order to release Dame Cunegonda. I also charged him with a letter to the Baroness explaining the whole affair, and entreating her good offices in reconciling Don Gaston to my union with his Daughter. I discovered to her my real name: I proved to her that my birth and expectations justified my pretending to her Niece, and assured her, though it was out of my power to return her love, that I would strive unceasingly to obtain her esteem and friendship.

I stepped into the Carriage, where Agnes was already seated. Theodore closed the door, and the Postillions drove away. At first I was delighted with the rapidity of our progress; But as soon as we were in no danger of pursuit, I called to the Drivers, and bad them moderate their pace. They strove in vain to obey me. The Horses refused to answer the rein, and continued to rush on with astonishing swiftness. The Postillions redoubled their efforts to stop them, but by kicking and plunging the Beasts soon released themselves from this restraint. Uttering a loud shriek, the Drivers were hurled upon the ground. Immediately thick clouds obscured the sky: The winds howled around us, the lightning flashed, and the Thunder roared tremendously. Never did I behold so frightful a Tempest! Terrified by the jar of contending elements, the Horses seemed every moment to increase their speed. Nothing could interrupt their career; They dragged the Carriage through Hedges and Ditches, dashed down the most dangerous precipices, and seemed to vye in swiftness with the rapidity of the winds.

All this while my Companion lay motionless in my arms. Truly alarmed by the magnitude of the danger, I was in vain attempting to recall her to her senses; when a loud crash announced, that a stop was put to our progress in the most disagreeable manner. The Carriage was shattered to pieces. In falling I struck my temple against a flint. The pain of the wound, the violence of the shock, and apprehension for the safety of Agnes combined to over-power me so compleatly, that my senses forsook me, and I lay without animation on the ground.

I probably remained for some time in this situation, since when I opened my eyes, it was broad day-light. Several Peasants were standing round me, and seemed disputing whether my recovery was possible. I spoke German tolerably well. As soon as I could utter an articulate sound, I enquired after Agnes. What was my surprise and distress, when assured by the Peasants, that nobody had been seen answering the description which I gave of her! They told me, that in going to their daily labour they had been alarmed by observing the fragments of my Carriage, and by hearing the groans of an Horse, the only one of the four which remained alive: The other Three lay dead by my side. Nobody was near me when they came up, and much time had been lost, before they succeeded in recovering me. Uneasy beyond expression respecting the fate of my Companion, I besought the Peasants to disperse themselves in search of her: I described her dress, and promised immense rewards to whoever brought me any intelligence. As for myself, it was impossible for me to join in the pursuit: I had broken two of my ribs in the fall: My arm being dislocated hung useless by my side; and my left leg was shattered so terribly, that I never expected to recover its use.

The Peasants complied with my request: All left me except Four, who made a litter of boughs, and prepared to convey me to the neighbouring Town. I enquired its name. It proved to be Ratisbon, and I could scarcely persuade myself that I had travelled to such a distance in a single night. I told the Countrymen, that at one o'clock that morning I had past through the Village of Rosenwald. They shook their heads wistfully, and made signs to each other, that I must certainly be delirious. I was conveyed to a decent Inn, and immediately put to bed. A Physician was sent for, who set my arm with success. He then examined my other hurts, and told me that I need be under no apprehension of the consequences of any of them; But ordered me to keep myself quiet, and be prepared for a tedious and painful cure. I answered him, that if He hoped to keep me quiet, He must first endeavour to procure me some news of a Lady, who had quitted Rosenwald in my company the night before, and had been with me at the moment when the Coach broke down. He smiled, and only replied by advising me to make myself easy, for that all proper care should be taken of me. As He quitted me, the Hostess met him at the door of the room.

'The Gentleman is not quite in his right senses,' I heard him say to her in a low voice; ' 'Tis the natural consequence of his fall, but that will soon be over.'

One after another the Peasants returned to the Inn, and informed me that no traces had been discovered of my unfortunate Mistress. Uneasiness now became despair. I entreated them to renew their search in the most urgent terms, doubling the promises which I had already made them. My wild and frantic manner confirmed the bye-standers in the idea of my being delirious. No signs of the Lady having appeared, they believed her to be a creature fabricated by my over-heated brain, and paid no attention to my entreaties. However, the Hostess assured me that a fresh enquiry should be made, but I found afterwards that her promise was only given to quiet me. No further steps were taken in the business.

Though my Baggage was left at Munich under the care of my French Servant, having prepared myself for a long journey, my purse was amply furnished: Besides my equipage proved me to be of distinction, and in consequence all possible attention was paid me at the Inn. The day passed away: Still no news arrived of Agnes. The anxiety of fear now gave place to despondency. I ceased to rave about her, and was plunged in the depth of melancholy reflections. Perceiving me to be silent and tranquil, my Attendants believed my delirium to have abated, and that my malady had taken a favourable turn. According to the Physician's order I swallowed a composing medicine; and as soon as the night shut in, my attendants withdrew, and left me to repose.

That repose I wooed in vain. The agitation of my bosom chased away sleep. Restless in my mind, in spite of the fatigue of my body I continued to toss about from side to side, till the Clock in a neighbouring Steeple struck 'One.' As I listened to the mournful hollow sound, and heard it die away in the wind, I felt a sudden chillness spread itself over my body. I shuddered without knowing wherefore; Cold dews poured down my forehead, and my hair stood bristling with alarm. Suddenly I heard slow and heavy steps ascending the stair-case. By an involuntary movement I started up in my bed, and drew back the curtain. A single rush-light, which glimmered upon the hearth shed a faint gleam through the apartment, which was hung with tapestry. The door was thrown open with violence. A figure entered, and drew near my Bed with solemn measured steps. With trembling apprehension I examined this midnight Visitor. God Almighty! It was the Bleeding Nun! It was my lost Companion! Her face was still veiled, but She no longer held her Lamp and dagger. She lifted up her veil slowly. What a sight presented itself to my startled eyes! I beheld before me an animated Corse. Her countenance was long and haggard; Her cheeks and lips were bloodless; The paleness of death was spread over her features, and her eye-balls fixed stedfastly upon me were lustreless and hollow.

I gazed upon the Spectre with horror too great to be described. My blood was frozen in my veins. I would have called for aid, but the sound expired, ere it could pass my lips. My nerves were bound up in impotence, and I remained in the same attitude inanimate as a Statue.

The visionary Nun looked upon me for some minutes in silence: There was something petrifying in her regard. At length in a low sepulchral voice She pronounced the following words.

> "Raymond! Raymond! Thou art mine!
> Raymond! Raymond! I am thine!
> In thy veins while blood shall roll,
> I am thine!
> Thou art mine!
> Mine thy body! Mine thy soul!——"

Breathless with fear, I listened while She repeated my own expressions. The Apparition seated herself opposite to me at the foot of the Bed, and was silent. Her eyes were fixed earnestly upon mine: They seemed endowed with the property of the Rattle-snake's, for I strove in vain to look off her. My eyes were fascinated, and I had not the power of withdrawing them from the Spectre's.

In this attitude She remained for a whole long hour without speaking or moving; nor was I able to do either. At length the Clock struck two. The Apparition rose from her seat, and approached the side of the bed. She grasped with her icy fingers my hand which hung lifeless upon the Coverture, and pressing her cold lips to mine, again repeated,

> *"Raymond! Raymond! Thou art mine!*
> *Raymond! Raymond! I am thine! &c.—"*

She then dropped my hand, quitted the chamber with slow steps, and the Door closed after her. Till that moment the faculties of my body had been all suspended; Those of my mind had alone been waking. The charm now ceased to operate: The blood which had been frozen in my veins rushed back to my heart with violence: I uttered a deep groan, and sank lifeless upon my pillow.

The adjoining room was only separated from mine by a thin partition: It was occupied by the Host and his Wife: The Former was rouzed by my groan, and immediately hastened to my chamber: The Hostess soon followed him. With some difficulty they succeeded in restoring me to my senses, and immediately sent for the Physician, who arrived in all diligence. He declared my fever to be very much increased, and that if I continued to suffer such violent agitation, He would not take upon him to ensure my life. Some medicines which He gave me, in some degree tranquillized my spirits. I fell into a sort of slumber towards day-break; But fearful dreams prevented me from deriving any benefit from my repose. Agnes and the Bleeding Nun presented themselves by turns to my fancy, and combined to harass and torment me. I awoke fatigued and unrefreshed. My fever seemed rather augmented than diminished; The agitation of my mind impeded my fractured bones from knitting: I had frequent fainting fits, and during the whole day the Physician judged it expedient not to quit me for two hours together.

The singularity of my adventure made me determine to conceal it from every one, since I could not expect that a circumstance so strange should gain credit. I was very uneasy about Agnes. I knew not what She would think at not finding me at the rendez-vous, and dreaded her entertaining suspicions of my fidelity. However, I depended upon Theodore's discretion, and trusted, that my letter to the Baroness would convince her of the rectitude of my intentions. These considerations somewhat lightened my inquietude upon her account: But the impression left upon my mind by my nocturnal Visitor, grew stronger with every succeeding moment. The night drew near; I dreaded its arrival. Yet I strove to persuade myself that the Ghost would appear no more, and at all events I desired, that a Servant might sit up in my chamber.

The fatigue of my body from not having slept on the former night co-operating with the strong opiates administered to me in profusion at length procured me that repose of which I was so much in need. I sank into a profound and tranquil slumber, and had already slept for some hours, when the neighbouring Clock rouzed me by striking 'One'. Its sound brought with it to my memory all the horrors of the night before. The same cold shivering seized me. I started up in my bed, and perceived the Servant fast asleep in an armed-Chair near me. I called him by his name: He made no answer. I shook him forcibly by the arm, and strove in vain to wake him. He was perfectly insensible to my efforts. I now heard the heavy steps ascending the stair-case; The Door was thrown open, and again the Bleeding Nun stood before me. Once more my limbs were chained in second infancy. Once more I heard those fatal words repeated,

> *"Raymond! Raymond! Thou art mine!*
> *Raymond! Raymond! I am thine! &c.—"*

The scene which had shocked me so sensibly on the former night, was again presented. The Spectre again pressed her lips to mine, again touched me with her rotting fingers, and as on her first appearance, quitted the chamber as soon as the Clock told 'Two.'

Even night was this repeated. Far from growing accustomed to the Ghost, every succeeding visit inspired me with greater horror. Her idea pursued me continually, and I became the prey of habitual melancholy. The constant agitation of my mind naturally retarded the re-establishment of my health. Several months elapsed before I was able to quit my bed; and when at length I was moved to a Sopha, I was so faint, spiritless, and emaciated, that I could not cross the room without assistance. The looks of my Attendants sufficiently denoted the little hope, which they entertained of my recovery. The profound sadness, which oppressed me without remission made the Physician consider me to be an Hypochondriac. The cause of my distress I carefully concealed in my own bosom, for I knew that no one could give me relief: The Ghost was not even visible to any eye but mine. I had frequently caused Attendants to sit up in my room: But the moment that the Clock struck 'One,' irresistible slumber seized them, nor left them till the departure of the Ghost.

You may be surprized, that during this time I made no enquiries after your Sister. Theodore, who with difficulty had discovered my abode, had quieted my apprehensions for her safety: At the same time He convinced me, that all attempts to release her from captivity must be fruitless, till I should be in a condition to return to Spain. The particulars of her adventure which I shall now relate to you, were partly communicated to me by Theodore, and partly by Agnes herself.

On the fatal night when her elopement was to have taken place, accident had not permitted her to quit her chamber at the appointed time. At length She ventured into the haunted room, descended the stair-case leading into the Hall, found the Gates open as She expected, and left the Castle unobserved. What was her surprize at not finding me ready to receive her! She examined the Cavern, ranged through every Alley of the neighbouring wood, and passed two full hours in this fruitless enquiry. She could discover no traces either of me or of the Carriage. Alarmed and disappointed, her only resource was to return to the Castle before the Baroness missed her: But here She found herself in a fresh embarrassment. The Bell had already tolled 'Two:' The Ghostly hour was past, and the careful Porter had locked the folding gates. After much irresolution She ventured to knock softly. Luckily for her Conrad was still awake: He heard the noise, and rose, murmuring at being called up a second time. No sooner had He opened one of the Doors, and beheld the supposed Apparition waiting there for admittance, than He uttered a loud cry, and sank upon his knees. Agnes profited by his terror. She glided by him, flew to her own apartment, and having thrown off her Spectre's trappings, retired to bed endeavouring in vain to account for my disappearing.

In the mean while Theodore having seen my Carriage drive off with the false Agnes, returned joyfully to the Village. The next morning He released Cunegonda from her confinement, and accompanied her to the Castle. There He found the Baron, his Lady, and Don Gaston, disputing together upon the Porter's relation. All of them agreed in believing the existence of Spectres: But the Latter contended, that for a Ghost to knock for admittance was a proceeding till then unwitnessed, and totally incompatible with the immaterial nature of a Spirit. They were still discussing this subject, when the Page appeared with Cunegonda, and cleared up the mystery. On hearing his deposition, it was agreed unanimously that the Agnes whom Theodore had seen step into my Carriage must have been the Bleeding Nun, and that the Ghost who had terrified Conrad was no other than Don Gaston's Daughter.

The first surprize which this discovery occasioned being over, the Baroness resolved to make it of use in persuading her Niece to take the veil. Fearing lest so advantageous an establishment for his Daughter should induce Don Gaston to renounce his resolution, She suppressed my letter, and continued to represent me as a needy unknown Adventurer. A childish vanity had led me to conceal my real name even from my Mistress; I wished to be loved for myself, not for being the Son and Heir of the Marquis de las

Cisternas. The consequence was, that my rank was known to no one in the Castle except the Baroness, and She took good care to confine the knowledge to her own breast. Don Gaston having approved his Sister's design, Agnes was summoned to appear before them. She was taxed with having meditated an elopement, obliged to make a full confession, and was amazed at the gentleness with which it was received: But what was her affliction, when informed that the failure of her project must be attributed to me! Cunegonda, tutored by the Baroness, told her that when I released her, I had desired her to inform her Lady that our connexion was at an end, that the whole affair was occasioned by a false report, and that it by no means suited my circumstances to marry a Woman without fortune or expectations.

To this account my sudden disappearing gave but too great an air of probability. Theodore, who could have contradicted the story, by Donna Rodolpha's order was kept out of her sight: What proved a still greater confirmation of my being an Impostor, was the arrival of a letter from yourself declaring, that you had no sort of acquaintance with Alphonso d'Alvarada. These seeming proofs of my perfidy, aided by the artful insinuations of her Aunt, by Cunegonda's flattery, and her Father's threats and anger, entirely conquered your Sister's repugnance to a Convent. Incensed at my behaviour, and disgusted with the world in general, She consented to receive the veil. She past another Month at the Castle of Lindenberg, during which my non-appearance confirmed her in her resolution, and then accompanied Don Gaston into Spain. Theodore was now set at liberty. He hastened to Munich, where I had promised to let him hear from me; But finding from Lucas that I had never arrived there, He pursued his search with indefatigable perseverance, and at length succeeded in rejoining me at Ratisbon.

So much was I altered, that scarcely could He recollect my features: The distress visible upon his sufficiently testified how lively was the interest which He felt for me. The society of this amiable Boy, whom I had always considered rather as a Companion than a Servant, was now my only comfort. His conversation was gay yet sensible, and his observations shrewd and entertaining: He had picked up much more knowledge than is usual at his Age: But what rendered him most agreeable to me, was his having a delightful voice, and some skill in Music. He had also acquired some taste in poetry, and even ventured sometimes to write verses himself. He occasionally composed little Ballads in Spanish, his compositions were but indifferent, I must confess; yet they were pleasing to me from their novelty, and hearing him sing them to his guitar was the only amusement, which I was capable of receiving. Theodore perceived well enough that something preyed upon my mind; But as I concealed the cause of my grief even from him, Respect would not permit him to pry into my secrets.

One Evening I was lying upon my Sopha, plunged in reflections very far from agreeable: Theodore amused himself by observing from the window a Battle between two Postillions, who were quarrelling in the Inn-yard.

'Ha! Ha!' cried He suddenly; 'Yonder is the Great Mogul.'

'Who?' said I.

'Only a Man, who made me a strange speech at Munich.'

'What was the purport of it?'

'Now you put me in mind of it, Segnor, it was a kind of message to you; but truly it was not worth delivering. I believe the Fellow to be mad for my part. When I came to Munich in search of you, I found him living at 'The King of the Romans,' and the Host gave me an odd account of him. By his accent He is supposed to be a Foreigner, but of what Country nobody can tell. He seemed to have no acquaintance in the Town, spoke very seldom, and never was seen to smile. He had neither Servants or Baggage; But his Purse seemed well-furnished, and He did much good in the Town. Some supposed him to be an Arabian Astrologer, Others to be a Travelling Mountebank, and many declared that He was Doctor Faustus, whom the Devil had sent back to Germany. The Landlord, however told me, that He had the best reasons to believe him to be the Great Mogul incognito.'

'But the strange speech, Theodore.'

'True, I had almost forgotten the speech: Indeed for that matter, it would not have been a great loss, if I had forgotten it altogether. You are to know, Segnor, that while I was enquiring about you of the Landlord, this Stranger passed by. He stopped, and looked at me earnestly. 'Youth!' said He in a solemn voice, 'He whom you seek, has found that, which He would fain lose. My hand alone can dry up the blood: Bid your Master wish for me, when the Clock strikes, 'One.'

'How?' cried I, starting from my Sopha. [The words which Theodore had repeated, seemed to imply the Stranger's knowledge of my secret] 'Fly to him, my Boy! Entreat him to grant me one moment's conversation!'

Theodore was surprised at the vivacity of my manner: However, He asked no questions, but hastened to obey me. I waited his return impatiently. But a short space of time had elapsed when He again appeared, and ushered the expected Guest into my chamber. He was a Man of majestic presence: His countenance was strongly marked, and his eyes were large, black, and sparkling: Yet there was a something in his look, which the moment that I saw him, inspired me with a secret awe, not to say horror. He was drest plainly, his hair was unpowdered, and a band of black velvet which encircled his fore-head, spread over his features an additional gloom. His countenance wore the marks of profound melancholy; his step was slow, and his manner grave, stately, and solemn.

He saluted me with politeness; and having replied to the usual compliments of introduction, He motioned to Theodore to quit the chamber. The Page instantly with-drew.

'I know your business,' said He, without giving me time to speak. 'I have the power of releasing you from your nightly Visitor; But this cannot be done before Sunday. On the hour when the Sabbath Morning breaks, Spirits of darkness have least influence over Mortals. After Saturday the Nun shall visit you no more.'

'May I not enquire,' said I, 'by what means you are in possession of a secret, which I have carefully concealed from the knowledge of every one?'

'How can I be ignorant of your distress, when their cause at this moment stands beside you?'

I started. The Stranger continued.

'Though to you only visible for one hour in the twenty-four, neither day or night does She ever quit you; Nor will She ever quit you till you have granted her request.'

'And what is that request?'

'That She must herself explain: It lies not in my knowledge. Wait with patience for the night of Saturday: All shall be then cleared up.'

I dared not press him further. He soon after changed the conversation, and talked of various matters. He named People who had ceased to exist for many Centuries, and yet with whom He appeared to have been personally acquainted. I could not mention a Country however distant which He had not visited, nor could I sufficiently admire the extent, and variety of his information. I remarked to him that having travelled, seen, and known so much, must have given him infinite pleasure. He shook his head mournfully.

'No one,' He replied, 'is adequate to comprehending the misery of my lot! Fate obliges me to be constantly in movement: I am not permitted to pass more than a fortnight in the same place. I have no Friend in the world, and from the restlessness of my destiny I never can acquire one. Fain would I lay down my miserable life, for I envy those who enjoy the quiet of the Grave: But Death eludes me, and flies from my embrace. In vain do I throw myself in the way of danger. I plunge into the Ocean; The Waves throw me back with abhorrence upon the shore: I rush into fire; The flames recoil at my approach: I oppose myself to the fury of Banditti; Their swords become blunted, and break against my breast: The hungry Tiger shudders at my approach, and the Alligator flies from a Monster more horrible than itself. God has set his seal upon me, and all his Creatures respect this fatal mark!'

He put his hand to the velvet, which was bound round his fore-head. There was in his eyes an expression of fury, despair, and malevolence, that struck horror to my very soul. An involuntary convulsion made me shudder. The Stranger perceived it.

'Such is the curse imposed on me,' he continued: 'I am doomed to inspire all who look on me with terror and detestation. You already feel the influence of the charm, and with every succeeding moment will feel it more. I will not add to your sufferings by my presence. Farewell till Saturday. As soon as the Clock strikes twelve, expect me at your chamber-door.'

Having said this He departed, leaving me in astonishment at the mysterious turn of his manner and conversation.

His assurances that I should soon be relieved from the Apparition's visits, produced a good effect upon my constitution. Theodore, whom I rather treated as an adopted Child than a Domestic, was surprized at his return to observe the amendment in my looks. He congratulated me on this symptom of returning health, and declared himself delighted at my having received so much benefit from my conference with the Great Mogul. Upon enquiry I found that the Stranger had already past eight days in Ratisbon: According to his own account, therefore, He was only to remain there six days longer. Saturday was still at the distance of Three. Oh! with what impatience did I expect its arrival! In the interim, the Bleeding Nun continued her nocturnal visits; But hoping soon to be released from them altogether, the effects which they produced on me became less violent than before.

The wished-for night arrived. To avoid creating suspicion I retired to bed at my usual hour: But as soon as my Attendants had left me, I dressed myself again, and prepared for the Stranger's reception. He entered my room upon the turn of midnight. A small Chest was in his hand, which He placed near the Stove. He saluted me without speaking; I returned the compliment, observing an equal silence. He then opened his Chest. The first thing which He produced, was a small wooden Crucifix: He sank upon his knees, gazed upon it mournfully, and cast his eyes towards heaven. He seemed to be praying devoutly. At length He bowed his head respectfully, kissed the Crucifix thrice, and quitted his kneeling posture. He next drew from the Chest a covered Goblet: With the liquor which it contained, and which appeared to be blood, He sprinkled the floor, and then dipping in it one end of the Crucifix, He described a circle in the middle of the room. Round about this He placed various reliques, sculls, thigh-bones &c; I observed, that He disposed them all in the forms of Crosses. Lastly He took out a large Bible, and beckoned me to follow him into the Circle. I obeyed.

'Be cautious not to utter a syllable!' whispered the Stranger; 'Step not out of the circle, and as you love yourself, dare not to look upon my face!'

Holding the Crucifix in one hand, the Bible in the other, He seemed to read with profound attention. The Clock struck 'One'! As usual I heard the Spectre's steps upon the Stair-case: But I was not seized with the accustomed shivering. I waited her approach with confidence. She entered the room, drew near the Circle, and stopped. The Stranger muttered some words, to me unintelligible. Then raising his head from the Book, and extending the Crucifix towards the Ghost, He pronounced in a voice distinct and solemn,

'Beatrice! Beatrice! Beatrice!'

'What wouldst Thou?' replied the Apparition in a hollow faltering tone.

'What disturbs thy sleep? Why dost thou afflict and torture this Youth? How can rest be restored to thy unquiet Spirit?'

'I dare not tell!—I must not tell!—Fain would I repose in my Grave, but stern commands force me to prolong my punishment!'

'Knowest Thou this blood? Knowest Thou in whose veins it flowed? Beatrice! Beatrice! In his name I charge thee to answer me!'

'I dare not disobey my taskers.'

'Darest Thou disobey Me?'

He spoke in a commanding tone, and drew the sable band from his fore-head. In spite of his injunctions to the contrary, Curiosity would not suffer me to keep my eyes off his face: I raised them, and beheld a burning Cross impressed upon his brow. For the horror with which this object inspired me I cannot account, but I never felt its equal! My senses left me for some moments; A mysterious dread overcame my courage, and had not the Exorciser caught my hand, I should have fallen out of the Circle.

When I recovered myself, I perceived that the burning Cross had produced an effect no less violent upon the Spectre. Her countenance expressed reverence, and horror, and her visionary limbs were shaken by fear.

'Yes!' She said at length; 'I tremble at that mark!—I respect it!—I obey you! Know then, that my bones lie still unburied: They rot in the obscurity of Lindenberg Hole. None but this Youth has the right of consigning them to the Grave. His own lips have made over to me his body and his soul: Never will I give back his promise, never shall He know a night devoid of terror, unless He engages to collect my mouldering bones, and deposit them in the family vault of his Andalusian Castle. Then let thirty Masses be said for the repose of my Spirit, and I trouble this world no more. Now let me depart! Those flames are scorching!'

He let the hand drop slowly which held the Crucifix, and which till then He had pointed towards her. The apparition bowed her head, and her form melted into air. The Exorciser led me out of the Circle. He replaced the Bible &c. in the Chest, and then addressed himself to me, who stood near him speechless from astonishment.

'Don Raymond, you have heard the conditions on which repose is promised you. Be it your business to fulfil them to the letter. For me nothing more remains than to clear up the darkness still spread over the Spectre's History, and inform you that when living Beatrice bore the name of las Cisternas. She was the great Aunt of your Grand-father: In quality of your relation, her ashes demand respect from you, though the enormity of her crimes must excite your abhorrence. The nature of those crimes no one is more capable of explaining to you than myself: I was personally acquainted with the holy Man who proscribed her nocturnal riots in the Castle of Lindenberg, and I hold this narrative from his own lips.

'Beatrice de las Cisternas took the veil at an early age, not by her own choice, but at the express command of her Parents. She was then too young to regret the pleasures, of which her profession deprived her: But no sooner did her warm and voluptuous character begin to be developed, than She abandoned herself freely to the impulse of her passions, and seized the first opportunity to procure their gratification. This opportunity was at length presented, after many obstacles which only added new force to her desires. She contrived to elope from the Convent, and fled to Germany with the Baron Lindenberg. She lived at his Castle several months as his avowed Concubine: All Bavaria was scandalized by her impudent and abandoned conduct. Her feasts vied in luxury with Cleopatra's, and Lindenberg became the Theatre of the most unbridled debauchery. Not satisfied with displaying the incontinence of a Prostitute, She professed herself an Atheist: She took every opportunity to scoff at her monastic vows, and loaded with ridicule the most sacred ceremonies of Religion.

'Possessed of a character so depraved, She did not long confine her affections to one object. Soon after her arrival at the Castle, the Baron's younger Brother attracted her notice by his strong-marked features, gigantic Stature, and Herculean limbs. She was not of an humour to keep her inclinations long unknown; But She found in Otto von Lindenberg her equal in depravity. He returned her passion just sufficiently to increase it; and when He had worked it up to the desired pitch, He fixed the price of his love at his Brother's murder. The Wretch consented to this horrible agreement. A night was pitched upon for perpetrating the deed. Otto, who resided on a small Estate a few miles distant from the Castle, promised that at One in the morning He would be waiting for her at Lindenberg Hole; that He would bring with him a party of chosen Friends, by whose aid He doubted not being able to make himself Master of the Castle; and that his next step should be the uniting her hand to his. It was this last promise, which overruled every scruple of Beatrice, since in spite of his affection for her, the Baron had declared positively, that He never would make her his Wife.

'The fatal night arrived. The Baron slept in the arms of his perfidious Mistress, when the Castle-Bell struck 'One.' Immediately Beatrice drew a dagger from underneath the pillow, and plunged it in her Paramour's heart. The Baron uttered a single dreadful groan, and expired. The Murderess quitted her bed hastily, took a Lamp in one hand, in the other the bloody dagger, and bent her course towards the cavern. The Porter dared not to refuse opening the Gates to one more dreaded in the Castle, than its Master. Beatrice reached Lindenberg Hole unopposed, where according to promise

She found Otto waiting for her. He received, and listened to her narrative with transport: But ere She had time to ask why He came unaccompanied, He convinced her that He wished for no witnesses to their interview. Anxious to conceal his share in the murder, and to free himself from a Woman, whose violent and atrocious character made him tremble with reason for his own safety, He had resolved on the destruction of his wretched Agent. Rushing upon her suddenly, He wrested the dagger from her hand: He plunged it still reeking with his Brother's blood in her bosom, and put an end to her existence by repeated blows.

'Otto now succeeded to the Barony of Lindenberg. The murder was attributed solely to the fugitive Nun, and no one suspected him to have persuaded her to the action. But though his crime was unpunished by Man, God's justice permitted him not to enjoy in peace his blood-stained honours. Her bones lying still unburied in the Cave, the restless soul of Beatrice continued to inhabit the Castle. Drest in her religious habit in memory of her vows broken to heaven, furnished with the dagger which had drank the blood of her Paramour, and holding the Lamp which had guided her flying steps, every night did She stand before the Bed of Otto. The most dreadful confusion reigned through the Castle; The vaulted chambers resounded with shrieks and groans; And the Spectre, as She ranged along the antique Galleries, uttered an incoherent mixture of prayers and blasphemies. Otto was unable to withstand the shock, which He felt at this fearful Vision: Its horror increased with every succeeding appearance: His alarm at length became so insupportable, that his heart burst, and one morning He was found in his bed totally deprived of warmth and animation. His death did not put an end to the nocturnal riots. The bones of Beatrice continued to lie unburied, and her Ghost continued to haunt the Castle.

'The domains of Lindenberg now fell to a distant Relation. But terrified by the accounts given him of the Bleeding Nun [So was the Spectre called by the multitude,] the new Baron called to his assistance a celebrated Exorciser. This holy Man succeeded in obliging her to temporary repose; But though She discovered to him her history, He was not permitted to reveal it to others, or cause her skeleton to be removed to hallowed ground. That Office was reserved for you, and till your coming her Ghost was doomed to wander about the Castle, and lament the crime which She had there committed. However, the Exorciser obliged her to silence during his lifetime. So long as He existed, the haunted chamber was shut up, and the Spectre was invisible. At his death which happened in five years after, She again appeared, but only once on every fifth year, on the same day and at the same hour when She plunged her Knife in the heart of her sleeping Lover: She then visited the Cavern which held her mouldering skeleton, returned to the Castle as soon as the Clock struck 'Two,' and was seen no more till the next five years had elapsed.

'She was doomed to suffer during the space of a Century. That period is past. Nothing now remains but to consign to the Grave the ashes of Beatrice. I have been the means of releasing you from your visionary Tormentor; and amidst all the sorrows which oppress me, to think that I have been of use to you, is some consolation. Youth, farewell! May the Ghost of your Relation enjoy that rest in the Tomb, which the Almighty's vengeance has denied to me for ever!'

Here the Stranger prepared to quit the apartment.

'Stay yet one moment!' said I; 'You have satisfied my curiosity with regard to the Spectre, but you leave me in prey to yet greater respecting yourself. Deign to inform me, to whom I am under such real obligations. You mention circumstances long past, and persons long dead: You were personally acquainted with the Exorciser, who by your own account has been deceased near a Century. How am I to account for this? What means that burning Cross upon your fore-head, and why did the sight of it strike such horror to my soul?'

On these points He for some time refused to satisfy me. At length overcome by my entreaties, He consented to clear up the whole, on condition that I would defer his explanation till the next day. With this request I was obliged to comply, and He left me. In the Morning my first care was to enquire after the mysterious Stranger. Conceive my disappointment, when informed that He had already quitted Ratisbon. I dispatched messengers in pursuit of him but in vain. No traces of the Fugitive were discovered. Since that moment I never have heard any more of him, and 'tis most probable that I never shall.'

[Lorenzo here interrupted his Friend's narrative.

'How?' said He; 'You have never discovered who He was, or even formed a guess?'

'Pardon me,' replied the Marquis; 'When I related this adventure to my Uncle, the Cardinal-Duke, He told me that He had no doubt of this singular Man's being the celebrated Character known universally by the name of '*the wandering Jew.*' His not being permitted to pass more than fourteen days on the same spot, the burning Cross impressed upon his fore-head, the effect which it produced upon the Beholders, and many other circumstances give this supposition the colour of truth. The Cardinal is fully persuaded of it; and for my own part I am inclined to adopt the only solution which offers itself to this riddle. I return to the narrative from which I have disgressed.']

From this period I recovered my health so rapidly as to astonish my Physicians. The Bleeding Nun appeared no more, and I was soon able to set out for Lindenberg. The Baron received me with open arms. I confided to him the sequel of my adventure; and He was not a little pleased to find, that his Mansion would be no longer troubled with the Phantom's quiennial visits. I was sorry to perceive, that absence had not weakened Donna

Rodolpha's imprudent passion. In a private conversation, which I had with her during my short stay at the Castle, She renewed her attempts to persuade me to return her affection. Regarding her as the primary cause of all my sufferings, I entertained for her no other sentiment than disgust. The Skeleton of Beatrice was found in the place which She had mentioned. This being all that I sought at Lindenberg, I hastened to quit the Baron's domains, equally anxious to perform the obsequies of the murdered Nun, and escape the importunity of a Woman whom I detested. I departed, followed by Donna Rodolpha's menaces that my contempt should not be long unpunished.

I now bent my course towards Spain with all diligence. Lucas with my Baggage had joined me during my abode at Lindenberg. I arrived in my native Country without any accident, and immediately proceeded to my Father's Castle in Andalusia. The remains of Beatrice were deposited in the family vault, all due ceremonies performed, and the number of Masses said which She had required. Nothing now hindered me from employing all my endeavours to discover the retreat of Agnes. The Baroness had assured me, that her Niece had already taken the veil: This intelligence I suspected to have been forged by jealousy, and hoped to find my Mistress still at liberty to accept my hand. I enquired after her family; I found that before her Daughter could reach Madrid, Donna Inesilla was no more: You, my dear Lorenzo, were said to be abroad, but where I could not discover: Your Father was in a distant Province on a visit to the Duke de Medina, and as to Agnes no one could or would inform me what was become of her. Theodore according to promise had returned to Strasbourg, where He found his Grand-father dead, and Marguerite in possession of his fortune. All her persuasions to remain with her were fruitless: He quitted her a second time, and followed me to Madrid. He exerted himself to the utmost in forwarding my search: But our united endeavours were unattended by success. The retreat, which concealed Agnes remained an impenetrable mystery, and I began to abandon all hopes of recovering her.

About eight months ago I was returning to my Hotel in a melancholy humour, having past the evening at the Play-House. The Night was dark, and I was unaccompanied. Plunged in reflections which were far from being agreeable, I perceived not that three Men had followed me from the Theatre; till, on turning into an unfrequented Street, they all attacked me at the same time with the utmost fury. I sprang back a few paces, drew my sword, and threw my cloak over my left arm. The obscurity of the night was in my favour. For the most part the blows of the Assassins, being aimed at random, failed to touch me. I at length was fortunate enough to lay one of my Adversaries at my feet; But before this I had already received so many wounds. and was so warmly pressed, that my destruction would have been inevitable, had not the clashing of swords called a Cavalier to my assistance.

He ran towards me with his sword drawn: Several Domestics followed him with torches. His arrival made the combat equal: Yet would not the Bravoes abandon their design, till the Servants were on the point of joining us. They then fled away, and we lost them in the obscurity.

The Stranger now addressed himself to me with politeness, and enquired whether I was wounded. Faint with the loss of blood, I could scarcely thank him for his seasonable aid, and entreat him to let some of his Servants convey me to the Hotel de las Cisternas. I no sooner mentioned the name than He profest himself an acquaintance of my Father's, and declared that He would not permit my being transported to such a distance, before my wounds had been examined. He added, that his House was hard by, and begged me to accompany him thither. His manner was so earnest, that I could not reject his offer, and leaning upon his arm, a few minutes brought me to the Porch of a magnificent Hotel.

On entering the House, an old grey-headed Domestic came to welcome my Conductor: He enquired when the Duke, his Master, meant to quit the Country, and was answered that He would remain there yet some months. My Deliverer then desired the family-Surgeon to be summoned without delay. His orders were obeyed. I was seated upon a Sopha in a noble apartment; and my wounds being examined, they were declared to be very slight. The Surgeon, however, advised me not to expose myself to the night-air; and the Stranger pressed me so earnestly to take a bed in his House, that I consented to remain where I was for the present.

Being now left alone with my Deliverer, I took the opportunity of thanking him in more express terms, than I had done hitherto: But He begged me to be silent upon the subject.

'I esteem myself happy,' said He, 'in having had it in my power to render you this little service; and I shall think myself eternally obliged to my Daughter for detaining me so late at the Convent of St Clare. The high esteem in which I have ever held the Marquis de las Cisternas, though accident has not permitted our being so intimate as I could wish, makes me rejoice in the opportunity of making his Son's acquaintance. I am certain that my Brother in whose House you now are, will lament his not being at Madrid to receive you himself: But in the Duke's absence I am Master of the family, and may assure you in his name, that every thing in the Hotel de Medina is perfectly at your disposal.'

Conceive my surprize, Lorenzo, at discovering in the person of my Preserver Don Gaston de Medina: It was only to be equalled by my secret satisfaction at the assurance, that Agnes inhabited the Convent of St Clare. This latter sensation was not a little weakened, when in answer to my seemingly indifferent questions He told me, that his Daughter had really taken the veil. I suffered not my grief at this circumstance to take root in my mind: I flattered myself with the idea that my Uncle's credit at the Court of

Rome would remove this obstacle, and that without difficulty I should obtain for my Mistress a dispensation from her vows. Buoyed up with this hope I calmed the uneasiness of my bosom; and I redoubled my endeavours to appear grateful for the attention, and pleased with the society of Don Gaston.

A Domestic now entered the room, and informed me that the Bravo whom I had wounded, discovered some signs of life. I desired that He might be carried to my Father's Hotel, and that as soon as He recovered his voice, I would examine him respecting his reasons for attempting my life. I was answered, that He was already able to speak, though with difficulty: Don Gaston's curiosity made him press me to interrogate the Assassin in his presence, but this curiosity I was by no means inclined to gratify. One reason was, that doubting from whence the blow came, I was unwilling to place before Don Gaston's eyes the guilt of a Sister: Another was, that I feared to be recognized for Alphonso d'Alvarada, and precautions taken in consequence to keep me from the sight of Agnes. To avow my passion for his Daughter, and endeavour to make him enter into my schemes, what I knew of Don Gaston's character convinced me would be an imprudent step: and considering it to be essential that He should know me for no other than the Condé de las Cisternas, I was determined not to let him hear the Bravo's confession. I insinuated to him, that as I suspected a Lady to be concerned in the Business, whose name might accidentally escape from the Assassin, it was necessary for me to examine the Man in private. Don Gaston's delicacy would not permit his urging the point any longer, and in consequence the Bravo was conveyed to my Hotel.

The next Morning I took leave of my Host, who was to return to the Duke on the same day. My wounds had been so trifling, that except being obliged to wear my arm in a sling for a short time, I felt no inconvenience from the night's adventure. The Surgeon who examined the Bravo's wound declared it to be mortal: He had just time to confess, that He had been instigated to murder me by the revengeful Donna Rodolpha, and expired in a few minutes after.

All my thoughts were now bent upon gettii.g to the speech of my lovely Nun. Theodore set himself to work, and for this time with better success. He attacked the Gardener of St Clare so forcibly with bribes and promises, that the Old Man was entirely gained over to my interests; and it was settled, that I should be introduced into the Convent in the character of his Assistant. The plan was put into execution without delay. Disguised in a common habit, and a black patch covering one of my eyes, I was presented to the Lady Prioress, who condescended to approve of the Gardener's choice. I immediately entered upon my employment. Botany having been a favourite study with me, I was by no means at a loss in my new station. For some days I continued to work in the Convent-Garden without meeting the

Object of my disguise: On the fourth Morning I was more successful. I heard the voice of Agnes, and was speeding towards the sound, when the sight of the Domina stopped me. I drew back with caution, and concealed myself behind a thick clump of Trees.

The Prioress advanced, and seated herself with Agnes on a Bench at no great distance. I heard her in an angry tone blame her Companion's continual melancholy: She told her that to weep the loss of any Lover in her situation was a crime; But that to weep the loss of a faithless one was folly and absurdity in the extreme. Agnes replied in so low a voice that I could not distinguish her words, but I perceived that She used terms of gentleness and submission. The conversation was interrupted by the arrival of a young Pensioner, who informed the Domina that She was waited for in the Parlour. The old Lady rose, kissed the cheek of Agnes, and retired. The new-comer remained. Agnes spoke much to her in praise of somebody whom I could not make out, but her Auditor seemed highly delighted, and interested by the conversation. The Nun showed her several letters; the Other perused them with evident pleasure, obtained permission to copy them, and withdrew for that purpose to my great satisfaction.

No sooner was She out of sight, than I quitted my concealment. Fearing to alarm my lovely Mistress, I drew near her gently, intending to discover myself by degrees. But who for a moment can deceive the eyes of love? She raised her head at my approach, and recognised me in spite of my disguise at a single glance. She rose hastily from her seat with an exclamation of surprize, and attempted to retire; But I followed her, detained her, and entreated to be heard. Persuaded of my falsehood She refused to listen to me, and ordered me positively to quit the Garden. It was now my turn to refuse. I protested, that however dangerous might be the consequences, I would not leave her till She had heard my justification. I assured her, that She had been deceived by the artifices of her Relations; that I could convince her beyond the power of doubt, that my passion had been pure and disinterested; and I asked her, what should induce me to seek her in the Convent, were I influenced by the selfish motives which my Enemies had ascribed to me.

My prayers, my arguments, and vows not to quit her, till She had promised to listen to me, united to her fears lest the Nuns should see me with her, to her natural curiosity, and to the effection which She still felt for me in spite of my supposed desertion, at length prevailed. She told me, that to grant my request at that moment was impossible; But She engaged to be in the same spot at eleven that night, and to converse with me for the last time. Having obtained this promise I released her hand, and She fled back with rapidity towards the Convent.

I communicated my success to my Ally, the old Gardener: He pointed out an hiding-place, where I might shelter myself till night without fear of a discovery. Thither I betook myself at the hour when I ought to have retired with my supposed Master, and waited impatiently for the appointed time. The chillness of the night was in my favour, since it kept the other Nuns confined to their Cells. Agnes alone was insensible of the inclemency of the Air, and before eleven joined me at the spot, which had witnessed our former interview. Secure from interruption I related to her the true cause of my disappearing on the fatal fifth of May. She was evidently much affected by my narrative: When it was concluded, She confessed the injustice of her suspicions, and blamed herself for having taken the veil through despair at my ingratitude.

'But now it is too late to repine!' She added; 'The die is thrown: I have pronounced my vows, and dedicated myself to the service of heaven. I am sensible, how ill I am calculated for a Convent. My disgust at a monastic life increases daily: Ennui and discontent are my constant Companions; and I will not conceal from you, that the passion which I formerly felt for one so near being my Husband is not yet extinguished in my bosom. But we must part! Insuperable Barriers divide us from each other, and on this side the Grave we must never meet again!'

I now exerted myself to prove, that our union was not so impossible as She seemed to think it. I vaunted to her the Cardinal-Duke of Lerma's influence at the Court of Rome: I assured her, that I should easily obtain a dispensation from her vows; and I doubted not but Don Gaston would coincide with my views, when informed of my real name and long attachment. Agnes replied, that since I encouraged such an hope, I could know but little of her Father. Liberal and kind in every other respect, Superstition formed the only stain upon his character. Upon this head He was inflexible; He sacrificed his dearest interests to his scruples, and would consider it an insult to suppose him capable, of authorising his daughter to break her vows to heaven.

'But suppose,' said I interrupting her; 'Suppose, that He should disapprove of our union; Let him remain ignorant of my proceedings, till I have rescued you from the prison, in which you are now confined. Once my Wife, you are free from his authority: I need from him no pecuniary assistance; and when He sees his resentment to be unavailing, He will doubtless restore you to his favour. But let the worst happen; Should Don Gaston be irreconcileable, my Relations will vie with each other in making you forget his loss: and you will find in my Father a substitute for the Parent of whom I shall deprive you.'

'Don Raymond,' replied Agnes in a firm and resolute voice, 'I love my Father: He has treated me harshly in this one instance; but I have received from him in every other so many proofs of love, that his affection is become necessary to my existence. Were I to quit the Convent, He never would forgive me; nor can I think that on his death-bed He would leave me his curse, without shuddering at the very idea. Besides, I am conscious myself, that my vows are binding: Wilfully did I contract my engagement with heaven; I cannot break it without a crime. Then banish from your mind the idea of our being ever united. I am devoted to religion; and however I may grieve at our separation, I would oppose obstacles myself, to what I feel would render me guilty.'

I strove to over-rule these ill-grounded scruples: We were still disputing upon the subject, when the Convent-Bell summoned the Nuns to Matins. Agnes was obliged to attend them; But She left me not, till I had compelled her to promise, that on the following night She would be at the same place at the same hour. These meetings continued for several Weeks uninterrupted; and 'tis now, Lorenzo, that I must implore your indulgence. Reflect upon our situation, our youth, our long attachment: Weigh all the circumstances which attended our assignations, and you will confess the temptation to have been irresistible; you will even pardon me when I acknowledge, that in an unguarded moment the honour of Agnes was sacrificed to my passion.'

[Lorenzo's eyes sparkled with fury: A deep crimson spread itself over his face. He started from his seat, and attempted to draw his sword. The Marquis was aware of his movement, and caught his hand: He pressed it affectionately.

'My Friend! My Brother! Hear me to the conclusion! Till then restrain your passion, and be at least convinced, that if what I have related is criminal, the blame must fall upon me, and not upon your Sister.'

Lorenzo suffered himself to be prevailed upon by Don Raymond's entreaties. He resumed his place, and listened to the rest of the narrative with a gloomy and impatient countenance. The Marquis thus continued.]

'Scarcely was the first burst of passion past, when Agnes recovering herself started from my arms with horror. She called me infamous Seducer, loaded me with the bitterest reproaches, and beat her bosom in all the wildness of delirium. Ashamed of my imprudence, I with difficulty found words to excuse myself. I endeavoured to console her; I threw myself at her feet, and entreated her forgiveness. She forced her hand from me, which I had taken, and would have prest to my lips.

'Touch me not!' She cried with a violence which terrified me; 'Monster of perfidy and ingratitude, how have I been deceived in you! I looked upon you as my Friend, my Protector: I trusted myself in your hands with confidence, and relying upon your honour thought that mine ran no risque. And 'tis by you, whom I adored, that I am covered with infamy! 'Tis by you that I have been seduced into breaking my vows to God, that I am reduced to a level with the basest of my sex! Shame upon you, Villain, you shall never see me more!'

She started from the Bank on which She was seated. I endeavoured to detain her; But She disengaged herself from me with violence, and took refuge in the Convent.

I retired, filled with confusion and inquietude. The next morning I failed not as usual to appear in the Garden; but Agnes was no where to be seen. At night I waited for her at the place where we generally met; I found no better success. Several days and nights passed away in the same manner. At length I saw my offended Mistress cross the walk, on whose borders I was working: She was accompanied by the same young Pensioner, on whose arm She seemed from weakness obliged to support herself. She looked upon me for a moment, but instantly turned her head away. I waited her return; But She passed on to the Convent without paying any attention to me, or the penitent looks with which I implored her forgiveness.

As soon as the Nuns were retired, the old Gardener joined me with a sorrowful air.

'Segnor,' said He, 'it grieves me to say, that I can be no longer of use to you. The Lady whom you used to meet, has just assured me, that if I admitted you again into the Garden, She would discover the whole business to the Lady Prioress. She bade me tell you also, that your presence was an insult, and that if you still possess the least respect for her, you will never attempt to see her more. Excuse me then for informing you, that I can favour your disguise no longer. Should the Prioress be acquainted with my conduct, She might not be contented with dismissing me her service: Out of revenge She might accuse me of having profaned the Convent, and cause me to be thrown into the Prisons of the Inquisition.'

Fruitless were my attempts to conquer his resolution. He denied me all future entrance into the Garden, and Agnes persevered in neither letting me see, or hear from her. In about a fortnight after a violent illness which had seized my Father, obliged me to set out for Andalusia. I hastened thither, and as I imagined, found the Marquis at the point of death. Though on its first appearance his complaint was declared mortal, He lingered out several Months; during which my attendance upon him during his malady, and the occupation of settling his affairs after his decease, permitted not my quitting Andalusia. Within these four days I returned to Madrid, and on arriving at my Hotel, I there found this letter waiting for me.

[Here the Marquis unlocked the drawer of a Cabinet: He took out a folded paper, which He presented to his Auditor. Lorenzo opened it, and recognised his Sister's hand. The Contents were as follows.

Into what an abyss of misery have you plunged me! Raymond, you force me to become as criminal as yourself. I had resolved never to see you more; if possible, to forget you; If not, only to remember you with hate. A Being for whom I already feel a Mother's tenderness, solicits me to pardon my Seducer, and apply to his love for the means of preservation. Raymond, your child lives in my bosom. I tremble at the vengeance of the Prioress; I tremble much for myself, yet more for the innocent Creature whose existence depends upon mine. Both of us are lost, should my situation be discovered. Advise me then what steps to take, but seek not to see me. The Gardener, who undertakes to deliver this, is dismissed, and we have nothing to hope from that quarter: The Man engaged in his place is of incorruptible fidelity. The best means of conveying to me your answer, is by concealing it under the great Statue of St Francis, which stands in the Capuchin-Cathedral. Thither I go every Thursday to confession, and shall easily have an opportunity of securing your letter. I hear, that you are now absent from Madrid; Need I entreat you to write the very moment of your return? I will not think it. Ah! Raymond! Mine is a cruel situation! Deceived by my nearest Relations, compelled to embrace a profession the duties of which I am ill-calculated to perform, conscious of the sanctity of those duties, and seduced into violating them by One whom I least suspected of perfidy, I am now obliged by circumstances to chuse between death and perjury. Woman's timidity, and maternal affection permit me not to balance in the choice. I feel all the guilt into which I plunge myself, when I yield to the plan which you before proposed to me. My poor Father's death which has taken place since we met, has removed one obstacle. He sleeps in his grave, and I no longer dread his anger. But from the anger of God, Oh! Raymond! who shall shield me? Who can protect me against my conscience, against myself? I dare not dwell upon these thoughts; They will drive me mad. I have taken my resolution: Procure a dispensation from my vows; I am ready to fly with you. Write to me, my Husband! Tell me, that absence has not abated your love, tell me that you will rescue from death your unborn Child, and its unhappy Mother. I live in all the agonies of terror: Every eye which is fixed upon me, seems to read my secret and my shame. And you are the cause of those agonies! Oh! When my heart first loved you, how little did it suspect you of making it feel such pangs!

Agnes.

Having perused the letter, Lorenzo restored it in silence. The Marquis replaced it in the Cabinet, and then proceeded.]

'Excessive was my joy at reading this intelligence so earnestly-desired, so little expected. My plan was soon arranged. When Don Gaston discovered to me his Daughter's retreat, I entertained no doubt of her readiness to quit the Convent: I had, therefore, entrusted the Cardinal-Duke of Lerma with the whole affair, who immediately busied himself in obtaining the necessary Bull. Fortunately I had afterwards neglected to stop his proceedings. Not long since I received a letter from him, stating that He expected daily to receive the order from the Court of Rome. Upon this I would willingly have relyed: But the Cardinal wrote me word, that I must find some means of conveying Agnes out of the Convent, unknown to the Prioress. He doubted not but this Latter would be much incensed by losing a Person of such high rank from her society, and consider the renunciation of Agnes as an insult to her House. He represented her as a Woman of a violent and revengeful character, capable of proceeding to the greatest extremities. It was therefore to be feared, lest by confining Agnes in the Convent She should frustrate my hopes, and render the Pope's mandate unavailing. Influenced by this consideration, I resolved to carry off my Mistress, and conceal her till the arrival of the expected Bull in the Cardinal-Duke's Estate. He approved of my design, and profest himself ready to give a shelter to the Fugitive. I next caused the new Gardener of St Clare to be seized privately, and confined in my Hotel. By this means I became Master of the Key to the Garden-door, and I had now nothing more to do than prepare Agnes for the elopement. This was done by the letter, which you saw me deliver this Evening. I told her in it, that I should be ready to receive her at twelve tomorrow night, that I had secured the Key of the Garden, and that She might depend upon a speedy release.

You have now, Lorenzo, heard the whole of my long narrative. I have nothing to say in my excuse, save that my intentions towards your Sister have been ever the most honourable: That it has always been, and still is my design to make her my Wife: And that I trust, when you consider these circumstances, our youth, and our attachment, you will not only forgive our momentary lapse from virtue, but will aid me in repairing my faults to Agnes, and securing a lawful title to her person and her heart.

CHAPTER II

O You! whom Vanity's light bark conveys
On Fame's mad voyage by the wind of praise,
With what a shifting gale your course you ply,
For ever sunk too low, or borne too high!
Who pants for glory finds but short repose,
A breath revives him, and a breath o'er-throws.

                                                      Pope.

HERE the Marquis concluded his adventures. Lorenzo, before He could determine on his reply, past some moments in reflection. At length He broke silence.

'Raymond,' said He taking his hand, 'strict honour would oblige me to wash off in your blood the stain thrown upon my family; But the circumstances of your case forbid me to consider you as an Enemy. The temptation was too great to be resisted. 'Tis the superstition of my Relations which has occasioned these misfortunes, and they are more the Offenders than yourself and Agnes. What has past between you cannot be recalled, but may yet be repaired by uniting you to my Sister. You have ever been, you still continue to be, my dearest and indeed my only Friend. I feel for Agnes the truest affection, and there is no one on whom I would bestow her more willingly than on yourself. Pursue then your design. I will accompany you tomorrow night, and conduct her myself to the House of the Cardinal. My presence will be a sanction for her conduct, and prevent her incurring blame by her flight from the Convent.'

The Marquis thanked him in terms by no means deficient in gratitude. Lorenzo then informed him, that He had nothing more to apprehend from Donna Rodolpha's enmity. Five Months had already elapsed, since in an excess of passion She broke a blood-vessel, and expired in the course of a few hours. He then proceeded to mention the interests of Antonia. The Marquis was much surprized at hearing of this new Relation: His Father had carried his hatred of Elvira to the Grave, and had never given the least hint, that He knew what was become of his eldest Son's Widow. Don Raymond assured his Friend, that He was not mistaken in supposing him ready to acknowledge his Sister-in-law, and her amiable Daughter. The preparations for the elopement would not permit his visiting them the next day; But in the mean while He desired Lorenzo to assure them of his friendship, and to supply Elvira upon his account with any sums which She might want. This the Youth promised to do, as soon as her abode should be known to him: He then took leave of his future Brother, and returned to the Palace de Medina.

The day was already on the point of breaking, when the Marquis retired to his chamber. Conscious that his narrative would take up some hours, and wishing to secure himself from interruption, on returning to the Hotel He ordered his Attendants not to sit up for him. Consequently, He was somewhat surprised on entering his Anti-room, to find Theodore established there. The Page sat near a Table with a pen in his hand, and was so totally occupied by his employment, that He perceived not his Lord's approach. The Marquis stopped to observe him. Theodore wrote a few lines, then paused, and scratched out a part of the writing: Then wrote again, smiled, and seemed highly pleased with what He had been about. At last He threw down his pen, sprang from his chair, and clapped his hands together joyfully.

'There it is!' cried He aloud: 'Now they are charming!'

His transports were interrupted by a laugh from the Marquis, who suspected the nature of his employment.

'What is so charming, Theodore?'

The Youth started, and looked round. He blushed, ran to the Table, seized the paper on which He had been writing, and concealed it in confusion.

'Oh! my Lord, I knew not that you were so near me. Can I be of use to you? Lucas is already gone to bed.'

'I shall follow his example when I have given my opinion of your verses.'

'My verses, my Lord?'

'Nay, I am sure that you have been writing some, for nothing else could have kept you awake till this time of the morning. Where are they, Theodore? I shall like to see your composition.'

Theodore's cheeks glowed with still deeper crimson: He longed to show his poetry, but first chose to be pressed for it.

'Indeed, my Lord, they are not worthy your attention.'

'Not these verses, which you just now declared to be so charming? Come, come, let me see whether our opinions are the same. I promise, that you shall find in me an indulgent Critic.'

The Boy produced his paper with seeming reluctance; but the satisfaction which sparkled in his dark expressive eyes betrayed the vanity of his little bosom. The Marquis smiled while He observed the emotions of an heart, as yet but little skilled in veiling its sentiments. He seated himself upon a Sopha: Theodore, while Hope and fear contended on his anxious countenance, waited with inquietude for his Master's decision, while the Marquis read the following lines.

LOVE AND AGE

The night was dark; The wind blew cold;
Anacreon, grown morose and old,
Sat by his fire, and fed the chearful flame:
Sudden the Cottage-door expands,
And lo! before him Cupid stands,
Casts round a friendly glance, and greets him by his name.

'What is it Thou?' the startled Sire
In sullen tone exclaimed, while ire
With crimson flushed his pale and wrinkled cheek:
'Wouldst Thou again with amorous rage
Inflame my bosom? Steeled by age,
Vain Boy, to pierce my breast thine arrows are too weak.

'What seek You in this desart drear?
No smiles or sports inhabit here;
Ne'er did these vallies witness dalliance sweet:
Eternal winter binds the plains;
Age in my house despotic reigns,
My Garden boasts no flower, my bosom boasts no heat.

'Begone, and seek the blooming bower,
Where some ripe Virgin courts thy power,

Or bid provoking dreams flit round her bed;
  On Damon's amorous breast repose;
  Wanton on Chloe's lip of rose,
Or make her blushing cheek a pillow for thy head.

  'Be such thy haunts; These regions cold
  Avoid! Nor think grown wise and old
This hoary head again thy yoke shall bear:
  Remembering that my fairest years
  By Thee were marked with sighs and tears,
I think thy friendship false, and shun the guileful snare.

  'I have not yet forgot the pains
  I felt, while bound in Julia's chains;
The ardent flames with which my bosom burned;
  The nights I passed deprived of rest;
  The jealous pangs which racked my breast;
My disappointed hopes, and passion unreturned.

  'Then fly, and curse mine eyes no more!
  Fly from my peaceful Cottage-door!
No day, no hour, no moment shalt Thou stay.
  I know thy falsehood, scorn thy arts,
  Distrust thy smiles, and fear thy darts;
Traitor, begone, and seek some other to betray!'

  'Does Age, old Man, your wits confound?'
  Replied the offended God, and frowned;
[His frown was sweet as is the Virgin's smile!]
  'Do You to Me these words address?
  To Me, who do not love you less,
Though You my friendship scorn, and pleasures past revile!

  'If one proud Fair you chanced to find,
  An hundred other Nymphs were kind,
Whose smiles might well for Julia's frowns atone:
  But such is Man! His partial hand
  Unnumbered favours writes on sand,
But stamps one little fault on solid lasting stone.

  'Ingrate! Who led Thee to the wave,
  At noon where Lesbia loved to lave?
Who named the bower alone where Daphne lay?
  And who, when Cælia shrieked for aid,
  Bad you with kisses hush the Maid?
What other was't than Love, Oh! false Anacreon, say!

'Then You could call me—"Gentle Boy!
  "My only bliss! my source of joy!"—
Then You could prize me dearer than your soul!
  Could kiss, and dance me on your knees;
  And swear, not wine itself would please,
Had not the lip of Love first touched the flowing bowl!

  'Must those sweet days return no more?
  Must I for aye your loss deplore,
Banished your heart, and from your favour driven?
  Ah! no; My fears that smile denies;
  That heaving breast, those sparkling eyes
Declare me ever dear and all my faults forgiven.

  'Again beloved, esteemed, carest,
  Cupid shall in thine arms be prest,
Sport on thy knees, or on thy bosom sleep:
  My Torch thine age-struck heart shall warm;
  My Hand pale Winter's rage disarm,
And Youth and Spring shall here once more their revels keep.'—

  A feather now of golden hue
  He smiling from his pinion drew;
This to the Poet's hand the Boy commits;
  And straight before Anacreon's eyes
  The fairest dreams of fancy rise,
  And round his favoured head wild inspiration flits.

  His bosom glows with amorous fire;
  Eager He grasps the magic lyre;
Swift o'er the tuneful chords his fingers move:
  The Feather plucked from Cupid's wing
  Sweeps the too-long-neglected string,
While soft Anacreon sings the power and praise of Love.

  Soon as that name was heard, the Woods
  Shook off their snows; The melting floods
Broke their cold chains, and Winter fled away.
  Once more the earth was deckt with flowers;
  Mild Zephyrs breathed through blooming bowers;
High towered the glorious Sun, and poured the blaze of day.

  Attracted by the harmonious sound,
  Sylvans and Fauns the Cot surround,
And curious crowd the Minstrel to behold:
  The Wood-nymphs haste the spell to prove;

Eager They run; They list, they love,
And while They hear the strain, forget the Man is old.

Cupid, to nothing constant long,
Perched on the Harp attends the song,
Or stifles with a kiss the dulcet notes:
Now on the Poet's breast reposes,
Now twines his hoary locks with roses,
Or borne on wings of gold in wanton circle floats.

Then thus Anacreon—'I no more
At other shrine my vows will pour,
Since Cupid deigns my numbers to inspire:
From Phœbus or the blue-eyed Maid
Now shall my verse request no aid,
For Love alone shall be the Patron of my Lyre.

'In lofty strain, of earlier days,
I spread the King's or Hero's praise,
And struck the martial Chords with epic fire:
But farewell, Hero! farewell, King!
Your deeds my lips no more shall sing,
For Love alone shall be the subject of my Lyre.

The Marquis returned the paper with a smile of encouragement.
'Your little poem pleases me much,' said He; 'However, you must not count my opinion for any-thing. I am no judge of verses, and for my own part, never composed more than six lines in my life: Those six produced so unlucky an effect, that I am fully resolved never to compose another. But I wander from my subject. I was going to say, that you cannot employ your time worse than in making verses. An Author, whether good or bad, or between both, is an Animal whom every body is privileged to attack; For though All are not able to write books, all conceive themselves able to judge them. A bad composition carries with it its own punishment, contempt and ridicule. A good one excites envy, and entails upon its Author a thousand mortifications. He finds himself assailed by partial and ill-humoured Criticism: One Man finds fault with the plan, Another with the style, a Third with the precept, which it strives to inculcate; and they who cannot succeed in finding fault with the Book, employ themselves in stigmatizing its Author. They maliciously rake out from obscurity every little circumstance, which may throw ridicule upon his private character or conduct, and aim at wounding the Man, since They cannot hurt the Writer. In short to enter the lists of literature is wilfully to expose yourself to the arrows of neglect, ridicule, envy, and disappointment. Whether you write well or ill, be assured

that you will not escape from blame; Indeed this circumstance contains a young Author's chief consolation: He remembers that Lope de Vega and Calderona had unjust and envious Critics, and He modestly conceives himself to be exactly in their predicament. But I am conscious, that all these sage observations are thrown away upon you. Authorship is a mania to conquer which no reasons are sufficiently strong; and you might as easily persuade me not to love, as I persuade you not to write. However, if you cannot help being occasionally seized with a poetical paroxysm, take at least the precaution of communicating your verses to none but those, whose partiality for you secures their approbation.'

'Then, my Lord, you do not think these lines tolerable?' said Theodore with an humble and dejected air.

'You mistake my meaning. As I said before, they have pleased me much; But my regard for you makes me partial, and Others might judge them less favourably. I must still remark, that even my prejudice in your favour does not blind me so much, as to prevent my observing several faults. For instance, you make a terrible confusion of metaphors; You are too apt to make the strength of your lines consist more in the words than sense; Some of the verses only seem introduced in order to rhyme with others; and most of the best ideas are borrowed from other Poets, though possibly you are unconscious of the theft yourself. These faults may occasionally be excused in a work of length; But a short Poem must be correct and perfect.'

'All this is true, Segnor; But you should consider that I only write for pleasure.'

'Your defects are the less excusable. Their incorrectness may be forgiven, who work for money, who are obliged to compleat a given task in a given time, and are paid according to the bulk, not value of their productions. But in those whom no necessity forces to turn Author, who merely write for fame, and have full leisure to polish their compositions, faults are impardonable, and merit the sharpest arrows of criticism.'

The Marquis rose from the Sopha; the Page looked discouraged and melancholy, and this did not escape his Master's observation.

'However' added He smiling, 'I think that these lines do you no discredit. Your versification is tolerably easy, and your ear seems to be just. The perusal of your little poem upon the whole gave me much pleasure; and if it is not asking too great a favour, I shall be highly obliged to you for a Copy.'

The Youth's countenance immediately cleared up. He perceived not the smile, half approving, half ironical, which accompanied the request, and He promised the Copy with great readiness. The Marquis with-drew to his chamber, much amused by the instantaneous effect produced upon Theodore's vanity by the conclusion of his Criticism. He threw himself upon his Couch; Sleep soon stole over him, and his dreams presented him with the most flattering pictures of happiness with Agnes.

On reaching the Hotel de Medina, Lorenzo's first care was to enquire for Letters. He found several waiting for him; but that which He sought, was not amongst them. Leonella had found it impossible to write that evening. However, her impatience to secure Don Christoval's heart, on which She flattered herself with having made no slight impression, permitted her not to pass another day, without informing him where She was to be found. On her return from the Capuchin-Church, She had related to her Sister with exultation, how attentive an handsome Cavalier had been to her; as also how his Companion had undertaken to plead Antonia's cause with the Marquis de las Cisternas. Elvira received this intelligence with sensations very different from those with which it was communicated. She blamed her Sister's imprudence in confiding her history to an absolute Stranger, and expressed her fears, lest this inconsiderate step should prejudice the Marquis against her. The greatest of her apprehensions She concealed in her own breast. She had observed with inquietude, that at the mention of Lorenzo a deep blush spread itself over her Daughter's cheek. The timid Antonia dared not to pronounce his name: Without knowing wherefore, She felt embarrassed when He was made the subject of discourse, and endeavoured to change the conversation to Ambrosio. Elvira perceived the emotions of this young bosom: In consequence, She insisted upon Leonella's breaking her promise to the Cavaliers. A sigh, which on hearing this order escaped from Antonia, confirmed the wary Mother in her resolution.

Through this resolution Leonella was determined to break: She conceived it to be inspired by envy, and that her Sister dreaded her being elevated above her. Without imparting her design to any one, She took an opportunity of dispatching the following note to Lorenzo; It was delivered to him as soon as He woke.

'Doubtless, Segnor Don Lorenzo, you have frequently accused me of ingratitude and forgetfulness: But on the word of a Virgin, it was out of my power to perform my promise yesterday. I know not in what words to inform you, how strange a reception my Sister gave your kind wish to visit her. She is an odd Woman, with many good points about her; But her jealousy of me frequently makes her conceive notions quite unaccountable. On hearing that your Friend had paid some little attention to me, She immediately took the alarm: She blamed my conduct, and has absolutely forbidden me to let you know our abode. My strong sense of gratitude for your kind offers of service, and . . . Shall I confess it? my desire to behold once more the too amiable Don Christoval, will not permit my obeying her injunctions. I have therefore stolen a moment to inform you, that we lodge in the Strada di San Iago, four doors from the Palace d'Albornos, and nearly opposite to the Barber's Miguel Coello. Enquire for Donna Elvira Dalfa, since in compliance with her Father-in-law's order, my Sister continues to be called by her maiden name. At eight this evening you will be sure of finding us: But let not a word drop, which may raise a suspicion of my having written this letter. Should you see the Condé d'Ossorio, tell him . . . I blush while I declare it . . . Tell him that his presence will be but too acceptable to the sympathetic

Leonella.

The latter sentences were written in red ink, to express the blushes of her cheek, while She committed an outrage upon her virgin modesty.

Lorenzo had no sooner perused this note, than He set out in search of Don Christoval. Not being able to find him in the course of the day, He proceeded to Donna Elvira's alone to Leonella's infinite disappointment. The Domestic, by whom He sent up his name, having already declared his Lady to be at home, She had no excuse for refusing his visit: Yet She consented to receive it with much reluctance. That reluctance was increased by the changes which his approach produced in Antonia's countenance; nor was it by any means abated, when the Youth himself appeared. The symmetry of his person, animation of his features, and natural elegance of his manners and address, convinced Elvira that such a Guest must be dangerous for her Daughter. She resolved to treat him with distant politeness, to decline his services with gratitude for the tender of them, and to make him feel, without offence, that his future visits would be far from acceptable.

On his entrance He found Elvira who was indisposed, reclining upon a Sopha: Antonia sat by her embroidery frame, and Leonella, in a pastoral dress, held '*Montemayor's Diana.*' In spite of her being the Mother of Antonia, Lorenzo could not help expecting to find in Elvira Leonella's true Sister, and the Daughter of 'as honest a pains-taking Shoe-maker, as any in Cordova.' A single glance was sufficient to undeceive him. He beheld a Woman whose features, though impaired by time and sorrow, still bore the marks of distinguished beauty: A serious dignity reigned upon her countenance, but was tempered by a grace and sweetness which rendered her truly enchanting. Lorenzo fancied that She must have resembled her Daughter in her youth, and readily excused the imprudence of the late Condé de las Cisternas. She desired him to be seated, and immediately resumed her place upon the Sopha.

Antonia received him with a simple reverence, and continued her work: Her cheeks were suffused with crimson, and She strove to conceal her emotion by leaning over her embroidery frame. Her Aunt also chose to play off her airs of modesty; She affected to blush and tremble, and waited with her eyes cast down to receive, as She expected, the compliments of Don Christoval. Finding after some time that no sign of his approach was given, She ventured to look round the room, and perceived with vexation that

Medina was unaccompanied. Impatience would not permit her waiting for an explanation: Interrupting Lorenzo, who was delivering Raymond's message, She desired to know what was become of his Friend.

He, who thought it necessary to maintain himself in her good graces, strove to console her under her disappointment by committing a little violence upon truth.

'Ah! Segnora,' He replied in a melancholy voice 'How grieved will He be at losing this opportunity of paying you his respects! A Relation's illness has obliged him to quit Madrid in haste: But on his return, He will doubtless seize the first moment with transport to throw himself at your feet!'

As He said this, his eyes met those of Elvira: She punished his falsehood sufficiently by darting at him a look expressive of displeasure and reproach. Neither did the deceit answer his intention. Vexed and disappointed Leonella rose from her seat, and retired in dudgeon to her own apartment.

Lorenzo hastened to repair the fault, which had injured him in Elvira's opinion. He related his conversation with the Marquis respecting her: He assured her that Raymond was prepared to acknowledge her for his Brother's Widow; and that till it was in his power to pay his compliments to her in person, Lorenzo was commissioned to supply his place. This intelligence relieved Elvira from an heavy weight of uneasiness: She had now found a Protector for the fatherless Antonia, for whose future fortunes She had suffered the greatest apprehensions. She was not sparing of her thanks to him, who had interfered so generously in her behalf; But still She gave him no invitation to repeat his visit. However, when upon rising to depart He requested permission to enquire after her health occasionally, the polite earnestness of his manner, gratitude for his services, and respect for his Friend the Marquis, would not admit of a refusal. She consented reluctantly to receive him: He promised not to abuse her goodness, and quitted the House.

Antonia was now left alone with her Mother: A temporary silence ensued. Both wished to speak upon the same subject, but Neither knew how to introduce it. The one felt a bashfulness which sealed up her lips, and for which She could not account: The other feared to find her apprehensions true, or to inspire her Daughter with notions to which She might be still a Stranger. At length Elvira began the conversation.

'That is a charming young Man, Antonia; I am much pleased with him. Was He long near you yesterday in the Cathedral?'

'He quitted me not for a moment while I staid in the Church: He gave me his seat, and was very obliging and attentive.'

'Indeed? Why then have you never mentioned his name to me? Your Aunt lanched out in praise of his Friend, and you vaunted Ambrosio's eloquence: But Neither said a word of Don Lorenzo's person and accomplishments. Had not Leonella spoken of his readiness to undertake our cause, I should not have known him to be in existence.'

She paused. Antonia coloured, but was silent.

'Perhaps you judge him less favourably than I do. In my opinion his figure is pleasing, his conversation sensible, and manners engaging. Still He may have struck you differently: You may think him disagreeable, and . . .'.

'Disagreeable? Oh! dear Mother, how should I possibly think him so? I should be very ungrateful, were I not sensible of his kindness yesterday, and very blind if his merits had escaped me. His figure is so graceful, so noble! His manners so gentle, yet so manly! I never yet saw so many accomplishments united in one person, and I doubt whether Madrid can produce his equal.'

'Why then were you so silent in praise of this Phœnix of Madrid? Why was it concealed from me, that his society had afforded you pleasure?'

'In truth, I know not: You ask me a question, which I cannot resolve myself. I was on the point of mentioning him a thousand times: His name was constantly upon my lips, but when I would have pronounced it, I wanted courage to execute my design. However, if I did not speak of him, it was not that I thought of him the less.'

'That I believe; But shall I tell you why you wanted courage? It was because accustomed to confide to me your most secret thoughts, you knew not how to conceal, yet feared to acknowledge, that your heart nourished a sentiment, which you were conscious I should disapprove. Come hither to me, my Child.'

Antonia quitted her embroidery frame, threw herself upon her knees by the Sopha, and hid her face in her Mother's lap.

'Fear not, my sweet Girl! Consider me equally as your Friend and Parent, and apprehend no reproof from me. I have read the emotions of your bosom; you are yet ill skilled in concealing them, and they could not escape my attentive eye. This Lorenzo is dangerous to your repose; He has already made an impression upon your heart. 'Tis true, that I perceive easily that your affection is returned; But what can be the consequences of this attachment? You are poor and friendless, my Antonia; Lorenzo is the Heir of the Duke of Medina Celi. Even should Himself mean honourably, his Uncle never will consent to your union; Nor without that Uncle's consent, will I. By sad experience I know what sorrows She must endure, who marries into a family unwilling to receive her. Then struggle with your affection: Whatever pains it may cost you, strive to conquer it. Your heart is tender and susceptible: It has already received a strong impression; But when once convinced that you should not encourage such sentiments, I trust, that you have sufficient fortitude to drive them from your bosom.'

Antonia kissed her hand, and promised implicit obedience. Elvira then continued.

'To prevent your passion from growing stronger, it will be needful to prohibit Lorenzo's visits. The service which He has rendered me permits not my forbidding them positively; But unless I judge too favourably of his character, He will discontinue them without taking offence, if I confess to him my reasons, and throw myself entirely on his generosity. The next time that I see him, I will honestly avow to him the embarrassment which his presence occasions. How say you, my Child? Is not this measure necessary?'

Antonia subscribed to every thing without hesitation, though not without regret. Her Mother kissed her affectionately, and retired to bed. Antonia followed her example, and vowed so frequently never more to think of Lorenzo, that till Sleep closed her eyes She thought of nothing else.

While this was passing at Elvira's, Lorenzo hastened to rejoin the Marquis. Every thing was ready for the second elopement of Agnes; and at twelve the two Friends with a Coach and four were at the Garden-wall of the Convent. Don Raymond drew out his Key, and unlocked the door. They entered, and waited for some time in expectation of being joined by Agnes. At length the Marquis grew impatient: Beginning to fear that his second attempt would succeed no better than the first, He proposed to reconnoitre the Convent. The Friends advanced towards it. Every thing was still and dark. The Prioress was anxious to keep the story a secret, fearing lest the crime of one of its members should bring disgrace upon the whole community, or that the interposition of powerful Relations should deprive her vengeance of its intended victim. She took care therefore to give the Lover of Agnes no cause to suppose, that his design was discovered, and his Mistress on the point of suffering the punishment of her fault. The same reason made her reject the idea of arresting the unknown Seducer in the Garden; Such a proceeding would have created much disturbance, and the disgrace of her Convent would have been noised about Madrid. She contented herself with confining Agnes closely; As to the Lover She left him at liberty to pursue his designs. What She had expected was the result. The Marquis and Lorenzo waited in vain till the break of day: They then retired without noise, alarmed at the failure of their plan, and ignorant of the cause of its ill-success.

The next morning Lorenzo went to the Convent, and requested to see his Sister. The Prioress appeared at the Grate with a melancholy countenance: She informed him that for several days Agnes had appeared much agitated; That She had been prest by the Nuns in vain to reveal the cause, and apply to their tenderness for advice and consolation; That She had obstinately persisted in concealing the cause of her distress; But that on Thursday Evening it had produced so violent an effect upon her constitution, that She had fallen ill, and was actually confined to her bed. Lorenzo did not credit a syllable of this account: He insisted upon seeing his Sister; If She was unable to come to the Grate, He desired to be admitted to her Cell. The Prioress crossed herself! She was shocked at the very idea of a Man's profane eye pervading the interior of her holy Mansion, and professed herself astonished that Lorenzo could think of such a thing. She told him that his request could not be granted; But that if He returned the next day, She hoped that her beloved Daughter would then be sufficiently recovered to join him at the Parlour-grate. With this answer Lorenzo was obliged to retire, unsatisfied and trembling for his Sister's safety.

He returned the next morning at an early hour. 'Agnes was worse; The Physician had pronounced her to be in imminent danger; She was ordered to remain quiet, and it was utterly impossible for her to receive her Brother's visit.' Lorenzo stormed at this answer, but there was no resource. He raved, He entreated, He threatened: No means were left untried to obtain a sight of Agnes. His endeavours were as fruitless as those of the day before, and He returned in despair to the Marquis. On his side, the Latter had spared no pains to discover what had occasioned his plot to fail: Don Christoval to whom the affair was now entrusted, endeavoured to worm out the secret from the Old Porteress of St Clare, with whom He had formed an acquaintance; But She was too much upon her guard, and He gained from her no intelligence. The Marquis was almost distracted, and Lorenzo felt scarcely less inquietude. Both were convinced, that the purposed elopement must have been discovered: They doubted not but the malady of Agnes was a pretence, But they knew not by what means to rescue her from the hands of the Prioress.

Regularly every day did Lorenzo visit the Convent: As regularly was He informed that his Sister rather grew worse than better. Certain that her indisposition was feigned, these accounts did not alarm him: But his ignorance of her fate, and of the motives which induced the Prioress to keep her from him, excited the most serious uneasiness. He was still uncertain what steps He ought to take, when the Marquis received a letter from the Cardinal-Duke of Lerma. It inclosed the Pope's expected Bull, ordering that Agnes should be released from her vows, and restored to her Relations. This essential paper decided at once the proceedings of her Friends: They resolved that Lorenzo should carry it to the Domina without delay, and demand that his Sister should be instantly given up to him. Against this mandate illness could not be pleaded: It gave her Brother the power of removing her instantly to the Palace de Medina, and He determined to use that power on the following day.

His mind relieved from inquietude respecting his Sister, and his Spirits raised by the hope of soon restoring her to freedom, He now had time to give a few moments to love and to Antonia. At the same hour as on his former visit He repaired to Donna Elvira's: She had given orders for his admission. As soon as He was announced, her Daughter retired with Leonella, and when He entered the chamber, He found the Lady of the House alone. She received him with less distance than before, and desired him to place himself near her upon the Sopha. She then without losing time opened her business, as had been agreed between herself and Antonia.

'You must not think me ungrateful, Don Lorenzo, or forgetful how essential are the services, which you have rendered me with the Marquis. I feel the weight of my obligations; Nothing under the Sun should induce my taking the step to which I am now compelled, but the interest of my Child, of my beloved Antonia. My health is declining; God only knows, how soon I may be summoned before his Throne. My Daughter will be left without Parents, and should She lose the protection of the Cisternas family, without Friends. She is young and artless, uninstructed in the world's perfidy, and with charms sufficient to render her an object of seduction. Judge then, how I must tremble at the prospect before her! Judge, how anxious I must be to keep her from their society, who may excite the yet dormant passions of her bosom. You are amiable, Don Lorenzo: Antonia has a susceptible, a loving heart, and is grateful for the favours conferred upon us by your interference with the Marquis. Your presence makes me tremble: I fear, lest it should inspire her with sentiments which may embitter the remainder of her life, or encourage her to cherish hopes in her situation unjustifiable and futile. Pardon me, when I avow my terrors, and let my frankness plead in my excuse. I cannot forbid you my House, for gratitude restrains me; I can only throw myself upon your generosity, and entreat you to spare the feelings of an anxious, of a doting Mother. Believe me when I assure you, that I lament the necessity of rejecting your acquaintance; But there is no remedy, and Antonia's interest obliges me to beg you to forbear your visits. By complying with my request, you will increase the esteem which I already feel for you, and of which every thing convinces me, that you are truly deserving.'

'Your frankness charms me,' replied Lorenzo; 'You shall find, that in your favourable opinion of me you were not deceived. Yet I hope, that the reasons now in my power to allege, will persuade you to withdraw a request, which I cannot obey without infinite reluctance. I love your Daughter, love her most sincerely: I wish for no greater happiness than to inspire her with the same sentiments, and receive her hand at the Altar as her Husband. 'Tis true, I am not rich myself; My Father's death has left me but little in my own possession; But my expectations justify my pretending to the Condé de las Cisternas' Daughter.'

He was proceeding, but Elvira interrupted him.

'Ah! Don Lorenzo, you forget in that pompous title the meanness of my origin. You forget, that I have now past fourteen years in Spain, disavowed by my Husband's family, and existing upon a stipend barely sufficient for the support and education of my Daughter. Nay, I have even been neglected by most of my own Relations, who out of envy affect to doubt the reality of my marriage. My allowance being dis-continued at my Father-in-law's death, I was reduced to the very brink of want. In this situation I was found by my Sister, who amongst all her foibles possesses a warm, generous, and affectionate heart. She aided me with the little fortune which my Father left her, persuaded me to visit Madrid, and has supported my Child and myself since our quitting Murcia. Then consider not Antonia as descended from the Condé de la Cisternas: Consider her as a poor and unprotected Orphan, as the Grand-child of the Tradesman Torribio Dalfa, as the needy Pensioner of that Tradesman's Daughter. Reflect upon the difference between such a situation, and that of the Nephew and Heir of the potent Duke of Medina. I believe your intentions to be honourable; But as there are no hopes that your Uncle will approve of the union, I fore-see that the consequences of your attachment must be fatal to my Child's repose.'

'Pardon me, Segnora; You are mis-informed if you suppose the Duke of Medina to resemble the generality of Men. His sentiments are liberal and disinterested: He loves me well; and I have no reason to dread his forbidding the marriage, when He perceives that my happiness depends upon Antonia. But supposing him to refuse his sanction, what have I still to fear? My Parents are no more; My little fortune is in my own possession: It will be sufficient to support Antonia, and I shall exchange for her hand Medina's Dukedom without one sigh of regret.'

'You are young and eager; It is natural for you to entertain such ideas. But Experience has taught me to my cost, that curses accompany an unequal alliance. I married the Condé de las Cisternas in opposition to the will of his Relations; Many an heart-pang has punished me for the imprudent step. Where-ever we bent our course, a Father's execration pursued Gonzalvo. Poverty over-took us, and no Friend was near to relieve our wants. Still our mutual affection existed, but alas! not without interruption. Accustomed to wealth and ease, ill could my Husband support the transition to distress and indigence. He looked back with repining to the comforts which He once enjoyed. He regretted the situation which for my sake He had quitted; and in moments when Despair possessed his mind, has reproached me with having made him the Companion of want and wretchedness! He has called me his bane! The source of his sorrows, the cause of his destruction! Ah God! He little knew, how much keener were my own heart's reproaches! He was ignorant that I suffered trebly, for myself, for my Children, and for him! 'Tis true that his anger seldom lasted long: His sincere affection for me soon revived in his heart; and then his repentance for the tears which He had made me shed, tortured me even more than his reproaches. He would throw himself on the ground, implore my forgiveness in the most frantic terms, and load himself with curses for being the Murderer of my repose. Taught by experience

that an union contracted against the inclinations of families on either
side must be unfortunate, I will save my Daughter from those miseries,
which I have suffered. Without your Uncle's consent, while I live, She
never shall be yours. Undoubtedly He will disapprove of the union; His
power is immense, and Antonia shall not be exposed to his anger and
persecution.'

'His persecution? How easily may that be avoided! Let the worst happen,
it is but quitting Spain. My wealth may easily be realised; The Indian
Islands will offer us a secure retreat; I have an estate, though not of value,
in Hispaniola: Thither will we fly, and I shall consider it to be my native
Country, if it gives me Antonia's undisturbed possession.'

'Ah! Youth, this is a fond romantic vision. Gonzalvo thought the same.
He fancied, that He could leave Spain without regret; But the moment of
parting undeceived him. You know not yet what it is to quit your native
land; to quit it, never to behold it more! You know not, what it is to
exchange the scenes where you have passed your infancy, for unknown
realms and barbarous climates! To be forgotten, utterly eternally forgotten
by the Companions of your Youth! To see your dearest Friends, the fondest
objects of your affection, perishing with diseases incidental to Indian
atmospheres, and find yourself unable to procure for them necessary
assistance! I have felt all this! My Husband and two sweet Babes found their
Graves in Cuba: Nothing would have saved my young Antonia but my
sudden return to Spain. Ah! Don Lorenzo, could you conceive what I
suffered during my absence! Could you know, how sorely I regretted all that
I left behind, and how dear to me was the very name of Spain! I envied the
winds which blew towards it: And when the Spanish Sailor chaunted some
well-known air as He past my window, tears filled my eyes, while I thought
upon my native land. Gonzalvo too . . . My Husband . . .'.

Elvira paused. Her voice faltered, and She concealed her face with her
hand-kerchief. After a short silence She rose from the Sopha, and proceeded.

'Excuse my quitting you for a few moments: The remembrance of what I
have suffered has much agitated me, and I need to be alone. Till I return
peruse these lines. After my Husband's death I found them among his
papers; Had I known sooner that He entertained such sentiments, Grief
would have killed me. He wrote these verses on his voyage to Cuba, when
his mind was clouded by sorrow, and He forgot that He had a Wife and
Children. What we are losing, ever seems to us the most precious: Gonzalvo
was quitting Spain for ever, and therefore was Spain dearer to his eyes, than
all else which the World contained. Read them, Don Lorenzo; They will
give you some idea of the feelings of a banished Man!'

Elvira put a paper into Lorenzo's hand, and retired from the chamber.
The Youth examined the contents, and found them to be as follows.

THE EXILE

Farewell, Oh! native Spain! Farewell for ever!
  These banished eyes shall view thy coasts no more;
A mournful presage tells my heart, that never
  Gonzalvo's steps again shall press thy shore.

Hushed are the winds; While soft the Vessel sailing
  With gentle motion plows the unruffled Main,
I feel my bosom's boasted courage failing,
  And curse the waves which bear me far from Spain.

I see it yet! Beneath yon blue clear Heaven
  Still do the Spires, so well beloved, appear;
From yonder craggy point the gale of Even
  Still wafts my native accents to mine ear:

Propped on some moss-crowned Rock, and gaily singing,
  There in the Sun his nets the Fisher dries;
Oft have I heard the plaintive Ballad, bringing
  Scenes of past joys before my sorrowing eyes.

Ah! Happy Swain! He waits the accustomed hour,
  When twilight-gloom obscures the closing sky;
Then gladly seeks his loved paternal bower,
  And shares the feast his native fields supply:

Friendship and Love, his Cottage Guests, receive him
  With honest welcome and with smile sincere;
No threatening woes of present joys bereave him,
  No sigh his bosom owns, his cheek no tear.

Ah! Happy Swain! Such bliss to me denying,
  Fortune thy lot with envy bids me view;
Me, who from home and Spain an Exile flying,
  Bid all I value, all I love, adieu.

No more mine ear shall list the well-known ditty
  Sung by some Mountain-Girl, who tends her Goats,
Some Village-Swain imploring amorous pity,
  Or Shepherd chaunting wild his rustic notes:

No more my arms a Parent's fond embraces,
  No more my heart domestic calm, must know;
Far from these joys, with sighs which Memory traces,
  To sultry skies, and distant climes I go.

Where Indian Suns engender new diseases,
  Where snakes and tigers breed, I bend my way

To brave the feverish thirst no art appeases,
   The yellow plague, and madding blaze of day:

But not to feel slow pangs consume my liver,
   To die by piece-meal in the bloom of age,
My boiling blood drank by insatiate fever,
   And brain delirious with the day-star's rage,

Can make me know such grief, as thus to sever
   With many a bitter sigh, Dear Land, from Thee;
To feel this heart must doat on thee for ever,
   And feel, that all thy joys are torn from me!

Ah me! How oft will Fancy's spells in slumber
   Recall my native Country to my mind!
How oft regret will bid me sadly number
   Each lost delight and dear Friend left behind!

Wild Murcia's Vales, and loved romantic bowers,
   The River on whose banks a Child I played,
My Castle's antient Halls, its frowning Towers,
   Each much-regretted wood, and well-known Glade,

Dreams of the land where all my wishes centre,
   Thy scenes, which I am doomed no more to know,
Full oft shall Memory trace, my soul's Tormentor,
   And turn each pleasure past to present woe.

But Lo! The Sun beneath the waves retires;
   Night speeds apace her empire to restore:
Clouds from my sight obscure the village-spires,
   Now seen but faintly, and now seen no more.

Oh! breathe not, Winds! Still be the Water's motion!
   Sleep, sleep, my Bark, in silence on the Main!
So when to-morrow's light shall gild the Ocean,
   Once more mine eyes shall see the coast of Spain.

Vain is the wish! My last petition scorning,
   Fresh blows the Gale, and high the Billows swell:
Far shall we be before the break of Morning;
   Oh! then for ever, native Spain, farewell!

Lorenzo had scarcely time to read these lines, when Elvira returned to him: The giving a free course to her tears had relieved her, and her spirits had regained their usual composure.

'I have nothing more to say, my Lord,' said She; 'You have heard ~~rehensions, and my reasons for begging you not to repeat your visits. I have thrown myself in full confidence upon your honour: I am certain, that you will not prove my opinion of you to have been too favourable.'

'But one question more, Segnora, and I leave you. Should the Duke of Medina approve my love, would my addresses be unacceptable to yourself and the fair Antonia?'

'I will be open with you, Don Lorenzo: There being little probability of such an union taking place, I fear that it is desired but too ardently by my Daughter. You have made an impression upon her young heart, which gives me the most serious alarm: To prevent that impression from growing stronger, I am obliged to decline your acquaintance. For me, you may be sure, that I should rejoice at establishing my Child so advantageously. Conscious that my constitution, impaired by grief and illness, forbids me to expect a long continuance in this world, I tremble at the thought of leaving her under the protection of a perfect Stranger. The Marquis de las Cisternas is totally unknown to me: He will marry; His Lady may look upon Antonia with an eye of displeasure, and deprive her of her only Friend. Should the Duke, your Uncle, give his consent, you need not doubt obtaining mine and my Daughter's: But without his, hope not for ours. At all events, what ever steps you may take, what ever may be the Duke's decision, till you know it let me beg your forbearing to strengthen by your presence Antonia's prepossession. If the sanction of your Relations authorises your addressing her as your Wife, my Doors fly open to you: If that sanction is refused, be satisfied to possess my esteem and gratitude, but remember, that we must meet no more.'

Lorenzo promised reluctantly to conform to this decree: But He added that He hoped soon to obtain that consent, which would give him a claim to the renewal of their acquaintance. He then explained to her why the Marquis had not called in person, and made no scruple of confiding to her his Sister's History. He concluded by saying, that He hoped to set Agnes at liberty the next day; and that as soon as Don Raymond's fears were quieted upon this subject, He would lose no time in assuring Donna Elvira of his friendship and protection.

The Lady shook her head.

'I tremble for your Sister,' said She; 'I have heard many traits of the Domina of St Clare's character, from a Friend who was educated in the same Convent with her. She reported her to be haughty, inflexible, superstitious, and revengeful. I have since heard, that She is infatuated with the idea of rendering her Convent the most regular in Madrid, and never forgave those whose imprudence threw upon it the slightest stain. Though naturally violent and severe, when her interests require it, She well knows how to assume an appearance of benignity. She leaves no means untried to persuade young Women of rank to become Members of her Community:

She is implacable when once incensed, and has too much intrepidity to shrink at taking the most rigorous measures for punishing the Offender. Doubtless, She will consider your Sister's quitting the Convent, as a disgrace thrown upon it: She will use every artifice to avoid obeying the mandate of his Holiness, and I shudder to think, that Donna Agnes is in the hands of this dangerous Woman.'

Lorenzo now rose to take leave. Elvira gave him her hand at parting, which He kissed respectfully; and telling her that He soon hoped for the permission to salute that of Antonia, He returned to his Hotel. The Lady was perfectly satisfied with the conversation, which had past between them. She looked forward with satisfaction to the prospect of his becoming her Son-in-law; But Prudence bad her conceal from her Daughter's knowledge, the flattering hopes which Herself now ventured to entertain.

Scarcely was it day, and already Lorenzo was at the Convent of St Clare, furnished with the necessary mandate. The Nuns were at Matins. He waited impatiently for the conclusion of the service, and at length the Prioress appeared at the Parlour-Grate. Agnes was demanded. The old Lady replied with a melancholy air, that the dear Child's situation grew hourly more dangerous; That the Physicians despaired of her life; But that they had declared, the only chance for her recovery to consist in keeping her quiet, and not to permit those to approach her whose presence was likely to agitate her. Not a word of all this was believed by Lorenzo, any more than He credited the expressions of grief and affection for Agnes, with which this account was interlarded. To end the business, He put the Pope's Bull into the hands of the Domina, and insisted, that ill or in health his Sister should be delivered to him without delay.

The Prioress received the paper with an air of humility: But no sooner had her eye glanced over the contents, than her resentment baffled all the efforts of Hypocrisy. A deep crimson spread itself over her face, and She darted upon Lorenzo looks of rage and menace.

'This order is positive,' said She in a voice of anger, which She in vain strove to disguise; 'Willingly would I obey it; But unfortunately it is out of my power.'

Lorenzo interrupted her by an exclamation of surprize.

'I repeat it, Segnor; to obey this order is totally out of my power. From tenderness to a Brother's feelings, I would have communicated the sad event to you by degrees, and have prepared you to hear it with fortitude. My measures are broken through: This order commands me to deliver up to you the Sister Agnes without delay; I am therefore obliged to inform you without circumlocution, that on Friday last She expired.'

Lorenzo started back with horror, and turned pale. A moment's recollection convinced him, that this assertion must be false, and it restored him to himself.

'You deceive me!' said He passionately; 'But five minutes past since you assured me, that though ill She was still alive. Produce her this instant! See her I must and will, and every attempt to keep her from me will be unavailing.'

'You forget yourself, Segnor; You owe respect to my age as well as my profession. Your Sister is no more. If I at first concealed her death, it was from dreading, lest an event so unexpected should produce on you too violent an effect. In truth, I am but ill repaid for my attention. And what interest, I pray you, should I have in detaining her? To know her wish of quitting our society is a sufficient reason for me to wish her absence, and think her a disgrace to the Sister-hood of St Clare: But She has forfeited my affection in a manner yet more culpable. Her crimes were great, and when you know the cause of her death, you will doubtless rejoice, Don Lorenzo, that such a Wretch is no longer in existence. She was taken ill on Thursday last on returning from confession in the Capuchin-Chapel. Her malady seemed attended with strange circumstances; But She persisted in concealing its cause: Thanks to the Virgin, we were too ignorant to suspect it! Judge then what must have been our consternation, our horror, when She was delivered the next day of a still-born Child, whom She immediately followed to the Grave. How, Segnor? Is it possible, that your countenance expresses no surprize, no indignation? Is it possible, that your Sister's infamy was known to you, and that still She possessed your affection? In that case, you have no need of my compassion. I can say nothing more, except repeat my inability of obeying the orders of his Holiness. Agnes is no more, and to convince you that what I say is true, I swear by our blessed Saviour, that three days have past since She was buried.'

Here She kissed a small crucifix, which hung at her girdle. She then rose from her chair, and quitted the Parlour. As She withdrew, She cast upon Lorenzo a scornful smile.

'Farewell, Segnor,' said She; 'I know no remedy for this accident: I fear that even a second Bull from the Pope will not procure your Sister's resurrection.'

Lorenzo also retired, penetrated with affliction: But Don Raymond's at the news of this event amounted to Madness. He would not be convinced that Agnes was really dead, and continued to insist, that the Walls of St Clare still confined her. No arguments could make him abandon his hopes of regaining her: Every day some fresh scheme was invented for procuring intelligence of her, and all of them were attended with the same success.

On his part, Medina gave up the idea of ever seeing his Sister more: Yet He believed, that She had been taken off by unfair means. Under this persuasion, He encouraged Don Raymond's researches, determined, should He discover the least warrant for his suspicions, to take a severe vengeance upon the unfeeling Prioress. The loss of his Sister affected him sincerely; Nor was it the least cause of his distress, that propriety obliged him for some time to defer mentioning Antonia to the Duke. In the mean while his emissaries constantly surrounded Elvira's Door. He had intelligence of all the movements of his Mistress: As She never failed every Thursday to attend the Sermon in the Capuchin Cathedral, He was secure of seeing her once a week, though in compliance with his promise, He carefully shunned her observation. Thus two long Months passed away. Still no information was procured of Agnes: All but the Marquis credited her death; and now Lorenzo determined to disclose his sentiments to his Uncle. He had already dropt some hints of his intention to marry; They had been as favourably received as He could expect, and He harboured no doubt of the success of his application.

CHAPTER III

> While in each other's arms entranced They lay,
> They blessed the night, and curst the coming day.
> > Lee.

THE burst of transport was past: Ambrosio's lust was satisfied; Pleasure fled, and Shame usurped her seat in his bosom. Confused and terrified at his weakness He drew himself from Matilda's arms. His perjury presented itself before him: He reflected on the scene which had just been acted, and trembled at the consequences of a discovery. He looked forward with horror; His heart was despondent, and became the abode of satiety and disgust. He avoided the eyes of his Partner in frailty; A melancholy silence prevailed, during which Both seemed busied with disagreeable reflections.

Matilda was the first to break it. She took his hand gently, and pressed it to her burning lips.

'Ambrosio!' She murmured in a soft and trembling voice.

The Abbot started at the sound. He turned his eyes upon Matilda's: They were filled with tears; Her cheeks were covered with blushes, and her supplicating looks seemed to solicit his compassion.

'Dangerous Woman!' said He; 'Into what an abyss of misery have you plunged me! Should your sex be discovered, my honour, nay my life, must pay for the pleasure of a few moments. Fool that I was, to trust myself to your seductions! What can now be done? How can my offence be expiated? What atonement can purchase the pardon of my crime? Wretched Matilda, you have destroyed my quiet for ever!'

'To me these reproaches, Ambrosio? To me, who have sacrificed for you the world's pleasures, the luxury of wealth, the delicacy of sex, my Friends, my fortune, and my fame? What have you lost, which I preserved? Have *I* not shared in *your* guilt? Have *you* not shared in *my* pleasure? Guilt, did I say? In what consists ours, unless in the opinion of an ill-judging World? Let that World be ignorant of them, and our joys become divine and blameless! Unnatural were your vows of Celibacy; Man was not created for such a state; And were Love a crime, God never would have made it so sweet, so irresistible! Then banish those clouds from your brow, my Ambrosio! Indulge in those pleasures freely, without which life is a worthless gift: Cease to reproach me with having taught you, what is bliss, and feel equal transports with the Woman who adores you!'

As She spoke, her eyes were filled with a delicious languor. Her bosom panted: She twined her arms voluptuously round him, drew him towards her, and glewed her lips to his. Ambrosio again raged with desire: The die was thrown: His vows were already broken; He had already committed the crime, and why should He refrain from enjoying its reward? He clasped her to his breast with redoubled ardour. No longer repressed by the sense of shame, He gave a loose to his intemperate appetites: While the fair Wanton put every invention of lust in practice, every refinement in the art of pleasure, which might heighten the bliss of her possession, and render her Lover's transports still more exquisite. Ambrosio rioted in delights till then unknown to him: Swift fled the night, and the Morning blushed to behold him still clasped in the embraces of Matilda.

Intoxicated with pleasure, the Monk rose from the Syren's luxurious Couch. He no longer reflected with shame upon his incontinence, or dreaded the vengeance of offended heaven. His only fear was, lest Death should rob him of enjoyments, for which his long Fast had only given a keener edge to his appetite. Matilda was still under the influence of poison, and the voluptuous Monk trembled less for his Preserver's life than his Concubine's. Deprived of her, He would not easily find another Mistress, with whom He could indulge his passions so fully, and so safely. He therefore pressed her with earnestness to use the means of preservation, which She had declared to be in her possession.

'Yes!' replied Matilda; 'Since you have made me feel that Life is valuable, I will rescue mine at any rate. No dangers shall appall me: I will look upon the consequences of my action boldly, nor shudder at the horrors which they present. I will think my sacrifice scarcely worthy to purchase your possession, and remember, that a moment past in your arms in *this* world, o'er-pays an age of punishment in the next. But before I take this step, Ambrosio, give me your solemn oath never to enquire, by what means I shall preserve myself.'

He did so in a manner the most binding.

'I thank you, my Beloved. This precaution is necessary, for though you know it not, you are under the command of vulgar prejudices: The Business on which I must be employed this night, might startle you from its singularity, and lower me in your opinion. Tell me; Are you possessed of the Key of the low door on the western side of the Garden?'

'The Door which opens into the burying-ground common to us and the Sister-hood of St Clare? I have not the Key, but can easily procure it.'

'You have only this to do. Admit me into the burying-ground at midnight; Watch while I descend into the vaults of St Clare, lest some prying eye should observe my actions; Leave me there alone for an hour, and that life is safe, which I dedicate to your pleasures. To prevent creating suspicion do not visit me during the day. Remember the Key, and that I expect you before twelve. Hark! I hear steps approaching! Leave me; I will pretend to sleep.'

The Friar obeyed, and left the Cell. As He opened the door, Father Pablos made his appearance.

'I come,' said the Latter 'to enquire after the health of my young Patient.'

'Hush!' replied Ambrosio, laying his finger upon his lip; 'Speak softly; I am just come from him. He has fallen into a profound slumber, which doubtless will be of service to him. Do not disturb him at present, for He wishes to repose.'

Father Pablos obeyed, and hearing the Bell ring, accompanied the Abbot to Matins. Ambrosio felt embarrassed, as He entered the Chapel. Guilt was new to him, and He fancied that every eye could read the transactions of the night upon his countenance. He strove to pray; His bosom no longer glowed with devotion; His thoughts insensibly wandered to Matilda's secret charms. But what He wanted in purity of heart, He supplied by exterior sanctity. The better to cloak his transgression, He redoubled his pretensions to the semblance of virtue, and never appeared more devoted to Heaven as since He had broken through his engagements. Thus did He unconsciously add Hypocrisy to perjury and incontinence; He had fallen into the latter errors from yielding to seduction almost irresistible; But he was now guilty of a voluntary fault by endeavouring to conceal those, into which Another had betrayed him.

The Matins concluded, Ambrosio retired to his Cell. The pleasures which He had just tasted for the first time were still impressed upon his mind. His brain was bewildered, and presented a confused Chaos of remorse, voluptuousness, inquietude, and fear. He looked back with regret to that peace of soul, that security of virtue, which till then had been his portion. He had indulged in excesses whose very idea but four and twenty hours before He had recoiled at with horror. He shuddered at reflecting, that a trifling indiscretion on his part, or on Matilda's, would overturn that fabric of reputation which it had cost him thirty years to erect, and render him the abhorrence of that People of whom He was then the Idol. Conscience painted to him in glaring colours his perjury and weakness; Apprehension magnified to him the horrors of punishment, and He already fancied himself in the prisons of the Inquisition. To these tormenting ideas, succeeded Matilda's beauty, and those delicious lessons, which once learnt can never be forgotten. A single glance thrown upon these reconciled him with himself. He considered the pleasures of the former night to have been purchased at an easy price by the sacrifice of innocence and honour. Their very remembrance filled his soul with ecstacy; He cursed his foolish vanity, which had induced him to waste in obscurity the bloom of life, ignorant of the blessings of Love and Woman. He determined at all events to continue his commerce with Matilda, and called every argument to his aid, which might confirm his resolution. He asked himself, provided his irregularity was unknown, in what would his fault consist, and what consequences He had to apprehend? By adhering strictly to every rule of his order save Chastity, He doubted not to retain the esteem of Men, and even the protection of heaven. He trusted easily to be forgiven so slight and natural a deviation from his vows: But He forgot that having pronounced those vows, Incontinence, in Lay-men the most venial of errors, became in his person the most heinous of crimes.

Once decided upon his future conduct, his mind became more easy. He threw himself upon his bed, and strove by sleeping to recruit his strength exhausted by his nocturnal excesses. He awoke refreshed, and eager for a repetition of his pleasures. Obedient to Matilda's order, He visited not her Cell during the day. Father Pablos mentioned in the Refectory, that Rosario had at length been prevailed upon to follow his prescription; But that the medicine had not produced the slightest effect, and that He believed no mortal skill could rescue him from the Grave. With this opinion the Abbot agreed, and affected to lament the untimely fate of a Youth, whose talents had appeared so promising.

The night arrived. Ambrosio had taken care to procure from the Porter the Key of the low door opening into the Cemetery. Furnished with this, when all was silent in the Monastery, He quitted his Cell, and hastened to Matilda's. She had left her bed, and was drest before his arrival.

'I have been expecting you with impatience,' said She; 'My life depends upon these moments. Have you the Key?'

'I have.'

'Away then to the garden. We have no time to lose. Follow me!'

She took a small covered Basket from the Table. Bearing this in one hand, and the Lamp, which was flaming upon the Hearth, in the other, She hastened from the Cell. Ambrosio followed her. Both maintained a profound silence. She moved on with quick but cautious steps, passed through the Cloisters, and reached the Western side of the Garden. Her eyes flashed with a fire and wildness, which impressed the Monk at once with awe and horror. A determined desperate courage reigned upon her brow. She gave the Lamp to Ambrosio; Then taking from him the Key, She unlocked the low Door, and entered the Cemetery. It was a vast and spacious Square planted with yew-trees: Half of it belonged to the Abbey; The other half was the property of the Sister-hood of St Clare, and was protected by a roof of Stone. The Division was marked by an iron railing, the wicket of which was generally left unlocked.

Thither Matilda bent her course. She opened the wicket, and sought for the door leading to the subterraneous Vaults, where reposed the mouldering Bodies of the Votaries of St Clare. The night was perfectly dark; Neither Moon or Stars were visible. Luckily there was not a breath of Wind, and the Friar bore his Lamp in full security: By the assistance of its beams, the door of the Sepulchre was soon discovered. It was sunk within the hollow of a wall, and almost concealed by thick festoons of ivy hanging over it. Three steps of rough-hewn Stone conducted to it, and Matilda was on the point of descending them, when She suddenly started back.

'There are People in the Vaults!' She whispered to the Monk; 'Conceal yourself till they are past.'

She took refuge behind a lofty and magnificent Tomb, erected in honour of the Convent's Foundress. Ambrosio followed her example, carefully hiding his Lamp, lest its beams should betray them. But a few moments had elapsed when the Door was pushed open leading to the subterraneous Caverns. Rays of light proceeded up the Stair-case: They enabled the concealed Spectators to observe two Females drest in religious habits, who seemed engaged in earnest conversation. The Abbot had no difficulty to recognize the Prioress of St Clare in the first, and one of the elder Nuns in her Companion.

'Every thing is prepared,' said the Prioress; 'Her fate shall be decided to-morrow. All her tears and sighs will be unavailing. No! In five and twenty years that I have been Superior of this Convent, never did I witness a transaction more infamous!'

'You must expect much opposition to your will;' the Other replied in a milder voice; 'Agnes has many Friends in the Convent, and in particular the Mother St Ursula will espouse her cause most warmly. In truth, She merits to have Friends; and I wish, I could prevail upon you to consider her youth, and her peculiar situation. She seems sensible of her fault; The excess of her grief proves her penitence, and I am convinced that her tears flow more from contrition, than fear of punishment. Reverend Mother, would you be persuaded to mitigate the severity of your sentence, would you but deign to over-look this first transgression, I offer myself as the pledge of her future conduct.'

'Over-look it, say you? Mother Camilla, you amaze me! What? After disgracing me in the presence of Madrid's Idol, of the very Man on whom I most wished to impress an idea of the strictness of my discipline? How despicable must I have appeared to the reverend Abbot! No, Mother, No! I never can forgive the insult. I cannot better convince Ambrosio that I abhor such crimes, than by punishing that of Agnes with all the rigour of which our severe laws admit. Cease then your supplications; They will all be unavailing. My resolution is taken: To-morrow Agnes shall be made a terrible example of my justice and resentment.'

The Mother Camilla seemed not to give up the point, but by this time the Nuns were out of hearing. The Prioress unlocked the door which communicated with St Clare's Chapel, and having entered with her Companion closed it again after them.

Matilda now asked, who was this Agnes with whom the Prioress was thus incensed, and what connexion She could have with Ambrosio. He related her adventure; and He added, that since that time his ideas having undergone a thorough revolution, He now felt much compassion for the unfortunate Nun.

'I design,' said He, 'to request an audience of the Domina to-morrow, and use every means of obtaining a mitigation of her sentence.'

'Beware of what you do!' interrupted Matilda; 'Your sudden change of sentiment may naturally create surprize, and may give birth to suspicions which it is most our interest to avoid. Rather redouble your outward austerity, and thunder out menaces against the errors of others, the better to conceal your own. Abandon the Nun to her fate. Your interfering might be dangerous, and her imprudence merits to be punished: She is unworthy to enjoy Love's pleasures, who has not wit enough to conceal them. But in discussing this trifling subject I waste moments which are precious. The night flies apace, and much must be done before morning. The Nuns are retired; All is safe. Give me the Lamp, Ambrosio. I must descend alone into these Caverns: Wait here, and if any one approaches, warn me by your voice; But as you value your existence, presume not to follow me. Your life would fall a victim to your imprudent curiosity.'

Thus saying She advanced towards the Sepulchre, still holding her Lamp in one hand, and her little Basket in the other. She touched the door: It turned slowly upon its grating hinges, and a narrow winding stair-case of black marble presented itself to her eyes. She descended it. Ambrosio remained above, watching the faint beams of the Lamp, as they still proceeded up the stairs. They disappeared, and He found himself in total darkness.

Left to himself He could not reflect without surprize on the sudden change in Matilda's character and sentiments. But a few days had past, since She appeared the mildest and softest of her sex, devoted to his will, and looking up to him as to a superior Being. Now She assumed a sort of courage and manliness in her manners and discourse but ill calculated to please him. She spoke no longer to insinuate, but command: He found himself unable to

cope with her in argument, and was unwillingly obliged to confess the
superiority of her judgment. Every moment convinced him of the
astonishing powers of her mind: But what She gained in the opinion of the
Man, She lost with interest in the affection of the Lover. He regretted
Rosario, the fond, the gentle, and submissive: He grieved, that Matilda
preferred the virtues of his sex to those of her own; and when He thought
of her expressions respecting the devoted Nun, He could not help blaming
them as cruel and unfeminine. Pity is a sentiment so natural, so appropriate
to the female character, that it is scarcely a merit for a Woman to possess
it, but to be without it is a grievous crime. Ambrosio could not easily forgive
his Mistress for being deficient in this amiable quality. However, though he
blamed her insensibility, He felt the truth of her observations; and though
He pitied sincerely the unfortunate Agnes, He resolved to drop the idea of
interposing in her behalf.

Near an hour had elapsed, since Matilda descended into the Caverns; Still
She returned not. Ambrosio's curiosity was excited. He drew near the
Stair-case. He listened. All was silent, except that at intervals He caught the
sound of Matilda's voice, as it wound along the subterraneous passages, and
was re-echoed by the Sepulchre's vaulted roofs. She was at too great a
distance for him to distinguish her words, and ere they reached him they
were deadened into a low murmur. He longed to penetrate into this
mystery. He resolved to disobey her injunctions, and follow her into the
Cavern. He advanced to the Stair-case; He had already descended some
steps, when his courage failed him. He remembered Matilda's menaces if
He infringed her orders, and his bosom was filled with a secret unaccountable awe. He returned up the stairs, resumed his former station, and waited
impatiently for the conclusion of this adventure.

Suddenly He was sensible of a violent shock: An earth-quake rocked the
ground. The Columns, which supported the roof under which He stood,
were so strongly shaken, that every moment menaced him with its fall, and
at the same moment He heard a loud and tremendous burst of thunder. It
ceased, and his eyes being fixed upon the Stair-case, He saw a bright column
of light flash along the Caverns beneath. It was seen but for an instant. No
sooner did it disappear, than all was once more quiet and obscure. Profound
Darkness again surrounded him, and the silence of night was only broken
by the whirring Bat, as She flitted slowly by him.

With every instant Ambrosio's amazement increased. Another hour
elapsed, after which the same light again appeared and was lost again as
suddenly. It was accompanied by a strain of sweet but solemn Music, which
as it stole through the Vaults below, inspired the Monk with mingled delight
and terror. It had not long been hushed, when He heard Matilda's steps
upon the Stair-case. She ascended from the Cavern; The most lively joy
animated her beautiful features.

'Did you see any thing?' She asked.

'Twice I saw a column of light flash up the Stair-case.'

'Nothing else?'

'Nothing.'

'The Morning is on the point of breaking. Let us retire to the Abbey, lest day-light should betray us.'

With a light step She hastened from the burying-ground. She regained her Cell, and the curious Abbot still accompanied her. She closed the door, and disembarrassed herself of her Lamp and Basket.

'I have succeeded!' She cried, throwing herself upon his bosom: 'Succeeded beyond my fondest hopes! I shall live, Ambrosio, shall live for you! The step, which I shuddered at taking, proves to me a source of joys inexpressible! Oh! that I dared communicate those joys to you! Oh! that I were permitted to share with you my power, and raise you as high above the level of your sex, as one bold deed has exalted me above mine!'

'And what prevents you, Matilda?' interrupted the Friar; 'Why is your business in the Cavern made a secret? Do you think me undeserving of your confidence? Matilda, I must doubt the truth of your affection, while you have joys in which I am forbidden to share.'

'You reproach me with injustice. I grieve sincerely, that I am obliged to conceal from you my happiness. But I am not to blame: The fault lies not in me, but in yourself, my Ambrosio! You are still too much the Monk. Your mind is enslaved by the prejudices of Education; And Superstition might make you shudder at the idea of that, which experience has taught me to prize and value. At present you are unfit to be trusted with a secret of such importance: But the strength of your judgment; and the curiosity which I rejoice to see sparkling in your eyes, makes me hope, that you will one day deserve my confidence. Till that period arrives, restrain your impatience. Remember that you have given me your solemn oath, never to enquire into this night's adventures. I insist upon your keeping this oath: For though' She added smiling, while She sealed his lips with a wanton kiss; 'Though I forgive your breaking your vows to heaven, I expect you to keep your vows to me.'

The Friar returned the embrace, which had set his blood on fire. The luxurious and unbounded excesses of the former night were renewed, and they separated not till the Bell rang for Matins.

The same pleasures were frequently repeated. The Monks rejoiced in the feigned Rosario's unexpected recovery, and none of them suspected his real sex. The Abbot possessed his Mistress in tranquillity, and perceiving his frailty unsuspected, abandoned himself to his passions in full security. Shame and remorse no longer tormented him. Frequent repetitions made him familiar with sin, and his bosom became proof against the stings of Conscience. In these sentiments He was encouraged by Matilda; But She soon was aware that She had satiated her Lover by the unbounded freedom of her caresses. Her charms becoming accustomed to him, they ceased to excite the same desires, which at first they had inspired. The delirium of passion being past, He had leisure to observe every trifling defect: Where none were to be found, Satiety made him fancy them. The Monk was glutted with the fullness of pleasure: A Week had scarcely elapsed, before He was wearied of his Paramour: His warm constitution still made him seek in her arms the gratification of his lust: But when the moment of passion was over, He quitted her with disgust, and his humour, naturally inconstant, made him sigh impatiently for variety.

Possession, which cloys Man, only increases the affection of Woman. Matilda with every succeeding day grew more attached to the Friar. Since He had obtained her favours, He was become dearer to her than ever, and She felt grateful to him for the pleasures, in which they had equally been Sharers. Unfortunately as her passion grew ardent, Ambrosio's grew cold; The very marks of her fondness excited his disgust, and its excess served to extinguish the flame, which already burned but feebly in his bosom. Matilda could not but remark that her society seemed to him daily less agreeable: He was inattentive while She spoke: her musical talents, which She possessed in perfection, had lost the power of amusing him; Or if He deigned to praise them, his compliments were evidently forced and cold. He no longer gazed upon her with affection, or applauded her sentiments with a Lover's partiality. This Matilda well perceived, and redoubled her efforts to revive those sentiments, which He once had felt. She could not but fail, since He considered as importunities, the pains which She took to please him, and was disgusted by the very means which She used to recall the Wanderer. Still, however, their illicit Commerce continued: But it was clear, that He was led to her arms, not by love, but the cravings of brutal appetite. His constitution made a Woman necessary to him, and Matilda was the only one with whom He could indulge his passions safely: In spite of her beauty, He gazed upon every other Female with more desire; But fearing that his Hypocrisy should be made public, He confined his inclinations to his own breast.

It was by no means his nature to be timid: But his education had impressed his mind with fear so strongly, that apprehension was now become part of his character. Had his Youth been passed in the world, He would have shown himself possessed of many brilliant and manly qualities. He was naturally enterprizing, firm, and fearless: He had a Warrior's heart, and He might have shone with splendour at the head of an Army. There was no want of generosity in his nature: The Wretched never failed to find in him a compassionate Auditor: His abilities were quick and shining, and his judgment vast, solid, and decisive. With such qualifications He would have been an ornament to his Country: That He possessed them, He had given proofs in his earliest infancy, and his Parents had beheld his dawning virtues with the fondest delight and admiration. Unfortunately, while yet a Child He was deprived of those Parents. He fell into the power of a Relation, whose only wish about him was never to hear of him more; For that purpose He gave him in charge to his Friend, the former Superior of the Capuchins. The Abbot, a very Monk, used all his endeavours to persuade the Boy, that happiness existed not without the walls of a Convent. He succeeded fully. To deserve admittance into the order of St Francis was Ambrosio's highest ambition. His Instructors carefully repressed those virtues, whose grandeur and disinterestedness were ill-suited to the Cloister. Instead of universal benevolence He adopted a selfish partiality for his own particular establishment: He was taught to consider compassion for the errors of Others as a crime of the blackest dye: The noble frankness of his temper was exchanged for servile humility; and in order to break his natural spirit, the Monks terrified his young mind, by placing before him all the horrors with which Superstition could furnish them: They painted to him the torments of the Damned in colours the most dark, terrible, and fantastic, and threatened him at the slightest fault with eternal perdition. No wonder, that his imagination constantly dwelling upon these fearful objects should have rendered his character timid and apprehensive. Add to this, that his long absence from the great world, and total unacquaintance with the common dangers of life made him form of them an idea far more dismal than the reality. While the Monks were busied in rooting out his virtues, and narrowing his sentiments, they allowed every vice which had fallen to his share, to arrive at full perfection. He was suffered to be proud, vain, ambitious, and disdainful: He was jealous of his Equals, and despised all merit but his own: He was implacable when offended, and cruel in his revenge. Still in spite of the pains taken to pervert them, his natural good qualities would occasionally break through the gloom cast over them so carefully: At such times the contest for superiority between his real and acquired character was striking and unaccountable to those unacquainted with his original disposition. He pronounced the most severe sentences upon Offenders, which the moment after Compassion induced him to mitigate: He undertook the most daring enterprizes, which the fear of their consequences soon obliged him to abandon: His in-born genius darted a brilliant light upon subjects the most obscure; and almost instantaneously his Superstition replunged them in darkness more profound than that from which they had just been rescued. His Brother Monks, regarding him as a Superior Being, remarked not this contradiction in their Idol's conduct. They were persuaded, that what He did must be right, and supposed him to have good reasons for changing his resolutions. The fact was, that the different sentiments, with which Education and Nature had inspired him, were combating in his bosom: It remained for his passions which as yet no opportunity had called into play, to decide the victory. Unfortunately his passions were the very worst Judges, to whom He could possibly have applied. His monastic seclusion had till now been in his favour, since it gave him no room for discovering his bad qualities. The superiority of his talents raised him too far above his Companions to permit his being jealous of them: His exemplary piety, persuasive eloquence, and pleasing manners had secured him universal Esteem, and consequently He had no injuries to revenge: His Ambition was justified by his acknowledged merit, and his pride considered as no more than proper confidence. He never saw, much less conversed with, the other sex: He was ignorant of the pleasures in Woman's power to bestow, and if He read in the course of his studies

'That Men were fond, He smiled, and wondered how!'

For a time spare diet, frequent watching, and severe penance cooled and represt the natural warmth of his constitution: But no sooner did opportunity present itself, no sooner did He catch a glimpse of joys to which He was still a Stranger, than Religion's barriers were too feeble to resist the over-whelming torrent of his desires. All impediments yielded before the force of his temperament, warm, sanguine, and voluptuous in the excess. As yet his other passions lay dormant; But they only needed to be once awakened, to display themselves with violence as great and irresistible.

He continued to be the admiration of Madrid. The Enthusiasm created by his eloquence seemed rather to increase than diminish. Every Thursday, which was the only day when He appeared in public, the Capuchin-Cathedral was crowded with Auditors, and his discourse was always received with the same approbation. He was named Confessor to all the chief families in Madrid; and no one was counted fashionable, who was injoined penance by any other than Ambrosio. In his resolution of never stirring out of his Convent He still persisted. This circumstance created a still greater opinion of his sanctity and self-denial. Above all the Women sang forth his praises loudly, less influenced by devotion than by his noble countenance, majestic air, and well-turned graceful figure. The Abbey-door was thronged with Carriages from morning to night; and the noblest and fairest Dames of Madrid confessed to the Abbot their secret peccadilloes. The eyes of the luxurious Friar devoured their charms. Had his Penitents consulted those Interpreters, He would have needed no other means of expressing his desires. For his misfortune, they were so strongly persuaded of his continence, that the possibility of his harbouring indecent thoughts never once entered their imaginations. The climate's heat, 'tis well known, operates with no small influence upon the constitutions of the Spanish Ladies: But the most abandoned would have thought it an easier task to inspire with passion the marble Statue of St Francis, than the cold and rigid heart of the immaculate Ambrosio.

On his part, the Friar was little acquainted with the depravity of the world; He suspected not, that but few of his Penitents would have rejected his addresses. Yet had He been better instructed on this head, the danger attending such an attempt would have sealed up his lips in silence. He knew that it would be difficult for a Woman to keep a secret so strange and so important as his frailty; and He even trembled, lest Matilda should betray him. Anxious to preserve a reputation which was infinitely dear to him, He saw all the risque of committing it to the power of some vain giddy Female; and as the Beauties of Madrid affected only his senses without touching his heart, He forgot them as soon as they were out of his sight. The danger of discovery, the fear of being repulsed, the loss of reputation, all these considerations counselled him to stifle his desires: And though He now felt for it the most perfect indifference, He was necessitated to confine himself to Matilda's person.

One morning, the confluence of Penitents was greater than usual. He was detained in the Confessional Chair till a late hour. At length the crowd was dispatched, and He prepared to quit the Chapel, when two Females entered, and drew near him with humility. They threw up their veils, and the youngest entreated him to listen to her for a few moments. The melody of her voice, of that voice to which no Man ever listened without interest, immediately caught Ambrosio's attention. He stopped. The Petitioner seemed bowed down with affliction: Her cheeks were pale, her eyes dimmed with tears, and her hair fell in disorder over her face and bosom. Still her countenance was so sweet, so innocent, so heavenly, as might have charmed an heart less susceptible, than that which panted in the Abbot's breast. With more than usual softness of manner He desired her to proceed, and heard her speak as follows with an emotion, which increased every moment.

'Reverend Father, you see an Unfortunate, threatened with the loss of her dearest, of almost her only Friend! My Mother, my excellent Mother lies upon the bed of sickness. A sudden and dreadful malady seized her last night; and so rapid has been its progress, that the Physicians despair of her life. Human aid fails me; Nothing remains for me but to implore the mercy of Heaven. Father, all Madrid rings with the report of your piety and virtue. Deign to remember my Mother in your prayers: Perhaps they may prevail on the Almighty to spare her; and should that be the case, I engage myself every Thursday in the next three Months to illuminate the Shrine of St Francis in his honour.'

'So!' thought the Monk; 'Here we have a second Vincentio della Ronda. Rosario's adventure began thus,' and He wished secretly, that this might have the same conclusion.

He acceded to the request. The Petitioner returned him thanks with every mark of gratitude, and then continued.

'I have yet another favour to ask. We are Strangers in Madrid; My Mother needs a Confessor, and knows not to whom She should apply. We understand that you never quit the Abbey, and Alas! my poor Mother is unable to come hither! If you would have the goodness, reverend Father, to name a proper person, whose wise and pious consolations may soften the agonies of my Parent's death-bed, you will confer an everlasting favour upon hearts not ungrateful.'

With this petition also the Monk complied. Indeed, what petition would He have refused, if urged in such enchanting accents? The suppliant was so interesting! Her voice was so sweet, so harmonious! Her very tears became her, and her affliction seemed to add new lustre to her charms. He promised to send to her a Confessor that same Evening, and begged her to leave her address. The Companion presented him with a Card on which it was written, and then with-drew with the fair Petitioner, who pronounced before her departure a thousand benedictions on the Abbot's goodness. His eyes followed her out of the Chapel. It was not till She was out of sight that He examined the Card, on which He read the following words.

'Donna Elvira Dalfa, Strada di San Iago, four doors from the Palace d'Albornos.'

The Suppliant was no other than Antonia, and Leonella was her Companion. The Latter had not consented without difficulty to accompany her Niece to the Abbey: Ambrosio had inspired her with such awe, that She trembled at the very sight of him. Her fears had conquered even her natural loquacity, and while in his presence She uttered not a single syllable.

The Monk retired to his Cell, whither He was pursued by Antonia's image. He felt a thousand new emotions springing in his bosom, and He trembled to examine into the cause which gave them birth. They were totally different from those inspired by Matilda, when She first declared her sex and her affection. He felt not the provocation of lust; No voluptuous desires rioted in his bosom; Nor did a burning imagination picture to him the charms, which Modesty had veiled from his eyes. On the contrary, what He now felt was a mingled sentiment of tenderness, admiration, and respect. A soft and delicious melancholy infused itself into his soul, and He would not have exchanged it for the most lively transports of joy. Society now disgusted him: He delighted in solitude, which permitted his indulging the visions of Fancy: His thoughts were all gentle, sad, and soothing, and the whole wide world presented him with no other object than Antonia.

'Happy Man!' He exclaimed in his romantic enthusiasm; 'Happy Man, who is destined to possess the heart of that lovely Girl! What delicacy in her features! What elegance in her form! How enchanting was the timid innocence of her eyes, and how different from the wanton expression, the wild luxurious fire, which sparkles in Matilda's! Oh! sweeter must one kiss be snatched from the rosy lips of the First, than all the full and lustful favours bestowed so freely by the Second. Matilda gluts me with enjoyment even to loathing, forces me to her arms, apes the Harlot, and glories in her prostitution. Disgusting! Did She know the inexpressible charm of Modesty, how irresistibly it enthralls the heart of Man, how firmly it chains him to the Throne of Beauty, She never would have thrown it off. What would be too dear a price for this lovely Girl's affections? What would I refuse to sacrifice, could I be released from my vows, and permitted to declare my love in the sight of earth and heaven? While I strove to inspire her with tenderness, with friendship and esteem, how tranquil and undisturbed would the hours roll away! Gracious God! To see her blue down-cast eyes beam upon mine with timid fondness! To sit for days, for years listening to that gentle voice! To acquire the right of obliging her, and hear the artless expressions of her gratitude! To watch the emotions of her spotless heart! To encourage each dawning virtue! To share in her joy when happy, to kiss away her tears when distrest, and to see her fly to my arms for comfort and support! Yes; If there is perfect bliss on earth, 'tis his lot alone, who becomes that Angel's Husband.'

While his fancy coined these ideas, He paced his Cell with a disordered air. His eyes were fixed upon vacancy: His head reclined upon his shoulder; A tear rolled down his cheek, while He reflected that the vision of happiness for him could never be realized.

'She is lost to me!' He continued; 'By marriage She cannot be mine: And to seduce such innocence, to use the confidence reposed in me to work her ruin. . . . Oh! it would be a crime, blacker than yet the world ever witnessed! Fear not, lovely Girl! Your virtue runs no risque from me. Not for Indies would I make that gentle bosom know the tortures of remorse.'

Again He paced his chamber hastily. Then stopping, his eye fell upon the picture of his once-admired Madona. He tore it with indignation from the wall: He threw it on the ground, and spurned it from him with his foot.

'The Prostitute!'

Unfortunate Matilda! Her Paramour forgot, that for his sake alone She had forfeited her claim to virtue; and his only reason for despising her was, that She had loved him much too well.

He threw himself into a Chair, which stood near the Table. He saw the card with Elvira's address. He took it up, and it brought to his recollection his promise respecting a Confessor. He passed a few minutes in doubt: But Antonia's Empire over him was already too much decided to permit his making a long resistance to the idea which struck him. He resolved to be the Confessor himself. He could leave the Abbey unobserved without difficulty: By wrapping up his head in his Cowl He hoped to pass through the Streets without being recognised: By taking these precautions, and by recommending secrecy to Elvira's family, He doubted not to keep Madrid in ignorance that He had broken his vow never to see the outside of the

Abbey-walls. Matilda was the only person whose vigilance He dreaded: But by informing her at the Refectory, that during the whole of that day Business would confine him to his Cell, He thought himself secure from her wakeful jealousy. Accordingly at the hours when the Spaniards are generally taking their Siesta, He ventured to quit the Abbey by a private door, the Key of which was in his possession. The Cowl of his habit was thrown over his face: From the heat of the weather the Streets were almost totally deserted: The Monk met with few people, found the Strada di San Iago, and arrived without accident at Donna Elvira's door. He rang, was admitted, and immediately ushered into an upper apartment.

It was here, that He ran the greatest risque of a discovery. Had Leonella been at home, She would have recognized him directly: Her communicative disposition would never have permitted her to rest, till all Madrid was informed that Ambrosio had ventured out of the Abbey, and visited her Sister. Fortune here stood the Monk's Friend. On Leonella's return home, She found a letter instructing her, that a Cousin was just dead, who had left what little He possessed between Herself and Elvira. To secure this bequest She was obliged to set out for Cordova without losing a moment. Amidst all her foibles her heart was truly warm and affectionate, and She was unwilling to quit her Sister in so dangerous a state. But Elvira insisted upon her taking the journey, conscious that in her Daughter's forlorn situation no increase of fortune, however trifling, ought to be neglected. Accordingly Leonella left Madrid, sincerely grieved at her Sister's illness, and giving some few sighs to the memory of the amiable but inconstant Don Christoval. She was fully persuaded, that at first She had made a terrible breach in his heart: But hearing nothing more of him, She supposed that He had quitted the pursuit, disgusted by the lowness of her origin, and knowing upon other terms than marriage He had nothing to hope from such a Dragon of Virtue as She professed herself; Or else, that being naturally capricious and changeable, the remembrance of her charms had been effaced from the Condé's heart by those of some newer Beauty. Whatever was the cause of her losing him, She lamented it sorely. She strove in vain, as She assured every body who was kind enough to listen to her, to tear his image from her too susceptible heart. She affected the airs of a love-sick Virgin, and carried them all to the most ridiculous excess. She heaved lamentable sighs, walked with her arms folded, uttered long soliloquies, and her discourse generally turned upon some forsaken Maid, who expired of a broken heart! Her fiery locks were always ornamented with a garland of willow; Every evening She was seen straying upon the Banks of a rivulet by Moon-light; and She declared herself a violent Admirer of murmuring Streams and Nightingales;

> 'Of lonely haunts, and twilight Groves,
> 'Places which pale Passion loves!'

Such was the state of Leonella's mind, when obliged to quit Madrid. Elvira was out of patience at all these follies, and endeavoured at persuading her to act like a reasonable Woman. Her advice was thrown away: Leonella assured her at parting, that nothing could make her forget the perfidious Don Christoval. In this point She was fortunately mistaken. An honest Youth of Cordova, Journeyman to an Apothecary, found that her fortune would be sufficient to set him up in a genteel Shop of his own: In consequence of this reflection He avowed himself her Admirer. Leonella was not inflexible. The ardour of his sighs melted her heart, and She soon consented to make him the happiest of Mankind. She wrote to inform her Sister of her marriage; But, for reasons which will be explained here-after, Elvira never answered her letter.

Ambrosio was conducted into the Anti-chamber to that, where Elvira was reposing. The Female Domestic who had admitted him, left him alone, while She announced his arrival to her Mistress. Antonia who had been by her Mother's Bed-side, immediately came to him.

'Pardon me, Father,' said She advancing towards him; when recognizing his features She stopped suddenly, and uttered a cry of joy. 'Is it possible!' She continued; 'Do not my eyes deceive me? Has the worthy Ambrosio broken through his resolution, that He may soften the agonies of the best of Women? What pleasure will this visit give my Mother! Let me not delay for a moment the comfort, which your piety and wisdom will afford her.'

Thus saying, She opened the chamber-door, presented to her Mother her distinguished Visitor, and having placed an armed-chair by the side of the Bed, withdrew into another department.

Elvira was highly gratified by this visit: Her expectations had been raised high by general report, but She found them far exceeded. Ambrosio, endowed by nature with powers of pleasing, exerted them to the utmost while conversing with Antonia's Mother. With persuasive eloquence He calmed every fear, and dissipated every scruple: He bad her reflect on the infinite mercy of her Judge, despoiled Death of his darts and terrors, and taught her to view without shrinking the abyss of eternity, on whose brink She then stood. Elvira was absorbed in attention and delight: While She listened to his exhortations, confidence and comfort stole insensibly into her mind. She unbosomed to him without hesitation her cares and apprehensions. The latter respecting a future life He had already quieted: And He now removed the former, which She felt for the concerns of this. She trembled for Antonia. She had none to whose care She could recommend her, save to the Marquis de las Cisternas, and her Sister Leonella. The protection of the One was very uncertain; and as to the Other, though fond of her Niece Leonella was so thoughtless and vain, as to make her an improper person to have the sole direction of a Girl so young and ignorant of the World. The Friar no sooner learnt the cause of her alarms, than He begged her to make herself easy upon that head. He doubted not being able to secure for Antonia a safe refuge in the House of one of his Penitents, the Marchioness of Villa-Franca: This was a Lady of acknowledged virtue, remarkable for strict principles and extensive charity. Should accident deprive her of this resource, He engaged to procure Antonia a reception in some respectable Convent: That is to say, in quality of boarder; for Elvira had declared herself no Friend to a monastic life, and the Monk was either candid or complaisant enough to allow, that her disapprobation was not unfounded.

These proofs of the interest which He felt for her, completely won Elvira's heart. In thanking him She exhausted every expression which Gratitude could furnish, and protested, that now She should resign herself with tranquillity to the Grave. Ambrosio rose to take leave: He promised to return the next day at the same hour, but requested that his visits might be kept secret.

'I am unwilling' said He, 'that my breaking through a rule imposed by necessity, should be generally known. Had I not resolved never to quit my Convent, except upon circumstances as urgent as that which has conducted me to your door, I should be frequently summoned upon insignificant occasions: That time would be engrossed by the Curious, the Unoccupied, and the fanciful, which I now pass at the Bed-side of the Sick, in comforting the expiring Penitent, and clearing the passage to Eternity from Thorns.'

Elvira commended equally his prudence and compassion, promising to conceal carefully the honour of his visits. The Monk then gave her his benediction, and retired from the chamber.

In the Anti-room He found Antonia: He could not refuse himself the pleasure of passing a few moments in her society. He bad her take comfort, for that her Mother seemed composed and tranquil, and He hoped that She might yet do well. He enquired who attended her, and engaged to send the Physician of his Convent to see her, one of the most skilful in Madrid. He then launched out in Elvira's commendation, praised her purity and fortitude of mind, and declared, that She had inspired him with the highest esteem and reverence. Antonia's innocent heart swelled with gratitude: Joy danced in her eyes, where a tear still sparkled. The hopes which He gave her of her Mother's recovery, the lively interest which He seemed to feel for her, and the flattering way in which She was mentioned by him, added to the report of his judgment and virtue, and to the impression made upon her by his eloquence, confirmed the favourable opinion with which his first appearance had inspired Antonia. She replied with diffidence, but without restraint: She feared not to relate to him all her little sorrows, all her little fears and anxieties; and She thanked him for his goodness with all the genuine warmth, which favours kindle in a young and innocent heart. Such alone know how to estimate benefits at their full value. They who are conscious of Mankind's perfidy and selfishness, ever receive an obligation with apprehension and distrust: They suspect, that some secret motive must lurk behind it: They express their thanks with restraint and caution, and fear to praise a kind action to its full extent, aware that some future day a return may be required. Not so Antonia; She thought, the world was composed only of those who resembled her, and that vice existed was to her still a secret. The Monk had been of service to her; He said, that He wished her well; She was grateful for his kindness, and thought that no terms were strong enough to be the vehicle of her thanks. With what delight did Ambrosio listen to the declaration of her artless gratitude! The natural grace of her manners, the unequalled sweetness of her voice, her modest vivacity, her unstudied elegance, her expressive countenance, and intelligent eyes united to inspire him with pleasure and admiration: While the solidity and correctness of her remarks received additional beauty from the unaffected simplicity of the language, in which they were conveyed.

Ambrosio was at length obliged to tear himself from this conversation, which possessed for him but too many charms. He repeated to Antonia his wishes, that his visits should not be made known, which desire She promised to observe. He then quitted the House, while his Enchantress hastened to her Mother, ignorant of the mischief which her Beauty had caused. She was eager to know Elvira's opinion of the Man whom She had praised in such enthusiastic terms, and was delighted to find it equally favourable, if not even more so, than her own.

'Even before He spoke,' said Elvira, 'I was prejudiced in his favour: The fervour of his exhortations, dignity of his manner, and closeness of his reasoning, were very far from inducing me to alter my opinion. His fine and full-toned voice struck me particularly; But surely, Antonia, I have heard it before. It seemed perfectly familiar to my ear. Either I must have known the Abbot in former times, or his voice bears a wonderful resemblance to that of some other, to whom I have often listened. There were certain tones which touched my very heart, and made me feel sensations so singular, that I strive in vain to account for them.'

'My dearest Mother, it produced the same effect upon me: Yet certainly neither of us ever heard his voice till we came to Madrid. I suspect, that what we attribute to his voice, really proceeds from his pleasant manners, which forbid our considering him as a Stranger. I know not why, but I feel more at my ease while conversing with him, than I usually do with people who are unknown to me. I feared not to repeat to him all my childish thoughts; and some-how I felt confident that He would hear my folly with indulgence. Oh! I was not deceived in him! He listened to me with such an air of kindness and attention! He answered me with such gentleness, such condescension! He did not call me an Infant, and treat me with contempt, as our cross old Confessor at the Castle used to do. I verily believe, that if I had lived in Murcia a thousand years, I never should have liked that fat old Father Dominic!'

'I confess, that Father Dominic had not the most pleasing manners in the world; But He was honest, friendly, and well-meaning.'

'Ah! my dear Mother, those qualities are so common!'

'God grant, my Child, that Experience may not teach you to think them rare and precious: I have found them but too much so! But tell me, Antonia; Why is it impossible for me to have seen the Abbot before?'

'Because since the moment when He entered the Abbey, He has never been on the outside of its walls. He told me just now, that from his ignorance of the Streets, He had some difficulty to find the Strada di San Iago, though so near the Abbey.'

'All this is possible, and still I may have seen him *before* He entered the Abbey: In order to come out, it was rather necessary that He should first go in.'

'Holy Virgin! As you say, that is very true.—Oh! But might He not have been born in the Abbey?'

Elvira smiled.

'Why not very easily.'

'Stay, Stay! Now I recollect how it was. He was put into the Abbey quite a Child; The common People say, that He fell from heaven, and was sent as a present to the Capuchins by the Virgin.'

'That was very kind of her. And so He fell from heaven, Antonia? He must have had a terrible tumble.'

'Many do not credit this, and I fancy, my dear Mother, that I must number you among the Unbelievers. Indeed, as our Land-lady told my Aunt, the general idea is, that his Parents, being poor and unable to maintain him, left him just born at the Abbey-door. The late Superior from pure charity had him educated in the Convent, and He proved to be a model of virtue, and piety, and learning, and I know not what else besides: In consequence, He was first received as a Brother of the order, and not long ago was chosen Abbot. However, whether this account or the other is the true one, at least all agree that when the Monks took him under their care, He could not speak: Therefore, you could not have heard his voice before He entered the Monastery, because at that time He had no voice at all.'

'Upon my word, Antonia, you argue very closely! Your conclusions are infallible! I did not suspect you of being so able a Logician.'

'Ah! You are mocking me! But so much the better. It delights me to see you in spirits: Besides you seem tranquil and easy, and I hope, that you will have no more convulsions. Oh! I was sure the Abbot's visit would do you good!'

'It has indeed done me good, my Child. He has quieted my mind upon some points which agitated me, and I already feel the effects of his attention. My eyes grow heavy, and I think I can sleep a little. Draw the curtains, my Antonia: But if I should not wake before midnight, do not sit up with me, I charge you.'

Antonia promised to obey her, and having received her blessing drew the curtains of the Bed. She then seated herself in silence at her embroidery frame, and beguiled the hours with building Castles in the air. Her spirits were enlivened by the evident change for the better in Elvira, and her fancy presented her with visions bright and pleasing. In these dreams Ambrosio made no despicable figure. She thought of him with joy and gratitude; But for every idea which fell to the Friar's share, at least two were unconsciously bestowed upon Lorenzo. Thus passed the time, till the Bell in the neighbouring Steeple of the Capuchin-Cathedral announced the hour of midnight. Antonia remembered her Mother's injunctions, and obeyed them, though with reluctance. She undrew the curtains with caution. Elvira was enjoying a profound and quiet slumber; Her cheek glowed with health's returning colours: A smile declared, that her dreams were pleasant, and as Antonia bent over her, She fancied that She heard her name pronounced. She kissed her Mother's fore-head softly, and retired to her chamber. There She knelt before a Statue of St Rosolia, her Patroness; She recommended herself to the protection of heaven, and as had been her custom from infancy, concluded her devotions by chaunting the following Stanzas.

MIDNIGHT HYMN

Now all is hushed; The solemn chime
No longer swells the nightly gale:
Thy awful presence, Hour sublime,
With spotless heart once more I hail.

'Tis now the moment still and dread,
When Sorcerers use their baleful power;
When Graves give up their buried dead
To profit by the sanctioned hour:

From guilt and guilty thoughts secure,
To duty and devotion true,
With bosom light and conscience pure,
Repose, thy gentle aid I woo.

Good Angels, take my thanks, that still
The snares of vice I view with scorn;
Thanks, that to-night as free from ill
I sleep, as when I woke at morn.

Yet may not my unconscious breast
Harbour some guilt to me unknown?
Some wish impure, which unreprest
You blush to see, and I to own?

If such there be, in gentle dream
Instruct my feet to shun the snare;
Bid truth upon my errors beam,
And deign to make me still your care.

Chase from my peaceful bed away
The witching Spell, a foe to rest,
The nightly Goblin, wanton Fay,
The Ghost in pain, and Fiend unblest:

Let not the Tempter in mine ear
Pour lessons of unhallowed joy;
Let not the Night-mare, wandering near
My Couch, the calm of sleep destroy;

Let not some horrid dream affright
With strange fantastic forms mine eyes;
But rather bid some vision bright
Display the bliss of yonder skies.

Show me the crystal Domes of Heaven,
The worlds of light where Angels lie;
Shew me the lot of Mortals given,
Who guiltless live, who guiltless die.

Then show me how a seat to gain
Amidst those blissful realms of Air;
Teach me to shun each guilty stain,
And guide me to the good and fair.

So every morn and night, my Voice
To heaven the grateful strain shall raise;
In You as Guardian Powers rejoice,
Good Angels, and exalt your praise:

So will I strive with zealous fire
Each vice to shun, each fault correct;
Will love the lessons you inspire,
And Prize the virtues you protect.

Then when at length by high command
My body seeks the Grave's repose,

When Death draws nigh with friendly hand
My failing Pilgrim eyes to close;

Pleased that my soul has 'scaped the wreck,
Sighless will I my life resign,
And yield to God my Spirit back,
As pure as when it first was mine.

Having finished her usual devotions, Antonia retired to bed. Sleep soon stole over her senses; and for several hours She enjoyed that calm repose which innocence alone can know, and for which many a Monarch with pleasure would exchange his Crown.

CHAPTER IV

——and Ah! how dark
These long-extended realms and rueful wastes;
Where nought but silence reigns, and night, dark night,
Dark as was Chaos ere the Infant Sun
Was rolled together, or had tried its beams
Athwart the gloom profound! The sickly Taper
By glimmering through thy low-browed misty vaults,
Furred round with mouldy damps, and ropy slime,
Lets fall a supernumerary horror,
And only serves to make Thy night more irksome!

                                                    Blair.

RETURNED undiscovered to the Abbey, Ambrosio's mind was filled with the most pleasing images. He was wilfully blind to the danger of exposing himself to Antonia's charms: He only remembered the pleasure which her society had afforded him, and rejoiced in the prospect of that pleasure being repeated. He failed not to profit by Elvira's indisposition to obtain a sight of her Daughter every day. At first He bounded his wishes to inspire Antonia with friendship: But no sooner was He convinced that She felt that sentiment in its fullest extent, than his aim became more decided, and his attentions assumed a warmer colour. The innocent familiarity with which She treated him, encouraged his desires: Grown used to her modesty, it no longer commanded the same respect and awe: He still admired it, but it only made him more anxious to deprive her of that quality, which formed her principal charm. Warmth of passion, and natural penetration, of which latter unfortunately both for himself and Antonia He possessed an ample share, supplied a knowledge of the arts of seduction. He easily distinguished the emotions which were favourable to his designs, and seized every means with avidity of infusing corruption into Antonia's bosom. This He found no easy matter. Extreme simplicity prevented her from perceiving the aim to which the Monk's insinuations tended; But the excellent morals which She owed to Elvira's care, the solidity and correctness of her understanding, and a strong sense of what was right implanted in her heart by Nature, made her feel that his precepts must be faulty. By a few simple words She frequently overthrew the whole bulk of his sophistical arguments, and made him conscious how weak they were when opposed to Virtue and Truth. On such occasion He took refuge in his eloquence; He over-powered her with a torrent of Philosophical paradoxes, to which, not understanding them, it was impossible for her to reply; And thus though He did not convince her that his reasoning was just, He at least prevented her from discovering it to be false. He perceived that her respect for his judgment augmented daily, and doubted not with time to bring her to the point desired.

He was not unconscious, that his attempts were highly criminal: He saw clearly the baseness of seducing the innocent Girl: But his passion was too violent to permit his abandoning his design. He resolved to pursue it, let the consequences be what they might. He depended upon finding Antonia in some unguarded moment; And seeing no other Man admitted into her society, nor hearing any mentioned either by her or by Elvira, He imagined that her young heart was still unoccupied. While He waited for the opportunity of satisfying his unwarrantable lust, every day increased his coldness for Matilda. Not a little was this occasioned by the consciousness of his faults to her. To hide them from her He was not sufficiently master of himself: Yet He dreaded, lest in a transport of jealous rage She should betray the secret, on which his character and even his life depended. Matilda could not but remark his indifference: He was conscious that She remarked it, and fearing her reproaches shunned her studiously. Yet when He could not avoid her, her mildness might have convinced him that He had nothing to dread from her resentment. She had resumed the character of the gentle interesting Rosario: She taxed him not with ingratitude; But her eyes filled with involuntary tears, and the soft melancholy of her countenance and voice uttered complaints far more touching than words could have conveyed. Ambrosio was not unmoved by her sorrow; But unable to remove its cause, He forbore to show that it affected him. As her conduct convinced him that He needed not fear her vengeance. He continued to neglect her, and avoided her company with care. Matilda saw, that She in vain attempted to regain his affections: Yet She stifled the impulse of resentment, and continued to treat her inconstant Lover with her former fondness and attention.

By degrees Elvira's constitution recovered itself. She was no longer troubled with convulsions, and Antonia ceased to tremble for her Mother. Ambrosio beheld this re-establishment with displeasure. He saw, that

Elvira's knowledge of the world would not be the Dupe of his sanctified demeanour, and that She would easily perceive his views upon her Daughter. He resolved therefore, before She quitted her chamber, to try the extent of his influence over the innocent Antonia.

One evening, when He had found Elvira almost perfectly restored to health, He quitted her earlier than was his usual custom. Not finding Antonia in the Anti-Chamber, He ventured to follow her to her own. It was only separated from her Mother's by a Closet, in which Flora, the Waiting-Woman, generally slept. Antonia sat upon a Sopha with her back towards the door, and read attentively. She heard not his approach, till He had seated himself by her. She started, and welcomed him with a look of pleasure: Then rising, She would have conducted him to the sitting-room; But Ambrosio taking her hand, obliged her by gentle violence to resume her place. She complied without difficulty: She knew not, that there was more impropriety in conversing with him in one room than another. She thought herself equally secure of his principles and her own, and having replaced herself upon the Sopha, She began to prattle to him with her usual ease and vivacity.

He examined the Book which She had been reading, and had now placed upon the Table. It was the Bible.

'How!' said the Friar to himself; 'Antonia reads the Bible, and is still so ignorant?'

But, upon a further inspection, He found that Elvira had made exactly the same remark. That prudent Mother, while She admired the beauties of the sacred writings, was convinced, that unrestricted no reading more improper could be permitted a young Woman. Many of the narratives can only tend to excite ideas the worst calculated for a female breast: Every thing is called plainly and roundly by its name; and the annals of a Brothel would scarcely furnish a greater choice of indecent expressions. Yet this is the Book, which young Women are recommended to study; which is put into the hands of Children, able to comprehend little more than those passages of which they had better remain ignorant; and which but too frequently inculcates the first rudiments of vice, and gives the first alarm to the still sleeping passions. Of this was Elvira so fully convinced, that She would have preferred putting into her Daughter's hands 'Amadis de Gaul,' or 'The Valiant Champion, Tirante the White;' and would sooner have authorised her studying the lewd exploits of 'Don Galaor,' or the lascivious jokes of the 'Damsel Plazer di mi vida.' She had in consequence made two resolutions respecting the Bible. The first was, that Antonia should not read it, till She was of an age to feel its beauties, and profit by its morality: The second, that it should be copied out with her own hand, and all improper passages either altered or omitted. She had adhered to this determination, and such was the Bible which Antonia was reading: It had been lately delivered to her, and She perused it with an avidity, with a delight that was inexpressible. Ambrosio perceived his mistake, and replaced the Book upon the Table.

Antonia spoke of her Mother's health with all the enthusiastic joy of a youthful heart.

'I admire your filial affection,' said the Abbot; 'It proves the excellence and sensibility of your character; It promises a treasure to him, whom Heaven has destined to possess your affections. The Breast, so capable of fondness for a Parent, what will it feel for a Lover? Nay, perhaps, what feels it for one even now? Tell me, my lovely Daughter; Have you known, what it is to love? Answer me with sincerity: Forget my habit, and consider me only as a Friend.'

'What it is to love?' said She, repeating his question; 'Oh! yes, undoubtedly; I have loved many, many People.'

'That is not what I mean. The love of which I speak, can be felt only for one. Have you never seen the Man, whom you wished to be your Husband?'

'Oh! No, indeed!'

This was an untruth, but She was unconscious of its falsehood: She knew not the nature of her sentiments for Lorenzo; and never having seen him since his first visit to Elvira, with every day his Image grew less feebly impressed upon her bosom. Besides, She thought of an Husband with all a Virgin's terror, and negatived the Friar's demand without a moment's hesitation.

'And do you not long to see that Man, Antonia? Do you feel no void in your heart, which you fain would have filled up? Do you heave no sighs for the absence of some one dear to you, but who that some one is, you know not? Perceive you not that what formerly could please, has charms for you no longer? That a thousand new wishes, new ideas, new sensations, have sprang in your bosom, only to be felt, never to be described? Or while you fill every other heart with passion, is it possible that your own remains insensible and cold? It cannot be! That melting eye, that blushing cheek, that enchanting voluptuous melancholy which at times over-spreads your features, all these marks belye your words. You love, Antonia, and in vain would hide it from me.'

'Father, you amaze me! What is this love of which you speak? I neither know its nature, nor if I felt it, why I should conceal the sentiment.'

'Have you seen no Man, Antonia, whom though never seen before, you seemed long to have sought? Whose form, though a Stranger's, was familiar to your eyes? The sound of whose voice soothed you, pleased you, penetrated to your very soul? In whose presence you rejoiced, for whose absence you lamented? With whom your heart seemed to expand, and in whose bosom with confidence unbounded you reposed the cares of your own? Have you not felt all this, Antonia?'

'Certainly I have: The first time that I saw you, I felt it.'

Ambrosio started. Scarcely dared He credit his hearing.

'Me, Antonia?' He cried, his eyes sparkling with delight and impatience, while He seized her hand, and pressed it rapturously to his lips. 'Me, Antonia? You felt these sentiments for me?'

'Even with more strength than you have described. The very moment that I beheld you, I felt so pleased, so interested! I waited so eagerly to catch the sound of your voice, and when I heard it, it seemed so sweet! It spoke to me a language till then so unknown! Methought, it told me a thousand things which I wished to hear! It seemed as if I had long known you; as if I had a right to your friendship, your advice, and your protection. I wept when you departed, and longed for the time which should restore you to my sight.'

'Antonia! my charming Antonia!' exclaimed the Monk, and caught her to his bosom; 'Can I believe my senses? Repeat it to me, my sweet Girl! Tell me again that you love me, that you love me truly and tenderly!'

'Indeed, I do: Let my Mother be excepted, and the world holds no one more dear to me!'

At this frank avowal Ambrosio no longer possessed himself; Wild with desire, He clasped the blushing Trembler in his arms. He fastened his lips greedily upon hers, sucked in her pure delicious breath, violated with his bold hand the treasures of her bosom, and wound around him her soft and yielding limbs. Startled, alarmed, and confused at his action, surprize at first deprived her of the power of resistance. At length recovering herself, She strove to escape from his embrace.

'Father! . . . . Ambrosio!' She cried; 'Release me, for God's sake!'

But the licentious Monk heeded not her prayers: He persisted in his design, and proceeded to take still greater liberties. Antonia prayed, wept, and struggled: Terrified to the extreme, though at what She knew not, She exerted all her strength to repulse the Friar, and was on the point of shrieking for assistance, when the chamber-door was suddenly thrown open. Ambrosio had just sufficient presence of mind to be sensible of his danger. Reluctantly He quitted his prey, and started hastily from the Couch. Antonia uttered an exclamation of joy, flew towards the door, and found herself clasped in the arms of her Mother.

Alarmed at some of the Abbot's speeches, which Antonia had innocently repeated, Elvira resolved to ascertain the truth of her suspicions. She had known enough of Mankind, not to be imposed upon by the Monk's reputed virtue. She reflected on several circumstances, which though trifling, on being put together seemed to authorize her fears. His frequent visits, which as far as She could see, were confined to her family; His evident emotion, whenever She spoke of Antonia; His being in the full prime and heat of Manhood; and above all, his pernicious philosophy communicated to her by Antonia, and which accorded but ill with his conversation in her presence, all these circumstances inspired her with doubts respecting the purity of

Ambrosio's friendship. In consequence, She resolved, when He should next be alone with Antonia, to endeavour at surprizing him. Her plan had succeeded. 'Tis true, that when She entered the room, He had already abandoned his prey; But the disorder of her Daughter's dress, and the shame and confusion stamped upon the Friar's countenance sufficed to prove, that her suspicions were but too well-founded. However, She was too prudent to make those suspicions known. She judged, that to unmask the Imposter would be no easy matter, the public being so much prejudiced in his favour: and having but few Friends, She thought it dangerous to make herself so powerful an Enemy. She affected therefore not to remark his agitation, seated herself tranquilly upon the Sopha, assigned some trifling reason for having quitted her room unexpectedly, and conversed on various subjects with seeming confidence and ease.

Re-assured by her behaviour, the Monk began to recover himself. He strove to answer Elvira without appearing embarrassed: But He was still too great a novice in dissimulation, and He felt, that He must look confused and awkward. He soon broke off the conversation, and rose to depart. What was his vexation, when on taking leave, Elvira told him in polite terms, that being now perfectly re-established, She thought it an injustice to deprive Others of his company, who might be more in need of it! She assured him of her eternal gratitude, for the benefit which during her illness She had derived from his society and exhortations: And She lamented that her domestic affairs, as well as the multitude of business which his situation must of necessity impose upon him, would in future deprive her of the pleasure of his visits. Though delivered in the mildest language this hint was too plain to be mistaken. Still He was preparing to put in a remonstrance, when an expressive look from Elvira stopped him short. He dared not press her to receive him, for her manner convinced him that He was discovered: He submitted without reply, took an hasty leave, and retired to the Abbey, his heart filled with rage and shame, with bitterness and disappointment.

Antonia's mind felt relieved by his departure; Yet She could not help lamenting, that She was never to see him more. Elvira also felt a secret sorrow; She had received too much pleasure from thinking him her Friend, not to regret the necessity of changing her opinion: But her mind was too much accustomed to the fallacy of worldly friendships to permit her present disappointment to weigh upon it long. She now endeavoured to make her Daughter aware of the risque, which She had ran: But She was obliged to treat the subject with caution, lest in removing the bandage of ignorance, the veil of innocence should be rent away. She therefore contented herself with warning Antonia to be upon her guard, and ordering her, should the Abbot persist in his visits, never to receive them but in company. With this injunction Antonia promised to comply.

Ambrosio hastened to his Cell. He closed the door after him, and threw himself upon the bed in despair. The impulse of desire, the stings of disappointment, the shame of detection, and the fear of being publicly unmasked, rendered his bosom a scene of the most horrible confusion. He knew not what course to pursue. Debarred the presence of Antonia, He had no hopes of satisfying that passion, which was now become a part of his existence. He reflected, that his secret was in a Woman's power: He trembled with apprehension when He beheld the precipice before him, and with rage, when He thought that had it not been for Elvira, He should now have possessed the object of his desires. With the direct imprecations He vowed vengeance against her; He swore, that cost what it would, He still would possess Antonia. Starting from the Bed He paced the chamber with disordered steps, howled with impotent fury, dashed himself violently against the walls, and indulged all the transports of rage and madness.

He was still under the influence of this storm of passions, when He heard a gentle knock at the door of his Cell. Conscious that his voice must have been heard, He dared not refuse admittance to the Importuner: He strove to compose himself, and to hide his agitation. Having in some degree succeeded, He drew back the bolt: The door opened, and Matilda appeared.

At this precise moment there was no one with whose presence He could better have dispensed. He had not sufficient command over himself to conceal his vexation. He started back, and frowned.

'I am busy,' said He in a stern and hasty tone; 'Leave me!'

Matilda heeded him not: She again fastened the door, and then advanced towards him with an air gentle and supplicating.

'Forgive me, Ambrosio,' said She; 'For your own sake I must not obey you. Fear no complaints from me; I come not to reproach you with your ingratitude. I pardon you from my heart, and since your love can no longer be mine, I request the next best gift, your confidence and friendship. We cannot force our inclinations; The little beauty which you once saw in me, has perished with its novelty, and if it can no longer excite desire, mine is the fault, not yours. But why persist in shunning me? Why such anxiety to fly my presence? You have sorrows, but will not permit me to share them; You have disappointments, but will not accept my comfort; You have wishes, but forbid my aiding your pursuits. 'Tis of this which I complain, not of your indifference to my person. I have given up the claims of the Mistress, but nothing shall prevail on me to give up those of the Friend.'

Her mildness had an instantaneous effect upon Ambrosio's feelings.

'Generous Matilda!' He replied, taking her hand, 'How far do you rise superior to the foibles of your sex! Yes, I accept your offer. I have need of an adviser, and a Confident: In you I find every needful quality united. But to aid my pursuits. . . . Ah! Matilda, it lies not in your power!'

'It lies in no one's power but mine. Ambrosio, your secret is none to me; Your every step, your every action has been observed by my attentive eye. You love.'

'Matilda!'

'Why conceal it from me? Fear not the little jealousy, which taints the generality of Women: My soul disdains so despicable a passion. You love, Ambrosio; Antonia Dalfa is the object of your flame. I know every circumstance respecting your passion: Every conversation has been repeated to me. I have been informed of your attempt to enjoy Antonia's person, your disappointment, and dismission from Elvira's House. You now despair of possessing your Mistress; But I come to revive your hopes, and point out the road to success.'

'To success? Oh! impossible!'

'To them who dare nothing is impossible. Rely upon me, and you may yet be happy. The time is come, Ambrosio, when regard for your comfort and tranquillity compels me to reveal a part of my History, with which you are still unacquainted. Listen, and do not interrupt me: Should my confession disgust you, remember that in making it my sole aim is to satisfy your wishes, and restore that peace to your heart, which at present has abandoned it. I formerly mentioned, that my Guardian was a Man of uncommon knowledge: He took pains to instil that knowledge into my infant mind. Among the various sciences which curiosity had induced him to explore, He neglected not that, which by most is esteemed impious, and by many chimerical. I speak of those arts, which relate to the world of Spirits. His deep researches into causes and effects, his unwearied application to the study of natural philosophy, his profound and unlimited knowledge of the properties and virtues of every gem which enriches the deep, of every herb which the earth produces, at length procured him the distinction, which He had sought so long, so earnestly. His curiosity was fully slaked, his ambition amply gratified. He gave laws to the elements; He could reverse the order of nature; His eye read the mandates of futurity, and the infernal Spirits were submissive to his commands. Why shrink you from me? I understand that enquiring look. Your suspicions are right, though your terrors are unfounded. My Guardian concealed not from me his most precious acquisition. Yet had I never seen *you*, I should never have exerted my power. Like you I shuddered at the thoughts of Magic: Like you I had formed a terrible idea of the consequences of raising a dæmon. To preserve that life which your love had taught me to prize, I had recourse to means which I trembled at employing. You remember that night, which I past in St Clare's Sepulchre? Then was it, that surrounded by mouldering bodies, I dared to perform those mystic rites, which summoned to my aid a fallen Angel. Judge what must have been my joy at discovering, that my terrors were imaginary: I saw the Dæmon obedient to my orders; I saw him trembling at my frown, and found, that instead of selling my soul to a Master, my courage had purchased for myself a Slave.'

'Rash Matilda! What have you done? You have doomed yourself to endless perdition; You have bartered for momentary power eternal happiness! If on witch-craft depends the fruition of my desires, I renounce your aid most absolutely. The consequences are too horrible: I doat upon Antonia, but am not so blinded by lust, as to sacrifice for her enjoyment my existence both in this world and the next.'

'Ridiculous prejudices! Oh! blus, Ambrosio, blush at being subjected to their dominion. Where is the risque of accepting my offers? What should induce my persuading you to this step, except the wish of restoring you to happiness and quiet. If there is danger, it must fall upon me: It is I, who invoke the ministry of the Spirits; Mine therefore will be the crime, and yours the profit. But danger there is none: The Enemy of Mankind is my Slave, not my Sovereign. Is there no difference between giving and receiving laws, between serving and commanding? Awake from your idle dreams, Ambrosio! Throw from you these terrors so ill-suited to a soul like yours; Leave them for common Men, and dare to be happy! Accompany me this night to St Clare's Sepulchre, witness my incantations, and Antonia is your own.'

'To obtain her by such means I neither can, or will. Cease then to persuade me, for I dare not employ Hell's agency.'

'You *dare* not? How have you deceived me! That mind which I esteemed so great and valiant, proves to be feeble, puerile, and grovelling, a slave to vulgar errors, and weaker than a Woman's.'

'What? Though conscious of the danger, wilfully shall I expose myself to the Seducer's arts? Shall I renounce for ever my title to salvation? Shall my eyes seek a sight, which I know will blast them? No, no, Matilda; I will not ally myself with God's Enemy.'

'Are you then God's Friend at present? Have you not broken your engagements with him, renounced his service, and abandoned yourself to the impulse of your passions? Are you not planning the destruction of innocence, the ruin of a Creature, whom He formed in the mould of Angels? If not of Dæmons, whose aid would you invoke to forward this laudable design? Will the Seraphims protect it, conduct Antonia to your arms, and sanction with their ministry your illicit pleasures? Absurd! But I am not deceived, Ambrosio! It is not virtue, which makes you reject my offer: You *would* accept it, but you *dare* not. 'Tis not the crime which holds your hand, but the punishment; 'Tis not respect for God which restrains you, but the terror of his vengeance! Fain would you offend him in secret, but you tremble to profess yourself his Foe. Now shame on the coward soul, which wants the courage either to be a firm Friend, or open Enemy!'

'To look upon guilt with horror, Matilda, is in itself a merit: In this respect I glory to confess myself a Coward. Though my passions have made me deviate from her laws, I still feel in my heart an innate love of virtue. But it ill becomes you to tax me with my perjury: You, who first seduced me to violate my vows; You, who first rouzed my sleeping vices, made me feel the weight of Religion's chains, and bad me be convinced that guilt had pleasures. Yet though my principles have yielded to the force of temperament, I still have sufficient grace to shudder at Sorcery, and avoid a crime so monstrous, so unpardonable!'

'Unpardonable, say you? Where then is your constant boast of the Almighty's infinite mercy? Has He of late set bounds to it? Receives He no longer a Sinner with joy? You injure him, Ambrosio; You will always have time to repent, and He have goodness to forgive. Afford him a glorious opportunity to exert that goodness: The greater your crime, the greater his merit in pardoning. Away then with these childish scruples: Be persuaded to your good, and follow me to the Sepulchre.'

'Oh! cease, Matilda! That scoffing tone, that bold and impious language is horrible in every mouth, but most so in a Woman's. Let us drop a conversation, which excites no other sentiments than horror and disgust. I will not follow you to the Sepulchre, or accept the services of your infernal Agents. Antonia shall be mine, but mine by human means.'

'Then yours She will never be! You are banished her presence; Her Mother has opened her eyes to your designs, and She is now upon her guard against them. Nay more, She loves another. A Youth of distinguished merit, possesses her heart, and unless you interfere, a few days will make her his Bride. This intelligence was brought me by my invisible Servants, to whom I had recourse on first perceiving your indifference. They watched your every action, related to me all that past at Elvira's, and inspired me with the idea of favouring your designs. Their reports have been my only comfort. Though you shunned my presence, all your proceedings were known to me: Nay, I was constantly with you in some degree, thanks to this precious gift!'

With these words She drew from beneath her habit a mirror of polished steel, the borders of which were marked with various strange and unknown characters.

'Amidst all my sorrows, amidst all my regrets for your coldness, I was sustained from despair by the virtues of this Talisman. On pronouncing certain words the Person appears in it, on whom the Observer's thoughts are bent: thus though *I* was exiled from *your* sight, you, Ambrosio, were ever present to mine.'

The Friar's curiosity was excited strongly.

'What you relate is incredible! Matilda, are you not amusing yourself with my credulity?'

'Be your own eyes the Judge.'

She put the Mirror into his hand. Curiosity induced him to take it, and Love, to wish that Antonia might appear. Matilda pronounced the magic words. Immediately, a thick smoke rose from the characters traced upon the borders, and spread itself over the surface. It dispersed again gradually; A confused mixture of colours and images presented themselves to the Friar's eyes, which at length arranging themselves in their proper places, He beheld in miniature Antonia's lovely form.

The scene was a small closet belonging to her apartment. She was undressing to bathe herself. The long tresses of her hair were already bound up. The amorous Monk had full opportunity to observe the voluptuous contours and admirable symmetry of her person. She threw off her last garment, and advancing to the Bath prepared for her, She put her foot into the water. It struck cold, and She drew it back again. Though unconscious of being observed, an in-bred sense of modesty induced her to veil her charms; and She stood hesitating upon the brink, in the attitude of the Venus de Medicis. At this moment a tame Linnet flew towards her, nestled its head between her breasts, and nibbled them in wanton play. The smiling Antonia strove in vain to shake off the Bird, and at length raised her hands to drive it from its delightful harbour. Ambrosio could bear no more: His desires were worked up to phrenzy.

'I yield!' He cried, dashing the mirror upon the ground: 'Matilda, I follow you! Do with me what you will!'

She waited not to hear his consent repeated. It was already midnight. She flew to her Cell, and soon returned with her little basket and the Key of the Cemetery, which had remained in her possession since her first visit to the Vaults. She gave the Monk no time for reflection.

'Come!' She said, and took his hand; 'Follow me, and witness the effects of your resolve!'

This said, She drew him hastily along. They passed into the Burying-ground unobserved, opened the door of the Sepulchre, and found themselves at the head of the subterraneous Stair-case. As yet the beams of the full Moon had guided their steps, but that resource now failed them. Matilda had neglected to provide herself with a Lamp. Still holding Ambrosio's hand She descended the marble steps; But the profound obscurity with which they were over-spread, obliged them to walk slow and cautiously.

'You tremble!' said Matilda to her Companion; 'Fear not; The destined spot is near.'

They reached the foot of the Stair-case, and continued to proceed, feeling their way along the Walls. On turning a corner suddenly, they descried faint gleams of light, which seemed burning at a distance. Thither they bent their steps: The rays proceeded from a small sepulchral Lamp, which flamed unceasingly before the Statue of St Clare. It tinged with dim and cheerless beams the massy Columns which supported the Roof, but was too feeble to dissipate the thick gloom, in which the Vaults above were buried.

Matilda took the Lamp.

'Wait for me!' said She to the Friar; 'In a few moments I am here again.'

With these words She hastened into one of the passages which branched in various directions from this spot, and formed a sort of Labyrinth. Ambrosio was now left alone: Darkness the most profound surrounded him, and encouraged the doubts, which began to revive in his bosom. He had been hurried away by the delirium of the moment: The shame of betraying his terrors, while in Matilda's presence, had induced him to repress them; But now that he was abandoned to himself, they resumed their former ascendancy. He trembled at the scene, which He was soon to witness. He knew not how far the delusions of Magic might operate upon his mind, and possibly might force him to some deed, whose commission would make the breach between himself and Heaven irreparable. In this fearful dilemma, He would have implored God's assistance, but was conscious that He had forfeited all claim to such protection. Gladly would He have returned to the Abbey; But as He had past through innumerable Caverns and winding passages, the attempt of regaining the Stairs was hopeless. His fate was determined: No possibility of escape presented itself: He therefore combated his apprehensions, and called every argument to his succour, which might enable him to support the trying scene with fortitude. He reflected, that Antonia would be the reward of his daring: He inflamed his imagination by enumerating her charms. He persuaded himself, that, [as Matilda had observed,] He always should have time sufficient for repentance, and that as He employed *her* assistance, not that of the Dæmons, the crime of Sorcery could not be laid to his charge. He had read much respecting witchcraft: He understood that unless a formal Act was signed renouncing his claim to salvation, Satan would have no power over him. He was fully determined not to execute any such act, whatever threats might be used, or advantages held out to him.

Such were his meditations, while waiting for Matilda. They were interrupted by a low murmur, which seemed at no great distance from him. He was startled. He listened. Some minutes past in silence, after which the murmur was repeated. It appeared to be the groaning of one in pain. In any other situation, this circumstance would only have excited his attention and curiosity: In the present, his predominant sensation was that of terror. His imagination totally engrossed by the ideas of sorcery and Spirits, He fancied that some unquiet Ghost was wandering near him; or else, that Matilda had fallen a Victim to her presumption, and was perishing under the cruel fangs of the Dæmons. The noise seemed not to approach, but continued to be heard at intervals. Sometimes it became more audible, doubtless, as the sufferings of the person who uttered the groans became more acute and insupportable. Ambrosio now and then thought, that He could distinguish accents; and once in particular He was almost convinced, that He heard a faint voice exclaim,

'God! Oh! God! No hope! No succour!'

Yet deeper groans followed these words. They died away gradually, and universal silence again prevailed.

'What can this mean?' thought the bewildered Monk.

At that moment an idea which flashed into his mind, almost petrified him with horror. He started, and shuddered at himself.

'Should it be possible!' He groaned involuntarily; 'Should it but be possible, Oh! what a Monster am I!'

He wished to resolve his doubts, and to repair his fault, if it were not too late already: But these generous and compassionate sentiments were soon put to flight by the return of Matilda. He forgot the groaning Sufferer, and remembered nothing but the danger and embarrassment of his own situation. The light of the returning Lamp gilded the walls, and in a few moments after Matilda stood beside him. She had quitted her religious habit: She was now cloathed in a long sable Robe, on which was traced in gold embroidery a variety of unknown characters: It was fastened by a girdle of precious stones, in which was fixed a poignard. Her neck and arms were uncovered. In her hand She bore a golden wand. Her hair was loose and flowed wildly upon her shoulders; Her eyes sparkled with terrific expression; and her whole Demeanour was calculated to inspire the beholder with awe and admiration.

'Follow me!' She said to the Monk in a low and solemn voice; 'All is ready!'

His limbs trembled, while He obeyed her. She led him through various narrow passages; and on every side as they past along, the beams of the Lamp displayed none but the most revolting objects; Skulls, Bones, Graves, and Images whose eyes seemed to glare on them with horror and surprize. At length they reached a spacious Cavern, whose lofty roof the eye sought in vain to discover. A profound obscurity hovered through the void. Damp vapours struck cold to the Friar's heart; and He listened sadly to the blast, while it howled along the lonely Vaults. Here Matilda stopped. She turned to Ambrosio. His cheeks and lips were pale with apprehension. By a glance of mingled scorn and anger She reproved his pusillanimity, but She spoke not. She placed the Lamp upon the ground, near the Basket. She motioned that Ambrosio should be silent, and began the mysterious rites. She drew a circle round him, another round herself, and then taking a small Phial from the Basket, poured a few drops upon the ground before her. She bent over the place, muttered some indistinct sentences, and immediately a pale sulphurous flame arose from the ground. It increased by degrees, and at length spread its waves over the whole surface, the circles alone excepted in which stood Matilda and the Monk. It then ascended the huge Columns of unhewn stone, glided along the roof, and formed the Cavern into an immense chamber totally covered with blue trembling fire. It emitted no heat: On the contrary, the extreme chillness of the place seemed to augment with every moment. Matilda continued her incantations: At intervals She took various articles from the Basket, the nature and name of most of which were unknown to the Friar: But among the few which He distinguished, He particularly observed three human fingers, and an Agnus Dei which She broke in pieces. She threw them all into the flames which burned before her, and they were instantly consumed.

The Monk beheld her with anxious curiosity. Suddenly She uttered a loud and piercing shriek. She appeared to be seized with an access of delirium; She tore her hair, beat her bosom, used the most frantic gestures, and drawing the poignard from her girdle plunged it into her left arm. The blood gushed out plentifully, and as She stood on the brink of the circle, She took care that it should fall on the outside. The flames retired from the spot on which the blood was pouring. A volume of dark clouds rose slowly from the ensanguined earth, and ascended gradually, till it reached the vault of the Cavern. At the same time a clap of thunder was heard: The echo pealed fearfully along the subterraneous passages, and the ground shook beneath the feet of the Enchantress.

It was now that Ambrosio repented of his rashness. The solemn singularity of the charm had prepared him for something strange and horrible. He waited with fear for the Spirit's appearance, whose coming was announced by thunder and earthquakes. He looked wildly round him, expecting that some dreadful Apparition would meet his eyes, the sight of which would drive him mad. A cold shivering seized his body, and He sank upon one knee, unable to support himself.

'He comes!' exclaimed Matilda in a joyful accent.

Ambrosio started, and expected the Dæmon with terror. What was his surprize, when the Thunder ceasing to roll, a full strain of melodious Music sounded in the air. At the same time the cloud dispersed, and He beheld a Figure more beautiful, than Fancy's pencil ever drew. It was a Youth seemingly scarce eighteen, the perfection of whose form and face was unrivalled. He was perfectly naked: A bright Star sparkled upon his fore-head; Two crimson wings extended themselves from his shoulders; and his silken locks were confined by a band of many-coloured fires, which played round his head, formed themselves into a variety of figures, and shone with a brilliance far surpassing that of precious Stones. Circlets of Diamonds were fastened round his arms and ankles, and in his right hand He bore a silver branch, imitating Myrtle. His form shone with dazzling glory: He was surrounded by clouds of rose-coloured light, and at the moment that He appeared, a refreshing air breathed perfumes through the

Cavern. Enchanted at a vision so contrary to his expectations, Ambrosio gazed upon the Spirit with delight and wonder: Yet however beautiful the Figure, He could not but remark a wildness in the Dæmon's eyes, and a mysterious melancholy impressed upon his features, betraying the Fallen Angel, and inspiring the Spectators with secret awe.

The Music ceased. Matilda addressed herself to the Spirit: She spoke in a language unintelligible to the Monk, and was answered in the same. She seemed to insist upon something, which the Dæmon was unwilling to grant. He frequently darted upon Ambrosio angry glances, and at such times the Friar's heart sank within him. Matilda appeared to grow incensed. She spoke in a loud and commanding tone, and her gestures declared, that She was threatening him with her vengeance. Her menaces had the desired effect: The Spirit sank upon his knee, and with a submissive air presented to her the branch of Myrtle. No sooner had She received it, than the Music was again heard; A thick cloud spread itself over the Apparition; The blue flames disappeared, and total obscurity reigned through the Cave. The Abbot moved not from his place: His faculties were all bound up in pleasure, anxiety, and surprize. At length the darkness dispersing, He perceived Matilda standing near him in her religious habit, with the Myrtle in her hand. No traces of the incantation, and the Vaults were only illuminated by the faint rays of the sepulchral Lamp.

'I have succeeded,' said Matilda, 'though with more difficulty than I expected. Lucifer, whom I summoned to my assistance, was at first unwilling to obey my commands: To enforce his compliance I was constrained to have recourse to my strongest charms. They have produced the desired effect, but I have engaged never more to invoke his agency in your favour. Beware then, how you employ an opportunity which never will return. My magic arts will now be of no use to you: In future you can only hope for supernatural aid, by invoking the Dæmons yourself, and accepting the conditions of their service. This you will never do: You want strength of mind to force them to obedience, and unless you pay their established price, they will not be your voluntary Servants. In this one instance they consent to obey you: I offer you the means of enjoying your Mistress, and be careful not to lose the opportunity. Receive this constellated Myrtle: While you bear this in your hand, every door will fly open to you. It will procure you access tomorrow night to Antonia's chamber: Then breathe upon it thrice, pronounce her name, and place it upon her pillow. A death-like slumber will immediately seize upon her, and deprive her of the power of resisting your attempts. Sleep will hold her till break of Morning. In this state you may satisfy your desires without danger of being discovered; since when day-light shall dispel the effects of the enchantment, Antonia will perceive her dishonour, but be ignorant of the Ravisher. Be happy then, my Ambrosio, and let this service convince you, that my friendship is disinterested and pure. The night must be near expiring: Let us return to the Abbey, lest our absence should create surprize.'

The Abbot received the talisman with silent gratitude. His ideas were too much bewildered by the adventures of the night, to permit his expressing his thanks audibly, or indeed as yet to feel the whole value of her present. Matilda took up her Lamp and Basket, and guided her Companion from the mysterious Cavern. She restored the Lamp to its former place, and continued her route in darkness, till She reached the foot of the Stair-case. The first beams of the rising Sun darting down it facilitated the ascent. Matilda and the Abbot hastened out of the Sepulchre, closed the door after them, and soon regained the Abbey's western Cloister. No one met them, and they retired unobserved to their respective Cells.

The confusion of Ambrosio's mind now began to appease. He rejoiced in the fortunate issue of his adventure, and reflecting upon the virtues of the Myrtle, looked upon Antonia as already in his power. Imagination retraced to him those secret charms, betrayed to him by the Enchanted Mirror, and He waited with impatience for the approach of midnight.

END OF THE SECOND VOLUME

VOLUME III

CHAPTER I

The crickets sing, and Man's o'er-laboured sense
Repairs itself by rest: Our Tarquin thus
Did softly press the rushes, ere He wakened
The chastity He wounded—Cytherea,
How bravely thou becom'st thy bed! Fresh Lily!
And whiter than the sheets!

Cymbeline

ALL the researches of the Marquis de las Cisternas proved vain: Agnes was lost to him for ever. Despair produced so violent an effect upon his constitution, that the consequence was a long and severe illness. This prevented him from visiting Elvira, as He had intended; and She being ignorant of the cause of his neglect, it gave her no trifling uneasiness. His Sister's death had prevented Lorenzo from communicating to his Uncle his designs respecting Antonia: The injunctions of her Mother forbad his presenting himself to her without the Duke's consent; and as She heard no more of him or his proposals, Elvira conjectured that He had either met with a better match, or had been commanded to give up all thoughts of her Daughter. Every day made her more uneasy respecting Antonia's fate: While She retained the Abbot's protection, She bore with fortitude the disappointment of her hopes with regard to Lorenzo and the Marquis. That resource now failed her. She was convinced that Ambrosio had meditated her Daughter's ruin: And when She reflected that her death would leave Antonia friendless, and unprotected in a world so base, so perfidious and depraved, her heart swelled with the bitterness of apprehension. At such times She would sit for hours gazing upon the lovely Girl; and seeming to listen to her innocent prattle, while in reality her thoughts dwelt upon the sorrows, into which a moment would suffice to plunge her. Then She would clasp her in her arms suddenly, lean her head upon her Daughter's bosom, and bedew it with her tears.

An event was in preparation, which had She known it, would have relieved her from her inquietude. Lorenzo now waited only for a favourable opportunity to inform the Duke of his intended marriage: However, a circumstance which occurred at this period, obliged him to delay his explanation for a few days longer.

Don Raymond's malady seemed to gain ground. Lorenzo was constantly at his bed-side, and treated him with a tenderness truly fraternal. Both the cause and effects of the disorder were highly afflicting to the Brother of Agnes: yet Theodore's grief was scarcely less sincere. That amiable Boy quitted not his Master for a moment, and put every means in practice to console and alleviate his sufferings. The Marquis had conceived so rooted an affection for his deceased Mistress, that it was evident to all that He never could survive her loss: Nothing could have prevented him from sinking under his grief, but the persuasion of her being still alive, and in need of his assistance. Though convinced of its falsehood, his Attendants encouraged him in a belief, which formed his only comfort. He was assured daily, that fresh perquisitions were making respecting the fate of Agnes: Stories were invented recounting the various attempts made to get admittance into the Convent; and circumstances were related, which though they did not promise her absolute recovery, at least were sufficient to keep his hopes alive. The Marquis constantly fell into the most terrible access of passion, when informed of the failure of these supposed attempts. Still He would not credit that the succeeding ones would have the same fate, but flattered himself that the next would prove more fortunate.

Theodore was the only one, who exerted himself to realize his Master's Chimœras. He was eternally busied in planning schemes for entering the Convent, or at least of obtaining from the Nuns some intelligence of Agnes. To execute these schemes was the only inducement, which could prevail on him to quit Don Raymond. He became a very Proteus, changing his shape every day; but all his metamorphoses were to very little purpose: He regularly returned to the Palace de las Cisternas without any intelligence to confirm his Master's hopes. One day He took it into his head to disguise himself as a Beggar. He put a patch over his left eye, took his Guitar in hand, and posted himself at the Gate of the Convent.

'If Agnes is really confined in the Convent,' thought He, 'and hears my voice, She will recollect it, and possibly may find means to let me know, that She is here.'

With this idea He mingled with a crowd of Beggars, who assembled daily at the Gate of St Clare to receive Soup, which the Nuns were accustomed to distribute at twelve o'clock. All were provided with jugs or bowls to carry it away; But as Theodore had no utensil of this kind, He begged leave to eat his portion at the Convent-door. This was granted without difficulty: His sweet voice, and in spite of his patched eye his engaging countenance, won the heart of the good old Porteress, who aided by a Lay-Sister was busied in serving to each his Mess. Theodore was bad to stay till the Others should depart, and promised that his request should then be granted. The Youth desired no better, since it was not to eat Soup that He presented himself at the Convent. He thanked the Porteress for her permission, retired from the Door, and seating himself upon a large stone, amused himself in tuning his Guitar while the Beggars were served.

As soon as the Crowd was gone, Theodore was beckoned to the Gate, and desired to come in. He obeyed with infinite readiness, but affected great respect at passing the hallowed Threshold, and to be much daunted by the presence of the Reverend Ladies. His feigned timidity flattered the vanity of the Nuns, who endeavoured to re-assure him. The Porteress took him into her own little Parlour: In the mean while, the Lay-Sister went to the Kitchen, and soon returned with a double portion of Soup, of better quality than what was given to the Beggars. His Hostess added some fruits and confections from her own private store, and Both encouraged the Youth to dine heartily. To all these attentions He replied with much seeming gratitude, and abundance of blessings upon his benefactresses. While He ate, the Nuns admired the delicacy of his features, the beauty of his hair, and the sweetness and grace which accompanied all his actions. They lamented to each other in whispers, that so charming a Youth should be exposed to the seductions of the World, and agreed, that He would be a worthy Pillar of the Catholic Church. They concluded their conference by resolving, that Heaven would be rendered a real service, if they entreated the Prioress to intercede with Ambrosio for the Beggar's admission into the order of Capuchins.

This being determined, the Porteress who was a person of great influence in the Convent, posted away in all haste to the Domina's Cell. Here She made so flaming a narrative of Theodore's merits, that the old Lady grew curious to see him. Accordingly the Porteress was commissioned to convey him to the Parlour-grate. In the interim, the supposed Beggar was sifting the Lay-Sister with respect to the fate of Agnes: Her evidence only corroborated the Domina's assertions. She said, that Agnes had been taken ill on returning from confession, had never quitted her bed from that moment, and that She had herself been present at the Funeral. She even attested having seen her dead body, and assisted with her own hands in adjusting it upon the Bier. This account discouraged Theodore: Yet as He had pushed the adventure so far, He resolved to witness its conclusion.

The Porteress now returned, and ordered him to follow her. He obeyed, and was conducted into the Parlour, where the Lady Prioress was already posted at the Grate. The Nuns surrounded her, who all flocked with eagerness to a scene which promised some diversion. Theodore saluted them with profound respect, and his presence had the power to smooth for a moment even the stern brow of the Superior. She asked several questions respecting his Parents, his religion, and what had reduced him to a state of Beggary. To these demands his answers were perfectly satisfactory and perfectly false. He was then asked his opinion of a monastic life: He replied in terms of high estimation and respect for it. Upon this, the Prioress told him, that his obtaining an entrance into a religious order was not impossible; that her recommendation would not permit his poverty to be an obstacle, and that if She found him deserving it, He might depend in future upon her protection. Theodore assured her that to merit her favour would be his highest ambition; and having ordered him to return next day, when She would talk with him further, the Domina quitted the Parlour.

The Nuns, whom respect for the Superior had till then kept silent, now crowded all together to the Grate, and assailed the Youth with a multitude of questions. He had already examined each with attention: Alas! Agnes was not amongst them. The Nuns heaped question upon question so thickly, that it was scarcely possible for him to reply. One asked where He was born, since his accent declared him to be a Foreigner: Another wanted to know, why He wore a patch upon his left eye: Sister Helena enquired whether He had not a Sister like him, because She should like such a Companion; and Sister Rachael was fully persuaded, that the Brother would be the pleasanter Companion of the Two. Theodore amused himself with retailing to the credulous Nuns for truths all the strange stories which his imagination could invent. He related to them his supposed adventures, and penetrated every Auditor with astonishment, while He talked of Giants, Savages, Ship-wrecks, and Islands inhabited

> 'By Anthropophagi, and Men whose heads
> Do grow beneath their shoulders,'

With many other circumstances to the full as remarkable. He said, that He was born in Terra Incognita, was educated at an Hottentot University, and had past two years among the Americans of Silesia.

'For what regards the loss of my eye' said He, 'it was a just punishment upon me for disrespect to the Virgin, when I made my second pilgrimage to Loretto. I stood near the Altar in the miraculous Chapel: The Monks were proceeding to array the Statue in her best apparel. The Pilgrims were ordered to close their eyes during this ceremony: But though by nature extremely religious, curiosity was too powerful. At the moment . . . . . I shall penetrate you with horror, reverend Ladies, when I reveal my crime! . . . . At the moment that the Monks were changing her shift, I ventured to open my left eye, and gave a little peep towards the Statue. That look was my last! The Glory which surrounded the Virgin was too great to be supported. I hastily shut my sacrilegious eye, and never have been able to unclose it since!'

At the relation of this miracle the Nuns all crossed themselves, and promised to intercede with the blessed Virgin for the recovery of his sight. They expressed their wonder at the extent of his travels, and at the strange adventures which He had met with at so early an age. They now remarked his Guitar, and enquired whether he was an adept in Music. He replied with modesty that it was not for him to decide upon his talents, but requested permission to appeal to them as Judges. This was granted without difficulty.

'But at least,' said the old Porteress, 'take care not to sing any thing profane.'

'You may depend upon my discretion,' replied Theodore: 'You shall hear, how dangerous it is for young Women to abandon themselves to their passions, illustrated by the adventure of a Damsel, who fell suddenly in love with an unknown Knight.'

'But is the adventure true?' enquired the Porteress.

'Every word of it. It happened in Denmark, and the Heroine was thought so beautiful, that She was known by no other name but that of "the lovely Maid".'

'In Denmark, say you?' mumbled an old Nun; 'Are not the People all Blacks in Denmark?'

'By no means, reverend Lady; They are of a delicate pea-green with flame-coloured hair and whiskers.'

'Mother of God! Pea-green?' exclaimed Sister Helena; 'Oh! 'tis impossible!'

'Impossible?' said the Porteress with a look of contempt and exultation: 'Not at all: When I was a young Woman, I remember seeing several of them myself.'

Theodore now put his instrument in proper order. He had read the story of a King of England, whose prison was discovered by a Minstrel; and He hoped that the same scheme would enable him to discover Agnes, should She be in the Convent. He chose a Ballad, which She had taught him herself in the Castle of Lindenberg: She might possibly catch the sound, and He hoped to hear her replying to some of the Stanzas. His Guitar was now in tune, and He prepared to strike it.

'But before I begin,' said He 'it is necessary to inform you, Ladies, that this same Denmark is terribly infested by Sorcerers, Witches, and Evil Spirits. Every element possesses its appropriate Dæmons. The Woods are haunted by a malignant power, called "the Erl- or Oak-King:" He it is who blights the Trees, spoils the Harvest, and commands the Imps and Goblins: He appears in the form of an old Man of majestic figure, with a golden Crown and long white beard: His principal amusement is to entice young Children from their Parents, and as soon as He gets them into his Cave, He tears them into a thousand pieces—The Rivers are governed by another Fiend, called "the Water-King:" His province is to agitate the deep, occasion ship-wrecks, and drag the drowning Sailors beneath the waves: He wears the appearance of a Warrior, and employs himself in luring young Virgins into his snare: What He does with them, when He catches them in the water,

Reverend Ladies, I leave for you to imagine—"The Fire-King" seems to be a Man all formed of flames: he raises the Meteors and wandering lights, which beguile Travellers into ponds and marshes, and He directs the lightning where it may do most mischief—The last of these elementary Dæmons is called "the Cloud-King;" His figure is that of a beautiful Youth, and He is distinguished by two large sable Wings: Though his outside is so enchanting, He is not a bit better disposed than the Others: He is continually employed in raising Storms, tearing up Forests by the roots, and blowing Castles and Convents about the ears of their Inhabitants—The First has a Daughter, who is Queen of the Elves and Fairies; The Second has a Mother, who is a powerful Enchantress: Neither of these Ladies are worth more than the Gentlemen: I do not remember to have heard any family assigned to the two other Dæmons, but at present I have no business with any of them, except the Fiend of the Waters. He is the Hero of my Ballad; but I thought it necessary before I began, to give you some account of his proceedings—'

Theodore then played a short symphony; After which, stretching his voice to its utmost extent to facilitate its reaching the ear of Agnes, He sang the following Stanzas.

THE WATER-KING
A DANISH BALLAD

> With gentle murmur flowed the Tide,
> While by the fragrant flowery side
> The lovely Maid with carols gay
> To Mary's Church pursued her way.
>
> The Water-Fiend's malignant eye
> Along the Banks beheld her hie;
> Straight to his Mother-witch He sped,
> And thus in suppliant accents said.
>
> 'Oh! Mother! Mother! now advise,
> How I may yonder Maid surprize:
> Oh! Mother! Mother! Now explain,
> How I may yonder Maid obtain.'
>
> The Witch She gave him armour white;
> She formed him like a gallant Knight;
> Of water clear next made her hand
> A Steed, whose housings were of sand.
>
> The Water-King then swift He went;
> To Mary's Church his steps He bent:

He bound his Courser to the Door,
And paced the Church-yard three times four.

His Courser to the door bound He,
And paced the Church-yard four time three:
Then hastened up the Aisle, where all
The People flocked, both great and small.

The Priest said, as the Knight drew near,
'And wherefore comes the white Chief here?'
The lovely Maid She smiled aside;
'Oh! would I were the white Chief's Bride!'

He stept o'er Benches one and two;
'Oh! lovely Maid, I die for You!'
He stept o'er Benches two and three;
'Oh! lovely Maiden, go with me!'

Then sweet She smiled, the lovely Maid,
And while She gave her hand, She said,
'Betide me joy, betide me woe,
O'er Hill, o'er dale, with thee I go.'

The Priest their hands together joins:
They dance, while clear the moon-beam shines;
And little thinks the Maiden bright,
Her Partner is the Water-spright.

Oh! had some spirit deigned to sing,
'Your Partner is the Water-King!'
The Maid had fear and hate confest,
And cursed the hand which then She prest.

But nothing giving cause to think,
How near She strayed to danger's brink,
Still on She went, and hand in hand
The Lovers reached the yellow sand.

'Ascend this Steed with me, my Dear;
We needs must cross the streamlet here;
Ride boldly in; It is not deep;
The winds are hushed, the billows sleep.'

Thus spoke the Water-King. The Maid
Her Traitor-Bride-groom's wish obeyed:
And soon She saw the Courser lave
Delighted in his parent wave.

'Stop! Stop! my Love! The waters blue
E'en now my shrinking foot bedew!'
'Oh! lay aside your fears, sweet Heart!
We now have reached the deepest part.'

'Stop! Stop! my Love! For now I see
The waters rise above my knee.'
'Oh! lay aside your fears, sweet Heart!
We now have reached the deepest part.'

'Stop! Stop! for God's sake, stop! For Oh!
The waters o'er my bosom flow!'—
Scarce was the word pronounced, when Knight
And Courser vanished from her sight.

She shrieks, but shrieks in vain; for high
The wild winds rising dull the cry;
The Fiend exults; The Billows dash,
And o'er their hapless Victim wash.

Three times while struggling with the stream,
The lovely Maid was heard to scream;
But when the Tempest's rage was o'er,
The lovely Maid was seen no more.

Warned by this Tale, ye Damsels fair,
To whom you give your love beware!
Believe not every handsome Knight,
And dance not with the Water-Spright!

The Youth ceased to sing. The Nuns were delighted with the sweetness of his voice, and masterly manner of touching the Instrument: But however acceptable this applause would have been at any other time, at present it was insipid to Theodore. His artifice had not succeeded. He paused in vain between the Stanzas: No voice replied to his, and He abandoned the hope of equalling Blondel.

The Convent-Bell now warned the Nuns, that it was time to assemble in the Refectory. They were obliged to quit the Grate; They thanked the Youth for the entertainment which his Music had afforded them, and charged him to return the next day. This He promised: The Nuns, to give him the greater inclination to keep his word, told him that He might always depend upon the Convent for his meals, and each of them made him some little present. One gave him a box of sweetmeats; Another, an Agnus Dei; Some brought reliques of Saints, waxen Images, and consecrated Crosses; and Others presented him with pieces of those works in which the Religious excel, such as embroidery, artificial flowers, lace, and needle-work. All these He was advised to sell, in order to put himself into better case; and He was assured that it would be easy to dispose of them, since the Spaniards hold the performances of the Nuns in high estimation. Having received these gifts with seeming respect and gratitude, He remarked, that having no Basket, He knew not how to convey them away. Several of the Nuns were hastening in search of one, when they were stopped by the return of an elderly Woman, whom Theodore had not till then observed: Her mild countenance, and respectable air prejudiced him immediately in her favour.

'Hah!' said the Porteress; 'Here comes the Mother St Ursula with a Basket.'

The Nun approached the Grate, and presented the Basket to Theodore: It was of willow, lined with blue satin, and upon the four sides were painted scenes from the legend of St Genevieve.

'Here is my gift,' said She, as She gave it into his hand; 'Good Youth, despise it not; Though its value seems insignificant, it has many hidden virtues.'

She accompanied these words with an expressive look. It was not lost upon Theodore; In receiving the present, He drew as near the Grate as possible.

'Agnes!' She whispered in a voice scarcely intelligible.

Theodore, however, caught the sound: He concluded that some mystery was concealed in the Basket, and his heart beat with impatience and joy. At this moment the Domina returned. Her air was gloomy and frowning, and She looked if possible more stern than ever.

'Mother St Ursula, I would speak with you in private.'

The Nun changed colour, and was evidently disconcerted.

'With me?' She replied in a faltering voice.

The Domina motioned that She must follow her, and retired. The Mother St Ursula obeyed her; Soon after the Refectory Bell ringing a second time, the Nuns quitted the Grate, and Theodore was left at liberty to carry off his prize. Delighted that at length He had obtained some intelligence for the Marquis, He flew rather than ran, till He reached the Hotel de las Cisternas. In a few minutes He stood by his Master's Bed with the Basket in his hand. Lorenzo was in the chamber, endeavouring to reconcile his Friend to a misfortune, which He felt himself but too severely. Theodore related his adventure, and the hopes which had been created by the Mother St Ursula's gift. The Marquis started from his pillow: That fire which since the death of Agnes had been extinguished, now revived in his bosom, and his eyes sparkled with the eagerness of expectation. The emotions which Lorenzo's countenance betrayed, were scarcely weaker, and He waited with inexpressible impatience for the solution of this mystery. Raymond caught the basket from the hands of his Page: He emptied the contents upon the bed, and examined them with minute attention. He hoped that a letter would be found at the bottom; Nothing of the kind appeared. The search was resumed, and still with no better success. At length Don Raymond observed, that one corner of the blue satin lining was unripped; He tore it open hastily, and drew forth a small scrap of paper neither folded or sealed. It was addressed to the Marquis de las Cisternas, and the contents were as follows.

Having recognised your Page, I venture to send these few lines. Procure an order from the Cardinal-Duke for seizing my Person, and that of the Domina; But let it not be executed till Friday at midnight. It is the Festival of St Clare: There will be a procession of Nuns by torch-light, and I shall be among them. Beware not to let your intention be known: Should a syllable be dropt to excite the Domina's suspicions, you will never hear of me more. Be cautious, if you prize the memory of Agnes, and wish to punish her Assassins. I have that to tell, will freeze your blood with horror.

St Ursula.

No sooner had the Marquis read the note, than He fell back upon his pillow deprived of sense or motion. The hope failed him which till now had supported his existence; and these lines convinced him but too positively that Agnes was indeed no more. Lorenzo felt this circumstance less forcibly, since it had always been his idea that his Sister had perished by unfair means. When He found by the Mother St Ursula's letter how true were his suspicions, the confirmation excited no other sentiment in his bosom, than a wish to punish the Murderers as they deserved. It was no easy task to recall the Marquis to himself. As soon as He recovered his speech, He broke out into execrations against the Assassins of his Beloved, and vowed to take upon them a signal vengeance. He continued to rave and torment himself with impotent passion, till his constitution enfeebled by grief and illness could support itself no longer, and He relapsed into insensibility. His melancholy situation sincerely affected Lorenzo, who would willingly have remained in the apartment of his Friend; But other cares now demanded his presence. It was necessary to procure the order for seizing the Prioress of St Clare. For this purpose, having committed Raymond to the care of the best Physicians in Madrid, He quitted the Hotel de las Cisternas, and bent his course towards the Palace of the Cardinal-Duke.

His disappointment was excessive, when He found that affairs of State had obliged the Cardinal to set out for a distant Province. It wanted but five to Friday: Yet by travelling day and night, He hoped to return in time for the Pilgrimage of St Clare. In this He succeeded. He found the Cardinal-Duke; and represented to him the supposed culpability of the Prioress, as also the violent effects which it had produced upon Don Raymond. He could have used no argument so forcible as this last. Of all his Nephews, the Marquis was the only one to whom the Cardinal-Duke was sincerely attached: He perfectly doated upon him, and the Prioress could have committed no greater crime in his eyes, than to have endangered the life of the Marquis. Consequently, He granted the order of arrest without difficulty: He also gave Lorenzo a letter to a principal Officer of the Inquisition, desiring him to see his mandate executed. Furnished with these papers, Medina hastened back to Madrid, which He reached on the Friday a few hours before dark. He found the Marquis somewhat easier, but so weak and exhausted, that without great exertion He could neither speak or more. Having past an hour by his Bed-side, Lorenzo left him to communicate his design to his Uncle, as also to give Don Ramirez de Mello the Cardinal's letter. The First was petrified with horror, when He learnt the fate of his unhappy Niece: He encouraged Lorenzo to punish her Assassins, and engaged to accompany him at night to St Clare's Convent. Don Ramirez promised his firmest support, and selected a band of trusty Archers to prevent opposition on the part of the Populace.

But while Lorenzo was anxious to unmask one religious Hypocrite, He was unconscious of the sorrows prepared for him by Another. Aided by Matilda's infernal Agents, Ambrosio had resolved upon the innocent Antonia's ruin. The moment destined to be so fatal to her arrived. She had taken leave of her Mother for the night. As She kissed her, She felt an unusual despondency infuse itself into her bosom. She left her, and returned to her instantly, threw herself into her maternal arms, and bathed her cheek with tears: She felt uneasy at quitting her, and a secret presentiment assured her that never must they meet again. Elvira observed, and tried to laugh her out of this childish prejudice: She chid her mildly for encouraging such ungrounded sadness, and warned her how dangerous it was to encourage such ideas.

To all her remonstrances She received no other answer, than,

'Mother! Dear Mother! Oh! would to God, it were Morning!'

Elvira, whose inquietude respecting her Daughter, was a great obstacle to her perfect re-establishment, was still labouring under the effects of her late severe illness. She was this Evening more than usually indisposed, and retired to bed before her accustomed hour. Antonia withdrew from her Mother's chamber with regret, and till the Door closed, kept her eyes fixed upon her with melancholy expression. She retired to her own apartment; Her heart was filled with bitterness: It seemed to her that all her prospects were blasted, and the world contained nothing for which it was worth existing. She sank into a Chair, reclined her head upon her arm, and gazed upon the floor with a vacant stare, while the most gloomy images floated before her fancy. She was still in this state of insensibility, when She was disturbed by hearing a strain of soft Music breathed beneath her window. She rose, drew near the Casement, and opened it to hear it more distinctly. Having thrown her veil over her face, She ventured to look out. By the light of the Moon She perceived several Men below with Guitars and Lutes in their hands; and at a little distance from them stood Another wrapped in his cloak, whose stature and appearance bore a strong resemblance to Lorenzo's. She was not deceived in this conjecture. It was indeed Lorenzo himself, who bound by his word not to present himself to Antonia without his Uncle's consent, endeavoured by occasional Serenades, to convince his Mistress that his attachment still existed. His stratagem had not the desired effect. Antonia was far from supposing, that this nightly music was intended as a compliment to her: She was too modest to think herself worthy such attentions; and concluding them to be addressed to some neighbouring Lady, She grieved to find that they were offered by Lorenzo.

The air which was played, was plaintive and melodious. It accorded with the state of Antonia's mind, and She listened with pleasure. After a symphony of some length, it was succeeded by the sound of voices, and Antonia distinguished the following words.

SERENADE

Chorus

Oh! Breathe in gentle strain, my Lyre!
'Tis here that Beauty loves to rest:
Describe the pangs of fond desire,
Which rend a faithful Lover's breast.

Song

In every heart to find a Slave,
In every Soul to fix his reign,
In bonds to lead the wise and brave,
And make the Captives kiss his chain,
Such is the power of Love, and Oh!
I grieve so well Love's power to know.

In sighs to pass the live-long day,
To taste a short and broken sleep,
For one dear Object far away,
All others scorned, to watch and weep,
Such are the pains of Love, and Oh!
I grieve so well Love's pains to know!

To read consent in virgin eyes,
To press the lip ne'er prest till then,
To hear the sigh of transport rise,
And kiss, and kiss, and kiss again,
Such are thy pleasures, Love; But Oh!
When shall my heart thy pleasures know?

Chorus

Now hush, my Lyre! My voice be still!
Sleep, gentle Maid! May fond desire
With amorous thoughts thy visions fill,
Though still my voice, and hushed my Lyre.

The Music ceased: The Performers dispersed, and silence prevailed through the Street. Antonia quitted the window with regret: She as usual recommended herself to the protection of St Rosolia, said her accustomed prayers, and retired to bed. Sleep was not long absent, and his presence relieved her from her terrors and inquietude.

It was almost two o'clock, before the lustful Monk ventured to bend his steps towards Antonia's dwelling. It has been already mentioned, that the Abbey was at no great distance from the Strada di San Iago. He reached the House unobserved. Here He stopped, and hesitated for a moment. He reflected on the enormity of the crime, the consequences of a discovery, and the probability, after what had passed, of Elvira's suspecting him to be her Daughter's Ravisher: On the other hand it was suggested, that She could do no more than suspect; that no proofs of his guilt could be produced; that it would seem impossible for the rape to have been committed without Antonia's knowing when, where, or by whom; and finally, He believed that his fame was too firmly established to be shaken by the unsupported accusations of two unknown Women. This latter argument was perfectly false: He knew not how uncertain is the air of popular applause, and that a moment suffices to make him to-day the detestation of the world, who yesterday was its Idol. The result of the Monk's deliberations was, that He should proceed in his enterprize. He ascended the steps leading to the House. No sooner did He touch the door with the silver Myrtle, than it flew open, and presented him with a free passage. He entered, and the door closed after him of its own accord.

Guided by the moon-beams, He proceeded up the Stair-case with slow and cautious steps. He looked round him every moment with apprehension and anxiety. He saw a Spy in every shadow, and heard a voice in every murmur of the night-breeze. Consciousness of the guilty business on which He was employed appalled his heart, and rendered it more timid than a Woman's. Yet still He proceeded. He reached the door of Antonia's chamber. He stopped, and listened. All was hushed within. The total silence persuaded him that his intended Victim was retired to rest, and He ventured to lift up the Latch. The door was fastened, and resisted his efforts: But no sooner was it touched by the Talisman, than the Bolt flew back. The Ravisher stept on, and found himself in the chamber, where slept the innocent Girl, unconscious how dangerous a Visitor was drawing near her Couch. The door closed after him, and the Bolt shot again into its fastening.

Ambrosio advanced with precaution. He took care that not a board should creak under his foot, and held in his breath as He approached the Bed. His first attention was to perform the magic ceremony, as Matilda had charged him: He breathed thrice upon the silver Myrtle, pronounced over it Antonia's name, and laid it upon her pillow. The effects which it had already produced, permitted not his doubting its success in prolonging the slumbers of his ·devoted Mistress. No sooner was the enchantment performed, than He considered her to be absolutely in his power, and his eyes flamed with lust and impatience. He now ventured to cast a glance upon the sleeping Beauty. A single Lamp, burning before the Statue of St Rosolia, shed a faint light through the room, and permitted him to examine all the charms of the lovely Object before him. The heat of the weather had obliged her to throw off part of the Bed-cloathes: Those which still covered her, Ambrosio's insolent hand hastened to remove. She lay with her cheek reclining upon one ivory arm; The Other rested on the side of the Bed with graceful indolence. A few tresses of her hair had escaped from beneath the Muslin which confined the rest, and fell carelessly over her bosom, as it heaved with slow and regular suspiration. The warm air had spread her cheek with higher colour than usual. A smile inexpressibly sweet played round her ripe and coral lips, from which every now and then escaped a gentle sigh or an half-pronounced sentence. An air of enchanting innocence and candour pervaded her whole form; and there was a sort of modesty in her very nakedness, which added fresh stings to the desires of the lustful Monk.

He remained for some moments devouring those charms with his eyes, which soon were to be subjected to his ill-regulated passions. Her mouth half-opened seemed to solicit a kiss: He bent over her; he joined his lips to hers, and drew in the fragrance of her breath with rapture. This momentary pleasure increased his longing for still greater. His desires were raised to that frantic height, by which Brutes are agitated. He resolved not to delay for one instant longer the accomplishment of his wishes, and hastily proceeded to tear off those garments, which impeded the gratification of his lust.

'Gracious God!' exclaimed a voice behind him; 'Am I not deceived? Is not this an illusion?'

Terror, confusion, and disappointment accompanied these words, as they struck Ambrosio's hearing. He started, and turned towards it. Elvira stood at the door of the chamber, and regarded the Monk with looks of surprize and detestation.

A frightful dream had represented to her Antonia on the verge of a precipice. She saw her trembling on the brink: Every moment seemed to threaten her fall, and She heard her exclaim with shrieks, 'Save me, Mother! Save me!—Yet a moment, and it will be too late!' Elvira woke in terror. The vision had made too strong an impression upon her mind, to permit her resting till assured of her Daughter's safety. She hastily started from her Bed, threw on a loose night-gown, and passing through the Closet in which slept the Waiting-woman, She reached Antonia's chamber just in time to rescue her from the grasp of the Ravisher.

His shame and her amazement seemed to have petrified into Statues both Elvira and the Monk: They remained gazing upon each other in silence. The Lady was the first to recover herself.

'It is no dream!' She cried; 'It is really Ambrosio, who stands before me! It is the Man whom Madrid esteems a Saint, that I find at this late hour near the Couch of my unhappy Child! Monster of Hypocrisy! I already suspected your designs, but forbore your accusation in pity to human frailty. Silence would now be criminal: The whole City shall be informed of your incontinence. I will unmask you, Villain, and convince the Church what a Viper She cherishes in her bosom.'

Pale and confused the baffled Culprit stood trembling before her. He would fain have extenuated his offence, but could find no apology for his conduct: He could produce nothing but broken sentences, and excuses which contradicted each other. Elvira was too justly incensed to grant the pardon which He requested. She protested that She would raise the neighbourhood, and make him an example to all future Hypocrites. Then hastening to the Bed, She called to Antonia to wake; and finding that her voice had no effect, She took her arm, and raised her forcibly from the pillow. The charm operated too powerfully. Antonia remained insensible, and on being released by her Mother, sank back upon the pillow.

'This slumber cannot be natural!' cried the amazed Elvira, whose indignation increased with every moment. 'Some mystery is concealed in it; But tremble, Hypocrite; all your villainy shall soon be unravelled! Help! Help!' She exclaimed aloud; 'Within there! Flora! Flora!'

'Hear me for one moment, Lady!' cried the Monk, restored to himself by the urgency of the danger; 'By all that is sacred and holy, I swear that your Daughter's honour is still unviolated. Forgive my transgression! Spare me the shame of a discovery, and permit me to regain the Abbey undisturbed. Grant me this request in mercy! I promise not only that Antonia shall be secure from me in future, but that the rest of my life shall prove . . . . . .'

Elvira interrupted him abruptly.

'Antonia secure from you? *I* will secure her! You shall betray no longer the confidence of Parents! Your iniquity shall be unveiled to the public eye: All Madrid shall shudder at your perfidy, your hypocrisy and incontinence. What Ho! there! Flora! Flora, I say!'

While She spoke thus, the remembrance of Agnes struck upon his mind. Thus had She sued to him for mercy, and thus had He refused her prayer! It was now his turn to suffer, and He could not but acknowledge that his punishment was just. In the mean while Elvira continued to call Flora to her assistance; but her voice was so choaked with passion, that the Servant who was buried in profound slumber, was insensible to all her cries: Elvira dared not go towards the Closet in which Flora slept, lest the Monk should take that opportunity to escape. Such indeed was his intention: He trusted, that could He reach the Abbey unobserved by any other than Elvira, her single testimony would not suffice to ruin a reputation, so well established as his was in Madrid. With this idea He gathered up such garments as He had already thrown off, and hastened towards the Door. Elvira was aware of his design; She followed him, and ere He could draw back the bolt, seized him by the arm, and detained him.

'Attempt not to fly!' said She; 'You quit not this room without Witnesses of your guilt.'

Ambrosio struggled in vain to disengage himself. Elvira quitted not her hold, but redoubled her cries for succour. The Friar's danger grew more urgent. He expected every moment to hear people assembling at her voice; And worked up to madness by the approach of ruin, He adopted a resolution equally desperate and savage. Turning round suddenly, with one hand He grasped Elvira's throat so as to prevent her continuing her clamour, and with the other, dashing her violently upon the ground, He dragged her towards the Bed. Confused by this unexpected attack, She scarcely had power to strive at forcing herself from his grasp: While the Monk, snatching the pillow from beneath her Daughter's head, covering with it Elvira's face, and pressing his knee upon her stomach with all his strength, endeavoured to put an end to her existence. He succeeded but too well. Her natural strength increased by the excess of anguish, long did the Sufferer struggle to disengage herself, but in vain. The Monk continued to kneel upon her breast, witnessed without mercy the convulsive trembling of her limbs beneath him, and sustained with inhuman firmness the spectacle of her agonies, when soul and body were on the point of separating. Those agonies at length were over. She ceased to struggle for life. The Monk took off the pillow, and gazed upon her. Her face was covered with a frightful blackness: Her limbs moved no more; The blood was chilled in her veins; Her heart had forgotten to beat, and her hands were stiff and frozen. Ambrosio beheld before him that once noble and majestic form, now become a Corse, cold, senseless and disgusting.

This horrible act was no sooner perpetrated, than the Friar beheld the enormity of his crime. A cold dew flowed over his limbs; his eyes closed; He staggered to a chair, and sank into it almost as lifeless, as the Unfortunate who lay extended at his feet. From this state He was rouzed by the necessity of flight, and the danger of being found in Antonia's apartment. He had no desire to profit by the execution of his crime. Antonia now appeared to him an object of disgust. A deadly cold had usurped the place of that warmth, which glowed in his bosom: No ideas offered themselves to his mind but those of death and guilt, of present shame and future punishment. Agitated by remorse and fear He prepared for flight: Yet his terrors did not so compleatly master his recollection, as to prevent his taking the precautions necessary for his safety. He replaced the pillow upon the bed, gathered up his garments, and with the fatal Talisman in his hand, bent his unsteady steps towards the door. Bewildered by fear, He fancied that his flight was opposed by Legions of Phantoms; Where-ever He turned, the disfigured Corse seemed to lie in his passage, and it was long before He succeeded in reaching the door. The enchanted Myrtle produced its former effect. The door opened, and He hastened down the stair-case. He entered the Abbey unobserved, and having shut himself into his Cell, He abandoned his soul to the tortures of unavailing remorse, and terrors of impending detection.

CHAPTER II

> Tell us, ye Dead, will none of you in pity
> To those you left behind disclose the secret?
> O! That some courteous Ghost would blab it out,
> What 'tis you are, and we must shortly be.
> I've heard, that Souls departed have sometimes
> Fore-warned Men of their deaths: 'Twas kindly done
> To knock, and give the alarum.
>
> Blair.

AMBROSIO shuddered at himself, when He reflected on his rapid advances in iniquity. The enormous crime which He had just committed, filled him with real horror. The murdered Elvira was continually before his eyes, and his guilt was already punished by the agonies of his conscience. Time, however, considerably weakened these impressions: One day passed away, another followed it, and still not the least suspicion was thrown upon him. Impunity reconciled him to his guilt: He began to resume his spirits; and as his fears of detection died away, He paid less attention to the reproaches of remorse. Matilda exerted herself to quiet his alarms. At the first intelligence of Elvira's death, She seemed greatly affected, and joined the Monk in deploring the unhappy catastrophe of his adventure: But when She found his agitation to be somewhat calmed, and himself better disposed to listen to her arguments, She proceeded to mention his offence in milder terms, and convince him that He was not so highly culpable as He appeared to consider himself. She represented, that He had only availed himself of the rights which Nature allows to every one, those of self-preservation: That either Elvira or himself must have perished, and that her inflexibility and resolution to ruin him had deservedly marked her out for the Victim. She next stated, that as He had before rendered himself suspected to Elvira, it was a fortunate event for him that her lips were closed by death; since without this last adventure, her suspicions if made public might have produced very disagreeable consequences. He had therefore freed himself from an Enemy, to whom the errors of his conduct were sufficiently known to make her dangerous, and who was the greatest obstacle to his designs upon Antonia. Those designs She encouraged him not to abandon. She assured him, that no longer protected by her Mother's watchful eye, the Daughter would fall an easy conquest; and by praising and enumerating Antonia's charms, She strove to rekindle the desires of the Monk. In this endeavour She succeeded but too well.

As if the crimes into which his passion had seduced him, had only increased its violence, He longed more eagerly than ever to enjoy Antonia. The same success in concealing his present guilt, He trusted, would attend his future. He was deaf to the murmurs of conscience, and resolved to satisfy his desires at any price. He waited only for an opportunity of repeating his former enterprize; But to procure that opportunity by the same means was now impracticable. In the first transports of despair He had dashed the enchanted Myrtle into a thousand pieces: Matilda told him plainly, that He must expect no further assistance from the infernal Powers, unless He was willing to subscribe to their established conditions. This Ambrosio was determined not to do: He persuaded himself that, however great might be his iniquity, so long as he preserved his claim to salvation, He need not despair of pardon. He therefore resolutely refused to enter into any bond or compact with the Fiends; and Matilda finding him obstinate upon this point, forbore to press him further. She exerted her invention to discover some means of putting Antonia into the Abbot's power: Nor was it long before that means presented itself.

While her ruin was thus meditating, the unhappy Girl herself suffered severely from the loss of her Mother. Every morning on waking, it was her first care to hasten to Elvira's chamber. On that which followed Ambrosio's fatal visit, She woke later than was her usual custom: Of this She was convinced by the Abbey-Chimes. She started from her bed, threw on a few loose garments hastily, and was speeding to enquire how her Mother had passed the night, when her foot struck against something which lay in her passage. She looked down. What was her horror at recognizing Elvira's livid Corse! She uttered a loud shriek, and threw herself upon the floor. She clasped the inanimate form to her bosom, felt that it was dead-cold, and with a movement of disgust, of which She was not the Mistress, let it fall again from her arms. The cry had alarmed Flora, who hastened to her assistance. The sight which She beheld penetrated her with horror; but her alarm was more audible than Antonia's. She made the House ring with her lamentations, while her Mistress almost suffocated with grief could only mark her distress by sobs and groans. Flora's shrieks soon reached the ears of the Hostess, whose terror and surprize were excessive on learning the cause of this disturbance. A Physician was immediately sent for: But on the first moment of beholding the Corse, He declared that Elvira's recovery was beyond the power of art. He proceeded therefore to give his assistance to Antonia, who by this time was truly in need of it. She was conveyed to bed, while the Landlady busied herself in giving orders for Elvira's Burial. Dame Jacintha was a plain good kind of Woman, charitable, generous, and devout: But her intellects were weak, and She was a Miserable Slave to fear and superstition. She shuddered at the idea of passing the night in the same House with a dead Body: She was persuaded that Elvira's Ghost would appear to her, and no less certain, that such a visit would kill her with fright. From this persuasion, She resolved to pass the night at a Neighbour's, and insisted that the Funeral should take place the next day. St Clare's Cemetery being the nearest, it was determined that Elvira should be buried there. Dame Jacintha engaged to defray every expence attending the burial. She knew not in what circumstances Antonia was left, but from the sparing manner in which the Family had lived, She concluded them to be indifferent. Consequently, She entertained very little hope of ever being recompensed; But this consideration prevented her not from taking care that the Interment was performed with decency, and from showing the unfortunate Antonia all possible respect.

Nobody dies of mere grief; Of this Antonia was an instance. Aided by her youth and healthy constitution, She shook off the malady, which her Mother's death had occasioned; But it was not so easy to remove the disease of her mind. Her eyes were constantly filled with tears: Every trifle affected her, and She evidently nourished in her bosom a profound and rooted melancholy. The slightest mention of Elvira, the most trivial circumstance recalling that beloved Parent to her memory, was sufficient to throw her into serious agitation. How much would her grief have been increased, had She known the agonies which terminated her Mother's existence! But of this no one entertained the least suspicion. Elvira was subject to strong convulsions: It was supposed, that aware of their approach, She had dragged herself to her Daughter's chamber in hopes of assistance; that a sudden access of her fits had seized her, too violent to be resisted by her already enfeebled state of health; and that She had expired, ere She had time to reach the medicine which generally relieved her, and which stood upon a shelf in Antonia's room. This idea was firmly credited by the few people, who interested themselves about Elvira: Her Death was esteemed a natural event, and soon forgotten by all save by her, who had but too much reason to deplore her loss.

In truth Antonia's situation was sufficiently embarrassing and unpleasant. She was alone in the midst of a dissipated and expensive City; She was ill provided with money, and worse with Friends. Her aunt Leonella was still at Cordova, and She knew not her direction. Of the Marquis de las Cisternas She heard no news: As to Lorenzo, She had long given up the idea of possessing any interest in his bosom. She knew not to whom She could address herself in her present dilemma. She wished to consult Ambrosio; But She remembered her Mother's injunctions to shun him as much as possible, and the last conversation which Elvira had held with her upon the subject, had given her sufficient lights respecting his designs, to put her upon her guard against him in future. Still all her Mother's warnings could not make her change her good opinion of the Friar. She continued to feel, that his friendship and society were requisite to her happiness: She looked upon his failings with a partial eye, and could not persuade herself, that He really had intended her ruin. However, Elvira had positively commanded her to drop his acquaintance, and She had too much respect for her orders to disobey them.

At length She resolved to address herself for advice and protection to the Marquis de las Cisternas, as being her nearest Relation. She wrote to him, briefly stating her desolate situation; She besought him to compassionate his Brother's Child, to continue to her Elvira's pension, and to authorise her retiring to his old Castle in Murcia, which till now had been her retreat. Having sealed her letter, She gave it to the trusty Flora, who immediately set out to execute her commission. But Antonia was born under an unlucky Star. Had She made her application to the Marquis but one day sooner, received as his Niece and placed at the head of his Family, She would have escaped all the misfortunes, with which She was now threatened. Raymond had always intended to execute this plan: But first, his hopes of making the proposal to Elvira through the lips of Agnes, and afterwards, his disappointment at losing his intended Bride, as well as the severe illness which for some time had confined him to his Bed, made him defer from day to day the giving an Asylum in his House to his Brother's Widow. He had commissioned Lorenzo to supply her liberally with money: But Elvira, unwilling to receive obligations from that Nobleman, had assured him that She needed no immediate pecuniary assistance. Consequently, the Marquis did not imagine, that a trifling delay on his part could create any embarrassment; and the distress and agitation of his mind might well excuse his negligence.

Had He been informed that Elvira's death had left her Daughter Friendless and unprotected, He would doubtless have taken such measures, as would have ensured her from every danger: But Antonia was not destined to be so fortunate. The day on which She sent her letter to the Palace de las Cisternas, was that following Lorenzo's departure from Madrid. The Marquis was in the first paroxysms of despair at the conviction, that Agnes was indeed no more: He was delirious, and his life being in danger, no one was suffered to approach him. Flora was informed, that He was incapable of attending to Letters, and that probably a few hours would decide his fate. With this unsatisfactory answer She was obliged to return to her Mistress, who now found herself plunged into greater difficulties than ever.

Flora and Dame Jacintha exerted themselves to console her. The Latter begged her to make herself easy, for that as long as She chose to stay with her, She would treat her like her own Child. Antonia, finding that the good Woman had taken a real affection for her, was somewhat comforted by thinking, that She had at least one Friend in the World. A Letter was now brought to her, directed to Elvira. She recognized Leonella's writing, and opening it with joy, found a detailed account of her Aunt's adventures at Cordova. She informed her Sister that She had recovered her Legacy, had lost her heart, and had received in exchange that of the most amiable of Apothecaries, past, present, and to come. She added, that She should be at Madrid on the Tuesday night, and meant to have the pleasure of presenting her Caro Sposo in form. Though her nuptials were far from pleasing Antonia, Leonella's speedy return gave her Niece much delight. She rejoiced in thinking, that She should once more be under a Relation's care. She could not but judge it to be highly improper, for a young Woman to be living among absolute Strangers, with no one to regulate her conduct, or protect her from the insults to which in her defenceless situation She was exposed. She therefore looked forward with impatience to the Tuesday night.

It arrived. Antonia listened anxiously to the Carriages, as they rolled along the Street. None of them stopped, and it grew late without Leonella's appearing. Still Antonia resolved to sit up till her Aunt's arrival, and in spite of all her remonstrances Dame Jacintha and Flora insisted upon doing the same. The hours passed on slow and tediously. Lorenzo's departure from Madrid had put a stop to the nightly Serenades: She hoped in vain to hear the usual sound of Guitars beneath her window. She took up her own, and struck a few chords: But Music that evening had lost its charms for her, and She soon replaced the Instrument in its case. She seated herself at her embroidery frame, but nothing went right: The silks were missing, the thread snapped every moment, and the needles were so expert at falling, that they seemed to be animated. At length a flake of wax fell from the Taper which stood near her upon a favourite wreath of Violets: This compleatly discomposed her; She threw down her needle, and quitted the frame. It was decreed, that for that night nothing should have the power of amusing her. She was the prey of Ennui, and employed herself in making fruitless wishes for the arrival of her Aunt.

As She walked with a listless air up and down the chamber, the Door caught her eye conducting to that which had been her Mother's. She remembered that Elvira's little Library was arranged there, and thought that She might possibly find in it, some Book to amuse her till Leonella should arrive. Accordingly She took her Taper from the table, passed through the little Closet, and entered the adjoining apartment. As She looked around her, the sight of this room brought to her recollection a thousand painful ideas. It was the first time of her entering it since her Mother's death. The total silence prevailing through the chamber, the Bed despoiled of its furniture, the cheerless hearth where stood an extinguished Lamp, and a few dying Plants in the window, which since Elvira's loss had been neglected, inspired Antonia with a melancholy awe. The gloom of night gave strength to this sensation. She placed her light upon the Table, and sank into a large chair, in which She had seen her Mother seated a thousand and a thousand times. She was never to see her seated there again! Tears unbidden streamed down her cheek, and She abandoned herself to the sadness, which grew deeper with every moment.

Ashamed of her weakness, She at length rose from her seat: She proceeded to seek for what had brought her to this melancholy scene. The small collection of Books was arranged upon several shelves in order. Antonia examined them without finding any thing likely to interest her, till She put her hand upon a volume of old Spanish Ballads. She read a few Stanzas of one of them: They excited her curiosity. She took down the Book, and seated herself to peruse it with more ease. She trimmed the Taper, which now drew towards its end, and then read the following Ballad.

ALONZO THE BRAVE

A Warrior so bold, and a Virgin so bright
   Conversed, as They sat on the green:
They gazed on each other with tender delight;
Alonzo the Brave was the name of the Knight,
   The Maid's was the Fair Imogine.

'And Oh!' said the Youth, 'since to-morrow I go
   To fight in a far distant land,
Your tears for my absence soon leaving to flow,
Some Other will court you, and you will bestow
   On a wealthier Suitor your hand.'

'Oh! hush these suspicions,' Fair Imogine said,
   'Offensive to Love and to me!
For if ye be living, or if ye be dead,
I swear by the Virgin, that none in your stead
   Shall Husband of Imogine be.

'If e'er I by lust or by wealth led aside
   Forget my Alonzo the Brave,
God grant, that to punish my falsehood and pride

Your Ghost at the Marriage may sit by my side,
May tax me with perjury, claim me as Bride,
  And bear me away to the Grave!'

To Palestine hastened the Hero so bold;
  His Love, She lamented him sore:
But scarce had a twelve-month elapsed, when behold,
A Baron all covered with jewels and gold
  Arrived at Fair Imogine's door.

His treasure, his presents, his spacious domain
  Soon made her untrue to her vows:
He dazzled her eyes; He bewildered her brain;
He caught her affections so light and so vain,
  And carried her home as his Spouse.

And now had the Marriage been blest by the Priest;
  The revelry now was begun:
The Tables, they groaned with the weight of the Feast;
Nor yet had the laughter and merriment ceased,
  When the Bell of the Castle told,—'One!'

Then first with amazement Fair Imogine found
  That a Stranger was placed by her side:
His air was terrific; He uttered no sound;
He spoke not, He moved not, He looked not around,
  But earnestly gazed on the Bride.

His vizor was closed, and gigantic his height;
  His armour was sable to view:
All pleasure and laughter were hushed at his sight;
The Dogs as They eyed him drew back in affright;
  The Lights in the chamber burned blue!

His presence all bosoms appeared to dismay;
  The Guests sat in silence and fear.
At length spoke the Bride, while She trembled; 'I pray,
Sir Knight, that your Helmet aside you would lay,
  And deign to partake of our chear.'

The Lady is silent: The Stranger complies.
  His vizor He slowly unclosed:
Oh! God! what a sight met Fair Imogine's eyes!
What words can express her dismay and surprize,
  When a Skeleton's head was exposed.

All present then uttered a terrified shout;
  All turned with disgust from the scene.

The worms, They crept in, and the worms, They crept out,
And sported his eyes and his temples about,
   While the Spectre addressed Imogine.

'Behold me, Thou false one! Behold me!' He cried;
   'Remember Alonzo the Brave!
God grants, that to punish thy falsehood and pride
My Ghost at thy marriage should sit by thy side,
Should tax thee with perjury, claim thee as Bride
   And bear thee away to the Grave!'

Thus saying, his arms round the Lady He wound,
   While loudly She shrieked in dismay;
Then sank with his prey through the wide-yawning ground:
Nor ever again was Fair Imogine found,
   Or the Spectre who bore her away.

Not long lived the Baron; and none since that time
   To inhabit the Castle presume:
For Chronicles tell, that by order sublime
There Imogine suffers the pain of her crime,
   And mourns her deplorable doom.

At midnight four times in each year does her Spright
   When Mortals in slumber are bound,
Arrayed in her bridal apparel of white,
Appear in the Hall with the Skeleton-Knight,
   And shriek, as He whirls her around.

While They drink out of skulls newly torn from the grave,
   Dancing round them the Spectres are seen:
Their liquor is blood, and this horrible Stave
They howl.—'To the health of Alonzo the Brave,
   And his Consort, the False Imogine!'

The perusal of this story was ill calculated to dispel Antonia's melancholy. She had naturally a strong inclination to the marvellous; and her Nurse who believed firmly in Apparitions, had related to her when an Infant so many horrible adventures of this kind, that all Elvira's attempts had failed to eradicate their impressions from her Daughter's mind. Antonia still nourished a superstitious prejudice in her bosom: She was often susceptible of terrors, which when She discovered their natural and insignificant cause made her blush at her own weakness. With such a turn of mind, the adventure which She had just been reading, sufficed to give her apprehensions the alarm. The hour and the scene combined to authorize them. It was the dead of night: She was alone, and in the chamber once occupied by her deceased Mother. The weather was comfortless and stormy: The wind howled around the House, the doors rattled in their frames, and the heavy rain pattered against the windows. No other sound was heard. The Taper, now burnt down to the socket, sometimes flaring upwards shot a gleam of light through the room, then sinking again seemed upon the point of expiring. Antonia's heart throbbed with agitation: Her eyes wandered fearfully over the objects around her, as the trembling flame illuminated them at intervals. She attempted to rise from her seat; But her limbs trembled so violently, that She was unable to proceed. She then called Flora, who was in a room at no great distance: But agitation choked her voice, and her cries died away in hollow murmurs.

She passed some minutes in this situation, after which her terrors began to diminish. She strove to recover herself, and acquire strength enough to quit the room: Suddenly She fancied, that She heard a low sigh drawn near her. This idea brought back her former weakness. She had already raised herself from her seat, and was on the point of taking the Lamp from the Table. The imaginary noise stopped her: She drew back her hand, and supported herself upon the back of a Chair. She listened anxiously, but nothing more was heard.

'Gracious God!' She said to herself; 'What could be that sound? Was I deceived, or did I really hear it?'

Her reflections were interrupted by a noise at the door scarcely audible: It seemed as if somebody was whispering. Antonia's alarm increased: Yet the Bolt She knew to be fastened, and this idea in some degree re-assured her. Presently the Latch was lifted up softly, and the Door moved with caution backwards and forwards. Excess of terror now supplied Antonia with that strength, of which She had till then been deprived. She started from her place, and made towards the Closet door, whence She might soon have reached the chamber where She expected to find Flora and Dame Jacintha. Scarcely had She reached the middle of the room, when the Latch was lifted up a second time. An involuntary movement obliged her to turn her head. Slowly and gradually the Door turned upon its hinges, and standing upon the Threshold She beheld a tall thin Figure, wrapped in a white shroud which covered it from head to foot.

This vision arrested her feet: She remained as if petrified in the middle of the apartment. The Stranger with measured and solemn steps drew near the Table. The dying Taper darted a blue and melancholy flame as the Figure advanced towards it. Over the Table was fixed a small Clock; The hand of it was upon the stroke of three. The Figure stopped opposite to the Clock: It raised its right arm, and pointed to the hour, at the same time looking earnestly upon Antonia, who waited for the conclusion of this scene, motionless and silent.

The figure remained in this posture for some moments. The clock struck. When the sound had ceased, the Stranger advanced yet a few steps nearer Antonia.

'Yet three days,' said a voice faint, hollow, and sepulchral; 'Yet three days, and we meet again!'

Antonia shuddered at the words.

'We meet again?' She pronounced at length with difficulty: 'Where shall we meet? Whom shall I meet?'

The figure pointed to the ground with one hand, and with the other raised the Linen which covered its face.

'Almighty God! My Mother!'

Antonia shrieked, and fell lifeless upon the floor.

Dame Jacintha who was at work in a neighbouring chamber, was alarmed by the cry: Flora was just gone down stairs to fetch fresh oil for the Lamp, by which they had been sitting. Jacintha therefore hastened alone to Antonia's assistance, and great was her amazement to find her extended upon the floor. She raised her in her arms, conveyed her to her apartment, and placed her upon the Bed still senseless. She then proceeded to bathe her temples, chafe her hands, and use all possible means of bringing her to herself. With some difficulty She succeeded. Antonia opened her eyes, and looked round her wildly.

'Where is She?' She cried in a trembling voice; 'Is She gone? Am I safe? Speak to me! Comfort me! Oh! speak to me for God's sake!'

'Safe from whom, my Child?' replied the astonished Jacintha; 'What alarms you? Of whom are you afraid?'

'In three days! She told me that we should meet in three days! I heard her say it! I saw her, Jacintha, I saw her but this moment!'

She threw herself upon Jacintha's bosom.

'You saw her? Saw whom?'

'My Mother's Ghost!'

'Christ Jesus! cried Jacintha, and starting from the Bed, let fall Antonia upon the pillow, and fled in consternation out of the room.

As She hastened down stairs, She met Flora ascending them.

'Go to your Mistress, Flora,' said She; 'Here are rare doings! Oh! I am the most unfortunate Woman alive! My House is filled with Ghosts and dead Bodies, and the Lord knows what besides; Yet I am sure, nobody likes such company, less than I do. But go your way to Donna Antonia, Flora, and let me go mine.'

Thus saying, She continued her course to the Street-door, which She opened, and without allowing herself time to throw on her veil, She made the best of her way to the Capuchin-Abbey. In the mean while, Flora hastened to her Lady's chamber, equally surprized and alarmed at Jacintha's consternation. She found Antonia lying upon the bed insensible. She used the same means for her recovery that Jacintha had already employed; But finding that her Mistress only recovered from one fit to fall into another, She sent in all haste for a Physician. While expecting his arrival, She undrest Antonia, and conveyed her to Bed.

Heedless of the storm, terrified almost out of her senses, Jacintha ran through the Streets, and stopped not till She reached the Gate of the Abbey. She rang loudly at the bell, and as soon as the Porter appeared, She desired permission to speak to the Superior. Ambrosio was then conferring with Matilda upon the means of procuring access to Antonia. The cause of Elvira's death remaining unknown, He was convinced that crimes were not so swiftly followed by punishment, as his Instructors the Monks had taught him, and as till then He had himself believed. This persuasion made him resolve upon Antonia's ruin, for the enjoyment of whose person dangers and difficulties only seemed to have increased his passion. The Monk had already made one attempt to gain admission to her presence; But Flora had refused him in such a manner as to convince him, that all future endeavours must be vain. Elvira had confided her suspicions to that trusty Servant: She had desired her never to leave Ambrosio alone with her Daughter, and if possible to prevent their meeting altogether. Flora promised to obey her, and had executed her orders to the very letter. Ambrosio's visit had been rejected that morning, though Antonia was ignorant of it. He saw that to obtain a sight of his Mistress by open means was out of the question; and both Himself and Matilda had consumed the night, in endeavouring to invent some plan, whose event might be more successful. Such was their employment, when a Lay-Brother entered the Abbot's Cell, and informed him, that a Woman calling herself Jacintha Zuniga requested audience for a few minutes.

Ambrosio was by no means disposed to grant the petition of his Visitor. He refused it positively, and bad the Lay-Brother tell the Stranger to return the next day. Matilda interrupted him.

'See this Woman,' said She in a low voice; 'I have my reasons.'

The Abbot obeyed her, and signified that He would go to the Parlour immediately. With this answer the Lay-Brother with-drew. As soon as they were alone Ambrosio enquired, why Matilda wished him to see this Jacintha.

'She is Antonia's Hostess,' replied Matilda; 'She may possibly be of use to you: but let us examine her, and learn what brings her hither.'

They proceeded together to the Parlour, where Jacintha was already waiting for the Abbot. She had conceived a great opinion of his piety and virtue; and supposing him to have much influence over the Devil, thought that it must be an easy matter for him to lay Elvira's Ghost in the Red Sea. Filled with this persuasion She had hastened to the Abbey. As soon as She saw the Monk enter the Parlour, She dropped upon her knees, and began her story as follows.

'Oh! Reverend Father! Such an accident! Such an adventure! I know not what course to take, and unless you can help me, I shall certainly go distracted. Well, to be sure, never was Woman so unfortunate, as myself! All in my power to keep clear of such abomination have I done, and yet that all is too little. What signifies my telling my beads four times a day, and observing every fast prescribed by the Calendar? What signifies my having made three Pilgrimages to St James of Compostella, and purchased as many pardons from the Pope, as would buy off Cain's punishment? Nothing prospers with me! All goes wrong, and God only knows, whether any thing will ever go right again! Why now, be your Holiness the Judge. My Lodger dies in convulsions; Out of pure kindness I bury her at my own expence; [Not that She is any Relation of mine, or that I shall be benefited a single pistole by her death: I got nothing by it, and therefore you know, reverend Father, that her living or dying was just the same to me. But that is nothing to the purpose; To return to what I was saying,] I took care of her funeral, had every thing performed decently and properly, and put myself to expence enough, God knows! And how do you think the Lady repays me for my kindness? Why truly by refusing to sleep quietly in her comfortable deal Coffin, as a peaceable well-disposed Spirit ought to do, and coming to plague me, who never wish to set eyes on her again. Forsooth, it well becomes her to go racketing about my House at midnight, popping into her Daughter's room through the Key-hole, and frightening the poor Child out of her wits! Though She be a Ghost, She might be more civil than to bolt into a Person's House, who likes her company so little. But as for me, reverend Father, the plain state of the case is this: If She walks into my House, I must walk out of it, for I cannot abide such Visitors, not I! Thus you see, your Sanctity, that without your assistance I am ruined and undone for ever. I shall be obliged to quit my House; Nobody will take it, when 'tis known that She haunts it, and then I shall find myself in a fine situation! Miserable Woman that I am! What shall I do! What will become of me!'

Here She wept bitterly, wrung her hands, and begged to know the Abbot's opinion of her case.

'In truth, good Woman,' replied He, 'It will be difficult for me to relieve you, without knowing what is the matter with you. You have forgotten to tell me what has happened, and what it is you want.'

'Let me die' cried Jacintha, 'but your Sanctity is in the right! This then is the fact stated briefly. A lodger of mine is lately dead, a very good sort of Woman that I must needs say for her as far as my knowledge of her went, though that was not a great way: She kept me too much at a distance; for indeed She was given to be upon the high ropes, and whenever I ventured to speak to her, She had a look with her, which always made me feel a little queerish, God forgive me for saying so. However, though She was more stately than needful, and affected to look down upon me [Though if I am well informed, I come of as good Parents as She could do for her ears, for her Father was a Shoe-maker at Cordova, and Mine was an Hatter at Madrid, aye, and a very creditable Hatter too, let me tell you,] Yet for all her pride, She was a quiet well-behaved Body, and I never wish to have a better Lodger. This makes me wonder the more at her not sleeping quietly in her Grave: But there is no trusting to people in this world! For my part, I never saw her do amiss, except on the Friday before her death. To be sure, I was then much scandalized by seeing her eat the wing of a Chicken! "How, Madona Flora!" quoth I; [Flora, may it please your Reverence, is the name of the waiting Maid]—"How, Madona Flora!" quoth I; "Does your Mistress eat flesh upon Fridays? Well! Well! See the event, and then remember, that Dame Jacintha warned you of it!" These were my very words, but Alas! I might as well have held my tongue! Nobody minded me; and Flora, who is somewhat pert and snappish, [More is the pity, say I] told me, that there was no more harm in eating a Chicken, than the egg from which it came. Nay She even declared, that if her Lady added a slice of bacon, She would not be an inch nearer Damnation, God protect us! A poor ignorant sinful soul! I protest to your Holiness, I trembled to hear her utter such blasphemies, and expected every moment to see the ground open and swallow her up, Chicken and all! For you must know, worshipful Father, that while She talked thus, She held the plate in her hand, on which lay the identical roast Fowl. And a fine Bird it was, that I must say for it! Done to a turn, for I super-intended the cooking of it myself: It was a little Gallician of my own raising, may it please your Holiness, and the flesh was as white as an egg-shell, as indeed Donna Elvira told me herself. "Dame Jacintha," said She, very good-humouredly, though to say the truth, She was always very polite to me . . . . .'

Here Ambrosio's patience failed him. Eager to know Jacintha's business in which Antonia seemed to be concerned, He was almost distracted while listening to the rambling of this prosing old Woman. He interrupted her, and protested that if She did not immediately tell her story and have done with it, He should quit the Parlour, and leave her to get out of her difficulties by herself. This threat had the desired effect. Jacintha related her business in as few words as She could manage; But her account was still so prolix that Ambrosio had need of his patience to bear him to the conclusion.

'And so, your Reverence,' said She, after relating Elvira's death and burial, with all their circumstances; 'And so, your Reverence, upon hearing the shriek, I put away my work, and away posted I to Donna Antonia's chamber. Finding nobody there, I past on to the next; But I must own, I was a little timorous at going in, for this was the very room, where Donna Elvira used to sleep. However, in I went, and sure enough there lay the young Lady at full length upon the floor, as cold as a stone, and as white as a sheet. I was surprized at this, as your Holiness may well suppose; But Oh me! how I shook, when I saw a great tall figure at my elbow whose head touched the ceiling! The face was Donna Elvira's, I must confess; But out of its mouth came clouds of fire, its arms were loaded with heavy chains which it rattled piteously, and every hair on its head was a Serpent as big as my arm! At this I was frightened enough, and began to say my Ave-Maria: But the Ghost interrupting me uttered three loud groans, and roared out in a terrible voice, "Oh! That Chicken's wing! My poor soul suffers for it!" As soon as Shè had said this, the Ground opened, the Spectre sank down, I heard a clap of thunder, and the room was filled with a smell of brimstone. When I recovered from my fright, and had brought Donna Antonia to herself, who told me that She had cried out upon seeing her Mother's Ghost, [And well might She cry, poor Soul! Had I been in her place, I should have cried ten times louder] it directly came into my head, that if any one had power to quiet this Spectre, it must be your Reverence. So hither I came in all diligence, to beg that you will sprinkle my House with holy water, and lay the Apparition in the Red Sea.'

Ambrosio stared at this strange story, which He could not credit.

'Did Donna Antonia also see the Ghost?' said He.

'As plain as I see you, Reverend Father!'

Ambrosio paused for a moment. Here was an opportunity offered him of gaining access to Antonia, but He hesitated to employ it. The reputation which He enjoyed in Madrid was still dear to him; and since He had lost the reality of virtue, it appeared as if its semblance was become more valuable. He was conscious, that publicly to break through the rule never to quit the Abbey-precincts, would derogate much from his supposed austerity. In visiting Elvira, He had always taken care to keep his features concealed from the Domestics. Except by the Lady, her Daughter, and the faithful Flora, He was known in the Family by no other name than that of Father Jerome. Should He comply with Jacintha's request, and accompany her to her House, He knew that the violation of his rule could not be kept a secret. However, his eagerness to see Antonia obtained the victory: He even hoped, that the singularity of this adventure would justify him in the eyes of Madrid: But whatever might be the consequences, He resolved to profit by the opportunity which chance had presented to him. An expressive look from Matilda confirmed him in this resolution.

'Good Woman,' said He to Jacintha, 'what you tell me is so extraordinary that I can scarcely credit your assertions. However, I will comply with your request. Tomorrow after Matins you may expect me at your House: I will then examine into what I can do for you, and if it is in my power, will free you from this unwelcome Visitor. Now then go home, and peace be with you!'

'Home?' exclaimed Jacintha; 'I go home? Not I by my troth! except under your protection, I set no foot of mine within the threshold. God help me, the Ghost may meet me upon the Stairs, and whisk me away with her to the devil! Oh! That I had accepted young Melchior Basco's offer! Then I should have had somebody to protect me; But now I am a lone Woman, and meet with nothing but crosses and misfortunes! Thank Heaven, it is not yet too late to repent! There is Simon Gonzalez will have me any day of the week, and if I live till day-break, I will marry him out of hand: An Husband I will have, that is determined, for now this Ghost is once in my House, I shall be frightened out of my wits to sleep alone. But for God's sake, reverend Father, come with me now. I shall have no rest till the House is purified, or the poor young Lady either. The dear Girl! She is in a piteous taking: I left her in strong convulsions, and I doubt, She will not easily recover her fright.'

The Friar started, and interrupted her hastily.

'In convulsions, say you? Antonia in convulsions? Lead on, good Woman! I follow you this moment!'

Jacintha insisted upon his stopping to furnish himself with the vessel of holy water: With this request He complied. Thinking herself safe under his protection should a Legion of Ghosts attack her, the old Woman returned the Monk a profusion of thanks, and they departed together for the Strada di San Iago.

So strong an impression had the Spectre made upon Antonia, that for the first two or three hours the Physician declared her life to be in danger. The fits at length becoming less frequent induced him to alter his opinion. He said, that to keep her quiet was all that was necessary; and He ordered a medicine to be prepared which would tranquillize her nerves, and procure her that repose, which at present She much wanted. The sight of Ambrosio, who now appeared with Jacintha at her Bed-side, contributed essentially to compose her ruffled spirits. Elvira had not sufficiently explained herself upon the nature of his designs, to make a Girl so ignorant of the world as her Daughter, aware how dangerous was his acquaintance. At this moment, when penetrated with horror at the scene which had just past, and dreading to contemplate the Ghost's prediction, her mind had need of all the succours of friendship and religion, Antonia regarded the Abbot with an eye doubly partial. That strong prepossession in his favour still existed, which She had felt for him at first sight: She fancied, yet knew not wherefore, that his presence was a safe-guard to her from every danger, insult, or misfortune. She thanked him gratefully for his visit, and related to him the adventure, which had alarmed her so seriously.

The Abbot strove to re-assure her, and convince her that the whole had been a deception of her over-heated fancy. The solitude in which She had passed the Evening, the gloom of night, the Book which She had been reading, and the Room in which She sat, were all calculated to place before her such a vision. He treated the idea of Ghosts with ridicule, and produced strong arguments to prove the fallacy of such a system. His conversation tranquillized and comforted her, but did not convince her. She could not believe, that the Spectre had been a mere creature of her imagination; Every circumstance was impressed upon her mind too forcibly, to permit her flattering herself with such an idea. She persisted in asserting, that She had really seen her Mother's Ghost, had heard the period of her dissolution announced and declared, that She never should quit her bed alive. Ambrosio advised her against encouraging these sentiments, and then quitted her chamber, having promised to repeat his visit on the morrow. Antonia received this assurance with every mark of joy: But the Monk easily perceived, that He was not equally acceptable to her Attendant. Flora obeyed Elvira's injunctions with the most scrupulous observance. She examined every circumstance with an anxious eye likely in the least to prejudice her young Mistress, to whom She had been attached for many years. She was a Native of Cuba, had followed Elvira to Spain, and loved the young Antonia with a Mother's affection. Flora quitted not the room for a moment, while the Abbot remained there: She watched his every word, his every look, his every action. He saw that her suspicious eye was always fixed upon him, and conscious that his designs would not bear inspection so minute, He felt frequently confused and disconcerted. He was aware, that She doubted the purity of his intentions; that She would never leave him alone with Antonia, and his Mistress defended by the presence of this vigilant Observer, He despaired of finding the means to gratify his passion.

As He quitted the House, Jacintha met him, and begged, that some Masses might be sung for the repose of Elvira's soul, which She doubted not was suffering in Purgatory. He promised not to forget her request; But He perfectly gained the old Woman's heart, by engaging to watch during the whole of the approaching night in the haunted chamber. Jacintha could find no terms sufficiently strong to express her gratitude, and the Monk departed loaded with her benedictions.

It was broad day, when He returned to the Abbey. His first care was to communicate what had past to his Confident. He felt too sincere a passion for Antonia to have heard unmoved the prediction of her speedy death, and He shuddered at the idea of losing an object so dear to him. Upon this head Matilda re-assured him. She confirmed the arguments, which Himself had already used: She declared Antonia to have been deceived by the wandering of her brain, by the Spleen which opprest her at the moment, and by the natural turn of her mind to superstition, and the marvellous. As to Jacintha's account, the absurdity refuted itself; The Abbot hesitated not to believe, that She had fabricated the whole story, either confused by terror, or hoping to make him comply more readily with her request. Having over-ruled the Monk's apprehensions, Matilda continued thus.

'The prediction and the Ghost are equally false; But it must be your care, Ambrosio, to verify the first. Antonia within three days must indeed be dead to the world; But She must live for you. Her present illness, and this fancy which She has taken into her head, will colour a plan, which I have long meditated, but which was impracticable without your procuring access to Antonia. She shall be yours, not for a single night, but for ever. All the vigilance of her Duenna shall not avail her: You shall riot unrestrained in the charms of your Mistress. This very day must the scheme be put in execution, for you have no time to lose. The Nephew of the Duke of Medina Celi prepares to demand Antonia for his Bride: In a few days She will be removed to the Palace of her Relation, the Marquis de las Cisternas, and there She will be secure from your attempts. Thus during your absence have I been informed by my Spies, who are ever employed in bringing me intelligence for your service. Now then listen to me. There is a juice extracted from certain herbs known but to few, which brings on the Person who drinks it the exact image of Death. Let this be administered to Antonia: You may easily find means to pour a few drops into her medicine. The effect will be throwing her into strong convulsions for an hour: After which her blood will gradually cease to flow, and heart to beat; A mortal paleness will spread itself over her features, and She will appear a Corse to every eye. She has no Friends about her: You may charge yourself unsuspected with the superintendence of her funeral, and cause her to be buried in the Vaults of St Clare. Their solitude and easy access render these Caverns favourable to your designs. Give Antonia the soporific draught this Evening: Eight and forty hours after She has drank it, Life will revive to her bosom. She will then be absolutely in your power: She will find all resistance unavailing, and necessity will compel her to receive you in her arms.'

'Antonia will be in my power!' exclaimed the Monk; 'Matilda, you transport me! At length then happiness will be mine, and that happiness will be Matilda's gift, will be the gift of friendship! I shall clasp Antonia in my arms, far from every prying eye, from every tormenting Intruder! I shall sigh out my soul upon her bosom; Shall teach her young heart the first rudiments of pleasure, and revel uncontrouled in the endless variety of her charms! And shall this delight indeed by mine? Shall I give the reins to my desires, and gratify every wild tumultuous wish? Oh! Matilda, how can I express to you my gratitude?'

'By profiting by my counsels. Ambrosio, I live but to serve you: Your interest and happiness are equally mine. Be your person Antonia's, but to your friendship and your heart I still assert my claim. Contributing to yours forms now my only pleasure. Should my exertions procure the gratification of your wishes, I shall consider my trouble to be amply repaid. But let us lose no time. The liquor of which I spoke, is only to be found in St Clare's Laboratory. Hasten then to the Prioress; Request of her admission to the Laboratory, and it will not be denied. There is a Closet at the lower end of the great Room, filled with liquids of different colours and qualities. The

Bottle in question stands by itself upon the third shelf on the left. It contains a greenish liquor: Fill a small phial with it when you are unobserved, and Antonia is your own.'

The Monk hesitated not to adopt this infamous plan. His desires, but too violent before, had acquired fresh vigour from the sight of Antonia. As He sat by her bedside, accident had discovered to him some of those charms, which till then had been concealed from him: He found them even more perfect, than his ardent imagination had pictured them. Sometimes her white and polished arm was displayed in arranging the pillow: Sometimes a sudden movement discovered part of her swelling bosom: But where-ever the new-found charm presented itself, there rested the Friar's gloating eyes. Scarcely could He master himself sufficiently to conceal his desires from Antonia and her vigilant Duenna. Inflamed by the remembrance of these beauties, He entered into Matilda's scheme without hesitation.

No sooner were Matins over, than He bent his course towards the Convent of St Clare: His arrival threw the whole Sisterhood into the utmost amazement. The Prioress was sensible of the honour done her Convent by his paying it his first visit, and strove to express her gratitude by every possible attention. He was paraded through the Garden, shown all the reliques of Saints and Martyrs, and treated with as much respect and distinction as had He been the Pope himself. On his part, Ambrosio received the Domina's civilities very graciously, and strove to remove her surprize at his having broken through his resolution. He stated, that among his penitents, illness prevented many from quitting their Houses. These were exactly the People, who most needed his advice and the comforts of Religion: Many representations had been made to him upon this account, and though highly repugnant to his own wishes, He had found it absolutely necessary for the service of heaven to change his determination, and quit his beloved retirement. The Prioress applauded his zeal in his profession and his charity towards Mankind: She declared, that Madrid was happy in possessing a Man so perfect and irreproachable. In such discourse, the Friar at length reached the Laboratory. He found the Closet: The Bottle stood in the place which Matilda had described, and the Monk seized an opportunity to fill his phial unobserved with the soporific liquor. Then having partaken of a Collation in the Refectory, He retired from the Convent pleased with the success of his visit, and leaving the Nuns delighted by the honour conferred upon them.

He waited till Evening, before He took the road to Antonia's dwelling. Jacintha welcomed him with transport, and besought him not to forget his promise to pass the night in the haunted Chamber: That promise He now repeated. He found Antonia tolerably well, but still harping upon the Ghost's prediction. Flora moved not from her Lady's Bed, and by symptoms yet stronger than on the former night testified her dislike to the Abbot's presence. Still Ambrosio affected not to observe them. The Physician arrived, while He was conversing with Antonia. It was dark already; Lights were called for, and Flora was compelled to descend for them herself. However, as She left a third Person in the room, and expected to be absent but a few minutes, She believed that She risqued nothing in quitting her post. No sooner had She left the room, than Ambrosio moved towards the Table, on which stood Antonia's medicine: It was placed in a recess of the window. The Physician seated in an armed-chair, and employed in questioning his Patient, paid no attention to the proceedings of the Monk. Ambrosio seized the opportunity: He drew out the fatal Phial, and let a few drops fall into the medicine. He then hastily left the Table, and returned to the seat which He had quitted. When Flora made her appearance with lights, every thing seemed to be exactly as She had left it.

The Physician declared, that Antonia might quit her chamber the next day with perfect safety. He recommended her following the same prescription, which on the night before had procured her a refreshing sleep: Flora replied, that the draught stood ready upon the Table: He advised the Patient to take it without delay, and then retired. Flora poured the medicine into a Cup, and presented it to her Mistress. At that moment Ambrosio's courage failed him. Might not Matilda have deceived him? Might not Jealousy have persuaded her to destroy her Rival, and substitute poison in the room of an opiate? This idea appeared so reasonable, that He was on the point of preventing her from swallowing the medicine. His resolution was adopted too late: The Cup was already emptied, and Antonia restored it into Flora's hands. No remedy was now to be found: Ambrosio could only expect the moment impatiently, destined to decide upon Antonia's life or death, upon his own happiness or despair.

Dreading to create suspicion by his stay, or betray himself by his mind's agitation, He took leave of his Victim, and withdrew from the room. Antonia parted from him with less cordiality than on the former night. Flora had represented to her Mistress, that to admit his visits was to disobey her Mother's orders: She described to her his emotion on entering the room, and the fire which sparkled in his eyes, while He gazed upon her. This had escaped Antonia's observation, but not her Attendant's; Who explaining the Monk's designs and their probable consequences in terms much clearer than Elvira's, though not quite so delicate, had succeeded in alarming her young Lady, and persuading her to treat him more distantly than She had done hitherto. The idea of obeying her Mother's will at once determined Antonia. Though She grieved at losing his society, She conquered herself sufficiently to receive the Monk with some degree of reserve and coldness. She thanked him with respect and gratitude for his former visits, but did not invite his repeating them in future. It now was not the Friar's interest to solicit admission to her presence, and He took leave of her, as if not designing to return. Fully persuaded that the acquaintance which She dreaded was now at an end, Flora was so much worked upon by his easy compliance, that She began to doubt the justice of her suspicions. As She lighted him down Stairs, She thanked him for having endeavoured to root out from Antonia's mind her superstitious terrors of the Spectre's prediction: She added, that as He seemed interested in Donna Antonia's welfare, should any change take place in her situation, She would be careful to let him know it. The Monk in replying took pains to raise his voice, hoping that Jacintha would hear it. In this He succeeded; As He reached the foot of the Stairs with his Conductress, the Landlady failed not to make her appearance.

'Why surely you are not going away, reverend Father?' cried She; 'Did you not promise to pass the night in the haunted Chamber? Christ Jesus! I shall be left alone with the Ghost, and a fine pickle I shall be in by morning! Do all I could, say all I could, that obstinate old Brute, Simon Gonzalez, refused to marry me to-day; And before to-morrow comes, I suppose, I shall be torn to pieces, by the Ghosts, and Goblins, and Devils, and what not! For God's sake, your Holiness, do not leave me in such a woeful condition! On my bended knees I beseech you to keep your promise: Watch this night in the haunted chamber; Lay the Apparition in the Red Sea, and Jacintha remembers you in her prayers to the last day of her existence!'

This request Ambrosio expected and desired; Yet He affected to raise objections, and to seem unwilling to keep his word. He told Jacintha that the Ghost existed no where but in her own brain, and that her insisting upon his staying all night in the House was ridiculous and useless. Jacintha was obstinate: She was not to be convinced, and pressed him so urgently not to leave her a prey to the Devil, that at length He granted her request. All this show of resistance imposed not upon Flora, who was naturally of a suspicious temper. She suspected the Monk to be acting a part very contrary to his own inclinations, and that He wished for no better than to remain where He was. She even went so far as to believe, that Jacintha was in his interest; and the poor old Woman was immediately set down, as no better than a Procuress. While She applauded herself for having penetrated into this plot against her Lady's honour, She resolved in secret to render it fruitless.

'So then,' said She to the Abbot with a look half-satirical and half indignant; 'So then you mean to stay here to-night? Do so, in God's name! Nobody will prevent you. Sit up to watch for the Ghost's arrival: I shall sit up too, and the Lord grant, that I may see nothing worse than a Ghost! I quit not Donna Antonia's Bed-side during this blessed night: Let me see any one dare to enter the room, and be He mortal or immortal, be He Ghost, Devil, or Man, I warrant his repenting that ever He crossed the threshold!'

This hint was sufficiently strong, and Ambrosio understood its meaning. But instead of showing that He perceived her suspicions; He replied mildly that He approved the Duenna's precautions, and advised her to persevere in her intention. This, She assured him faithfully, that He might depend upon her doing. Jacintha then conducted him into the chamber where the Ghost had appeared, and Flora returned to her Lady's.

Jacintha opened the door of the haunted room with a trembling hand: She ventured to peep in; But the wealth of India would not have tempted her to cross the threshold. She gave the Taper to the Monk, wished him well through the adventure, and hastened to be gone. Ambrosio entered. He bolted the door, placed the light upon the Table, and seated himself in the Chair which on the former night had sustained Antonia. In spite of Matilda's assurances that the Spectre was a mere creation of fancy, his mind was impressed with a certain mysterious horror. He in vain endeavoured to shake it off. The silence of the night, the story of the Apparition, the chamber wainscotted with dark oak pannells, the recollection which it brought with it of the murdered Elvira, and his incertitude respecting the nature of the drops given by him to Antonia, made him feel uneasy at his present situation. But He thought much less of the Spectre, than of the poison. Should He have destroyed the only object, which rendered life dear to him; Should the Ghost's prediction prove true; Should Antonia in three days be no more, and He the wretched cause of her death . . . . . . The supposition was too horrible to dwell upon. He drove away these dreadful images, and as often they presented themselves again before him. Matilda had assured him, that the effects of the Opiate would be speedy. He listened with fear, yet with eagerness, expecting to hear some disturbance in the adjoining chamber. All was still silent. He concluded, that the drops had not begun to operate. Great was the stake, for which He now played: A moment would suffice to decide upon his misery or happiness. Matilda had taught him the means of ascertaining, that life was not extinct for ever: Upon this assay depended all his hopes. With every instant his impatience redoubled; His terrors grew more lively, his anxiety more awake. Unable to bear this state of incertitude, He endeavoured to divert it by substituting the thoughts of Others to his own. The Books, as was before mentioned, were ranged upon shelves near the Table: This stood exactly opposite to the Bed, which was placed in an Alcove near the Closet-door. Ambrosio took down a Volume, and seated himself by the Table: But his attention wandered from the Pages before him. Antonia's image and that of the murdered Elvira persisted to force themselves before his imagination. Still He continued to read, though his eyes ran over the characters, without his mind being conscious of their import.

Such was his occupation, when He fancied that He heard a foot-step. He turned his head, but nobody was to be seen. He resumed his Book; But in a few minutes after the same sound was repeated, and followed by a rustling noise close behind him. He now started from his seat, and looking round him, perceived the Closet-door standing half-unclosed. On his first entering the room He had tried to open it, but found it bolted on the inside.

'How is this?' said He to himself; 'How comes this door unfastened?'

He advanced towards it: He pushed it open, and looked into the closet: No one was there. While He stood irresolute, He thought, that He distinguished a groaning in the adjacent chamber: It was Antonia's, and He supposed, that the drops began to take effect: But upon listening more attentively, He found the noise to be caused by Jacintha, who had fallen asleep by the Lady's Bed-side, and was snoring most lustily. Ambrosio drew back, and returned to the other room, musing upon the sudden opening of the Closet-door, for which He strove in vain to account.

He paced the chamber up and down in silence. At length He stopped, and the Bed attracted his attention. The curtain of the Recess was but half-drawn. He sighed involuntarily.

'That Bed,' said He in a low voice, 'That Bed was Elvira's! There has She past many a quiet night, for She was good and innocent. How sound must have been her sleep! And yet now She sleeps sounder! Does She indeed sleep? Oh! God grant, that She may! What if She rose from her Grave at this sad and silent hour? What if She broke the bonds of the Tomb, and glided angrily before my blasted eyes? Oh! I never could support the sight! Again to see her form distorted by dying agonies, her blood-swollen veins, her livid countenance, her eyes bursting from their sockets with pain! To hear her speak of future punishment, menace me with Heaven's vengeance, tax me with the crimes I have committed, with those I am going to commit . . . . . Great God! What is that?'

As He uttered these words, his eyes which were fixed upon the Bed, saw the curtain shaken gently backwards and forwards. The Apparition was recalled to his mind, and He almost fancied that He beheld Elvira's visionary form reclining upon the Bed. A few moments consideration sufficed to re-assure him.

'It was only the wind,' said He, recovering himself.

Again He paced the chamber; But an involuntary movement of awe and inquietude constantly led his eye towards the Alcove. He drew near it with irresolution. He paused before He ascended the few steps which led to it. He put out his hand thrice to remove the curtain, and as often drew it back.

'Absurd terrors!' He cried at length, ashamed of his own weakness——

Hastily he mounted the steps; When a Figure drest in white started from the Alcove, and gliding by him, made with precipitation towards the Closet. Madness and despair now supplied the Monk with that courage, of which He had till then been destitute. He flew down the steps, pursued the Apparition, and attempted to grasp it.

'Ghost, or Devil, I hold you!' He exclaimed, and seized the Spectre by the arm.

'Oh! Christ Jesus!' cried a shrill voice; 'Holy Father, how you gripe me! I protest, that I meant no harm!'

This address, as well as the arm which He held, convinced the Abbot that the supposed Ghost was substantial flesh and blood. He drew the Intruder towards the Table, and holding up the light, discovered the features of . . . . . . Madona Flora!

Incensed at having been betrayed by this trifling cause into fears so ridiculous, He asked her sternly, what business had brought her to that chamber. Flora, ashamed at being found out, and terrified at the severity of Ambrosio's looks, fell upon her knees, and promised to make a full confession.

'I protest, reverend Father,' said She, 'that I am quite grieved at having disturbed you: Nothing was further from my intention. I meant to get out of the room as quietly as I got in; and had you been ignorant that I watched you, you know, it would have been the same thing, as if I had not watched you at all. To be sure, I did very wrong in being a Spy upon you, that I cannot deny; But Lord! your Reverence, how can a poor weak Woman resist curiosity? Mine was so strong to know what you were doing, that I could not but try to get a little peep, without any body knowing any thing about it. So with that I left old Dame Jacintha sitting by my Lady's Bed, and I ventured to steal into the Closet. Being unwilling to interrupt you, I contented myself at first with putting my eye to the Key-hole; But as I could see nothing by this means, I undrew the bolt, and while your back was turned to the Alcove, I whipt me in softly and silently. Here I lay snug behind the curtain, till your Reverence found me out, and seized me ere I had time to regain the Closet-door. This is the whole truth, I assure you, Holy Father, and I beg your pardon a thousand times for my impertinence.'

During this speech the Abbot had time to recollect himself: He was satisfied with reading the penitent Spy a lecture upon the dangers of curiosity, and the meanness of the action in which She had been just discovered. Flora declared herself fully persuaded, that She had done wrong; She promised never to be guilty of the same fault again, and was retiring very humble and contrite to Antonia's chamber, when the Closet-door was suddenly thrown open, and in rushed Jacintha pale and out of breath.

'Oh! Father! Father!' She cried in a voice almost choaked with terror; 'What shall I do! What shall I do! Here is a fine piece of work! Nothing but misfortunes! Nothing but dead people, and dying people! Oh! I shall go distracted! I shall go distracted!'

'Speak! Speak!' cried Flora and the Monk at the same time; 'What has happened? What is the matter?'

'Oh! I shall have another Corse in my House! Some Witch has certainly cast a spell upon it, upon me, and upon all about me! Poor Donna Antonia! There She lies in just such convulsions, as killed her Mother! The Ghost told her true! I am sure, the Ghost has told her true!'

Flora ran, or rather flew to her Lady's chamber; Ambrosio followed her, his bosom trembling with hope and apprehension. They found Antonia as Jacintha had described, torn by racking convulsions from which they in vain endeavoured to relieve her. The Monk dispatched Jacintha to the Abbey in all haste, and commissioned her to bring Father Pablos back with her, without losing a moment.

'I will go for him,' replied Jacintha, 'and tell him to come hither; But as to bringing him myself, I shall do no such thing. I am sure that the House is bewitched, and burn me if ever I set foot in it again.'

With this resolution She set out for the Monastery, and delivered to Father Pablos the Abbot's orders. She then betook herself to the House of old Simon Gonzalez, whom She resolved never to quit, till She had made him her Husband, and his dwelling her own.

Father Pablos had no sooner beheld Antonia, than He pronounced her incurable. The convulsions continued for an hour: During that time her agonies were much milder than those, which her groans created in the Abbot's heart. Her every pang seemed a dagger in his bosom, and He cursed himself a thousand times for having adopted so barbarous a project. The hour being expired, by degrees the Fits became less frequent, and Antonia less agitated. She felt that her dissolution was approaching, and that nothing could save her.

'Worthy Ambrosio,' She said in a feeble voice, while She pressed his hand to her lips; 'I am now at liberty to express, how grateful is my heart for your attention and kindness. I am upon the bed of death; Yet an hour, and I shall be no more. I may therefore acknowledge without restraint, that to relinquish your society was very painful to me: But such was the will of a Parent, and I dared not disobey. I die without repugnance: There are few, whom I lament to leave. Among those few, I lament for none more than for yourself; But we shall meet again, Ambrosio! We shall one day meet in heaven: There shall our friendship be renewed, and my Mother shall view it with pleasure!'

She paused. The Abbot shuddered when She mentioned Elvira: Antonia imputed his emotion to pity and concern for her.

'You are grieved for me, Father,' She continued; 'Ah! sigh not for my loss. I have no crimes to repent, at least none of which I am conscious, and I restore my soul without fear to him from whom I received it. I have but few requests to make: Yet let me hope that what few I have shall be granted. Let a solemn Mass be said for my soul's repose, and another for that of my beloved Mother. Not, that I doubt her resting in her Grave: I am now convinced that my reason wandered, and the falsehood of the Ghost's prediction is sufficient to prove my error. But every one has some failing: My Mother may have had hers, though I knew them not: I therefore wish a Mass to be celebrated for her repose, and the expence may be defrayed by the little wealth of which I am possessed. Whatever may then remain, I bequeath to my Aunt Leonella. When I am dead, let the Marquis de las Cisternas know, that his Brother's unhappy family can no longer importune him. But disappointment makes me unjust: They tell me, that He is ill, and perhaps had it been in his power, He wished to have protected me. Tell him then, Father, only that I am dead, and that if He had any faults to me, I forgave him from my heart. This done, I have nothing more to ask for, than your prayers: Promise to remember my requests, and I shall resign my life without a pang or sorrow.'

Ambrosio engaged to comply with her desires, and proceeded to give her absolution. Every moment announced the approach of Antonia's fate: Her sight failed; Her heart beat sluggishly; Her fingers stiffened, and grew cold, and at two in the morning She expired without a groan. As soon as the breath had forsaken her body, Father Pablos retired, sincerely affected at the melancholy scene. On her part, Flora gave way to the most unbridled sorrow. Far different concerns employed Ambrosio: He sought for the pulse whose throbbing, so Matilda had assured him, would prove Antonia's death but temporal. He found it; He pressed it; It palpitated beneath his hand, and his heart was filled with ecstacy. However, He carefully concealed his satisfaction at the success of his plan. He assumed a melancholy air, and addressing himself to Flora, warned her against abandoning herself to fruitless sorrow. Her tears were too sincere to permit her listening to his counsels, and She continued to weep unceasingly. The Friar withdrew, first promising to give orders himself about the Funeral, which, out of consideration for Jacintha as He pretended, should take place with all expedition. Plunged in grief for the loss of her beloved Mistress, Flora scarcely attended to what He said. Ambrosio hastened to command the Burial. He obtained permission from the Prioress, that the Corse should be deposited in St Clare's Sepulchre: and on the Friday Morning, every proper and needful ceremony being performed, Antonia's body was committed to the Tomb.

On the same day Leonella arrived at Madrid, intending to present her young Husband to Elvira. Various circumstances had obliged her to defer her journey from Tuesday to Friday, and She had no opportunity of making this alteration in her plans known to her Sister. As her heart was truly affectionate, and as She had ever entertained a sincere regard for Elvira and her Daughter, her surprize at hearing of their sudden and melancholy fate was fully equalled by her sorrow and disappointment. Ambrosio sent to inform her of Antonia's bequest: At her solication, He promised, as soon as Elvira's trifling debts were discharged, to transmit to her the remainder. This being settled, no other business detained Leonella in Madrid, and She returned to Cordova with all diligence.

CHAPTER III

Oh! could I worship aught beneath the skies,
That earth hath seen or fancy could devise,
Thine altar, sacred Liberty, should stand,
Built by no mercenary vulgar hand,
With fragrant turf, and flowers as wild and fair,
As ever dressed a bank, or cented summer air.
                                        Cowper.

HIS whole attention bent upon bringing to justice the Assassins of his Sister, Lorenzo little thought, how severely his interest was suffering in another quarter. As was before mentioned, He returned not to Madrid till the evening of that day, on which Antonia was buried. Signifying to the Grand Inquisitor the order of the Cardinal-Duke [a ceremony not to be neglected, when a Member of the Church was to be arrested publicly] communicating his design to his Uncle and Don Ramirez, and assembling a troop of Attendants sufficiently to prevent opposition, furnished him with full occupation during the few hours preceding midnight. Consequently, He had no opportunity to enquire about his Mistress, and was perfectly ignorant both of her death and her Mother's.

The Marquis was by no means out of danger: His delirium was gone, but had left him so much exhausted, that the Physicians declined pronouncing upon the consequences likely to ensue. As for Raymond himself, He wished for nothing more earnestly than to join Agnes in the grave. Existence was hateful to him: He saw nothing in the world deserving his attention; and He hoped to hear that Agnes was revenged, and himself given over in the same moment.

Followed by Raymond's ardent prayers for success, Lorenzo was at the Gates of St Clare a full hour before the time appointed by the Mother St Ursula. He was accompanied by his Uncle, by Don Ramirez de Mello, and a party of chosen Archers. Though in considerable numbers their appearance created no surprize: A great Crowd was already assembled before the Convent-doors, in order to witness the Procession. It was naturally supposed, that Lorenzo and his Attendants were conducted thither by the same design. The Duke of Medina being recognised, the People drew back, and made way for his party to advance. Lorenzo placed himself opposite to the great Gate, through which the Pilgrims were to pass. Convinced that the Prioress could not escape him, He waited patiently for her appearance, which She was expected to make exactly at Midnight.

The Nuns were employed in religious duties established in honour of St Clare, and to which no Prophane was ever admitted. The Chapel-windows

were illuminated. As they stood on the outside, the Auditors heard the full
swell of the organ, accompanied by a chorus of female voices, rise upon the
stillness of the night. This died away, and was succeeded by a single strain
of harmony: It was the voice of her who was destined to sustain in the
procession the character of St Clare. For this office the most beautiful Virgin
of Madrid was always selected, and She upon whom the choice fell,
esteemed it as the highest of honours. While listening to the Music, whose
melody distance only seemed to render sweeter, the Audience was wrapped
up in profound attention. Universal silence prevailed through the Crowd,
and every heart was filled with reverence for religion. Every heart but
Lorenzo's. Conscious that among those who chaunted the praises of their
God so sweetly, there were some who cloaked with devotion the foulest sins,
their hymns inspired him with detastation at their Hypocrisy. He had long
observed with disapprobation and contempt the superstition, which governed Madrid's Inhabitants. His good sense had pointed out to him the
artifices of the Monks, and the gross absurdity of their miracles, wonders,
and suppositious reliques. He blushed to see his Countrymen the Dupes of
deceptions so ridiculous, and only wished for an opportunity to free them
from their monkish fetters. That opportunity, so long desired in vain, was at
length presented to him. He resolved not to let it slip, but to set before the
People in glaring colours, how enormous were the abuses but too frequently
practised in Monasteries, and how unjustly public esteem was bestowed
indiscriminately upon all who wore a religious habit. He longed for the
moment destined to unmask the Hypocrites, and convince his Countrymen,
that a sanctified exterior does not always hide a virtuous heart.

   The service lasted, till Midnight was announced by the Convent-Bell.
That sound being heard, the Music ceased: The voices died away softly, and
soon after the lights disappeared from the Chapel-windows. Lorenzo's heart
beat high, when He found the execution of his plan to be at hand. From the
natural superstition of the People He had prepared himself for some
resistance. But He trusted that the Mother St Ursula would bring good
reasons to justify his proceeding. He had force with him to repel the first
impulse of the Populace, till his arguments should be heard: His only fear
was, lest the Domina, suspecting his design, should have spirited away the
Nun, on whose deposition every thing depended. Unless the Mother St
Ursula should be present, He could only accuse the Prioress upon suspicion;
and this reflection gave him some little apprehension for the success of his
enterprize. The tranquillity which seemed to reign through the Convent, in
some degree re-assured him: Still He expected the moment eagerly, when
the presence of his Ally should deprive him of the power of doubting.

   The Abbey of Capuchins was only separated from the Convent by the
Garden and Cemetery. The Monks had been invited to assist at the
Pilgrimage. They now arrived, marching two by two with lighted Torches

in their hands, and chaunting Hymns in honour of St Clare. Father Pablos was at their head, the Abbot having excused himself from attending. The people made way for the holy Train, and the Friars placed themselves in ranks on either side of the great Gates. A few minutes sufficed to arrange the order of the Procession. This being settled, the Convent-doors were thrown open, and again the female Chorus sounded in full melody. First appeared a Band of Choristers: As soon as they had passed, the Monks fell in two by two, and followed with steps slow and measured. Next came the Novices; They bore no Tapers, as did the Professed, but moved on with eyes bent downwards, and seemed to be occupied by telling their Beads. To them succeeded a young and lovely Girl, who represented St Lucia: She held a golden bason in which were two eyes: Her own were covered by a velvet bandage, and She was conducted by another Nun habited as an Angel. She was followed by St Catherine, a palm-branch in one hand, a flaming Sword in the other: She was robed in white, and her brow was ornamented with a sparkling Diadem. After her appeared St Genevieve, surrounded by a number of Imps, who putting themselves into grotesque attitudes, drawing her by the robe, and sporting round her with antic gestures, endeavoured to distract her attention from the Book, on which her eyes were constantly fixed. These merry Devils greatly entertained the Spectators, who testified their pleasure by repeated bursts of Laughter. The Prioress had been careful to select a Nun whose disposition was naturally solemn and saturnine. She had every reason to be satisfied with her choice: The drolleries of the Imps were entirely thrown away, and St Genevieve moved on without discomposing a muscle.

Each of these Saints was separated from the Other by a band of Choristers, exalting her praise in their Hymns, but declaring her to be very much inferior to St Clare, the Convent's avowed Patroness. These having passed, a long train of Nuns appeared, bearing like the Choristers each a burning Taper. Next came the reliques of St Clare, inclosed in vases equally precious for their materials and workmanship: But they attracted not Lorenzo's attention. The Nun who bore the heart, occupied him entirely. According to Theodore's description, He doubted not her being the Mother St Ursula. She seemed to look round with anxiety. As He stood foremost in the rank by which the procession past, her eye caught Lorenzo's. A flush of joy overspread her till then pallid cheek. She turned to her Companion eagerly.

'We are safe!' He heard her whisper; ''tis her Brother!'

His heart being now at ease, Lorenzo gazed with tranquillity upon the remainder of the show. Now appeared its most brilliant ornament. It was a Machine fashioned like a throne, rich with jewels, and dazzling with light. It rolled onwards upon concealed wheels, and was guided by several lovely Children, dressed as Seraphs. The summit was covered with silver clouds, upon which reclined the most beautiful form that eyes ever witnessed. It was a Damsel representing St Clare: Her dress was of inestimable price, and round her head a wreath of Diamonds formed an artificial glory: But all these ornaments yielded to the lustre of her charms. As She advanced, a murmur of delight ran through the Crowd. Even Lorenzo confessed secretly, that He never beheld more perfect beauty, and had not his heart been Antonia's, it must have fallen a sacrifice to this enchanting Girl. As it was, He considered her only as a fine Statue: She obtained from him no tribute save cold admiration, and when She had passed him, He thought of her no more.

'Who is She?' asked a By-stander in Lorenzo's hearing.

'One, whose beauty you must often have heard celebrated. Her name is Virginia de Villa-Franca: She is a Pensioner of St Clare's Convent, a Relation of the Prioress, and has been selected with justice as the ornament of the Procession.'

The Throne moved onwards. It was followed by the Prioress herself: She marched at the head of the remaining Nuns with a devout and sanctified air, and closed the procession. She moved on slowly: Her eyes were raised to heaven: Her countenance calm and tranquil seemed abstracted from all sublunary things, and no feature betrayed her secret pride at displaying the pomp and opulence of her Convent. She passed along, accompanied by the prayers and benedictions of the Populace: But how great was the general confusion and surprize, when Don Ramirez starting forward, challenged her as his Prisoner.

For a moment amazement held the Domina silent and immoveable: But no sooner did She recover herself, than She exclaimed against sacrilege and impiety, and called the People to rescue a Daughter of the Church. They were eagerly preparing to obey her; when Don Ramirez, protected by the Archers from their rage, commanded them to forbear, and threatened them with the severest vengeance of the Inquisition. At that dreaded word every arm fell, every sword shrunk back into its scabbard. The Prioress herself turned pale, and trembled. The general silence convinced her that She had nothing to hope but from innocence, and She besought Don Ramirez in a faultering voice, to inform her of what crime She was accused.

'That you shall know in time,' replied He; 'But first I must secure the Mother St Ursula.'

'The Mother St Ursula?' repeated the Domina faintly.

At this moment casting her eyes round, She saw near her Lorenzo and the Duke, who had followed Don Ramirez.

'Ah! great God!' She cried, clasping her hands together with a frantic air; 'I am betrayed!'

'Betrayed?' replied St Ursula, who now arrived conducted by some of the Archers, and followed by the Nun her Companion in the procession: 'Not betrayed, but discovered. In me recognise your Accuser: You know not, how well I am instructed in your guilt!—Segnor!' She continued, turning to Don Ramirez; 'I commit myself to your custody. I charge the Prioress of St Clare with murder, and stake my life for the justice of my accusation.'

A general cry of surprize was uttered by the whole Audience, and an explanation was demanded loudly. The trembling Nuns, terrified at the noise and universal confusion, had dispersed, and fled different ways. Some regained the Convent; Others sought refuge in the dwellings of their Relations; and Many, only sensible of their present danger, and anxious to escape from the tumult, ran through the Streets, and wandered, they knew not whither. The lovely Virginia was one of the first to fly: And in order that She might be better seen and heard, the People desired that St Ursula should harangue them from the vacant Throne. The Nun complied; She ascended the glittering Machine, and then addressed the surrounding multitude as follows.

'However strange and unseemly may appear my conduct, when considered to be adopted by a Female and a Nun, necessity will justify it most fully. A secret, an horrible secret weighs heavy upon my soul: No rest can be mine till I have revealed it to the world, and satisfied that innocent blood which calls from the Grave for vengeance. Much have I dared to gain this opportunity of lightening my conscience. Had I failed in my attempt to reveal the crime, had the Domina but suspected that the mystery was none to me, my ruin was inevitable. Angels who watch unceasingly over those who deserve their favour, have enabled me to escape detection: I am now at liberty to relate a Tale, whose circumstances will freeze every honest soul with horror. Mine is the task to rend the veil from Hypocrisy, and show misguided Parents to what dangers the Woman is exposed, who falls under the sway of a monastic Tyrant.

'Among the Votaries of St Clare, none was more lovely, none more gentle, than Agnes de Medina. I knew her well; She entrusted to me every secret of her heart; I was her Friend and Confident, and I loved her with sincere affection. Nor was I singular in my attachment. Her piety unfeigned, her willingness to oblige, and her angelic disposition, rendered her the Darling of all that was estimable in the Convent. The Prioress herself, proud, scrupulous and forbidding, could not refuse Agnes that tribute of approbation, which She bestowed upon no one else. Every one has some fault: Alas! Agnes had her weakness! She violated the laws of our order, and incurred the inveterate hate of the unforgiving Domina. St Clare's rules are severe: But grown antiquated and neglected, many of late years have either been forgotten, or changed by universal consent into milder punishments. The penance, adjudged to the crime of Agnes, was most cruel, most inhuman! The law had been long exploded: Alas! It still existed, and the revengeful Prioress now determined to revive it. This law decreed, that the

Offender should be plunged into a private dungeon, expressly constituted to hide from the world for ever the Victim of Cruelty and tyrannic superstition. In this dreadful abode She was to lead a perpetual solitude, deprived of all society, and believed to be dead by those, whom affection might have prompted to attempt her rescue. Thus was She to languish out the remainder of her days, with no other food than bread and water, and no other comfort than the free indulgence of her tears.'

The indignation created by this account was so violent, as for some moments to interrupt St Ursula's narrative. When the disturbance ceased, and silence again prevailed through the Assembly, She continued her discourse, while at every word the Domina's countenance betrayed her increasing terrors.

'A Council of the twelve elder Nuns was called: I was of the number. The Prioress in exaggerated colours described the offence of Agnes, and scrupled not to propose the revival of this almost forgotten law. To the shame of our sex be it spoken, that either so absolute was the Domina's will in the Convent, or so much had disappointment, solitude, and self-denial hardened their hearts and sowered their tempers, that this barbarous proposal was assented to by nine voices out of the twelve. I was not one of the nine. Frequent opportunities had convinced me of the virtues of Agnes, and I loved and pitied her most sincerely. The Mothers Bertha and Cornelia joined my party: We made the strongest opposition possible, and the Superior found herself compelled to change her intention. In spite of the majority in her favour, She feared to break with us openly. She knew, that supported by the Medina family, our forces would be too strong for her to cope with: And She also knew, that after being once imprisoned and supposed dead, should Agnes be discovered, her ruin would be inevitable. She therefore gave up her design, though with much reluctance. She demanded some days to reflect upon a mode of punishment, which might be agreeable to the whole Community; and She promised, that as soon as her resolution was fixed, the same Council should be again summoned. Two days passed away: On the Evening of the Third it was announced, that on the next day Agnes should be examined; and that according to her behaviour on that occasion, her punishment should be either strengthened or mitigated.

'On the night preceding this examination, I stole to the Cell of Agnes at an hour, when I supposed the other Nuns to be buried in sleep. I comforted her to the best of my power: I bad her take courage, told her to rely upon the support of her friends, and taught her certain signs, by which I might instruct her to answer the Domina's questions by an assent or negative. Conscious, that her Enemy would strive to confuse, embarrass, and daunt her, I feared her being ensnared into some confession prejudicial to her interests. Being anxious to keep my visit secret, I stayed with Agnes but a short time. I bad her not let her spirits be cast down; I mingled my tears with those, which streamed down her cheek, embraced her fondly, and was on the point of retiring, when I heard the sound of steps approaching the Cell. I started back. A Curtain which veiled a large Crucifix offered me a retreat, and I hastened to place myself behind it. The door opened. The Prioress entered, followed by four other Nuns. They advanced towards the bed of Agnes. The Superior reproached her with her errors in the bitterest terms: She told her, that She was a disgrace to the Convent, that She was resolved to deliver the world and herself from such a Monster, and commanded her to drink the contents of a Goblet now presented to her by one of the Nuns. Aware of the fatal properties of the liquor, and trembling to find herself upon the brink of Eternity, the unhappy Girl strove to excite the Domina's pity by the most affecting prayers. She sued for life in terms which might have melted the heart of a Fiend: She promised to submit patiently to any punishment, to shame, imprisonment, and torture, might She but be permitted to live! Oh! might She but live another month, or week, or day! Her merciless Enemy listened to her complaints unmoved: She told her, that at first She meant to have spared her life, and that if She had altered her intention, She had to thank the opposition of her Friends. She continued to insist upon her swallowing the poison: She bad her recommend herself to the Almighty's mercy, not to hers, and assured her that in an hour She would be numbered with the Dead. Perceiving that it was vain to implore this unfeeling Woman, She attempted to spring from her bed, and call for assistance: She hoped, if She could not escape the fate announced to her, at least to have witnesses of the violence committed. The Prioress guessed her design. She seized her forcibly by the arm, and pushed her back upon her pillow. At the same time drawing a dagger, and placing it at the breast of the unfortunate Agnes, She protested that if She uttered a single cry, or hesitated a single moment to drink the poison, She would pierce her heart that instant. Already half-dead with fear, She could make no further resistance. The Nun approached with the fatal Goblet. The Domina obliged her to take it, and swallow the contents. She drank, and the horrid deed was accomplished. The Nuns then seated themselves round the Bed. They answered her groans with reproaches; They interrupted with sarcasms the prayers in which She recommended her parting soul to mercy: They threatened her with heaven's vengeance and eternal perdition: They bad her despair of pardon, and strowed with yet sharper thorns Death's painful pillow. Such were the sufferings of this young Unfortunate, till released by fate from the malice of her Tormentors. She expired in horror of the past, in fears for the future; and her agonies were such as must have amply gratified the hate and vengeance of her Enemies. As soon as her Victim ceased to breathe, the Domina retired, and was followed by her Accomplices.

'It was now that I ventured from my concealment. I dared not to assist my unhappy Friend, aware, that without preserving her, I should only have brought on myself the same destruction. Shocked and terrified beyond expression at this horrid scene, scarcely had I sufficient strength to regain my Cell. As I reached the door of that of Agnes, I ventured to look towards the bed, on which lay her lifeless body, once so lovely and so sweet! I breathed a prayer for her departed Spirit, and vowed to revenge her death by the shame and punishment of her Assassins. With danger and difficulty have I kept my oath. I unwarily dropped some words at the funeral of Agnes, while thrown off my guard by excessive grief, which alarmed the guilty conscience of the Prioress. My every action was observed; My every step was traced. I was constantly surrounded by the Superior's spies. It was long before I could find the means of conveying to the unhappy Girl's Relations an intimation of my secret. It was given out, that Agnes had expired suddenly: This account was credited not only by her Friends in Madrid, but even by those within the Convent. The poison had left no marks upon her body: No one suspected the true cause of her death, and it remained unknown to all, save the Assassins and Myself.

'I have no more to say: For what I have already said, I will answer with my life. I repeat, that the Prioress is a Murderess; That She has driven from the world, perhaps from heaven, an Unfortunate whose offence was light and venial; that She has abused the power intrusted to her hands, and has been a Tyrant, a Barbarian, and an Hypocrite. I also accuse the four Nuns, Violante, Camilla, Alix, and Mariana, as being her Accomplices, and equally criminal.'

Here St Ursula ended her narrative. It created horror and surprize throughout: But when She related the inhuman murder of Agnes, the indignation of the Mob was so audibly testified, that it was scarcely possible to hear the conclusion. This confusion increased with every moment: At length a multitude of voices exclaimed, that the Prioress should be given up to their fury. To this Don Ramirez refused to consent positively. Even Lorenzo bad the People remember, that She had undergone no trial, and advised them to leave her punishment to the Inquisition. All representations were fruitless: The disturbance grew still more violent, and the Populace more exasperated. In vain did Ramirez attempt to convey his Prisoner out of the Throng. Wherever He turned, a band of Rioters barred his passage, and demanded her being delivered over to them more loudly than before. Ramirez ordered his Attendants to cut their way through the multitude: Oppressed by numbers, it was impossible for them to draw their swords. He threatened the Mob with the vengeance of the Inquisition: But in this moment of popular phrenzy even this dreadful name had lost its effect. Though regret for his Sister made him look upon the Prioress with abhorrence, Lorenzo could not help pitying a Woman in a situation so terrible: But in spite of all his exertions, and those of the Duke, of Don Ramirez, and the Archers, the People continued to press onwards. They forced a passage through the Guards who protected their destined Victim, dragged her from her shelter, and proceeded to take upon her a most summary and cruel vengeance. Wild with terror, and scarcely knowing what She said, the wretched Woman shrieked for a moment's mercy: She protested that She was innocent of the death of Agnes, and could clear herself from the suspicion beyond the power of doubt. The Rioters heeded nothing but the gratification of their barbarous vengeance. They refused to listen to her: They showed her every sort of insult, loaded her with mud and filth, and called her by the most opprobrious appellations. They tore her one from another, and each new Tormentor was more savage than the former. They stifled with howls and execrations her shrill cries for mercy; and dragged her through the Streets, spurning her, trampling her, and treating her with every species of cruelty which hate or vindictive fury could invent. At length a Flint, aimed by some well-directing hand, struck her full upon the temple. She sank upon the ground bathed in blood, and in a few minutes terminated her miserable existence. Yet though She no longer felt their insults, the Rioters still exercised their impotent rage upon her lifeless body. They beat it, trod upon it, and ill-used it, till it became no more than a mass of flesh, unsightly, shapeless, and disgusting.

Unable to prevent this shocking event, Lorenzo and his Friends had beheld it with the utmost horror: But they were rouzed from their compelled inactivity, on hearing that the Mob was attacking the Convent of St Clare. The incensed Populace, confounding the innocent with the guilty, had resolved to sacrifice all the Nuns of that order to their rage, and not to leave one stone of the building upon another. Alarmed at this intelligence, they hastened to the Convent, resolved to defend it if possible, or at least to rescue the Inhabitants from the fury of the Rioters. Most of the Nuns had fled, but a few still remained in their habitation. Their situation was truly dangerous. However, as they had taken the precaution of fastening the inner Gates, with this assistance Lorenzo hoped to repel the Mob, till Don Ramirez should return to him with a more sufficient force.

Having been conducted by the former disturbance to the distance of some Streets from the Convent, He did not immediately reach it: When He arrived, the throng surrounding it was so excessive, as to prevent his approaching the Gates. In the interim, the Populace besieged the Building with persevering rage: They battered the walls, threw lighted torches in at the windows, and swore that by break of day not a Nun of St Clare's order should be left alive. Lorenzo had just succeeded in piercing his way through the Crowd, when one of the Gates was forced open. The Rioters poured into the interior part of the Building, where they exercised their vengeance upon every thing which found itself in their passage. They broke the furniture into pieces, tore down the pictures, destroyed the reliques, and in their hatred of her Servant forgot all respect to the Saint. Some employed themselves in searching out the Nuns, Others in pulling down parts of the Convent, and Others again in setting fire to the pictures and valuable furniture, which it contained. These Latter produced the most decisive desolation: Indeed the consequences of their action were more sudden, than themselves had expected or wished. The Flames rising from the burning piles caught part of the Building, which being old and dry, the conflagration spread with rapidity from room to room. The Walls were soon shaken by the devouring element: The Columns gave way: The Roofs came tumbling down upon the Rioters, and crushed many of them beneath their weight. Nothing was to be heard but shrieks and groans; The Convent was wrapped in flames, and the whole presented a scene of devastation and horror.

Lorenzo was shocked at having been the cause, however innocent, of this frightful disturbance: He endeavoured to repair his fault by protecting the helpless Inhabitants of the Convent. He entered it with the Mob, and exerted himself to repress the prevailing Fury, till the sudden and alarming progress of the flames compelled him to provide for his own safety. The People now hurried out, as eagerly as they had before thronged in; But their numbers clogging up the door-way, and the fire gaining upon them rapidly, many of them perished ere they had time to effect their escape. Lorenzo's good fortune directed him to a small door in a farther Aisle of the Chapel. The bolt was already undrawn: He opened the door, and found himself at the foot of St Clare's Sepulchre.

Here He stopped to breathe. The Duke and some of his Attendants had followed him, and thus were in security for the present. They now consulted, what steps they should take to escape from this scene of disturbance: But their deliberations were considerably interrupted by the sight of volumes of fire rising from amidst the Convent's massy walls, by the noise of some heavy Arch tumbling down in ruins, or by the mingled shrieks of the Nuns and Rioters, either suffocating in the press, perishing in the flames, or crushed beneath the weight of the falling Mansion.

Lorenzo enquired, whither the Wicket led? He was answered, to the Garden of the Capuchins, and it was resolved to explore an out-let upon that side. Accordingly the Duke raised the Latch, and passed into the adjoining Cemetery. The Attendants followed without ceremony. Lorenzo, being the last, was also on the point of quitting the Colonnade, when He saw the door of the Sepulchre opened softly. Some-one looked out, but on perceiving Strangers uttered a loud shriek, started back again, and flew down the marble Stairs.

'What can this mean?' cried Lorenzo; 'Here is some mystery concealed. Follow me without delay!'

Thus saying, He hastened into the Sepulchre, and pursued the person who continued to fly before him. The Duke knew not the cause of his exclamation, but supposing that He had good reasons for it, he followed him without hesitation. The Others did the same, and the whole Party soon arrived at the foot of the Stairs. The upper door having been left open, the neighbouring flames darted from above a sufficient light to enable Lorenzo's catching a glance of the Fugitive running through the long passages and distant Vaults: But when a sudden turn deprived him of this assistance, total darkness succeeded, and He could only trace the object of his enquiry by the faint echo of retiring feet. The Pursuers were now compelled to proceed with caution: As well as they could judge, the Fugitive also seemed to slacken pace, for they heard the steps follow each other at longer intervals. They at length were bewildered by the Labyrinth of passages, and dispersed in various directions. Carried away by his eagerness to clear up this mystery, and to penetrate into which He was impelled by a movement secret and unaccountable, Lorenzo heeded not this circumstance till He found himself in total solitude. The noise of foot-steps had ceased. All was silent around, and no clue offered itself to guide him to the flying Person. He stopped to reflect on the means most likely to aid his pursuit. He was persuaded, that no common cause would have induced the Fugitive to seek that dreary place at an hour so unusual: The cry which He had heard, seemed uttered in a voice of terror, and He was convinced that some mystery was attached to this event. After some minutes past in hesitation He continued to proceed, feeling his way along the walls of the passage. He had already past some time in this slow progress, when He descried a spark of light glimmering at a distance. Guided by this observation, and having drawn his sword, He bent his steps towards the place, whence the beam seemed to be emitted.

It proceeded from the Lamp, which flamed before St Clare's Statue. Before it stood several Females, their white Garments streaming in the blast, as it howled along the vaulted dungeons. Curious to know what had brought them together in this melancholy spot, Lorenzo drew near with precaution. The Strangers seemed earnestly engaged in conversation. They heard not Lorenzo's steps, and He approached unobserved, till He could hear their voices distinctly.

'I protest,' continued She who was speaking when He arrived, and to whom the rest were listening with great attention; 'I protest, that I saw them with my own eyes. I flew down the steps; They pursued me, and I escaped falling into their hands with difficulty. Had it not been for the Lamp, I should never have found you.'

'And what could bring them hither?' said another in a trembling voice; 'Do you think, that they were looking for us?'

'God grant, that my fears may be false,' rejoined the First; 'But I doubt they are Murderers! If they discover us, we are lost! As for me, my fate is certain: My affinity to the Prioress will be a sufficient crime to condemn me; and though till now these Vaults have afforded me a retreat. . . . . . .'

Here looking up, her eye fell upon Lorenzo, who had continued to approach softly.

'The Murderers!' She cried—

She started away from the Statue's Pedestal on which She had been seated, and attempted to escape by flight. Her Companions at the same moment uttered a terrified scream, while Lorenzo arrested the Fugitive by the arm. Frightened and desperate She sank upon her knees before him.

'Spare me!' She exclaimed; 'For Christ's sake, spare me! I am innocent, indeed, I am!'

While She spoke, her voice was almost choaked with fear. The beams of the Lamp darting full upon her face which was unveiled, Lorenzo recognized the beautiful Virginia de Villa-Franca. He hastened to raise her from the ground, and besought her to take courage. He promised to protect her from the Rioters, assured her that her retreat was still a secret, and that She might depend upon his readiness to defend her to the last drop of his blood. During this conversation, the Nuns had thrown themselves into various attitudes: One knelt, and addressed herself to heaven; Another hid her face in the lap of her Neighbour; Some listened motionless with fear to the discourse of the supposed Assassin; while Others embraced the Statue of St Clare, and implored her protection with frantic cries. On perceiving their mistake, they crowded round Lorenzo, and heaped benedictions on him by dozens. He found, that on hearing the threats of the Mob, and terrified by the cruelties, which from the Convent Towers they had seen inflicted on the Superior, many of the Pensioners and Nuns had taken refuge in the Sepulchre. Among the former was to be reckoned the lovely Virginia. Nearly related to the Prioress, She had more reason than the rest to dread the Rioters, and now besought Lorenzo earnestly not to abandon her to their rage. Her Companions, most of whom were Women of noble family, made the same request, which He readily granted. He promised not to quit them, till He had seen each of them safe in the arms of her Relations: But He advised their deferring to quit the Sepulchre for some time longer, when the popular fury should be somewhat calmed, and the arrival of military force have dispersed the multitude.

'Would to God!' cried Virginia, 'That I were already safe in my Mother's embraces! How say you, Segnor; Will it be long, ere we may leave this place? Every moment that I pass here, I pass in torture!'

'I hope, not long,' said He; 'But till you can can proceed with security, this Sepulchre will prove an impenetrable asylum. Here you run no risque of a discovery, and I would advise your remaining quiet for the next two or three hours.'

'Two or three hours?' exclaimed Sister Helena; 'If I stay another hour in these vaults, I shall expire with fear! Not the wealth of worlds should bribe me to undergo again, what I have suffered since my coming hither. Blessed Virgin! To be in this melancholy place in the middle of night, surrounded by the mouldering bodies of my deceased Companions, and expecting every moment to be torn in pieces by their Ghosts who wander about me, and complain, and groan, and wail in accents that make my blood run cold, ... Christ Jesus! It is enough to drive me to madness!'

'Excuse me,' replied Lorenzo, 'if I am surprized, that while menaced by real woes you are capable of yielding to imaginary dangers. These terrors are puerile and groundless: Combat them, holy Sister; I have promised to guard you from the Rioters, but against the attacks of superstition you must depend for protection upon yourself. The idea of Ghosts is ridiculous in the extreme; And if you continue to be swayed by ideal terrors . . . . . .'

'Ideal?' exclaimed the Nuns with one voice; 'Why we heard it ourselves, Segnor! Every one of us heard it! It was frequently repeated, and it sounded every time more melancholy and deep. You will never persuade me, that we could all have been deceived. Not we, indeed; No, no; Had the noise been merely created by fancy. . . .'

'Hark! Hark!' interrupted Virginia in a voice of terror; 'God preserve us! There it is again!'

The Nuns clasped their hands together, and sank upon their knees. Lorenzo looked round him eagerly, and was on the point of yielding to the fears, which already had possessed the Women. Universal silence prevailed. He examined the Vault, but nothing was to be seen. He now prepared to address the Nuns, and ridicule their childish apprehensions, when his attention was arrested by a deep and long-drawn groan.

'What was that?' He cried, and started.

'There, Segnor!' said Helena; 'Now you must be convinced! You have heard the noise yourself! Now judge, whether our terrors are imaginary. Since we have been here, that groaning has been repeated almost every five minutes. Doubtless, it proceeds from some Soul in pain, who wishes to be prayed out of purgatory: But none of us here dares ask it the question. As for me, were I to see an Apparition, the fright, I am very certain, would kill me out of hand.'

As She said this, a second groan was heard yet more distinctly. The Nuns crossed themselves, and hastened to repeat their prayers against evil Spirits. Lorenzo listened attentively. He even thought, that He could distinguish sounds, as of one speaking in complaint; But distance rendered them inarticulate. The noise seemed to come from the midst of the small Vault in which He and the Nuns then were, and which a multitude of passages branching out in various directions, formed into à sort of Star. Lorenzo's curiosity which was ever awake, made him anxious to solve this mystery. He desired that silence might be kept. The Nuns obeyed him. All was hushed, till the general stillness was again disturbed by the groaning, which was repeated several times successively. He perceived it to be most audible, when upon following the sound He was conducted close to the shrine of St Clare.

'The noise comes from hence,' said He; 'Whose is this Statue?'

Helena, to whom He addressed the question, paused for a moment. Suddenly She clapped her hands together.

'Aye!' cried She, 'it must be so. I have discovered the meaning of these groans.'

The Nuns crowded round her, and besought her eagerly to explain herself. She gravely replied, that for time immemorial the Statue had been famous for performing miracles: From this She inferred, that the Saint was concerned at the conflagration of a Convent which She protected, and expressed her grief by audible lamentations. Not having equal faith in the miraculous Saint, Lorenzo did not think this solution of the mystery quite so satisfactory, as the Nuns, who subscribed to it without hesitation. In one point, 'tis true, that He agreed with Helena. He suspected that the groans proceeded from the Statue: The more He listened, the more was He confirmed in this idea. He drew nearer to the Image, designing to inspect it more closely: But perceiving his intention, the Nuns besought him for God's sake to desist, since if He touched the Statue, his death was, inevitable.

'And in what consists the danger?' said He.

'Mother of God! In what?' replied Helena, ever eager to relate a miraculous adventure; 'If you had only heard the hundredth part of those marvellous Stories about this Statue, which the Domina used to recount! She assured us often and often, that if we only dared to lay a finger upon it, we might expect the most fatal consequences. Among other things She told us, that a Robber having entered these Vaults by night, He observed yonder Ruby, whose value is inestimable. Do you see it, Segnor? It sparkles upon the third finger of the hand, in which She holds a crown of Thorns. This Jewel naturally excited the Villain's cupidity. He resolved to make himself Master of it. For this purpose He ascended the Pedestal: He supported himself by grasping the Saint's right arm, and extended his own towards the Ring. What was his surprize, when He saw the Statue's hand raised in a posture of menace, and heard her lips pronounce his eternal perdition! Penetrated with awe and consternation, He desisted from his attempt, and prepared to quit the Sepulchre. In this He also failed. Flight was denied him. He found it impossible to disengage the hand, which rested upon the right arm of the Statue. In vain did He struggle: He remained fixed to the Image, till the insupportable and fiery anguish which darted itself through his veins, compelled his shrieking for assistance. The Sepulchre was now filled with Spectators. The Villain confessed his sacrilege, and was only released by the separation of his hand from his body. It has remained ever since fastened to the Image. The Robber turned Hermit, and led ever after an exemplary life: But yet the Saint's decree was performed, and Tradition says, that He continues to haunt this Sepulchre, and implore St Clare's pardon with groans and lamentations. Now I think of it, those which we have just heard, may very possibly have been uttered by the Ghost of this Sinner: But of this I will not be positive. All that I can say is, that since that time no one has ever dared to touch the Statue: Then do not be fool-hardy, good Segnor! For the love of heaven, give up your design, nor expose yourself unnecessarily to certain destruction.'

Not being convinced that his destruction would be so certain, as Helena seemed to think it, Lorenzo persisted in his resolution. The Nuns besought him to desist in piteous terms, and even pointed out the Robber's hand, which in effect was still visible upon the arm of the Statue. This proof, as they imagined, must convince him. It was very far from doing so; and they were greatly scandalized when he declared his suspicion, that the dried and shrivelled fingers had been placed there by order of the Prioress. In spite of their prayers and threats He approached the Statue. He sprang over the iron Rails which defended it, and the Saint under-went a thorough examination. The Image at first appeared to be of Stone, but proved on further inspection to be formed of no more solid materials than coloured Wood. He shook it, and attempted to move it; But it appeared to be of a piece with the Base which it stood upon. He examined it over and over: Still no clue guided him to the solution of this mystery, for which the Nuns were become equally solicitous, when they saw that He touched the Statue with impunity. He paused, and listened: The groans were repeated at intervals, and He was convinced of being in the spot nearest to them. He mused upon this singular event, and ran over the Statue with enquiring eyes. Suddenly they rested upon the shrivelled hand. It struck him, that so particular an injunction was not given without cause, not to touch the arm of the Image. He again ascended the Pedestal; He examined the object of his attention, and discovered a small knob of iron concealed between the Saint's shoulder, and what was supposed to have been the hand of the Robber. This observation delighted him. He applied his fingers to the knob, and pressed it down forcibly. Immediately a rumbling noise was heard within the Statue, as if a chain tightly stretched was flying back. Startled at the sound the timid Nuns started away, prepared to hasten from the Vault at the first appearance of danger. All remaining quiet and still, they again gathered round Lorenzo, and beheld his proceedings with anxious curiosity.

Finding that nothing followed this discovery, He descended. As He took his hand from the Saint, She trembled beneath his touch. This created new terrors in the Spectators, who believed the Statue to be animated. Lorenzo's ideas upon the subject were widely different. He easily comprehended, that the noise which He had heard, was occasioned by his having loosened a chain, which attached the Image to its Pedestal. He once more attempted to move it, and succeeded without much exertion. He placed it upon the ground, and then perceived the Pedestal to be hollow, and covered at the opening with an heavy iron grate.

This excited such general curiosity, that the Sisters forgot both their real and imaginary dangers. Lorenzo proceeded to raise the Grate, in which the Nuns assisted him to the utmost of their strength. The attempt was accomplished, with little difficulty. A deep abyss now presented itself before them, whose thick obscurity the eye strove in vain to pierce. The rays of the Lamp were too feeble to be of much assistance. Nothing was discernible, save a flight of rough unshapen steps, which sank into the yawning Gulph, and were soon lost in darkness. The groans were heard no more; But All believed them to have ascended from this Cavern. As He bent over it, Lorenzo fancied, that He distinguished something bright twinkling through the gloom. He gazed attentively upon the spot where it showed itself, and was convinced, that He saw a small spark of light, now visible, now disappearing. He communicated this circumstance to the Nuns: They also perceived the spark; But when He declared his intention to descend into the Cave, they united to oppose his resolution. All their remonstrances could not prevail on him to alter it. None of them had courage enough to accompany him; neither could He think of depriving them of the Lamp. Alone therefore and in darkness, He prepared to pursue his design, while the Nuns were contented to offer up prayers for his success and safety.

The steps were so narrow and uneven, that to descend them was like walking down the side of a precipice. The obscurity by which He was surrounded, rendered his footing insecure. He was obliged to proceed with great caution, lest He should miss the steps, and fall into the Gulph below him. This He was several times on the point of doing. However, He arrived sooner upon solid ground than He had expected. He now found, that the thick darkness and impenetrable mists which reigned through the Cavern, had deceived him into the belief of its being much more profound, than it proved upon inspection. He reached the foot of the Stairs unhurt: He now stopped, and looked round for the spark, which had before caught his attention. He sought it in vain: All was dark and gloomy. He listened for the groans; But his ear caught no sound, except the distant murmur of the Nuns above, as in low voices they repeated their Ave-Marias. He stood irresolute to which side He should address his steps. At all events He determined to proceed: He did so, but slowly, fearing lest instead of approaching, He should be retiring from the object of his search. The groans seemed to announce one in pain, or at least in sorrow, and He hoped to have the power of relieving the Mourner's calamities. A plaintive tone, sounding at no great distance, at length reached his hearing; He bent his course joyfully towards it. It became more audible as He advanced; and He soon beheld again the spark of light, which a low projecting Wall had hitherto concealed from him.

It proceeded from a small Lamp which was placed upon an heap of stones, and whose faint and melancholy rays served rather to point out, than dispell the horrors of a narrow gloomy dungeon formed in one side of the Cavern; It also showed several other recesses of similar construction, but whose depth was buried in obscurity. Coldly played the light upon the damp walls, whose dew-stained surface gave back a feeble reflection. A thick and pestilential fog clouded the height of the vaulted dungeon. As Lorenzo advanced, He felt a piercing chillness spread itself through his veins. The frequent groans still engaged him to move forwards. He turned towards them, and by the Lamp's glimmering beams beheld in a corner of this loathsome abode, a Creature stretched upon a bed of straw, so wretched, so emaciated, so pale, that He doubted to think her Woman. She was half-naked: Her long dishevelled hair fell in disorder over her face, and almost entirely concealed it. One wasted Arm hung listlessly upon a tattered rug, which covered her convulsed and shivering limbs: The Other was wrapped round a small bundle, and held it closely to her bosom. A large Rosary lay near her: Opposite to her was a Crucifix, on which She bent her sunk eyes fixedly, and by her side stood a Basket and a small Earthen Pitcher.

Lorenzo stopped: He was petrified with horror. He gazed upon the miserable Object with disgust and pity. He trembled at the spectacle; He grew sick at heart: His strength failed him, and his limbs were unable to support his weight. He was obliged to lean against the low Wall which was near him, unable to go forward, or to address the Sufferer. She cast her eyes towards the Stair-case: The Wall concealed Lorenzo, and She observed him not.

'No one comes!' She at length murmured.

As She spoke, her voice was hollow, and rattled in her throat: She signed bitterly.

'No one comes!' She repeated; 'No! They have forgotten me! They will come no more!'

She paused for a moment: Then continued mournfully.

'Two days! Two long, long days, and yet no food! And yet no hope, no comfort! Foolish Woman! How can I wish to lengthen a life so wretched! Yet such a death! O! God! To perish by such a death! To linger out such ages in torture! Till now, I knew not what it was to hunger! Hark! No. No one comes! They will come no more!'

She was silent. She shivered, and drew the rug over her naked shoulders.

'I am very cold! I am still unused to the damps of this dungeon! 'Tis strange: But no matter. Colder shall I soon be, and yet not feel it—I shall be cold, cold as Thou art!'

She looked at the bundle, which lay upon her breast. She bent over it, and kissed it: Then drew back hastily, and shuddered with disgust.

'It was once so sweet! It would have been so lovely, so like him! I have lost it for ever! How a few days have changed it! I should not know it again myself! Yet it is dear to me! God! how dear! I will forget what it is: I will only remember what it was, and love it as well, as when it was so sweet! so lovely! so like him! I thought, that I had wept away all my tears, but here is one still lingering.'

She wiped her eyes with a tress of her hair. She put out her hand for the Pitcher, and reached it with difficulty. She cast into it a look of hopeless enquiry. She sighed, and replaced it upon the ground.

'Quite a void! Not a drop! Not one drop left to cool my scorched-up burning palate! Now would I give treasures for a draught of water! And they are God's Servants, who make me suffer thus! They think themselves holy, while they torture me like Fiends! They are cruel and unfeeling; And 'tis they who bid me repent; And 'tis they, who threaten me with eternal perdition! Saviour, Saviour! You think not so!'

She again fixed her eyes upon the Crucifix, took her Rosary, and while She told her beads, the quick motion of her lips declared her to be praying with fervency.

While He listened to her melancholy accents, Lorenzo's sensibility became yet more violently affected. The first sight of such misery had given a sensible shock to his feelings: But that being past, He now advanced towards the Captive. She heard his steps, and uttering a cry of joy, dropped the Rosary.

'Hark! Hark! Hark!' She cried: 'Some one comes!'

She strove to raise herself, but her strength was unequal to the attempt: She fell back, and as She sank again upon the bed of straw, Lorenzo heard the rattling of heavy chains. He still approached, while the Prisoner thus continued.

'Is it you, Camilla? You are come then at last? Oh! it was time! I thought that you had forsaken me; that I was doomed to perish of hunger. Give me to drink, Camilla, for pity's sake! I am faint with long fasting, and grown so weak that I cannot raise myself from the ground. Good Camilla, give me to drink, lest I expire before you!'

Fearing that surprize in her enfeebled state might be fatal, Lorenzo was at a loss how to address her.

'It is not Camilla,' said He at length, speaking in a slow and gentle voice.

'Who is it then?' replied the Sufferer: 'Alix, perhaps, or Violante. My eyes are grown so dim and feeble, that I cannot distinguish your features. But which-ever it is, if your breast is sensible of the least compassion, if you are not more cruel than Wolves and Tigers, take pity on my sufferings. You know, that I am dying for want of sustenance. This is the third day, since these lips have received nourishment. Do you bring me food? Or come you only to announce my death, and learn how long I have yet to exist in agony?'

'You mistake my business,' replied Lorenzo; 'I am no Emissary of the cruel Prioress. I pity your sorrows, and come hither to relieve them.'

'To relieve them?' repeated the Captive; 'Said you, to relieve them?'

At the same time starting from the ground, and supporting herself upon her hands, She gazed upon the Stranger earnestly.

'Great God! It is no illusion! A Man! Speak! Who are you? What brings you hither? Come you to save me, to restore me to liberty, to life and light? Oh! speak, speak quickly, lest I encourage an hope whose disappointment will destroy me.'

'Be calm!' replied Lorenzo in a voice soothing and compassionate; 'The Domina of whose cruelty you complain, has already paid the forfeit of her offences: You have nothing more to fear from her. A few minutes will restore you to liberty, and the embraces of your Friends from whom you have been secluded. You may rely upon my protection. Give me your hand, and be not fearful. Let me conduct you where you may receive those attentions which your feeble state requires.'

'Oh! Yes! Yes! Yes!' cried the Prisoner with an exulting shriek; 'There is a God then, and a just one! Joy! Joy! I shall once more breath the fresh air, and view the light of the glorious sun-beams! I will go with you! Stranger, I will go with you! Oh! Heaven will bless you for pitying an Unfortunate! But this too must go with me,' She added pointing to the small bundle, which She still clasped to her bosom; 'I cannot part with this. I will bear it away: It shall convince the world, how dreadful are the abodes so falsely termed religious. Good Stranger, lend me your hand to rise: I am faint with want, and sorrow, and sickness, and my forces have quite forsaken me! So, that is well!'

As Lorenzo stooped to raise her, the beams of the Lamp struck full upon his face.

'Almighty God!' She exclaimed; 'Is it possible! That look! Those features! Oh! Yes, it is, it is . . . . .'

She extended her arms to throw them round him; But her enfeebled frame was unable to sustain the emotions, which agitated her bosom. She fainted, and again sank upon the bed of straw.

Lorenzo was surprised at her last exclamation. He thought that He had before heard such accents as her hollow voice had just formed, but where He could not remember. He saw, that in her dangerous situation immediate physical aid was absolutely necessary, and He hastened to convey her from the dungeon. He was at first prevented from doing so by a strong chain fastened round the prisoner's body, and fixing her to the neighbouring Wall. However, his natural strength being aided by anxiety to relieve the Unfortunate, He soon forced out the Staple, to which one end of the Chain was attached. Then taking the Captive in his arms, He bent his course towards the Stair-case. The rays of the Lamp above, as well as the murmur of female voices, guided his steps. He gained the Stairs, and in a few minutes after arrived at the iron-grate.

The Nuns during his absence had been terribly tormented by curiosity and apprehension: They were equally surprized and delighted on seeing him suddenly emerge from the Cave. Every heart was filled with compassion for the miserable Creature, whom He bore in his arms. While the Nuns, and Virginia in particular employed themselves in striving to re-call her to her senses, Lorenzo related in few words the manner of his finding her. He then observed to them that by this time the tumult must have been quelled, and that He could now conduct them to their Friends without danger. All were eager to quit the Sepulchre: Still to prevent all possibility of ill-usage, they besought Lorenzo to venture out first alone, and examine, whether the Coast was clear. With this request He complied. Helena offered to conduct him to the Stair-case, and they were on the point of departing, when a strong light flashed from several passages upon the adjacent walls. At the same time Steps were heard of people approaching hastily, and whose number seemed to be considerable. The Nuns were greatly alarmed at this circumstance: They supposed their retreat to be discovered, and the Rioters to be advancing in pursuit of them. Hastily quitting the Prisoner who remained insensible, they crowded round Lorenzo, and claimed his promise to protect them. Virginia alone forgot her own danger by striving to relieve the sorrows of Another. She supported the Sufferer's head upon her knees, bathing her temples with rose-water, chafing her cold hands, and sprinkling her face with tears which were drawn from her by compassion. The Strangers approaching nearer, Lorenzo was enabled to dispel the fears of the Suppliants. His name, pronounced by a number of voices among which He distinguished the Duke's, pealed along the Vaults, and convinced him that He was the object of their search. He communicated this intelligence to the Nuns, who received it with rapture. A few moments after confirmed his idea. Don Ramirez, as well as the Duke, appeared, followed by Attendants with Torches. They had been seeking him through the Vaults, in order to let him know that the Mob was dispersed, and the riot entirely over. Lorenzo recounted briefly his adventure in the Cavern, and explained, how much the Unknown was in want of medical assistance. He besought the Duke to take charge of her, as well as of the Nuns and Pensioners.

'As for me,' said He, 'Other cares demand my attention. While you with one half of the Archers convey these Ladies to their respective homes, I wish the other half to be left with me. I will examine the Cavern below, and pervade the most secret recesses of the Sepulchre. I cannot rest till convinced, that yonder wretched Victim was the only one confined by Superstition in these vaults.'

The Duke applauded his intention. Don Ramirez offered to assist him in his enquiry, and his proposal was accepted with gratitude. The Nuns having made their acknowledgments to Lorenzo, committed themselves to the care of his Uncle, and were conducted from the Sepulchre. Virginia requested that the Unknown might be given to her in charge, and promised to let Lorenzo know, whenever She was sufficiently recovered to accept his visits. In truth, She made this promise more from consideration for herself, than for either Lorenzo or the Captive. She had witnessed his politeness, gentleness, and intrepidity with sensible emotion. She wished earnestly to preserve his acquaintance; and in addition to the sentiments of pity which the Prisoner excited, She hoped that her attention to this Unfortunate would raise her a degree in the esteem of Lorenzo. She had no occasion to trouble herself upon this head. The kindness already displayed by her, and the tender concern which She had shown for the Sufferer had gained her an exalted place in his good graces. While occupied in alleviating the Captive's sorrows, the nature of her employment adorned her with new charms, and rendered her beauty a thousand times more interesting. Lorenzo viewed her with admiration and delight: He considered her as a ministering Angel descended to the aid of afflicted innocence; nor could his heart have resisted her attractions, had it not been steeled by the remembrance of Antonia.

The Duke now conveyed the Nuns in safety to the Dwellings of their respective Friends. The rescued Prisoner was still insensible, and gave no signs of life, except by occasional groans. She was borne upon a sort of litter; Virginia who was constantly by the side of it, was apprehensive that exhausted by long abstinence, and shaken by the sudden change from bonds and darkness to liberty and light, her frame would never get the better of the shock. Lorenzo and Don Ramirez still remained in the Sepulchre. After deliberating upon their proceedings, it was resolved that to prevent losing time, the Archers should be divided into two Bodies: That with one Don Ramirez should examine the cavern, while Lorenzo with the other might penetrate into the further Vaults. This being arranged, and his Followers being provided with Torches, Don Ramirez advanced to the Cavern. He had already descended some steps, when He heard People approaching hastily from the interior part of the Sepulchre. This surprised him, and He quitted the Cave precipitately.

'Do you hear foot-steps?' said Lorenzo; 'Let us bend our course towards them. 'Tis from this side, that they seem to proceed.'

At that moment a loud and piercing shriek induced him to quicken his steps.

'Help! Help, for God's sake!' cried a voice, whose melodious tone penetrated Lorenzo's heart with terror.

He flew towards the cry with the rapidity of lightning, and was followed by Don Ramirez with equal swiftness.

CHAPTER IV

Great Heaven! How frail thy creature Man is made!
How by himself insensibly betrayed!
In our own strength unhappily secure,
Too little cautious of the adverse power,
On pleasure's flowery brink we idly stray,
Masters as yet of our returning way:
Till the strong gusts of raging passion rise,
Till the dire Tempest mingles earth and skies,
And swift into the boundless Ocean borne,
Our foolish confidence too late we mourn:
Round our devoted heads the billows beat,
And from our troubled view the lessening lands retreat.

Prior.

ALL this while, Ambrosio was unconscious of the dreadful scenes which were passing so near. The execution of his designs upon Antonia employed his every thought. Hitherto, He was satisfied with the success of his plans. Antonia had drank the opiate, was buried in the vaults of St Clare, and absolutely in his disposal. Matilda, who was well acquainted with the nature and effects of the soporific medicine, had computed that it would not cease to operate till one in the Morning. For that hour He waited with impatience. The Festival of St Clare presented him with a favourable opportunity of consummating his crime. He was certain that the Friars and Nuns would be engaged in the Procession, and that He had no cause to dread an interruption: From appearing himself at the head of his Monks, He had desired to be excused. He doubted not, that being beyond the reach of help, cut off from all the world, and totally in his power, Antonia would comply with his desires. The affection which She had ever exprest for him, warranted this persuasion: But He resolved that should She prove obstinate, no consideration whatever should prevent him from enjoying her. Secure from a discovery, He shuddered not at the idea of employing force: Of if He felt any repugnance, it arose not from a principle of shame or compassion, but from his feeling for Antonia the most sincere and ardent affection, and wishing to owe her favours to no one but herself.

The Monks quitted the Abbey at midnight. Matilda was among the Choristers, and led the chaunt. Ambrosio was left by himself, and at liberty to pursue his own inclinations. Convinced that no one remained behind to watch his motions, or disturb his pleasures, He now hastened to the Western Aisles. His heart beating with hope not unmingled with anxiety, He crossed the Garden, unlocked the door which admitted him into the Cemetery, and in a few minutes He stood before the Vaults. Here He paused. He looked round him with suspicion, conscious that his business was unfit for any other eye. As He stood in hesitation, He heard the melancholy shriek of the screech-Owl: The wind rattled loudly against the windows of the adjacent Convent, and as the current swept by him, bore with it the faint notes of the chaunt of Choristers. He opened the door cautiously, as if fearing to be over-heard: He entered; and closed it again after him. Guided by his Lamp, He threaded the long passages, in whose windings Matilda had instructed him, and reached the private Vault which contained his sleeping Mistress.

Its entrance was by no means easy to discover: But this was no obstacle to Ambrosio, who at the time of Antonia's Funeral had observed it too carefully to be deceived. He found the door, which was unfastened, pushed it open, and descended into the dungeon. He approached the humble Tomb, in which Antonia reposed. He had provided himself with an iron crow and a pick-axe; But this precaution was unnecessary. The Grate was slightly fastened on the outside: He raised it, and placing the Lamp upon its ridge, bent silently over the Tomb. By the side of three putrid half-corrupted Bodies lay the sleeping Beauty. A lively red, the fore-runner of returning animation, had already spread itself over her cheek; and as wrapped in her shroud She reclined upon her funeral Bier, She seemed to smile at the Images of Death around her. While He gazed upon their rotting bones and disgusting figures, who perhaps were once as sweet and lovely, Ambrosio thought upon Elvira, by him reduced to the same state. As the memory of that horrid act glanced upon his mind, it was clouded with a gloomy horror. Yet it served but to strengthen his resolution to destroy Antonia's honour.

'For your sake, Fatal Beauty!' murmured the Monk, while gazing on his devoted prey; 'For your sake, have I committed this murder, and sold myself to eternal tortures. Now you are in my power: The produce of my guilt will at least be mine. Hope not that your prayers breathed in tones of unequalled melody, your bright eyes filled with tears, and your hands lifted in supplication, as when seeking in penitence the Virgin's pardon; Hope not, that your moving innocence, your beauteous grief, or all your suppliant arts shall ransom you from my embraces. Before the break of day, mine you must, and mine you shall be!'

He lifted her still motionless from the Tomb: He seated himself upon a bank of Stone, and supporting her in his arms, watched impatiently for the symptoms of returning animation. Scarcely could He command his passions sufficiently, to restrain himself from enjoying her while yet insensible. His natural lust was increased in ardour by the difficulties, which had opposed his satisfying it: As also by his long abstinence from Woman, since from the moment of resigning her claim to his love, Matilda had exiled him from her arms for ever.

'I am no Prostitute, Ambrosio;' Had She told him, when in the fullness of his lust He demanded her favours with more than usual earnestness; 'I am now no more than your Friend, and will not be your Mistress. Cease then to solicit my complying with desires, which insult me. While your heart was mine, I gloried in your embraces: Those happy times are past: My person is become indifferent to you, and 'tis necessity, not love, which makes you seek my enjoyment. I cannot yield to a request, so humiliating to my pride.'

Suddenly deprived of pleasures, the use of which had made them an absolute want, the Monk felt this restraint severely. Naturally addicted to the gratification of the senses, in the full vigour of manhood, and heat of blood, He had suffered his temperament to acquire such ascendency, that his lust was become madness. Of his fondness for Antonia, none but the grosser particles remained: He longed for the possession of her person; and even the gloom of the vault, the surrounding silence, and the resistance which He expected from her, seemed to give a fresh edge to his fierce and unbridled desires.

Gradually He felt the bosom which rested against his, glow with returning warmth. Her heart throbbed again; Her blood flowed swifter, and her lips moved. At length She opened her eyes, but still opprest and bewildered by the effects of the strong opiate, She closed them again immediately. Ambrosio watched her narrowly, nor permitted a movement to escape him. Perceiving that She was fully restored to existence, He caught her in rapture to his bosom, and closely pressed his lips to hers. The suddenness of his action sufficed to dissipate the fumes, which obscured Antonia's reason. She hastily raised herself, and cast a wild look round her. The strange Images which presented themselves on every side contributed to confuse her. She put her hand to her head, as if to settle her disordered imagination. At length She took it away, and threw her eyes through the dungeon a second time. They fixed upon the Abbot's face.

'Where am I?' She said abruptly. 'How came I here? Where is my Mother? Methought, I saw her! Oh! a dream, a dreadful dreadful dream told me . . . . . . But where am I? Let me go! I cannot stay here!'

She attempted to rise, but the Monk prevented her.

'Be calm, lovely Antonia!' He replied; 'No danger is near you: Confide in my protection. Why do you gaze on me so earnestly? Do you not know me? Not know your Friend? Ambrosio?'

'Ambrosio? My Friend? Oh! yes, yes; I remember . . . . . . But why am I here? Who has brought me? Why are you with me? Oh! Flora bad me beware . . . . . ! Here are nothing but Graves, and Tombs, and Skeletons! This place frightens me! Good Ambrosio take me away from it, for it recalls my fearful dream! Methought I was dead, and laid in my grave! Good

Ambrosio, take me from hence. Will you not? Oh! will you not? Do not look on me thus! Your flaming eyes terrify me! Spare me, Father! Oh! spare me for God's sake!'

'Why these terrors, Antonia?' rejoined the Abbot, folding her in his arms, and covering her bosom with kisses which She in vain struggled to avoid: 'What fear you from me, from one who adores you? What matters it where you are? This Sepulchre seems to me Love's bower; This gloom is the friendly night of mystery, which He spreads over our delights! Such do I think it, and such must my Antonia. Yes, my sweet Girl! Yes! Your veins shall glow with fire, which circles in mine, and my transports shall be doubled by your sharing them!'

While He spoke thus, He repeated his embraces, and permitted himself the most indecent liberties. Even Antonia's ignorance was not proof against the freedom of his behaviour. She was sensible of her danger, forced herself from his arms, and her shroud being her only garment, She wrapped it closely round her.

'Unhand me, Father!' She cried, her honest indignation tempered by alarm at her unprotected position; 'Why have you brought me to this place? Its appearance freezes me with horror! Convey me from hence, if you have the least sense of pity and humanity! Let me return to the House, which I have quitted I know not how; But stay here one moment longer, I neither will, or ought.'

Though the Monk was somewhat startled by the resolute tone in which this speech was delivered, it produced upon him no other effect than surprize. He caught her hand, forced her upon his knee, and gazing upon her with gloting eyes, He thus replied to her.

'Compose yourself, Antonia. Resistance is unavailing, and I need disavow my passion for you no longer. You are imagined dead: Society is for ever lost to you. I possess you here alone; You are absolutely in my power, and I burn with desires, which I must either gratify, or die: But I would owe my happiness to yourself. My lovely Girl! My adorable Antonia! Let me instruct you in joys to which you are still a Stranger, and teach you to feel those pleasures in my arms, which I must soon enjoy in yours. Nay, this struggling is childish,' He continued, seeing her repell his caresses, and endeavour to escape from his grasp; 'No aid is near: Neither heaven or earth shall save you from my embraces. Yet why reject pleasures so sweet, so rapturous? No one observes us: Our loves will be a secret to all the world: Love and opportunity invite your giving loose to your passions. Yield to them, my Antonia! Yield to them, my lovely Girl! Throw your arms thus fondly round me; Join your lips thus closely to mine! Amidst all her gifts, has Nature denied her most precious, the sensibility of Pleasure? Oh! impossible! Every feature, look, and motion declares you formed to bless, and to be blessed yourself! Turn not on me those supplicating eyes: Consult your own charms;

They will tell you, that I am proof against entreaty. Can I relinquish these limbs so white, so soft, so delicate; These swelling breasts, round, full, and elastic! These lips fraught with such inexhaustible sweetness? Can I relinquish these treasures, and leave them to another's enjoyment? No, Antonia; never, never! I swear it by this kiss, and this! and this!'

With every moment the Friar's passion became more ardent, and Antonia's terror more intense. She struggled to disengage herself from his arms: Her exertions were unsuccessful; and finding that Ambrosio's conduct became still freer, She shrieked for assistance with all her strength. The aspect of the Vault, the pale glimmering of the Lamp, the surrounding obscurity, the sight of the Tomb, and the objects of mortality which met her eyes on either side, were ill-calculated to inspire her with those emotions, by which the Friar was agitated. Even his caresses terrified her from their fury, and created no other sentiment than fear. On the contrary, her alarm, her evident disgust, and incessant opposition, seemed only to inflame the Monk's desires, and supply his brutality with additional strength. Antonia's shrieks were unheard: Yet She continued them, nor abandoned her endeavours to escape, till exhausted and out of breath She sank from his arms upon her knees, and once more had recourse to prayers and supplications. This attempt had no better success than the former. On the contrary, taking advantage of her situation, the Ravisher threw himself by her side: He clasped her to his bosom almost lifeless with terror, and faint with struggling. He stifled her cries with kisses, treated her with the rudeness of an unprincipled Barbarian, proceeded from freedom to freedom, and in the violence of his lustful delirium, wounded and bruised her tender limbs. Heedless of her tears, cries and entreaties, He gradually made himself Master of her person, and desisted not from his prey, till He had accomplished his crime and the dishonour of Antonia.

Scarcely had He succeeded in his design, than He shuddered at himself and the means by which it was effected. The very excess of his former eagerness to possess Antonia now contributed to inspire him with disgust; and a secret impulse made him feel, how base and unmanly was the crime, which He had just committed. He started hastily from her arms. She, who so lately had been the object of his adoration, now raised no other sentiment in his heart than aversion and rage. He turned away from her; or if his eyes rested upon her figure involuntarily, it was only to dart upon her looks of hate. The Unfortunate had fainted ere the completion of her disgrace: She only recovered life to be sensible of her misfortune. She remained stretched upon the earth in silent despair: The tears chased each other slowly down her cheeks, and her bosom heaved with frequent sobs. Oppressed with grief, She continued for some time in this state of torpidity. At length She rose with difficulty, and dragging her feeble steps towards the door, prepared to quit the dungeon.

The sound of her foot-steps rouzed the Monk from his sullen apathy. Starting from the Tomb against which He reclined, while his eyes wandered over the images of corruption contained in it, He pursued the Victim of his brutality, and soon over-took her. He seized her by the arm, and violently forced her back into the dungeon.

'Whither go you?' He cried in a stern voice; 'Return this instant!'

Antonia trembled at the fury of his countenance.

'What would you more?' She said with timidity: 'Is not my ruin compleated? Am I not undone, undone for ever? Is not your cruelty contented, or have I yet more to suffer? Let me depart. Let me return to my home, and weep unrestrained my shame and my affliction!'

'Return to your home?' repeated the Monk, with bitter and contemptuous mockery; Then suddenly his eyes flaming with passion, 'What? That you may denounce me to the world? That you may proclaim me an Hypocrite, a Ravisher, a Betrayer, a Monster of cruelty, lust, and ingratitude? No, no, no! I know well the whole weight of my offences; Well, that your complaints would be too just, and my crimes too notorious! You shall not from hence to tell Madrid that I am a Villain; that my conscience is loaded with sins, which make me despair of Heaven's pardon. Wretched Girl, you must stay here with me! Here amidst these lonely Tombs, these images of Death, these rotting loathsome corrupted bodies! Here shall you stay, and witness my sufferings; witness, what it is to die in the horrors of despondency, and breathe the last groan in blasphemy and curses! And who am I to thank for this? What seduced me into crimes, whose bare remembrance makes me shudder? Fatal Witch! was it not thy beauty? Have you not plunged my soul into infamy? Have you not made me a perjured Hypocrite, a Ravisher, an Assassin! Nay, at this moment, does not that angel look bid me despair of God's forgiveness? Oh! when I stand before his judgment-throne, that look will suffice to damn me! You will tell my Judge, that you were happy, till *I* saw you; that you were innocent, till *I* polluted you! You will come with those tearful eyes, those cheeks pale and ghastly, those hands lifted in supplication, as when you sought from me that mercy which I gave not! Then will my perdition be certain! Then will come your Mother's Ghost, and hurl me down into the dwellings of Fiends, and flames, and Furies, and everlasting torments! And 'tis you, who will accuse me! 'Tis you, who will cause my eternal anguish! You, wretched Girl! You! You!'

As He thundered out these words, He violently grasped Antonia's arm, and spurned the earth with delirious fury.

Supposing his brain to be turned, Antonia sank in terror upon her knees: She lifted up her hands, and her voice almost died away, ere She could give it utterance.

'Spare me! Spare me!' She murmured with difficulty.

'Silence!' cried the Friar madly, and dashed her upon the ground——

He quitted her, and paced the dungeon with a wild and disordered air. His eyes rolled fearfully: Antonia trembled, whenever She met their gaze. He seemed to meditate on something horrible, and She gave up all hopes of escaping from the Sepulchre with life. Yet in harbouring this idea, She did him injustice. Amidst the horror and disgust to which his soul was a prey, pity for his Victim still held a place in it. The storm of passion once over, He would have given worlds had He possest them, to have restored to her that innocence, of which his unbridled lust had deprived her. Of the desires which had urged him to the crime, no trace was left in his bosom: The wealth of India would not have tempted him to a second enjoyment of her person. His nature seemed to revolt at the very idea, and fain would He have wiped from his memory the scene which had just past. As his gloomy rage abated, in proportion did his compassion augment for Antonia. He stopped, and would have spoken to her words of comfort; But He knew not from whence to draw them, and remained gazing upon her with mournful wildness. Her situation seemed so hopeless, so woe-begone, as to baffle mortal power to relieve her. What could He do for her? Her peace of mind was lost, her honour irreparably ruined. She was cut off for ever from society, nor dared He give her back to it. He was conscious, that were She to appear in the world again, his guilt would be revealed, and his punishment inevitable. To one so laden with crimes, Death came armed with double terrors. Yet should He restore Antonia to light, and stand the chance of her betraying him, how miserable a prospect would present itself before her. She could never hope to be creditably established; She would be marked with infamy, and condemned to sorrow and solitude for the remainder of her existence. What was the alternative? A resolution far more terrible for Antonia, but which at least would insure the Abbot's safety. He determined to leave the world persuaded of her death, and to retain her a captive in this gloomy prison: There He proposed to visit her every night, to bring her food, to profess his penitence, and mingle his tears with hers. The Monk felt that this resolution was unjust and cruel; but it was his only means to prevent Antonia, from publishing his guilt and her own infamy. Should He release her, He could not depend upon her silence: His offence was too flagrant to permit his hoping for her forgiveness. Besides, her re-appearing would excite universal curiosity, and the violence of her affliction would prevent her from concealing its cause. He determined therefore, that Antonia should remain a Prisoner in the dungeon.

He approached her with confusion painted on his countenance. He raised her from the ground. Her hand trembled, as He took it, and He dropped it again as if He had touched a Serpent. Nature seemed to recoil at the touch. He felt himself at once repulsed from and attracted towards her, yet could account for neither sentiment. There was something in her look which penetrated him with horror; and though his understanding was still ignorant of it, Conscience pointed out to him the whole extent of his crime. In hurried accents yet the gentlest He could find, while his eye was averted, and his voice scarcely audible, He strove to console her under a misfortune which now could not be avoided. He declared himself sincerely penitent, and that He would gladly shed a drop of his blood, for every tear which his barbarity had forced from her. Wretched and hopeless, Antonia listened to him in silent grief: But when He announced her confinement in the Sepulchre, that dreadful doom to which even death seemed preferable, roused her from her insensibility at once. To linger out a life of misery in a narrow loathsome Cell, known to exist by no human Being save her Ravisher, surrounded by mouldering Corses, breathing the pestilential air of corruption, never more to behold the light, òr drink the pure gale of heaven, the idea was more terrible than She could support. It conquered even her abhorrence of the Friar. Again She sank upon her knees: She besought his compassion in terms the most pathetic and urgent. She promised, would He but restore her to liberty, to conceal her injuries from the world; to assign any reason for her re-appearance, which He might judge proper; and in order to prevent the least suspicion from falling upon him, She offered to quit Madrid immediately. Her entreaties were so urgent, as to make a considerable impression upon the Monk. He reflected, that as her person no longer excited his desires, He had no interest in keeping her concealed as He had at first intended; that He was adding a fresh injury, to those which She had already suffered; and that if She adhered to her promises, whether She was confined or at liberty, his life and reputation were equally secure. On the other hand, He trembled lest in her affliction Antonia should unintentionally break her engagement; or that her excessive simplicity and ignorance of deceit should permit some one more artful to surprize her secret. However well-founded were these apprehensions, compassion, and a sincere wish to repair his fault as much as possible solicited his complying with the prayers of his Suppliant. The difficulty of colouring Antonia's unexpected return to life, after her supposed death and public interment, was the only point which kept him irresolute. He was still pondering on the means of removing this obstacle, when He heard the sound of feet approaching with precipitation. The door of the Vault was thrown open, and Matilda rushed in, evidently much confused and terrified.

On seeing a Stranger enter, Antonia uttered a cry of joy: But her hopes of receiving succour from him were soon dissipated. The supposed Novice, without expressing the least surprize at finding a Woman alone with the Monk, in so strange a place, and at so late an hour, addressed him thus without losing a moment.

'What is to be done, Ambrosio? We are lost, unless some speedy means is found of dispelling the Rioters. Ambrosio, the Convent of St Clare is on fire; The Prioress has fallen a victim to the fury of the Mob. Already is the Abbey menaced with a similar fate. Alarmed at the threats of the People, the Monks seek for you everywhere. They imagine, that your authority alone will suffice to calm this disturbance. No one knows, what is become of you, and your absence creates universal astonishment and despair. I profited by the confusion, and fled hither to warn you of the danger.'

'This will soon be remedied,' answered the Abbot; 'I will hasten back to my Cell: a trivial reason will account for my having been missed.'

'Impossible!' rejoined Matilda: 'The Sepulchre is filled with Archers. Lorenzo de Medina, with several Officers of the Inquisition, searches through the Vaults, and pervades every passage. You will be intercepted in your flight; Your reasons for being at this late hour in the Sepulchre will be examined; Antonia will be found, and then you are undone for ever!'

'Lorenzo de Medina? Officers of the Inquisition? What brings them here? Seek they for me? Am I then suspected? Oh! speak, Matilda! Answer me, in pity!'

'As yet they do not think of you, but I fear, that they will ere long. Your only chance of escaping their notice rests upon the difficulty of exploring this Vault. The door is artfully hidden: Haply it may not be observed, and we may remain concealed till the search is over.'

'But Antonia . . . . . Should the Inquisitors draw near, and her cries be heard . . . .'

'Thus I remove that danger!' interrupted Matilda.

At the same time drawing a poignard, She rushed upon her devoted prey.

'Hold! Hold!' cried Ambrosio, seizing her hand, and wresting from it the already lifted weapon. 'What would you do, cruel Woman? The Unfortunate has already suffered but too much, thanks to your pernicious counsels! Would to God, that I had never followed them! Would to God, that I had never seen your face!'

Matilda darted upon him a look of scorn.

'Absurd!' She exclaimed with an air of passion and majesty, which impressed the Monk with awe. 'After robbing her of all that made it dear, can you fear to deprive her of a life so miserable? But 'tis well! Let her live to convince you of your folly. I abandon you to your evil destiny! I disclaim your alliance! Who trembles to commit so insignificant a crime, deserves not my protection. Hark! Hark! Ambrosio; Hear you not the Archers? They come, and your destruction is inevitable!'

At this moment the Abbot heard the sound of distant voices. He flew to close the door on whose concealment his safety depended, and which Matilda had neglected to fasten. Ere He could reach it, He saw Antonia glide suddenly by him, rush through the door, and fly towards the noise with the swiftness of an arrow. She had listened attentively to Matilda: She heard Lorenzo's name mentioned, and resolved to risque every thing to throw herself under his protection. The door was open. The sounds convinced her, that the Archers could be at no great distance. She mustered up her little remaining strength, rushed by the Monk ere He perceived her design, and bent her course rapidly towards the voices. As soon as He recovered from his first surprize, the Abbot failed not to pursue her. In vain did Antonia redouble her speed, and stretch every nerve to the utmost. Her Enemy gained upon her every moment: She heard his steps close after her, and felt the heat of his breath glow upon her neck. He over-took her; He twisted his hand in the ringlets of her streaming hair, and attempted to drag her back with him to the dungeon. Antonia resisted with all her strength: She folded her arms round a Pillar which supported the roof, and shrieked loudly for assistance. In vain did the Monk strive to threaten her to silence.

'Help!' She continued to exclaim; 'Help! Help! for God's sake!'

Quickened by her cries, the sound of foot-steps was heard approaching. The Abbot expected every moment to see the Inquisitors arrive. Antonia still resisted, and He now enforced her silence by means the most horrible and inhuman. He still grasped Matilda's dagger: Without allowing himself a moment's reflection, He raised it, and plunged it twice in the bosom of Antonia! She shrieked, and sank upon the ground. The Monk endeavoured to bear her away with him, but She still embraced the Pillar firmly. At that instant the light of approaching Torches flashed upon the Walls. Dreading a discovery, Ambrosio was compelled to abandon his Victim, and hastily fled back to the Vault, where He had left Matilda.

He fled not unobserved. Don Ramirez happening to arrive the first, perceived a Female bleeding upon the ground, and a Man flying from the spot, whose confusion betrayed him for the Murderer. He instantly pursued the Fugitive with some part of the Archers, while the Others remained with Lorenzo to protect the wounded Stranger. They raised her, and supported her in their arms. She had fainted from excess of pain, but soon gave signs of returning life. She opened her eyes, and on lifting up her head, the quantity of fair hair fell back which till then had obscured her features.

'God Almighty! It is Antonia!'

Such was Lorenzo's exclamation, while He snatched her from the Attendant's arms, and clasped her in his own.

Though aimed by an uncertain hand, the poignard had answered but too well the purpose of its Employer. The wounds were mortal, and Antonia was conscious, that She never could recover. Yet the few moments which remained for her, were moments of happiness. The concern exprest upon Lorenzo's countenance, the frantic fondness of his complaints, and his earnest enquiries respecting her wounds, convinced her beyond a doubt that his affections were her own. She would not be removed from the Vaults, fearing lest motion should only hasten her death; and She was unwilling to lose those moments, which She past in receiving proofs of Lorenzo's love, and assuring him of her own. She told him, that had She still been undefiled

She might have lamented the loss of life; But that deprived of honour and branded with shame, Death was to her a blessing: She could not have been his Wife, and that hope being denied her, She resigned herself to the Grave without one sigh of regret. She bad him take courage, conjured him not to abandon himself to fruitless sorrow, and declared that She mourned to leave nothing in the whole world, but him. While every sweet accent increased rather than lightened Lorenzo's grief, She continued to converse with him till the moment of dissolution. Her voice grew faint and scarcely audible; A thick cloud spread itself over her eyes; Her heart beat slow and irregular, and every instant seemed to announce that her fate was near at hand.

She lay, her head reclining upon Lorenzo's bosom, and her lips still murmuring to him words of comfort. She was interrupted by the Convent-Bell, as tolling at a distance, it struck the hour. Suddenly Antonia's eyes sparkled with celestial brightness: Her frame seemed to have received new strength and animation. She started from her Lover's arms.

'Three o'clock!' She cried; 'Mother, I come!'

She clasped her hands, and sank lifeless upon the ground. Lorenzo in agony threw himself beside her: He tore his hair, beat his breast, and refused to be separated from the Corse. At length his force being exhausted, He suffered himself to be led from the Vault, and was conveyed to the Palace de Medina scarcely more alive than the unfortunate Antonia.

In the mean while, though closely pursued, Ambrosio succeeded in regaining the Vault. The Door was already fastened when Don Ramirez arrived, and much time elapsed, ere the Fugitive's retreat was discovered. But nothing can resist perseverance. Though so artfully concealed, the Door could not escape the vigilance of the Archers. They forced it open, and entered the Vault to the infinite dismay of Ambrosio and his Companion. The Monk's confusion, his attempt to hide himself, his rapid flight, and the blood sprinkled upon his cloaths, left no room to doubt his being Antonia's Murderer. But when He was recognized for the immaculate Ambrosio, 'The Man of Holiness,' the Idol of Madrid, the faculties of the Spectators were chained up in surprize, and scarcely could they persuade themselves that what they saw was no vision. The Abbot strove not to vindicate himself, but preserved a sullen silence. He was secured and bound. The same precaution was taken with Matilda: Her Cowl being removed, the delicacy of her features and profusion of her golden hair betrayed her sex, and this incident created fresh amazement. The dagger was also found in the Tomb, where the Monk had thrown it; and the dungeon having undergone a thorough search, the two Culprits were conveyed to the prisons of the Inquisition.

Don Ramirez took care, that the populace should remain ignorant both of the crimes and profession of the Captives. He feared a repetition of the riots, which had followed the apprehending the Prioress of St Clare. He contented himself with stating to the Capuchins, the guilt of their Superior.

To avoid the shame of a public accusation, and dreading the popular fury from which they had already saved their Abbey with much difficulty, the Monks readily permitted the Inquisitors to search their Mansion without noise. No fresh discoveries were made. The effects found in the Abbot's and Matilda's Cells were seized, and carried to the Inquisition to be produced in evidence. Every thing else remained in its former position, and order and tranquillity once more prevailed through Madrid.

St Clare's Convent was completely ruined by the united ravages of the Mob and conflagration. Nothing remained of it but the principal Walls, whose thickness and solidity had preserved them from the flames. The Nuns who had belonged to it, were obliged in consequence to disperse themselves into other Societies: But the prejudice against them ran high, and the Superiors were very unwilling to admit them. However, most of them being related to Families the most distinguished for their riches, birth and power, the several Convents were compelled to receive them, though they did it with a very ill grace. This prejudice was extremely false and unjustifiable: After a close investigation, it was proved that All in the Convent were persuaded of the death of Agnes, except the four Nuns whom St Ursula had pointed out. These had fallen Victims to the popular fury; as had also several who were perfectly innocent and unconscious of the whole affair. Blinded by resentment, the Mob had sacrificed every Nun who fell into their hands: They who escaped were entirely indebted to the Duke de Medina's prudence and moderation. Of this they were conscious, and felt for that Nobleman a proper sense of gratitude.

Virginia was not the most sparing of her thanks: She wished equally to make a proper return for his attentions, and to obtain the good graces of Lorenzo's Uncle. In this She easily succeeded. The Duke beheld her beauty with wonder and admiration; and while his eyes were enchanted with her Form, the sweetness of her manners and her tender concern for the suffering Nun prepossessed his heart in her favour. This Virginia had discernment enough to perceive, and She redoubled her attention to the Invalid. When He parted from her at the door of her Father's Palace, the Duke entreated permission to enquire occasionally after her health. His request was readily granted: Virginia assured him, that the Marquis de Villa-Franca would be proud of an opportunity to thank him in person for the protection afforded to her. They now separated, He enchanted with her beauty and gentleness, and She much pleased with him and more with his Nephew.

On entering the Palace, Virginia's first care was to summon the family Physician, and take care of her unknown charge. Her Mother hastened to share with her the charitable office. Alarmed by the riots, and trembling for his Daughter's safety, who was his only child, the Marquis had flown to St Clare's Convent, and was still employed in seeking her. Messengers were now dispatched on all sides to inform him, that He would find her safe at his Hotel, and desire him to hasten thither immediately. His absence gave Virginia liberty to bestow her whole attention upon her Patient; and though much disordered herself by the adventures of the night, no persuasion could induce her to quit the bed-side of the Sufferer. Her constitution being much enfeebled by want and sorrow, it was some time before the Stranger was restored to her senses. She found great difficulty in swallowing the medicines prescribed to her: But this obstacle being removed, She easily conquered her disease which proceeded from nothing but weakness. The attention which was paid her, the wholesome food to which She had been long a Stranger, and her joy at being restored to liberty, to society, and, as She dared to hope, to Love, all this combined to her speedy re-establishment. From the first moment of knowing her, her melancholy situation, her sufferings almost unparalleled had engaged the affections of her amiable Hostess: Virginia felt for her the most lively interest; But how was She delighted, when her Guest being sufficiently recovered to relate her History, She recognized in the captive Nun the Sister of Lorenzo!

This victim of monastic cruelty was indeed no other than the unfortunate Agnes. During her abode in the Convent, She had been well known to Virginia: But her emaciated form, her features altered by affliction, her death universally credited, and her over-grown and matted hair which hung over her face and bosom in disorder, at first had prevented her being recollected. The Prioress had put every artifice in practice to induce Virginia to take the veil; for the Heiress of Villa-Franca would have been no despicable acquisition. Her seeming kindness and unremitted attention so far succeeded, that her young Relation began to think seriously upon compliance. Better instructed in the disgust and ennui of a monastic life, Agnes had penetrated the designs of the Domina: She trembled for the innocent Girl, and endeavoured to make her sensible of her error. She painted in their true colours the numerous inconveniencies attached to a Convent, the continued restraint, the low jealousies, the petty intrigues, the servile court and gross flattery expected by the Superior. She then bad Virginia reflect on the brilliant prospect which presented itself before her: The Idol of her Parents, the admiration of Madrid, endowed by nature and education with every perfection of person and mind, She might look forward to an establishment the most fortunate. Her riches furnished her with the means of exercising in their fullest extent, charity and benevolence, those virtues so dear to her; and her stay in the world, would enable her discovering Objects worthy her protection, which could not be done in the seclusion of a Convent.

Her persuasions induced Virginia to lay aside all thoughts of the Veil: But another argument, not used by Agnes, had more weight with her than all the others put together. She had seen Lorenzo, when He visited his Sister at the Grate. His Person pleased her, and her conversations with Agnes generally used to terminate in some question about her Brother. She, who doted upon Lorenzo, wished for no better than an opportunity to trumpet out his praise. She spoke of him in terms of rapture; and to convince her Auditor, how just were his sentiments, how cultivated his mind, and elegant his expressions, She showed her at different times the letters, which She received from him. She soon perceived that from these communications the heart of her young Friend had imbibed impressions, which She was far from intending to give, but was truly happy to discover. She could not have wished her Brother a more desirable union: Heiress of Villa-Franca, virtuous, affectionate, beautiful, and accomplished, Virginia seemed calculated to make him happy. She sounded her Brother upon the subject, though without mentioning names or circumstances. He assured her in his answers that his heart and hand were totally disengaged, and She thought, that upon these grounds She might proceed without danger. She in consequence endeavoured to strengthen the dawning passion of her Friend. Lorenzo was made the constant topic of her discourse; and the avidity with which her Auditor listened, the sighs which frequently escaped from her bosom, and the eagerness with which upon any digression She brought back the conversation to the subject whence it had wandered, sufficed to convince Agnes, that her Brother's addresses would be far from disagreeable. She at length ventured to mention her wishes to the Duke: Though a Stranger to the Lady herself, He knew enough of her situation to think her worthy his Nephew's hand. It was agreed between him and his Niece, that She should insinuate the idea to Lorenzo, and She only waited his return to Madrid to propose her Friend to him as his Bride. The unfortunate events which took place in the interim, prevented her from executing her design. Virginia wept her loss sincerely, both as a Companion, and as the only Person to whom She could speak of Lorenzo. Her passion continued to prey upon her heart in secret, and She had almost determined to confess her sentiments to her Mother, when accident once more threw their object in her way. The sight of him so near her, his politeness, his compassion, his intrepidity, had combined to give new ardour to her affection. When She now found her Friend and Advocate restored to her, She looked upon her as a Gift from Heaven; She ventured to cherish the hope of being united to Lorenzo, and resolved to use with him his Sister's influence.

Supposing that before her death Agnes might possibly have made the proposal, the Duke had placed all his Nephew's hints of marriage to Virginia's account: Consequently, He gave them the most favourable reception. On returning to his Hotel, the relation given him of Antonia's death, and Lorenzo's behaviour on the occasion, made evident his mistake. He lamented the circumstances; But the unhappy Girl being effectually out of the way, He trusted that his designs would yet be executed. 'Tis true, that Lorenzo's situation just then ill-suited him for a Bridegroom. His hopes disappointed at the moment when He expected to realize them, and the dreadful and sudden death of his Mistress had affected him very severely. The Duke found him upon the Bed of sickness. His Attendants expressed serious apprehensions for his life; But the Uncle entertained not the same fears. He was of opinion, and not unwisely, that 'Men have died, and worms have eat them; but not for Love!' He therefore flattered himself, that however deep might be the impression made upon his Nephew's heart, Time and Virginia would be able to efface it. He now hastened to the afflicted Youth, and endeavoured to console him: He sympathised in his distress, but encouraged him to resist the encroachments of despair. He allowed that He could not but feel shocked at an event so terrible, nor could He blame his sensibility; But He besought him not to torment himself with vain regrets, and rather to struggle with affliction, and preserve his life, if not for his own sake, at least for the sake of those who were fondly attached to him. While He laboured thus to make Lorenzo forget Antonia's loss, the Duke paid his court assiduously to Virginia, and seized every opportunity to advance his Nephew's interest in her heart.

It may easily be expected, that Agnes was not long without enquiring after Don Raymond. She was shocked to hear the wretched situation to which grief had reduced him; Yet She could not help exulting secretly, when She reflected, that his illness proved the sincerity of his love. The Duke undertook the office himself, of announcing to the Invalid the happiness which awaited him. Though He omitted no precaution to prepare him for such an event, at this sudden change from despair to happiness Raymond's transports were so violent, as nearly to have proved fatal to him. These once passed, the tranquillity of his mind, the assurance of felicity, and above all the presence of Agnes, [Who was no sooner re-established by the care of Virginia and the Marchioness, than She hastened to attend her Lover] soon enabled him to overcome the effects of his late dreadful malady. The calm of his soul communicated itself to his body, and He recovered with such rapidity as to create universal surprize.

Not so Lorenzo. Antonia's death accompanied with such terrible circumstances weighed upon his mind heavily. He was worn down to a shadow. Nothing could give him pleasure. He was persuaded with difficulty to swallow nourishment sufficient for the support of life, and a consumption was apprehended. The society of Agnes formed his only comfort. Though accident had never permitted their being much together, He entertained for her a sincere friendship and attachment. Perceiving how necessary She was to him, She seldom quitted his chamber. She listened to his complaints with unwearied attention, and soothed him by the gentleness of her manners, and by sympathising with his distress. She still inhabited the Palace de Villa-Franca, the Possessors of which treated her with marked affection. The Duke had intimated to the Marquis his wishes respecting Virginia. The match was unexceptionable: Lorenzo was Heir to his Uncle's immense property, and was distinguished in Madrid for his agreeable person, extensive knowledge, and propriety of conduct: Add to this, that the Marchioness had discovered, how strong was her Daughter's prepossession in his favour.

In consequence the Duke's proposal was accepted without hesitation: Every precaution was taken, to induce Lorenzo's seeing the Lady with those sentiments, which She so well merited to excite. In her visits to her Brother Agnes was frequently accompanied by the Marchioness; and as soon as He was able to move into his Anti-chamber, Virginia under her mother's protection was sometimes permitted to express her wishes for his recovery. This She did with such delicacy, the manner in which She mentioned Antonia was so tender and soothing, and when She lamented her Rival's melancholy fate, her bright eyes shone so beautiful through her tears, that Lorenzo could not behold, or listen to her without emotion. His Relations, as well as the Lady, perceived that with every day her society seemed to give him fresh pleasure, and that He spoke of her in terms of stronger admiration. However, they prudently kept their observations to themselves. No word was dropped, which might lead him to suspect their designs. They continued their former conduct and attention, and left Time to ripen into a warmer sentiment, the friendship which He already felt for Virginia.

In the mean while, her visits became more frequent; and latterly there was scarce a day, of which She did not pass some part by the side of Lorenzo's Couch. He gradually regained his strength, but the progress of his recovery was slow and doubtful. One evening He seemed to be in better spirits than usual: Agnes and her Lover, the Duke, Virginia, and her Parents were sitting round him. He now for the first time entreated his Sister to inform him, how She had escaped the effects of the poison, which St Ursula had seen her swallow. Fearful of recalling those scenes to his mind in which Antonia had perished, She had hitherto concealed from him the history of her sufferings. As He now started the subject himself, and thinking that perhaps the narrative of her sorrows might draw him from the contemplation of those on which He dwelt too constantly, She immediately complied with his request. The rest of the company had already heard her story; But the interest which all present felt for its Heroine made them anxious to hear it repeated. The whole society seconding Lorenzo's entreaties, Agnes obeyed. She first recounted the discovery which had taken place in the Abbey-Chapel, the Domina's resentment, and the mid-night scene of which St Ursula had been a concealed witness. Though the Nun had already described this latter event, Agnes now related it more circumstantially and at large: After which She proceeded in her narrative as follows.

Conclusion of the History of Agnes de Medina

My supposed death was attended with the greatest agonies. Those moments which I believed my last, were embittered by the Domina's assurances, that I could not escape perdition; and as my eyes closed, I heard her rage exhale itself in curses, on my offence. The horror of this situation, of a death-bed from which hope was banished, of a sleep from which I was only to wake to find myself the prey of flames and Furies, was more dreadful than I can describe. When animation revived in me, my soul was still impressed with these terrible ideas: I looked round with fear, expecting to behold the Ministers of divine vengeance. For the first hour, my senses were so bewildered, and my brain so dizzy, that I strove in vain to arrange the strange images which floated in wild confusion before me. If I endeavoured to raise myself from the ground, the wandering of my head deceived me. Every thing around me seemed to rock, and I sank once more upon the earth. My weak and dazzled eyes were unable to bear a nearer approach to a gleam of light, which I saw trembling above me. I was compelled to close them again, and remain motionless in the same posture.

A full hour elapsed, before I was sufficiently myself to examine the surrounding Objects. When I did examine them, what terror filled my bosom I found myself extended upon a sort of wicker Couch: It had six handles to it, which doubtless had served the Nuns to convey me to my grave. I was covered with a linen cloth: Several faded flowers were strown over me: On one side lay a small wooden Crucifix; On the other, a Rosary of large Beads. Four low narrow walls confined me. The top was also covered, and in it was practised a small grated Door: Through this was admitted the little air, which circulated in this miserable place. A faint glimmering of light which streamed through the Bars, permitted me to distinguish the surrounding horrors. I was opprest by a noisome suffocating smell; and perceiving that the grated door was unfastened, I thought that I might possibly effect my escape. As I raised myself with this design, my hand rested upon something soft: I grasped it, and advanced it towards the light. Almighty God! What was my disgust, my consternation! In spite of its putridity, and the worms which preyed upon it, I perceived a corrupted human head, and recognised the features of a Nun who had died some months before! I threw it from me, and sank almost lifeless upon my Bier.

When my strength returned, this circumstance, and the consciousness of being surrounded by the loathsome and mouldering Bodies of my Companions, increased my desire to escape from my fearful prison. I again moved towards the light. The grated door was within my reach: I lifted it without difficulty; Probably it had been left unclosed to facilitate my quitting the dungeon. Aiding myself by the irregularity of the Walls some of whose stones projected beyond the rest, I contrived to ascend them, and drag myself out of my prison. I now found Myself in a Vault tolerably spacious. Several Tombs, similar in appearance to that whence I had just escaped, were ranged along the sides in order, and seemed to be considerably sunk within the earth. A sepulchral Lamp was suspended from the roof by an iron chain, and shed a gloomy light through the dungeon. Emblems of Death were seen on every side: Skulls, shoulder-blades, thighbones, and other leavings of Mortality were scattered upon the dewy ground. Each Tomb was ornamented with a large Crucifix, and in one corner stood a wooden Statue of St Clare. To these objects I at first paid no attention: A Door, the only outlet from the Vault, had attracted my eyes. I hastened towards it, having wrapped my winding-sheet closely round me. I pushed against the door, and to my inexpressible terror found that it was fastened on the outside.

I guessed immediately, that the Prioress mistaking the nature of the liquor which She had compelled me to drink, instead of poison had administered a strong Opiate. From this I concluded, that being to all appearance dead I had received the rites of burial; and that deprived of the power of making my existence known, it would be my fate to expire of hunger. This idea penetrated me with horror, not merely for my own sake, but that of the innocent Creature, who still lived within my bosom. I again endeavoured to open the door, but it resisted all my efforts. I stretched my voice to the extent of its compass, and shrieked for aid: I was remote from the hearing of every one: No friendly voice replied to mine. A profound and melancholy silence prevailed through the Vault, and I despaired of liberty. My long abstinence from food now began to torment me. The tortures which hunger inflicted on me, were the most painful and insupportable: Yet they seemed to increase with every hour which past over my head. Sometimes I threw myself upon the ground, and rolled upon it wild and desperate: Sometimes starting up, I returned to the door, again strove to force it open, and repeated my fruitless cries for succour. Often was I on the point of striking my temple against the sharp corner of some Monument, dashing out my brains, and thus terminating my woes at once; But still the remembrance of my Baby vanquished my resolution: I trembled at a deed, which equally endangered my Child's existence and my own. Then would I vent my anguish in loud exclamations and passionate complaints; and then again my strength failing me, silent and hopeless I would sit me down upon the base of St Clare's Statue, fold my arms, and abandon myself to sullen despair. Thus passed several wretched hours. Death advanced towards me with rapid strides, and I expected that every succeeding moment would be that of my dissolution. Suddenly a neighbouring Tomb caught my eye: A Basket stood upon it, which till then I had not observed. I started from my seat: I made towards it as swiftly as my exhausted frame would permit. How eagerly did I seize the Basket, on finding it to contain a loaf of coarse bread and a small bottle of water.

I threw myself with avidity upon these humble aliments. They had to all appearance been placed in the Vault for several days; The bread was hard, and the water tainted; Yet never did I taste food to me so delicious. When the cravings of appetite were satisfied, I busied myself with conjectures upon this new circumstance: I debated whether the Basket had been placed there with a view to my necessity. Hope answered my doubts in the affirmative. Yet who could guess me to be in need of such assistance? If my existence was known, why was I detained in this gloomy Vault? If I was kept a Prisoner, what meant the ceremony of committing me to the Tomb? Or if I was doomed to perish with hunger, to whose pity was I indebted for provisions placed within my reach? A Friend would not have kept my dreadful punishment a secret; Neither did it seem probable, that an Enemy would have taken pains to supply me with the means of existence. Upon the whole I was inclined to think, that the Domina's designs upon my life had been discovered by some one of my Partizans in the Convent, who had found means to substitute an opiate for poison: That She had furnished me with food to support me, till She could effect my delivery: And that She was then employed in giving intelligence to my Relations of my danger, and pointing out a way to release me from captivity. Yet why then was the quality of my provisions so coarse? How could my Friend have entered the Vault without the Domina's knowledge? And if She had entered, why was the Door fastened so carefully? These reflections staggered me: Yet still this idea was the most favourable to my hopes, and I dwelt upon it in preference.

My meditations were interrupted by the sound of distant foot-steps. They approached, but slowly. Rays of light now darted through the crevices of the Door. Uncertain whether the Persons who advanced, came to relieve me, or were conducted by some other motive to the Vault, I failed not to attract their notice by loud cries for help. Still the sounds drew near: The light grew stronger: At length with inexpressible pleasure I heard the Key turning in the Lock. Persuaded that my deliverance was at hand, I flew towards the Door with a shriek of joy. It opened: But all my hopes of escape died away, when the Prioress appeared followed by the same four Nuns, who had been witnesses of my supposed death. They bore torches in their hands, and gazed upon me in fearful silence.

I started back in terror. The Domina descended into the Vault, as did also her Companions. She bent upon me a stern resentful eye, but expressed no surprize at finding me still living. She took the seat which I had just quitted: The door was again closed, and the Nuns ranged themselves behind their Superior, while the glare of their torches, dimmed by the vapours and dampness of the Vault, gilded with cold beams the surrounding Monuments. For some moments all preserved a dead and solemn silence. I stood at some distance from the Prioress. At length She beckoned me to advance. Trembling at the severity of her aspect my strength scarce sufficed me to obey

her. I drew near, but my limbs were unable to support their burthen. I sank
upon my knees; I clasped my hands, and lifted them up to her for mercy,
but had no power to articulate a syllable.

She gazed upon me with angry eyes.

'Do I see a Penitent, or a Criminal?' She said at length; 'Are those hands
raised in contrition for your crimes, or in fear of meeting their punishment?
Do those tears acknowledge the justice of your doom, or only solicit
mitigation of your sufferings? I fear me, 'tis the latter!'

She paused, but kept her eye still fixt upon mine.

'Take courage;' She continued: 'I wish not for your death, but your
repentance. The draught which I administered, was no poison, but an
opiate. My intention in deceiving you, was to make you feel the agonies of
a guilty conscience, had Death overtaken you suddenly, while your crimes
were still unrepented. You have suffered those agonies: I have brought you
to be familiar with the sharpness of death, and I trust, that your momentary
anguish will prove to you an eternal benefit. It is not my design to destroy
your immortal soul; or bid you seek the grave, burthened with the weight of
sins unexpiated. No, Daughter, far from it: I will purify you with wholesome
chastisement, and furnish you with full leisure for contrition and remorse.
Hear then my sentence; The ill-judged zeal of your Friends delayed its
execution, but cannot now prevent it. All Madrid believes you to be no
more; Your Relations are thoroughly persuaded of your death, and the
Nuns your Partizans have assisted at your funeral. Your existence can never
be suspected: I have taken such precautions, as must render it an impenetrable mystery. Then abandon all thoughts of a World from which you are
eternally separated, and employ the few hours which are allowed you, in
preparing for the next.'

This exordium led me to expect something terrible. I trembled, and would
have spoken to deprecate her wrath: but a motion of the Domina commanded me to be silent. She proceeded.

'Though of late years unjustly neglected, and now opposed by many of
our mis-guided Sisters, [whom Heaven convert!] it is my intention to revive
the laws of our order in their full force. That against incontinence is severe,
but no more than so monstrous an offence demands: Submit to it, Daughter,
without resistance; You will find the benefit of patience and resignation in
a better life than this. Listen then to the sentence of St Clare. Beneath these
Vaults there exist Prisons, intended to receive such criminals as yourself:
Artfully is their entrance concealed, and She who enters them, must resign
all hopes of liberty. Thither must you now be conveyed. Food shall be
supplied you, but not sufficient for the indulgence of appetite: You shall
have just enough to keep together body and soul, and its quality shall be the
simplest and coarsest. Weep, Daughter, weep, and moisten your bread with
your tears: God knows, that you have ample cause for sorrow! Chained

down in one of these secret dungeons, shut out from the world and light for ever, with no comfort but religion, no society but repentance, thus must you groan away the remainder of your days. Such are St Clare's orders; Submit to them without repining. Follow me!'

Thunder-struck at this barbarous decree, my little remaining strength abandoned me. I answered only by falling at her feet, and bathing them with tears. The Domina, unmoved by my affliction, rose from her seat with a stately air. She repeated her commands in an absolute tone: But my excessive faintness made me unable to obey her. Mariana and Alix raised me from the ground, and carried me forwards in their arms. The Prioress moved on, leaning upon Violante, and Camilla preceded her with a Torch. Thus passed our sad procession along the passages, in silence only broken by my sighs and groans. We stopped before the principal shrine of St Clare. The Statue was removed from its Pedestal, though how I knew not. The Nuns afterwards raised an iron grate till then concealed by the Image, and let it fall on the other side with a loud crash. The awful sound, repeated by the vaults above, and Caverns below me, rouzed me from the despondent apathy in which I had been plunged. I looked before me: An abyss presented itself to my affrighted eyes, and a steep and narrow Staircase, whither my Conductors were leading me. I shrieked, and started back. I implored compassion, rent the air with my cries, and summoned both heaven and earth to my assistance. In vain! I was hurried down the Staircase, and forced into one of the Cells which lined the Cavern's sides.

My blood ran cold, as I gazed upon this melancholy abode. The cold vapours hovering in the air, the walls green with damp, the bed of Straw so forlorn and comfortless, the Chain destined to bind me for ever to my prison, and the Reptiles of every description which as the torches advanced towards them, I descried hurrying to their retreats, struck my heart with terrors almost too exquisite for nature to bear. Driven by despair to madness, I burst suddenly from the Nuns who held me: I threw myself upon my knees before the Prioress, and besought her mercy in the most passionate and frantic terms.

'If not on me,' said I, 'look at least with pity on that innocent Being, whose life is attached to mine! Great is my crime, but let not my Child suffer for it! My Baby has committed no fault: Oh! spare me for the sake of my unborn Offspring, whom ere it tastes life your severity dooms to destruction!'

The Prioress drew back haughtily: She forced her habit from my grasp, as if my touch had been contagious.

'What?' She exclaimed with an exasperated air; 'What? Dare you plead for the produce of your shame? Shall a Creature be permitted to live, conceived in guilt so monstrous? Abandoned Woman, speak for him no more! Better that the Wretch should perish than live: Begotten in perjury, incontinence, and pollution, It cannot fail to prove a Prodigy of vice. Hear me, thou Guilty! Expect no mercy from me either for yourself, or Brat. Rather pray, that Death may seize you before you produce it; Or if it must see the light, that its eyes may immediately be closed again for ever! No aid shall be given you in your labour; Bring your Offspring into the world yourself, Feed it yourself, Nurse it yourself, Bury it yourself: God grant that the latter may happen soon, lest you receive comfort from the fruit of your iniquity!'

This inhuman speech, the threats which it contained, the dreadful sufferings foretold to me by the Domina, and her prayers for my Infant's death, on whom though unborn I already doated, were more than my exhausted frame could support. Uttering a deep groan, I fell senseless at the feet of my unrelenting Enemy. I know not how long I remained in this situation; But I imagine, that some time must have elapsed before my recovery, since it sufficed the Prioress and her Nuns to quit the Cavern. When my senses returned, I found myself in silence and solitude. I heard not even the retiring foot-steps of my Persecutors. All was hushed, and all was dreadful! I had been thrown upon the bed of Straw: The heavy Chain which I had already eyed with terror, was wound around my waist, and fastened me to the Wall. A Lamp glimmering with dull, melancholy rays through my dungeon, permitted my distinguishing all its horrors: It was separated from the Cavern by a low and irregular Wall of Stone: A large Chasm was left open in it which formed the entrance, for door there was none. A leaden Crucifix was in front of my straw Couch. A tattered rug lay near me, as did also a Chaplet of Beads; and not far from me stood a pitcher of water, and a wicker-Basket containing a small loaf, and a bottle of oil to supply my Lamp.

With a despondent eye did I examine this scene of suffering: When I reflected, that I was doomed to pass in it the remainder of my days, my heart was rent with bitter anguish. I had once been taught to look forward to a lot so different! At one time my prospects had appeared so bright, so flattering! Now all was lost to me. Friends, comfort, society, happiness, in one moment I was deprived of all! Dead to the world, Dead to pleasure, I lived to nothing but the sense of misery. How fair did that world seem to me, from which I was for ever excluded! How many loved objects did it contain, whom I never should behold again! As I threw a look of terror round my prison, as I shrunk from the cutting wind, which howled through my subterraneous dwelling, the change seemed so striking, so abrupt, that I doubted its reality. That the Duke de Medina's Niece, that the destined Bride of the Marquis de las Cisternas, One bred up in affluence, related to the noblest families in Spain, and rich in a multitude of affectionate Friends, that She should in one moment become a Captive, separated from the world ever, weighed down with chains, and reduced to support life with the coarsest aliments, appeared a change so sudden and incredible, that I believed myself the sport of some frightful vision. Its continuance convinced me of my mistake with but too much certainty. Every morning my hopes were disappointed. At length I abandoned all idea of escaping: I resigned myself to my fate, and only expected Liberty when She came the Companion of Death.

My mental anguish, and the dreadful scenes in which I had been an Actress, advanced the period of my labour. In solitude and misery, abandoned by all, unassisted by Art, uncomforted by Friendship, with pangs which if witnessed would have touched the hardest heart, was I delivered of my wretched burthen. It came alive into the world; But I knew not how to treat it, or by what means to preserve its existence. I could only bathe it with tears, warm it in my bosom, and offer up prayers for its safety. I was soon deprived of this mournful employment: The want of proper attendance, my ignorance how to nurse it, the bitter cold of the dungeon, and the unwholesome air which inflated its lungs, terminated my sweet Babe's short and painful existence. It expired in a few hours after its birth, and I witnessed its death with agonies which beggar all description.

But my grief was unavailing. My Infant was no more; nor could all my sighs impart to its little tender frame the breath of a moment. I rent my winding-sheet, and wrapped in it my lovely Child. I placed it on my bosom, its soft arm folded round my neck, and its pale cold cheek resting upon mine. Thus did its lifeless limbs repose, while I covered it with kisses, talked to it, wept, and moaned over it without remission, day or night. Camilla entered my prison regularly once every twenty-four hours, to bring me food. In spite of her flinty nature, She could not behold this spectacle unmoved. She feared, that grief so excessive would at length turn my brain, and in truth I was not always in my proper senses. From a principle of compassion She urged me to permit the Corse to be buried: But to this I never would consent. I vowed not to part with it while I had life: Its presence was my only comfort, and no persuasion could induce me to give it up. It soon became a mass of putridity, and to every eye was a loathsome and disgusting Object; To every eye, but a Mother's. In vain did human feelings bid me recoil from this emblem of mortality with repugnance: I with-stood, and vanquished that repugnance. I persisted in holding my Infant to my bosom, in lamenting it, loving it, adoring it! Hour after hour have I passed upon my sorry Couch, contemplating what had once been my Child: I endeavoured to retrace its features through the livid corruption, with which they were over-spread: During my confinement this sad occupation was my only delight; and at that time Worlds should not have bribed me to give it up. Even when released from my prison, I brought away my Child in my arms. The representations of my two kind Friends,"—[Here She took the hands of the Marchioness and Virginia, and pressed them alternately to her lips]   "at length persuaded me to resign my unhappy Infant to the Grave. Yet I parted from it with reluctance: However, reason at length prevailed; I suffered it to be taken from me, and it now reposes in consecrated ground.

I before mentioned, that regularly once a day Camilla brought me food. She sought not to embitter my sorrows with reproach: She bad me, 'tis true, resign all hopes of liberty and worldly happiness; But She encouraged me to bear with patience my temporary distress, and advised me to draw comfort from religion. My situation evidently affected her more, than She ventured to express: But She believed, that to extenuate my fault would make me less anxious to repent it. Often while her lips painted the enormity of my guilt in glaring colours, her eyes betrayed, how sensible She was to my sufferings. In fact I am certain that none of my Tormentors, [for the three other Nuns entered my prison occasionally] were so much actuated by the spirit of oppressive cruelty, as by the idea that to afflict my body was the only way to preserve my soul. Nay, even this persuasion might not have had such weight with them, and they might have thought my punishment too severe, had not their good dispositions been represt by blind obedience to their Superior. Her resentment existed in full force. My project of elopement having been discovered by the Abbot of the Capuchins, She supposed herself lowered in his opinion by my disgrace, and in consequence her hate was inveterate. She told the Nuns to whose custody I was committed, that my fault was of the most heinous nature, that no sufferings could equal the offence, and that nothing could save me from eternal perdition, but punishing my guilt with the utmost severity. The Superior's word is an oracle to but too many of a Convent's Inhabitants. The Nuns believed whatever the Prioress chose to assert: Though contradicted by reason and charity, they hesitated not to admit the truth of her arguments. They followed her injunctions to the very letter, and were fully persuaded, that to treat me with lenity, or to show the least pity for my woes, would be a direct means to destroy my chance for salvation.

Camilla being most employed about me, was particularly charged by the Prioress to treat me with harshness. In compliance with these orders, She frequently strove to convince me, how just was my punishment, and how enormous was my crime: She bad me think myself too happy in saving my soul by mortifying my body, and even threatened me sometimes with eternal perdition. Yet as I before observed, She always concluded by words of encouragement and comfort; and though uttered by Camilla's lips, I easily recognised the Domina's expressions. Once, and once only, the Prioress visited me in my dungeon. She then treated me with the most unrelenting cruelty: She loaded me with reproaches, taunted me with my frailty, and when I implored her mercy, told me to ask it of heaven, since I deserved none on earth. She even gazed upon my lifeless Infant without emotion; and when She left me, I heard her charge Camilla to increase the hardships of my Captivity. Unfeeling Woman! But let me check my resentment: She has expiated her errors by her sad and unexpected death. Peace be with her; and may her crimes be forgiven in heaven, as I forgive her my sufferings on earth!

Thus did I drag on a miserable existence. Far from growing familiar with my prison, I beheld it every moment with new horror. The cold seemed more piercing and bitter, the air more thick and pestilential. My frame became weak, feverish, and emaciated. I was unable to rise from the bed of Straw, and exercise my limbs in the narrow limits, to which the length of my chain permitted me to move. Though exhausted, faint, and weary, I trembled to profit by the approach of Sleep: My slumbers were constantly interrupted by some obnoxious Insect crawling over me. Sometimes I felt the bloated Toad, hideous and pampered with the poisonous vapours of the dungeon, dragging his loathsome length along my bosom: Sometimes the quick cold Lizard rouzed me leaving his slimy track upon my face, and entangling itself in the tresses of my wild and matted hair: Often have I at waking found my fingers ringed with the long worms, which bred in the corrupted flesh of my Infant. At such times I shrieked with terror and disgust, and while I shook off the reptile, trembled with all a Woman's weakness.

Such was my situation, when Camilla was suddenly taken ill. A dangerous fever, supposed to be infectious, confined her to her bed. Every one except the Lay-Sister appointed to nurse her, avoided her with caution, and feared to catch the disease. She was perfectly delirious, and by no means capable of attending to me. The Domina and the Nuns admitted to the mystery, had latterly given me over entirely to Camilla's care: In consequence, they busied themselves no more about me; and occupied by preparing for the approaching Festival, it is more than probable, that I never once entered into their thoughts. Of the reason of Camilla's negligence, I have been informed since my release by the Mother St Ursula; At that time I was very far from suspecting its cause. On the contrary, I waited for my Gaoler's appearance at first with impatience, and afterwards with despair. One day passed away; Another followed it; The Third arrived. Still no Camilla! Still no food! I knew the lapse of time by the wasting of my Lamp, to supply which fortunately a week's supply of Oil had been left me. I supposed, either that the Nuns had forgotten me, or that the Domina had ordered them to let me perish. The latter idea seemed the most probable; Yet so natural is the love of life, that I trembled to find it true. Though embittered by every species of misery, my existence was still dear to me, and I dreaded to lose it. Every succeeding minute proved to me, that I must abandon all hopes of relief. I was become an absolute skeleton: My eyes already failed me, and my limbs were beginning to stiffen. I could only express my anguish, and the pangs of that hunger which gnawed my heart-strings, by frequent groans, whose melancholy sound the vaulted roof of the dungeon re-echoed. I resigned myself to my fate: I already expected the moment of dissolution, when my Guardian Angel, when my beloved Brother arrived in time to save me. My sight grown him and feeble at first refused to recognize him; and when I did distinguish his features, the sudden burst of rapture was too much for me to bear. I was overpowered by the swell of joy at once more beholding a Friend, and that a Friend so dear to me. Nature could not support my emotions, and took her refuge in insensibility.

You already know, what are my obligations to the Family of Villa-Franca: But what you cannot know is the extent of my gratitude, boundless as the excellence of my Benefactors. Lorenzo! Raymond! Names so dear to me! Teach me to bear with fortitude this sudden transition from misery to bliss. So lately a Captive, opprest with chains, perishing with hunger, suffering every inconvenience of cold and want, hidden from the light, excluded from society, hopeless, neglected, and as I feared, forgotten; Now restored to life and liberty, enjoying all the comforts of affluence and ease, surrounded by those who are most loved by me, and on the point of becoming his Bride who has long been wedded to my heart, my happiness is so exquisite, so perfect, that scarcely can my brain sustain the weight. One only wish remains ungratified: It is to see my Brother in his former health, and to know that Antonia's memory is buried in her grave. Granted this prayer, I have nothing more to desire. I trust, that my past sufferings have purchased from heaven the pardon of my momentary weakness. That I have offended, offended greatly and grievously, I am fully conscious; But let not my Husband, because He once conquered my virtue, doubt the propriety of my future conduct. I have been frail and full of error: But I yielded not to the warmth of constitution; Raymond, affection for you betrayed me. I was too confident of my strength; But I depended no less on your honour than my own. I had vowed never to see you more: Had it not been for the consequences of that unguarded moment, my resolution had been kept. Fate willed it otherwise, and I cannot but rejoice at its decree. Still my conduct has been highly blameable, and while I attempt to justify myself, I blush at recollecting my imprudence. Let me then dismiss the ungrateful subject; First assuring you, Raymond, that you shall have no cause to repent our union, and that the more culpable have been the errors of your Mistress, the more exemplary shall be the conduct of your Wife.

Here Agnes ceased, and the Marquis replied to her address in terms equally sincere and affectionate. Lorenzo expressed his satisfaction at the prospect of being so closely connected with a Man, for whom He had ever entertained the highest esteem. The Pope's Bull had fully and effectually released Agnes from her religious engagements: The marriage was therefore celebrated as soon as the needful preparations had been made, for the

Marquis wished to have the ceremony performed with all possible splendour and publicity. This being over, and the Bride having received the compliments of Madrid, She departed with Don Raymond for his Castle in Andalusia: Lorenzo accompanied them, as did also the Marchioness de Villa-Franca and her lovely Daughter. It is needless to say, that Theodore was of the party, and it would be impossible to describe his joy at his Master's marriage. Previous to his departure, the Marquis to atone in some measure for his past neglect, made some enquiries relative to Elvira. Finding that She as well as her Daughter had received many services from Leonella and Jacintha, He showed his respect to the memory of his Sister-in-law by making the two Women handsome presents. Lorenzo followed his example— Leonella was highly flattered by the attentions of Noblemen so distinguished, and Jacintha blessed the hour on which her House was bewitched.

On her side, Agnes failed not to reward her Convent-Friends. The worthy Mother St Ursula, to whom She owed her liberty, was named at her request Superintendent of 'The Ladies of Charity:' This was one of the best and most opulent Societies throughout Spain. Bertha and Cornelia not chusing to quit their Friend, were appointed to principal charges in the same establishment. As to the Nuns who had aided the Domina in persecuting Agnes, Camilla being confined by illness to her bed, had perished in the flames which consumed St Clare's Convent. Mariana, Alix, and Violante, as well as two more, had fallen victims to the popular rage. The three Others who in Council had supported the Domina's sentence, were severely reprimanded, and banished to religious Houses in obscure and distant Provinces: Here they languished away a few years, ashamed of their former weakness, and shunned by their Companions with aversion and contempt.

Nor was the fidelity of Flora permitted to go unrewarded. Her wishes being consulted, She declared herself impatient to revisit her native land. In consequence, a passage was procured for her to Cuba, where She arrived in safety, loaded with the presents of Raymond and Lorenzo.

The debts of gratitude discharged, Agnes was at liberty to pursue her favourite plan. Lodged in the same House, Lorenzo and Virginia were eternally together. The more He saw of her, the more was He convinced of her merit. On her part, She laid herself out to please, and not to succeed was for her impossible. Lorenzo witnessed with admiration her beautiful person, elegant manners, innumerable talents, and sweet disposition: He was also much flattered by her prejudice in his favour, which She had not sufficient art to conceal. However, his sentiments partook not of that ardent character, which had marked his affection for Antonia. The image of that lovely and unfortunate Girl still lived in his heart, and baffled all Virginia's efforts to displace it. Still when the Duke proposed to him the match, which He wished so earnestly to take place, his Nephew did not reject the offer. The urgent supplications of his Friends, and the Lady's merit conquered his repugnance to entering into new engagements. He proposed himself to the Marquis de Villa-Franca, and was accepted with joy and gratitude. Virginia became his Wife, nor did She ever give him cause to repent his choice. His esteem increased for her daily. Her unremitted endeavours to please him could not but succeed. His affection assumed stronger and warmer colours. Antonia's image was gradually effaced from his bosom; and Virginia became sole Mistress of that heart, which She well deserved to possess without a Partner.

The remaining years of Raymond and Agnes, of Lorenzo and Virginia, were happy as can be those allotted to Mortals, born to be the prey of grief, and sport of disappointment. The exquisite sorrows with which they had been afflicted, made them think lightly of every succeeding woe. They had felt the sharpest darts in misfortune's quiver; Those which remained appeared blunt in comparison. Having weathered Fate's heaviest Storms, they looked calmly upon its terrors: or if ever they felt Affliction's casual gales, they seemed to them gentle as Zephyrs, which breathe over summer-seas.

CHAPTER V

⸻He was a fell despightful Fiend:
Hell holds none worse in baleful bower below:
By pride, and wit, and rage, and rancor keened;
Of Man alike, if good or bad the Foe.
                                        Thomson.

ON the day following Antonia's death, all Madrid was a scene of consternation and amazement. An Archer who had witnessed the adventure in the Sepulchre, had indiscreetly related the circumstances of the murder: He had also named the perpetrator. The confusion was without example, which this intelligence raised among the Devotees. Most of them disbelieved it, and went themselves to the Abbey to ascertain the fact. Anxious to avoid the shame to which their Superior's ill-conduct exposed the whole Brotherhood, the Monks assured the Visitors, that Ambrosio was prevented from receiving them as usual by nothing but illness. This attempt was unsuccessful: The same excuse being repeated day after day, the Archer's story gradually obtained confidence. His Partizans abandoned him: No one entertained a doubt of his guilt; and they who before had been the warmest in his praise, were now the most vociferous in his condemnation.

While his innocence or guilt was debated in Madrid with the utmost acrimony, Ambrosio was a prey to the pangs of conscious villainy, and the terrors of punishment impending over him. When He looked back to the eminence on which He had lately stood, universally honoured and respected, at peace with the world and with himself, scarcely could He believe that He was indeed the culprit, whose crimes and whose fate He trembled to envisage. But a few weeks had elapsed, since He was pure and virtuous, courted by the wisest and noblest in Madrid, and regarded by the People with a reverence that approached idolatory: He now saw himself stained with the most loathed and monstrous sins, the object of universal execration, a Prisoner of the Holy Office, and probably doomed to perish in tortures the most severe. He could not hope to deceive his Judges: The proofs of his guilt were too strong. His being in the Sepulchre at so late an hour, his confusion at the discovery, the dagger which in his first alarm He owned had been concealed by him, and the blood which had spirted upon his habit from Antonia's wound, sufficiently marked him out for the Assassin. He waited with agony for the day of examination: He had no resource to comfort him in his distress. Religion could not inspire him with fortitude: If He read the Books of morality which were put into his hands, He saw in them nothing but the enormity of his offences; If he attempted to pray, He recollected that He deserved not heaven's protection, and believed his crimes so monstrous, as to baffle even God's infinite goodness. For every other Sinner, He thought there might be hope, but for him there could be none. Shuddering at the past, anguished by the present, and dreading the future, thus passed He the few days preceding that which was marked for his Trial.

That day arrived. At nine in the morning his prison door was unlocked, and his Gaoler entering, commanded him to follow him. He obeyed with trembling. He was conducted into a spacious Hall, hung with black cloth. At the Table sat three grave stern-looking Men, also habited in black: One was the Grand Inquisitor, whom the importance of this cause had induced to examine into it himself. As a smaller table at a little distance sat the Secretary, provided with all necessary implements for writing Ambrosio was beckoned to advance, and take his station at the lower end of the Table. As his eye glanced downwards, He perceived various iron instruments lying scattered upon the floor. Their forms were unknown to him, but apprehension immediately guessed them to be engines of torture. He turned pale, and with difficulty prevented himself from sinking upon the ground.

Profound silence prevailed, except when the Inquisitors whispered a few words among themselves mysteriously. Near an hour past away, and with every second of it Ambrosio's fears grew more poignant. At length a small Door, opposite to that by which He had entered the Hall, grated heavily upon its hinges. An Officer appeared, and was immediately followed by the beautiful Matilda. Her hair hung about her face wildly; Her cheeks were pale, and her eyes sunk and hollow. She threw a melancholy look upon Ambrosio: He replied by one of aversion and reproach. She was placed opposite to him. A Bell then sounded thrice. It was the signal for opening the Court, and the Inquisitors entered upon their office.

In these trials neither the accusation is mentioned, or the name of the Accuser. The Prisoners are only asked, whether they will confess: If they reply that having no crime they can make no confession, they are put to the torture without delay. This is repeated at intervals, either till the suspected avow themselves culpable, or the perseverance of the examinants is worn out and exhausted: But without a direct acknowledgment of their guilt, the Inquisition never pronounces the final doom of its Prisoners. In general much time is suffered to elapse without their being questioned: But Ambrosio's trial had been hastened, on account of a solemn Auto da Fé which would take place in a few days, and in which the Inquisitors meant this distinguished Culprit to perform a part, and give a striking testimony of their vigilance.

The Abbot was not merely accused of rape and murder: The crime of Sorcery was laid to his charge, as well as to Matilda's. She had been seized as an Accomplice in Antonia's assassination. On searching her Cell, various suspicious books and instruments were found, which justified the accusation brought against her. To criminate the Monk, the constellated Mirror was produced, which Matilda had accidentally left in his chamber. The strange figures engraved upon it caught the attention of Don Ramirez, while searching the Abbot's Cell: In consequence, He carried it away with him. It was shown to the Grand Inquisitor, who having considered it for some time, took off a small golden Cross which hung at his girdle, and laid it upon the Mirror. Instantly a loud noise was heard, resembling a clap of thunder, and the steel shivered into a thousand pieces. This circumstance confirmed the suspicion of the Monk's having dealt in Magic: It was even supposed, that his former influence over the minds of the People was entirely to be ascribed to witch-craft.

Determined to make him confess not only the crimes which He had committed, but those also of which He was innocent, the Inquisitors began their examination. Though dreading the tortures, as He dreaded death still more which would consign him to eternal torments, the Abbot asserted his purity in a voice bold and resolute. Matilda followed his example, but spoke with fear and trembling. Having in vain exhorted him to confess, the Inquisitors ordered the Monk to be put to the question. The Decree was immediately executed. Ambrosio suffered the most excruciating pangs, that ever were invented by human cruelty: Yet so dreadful is Death when guilt accompanies it, that He had sufficient fortitude to persist in his disavowal. His agonies were redoubled in consequence: Nor was He released till fainting from excess of pain, insensibility rescued him from the hands of his Tormentors.

Matilda was next ordered to the torture: But terrified by the sight of the Friar's sufferings, her courage totally deserted her. She sank upon her knees, acknowledged her corresponding with infernal Spirits, and that She had witnessed the Monk's assassination of Antonia: But as to the crime of Sorcery, She declared herself the sole criminal, and Ambrosio perfectly innocent. The latter assertion met with no credit. The Abbot had recovered his senses in time to hear the confession of his Accomplice: But He was too much enfeebled by what He had already undergone, to be capable at that time of sustaining new torments. He was commanded back to his Cell, but first informed, that as soon as He had gained strength sufficient, He must prepare himself for a second examination: The Inquisitors hoped, that He would then be less hardened and obstinate. To Matilda it was announced, that She must expiate her crime in fire on the approaching Auto da Fé. All her tears and entreaties could procure no mitigation of her doom, and She was dragged by force from the Hall of Trial.

Returned to his dungeon, the sufferings of Ambrosio's body were far more supportable than those of his mind. His dislocated limbs, the nails torn from his hands and feet, and his fingers mashed and broken by the pressure of screws, were far surpassed in anguish by the agitation of his soul, and vehemence of his terrors. He saw, that guilty or innocent his Judges were bent upon condemning him: The remembrance of what his denial had already cost him, terrified him at the idea of being again applied to the question, and almost engaged him to confess his crimes. Then again the consequences of his confession flashed before him, and rendered him once more irresolute. His death would be inevitable, and that a death the most dreadful: He had listened to Matilda's doom, and doubted not that a similar was reserved for him. He shuddered at the approaching Auto da Fé, at the idea of perishing in flames, and only escaping from indurable torments to pass into others more subtile and ever-lasting! With affright did He bend his mind's eye on the space beyond the grave; nor could hide from himself, how justly he ought to dread Heaven's vengeance. In this Labyrinth of terrors, fain would He have taken his refuge in the gloom of Atheism: Fain would He have denied the soul's immortality; have persuaded himself that when his eyes once closed, they would never more open, and that the same moment would annihilate his soul and body. Even this resource was refused to him. To permit his being blind to the fallacy of this belief, his knowledge was too extensive, his understanding too solid and just. He could not help feeling the existence of a God. Those truths, once his comfort, now presented themselves before him in the clearest light; But they only served to drive him to distraction. They destroyed his ill-grounded hopes of escaping punishment; and dispelled by the irresistible brightness of Truth and conviction, Philosophy's deceitful vapours faded away like a dream.

In anguish almost too great for mortal frame to bear, He expected the time, when He was again to be examined. He busied himself in planning ineffectual schemes for escaping both present and future punishment. Of the first there was no possibility; Of the second Despair made him neglect the only means. While Reason forced him to acknowledge a God's existence, Conscience made him doubt the infinity of his goodness. He disbelieved, that a Sinner like him could find mercy. He had not been deceived into error: Ignorance could furnish him with no excuse. He had seen vice in her true colours; Before He committed his crimes, He had computed every scruple of their weight; and yet he had committed them.

'Pardon?' He would cry in an access of phrenzy; 'Oh! there can be none for me!'

Persuaded of this, instead of humbling himself in penitence, of deploring his guilt, and employing his few remaining hours in deprecating Heaven's wrath, He abandoned himself to the transports of desperate rage; He sorrowed for the punishment of his crimes, not their commission; and exhaled his bosom's anguish in idle sighs, in vain lamentations, in blasphemy and despair. As the few beams of day, which pierced through the bars of his prison-window, gradually disappeared, and their place was supplied by the pale and glimmering Lamp, He felt his terrors redouble, and his ideas become more gloomy, more solemn, more despondent. He dreaded the approach of sleep: No sooner did his eyes close, wearied with tears and watching, than the dreadful visions seemed to be realised, on which his mind had dwelt during the day. He found himself in sulphurous realms and burning Caverns, surrounded by Fiends appointed his Tormentors, and who drove him through a variety of tortures, each of which was more dreadful than the former. Amidst these dismal scenes wandered the Ghosts of Elvira and her Daughter. They reproached him with their deaths, recounted his crimes to the Dæmons, and urged them to inflict torments of cruelty yet more refined. Such were the pictures, which floated before his eyes in sleep: They vanished not till his repose was disturbed by excess of agony. Then would He start from the ground on which He had stretched himself, his brows running down with cold sweat, his eyes wild and phrenzied; and He only exchanged the terrible certainty for surmizes scarcely more supportable. He paced his dungeon with disordered steps; He gazed with terror upon the surrounding darkness, and often did He cry,

'Oh! fearful is night to the Guilty!'

The day of his second examination was at hand. He had been compelled to swallow cordials, whose virtues were calculated to restore his bodily strength, and enable him to support the question longer. On the night preceding this dreaded day, his fears for the morrow permitted him not to sleep. His terrors were so violent, as nearly to annihilate his mental powers. He sat like one stupefied near the Table on which his Lamp was burning dimly. Despair chained up his faculties in Idiotism, and He remained for some hours, unable to speak or move, or indeed to think.

'Look up, Ambrosio!' said a Voice in accents well-known to him—

The Monk started, and raised his melancholy eyes. Matilda stood before him. She had quitted her religious habit. She now wore a female dress, at once elegant and splendid: A profusion of diamonds blazed upon her robes, and her hair was confined by a coronet of Roses. In her right hand She held a small Book: A lively expression of pleasure beamed upon her countenance; But still it was mingled with a wild imperious majesty, which inspired the Monk with awe, and represt in some measure his transports at seeing her.

'You here, Matilda?' He at length exclaimed; 'How have you gained entrance? Where are your Chains? What means this magnificence, and the joy which sparkles in your eyes? Have our Judges relented? Is there a chance of my escaping? Answer me for pity, and tell me, what I have to hope, or fear.'

'Ambrosio!' She replied with an air of commanding dignity; 'I have baffled the Inquisition's fury. I am free: A few moments will place kingdoms between these dungeons and me. Yet I purchase my liberty at a dear, at a dreadful price! Dare you pay the same, Ambrosio? Dare you spring without fear over the bounds, which separate Men from Angels?—You are silent.— You look upon me with eyes of suspicion and alarm—I read your thoughts and confess their justice. Yes, Ambrosio; I have sacrificed all for life and liberty. I am no longer a candidate for heaven! I have renounced God's service, and am enlisted beneath the banners of his Foes. The deed is past recall: Yet were it in my power to go back, I would not. Oh! my Friend, to expire in such torments! To die amidst curses and execrations! To bear the insults of an exasperated Mob! To be exposed to all the mortifications of shame and infamy! Who can reflect without horror on such a doom? Let me then exult in my exchange. I have sold distant and uncertain happiness for present and secure: I have preserved a life, which otherwise I had lost in torture; and I have obtained the power of procuring every bliss, which can make that life delicious! The Infernal Spirits obey me as their Sovereign: By their aid shall my days be past in every refinement of luxury and voluptuousness. I will enjoy unrestrained the gratification of my senses: Every passion shall be indulged, even to satiety; Then will I bid my Servants invent new pleasures, to revive and stimulate my glutted appetites! I go impatient to exercise my newly-gained dominion. I pant to be at liberty. Nothing should hold me one moment longer in this abhorred abode, but the hope of persuading you to follow my example. Ambrosio, I still love you: Our mutual guilt and danger have rendered you dearer to me, than ever and I would fain save you from impending destruction. Summon then your resolution to your aid; and renounce for immediate and certain benefits the hopes of a salvation, difficult to obtain, and perhaps altogether erroneous. Shake off the prejudice of vulgar souls; Abandon a God, who has abandoned you, and raise yourself to the level of superior Beings!'

She paused for the Monk's reply: He shuddered, while He gave it.

'Matilda!' He said after a long silence in a low and unsteady voice; 'What price gave you for liberty?'

She answered him firm and dauntless.

'Ambrosio, it was my Soul!'

'Wretched Woman, what have you done? Pass but a few years, and how dreadful will be your sufferings!'

'Weak Man, pass but this night, and how dreadful will be your own! Do you remember what you have already endured? To-morrow you must bear torments doubly exquisite. Do you remember the horrors of a fiery punishment? In two days you must be led a Victim to the Stake! What then will become of you? Still dare you hope for pardon? Still are you beguiled with visions of salvation? Think upon your crimes! Think upon your lust, your perjury, inhumanity, and hypocrisy! Think upon the innocent blood, which cries to the Throne of God for vengeance, and then hope for mercy! Then dream of heaven, and sigh for worlds of light, and realms of peace and pleasure! Absurd! Open your eyes, Ambrosio, and be prudent. Hell is your lot; You are doomed to eternal perdition; Nought lies beyond your grave, but a gulph of devouring flames. And will you then speed towards that Hell? Will you clasp that perdition in your arms, ere 'tis needful? Will you plunge into those flames, while you still have the power to shun them? 'Tis a Madman's action. No, no, Ambrosio: Let us for awhile fly from divine vengeance. Be advised by me; Purchase by one moment's courage the bliss of years; Enjoy the present, and forget that a future lags behind.'

'Matilda, your counsels are dangerous: I dare not, I will not follow them. I must not give up my claim to salvation. Monstrous are my crimes; But God is merciful, and I will not despair of pardon.'

'Is such your resolution? I have no more to say. I speed to joy and liberty, and abandon you to death and eternal torments.'

'Yet stay one moment, Matilda! You command the infernal Dæmons: You can force open these prison-doors; You can release me from these chains, which weigh me down. Save me, I conjure you, and bear me from these fearful abodes!'

'You ask the only boon beyond my power to bestow. I am forbidden to assist a Churchman and a Partizan of God: Renounce those titles, and command me.'

'I will not sell my soul to perdition.'

'Persist in your obstinacy, till you find yourself at the Stake: Then will you repent your error, and sigh for escape when the moment is gone by. I quit you.—Yet ere the hour of death arrives should wisdom enlighten you, listen to the means of repairing your present fault. I leave with you this Book. Read the four first lines of the seventh page backwards: The Spirit whom you have already once beheld, will immediately appear to you. If you are wise, we shall meet again: If not, farewell for ever!'

She let the Book fall upon the ground. A cloud of blue fire wrapped itself round her: She waved her hand to Ambrosio, and disappeared. The momentary glare which the flames poured through the dungeon, on dissipating suddenly, seemed to have increased its natural gloom. The solitary Lamp scarcely gave light sufficient to guide the Monk to a Chair. He threw himself into his seat, folded his arms, and leaning his head upon the table, sank into reflections perplexing and unconnected.

He was still in this attitude, when the opening of the prison-door rouzed him from his stupor. He was summoned to appear before the Grand Inquisitor. He rose, and followed his Gaoler with painful steps. He was led into the same Hall, placed before the same Examiners, and was again interrogated, whether He would confess. He replied as before, that having no crimes, He could acknowledge none: But when the Executioners prepared to put him to the question, when He saw the engines of torture, and remembered the pangs, which they had already inflicted, his resolution failed him entirely. Forgetting the consequences, and only anxious to escape the terrors of the present moment, He made an ample confession. He disclosed every circumstance of his guilt, and owned not merely the crimes with which He was charged, but those of which He had never been suspected. Being interrogated as to Matilda's flight which had created much confusion, He confessed that She had sold herself to Satan, and that She was indebted to Sorcery for her escape. He still assured his Judges, that for his own part He had never entered into any compact with the infernal Spirits; But the threat of being tortured made him declare himself to be a Sorcerer, and Heretic, and whatever other title the Inquisitors chose to fix upon him. In consequence of this avowal, his sentence was immediately pronounced. He was ordered to prepare himself to perish in the Auto da Fé, which was to be solemnized at twelve o'clock that night. This hour was chosen from the idea, that the horror of the flames being heightened by the gloom of midnight, the execution would have a greater effect upon the mind of the People.

Ambrosio rather dead than alive was left alone in his dungeon. The moment in which this terrible decree was pronounced, had nearly proved that of his dissolution. He looked forward to the morrow with despair, and his terrors increased with the approach of midnight. Sometimes He was buried in gloomy silence: At others He raved with delirious passion, wrung his hands, and cursed the hour, when He first beheld the light. In one of these moments his eye rested upon Matilda's mysterious gift. His transports of rage were instantly suspended. He looked earnestly at the Book; He took it up, but immediately threw it from him with horror. He walked rapidly up and down his dungeon: Then stopped, and again fixed his eyes on the spot where the Book had fallen. He reflected, that here at least was a resource from the fate which He dreaded. He stooped, and took it up a second time.

He remained for some time trembling and irresolute: He longed to try the charm, yet feared its consequences. The recollection of his sentence at length fixed his indecision. He opened the Volume; but his agitation was so great, that He at first sought in vain for the page mentioned by Matilda. Ashamed of himself, He called all his courage to his aid. He turned to the seventh leaf. He began to read it aloud; But his eyes frequently wandered from the Book, while He anxiously cast them round in search of the Spirit, whom He wished, yet dreaded to behold. Still He persisted in his design; and with a voice unassured and frequent interruptions, He contrived to finish the four first lines of the page.

They were in a language, whose import was totally unknown to him. Scarce had He pronounced the last word, when the effects of the charm were evident. A loud burst of Thunder was heard; The prison shook to its very foundations; A blaze of lightning flashed through the Cell; and in the next moment, borne upon sulphurous whirl-winds, Lucifer stood before him a second time. But He came not, as when at Matilda's summons He borrowed the Seraph's form to deceive Ambrosio. He appeared in all that ugliness, which since his fall from heaven had been his portion: His blasted limbs still bore marks of the Almighty's thunder: A swarthy darkness spread itself over his gigantic form: His hands and feet were armed with long Talons: Fury glared in his eyes, which might have struck the bravest heart with terror: Over his huge shoulders waved two enormous sable wings; and his hair was supplied by living snakes, which twined themselves round his brows with frightful hissings. In one hand He held a roll of parchment, and in the other an iron pen. Still the lightning flashed around him, and the Thunder with repeated bursts, seemed to announce the dissolution of Nature.

Terrified at an Apparition so different from what He had expected, Ambrosio remained gazing upon the Fiend, deprived of the power of utterance. The Thunder had ceased to roll: Universal silence reigned through the dungeon.

'For what am I summoned hither?' said the Dæmon, in a voice which *sulphurous fogs had damped to hoarseness*—

At the sound Nature seemed to tremble: A violent earth-quake rocked the ground, accompanied by a fresh burst of Thunder, louder and more appalling than the first.

Ambrosio was long unable to answer the Dæmon's demand.

'I am condemned to die;' He said with a faint voice, his blood running cold, while He gazed upon his dreadful Visitor. 'Save me! Bear me from hence!'

'Shall the reward of my services be paid me? Dare you embrace my cause? Will you be mine, body and soul? Are you prepared to renounce him who made you, and him who died for you? Answer but "Yes" and Lucifer is your Slave.'

'Will no less price content you? Can nothing satisfy you but my eternal ruin? Spirit, you ask too much. Yet convey me from this dungeon: Be my Servant for one hour, and I will be yours for a thousand years. Will not this offer suffice?'

'It will not. I must have your soul; must have it mine, and mine for ever.'

'Insatiate Dæmon, I will not doom myself to endless torments. I will not give up my hopes of being one day pardoned.'

'You will not? On what Chimæra rest then your hopes? Short-sighted Mortal! Miserable Wretch! Are you not guilty? Are you not infamous in the eyes of Men and Angels. Can such enormous sins be forgiven? Hope you to escape my power? Your fate is already pronounced. The Eternal has abandoned you; Mine you are marked in the book of destiny, and mine you must and shall be!'

'Fiend, 'tis false! Infinite is the Almighty's mercy, and the Penitent shall meet his forgiveness. My crimes are monstrous, but I will not despair of pardon: Haply, when they have received due chastisement . . . .'

'Chastisement? Was Purgatory meant for guilt like yours? Hope you that your offences shall be bought off by prayers of superstitious dotards and droning Monks? Ambrosio, be wise! Mine you must be: You are doomed to flames, but may shun them for the present. Sign this parchment: I will bear you from hence, and you may pass your remaining years in bliss and liberty. Enjoy your existence: Indulge in every pleasure to which appetite may lead you: But from the moment that it quits your body, remember that your soul belongs to me, and that I will not be defrauded of my right.'

The Monk was silent; But his looks declared, that the Tempter's words were not thrown away. He reflected on the conditions proposed with horror: On the other hand, He believed himself doomed to perdition, and that, by refusing the Dæmon's succour, He only hastened tortures which He never could escape. The Fiend saw, that his resolution was shaken: He renewed his instances, and endeavoured to fix the Abbot's indecision. He described the agonies of death in the most terrific colours; and He worked so powerfully upon Ambrosio's despair and fears, that He prevailed upon him to receive the Parchment. He then struck the iron Pen which He held into a vein of the Monk's left-hand. It pierced deep, and was instantly filled with blood; Yet Ambrosio felt no pain from the wound. The Pen was put into his hand: It trembled. The Wretch placed the Parchment on the Table before him, and prepared to sign it. Suddenly He held his hand: He started away hastily, and threw the Pen upon the table.

'What am I doing?' He cried—Then turning to the Fiend with a desperate air, 'Leave me! Begone! I will not sign the Parchment.'

'Fool!' exclaimed the disappointed Dæmon, darting looks so furious as penetrated the Friar's soul with horror; 'Thus am I trifled with? Go then!

Rave in agony, expire in tortures, and then learn the extent of the Eternal's mercy! But beware how you make me again your mock! Call me no more, till resolved to accept my offers! Summon me a second time to dismiss me thus idly, and these Talons shall rend you into a thousand pieces! Speak yet again; Will you sign the Parchment?'

'I will not! Leave me! Away!'

Instantly the Thunder was heard to roll horribly: Once more the earth trembled with violence: The Dungeon resounded with loud shrieks, and the Dæmon fled with blasphemy and curses.

At first, the Monk rejoiced at having resisted the Seducer's arts, and obtained a triumph over Mankind's Enemy: But as the hour of punishment drew near, his former terrors revived in his heart. Their momentary repose seemed to have given them fresh vigour. The nearer that the time approached, the more did He dread appearing before the Throne of God. He shuddered to think how soon He must be plunged into eternity; How soon meet the eyes of his Creator, whom He had so grievously offended. The Bell announced mid-night: It was the signal for being led to the Stake! As He listened to the first stroke, the blood ceased to circulate in the Abbot's veins: He heard death and torture murmured in each succeeding sound. He expected to see the Archers entering his prison; and as the Bell forbore to toll, he seized the magic volume in a fit of despair. He opened it, turned hastily to the seventh page, and as if fearing to allow himself a moment's thought ran over the fatal lines with rapidity. Accompanied by his former terrors, Lucifer again stood before the Trembler.

'You have summoned me,' said the Fiend; 'Are you determined to be wise? Will you accept my conditions? You know them already. Renounce your claim to salvation, make over to me your soul, and I bear you from this dungeon instantly. Yet is it time. Resolve, or it will be too late. Will you sign the Parchment?'

'I must!—Fate urges me!—I accept your conditions.'

'Sign the Parchment!' replied the Dæmon in an exulting tone.

The Contract and the bloody Pen still lay upon the Table. Ambrosio drew near it. He prepared to sign his name. A moment's reflection made him hesitate.

'Hark!' cried the Tempter; 'They come! Be quick! Sign the Parchment, and I bear you from hence this moment.'

In effect, the Archers were heard approaching, appointed to lead Ambrosio to the Stake. The sound encouraged the Monk in his resolution.

'What is the import of this writing?' said He.

'It makes your soul over to me for ever, and without reserve.'

'What am I to receive in exchange?'

'My protection, and release from this dungeon. Sign it, and this instant I bear you away.'

Ambrosio took up the Pen; He set it to the Parchment. Again his courage failed him: He felt a pang of terror at his heart, and once more threw the Pen upon the Table.

'Weak and Puerile!' cried the exasperated Fiend: 'Away with this folly! Sign the writing this instant, or I sacrifice you to my rage!'

At this moment the bolt of the outward Door was drawn back. The Prisoner heard the rattling of Chains; The heavy Bar fell; The Archers were on the point of entering. Worked up to phrenzy by the urgent danger, shrinking from the approach of death, terrified by the Dæmon's threats, and seeing no other means to escape destruction, the wretched Monk complied. He signed the fatal contract, and gave it hastily into the evil Spirit's hands, whose eyes, as He received the gift, glared with malicious rapture.

'Take it!' said the God-abandoned; 'Now then save me! Snatch me from hence!'

'Hold! Do you freely and absolutely renounce your Creator and his Son?'

'I do! I do!'

'Do you make over your soul to me for ever?'

'For ever!'

'Without reserve or subterfuge? Without future appeal to the divine mercy?'

The last Chain fell from the door of the prison: The key was heard turning in the Lock: Already the iron door grated heavily upon its rusty hinges.

'I am yours for ever and irrevocably!' cried the Monk wild with terror: 'I abandon all claim to salvation! I own no power but yours! Hark! Hark! They come! Oh! save me! Bear me away!'

'I have triumphed! You are mine past reprieve, and I fulfil my promise.'

While He spoke, the Door unclosed. Instantly the Dæmon grasped one of Ambrosio's arms, spread his broad pinions, and sprang with him into the air. The roof opened as they soared upwards, and closed again when they had quitted the Dungeon.

In the mean while, the Gaoler was thrown into the utmost surprize by the disappearance of his Prisoner. Though neither He nor the Archers were in time to witness the Monk's escape, a sulphurous smell prevailing through the prison sufficiently informed them by whose aid He had been liberated. They hastened to make their report to the Grand Inquisitor. The story, how a Sorcerer had been carried away by the Devil, was soon noised about Madrid; and for some days the whole City was employed in discussing the subject. Gradually it ceased to be the topic of conversation: Other adventures arose whose novelty engaged universal attention; and Ambrosio was soon forgotten as totally, as if He never had existed. While this was passing, the Monk supported by his infernal guide, traversed the air with the rapidity of an arrow, and a few moments placed him upon a Precipice's brink, the steepest in Sierra Morena.

Though rescued from the Inquisition, Ambrosio as yet was insensible of the blessings of liberty. The damning contract weighed heavy upon his mind; and the scenes in which He had been a principal actor, had left behind them such impressions, as rendered his heart the seat of anarchy and confusion. The Objects now before his eyes, and which the full Moon sailing through clouds permitted him to examine, were ill-calculated to inspire that calm, of which He stood so much in need. The disorder of his imagination was increased by the wildness of the surrounding scenery; By the gloomy Caverns and steep rocks, rising above each other, and dividing the passing clouds; solitary clusters of Trees scattered here and there, among whose thick-twined branches the wind of night sighed hoarsely and mournfully; the shrill cry of mountain Eagles, who had built their nests among these lonely Desarts; the stunning roar of torrents, as swelled by late rains they rushed violently down tremendous precipices; and the dark waters of a silent sluggish stream which faintly reflected the moon-beams, and bathed the Rock's base on which Ambrosio stood. The Abbot cast round him a look of terror. His infernal Conductor was still by his side, and eyed him with a look of mingled malice, exultation, and contempt.

'Whither have you brought me?' said the Monk at length in an hollow trembling voice: 'Why am I placed in this melancholy scene? Bear me from it quickly! Carry me to Matilda!'

The Fiend replied not, but continued to gaze upon him in silence. Ambrosio could not sustain his glance; He turned away his eyes, while thus spoke the Dæmon:

'I have him then in my power! This model of piety! This being without reproach! This Mortal who placed his puny virtues on a level with those of Angels. He is mine! Irrevocably, eternally mine! Companions of my sufferings! Denizens of hell! How grateful will be my present!'

He paused; then addressed himself to the Monk——

'Carry you to Matilda?' He continued, repeating Ambrosio's words: 'Wretch! you shall soon be with her! You well deserve a place near her, for hell boasts no miscreant more guilty than yourself. Hark, Ambrosio, while I unveil your crimes! You have shed the blood of two innocents; Antonia and Elvira perished by your hand. That Antonia whom you violated, was your Sister! That Elvira whom you murdered, gave you birth! Tremble, abandoned Hypocrite! Inhuman Parricide! Incestuous Ravisher! Tremble at the extent of your offences! And you it was who thought yourself proof against temptation, absolved from human frailties, and free from error and vice! Is pride then a virtue? Is inhumanity no fault? Know, vain Man! That I long have marked you for my prey: I watched the movements of your heart; I saw that you were virtuous from vanity, not principle, and I seized the fit moment of seduction. I observed your blind idolatry of the Madona's picture. I bad a subordinate but crafty spirit assume a similar form, and you eagerly yielded to the blandishments of Matilda. Your pride was gratified by her flattery; Your lust only needed an opportunity to break forth; You ran into the snare blindly, and scrupled not to commit a crime, which you blamed in another with unfeeling severity. It was I who threw Matilda in your way; It was I who gave you entrance to Antonia's chamber; It was I who caused the dagger to be given you which pierced your Sister's bosom; and it was I who warned Elvira in dreams of your designs upon her Daughter, and thus, by preventing your profiting by her sleep, compelled you to add rape as well as incest to the catalogue of your crimes. Hear, hear, Ambrosio! Had you resisted me one minute longer, you had saved your body and soul. The guards whom you heard at your prison-door, came to signify your pardon. But I had already triumphed: My plots had already succeeded. Scarcely could I propose crimes so quick as you performed them. You are mine, and Heaven itself cannot rescue you from my power. Hope not that your penitence will make void our contract. Here is your bond signed with your blood; You have given up your claim to mercy, and nothing can restore to you the rights which you have foolishly resigned. Believe you, that your secret thoughts escaped me? No, no, I read them all! You trusted that you should still have time for repentance. I saw your artifice, knew its falsity, and rejoiced in deceiving the deceiver! You are mine beyond reprieve: I burn to possess my right, and alive you quit not these mountains.'

During the Dæmon's speech, Ambrosio had been stupefied by terror and surprize. This last declaration rouzed him.

'Not quit these mountains alive?' He exclaimed: 'Perfidious, what mean you? Have you forgotten our contract?'

The Fiend answered by a malicious laugh:

'Our contract? Have I not performed my part? What more did I promise than to save you from your prison? Have I not done so? Are you not safe from the Inquisition—safe from all but from me? Fool that you were to confide yourself to a Devil! Why did you not stipulate for life, and power, and pleasure? Then all would have been granted: Now, your reflections come too late. Miscreant, prepare for death; You have not many hours to live!'

On hearing this sentence, dreadful were the feelings of the devoted Wretch! He sank upon his knees, and raised his hands towards heaven. The Fiend read his intention and prevented it—

'What?' He cried, darting at him a look of fury: 'Dare you still implore the Eternal's mercy? Would you feign penitence, and again act an Hypocrite's part? Villain, resign your hopes of pardon. Thus I secure my prey!'

As He said this, darting his talons into the Monk's shaven crown, He sprang with him from the rock. The Caves and mountains rang with Ambrosio's shrieks. The Dæmon continued to soar aloft, till reaching a dreadful height, He released the sufferer. Headlong fell the Monk through the airy waste; The sharp point of a rock received him; and He rolled from precipice to precipice, till bruised and mangled He rested on the river's banks. Life still existed in his miserable frame. He attempted in vain to raise himself; His broken and dislocated limbs refused to perform their office, nor was He able to quit the spot where He had first fallen. The Sun now rose above the horizon; Its scorching beams darted full upon the head of the expiring Sinner. Myriads of insects were called forth by the warmth; They drank the blood which trickled from Ambrosio's wounds; He had no power to drive them from him, and they fastened upon his sores, darted their stings into his body, covered him with their multitudes, and inflicted on him tortures the most exquisite and insupportable. The Eagles of the rock tore his flesh piecemeal, and dug out his eye-balls with their crooked beaks. A burning thirst tormented him; He heard the river's murmur as it rolled beside him, but strove in vain to drag himself towards the sound. Blind, maimed, helpless, and despairing, venting his rage in blasphemy and curses, execrating his existence, yet dreading the arrival of death destined to yield him up to greater torments, six miserable days did the Villain languish. On the Seventh a violent storm arose: The winds in fury rent up rocks and forests: The sky was now black with clouds, now sheeted with fire: The rain fell in torrents; It swelled the stream; The waves over-flowed their banks; They reached the spot where Ambrosio lay, and when they abated carried with them into the river the Corse of the despairing Monk.

MARY SHELLEY

Frankenstein

A CHRONOLOGY OF MARY SHELLEY

1797   (30 August) Mary Wollstonecraft Godwin born at The Polygon, Somers Town, daughter of William Godwin and Mary Wollstonecraft, who dies ten days later

1807   Godwin family move to Skinner Street, Holborn

1812   (June) Goes to stay with the Baxter family at Dundee. Beginning of friendship between Godwin and Percy Bysshe Shelley

1814   (May) Returns to Skinner Street; meets Shelley again
        (28 July) Mary, accompanied by her step-sister, Claire Clairmont, elopes with Shelley. Travel through France and Switzerland, and return to England (August–September)

1815   (February) A daughter born prematurely to Mary and Shelley, but dies a few days later
        (August) Settled with Shelley at Bishops Gate, Windsor

1816   (January) A son, William, born
        (May) Mary and Shelley, with Claire Clairmont, leave England for Geneva, where they meet Lord Byron (who has already formed a liaison with Claire) and his physician Dr Polidori
        (June) Mary, Shelley, and Claire settle at the Maison Chapuis, at Montalègre, close to Byron at the Villa Diodati at Cologny, near Geneva. *Frankenstein* begun
        (July) Expedition to Chamonix and the Mer de Glace
        (September) Return to England
        (October) Suicide of Fanny Imlay, Mary's half-sister
        (December) Suicide of Shelley's first wife, Harriet. Mary and Shelley married at St Mildred's Church, Bread Street, London (30 December)

1817   (March) Move to Marlow. Shelley refused custody of his children by his first marriage
        (May) *Frankenstein* completed
        (September) Daughter Clara born
        History of a Six-Weeks' Tour published

1818   (March) Mary and Shelley, with Claire and the children, leave for Italy. *Frankenstein* published
        (June) Settled for two months at Bagni di Lucca
        (September) Move to Este. The baby Clara dies in Venice. Visits to Byron in Venice
        (November) Journey south to Rome
        (December) Settle in Naples for the winter

1819   (March) Return to Rome, where her son William dies
        (June) Departure for Leghorn
        (September) Move to Florence for approaching confinement
        (November) A son, Percy Florence, born

1820   (January) Move to Pisa and (June) to Leghorn

	(August) Move to Bagni di San Giuliano, near Pisa
	(October) Driven out of San Giuliano by floods, the Shelleys move to Pisa.
1821	(April) Return to Bagni di San Giuliano for the summer
	(October) The Shelleys move to Pisa, with Edward and Jane Williams and with Byron as near neighbour
1822	(May) The Shelleys settle with the Williamses at Casa Magni, near Lerici
	(July) Shelley and Williams sail to Leghorn to meet Leigh Hunt but are lost at sea on the return journey
	(September) Mary joins the Hunts and Byron at Genoa
1823	(February) *Valperga* published
	(August) Returns to London
1824	(June) Shelley's *Posthumous Poems* published, but withdrawn on the insistence of Shelley's father, Sir Timothy
1826	(February) *The Last Man* published
	(September) Percy Florence becomes heir to the Shelley title and estate on the death of Charles Bysshe, Shelley's son by his first wife Harriet
1830	*Perkin Warbeck* published
1832	(September) Percy Florence entered at Harrow
1835	*Lodore* published
1837	*Falkner*, her last novel, published
	(July) Percy Florence entered at Trinity College, Cambridge
1839	Publication of Shelley's *Poetical Works*, with notes partly replacing the unwritten biography
	Publication of Shelley's *Essays and Letters*
1840	(June–November) Continental tour with Percy Florence and friends
1841	(February) Percy Florence graduates
1842–3	Another continental tour
1844	*Rambles in Germany and Italy* published
	(April) Death of Sir Timothy Shelley; Percy Florence succeeds to title and estate
1851	(February) Mary Wollstonecraft Shelley dies at Chester Square, London; buried in Bournemouth churchyard

Frankenstein

or
The Modern Prometheus

Did I request thee, Maker, from my clay
To mould Me man? Did I solicit thee
From darkness to promote me?—
Paradise Lost [X. 743–5]

INTRODUCTION

[1831]

THE Publishers of the Standard Novels, in selecting 'Frankenstein' for one of their series, expressed a wish that I should furnish them with some account of the origin of the story. I am the more willing to comply, because I shall thus give a general answer to the question, so very frequently asked me—'How I, then a young girl, came to think of, and to dilate upon, so very hideous an idea?' It is true that I am very averse to bringing myself forward in print; but as my account will only appear as an appendage to a former production, and as it will be confined to such topics as have connection with my authorship alone, I can scarcely accuse myself of a personal intrusion.

It is not singular that, as the daughter of two persons of distinguished literary celebrity, I should very early in life have thought of writing. As a child I scribbled; and my favourite pastime, during the hours given me for recreation, was to 'write stories.' Still I had a dearer pleasure than this, which was the formation of castles in the air—the indulging in waking dreams—the following up trains of thought, which had for their subject the formation of a succession of imaginary incidents. My dreams were at once more fantastic and agreeable than my writings. In the latter I was a close imitator—rather doing as others had done, than putting down the suggestions of my own mind. What I wrote was intended at least for one other eye—my childhood's companion and friend; but my dreams were all my own; I accounted for them to nobody; they were my refuge when annoyed—my dearest pleasure when free.

I lived principally in the country as a girl, and passed a considerable time in Scotland. I made occasional visits to the more picturesque parts; but my habitual residence was on the blank and dreary northern shores of the Tay, near Dundee. Blank and dreary on retrospection I call them; they were not so to me then. They were the eyry of freedom, and the pleasant region where unheeded I could commune with the creatures of my fancy. I wrote then—but in a most common-place style. It was beneath the trees of the grounds belonging to our house, or on the bleak sides of the woodless mountains near, that my true compositions, the airy flights of my imagination, were born and fostered. I did not make myself the heroine of my tales. Life appeared to me too common-place an affair as regarded myself. I could not figure to myself that romantic woes or wonderful events would ever by my lot; but I was not confined to my own identity, and I could people the hours with creations far more interesting to me at that age, than my own sensations.

After this my life became busier, and reality stood in place of fiction. My husband, however, was, from the first, very anxious that I should prove myself worthy of my parentage, and enrol myself on the page of fame. He was for ever inciting me to obtain literary reputation, which even on my own part I cared for then, though since I have become infinitely indifferent to it. At this time he desired that I should write, not so much with the idea that I could produce any thing worthy of notice, but that he might himself judge how far I possessed the promise of better things hereafter. Still I did nothing. Travelling, and the cares of a family, occupied my time; and study, in the way of reading, or improving my ideas in communication with his far more cultivated mind, was all of literary employment that engaged my attention.

In the summer of 1816, we visited Switzerland, and became the neighbours of Lord Byron. At first we spent our pleasant hours on the lake, or wandering on its shores; and Lord Byron, who was writing the third canto of Childe Harold, was the only one among us who put his thoughts upon paper. These, as he brought them successively to us, clothed in all the light and harmony of poetry, seemed to stamp as divine the glories of heaven and earth, whose influences we partook with him.

But it proved a wet, ungenial summer, and incessant rain often confined us for days to the house. Some volumes of ghost stories, translated from the German into French, fell into our hands. There was the History of the Inconstant Lover, who, when he thought to clasp the bride to whom he had pledged his vows, found himself in the arms of the pale ghost of her whom he had deserted. There was the tale of the sinful founder of his race, whose miserable doom it was to bestow the kiss of death on all the younger sons of his fated house, just when they reached the age of promise. His gigantic, shadowy form, clothed like the ghost in Hamlet, in complete armour, but with the beaver up, was seen at midnight, by the moon's fitful beams, to advance slowly along the gloomy avenue. The shape was lost beneath the shadow of the castle walls; but soon a gate swung back, a step was heard, the door of the chamber opened, and he advanced to the couch of the blooming youths, cradled in healthy sleep. Eternal sorrow sat upon his face as he bent down and kissed the forehead of the boys, who from that hour withered like flowers snapt upon the stalk. I have not seen these stories since then; but their incidents are as fresh in my mind as if I had read them yesterday.

'We will each write a ghost story,' said Lord Byron; and his proposition was acceded to. There were four of us. The noble author began a tale, a fragment of which he printed at the end of his poem of Mazeppa. Shelley, more apt to embody ideas and sentiments in the radiance of brilliant imagery, and in the music of the most melodious verse that adorns our language, than to invent the machinery of a story, commenced one founded on the experiences of his early life. Poor Polidori had some terrible idea about a skull-headed lady, who was so punished for peeping through a key-hole—what to see I forget—something very shocking and wrong of course; but when she was reduced to a worse condition than the renowned Tom of Coventry, he did not know what to do with her, and was obliged to despatch her to the tomb of the Capulets, the only place for which she was fitted. The illustrious poets also, annoyed by the platitude of prose, speedily relinquished their uncongenial task.

I busied myself *to think of a story,*—a story to rival those which had excited us to this task. One which would speak to the mysterious fears of our nature, and awaken thrilling horror—one to make the reader dread to look round, to curdle the blood, and quicken the beatings of the heart. If I did not accomplish these things, my ghost story would be unworthy of its name. I thought and pondered—vainly. I felt that blank incapability of invention which is the greatest misery of authorship, when dull Nothing replies to our anxious invocations. *Have you thought of a story?* I was asked each morning, and each morning I was forced to reply with a mortifying negative.

Every thing must have a beginning, to speak in Sanchean phrase; and that beginning must be linked to something that went before. The Hindoos give the world an elephant to support it, but, they make the elephant stand upon a tortoise. Invention, it must be humbly admitted, does not consist in creating out of void, but out of chaos; the materials must, in the first place, be afforded: it can give form to dark, shapeless substances, but cannot bring into being the substance itself. In all matters of discovery and invention, even of those that appertain to the imagination, we are continually reminded of the story of Columbus and his egg. Invention consists in the capacity of seizing on the capabilities of a subject, and in the power of moulding and fashioning ideas suggested to it.

Many and long were the conversations between Lord Byron and Shelley, to which I was a devout but nearly silent listener. During one of these, various philosophical doctrines were discussed, and among others the nature of the principle of life, and whether there was any probability of its ever being discovered and communicated. They talked of the experiments of Dr Darwin, (I speak not of what the Doctor really did, or said that he did, but, as more to my purpose, of what was then spoken of as having been done by him,) who preserved a piece of vermicelli in a glass case, till by some extraordinary means it began to move with voluntary motion. Not thus, after all, would life be given. Perhaps a corpse would be re-animated; galvanism had given token of such things: perhaps the component parts of a creature might be manufactured, brought together, and endued with vital warmth.

Night waned upon this talk, and even the witching hour had gone by, before we retired to rest. When I placed my head on my pillow, I did not sleep, nor could I be said to think. My imagination, unbidden, possessed and guided me, gifting the successive images that arose in my mind with a vividness far beyond the usual bounds of reverie. I saw—with shut eyes, but acute mental vision,—I saw the pale student of unhallowed arts kneeling beside the thing he had put together. I saw the hideous phantasm of a man stretched out, and then, on the working of some powerful engine, show signs of life, and stir with an uneasy, half vital motion. Frightful must it be; for supremely frightful would be the effect of any human endeavour to mock the stupendous mechanism of the Creator of the world. His success would terrify the artist; he would rush away from his odious handywork, horror-stricken. He would hope that, left to itself, the slight spark of life which he had communicated would fade; that this thing, which had received such imperfect animation, would subside into dead matter; and he might sleep in the belief that the silence of the grave would quench for ever the transient existence of the hideous corpse which he had looked upon as the cradle of life. He sleeps; but he is awakened; he opens his eyes; behold the horrid thing stands at his bedside, opening his curtains, and looking on him with yellow, watery, but speculative eyes.

I opened mine in terror. The idea so possessed my mind, that a thrill of fear ran through me, and I wished to exchange the ghastly image of my fancy for the realities around. I see them still; the very room, the dark *parquet*, the closed shutters, with the moonlight struggling through, and the sense I had that the glassy lake and white high Alps were beyond. I could not so easily get rid of my hideous phantom; still it haunted me. I must try to think of something else. I recurred to my ghost story,—my tiresome unlucky ghost story! O! if I could only contrive one which would frighten my reader as I myself had been frightened that night!

Swift as light and as cheering was the idea that broke in upon me. 'I have found it! What terrified me will terrify others; and I need only describe the spectre which had haunted my midnight pillow.' On the morrow I announced that I had *thought of a story*. I began that day with the words, *It was on a dreary night of November*, making only a transcript of the grim terrors of my waking dream.

At first I thought but of a few pages—of a short tale; but Shelley urged me to develope the idea at greater length. I certainly did not owe the suggestion of one incident, nor scarcely of one train of feeling, to my husband, and yet but for his incitement, it would never have taken the form in which it was presented to the world. From this declaration I must except the preface. As far as I can recollect, it was entirely written by him.

And now, once again, I bid my hideous progeny go forth and prosper. I have an affection for it, for it was the offspring of happy days, when death and grief were but words, which found no true echo in my heart. Its several pages speak of many a walk, many a drive, and many a conversation, when I was not alone; and my companion was one who, in this world, I shall never see more. But this is for myself; my readers have nothing to do with these associations.

I will add but one word as to the alterations I have made. They are principally those of style. I have changed no portion of the story, nor introduced any new ideas or circumstances. I have mended the language where it was so bald as to interfere with the interest of the narrative; and these changes occur almost exclusively in the beginning of the first volume. Throughout they are entirely confined to such parts as are mere adjuncts to the story, leaving the core and substance of it untouched.

M.W.S.

London, October 15, 1831

PREFACE

[1818]

THE event on which this fiction is founded, has been supposed, by Dr Darwin, and some of the physiological writers of Germany, as not of impossible occurrence. I shall not be supposed as according the remotest degree of serious faith to such an imagination; yet, in assuming it as the basis of a work of fancy. I have not considered myself as merely weaving a series of supernatural terrors. The event on which the interest of the story depends is exempt from the disadvantages of a mere tale of spectres or enchantment. It was recommended by the novelty of the situations which it developes; and, however impossible as a physical fact, affords a point of view to the imagination for the delineating of human passions more comprehensive and commanding than any which the ordinary relations of existing events can yield.

I have thus endeavoured to preserve the truth of the elementary principles of human nature, while I have not scrupled to innovate upon their combinations. The Iliad, the tragic poetry of Greece,—Shakespeare, in the Tempest and Midsummer Night's Dream,—and most especially Milton, in Paradise Lost, conform to this rule; and the most humble novelist, who seeks to confer or receive amusement from his labours, may, without presumption, apply to prose fiction a licence, or rather a rule, from the adoption of which so many exquisite combinations of human feeling have resulted in the highest specimens of poetry.

The circumstance on which my story rests was suggested in casual conversation. It was commenced partly as a source of amusement, and partly as an expedient for exercising any untried resources of mind. Other motives were mingled with these, as the work proceeded. I am by no means indifferent to the manner in which whatever moral tendencies exist in the sentiments or characters it contains shall affect the reader; yet my chief concern in this respect has been limited to the avoiding the enervating effects of the novels of the present day, and to the exhibition of the amiableness of domestic affection, and the excellence of universal virtue. The opinions which naturally spring from the character and situation of the hero are by no means to be conceived as existing always in my own conviction; nor is any inference justly to be drawn from the following pages as prejudicing any philosophical doctrine of whatever kind.

It is a subject also of additional interest to the author, that this story was begun in the majestic region where the scene is principally laid, and in society which cannot cease to be regretted. I passed the summer of 1816 in the environs of Geneva. The season was cold and rainy, and in the evenings we crowded around a blazing wood fire, and occasionally amused ourselves with some German stories of ghosts, which happened to fall into our hands. These tales excited in us a playful desire of imitation. Two other friends (a tale from the pen of one of whom would be far more acceptable to the public than any thing I can ever hope to produce) and myself agreed to write each a story, founded on some supernatural occurence.

The weather, however, suddenly became serene; and my two friends left me on a journey among the Alps, and lost, in the magnificent scenes which they present, all memory of their ghostly visions. The following tale is the only one which has been completed.

Marlow, September, 1817.

FRANKENSTEIN

OR

THE MODERN PROMETHEUS

———

LETTER I

To Mrs Saville, England

St Petersburgh, Dec. 11th, 17—.

YOU will rejoice to hear that no disaster has accompanied the commencement of an enterprise which you have regarded with such evil forebodings.
I arrived here yesterday; and my first task is to assure my dear sister of my
welfare, and increasing confidence in the success of my undertaking.

I am already far north of London; and as I walk in the streets of
Petersburgh, I feel a cold northern breeze play upon my cheeks, which
braces my nerves, and fills me with delight. Do you understand this feeling?
This breeze, which has travelled from the regions towards which I am
advancing, gives me a foretaste of those icy climes. Inspirited by this wind
of promise, my day dreams become more fervent and vivid. I try in vain to
be persuaded that the pole is the seat of frost and desolation; it ever presents
itself to my imagination as the region of beauty and delight. There,
Margaret, the sun is for ever visible; its broad disk just skirting the horizon,
and diffusing a perpetual splendour. There—for with your leave, my sister,
I will put some trust in preceding navigators—there snow and frost are
banished; and, sailing over a calm sea, we may be wafted to a land
surpassing in wonders and in beauty every region hitherto discovered on the
habitable globe. Its productions and features may be without example, as
the phenomena of the heavenly bodies undoubtedly are in those undiscovered solitudes. What may not be expected in a country of eternal light?
I may there discover the wondrous power which attracts the needle; and
may regulate a thousand celestial observations, that require only this voyage
to render their seeming eccentricities consistent for ever. I shall satiate my
ardent curiosity with the sight of a part of the world never before visited,
and may tread a land never before imprinted by the foot of man. These are
my enticements, and they are sufficient to conquer all fear of danger or
death, and to induce me to commence this laborious voyage with the joy a

child feels when he embarks in a little boat, with his holiday mates, on an expedition of discovery up his native river. But, supposing all these conjectures to be false, you cannot contest the inestimable benefit which I shall confer on all mankind to the last generation, by discovering a passage near the pole to those countries, to reach which at present so many months are requisite; or by ascertaining the secret of the magnet, which, if at all possible, can only be effected by an undertaking such as mine.

These reflections have dispelled the agitation with which I began my letter, and I feel my heart glow with an enthusiasm which elevates me to heaven; for nothing contributes so much to tranquillise the mind as a steady purpose,—a point on which the soul may fix its intellectual eye. This expedition has been the favourite dream of my early years. I have read with ardour the accounts of the various voyages which have been made in the prospect of arriving at the North Pacific Ocean through the seas which surround the pole. You may remember, that a history of all the voyages made for purposes of discovery composed the whole of our good uncle Thomas's library. My education was neglected, yet I was passionately fond of reading. These volumes were my study day and night, and my familiarity with them increased that regret which I had felt, as a child, on learning that my father's dying injunction had forbidden my uncle to allow me to embark in a seafaring life.

These visions faded when I perused, for the first time, those poets whose effusions entranced my soul, and lifted it to heaven. I also became a poet, and for one year lived in a Paradise of my own creation; I imagined that I also might obtain a niche in the temple where the names of Homer and Shakespeare are consecrated. You are well acquainted with my failure, and how heavily I bore the disappointment. But just at that time I inherited the fortune of my cousin, and my thoughts were turned into the channel of their earlier bent.

Six years have passed since I resolved on my present undertaking. I can, even now, remember the hour from which I dedicated myself to this great enterprise. I commenced by inuring my body to hardship. I accompanied the whale-fishers on several expeditions to the North Sea; I voluntarily endured cold, famine, thirst, and want of sleep; I often worked harder than the common sailors during the day, and devoted my nights to the study of mathematics, the theory of medicine, and those branches of physical science from which a naval adventurer might derive the greatest practical advantage. Twice I actually hired myself as an under-mate in a Greenland whaler, and acquitted myself to admiration. I must own I felt a little proud, when my captain offered me the second dignity in the vessel, and entreated me to remain with the greatest earnestness; so valuable did he consider my services.

And now, dear Margaret, do I not deserve to accomplish some great purpose? My life might have been passed in ease and luxury; but I preferred glory to every enticement that wealth placed in my path. Oh, that some encouraging voice would answer in the affirmative! My courage and my resolution is firm; but my hopes fluctuate, and my spirits are often depressed. I am about to proceed on a long and difficult voyage, the emergencies of which will demand all my fortitude: I am required not only to raise the spirits of others, but sometimes to sustain my own, when theirs are failing.

This is the most favourable period for travelling in Russia. They fly quickly over the snow in their sledges; the motion is pleasant, and, in my opinion, far more agreeable than that of an English stage-coach. The cold is not excessive, if you are wrapped in furs,—a dress which I have already adopted; for there is a great difference between walking the deck and remaining seated motionless for hours, when no exercise prevents the blood from actually freezing in your veins. I have no ambition to lose my life on the post-road between St Petersburgh and Archangel.

I shall depart for the latter town in a fortnight or three weeks; and my intention is to hire a ship there, which can easily be done by paying the insurance for the owner, and to engage as many sailors as I think necessary among those who are accustomed to the whale-fishing. I do not intend to sail until the month of June; and when shall I return? Ah, dear sister, how can I answer this question? If I succeed, many, many months, perhaps years, will pass before you and I may meet. If I fail, you will see me again soon, or never.

Farewell, my dear, excellent Margaret. Heaven shower down blessings on you, and save me, that I may again and again testify my gratitude for all your love and kindness.

Your affectionate brother,
R. WALTON.

LETTER II

To Mrs Saville, England

Archangel, 28th March, 17—.

HOW slowly the time passes here, encompassed as I am by frost and snow! yet a second step is taken towards my enterprise. I have hired a vessel, and am occupied in collecting my sailors; those whom I have already engaged appear to be men on whom I can depend, and are certainly possessed of dauntless courage.

But I have one want which I have never yet been able to satisfy; and the absence of the object of which I now feel as a most severe evil. I have no friend, Margaret: when I am glowing with the enthusiasm of success, there will be none to participate my joy; if I am assailed by disappointment, no one will endeavour to sustain me in dejection. I shall commit my thoughts to paper, it is true; but that is a poor medium for the communication of feeling. I desire the company of a man who could sympathise with me; whose eyes would reply to mine. You may deem me romantic, my dear sister, but I bitterly feel the want of a friend. I have no one near me, gentle yet courageous, possessed of a cultivated as well as of a capacious mind, whose tastes are like my own, to approve or amend my plans. How would such a friend repair the faults of your poor brother! I am too ardent in execution, and too impatient of difficulties. But it is a still greater evil to me that I am self-educated: for the first fourteen years of my life I ran wild on a common, and read nothing but our uncle Thomas's books of voyages. At that age I became acquainted with the celebrated poets of our own country; but it was only when it had ceased to be in my power to derive its most important benefits from such a conviction, that I perceived the necessity of becoming acquainted with more languages than that of my native country. Now I am twenty-eight, and am in reality more illiterate than many schoolboys of fifteen. It is true that I have thought more, and that my day dreams are more extended and magnificent; but they want (as the painters call it) *keeping*; and I greatly need a friend who would have sense enough not to despise me as romantic, and affection enough for me to endeavour to regulate my mind.

Well, these are useless complaints; I shall certainly find no friend on the wide ocean, nor even here in Archangel, among merchants and seamen. Yet some feelings, unallied to the dross of human nature, beat even in these rugged bosoms. My lieutenant, for instance, is a man of wonderful courage and enterprise; he is madly desirous of glory: or rather, to word my phrase more characteristically, of advancement in his profession. He is an Englishman, and in the midst of national and professional prejudices, unsoftened by cultivation, retains some of the noblest endowments of humanity. I first became acquainted with him on board a whale vessel: finding that he was unemployed in this city, I easily engaged him to assist in my enterprise.

The master is a person of an excellent disposition, and is remarkable in the ship for his gentleness and the mildness of his discipline. This circumstance, added to his well known integrity and dauntless courage, made me very desirous to engage him. A youth passed in solitude, my best years spent under your gentle and feminine fosterage, has so refined the groundwork of my character, that I cannot overcome an intense distaste to the usual brutality exercised on board ship: I have never believed it to be necessary; and when I heard of a mariner equally noted for his kindliness of heart, and the respect and obedience paid to him by his crew, I felt myself peculiarly fortunate in being able to secure his services. I heard of him first in rather a romantic manner, from a lady who owes to him the happiness of her life.

This, briefly, is his story. Some years ago, he loved a young Russian lady, of moderate fortune; and having amassed a considerable sum in prize-money, the father of the girl consented to the match. He saw his mistress once before the destined ceremony; but she was bathed in tears, and, throwing herself at his feet, entreated him to spare her, confessing at the same time that she loved another, but that he was poor, and that her father would never consent to the union. My generous friend reassured the suppliant, and on being informed of the name of her lover, instantly abandoned his pursuit. He had already bought a farm with his money, on which he had designed to pass the remainder of his life; but he bestowed the whole on his rival, together with the remains of his prize-money to purchase stock, and then himself solicited the young woman's father to consent to her marriage with her lover. But the old man decidedly refused, thinking himself bound in honour to my friend; who, when he found the father inexorable, quitted his country, nor returned until he heard that his former mistress was married according to her inclinations. 'What a noble fellow!' you will exclaim. He is so; but then he is wholly uneducated: he is as silent as a Turk, and a kind of ignorant carelessness attends him, which, while it renders his conduct the more astonishing, detracts from the interest and sympathy which otherwise he would command.

Yet do not suppose, because I complain a little, or because I can conceive a consolation for my toils which I may never know, that I am wavering in my resolutions. Those are as fixed as fate; and my voyage is only now delayed until the weather shall permit my embarkation. The winter has been dreadfully severe; but the spring promises well, and it is considered as a remarkably early season; so that perhaps I may sail sooner than I expected. I shall do nothing rashly: you know me sufficiently to confide in my prudence and considerateness, whenever the safety of others is committed to my care.

I cannot describe to you my sensations on the near prospect of my undertaking. It is impossible to communicate to you a conception of the trembling sensation, half pleasurable and half fearful, with which I am preparing to depart. I am going to unexplored regions, to 'the land of mist and snow;' but I shall kill no albatross, therefore do not be alarmed for my safety, or if I should come back to you as worn and woful as the 'Ancient Mariner?' You will smile at my allusion; but I will disclose a secret. I have often attributed my attachment to, my passionate enthusiasm for, the dangerous mysteries of ocean, to that production of the most imaginative of modern poets. There is something at work in my soul, which I do not understand. I am practically industrious—pains-taking;—a workman to execute with perseverance and labour:—but besides this, there is a love for the marvellous, a belief in the marvellous, intertwined in all my projects, which hurries me out of the common pathways of men, even to the wild sea and unvisited regions I am about to explore.

But to return to dearer considerations. Shall I meet you again, after having traversed immense seas, and returned by the most southern cape of Africa or America? I dare not expect such success, yet I cannot bear to look on the reverse of the picture. Continue for the present to write to me by every opportunity: I may receive your letters on some occasions when I need them most to support my spirits. I love you very tenderly. Remember me with affection, should you never hear from me again.

Your affectionate brother,
ROBERT WALTON.

LETTER III

To Mrs Saville, England

MY DEAR SISTER,   July 7th, 17—.

I write a few lines in haste, to say that I am safe, and well advanced on my voyage. This letter will reach England by a merchantman now on its homeward voyage from Archangel; more fortunate than I, who may not see my native land, perhaps, for many years. I am, however, in good spirits: my men are bold, and apparently firm of purpose; nor do the floating sheets of ice that continually pass us, indicating the dangers of the region towards which we are advancing, appear to dismay them. We have already reached a very high latitude; but it is the height of summer, and although not so warm as in England, the southern gales, which blow us speedily towards those shores which I so ardently desire to attain, breathe a degree of renovating warmth which I had not expected.

No incidents have hitherto befallen us that would make a figure in a letter. One or two stiff gales, and the springing of a leak, are accidents which experienced navigators scarcely remember to record; and I shall be well content if nothing worse happen to us during our voyage.

Adieu, my dear Margaret. Be assured, that for my own sake, as well as yours, I will not rashly encounter danger. I will be cool, persevering, and prudent.

But success *shall* crown my endeavours. Wherefore not? Thus far I have gone, tracing a secure way over the pathless seas: the very stars themselves being witnesses and testimonies of my triumph. Why not still proceed over the untamed yet obedient element? What can stop the determined heart and resolved will of man?

My swelling heart involuntarily pours itself out thus. But I must finish. Heaven bless my beloved sister!

R.W.

LETTER IV

To Mrs Saville, England

August 5th, 17—.

SO strange an accident has happened to us, that I cannot forbear recording it, although it is very probable that you will see me before these papers can come into your possession.

Last Monday (July 31st), we were nearly surrounded by ice, which closed in the ship on all sides, scarcely leaving her the sea-room in which she floated. Our situation was somewhat dangerous, especially as we were compassed round by a very thick fog. We accordingly lay to, hoping that some change would take place in the atmosphere and weather.

About two o'clock the mist cleared away, and we beheld, stretched out in every direction, vast and irregular plains of ice, which seemed to have no end. Some of my comrades groaned, and my own mind began to grow watchful with anxious thoughts, when a strange sight suddenly attracted our attention, and diverted our solicitude from our own situation. We perceived a low carriage, fixed on a sledge and drawn by dogs, pass on towards the north, at the distance of half a mile: a being which had the shape of a man, but apparently of gigantic stature, sat in the sledge, and guided the dogs. We watched the rapid progress of the traveller with our telescopes, until he was lost among the distant inequalities of the ice.

This appearance excited our unqualified wonder. We were, as we believed, many hundred miles from any land; but this apparition seemed to denote that it was not, in reality, so distant as we had supposed. Shut in, however, by ice, it was impossible to follow his track, which we had observed with the greatest attention.

About two hours after this occurrence, we heard the ground sea; and before night the ice broke, and freed our ship. We, however, lay to until the morning, fearing to encounter in the dark those large loose masses which float about after the breaking up of the ice. I profited of this time to rest for a few hours.

In the morning, however, as soon as it was light, I went upon deck, and found all the sailors busy on one side of the vessel, apparently talking to some one in the sea. It was, in fact, a sledge, like that we had seen before, which had drifted towards us in the night, on a large fragment of ice. Only one dog remained alive; but there was a human being within it, whom the sailors were persuading to enter the vessel. He was not, as the other traveller seemed to be, a savage inhabitant of some undiscovered island, but an European. When I appeared on deck, the master said, 'Here is our captain, and he will not allow you to perish on the open sea.'

On perceiving me, the stranger addressed me in English, although with a foreign accent. 'Before I come on board your vessel,' said he, 'will you have the kindness to inform me whither you are bound?'

You may conceive my astonishment on hearing such a question addressed to me from a man on the brink of destruction, and to whom I should have supposed that my vessel would have been a resource which he would not have exchanged for the most precious wealth the earth can afford. I replied, however, that we were on a voyage of discovery towards the northern pole.

Upon hearing this he appeared satisfied, and consented to come on board. Good God! Margaret, if you had seen the man who thus capitulated for his safety, your surprise would have been boundless. His limbs were nearly frozen, and his body dreadfully emaciated by fatigue and suffering. I never saw a man in so wretched a condition. We attempted to carry him into the cabin; but as soon as he had quitted the fresh air, he fainted. We accordingly brought him back to the deck, and restored him to animation by rubbing him with brandy, and forcing him to swallow a small quantity. As soon as he showed signs of life we wrapped him up in blankets, and placed him near the chimney of the kitchen stove. By slow degrees he recovered, and ate a little soup, which restored him wonderfully.

Two days passed in this manner before he was able to speak; and I often feared that his suffering had deprived him of understanding. When he had in some measure recovered, I removed him to my own cabin, and attended on him as much as my duty would permit. I never saw a more interesting creature: his eyes have generally an expression of wildness, and even madness; but there are moments when, if any one performs an act of kindness towards him, or does him any the most trifling service, his whole countenance is lighted up, as it were, with a beam of benevolence and sweetness that I never saw equalled. But he is generally melancholy and despairing; and sometimes he gnashes his teeth, as if impatient of the weight of woes that oppresses him.

When my guest was a little recovered, I had great trouble to keep off the men, who wished to ask him a thousand questions; but I would not allow him to be tormented by their idle curiosity, in a state of body and mind whose restoration evidently depended upon entire repose. Once, however, the lieutenant asked, Why he had come so far upon the ice in so strange a vehicle?

His countenance instantly assumed an aspect of the deepest gloom; and he replied, 'To seek one who fled from me.'

'And did the man whom you pursued travel in the same fashion?'

'Yes.'

'Then I fancy we have seen him; for the day before we picked you up, we saw some dogs drawing a sledge, with a man in it, across the ice.'

This aroused the stranger's attention; and he asked a multitude of questions concerning the route which the dæmon, as he called him, had pursued. Soon after, when he was alone with me, he said,—'I have, doubtless, excited your curiosity, as well as that of these good people; but you are too considerate to make enquiries.'

'Certainly; it would indeed be very impertinent and inhuman in me to trouble you with any inquisitiveness of mine.'

'And yet you rescued me from a strange and perilous situation; you have benevolently restored me to life.'

Soon after this he enquired if I thought that the breaking up of the ice had destroyed the other sledge? I replied, that I could not answer with any degree of certainty; for the ice had not broken until near midnight, and the traveller might have arrived at a place of safety before that time; but of this I could not judge.

From this time a new spirit of life animated the decaying frame of the stranger. He manifested the greatest eagerness to be upon deck, to watch for the sledge which had before appeared; but I have persuaded him to remain in the cabin, for he is far too weak to sustain the rawness of the atmosphere. I have promised that some one should watch for him, and give him instant notice if any new object should appear in sight.

Such is my journal of what relates to this strange occurrence up to the present day. The stranger has gradually improved in health, but is very silent, and appears uneasy when any one except myself enters his cabin. Yet his manners are so conciliating and gentle, that the sailors are all interested in him, although they have had very little communication with him. For my own part, I begin to love him as a brother; and his constant and deep grief fills me with sympathy and compassion. He must have been a noble creature in his better days, being even now in wreck so attractive and amiable.

I said in one of my letters, my dear Margaret, that I should find no friend on the wide ocean; yet I have found a man who, before his spirit had been broken by misery, I should have been happy to have possessed as the brother of my heart.

I shall continue my journal concerning the stranger at intervals, should I have any fresh incidents to record.

August 13th, 17—.

My affection for my guest increases every day. He excites at once my admiration and my pity to an astonishing degree. How can I see so noble a creature destroyed by misery, without feeling the most poignant grief? He is so gentle, yet so wise; his mind is so cultivated; and when he speaks, although his words are culled with the choicest art, yet they flow with rapidity and unparalleled eloquence.

He is now much recovered from his illness, and is continually on the deck, apparently watching for the sledge that preceded his own. Yet, although unhappy, he is not so utterly occupied by his own misery, but that he interests himself deeply in the projects of others. He has frequently conversed with me on mine, which I have communicated to him without disguise. He entered attentively into all my arguments in favour of my eventual success, and into every minute detail of the measures I had taken to secure it. I was easily led by the sympathy which he evinced, to use the language of my heart; to give utterance to the burning ardour of my soul; and to say, with all the fervour that warmed me, how gladly I would sacrifice my fortune, my existence, my every hope, to the furtherance of my enterprise. One man's life or death were but a small price to pay for the acquirement of the knowledge which I sought; for the dominion I should acquire and transmit over the elemental foes of our race. As I spoke, a dark gloom spread over my listener's countenance. At first I perceived that he tried to suppress his emotion; he placed his hands before his eyes; and my voice quivered and failed me, as I beheld tears trickle fast from between his fingers,—a groan burst from his heaving breast. I paused;—at length he spoke, in broken accents:—'Unhappy man! Do you share my madness? Have you drank also of the intoxicating draught? Hear me,—let me reveal my tale, and you will dash the cup from your lips!'

Such words, you may imagine, strongly excited my curiosity; but the paroxysm of grief that had seized the stranger overcame his weakened powers, and many hours of repose and tranquil conversation were necessary to restore his composure.

Having conquered the violence of his feelings, he appeared to despise himself for being the slave of passion; and quelling the dark tyranny of despair, he led me again to converse concerning myself personally. He asked me the history of my earlier years. The tale was quickly told: but it awakened various trains of reflection. I spoke of my desire of finding a friend—of my thirst for a more intimate sympathy with a fellow mind than had ever fallen to my lot; and expressed my conviction that a man could boast of little happiness, who did not enjoy this blessing.

'I agree with you,' replied the stranger; 'we are unfashioned creatures, but half made up, if one wiser, better, dearer than ourselves—such a friend ought to be—do not lend his aid to perfectionate our weak and faulty natures. I once had a friend, the most noble of human creatures, and am entitled, therefore, to judge respecting friendship. You have hope, and the world before you, and have no cause for despair. But I—I have lost every thing, and cannot begin life anew.'

As he said this, his countenance became expressive of a calm settled grief, that touched me to the heart. But he was silent, and presently retired to his cabin.

Even broken in spirit as he is, no one can feel more deeply than he does the beauties of nature. The starry sky, the sea, and every sight afforded by these wonderful regions, seems still to have the power of elevating his soul from earth. Such a man has a double existence: he may suffer misery, and be overwhelmed by disappointments; yet, when he has retired into himself, he will be like a celestial spirit, that has a halo around him, within whose circle no grief or folly ventures.

Will you smile at the enthusiasm I express concerning this divine wanderer? You would not, if you saw him. You have been tutored and refined by books and retirement from the world, and you are, therefore, somewhat fastidious; but this only renders you the more fit to appreciate the extraordinary merits of this wonderful man. Sometimes I have endeavoured to discover what quality it is which he possesses, that elevates him so immeasurably above any other person I ever knew. I believe it to be an intuitive discernment; a quick but never-failing power of judgment; a penetration into the causes of things, unequalled for clearness and precision; add to this a facility of expression, and a voice whose varied intonations are soul-subduing music.

August 19. 17——.

Yesterday the stranger said to me, 'You may easily perceive, Captain Walton, that I have suffered great and unparalleled misfortunes. I had determined, at one time, that the memory of these evils should die with me; but you have won me to alter my determination. You seek for knowledge and wisdom, as I once did; and I ardently hope that the gratification of your wishes may not be a serpent to sting you, as mine has been. I do not know that the relation of my disasters will be useful to you; yet, when I reflect that you are pursuing the same course, exposing yourself to the same dangers which have rendered me what I am, I imagine that you may deduce an apt moral from my tale; one that may direct you if you succeed in your undertaking, and console you in case of failure. Prepare to hear of occurrences which are usually deemed marvellous. Were we among the tamer scenes of nature, I might fear to encounter your unbelief, perhaps your ridicule; but many things will appear possible in these wild and mysterious regions, which would provoke the laughter of those unacquainted with the ever-varied powers of nature:—nor can I doubt but that my tale conveys in its series internal evidence of the truth of the events of which it is composed.'

You may easily imagine that I was much gratified by the offered communication; yet I could not endure that he should renew his grief by a recital of his misfortunes. I felt the greatest eagerness to hear the promised narrative, partly from curiosity, and partly from a strong desire to ameliorate his fate, if it were in my power. I expressed these feelings in my answer.

'I thank you,' he replied, 'for your sympathy, but it is useless; my fate is nearly fulfilled. I wait but for one event, and then I shall repose in peace. I understand your feeling,' continued he, perceiving that I wished to interrupt him; 'but you are mistaken, my friend, if thus you will allow me to name you; nothing can alter my destiny: listen to my history, and you will perceive how irrevocably it is determined.'

He then told me, that he would commence his narrative the next day when I should be at leisure. This promise drew from me the warmest thanks. I have resolved every night, when I am not imperatively occupied by my duties, to record, as nearly as possible in his own words, what he has related during the day. If I should be engaged, I will at least make notes. This manuscript will doubtless afford you the greatest pleasure: but to me, who know him, and who hear it from his own lips, with what interest and sympathy shall I read it in some future day! Even now, as I commence my task, his full-toned voice swells in my ears; his lustrous eyes dwell on me with all their melancholy sweetness; I see his thin hand raised in animation, while the lineaments of his face are irradiated by the soul within. Strange and harrowing must be his story; frightful the storm which embraced the gallant vessel on its course, and wrecked it—thus!

CHAPTER I

I AM by birth a Genevese; and my family is one of the most distinguished of that republic. My ancestors had been for many years counsellors and syndics; and my father had filled several public situations with honour and reputation. He was respected by all who knew him, for his integrity and indefatigable attention to public business. He passed his younger days perpetually occupied by the affairs of his country; a variety of circumstances had prevented his marrying early, nor was it until the decline of life that he became a husband and the father of a family.

As the circumstances of his marriage illustrate his character, I cannot refrain from relating them. One of his most intimate friends was a merchant, who, from a flourishing state, fell, through numerous mischances, into poverty. This man, whose name was Beaufort, was of a proud and unbending disposition, and could not bear to live in poverty and oblivion in the same country where he had formerly been distinguished for his rank and magnificence. Having paid his debts, therefore, in the most honourable manner, he retreated with his daughter to the town of Lucerne, where he lived unknown and in wretchedness. My father loved Beaufort with the truest friendship, and was deeply grieved by his retreat in these unfortunate circumstances. He bitterly deplored the false pride which led his friend to a conduct so little worthy of the affection that united them. He lost no time in endeavouring to seek him out, with the hope of persuading him to begin the world again through his credit and assistance.

Beaufort had taken effectual measures to conceal himself; and it was ten months before my father discovered his abode. Overjoyed at this discovery, he hastened to the house, which was situated in a mean street, near the Reuss. But when he entered, misery and despair alone welcomed him. Beaufort had saved but a very small sum of money from the wreck of his fortunes; but it was sufficient to provide him with sustenance for some months, and in the mean time he hoped to procure some respectable employment in a merchant's house. The interval was, consequently, spent in inaction; his grief only became more deep and rankling, when he had leisure for reflection; and at length it took so fast hold of his mind, that at the end of three months he lay on a bed of sickness, incapable of any exertion.

His daughter attended him with the greatest tenderness; but she saw with despair that their little fund was rapidly decreasing, and that there was no other prospect of support. But Caroline Beaufort possessed a mind of an uncommon mould; and her courage rose to support her in her adversity. She procured plain work; she plaited straw; and by various means contrived to earn a pittance scarcely sufficient to support life.

Several months passed in this manner. Her father grew worse; her time was more entirely occupied in attending him; her means of subsistence decreased; and in the tenth month her father died in her arms, leaving her an orphan and a beggar. This last blow overcame her; and she knelt by Beaufort's coffin, weeping bitterly, when my father entered the chamber. He came like a protecting spirit to the poor girl, who committed herself to his care; and after the interment of his friend, he conducted her to Geneva, and placed her under the protection of a relation. Two years after this event Caroline became his wife.

There was a considerable difference between the ages of my parents, but this circumstance seemed to unite them only closer in bonds of devoted affection. There was a sense of justice in my father's upright mind, which rendered it necessary that he should approve highly to love strongly. Perhaps during former years he had suffered from the late-discovered unworthiness of one beloved, and so was disposed to set a greater value on tried worth. There was a show of gratitude and worship in his attachment to my mother, differing wholly from the doating fondness of age, for it was inspired by reverence for her virtues, and a desire to be the means of, in some degree, recompensing her for the sorrows she had endured, but which gave inexpressible grace to his behaviour to her. Every thing was made to yield to her wishes and her convenience. He strove to shelter her, as a fair exotic is sheltered by the gardener, from every rougher wind, and to surround her with all that could tend to excite pleasurable emotion in her soft and benevolent mind. Her health, and even the tranquillity of her hitherto constant spirit, had been shaken by what she had gone through. During the two years that had elapsed previous to their marriage my father had gradually relinquished all his public functions; and immediately after their union they sought the pleasant climate of Italy, and the change of scene and interest attendant on a tour through that land of wonders, as a restorative for her weakened frame.

From Italy they visited Germany and France. I, their eldest child, was born at Naples, and as an infant accompanied them in their rambles. I remained for several years their only child. Much as they were attached to each other, they seemed to draw inexhaustible stores of affection from a very mine of love to bestow them upon me. My mother's tender caresses, and my father's smile of benevolent pleasure while regarding me, are my first recollections. I was their plaything and their idol, and something better— their child, the innocent and helpless creature bestowed on them by Heaven, whom to bring up to good, and whose future lot it was in their hands to direct to happiness or misery, according as they fulfilled their duties towards me. With this deep consciousness of what they owed towards the being to which they had given life, added to the active spirit of tenderness that animated both, it may be imagined that while during every hour of my infant life I received a lesson of patience, of charity, and of self-control, I was so guided by a silken cord, that all seemed but one train of enjoyment to me.

For a long time I was their only care. My mother had much desired to have a daughter, but I continued their single offspring. When I was about five years old, while making an excursion beyond the frontiers of Italy, they passed a week on the shores of the Lake of Como. Their benevolent disposition often made them enter the cottages of the poor. This, to my mother, was more than a duty; it was a necessity, a passion,—remembering what she had suffered, and how she had been relieved,—for her to act in her turn the guardian angel to the afflicted. During one of their walks a poor cot in the foldings of a vale attracted their notice, as being singularly disconsolate, while the number of half-clothed children gathered about it, spoke of penury in its worst shape. One day, when my father had gone by himself to Milan, my mother, accompanied by me, visited this abode. She found a peasant and his wife, hard working, bent down by care and labour, distributing a scanty meal to five hungry babes. Among these there was one which attracted my mother far above all the rest. She appeared of a different stock. The four others were dark-eyed, hardly little vagrants; this child was thin, and very fair. Her hair was the brightest living gold, and, despite the poverty of her clothing, seemed to set a crown of distinction on her head. Her brow was clear and ample, her blue eyes cloudless, and her lips and the moulding of her face so expressive of sensibility and sweetness, that none could behold her without looking on her as of a distinct species, a being heaven-sent, and bearing a celestial stamp in all her features.

The peasant woman, perceiving that my mother fixed eyes of wonder and admiration on this lovely girl, eagerly communicated her history. She was not her child, but the daughter of a Milanese nobleman. Her mother was a German, and had died on giving her birth. The infant had been placed with these good people to nurse: they were better off then. They had not been long married, and their eldest child was but just born. The father of their charge was one of those Italians nursed in the memory of the antique glory of Italy,—one among the *schiavi ognor frementi*, who exerted himself to obtain the liberty of his country. He became the victim of its weakness. Whether he had died, or still lingered in the dungeons of Austria, was not known. His property was confiscated, his child became an orphan and a beggar. She continued with her foster parents, and bloomed in their rude abode, fairer than a garden rose among dark-leaved brambles.

When my father returned from Milan, he found playing with me in the hall of our villa, a child fairer than pictured cherub—a creature who seemed to shed radiance from her looks, and whose form and motions were lighter than the chamois of the hills. The apparition was soon explained. With his permission my mother prevailed on her rustic guardians to yield their charge to her. They were fond of the sweet orphan. Her presence had seemed a blessing to them; but it would be unfair to her to keep her in poverty and want, when Providence afforded her such powerful protection. They consulted their village priest, and the result was, that Elizabeth Lavenza became the inmate of my parents' house—my more than sister—the beautiful and adored companion of all my occupations and my pleasures.

Every one loved Elizabeth. The passionate and almost reverential attachment with which all regarded her became, while I shared it, my pride and my delight. On the evening previous to her being brought to my home, my mother had said playfully,—'I have a pretty present for my Victor—to-morrow he shall have it.' And when, on the morrow, she presented Elizabeth to me as her promised gift, I, with childish seriousness, interpreted her words literally, and looked upon Elizabeth as mine—mine to protect, love, and cherish. All praises bestowed on her, I received as made to a possession of my own. We called each other familiarly by the name of cousin. No word, no expression could body forth the kind of relation in which she stood to me—my more than sister, since till death she was to be mine only.

CHAPTER II

WE were brought up together; there was not quite a year difference in our ages. I need not say that we were strangers to any species of disunion or dispute. Harmony was the soul of our companionship, and the diversity and contrast that subsisted in our characters drew us nearer together. Elizabeth was of a calmer and more concentrated disposition; but, with all my ardour, I was capable of a more intense application, and was more deeply smitten with the thirst for knowledge. She busied herself with following the aerial creations of the poets; and in the majestic and wondrous scenes which surrounded our Swiss home—the sublime shapes of the mountains; the changes of the seasons; tempest and calm; the silence of winter, and the life and turbulence of our Alpine summers,—she found ample scope for admiration and delight. While my companion contemplated with a serious and satisfied spirit the magnificent appearances of things, I delighted in investigating their causes. The world was to me a secret which I desired to divine. Curiosity, earnest research to learn the hidden laws of nature, gladness akin to rapture, as they were unfolded to me, are among the earliest sensations I can remember.

On the birth of a second son, my junior by seven years, my parents gave up entirely their wandering life, and fixed themselves in their native country. We possessed a house in Geneva, and a *campagne* on Belrive, the eastern shore of the lake, at the distance of rather more than a league from the city. We resided principally in the latter, and the lives of my parents were passed in considerable seclusion. It was my temper to avoid a crowd, and to attach myself fervently to a few. I was indifferent, therefore, to my schoolfellows in general; but I united myself in the bonds of the closest friendship to one among them. Henry Clerval was the son of a merchant of Geneva. He was a boy of singular talent and fancy. He loved enterprise, hardship, and even danger, for its own sake. He was deeply read in books of chivalry and romance. He composed heroic songs, and began to write many a tale of enchantment and knightly adventure. He tried to make us act plays, and to enter into masquerades, in which the characters were drawn from the heroes of Roncesvalles, of the Round Table of King Arthur, and the chivalrous train who shed their blood to redeem the holy sepulchre from the hands of the infidels.

No human being could have passed a happier childhood than myself. My parents were possessed by the very spirit of kindness and indulgence. We felt that they were not the tyrants to rule our lot according to their caprice, but the agents and creators of all the many delights which we enjoyed. When I mingled with other families, I distinctly discerned how peculiarly fortunate my lot was, and gratitude assisted the development of filial love.

My temper was sometimes violent, and my passions vehement; but by some law in my temperature they were turned, not towards childish pursuits, but to an eager desire to learn, and not to learn all things indiscriminately. I confess that neither the structure of languages, nor the code of governments, nor the politics of various states, possessed attractions for me. It was the secrets of heaven and earth that I desired to learn; and whether it was the outward substance of things, or the inner spirit of nature and the mysterious soul of man that occupied me, still my enquiries were directed to the metaphysical, or, in its highest sense, the physical secrets of the world.

Meanwhile Clerval occupied himself, so to speak, with the moral relations of things. The busy stage of life, the virtues of heroes, and the actions of men, were his theme; and his hope and his dream was to become one among those whose names are recorded in story, as the gallant and adventurous benefactors of our species. The saintly soul of Elizabeth shone like a shrine-dedicated lamp in our peaceful home. Her sympathy was ours; her smile, her soft voice, the sweet glance of her celestial eyes, were ever there to bless and animate us. She was the living spirit of love to soften and attract: I might have become sullen in my study, rough through the ardour of my nature, but that she was there to subdue me to a semblance of her own gentleness. And Clerval—could aught ill entrench on the noble spirit of Clerval?—yet he might not have been so perfectly humane, so thoughtful in his generosity—so full of kindness and tenderness amidst his passion for adventurous exploit, had she not unfolded to him the real loveliness of beneficence, and made the doing good the end and aim of his soaring ambition.

I feel exquisite pleasure in dwelling on the recollections of childhood, before misfortune had tainted my mind, and changed its bright visions of extensive usefulness into gloomy and narrow reflections upon self. Besides, in drawing the picture of my early days, I also record those events which led, by insensible steps, to my after tale of misery: for when I would account to myself for the birth of that passion, which afterwards ruled my destiny, I find it arise, like a mountain river, from ignoble and almost forgotten sources; but, swelling as it proceeded, it became the torrent which, in its course, has swept away all my hopes and joys.

Natural philosophy is the genius that has regulated my fate; I desire, therefore, in this narration, to state those facts which led to my predilection for that science. When I was thirteen years of age, we all went on a party of pleasure to the baths near Thonon; the inclemency of the weather obliged us to remain a day confined to the inn. In this house I chanced to find a volume of the works of Cornelius Agrippa. I opened it with apathy; the theory which he attempts to demonstrate, and the wonderful facts which he relates, soon changed this feeling into enthusiasm. A new light seemed to dawn upon my mind; and, bounding with joy, I communicated my discovery to my father. My fahter looked carelessly at the titlepage of my book, and said, 'Ah! Cornelius Agrippa! My dear Victor, do not waste your time upon this; it is sad trash.'

If, instead of this remark, my father had taken the pains to explain to me, that the principles of Agrippa had been entirely exploded, and that a modern system of science had been introduced, which possessed much greater powers than the ancient, because the powers of the latter were chimerical, while those of the former were real and practical; under such circumstances, I should certainly have thrown Agrippa aside, and have contented my imagination, warmed as it was, by returning with greater ardour to my former studies. It is even possible, that the train of my ideas would never have received the fatal impulse that led to my ruin. But the cursory glance my father had taken of my volume by no means assured me that he was acquainted with its contents; and I continued to read with the greatest avidity.

When I returned home, my first care was to procure the whole works of this author, and afterwards of Paracelsus and Albertus Magnus. I read and studied the wild fancies of these writers with delight; they appeared to me treasures known to few beside myself. I have described myself as always having been embued with a fervent longing to penetrate the secrets of nature. In spite of the intense labour and wonderful discoveries of modern philosophers, I always came from my studies discontented and unsatisfied. Sir Isaac Newton is said to have avowed that he felt like a child picking up shells beside the great and unexplored ocean of truth. Those of his successors in each branch of natural philosophy with whom I was acquainted, appeared even to my boy's apprehensions, as tyros engaged in the same pursuit.

The untaught peasant beheld the elements around him, and was acquainted with their practical uses. The most learned philosopher knew little more. He had partially unveiled the face of Nature, but her immortal lineaments were still a wonder and a mystery. He might dissect, anatomise, and give names; but, not to speak of a final caue, causes in their secondary and tertiary grades were utterly unknown to him. I had gazed upon the fortifications and impediments that seemed to keep human beings from entering the citadel of nature, and rashly and ignorantly I had repined.

But here were books, and here were men who had penetrated deeper and knew more. I took their word for all that they averred, and I became their disciple. It may appear strange that such should arise in the eighteenth century; but while I followed the routine of education in the schools of Geneva, I was, to a great degree, self taught with regard to my favourite studies. My father was not scientific, and I was left to struggle with a child's blindness, added to a student's thirst for knowledge. Under the guidance of my new preceptors, I entered with the greatest diligence into the search of the philosopher's stone and the elixir of life; but the latter soon obtained my undivided attention. Wealth was an inferior object; but what glory would attend the discovery, if I could banish disease from the human frame, and render man invulnerable to any but a violent death!

Nor were these my only visions. The raising of ghosts or devils was a promise liberally accorded by my favourite authors, the fulfilment of which

I most eagerly sought; and if my incantations were always unsuccessful, I attributed the failure rather to my own inexperience and mistake, than to a want of skill or fidelity in my instructors. And thus for a time I was occupied by exploded systems, mingling, like an unadept, a thousand contradictory theories, and floundering desperately in a very slough of multifarious knowledge, guided by an ardent imagination and childish reasoning, till an accident again changed the current of my ideas.

When I was about fifteen years old we had retired to our house near Belrive, when we witnessed a most violent and terrible thunder-storm. It advanced from behind the mountains of Jura; and the thunder burst at once with frightful loudness from various quarters of the heavens. I remained, while the storm lasted, watching its progress with curiosity and delight. As I stood at the door, on a sudden I beheld a stream of fire issue from an old and beautiful oak, which stood about twenty yards from our house; and so soon as the dazzling light vanished, the oak had disappeared, and nothing remained but a blasted stump. When we visited it the next morning, we found the tree shattered in a singular manner. It was not splintered by the shock, but entirely reduced to thin ribands of wood. I never beheld any thing so utterly destroyed.

Before this I was not unacquainted with the more obvious laws of electricity. On this occasion a man of great research in natural philosophy was with us, and, excited by this catastrophe, he entered on the explanation of a theory which he had formed on the subject of electricity and galvanism, which was at once new and astonishing to me. All that he said threw greatly into the shade Cornelius Agrippa, Albertus Magnus, and Paracelsus, the lords of my imagination; but by some fatality the overthrow of these men disinclined me to pursue my accustomed studies. It seemed to me as if nothing would or could ever be known. All that had so long engaged my attention suddenly grew despicable. By one of those caprices of the mind, which we are perhaps most subject to in early youth, I at once gave up my former occupations; set down natural history and all its progeny as a deformed and abortive creation; and entertained the greatest disdain for a would-be science, which could never even step within the threshold of real knowledge. In this mood of mind I betook myself to the mathematics, and the branches of study appertaining to that science, as being built upon secure foundations, and so worthy of my consideration.

Thus strangely are our souls constructed, and by such slight ligaments are we bound to prosperity or ruin. When I look back, it seems to me as if this almost miraculous change of inclination and will was the immediate suggestion of the guardian angel of my life—the last effort made by the spirit of preservation to avert the storm that was even then hanging in the stars, and ready to envelope me. Her victory was announced by an unusual tranquillity and gladness of soul, which followed the relinquishing of my ancient and

latterly tormenting studies. It was thus that I was to be taught to associate
evil with their prosecution, happiness with their disregard.

It was a strong effort of the spirit of good; but it was ineffectual. Destiny
was too potent, and her immutable laws had decreed my utter and terrible
destruction.

CHAPTER III

WHEN I had attained the age of seventeen, my parents resolved that I
should become a student at the university of Ingolstadt. I had hitherto
attended the schools of Geneva; but my father thought it necessary, for the
completion of my education, that I should be made acquainted with other
customs than those of my native country. My departure was therefore fixed
at an early date; but, before the day resolved upon could arrive, the first
misfortune of my life occurred—an omen, as it were, of my future misery.

Elizabeth had caught the scarlet fever; her illness was severe, and she was
in the greatest danger. During her illness, many arguments had been urged
to persuade my mother to refrain from attending upon her. She had, at first,
yielded to our entreaties; but when she heard that the life of her favourite
was menaced, she could no longer control her anxiety. She attended her sick
bed,—her watchful attentions triumphed over the malignity of the distem-
per,—Elizabeth was saved, but the consequences of this imprudence were
fatal to her preserver. On the third day my mother sickened; her fever was
accompanied by the most alarming symptoms, and the looks of her medical
attendants prognosticated the worst event. On her death-bed the fortitude
and benignity of this best of women did not desert her. She joined the hands
of Elizabeth and myself:—'My children,' she said, 'my firmest hopes of
future happiness were placed on the prospect of your union. This expectation will now be the consolation of your father. Elizabeth, my love, you must
supply my place to my younger children. Alas! I regret that I am taken from
you; and, happy and beloved as I have been, is it not hard to quit you all?
But these are not thoughts befitting me; I will endeavour to resign myself
cheerfully to death, and will indulge a hope of meeting you in another
world.'

She died calmly; and her countenance expressed affection even in death.
I need not describe the feelings of those whose dearest ties are rent by that
most irreparable evil; the void that presents itself to the soul; and the despair
that is exhibited on the countenance. It is so long before the mind can
persuade itself that she, whom we saw every day, and whose very existence
appeared a part of our own, can have departed for ever—that the brightness
of a beloved eye can have been extinguished, and the sound of a voice so

familiar, and dear to the ear, can be hushed, never more to be heard. These are the reflections of the first days; but when the lapse of time proves the reality of the evil, then the actual bitterness of grief commences. Yet from whom has not that rude hand rent away some dear connection? and why should I describe a sorrow which all have felt, and must feel? The time at length arrives, when grief is rather an indulgence than a necessity; and the smile that plays upon the lips, although it may be deemed a sacrilege, is not banished. My mother was dead, but we had still duties which we ought to perform; we must continue our course with the rest, and learn to think ourselves fortunate, whilst one remains whom the spoiler has not seized.

My departure for Ingolstadt, which had been deferred by these events, was now again determined upon. I obtained from my father a respite of some weeks. It appeared to me sacrilege so soon to leave the repose, akin to death, of the house of mourning, and to rush into the thick of life. I was new to sorrow, but it did not the less alarm me. I was unwilling to quit the sight of those that remained to me; and, above all, I desired to see my sweet Elizabeth in some degree consoled.

She indeed veiled her grief, and strove to act the comforter to us all. She looked steadily on life, and assumed its duties with courage and zeal. She devoted herself to those whom she had been taught to call her uncle and cousins. Never was she so enchanting as at this time, when she recalled the sunshine of her smiles and spent them upon us. She forgot even her own regret in her endeavours to make us forget.

The day of my departure at length arrived. Clerval spent the last evening with us. He had endeavoured to persuade his father to permit him to accompany me, and to become my fellow student; but in vain. His father was a narrow-minded trader, and saw idleness and ruin in the aspirations and ambition of his son. Henry deeply felt the misfortune of being debarred from a liberal education. He said little; but when he spoke, I read in his kindling eye and in his animated glance a restrained but firm resolve, not to be chained to the miserable details of commerce.

We sat late. We could not tear ourselves away from each other, nor persuade ourselves to say the word 'Farewell!' It was said; and we retired under the pretence of seeking repose, each fancying that the other was deceived: but when at morning's dawn I descended to the carriage which was to convey me away, they were all there—my father again to bless me, Clerval to press my hand once more, my Elizabeth to renew her entreaties that I would write often, and to bestow the last feminine attentions on her playmate and friend.

I threw myself into the chaise that was to convey me away, and indulged in the most melancholy reflections. I, who had ever been surrounded by amiable companions, continually engaged in endeavouring to bestow mutual pleasure, I was now alone. In the university, whither I was going, I must form my own friends, and be my own protector. My life had hitherto been remarkably secluded and domestic; and this had given me invincible repugnance to new countenances. I loved my brothers, Elizabeth, and Clerval; these were 'old familiar faces;' but I believed myself totally unfitted for the company of strangers. Such were my reflections as I commenced my journey; but as I proceeded, my spirits and hopes rose. I ardently desired the acquisition of knowledge. I had often, when at home, thought it hard to remain during my youth cooped up in one place, and had longed to enter the world, and take my station among other human beings. Now my desires were complied with, and it would, indeed, have been folly to repent.

I had sufficient leisure for these and many other reflections during my journey to Ingolstadt, which was long and fatiguing. At length the high white steeple of the town met my eyes. I alighted, and was conducted to my solitary apartment, to spend the evening as I pleased.

The next morning I delivered my letters of introduction, and paid a visit to some of the principal professors. Chance—or rather the evil influence, the Angel of Destruction, which asserted omnipotent sway over me from the moment I turned my reluctant steps from my father's door—led me first to M. Krempe, professor of natural philosophy. He was an uncouth man, but deeply embued in the secrets of his science. He asked me several questions concerning my progress in the different branches of science appertaining to natural philosophy. I replied carelessly; and, partly in contempt, mentioned the names of my alchymists as the principal authors I had studied. The professor stared: 'Have you,' he said, 'really spent your time in studying such nonsense?'

I replied in the affirmative. 'Every minute,' continued M. Krempe with warmth, 'every instant that you have wasted on those books is utterly and entirely lost. You have burdened your memory with exploded systems and useless names. Good God! in what desert land have you lived, where no one was kind enough to inform you that these fancies, which you have so greedily imbibed, are a thousand years old, and as musty as they are ancient? I little expected, in this enlightened and scientific age, to find a disciple of Albertus Magnus and Paracelsus. My dear sir, you must begin your studies entirely anew.'

So saying, he stept aside, and wrote down a list of several books treating of natural philosophy, which he desired me to procure; and dismissed me, after mentioning that in the beginning of the following week he intended to commence a course of lectures upon natural philosophy in its general relations, and that M. Waldman, a fellow-professor, would lecture upon chemistry the alternate days that he omitted.

I returned home, not disappointed, for I have said that I had long considered those authors useless whom the professor reprobated; but I returned, not at all the more inclined to recur to these studies in any shape.

M. Krempe was a little squat man, with a gruff voice and a repulsive countenance; the teacher, therefore, did not prepossess me in favour of his pursuits. In rather a too philosophical and connected a strain, perhaps, I have given an account of the conclusions I had come to concerning them in my early years. As a child, I had not been content with the results promised by the modern professors of natural science. With a confusion of ideas only to be accounted for by my extreme youth, and my want of a guide on such matters, I had retrod the steps of knowledge along the paths of time, and exchanged the discoveries of recent enquirers for the dreams of forgotten alchymists. Besides, I had a contempt for the uses of modern natural philosophy. It was very different, when the masters of the science sought immortality and power; such views, although futile, were grand: but now the scene was changed. The ambition of the enquirer seemed to limit itself to the annihilation of those visions on which my interest in science was chiefly founded. I was required to exchange chimeras of boundless grandeur for realities of little worth.

Such were my reflections during the first two or three days of my residence at Ingolstadt, which were chiefly spent in becoming acquainted with the localities, and the principal residents in my new abode. But as the ensuing week commenced, I thought of the information which M. Krempe had given me concerning the lectures. And although I could not consent to go and hear that little conceited fellow deliver sentences out of a pulpit, I recollected what he had said of M. Waldman, whom I had never seen, as he had hitherto been out of town.

Partly from curiosity, and partly from idleness, I went into the lecturing room, which M. Waldman entered shortly after. This professor was very unlike his colleague. He appeared about fifty years of age, but with an aspect expressive of the greatest benevolence; a few grey hairs covered his temples, but those at the back of his head were nearly black. His person was short, but remarkably erect; and his voice the sweetest I had ever heard. He began his lecture by a recapitulation of the history of chemistry, and the various improvements made by different men of learning, pronouncing with fervour the names of the most distinguished discoverers. He then took a cursory view of the present state of the science, and explained many of its elementary terms. After having made a few preparatory experiments, he concluded with a panegyric upon modern chemistry, the terms of which I shall never forget:—

'The ancient teachers of this science,' said he, 'promised impossibilities, and performed nothing. The modern masters promise very little; they know that metals cannot be transmuted, and that the elixir of life is a chimera. But these philosophers, whose hands seem only made to dabble in dirt, and their eyes to pore over the microscope or crucible, have indeed performed miracles. They penetrate into the recesses of nature, and show how she works in her hiding places. They ascend into the heavens: they have discovered how the blood circulates, and the nature of the air we breathe. They have acquired new and almost unlimited powers; they can command the thunders of heaven, mimic the earthquake, and even mock the invisible world with its own shadows.'

Such were the professor's words—rather let me say such the words of fate, enounced to destroy me. As he went on, I felt as if my soul were grappling with a palpable enemy; one by one the various keys were touched which formed the mechanism of my being: chord after chord was sounded, and soon my mind was filled with one thought, one conception, one purpose. So much has been done, exclaimed the soul of Frankenstein,—more, far more, will I achieve: treading in the steps already marked, I will pioneer a new way, explore unknown powers, and unfold to the world the deepest mysteries of creation.

I closed not my eyes that night. My internal being was in a state of insurrection and turmoil; I felt that order would thence arise, but I had no power to produce it. By degrees, after the morning's dawn, sleep came. I awoke, and my yesternight's thoughts were as a dream. There only remained a resolution to return to my ancient studies, and to devote myself to a science for which I believed myself to possess a natural talent. On the same day, I paid M. Waldman a visit. His manners in private were even more mild and attractive than in public; for there was a certain dignity in his mien during his lecture, which in his own house was replaced by the greatest affability and kindness. I gave him pretty nearly the same account of my former pursuits as I had given to his fellow-professor. He heard with attention the little narration concerning my studies, and smiled at the names of Cornelius Agrippa and Paracelsus, but without the contempt that M. Krempe had exhibited. He said, that 'these were men to whose indefatigable zeal modern philosophers were indebted for most of the foundations of their knowledge. They had left to us, as an easier task, to give new names, and arrange in connected classifications, the facts which they in a great degree had been the instruments of bringing to light. The labours of men of genius, however erroneously directed, scarcely ever fail in ultimately turning to the solid advantage of mankind.' I listened to his statement, which was delivered without any presumption or affectation; and then added, that his lecture had removed my prejudices against modern chemists; I expressed myself in measured terms, with the modesty and deference due from a youth to his instructor, without letting escape (inexperience in life would have made me ashamed) any of the enthusiasm which stimulated my intended labours. I requested his advice concerning the books I ought to procure.

'I am happy,' said M. Waldman, 'to have gained a disciple; and if your application equals your ability, I have no doubt of your success. Chemistry is that branch of natural philosophy in which the greatest improvements have been and may be made: it is on that account that I have made it my peculiar study; but at the same time I have not neglected the other branches of science. A man would make but a very sorry chemist if he attended to that department of human knowledge alone. If your wish is to become really a man of science, and not merely a petty experimentalist, I should advise you to apply to every branch of natural philosophy, including mathematics.'

He then took me into his laboratory, and explained to me the uses of his various machines; instructing me as to what I ought to procure, and promising me the use of his own when I should have advanced far enough in the science not to derange their mechanism. He also gave me the list of books which I had requested; and I took my leave.

Thus ended a day memorable to me: it decided my future destiny.

CHAPTER IV

FROM this day natural philosophy, and particularly chemistry, in the most comprehensive sense of the term, became nearly my sole occupation. I read with ardour those works, so full of genius and discrimination, which modern enquirers have written on these subjects. I attended the lectures, and cultivated the acquaintance, of the men of science of the university; and I found even in M. Krempe a great deal of sound sense and real information, combined, it is true, with a repulsive physiognomy and manners, but not on that account the less valuable. In M. Waldman I found a true friend. His gentleness was never tinged by dogmatism; and his instructions were given with an air of frankness and good nature, that banished every idea of pedantry. In a thousand ways he smoothed for me the path of knowledge, and made the most abstruse enquiries clear and facile to my apprehension. My application was at first fluctuating and uncertain; it gained strength as I proceeded, and soon became so ardent and eager, that the stars often disappeared in the light of morning whilst I was yet engaged in my laboratory.

As I applied so closely, it may be easily conceived that my progress was rapid. My ardour was indeed the astonishment of the students, and my proficiency that of the masters. Professor Krempe often asked me, with a sly smile, how Cornelius Agrippa went on? whilst M. Waldman expressed the most heartfelt exultation in my progress. Two years passed in this manner, during which I paid no visit to Geneva, but was engaged, heart and soul, in the pursuit of some discoveries, which I hoped to make. None but those who have experienced them can conceive of the enticements of science. In other studies you go as far as others have gone before you, and there is nothing more to know; but in a scientific pursuit there is continual food for discovery and wonder. A mind of moderate capacity, which closely pursues one study, must infallibly arrive at great proficiency in that study; and I, who continually sought the attainment of one object of pursuit, and was solely wrapt up in this, improved so rapidly, that, at the end of two years, I made some discoveries in the improvement of some chemical instruments, which procured me great esteem and admiration at the university. When I had arrived at this point, and had become as well acquainted with the theory and practice of natural philosophy as depended on the lessons of any of the professors at Ingolstadt, my residence there being no longer conducive to my improvements, I thought of returning to my friends and my native town, when an incident happened that protracted my stay.

One of the phenomena which had peculiarly attracted my attention was the structure of the human frame, and, indeed, any animal endued with life. Whence, I often asked myself, did the principle of life proceed? It was a bold question, and one which has ever been considered as a mystery; yet with how many things are we upon the brink of becoming acquainted, if cowardice or carelessness did not restrain our enquiries. I revolved these circumstances in my mind, and determined thenceforth to apply myself more particularly to those branches of natural philosophy which relate to physiology. Unless I had been animated by an almost supernatural enthusiasm, my application to this study would have been irksome, and almost intolerable. To examine the causes of life, we must first have recourse to death. I became acquainted with the science of anatomy: but this was not sufficient; I must also observe the natural decay and corruption of the human body. In my education my father had taken the greatest precautions that my mind should be impressed with no supernatural horrors. I do not ever remember to have trembled at a tale of superstition, or to have feared the apparition of a spirit. Darkness had no effect upon my fancy; and a churchyard was to me merely the receptacle of bodies deprived of life, which, from being the seat of beauty and strength, had become food for the worm. Now I was led to examine the cause and progress of this decay, and forced to spend days and nights in vaults and charnel-houses. My attention was fixed upon every object the most insupportable to the delicacy of the human feelings. I saw how the fine form of man was degraded and wasted; I beheld the corruption of death succeed to the blooming cheek of life; I saw how the worm inherited the wonders of the eye and brain. I paused, examining and analysing all the minutiæ of causation, as exemplified in the change from life to death, and death to life, until from the midst of this darkness a sudden light broke in upon me—a light so brilliant and wondrous, yet so simple, that while I became dizzy with the immensity of the prospect which it illustrated, I was surprised, that among so many men of genius who had directed their enquiries towards the same science, that I alone should be reserved to discover so astonishing a secret.

Remember, I am not recording the vision of a madman. The sun does not more certainly shine in the heavens, than that which I now affirm is true. Some miracle might have produced it, yet the stages of the discovery were distinct and probable. After days and nights of incredible labour and fatigue, I succeeded in discovering the cause of generation and life; nay, more, I became myself capable of bestowing animation upon lifeless matter.

The astonishment which I had at first experienced on this discovery soon gave place to delight and rapture. After so much time spent in painful labour, to arrive at once at the summit of my desires, was the most gratifying consummation of my toils. But this discovery was so great and overwhelming, that all the steps by which I had been progressively led to it were obliterated, and I beheld only the result. What had been the study and desire of the wisest men since the creation of the world was now within my grasp. Not that, like a magic scene, it all opened upon me at once: the information I had obtained was of a nature rather to direct my endeavours so soon as I should point them towards the object of my search, than to exhibit that object already accomplished. I was like the Arabian who had been buried with the dead, and found a passage to life, aided only by one glimmering, and seemingly ineffectual, light.

I see by your eagerness, and the wonder and hope which your eyes express, my friend, that you expect to be informed of the secret with which I am acquainted; that cannot be: listen patiently until the end of my story, and you will easily perceive why I am reserved upon that subject. I will not lead you on, unguarded and ardent as I then was, to your destruction and infallible misery. Learn from me, if not by my precepts, at least by my example, how dangerous is the acquirement of knowledge, and how much happier that man is who believes his native town to be the world, than he who aspires to become greater than his nature will allow.

When I found so astonishing a power placed within my hands, I hesitated a long time concerning the manner in which I should employ it. Although I possessed the capacity of bestowing animation, yet to prepare a frame for the reception of it, with all its intricacies of fibres, muscles, and veins, still remained a work of inconceivable difficulty and labour. I doubted at first whether I should attempt the creation of a being like myself, or one of simpler organization; but my imagination was too much exalted by my first success to permit me to doubt of my ability to give life to an animal as complex and wonderful as man. The materials at present within my command hardly appeared adequate to so arduous an undertaking; but I doubted not that I should ultimately succeed. I prepared myself for a multitude of reverses; my operations might be incessantly baffled, and at last my work be imperfect: yet, when I considered the improvement which every day takes place in science and mechanics, I was encouraged to hope my present attempts would at least lay the foundations of future success. Nor could I consider the magnitude and complexity of my plan as any argument of its impracticability. It was with these feelings that I began the creation of a human being. As the minuteness of the parts formed a great hindrance to my speed, I resolved, contrary to my first intention, to make the being of a gigantic stature; that is to say, about eight feet in height, and proportionably large. After having formed this determination, and having spent some months in successfully collecting and arranging my materials, I began.

No one can conceive the variety of feelings which bore me onwards, like a hurricane, in the first enthusiasm of success. Life and death appeared to me ideal bounds, which I should first break through, and pour a torrent of light into our dark world. A new species would bless me as its creator and source; many happy and excellent natures would owe their being to me. No father could claim the gratitude of his child so completely as I should deserve theirs. Pursuing these reflections, I thought, that if I could bestow animation upon lifeless matter, I might in process of time (although I now found it impossible) renew life where death had apparently devoted the body to corruption.

These thoughts supported my spirits, while I pursued my undertaking with unremitting ardour. My cheek had grown pale with study, and my person had become emaciated with confinement. Sometimes, on the very brink of certainty, I failed; yet still I clung to the hope which the next day or the next hour might realise. One secret which I alone possessed was the hope to which I had dedicated myself; and the moon gazed on my midnight labours, while, with unrelaxed and breathless eagerness, I pursued nature to her hiding-places. Who shall conceive the horrors of my secret toil, as I dabbled among the unhallowed damps of the grave, or tortured the living animal to animate the lifeless clay? My limbs now tremble, and my eyes swim with the remembrance; but then a resistless, and almost frantic, impulse, urged me forward; I seemed to have lost all soul or sensation but for this one pursuit. It was indeed but a passing trance, that only made me feel with renewed acuteness so soon as, the unnatural stimulus ceasing to operate, I had returned to my old habits. I collected bones from charnel-houses; and disturbed, with profane fingers, the tremendous secrets of the human frame. In a solitary chamber, or rather cell, at the top of the house, and separated from all the other apartments by a gallery and staircase, I kept my workshop of filthy creation: my eye-balls were starting from their sockets in attending to the details of my employment. The dissecting room and the slaughter-house furnished many of my materials; and often did my human nature turn with loathing from my occupation, whilst, still urged on by an eagerness which perpetually increased, I brought my work near to a conclusion.

The summer months passed while I was thus engaged, heart and soul, in one pursuit. It was a most beautiful season; never did the fields bestow a more plentiful harvest, or the vines yield a more luxuriant vintage: but my eyes were insensible to the charms of nature. And the same feelings which made me neglect the scenes around me caused me also to forget those friends who were so many miles absent, and whom I had not seen for so long a time. I knew my silence disquieted them; and I well remembered the words of my father: 'I know that while you are pleased with yourself, you will think of us with affection, and we shall hear regularly from you. You must pardon me if I regard any interruption in your correspondence as a proof that your other duties are equally neglected.'

I knew well therefore what would be my father's feelings; but I could not tear my thoughts from my employment, loathsome in itself, but which had taken an irresistible hold of my imagination. I wished, as it were, to procrastinate all that related to my feelings of affection until the great object, which swallowed up every habit of my nature, should be completed.

I then thought that my father would be unjust if he ascribed my neglect to vice, or faultiness on my part; but I am now convinced that he was justified in conceiving that I should not be altogether free from blame. A human being in perfection ought always to preserve a calm and peaceful mind, and never to allow passion or a transitory desire to disturb his tranquillity. I do not think that the pursuit of knowledge is an exception to this rule. If the study to which you apply yourself has a tendency to weaken your affections, and to destroy your taste for those simple pleasures in which no alloy can possibly mix, then that study is certainly unlawful, that is to say, not befitting the human mind. If this rule were always observed; if no man allowed any pursuit whatsoever to interfere with the tranquillity of his domestic affections, Greece had not been enslaved; Cæsar would have spared his country; America would have been discovered more gradually; and the empires of Mexico and Peru had not been destroyed.

But I forget that I am moralising in the most interesting part of my tale; and your looks remind me to proceed.

My father made no reproach in his letters, and only took notice of my silence by enquiring into my occupations more particularly than before. Winter, spring, and summer passed away during my labours; but I did not watch the blossom or the expanding leaves—sights which before always yielded me supreme delight—so deeply was I engrossed in my occupation. The leaves of that year had withered before my work drew near to a close; and now every day showed me more plainly how well I had succeeded. But my enthusiasm was checked by my anxiety, and I appeared rather like one doomed by slavery to toil in the mines, or any other unwholesome trade, than an artist occupied by his favourite employment. Every night I was oppressed by a slow fever, and I became nervous to a most painful degree; the fall of a leaf startled me, and I shunned my fellow-creatures as if I had been guilty of a crime. Sometimes I grew alarmed at the wreck I perceived that I had become; the energy of my purpose alone sustained me: my labours would soon end, and I believed that exercise and amusement would

then drive away incipient disease; and I promised myself both of these when
my creation should be complete.

CHAPTER V

IT was on a dreary night of November, that I beheld the accomplishment
of my toils. With an anxiety that almost amounted to agony, I collected the
instruments of life around me, that I might infuse a spark of being into the
lifeless thing that lay at my feet. It was already one in the morning; the rain
pattered dismally against the panes, and my candle was nearly burnt out,
when, by the glimmer of the half-extinguished light, I saw the dull yellow
eye of the creature open; it breathed hard, and a convulsive motion agitated
its limbs.

How can I describe my emotions at this catastrophe, or how delineate the
wretch whom with such infinite pains and care I had endeavoured to form?
His limbs were in proportion, and I had selected his features as beautiful.
Beautiful!—Great God! His yellow skin scarcely covered the work of muscles
and arteries beneath; his hair was of a lustrous black, and flowing; his teeth
of a pearly whiteness; but these luxuriances only formed a more horrid
contrast with his watery eyes, that seemed almost of the same colour as the
dun white sockets in which they were set, his shrivelled complexion and
straight black lips.

The different accidents of life are not so changeable as the feelings of
human nature. I had worked hard for nearly two years, for the sole purpose
of infusing life into an inanimate body. For this I had deprived myself of rest
and health. I had desired it with an ardour that far exceeded moderation;
but now that I had finished, the beauty of the dream vanished, and
breathless horror and disgust filled my heart. Unable to endure the aspect
of the being I had created, I rushed out of the room, and continued a long
time traversing my bed-chamber, unable to compose my mind to sleep. At
length lassitude succeeded to the tumult I had before endured; and I threw
myself on the bed in my clothes, endeavouring to seek a few moments of
forgetfulness. But it was in vain: I slept, indeed, but I was disturbed by the
wildest dreams. I thought I saw Elizabeth, in the bloom of health, walking
in the streets of Ingolstadt. Delighted and surprised, I embraced her; but as
I imprinted the first kiss on her lips, they became livid with the hue of death;
her features appeared to change, and I thought that I held the corpse of my
dead mother in my arms; a shroud enveloped her form, and I saw the
grave-worms crawling in the folds of the flannel. I started from my sleep with
horror; a cold dew covered my forehead, my teeth chattered, and every limb
became convulsed: when, by the dim and yellow light of the moon, as it

forced its way through the window shutters, I beheld the wretch—the miserable monster whom I had created. He held up the curtain of the bed; and his eyes, if eyes they may be called, were fixed on me. His jaws opened, and he muttered some inarticulate sounds, while a grin wrinkled his cheeks. He might have spoken, but I did not hear; one hand was stretched out, seemingly to detain me, but I escaped, and rushed down stairs. I took refuge in the courtyard belonging to the house which I inhabited; where I remained during the rest of the night, walking up and down in the greatest agitation, listening attentively, catching and fearing each sound as if it were to announce the approach of the demoniacal corpse to which I had so miserably given life.

Oh! no mortal could support the horror of that countenance. A mummy again endued with animation could not be so hideous as that wretch. I had gazed on him while unfinished; he was ugly then; but when those muscles and joints were rendered capable of motion, it became a thing such as even Dante could not have conceived.

I passed the night wretchedly. Sometimes my pulse beat so quickly and hardly, that I felt the palpitation of every artery; at others, I nearly sank to the ground through languor and extreme weakness. Mingled with this horror, I felt the bitterness of disappointment; dreams that had been my food and pleasant rest for so long a space were now become a hell to me; and the change was so rapid, the overthrow so complete!

Morning, dismal and wet, at length dawned, and discovered to my sleepless and aching eyes the church of Ingolstadt, its white steeple and clock, which indicated the sixth hour. The porter opened the gates of the court, which had that night been my asylum, and I issued into the streets, pacing them with quick steps, as if I sought to avoid the wretch whom I feared every turning of the street would present to my view. I did not dare return to the apartment which I inhabited, but felt impelled to hurry on, although drenched by the rain which poured from a black and comfortless sky.

I continued walking in this manner for some time, endeavouring, by bodily exercise, to ease the load that weighed upon my mind. I traversed the streets, without any clear conception of where I was, or what I was doing. My heart palpitated in the sickness of fear; and I hurried on with irregular steps, not daring to look about me:—

> 'Like one who, on a lonely road,
>   Doth walk in fear and dread,
> And, having once turned round, walks on,
>   And turns no more his head;
> Because he knows a frightful fiend
>   Doth close behind him tread.'*

* Coleridge's Ancient Mariner'.

Continuing thus, I came at length opposite to the inn at which the various diligences and carriages usually stopped. Here I paused, I knew not why; but I remained some minutes with my eyes fixed on a coach that was coming towards me from the other end of the street. As it drew nearer, I observed that it was the Swiss diligence: it stopped just where I was standing; and, on the door being opened, I perceived Henry Clerval, who, on seeing me, instantly sprung out. 'My dear Frankenstein,' exclaimed he, 'how glad I am to see you! how fortunate that you should be here at the very moment of my alighting!'

Nothing could equal my delight on seeing Clerval; his presence brought back to my thoughts my father, Elizabeth, and all those scenes of home so dear to my recollection. I grasped his hand, and in a moment forgot my horror and misfortune; I felt suddenly, and for the first time during many months, calm and serene joy. I welcomed my friend, therefore, in the most cordial manner, and we walked towards my college. Clerval continued talking for some time about our mutual friends, and his own good fortune in being permitted to come to Ingolstadt. 'You may easily believe,' said he, 'how great was the difficulty to persuade my father that all necessary knowledge was not comprised in the noble art of book-keeping; and, indeed, I believe I left him incredulous to the last, for his constant answer to my unwearied entreaties was the same as that of the Dutch schoolmaster in the Vicar of Wakefield:—"I have ten thousand florins a year without Greek, I eat heartily without Greek." But his affection for me at length overcame his dislike of learning, and he has permitted me to undertake a voyage of discovery to the land of knowledge.'

'It gives me the greatest delight to see you; but tell me how you left my father, brothers, and Elizabeth.'

'Very well, and very happy, only a little uneasy that they hear from you so seldom. By the by, I mean to lecture you a little upon their account myself.—But, my dear Frankenstein,' continued he, stopping short, and gazing full in my face, 'I did not before remark how very ill you appear; so thin and pale; you look as if you had been watching for several nights.'

'You have guessed right; I have lately been so deeply engaged in one occupation, that I have not allowed myself sufficient rest, as you see: but I hope, I sincerely hope, that all these employments are now at an end, and that I am at length free.'

I trembled excessively; I could not endure to think of, and far less to allude to, the occurrences of the preceding night. I walked with a quick pace, and we soon arrived at my college. I then reflected, and the thought made me shiver, that the creature whom I had left in my apartment might still be there, alive, and walking about. I dreaded to behold this monster; but I feared still more that Henry should see him. Entreating him, therefore, to remain a few minutes at the bottom of the stairs, I darted up towards my own room. My hand was already on the lock of the door before I recollected myself. I then paused; and a cold shivering came over me. I threw the door forcibly open, as children are accustomed to do when they expect a spectre to stand in waiting for them on the other side; but nothing appeared. I stepped fearfully in: the apartment was empty; and my bedroom was also freed from its hideous guest. I could hardly believe that so great a good fortune could have befallen me; but when I became assured that my enemy had indeed fled, I clapped my hands for joy, and ran down to Clerval.

We ascended into my room, and the servant presently brought breakfast; but I was unable to contain myself. It was not joy only that possessed me; I felt my flesh tingle with excess of sensitiveness, and my pulse beat rapidly. I was unable to remain for a single instant in the same place; I jumped over the chairs, clapped my hands, and laughed aloud. Clerval at first attributed my unusual spirits to joy on his arrival; but when he observed me more attentively, he saw a wildness in my eyes for which he could not account; and my loud, unrestrained, heartless laughter, frightened and astonished him.

'My dear Victor,' cried he, 'what, for God's sake, is the matter? Do not laugh in that manner. How ill you are! What is the cause of all this?'

'Do not ask me,' cried I, putting my hands before my eyes, for I thought I saw the dreaded spectre glide into the room; '*he* can tell.—Oh, save me! save me!' I imagined that the monster seized me; I struggled furiously, and fell down in a fit.

Poor Clerval! what must have been his feelings? A meeting, which he anticipated with such joy, so strangely turned to bitterness. But I was not the witness of his grief; for I was lifeless, and did not recover my senses for a long, long time.

This was the commencement of a nervous fever, which confined me for several months. During all that time Henry was my only nurse. I afterwards learned that, knowing my father's advanced age, and unfitness for so long a journey, and how wretched my sickness would make Elizabeth, he spared them this grief by concealing the extent of my disorder. He knew that I could not have a more kind and attentive nurse than himself; and, firm in the hope he felt of my recovery, he did not doubt that, instead of doing harm, he performed the kindest action that he could towards them.

But I was in reality very ill; and surely nothing but the unbounded and unremitting attentions of my friend could have restored me to life. The form of the monster on whom I had bestowed existence was for ever before my eyes, and I raved incessantly concerning him. Doubtless my words surprised Henry: he at first believed them to be the wanderings of my disturbed imagination; but the pertinacity with which I continually recurred to the same subject persuaded him that my disorder indeed owed its origin to some uncommon and terrible event.

By very slow degrees, and with frequent relapses, that alarmed and grieved my friend, I recovered. I remember the first time I became capable of observing outward objects with any kind of pleasure, I perceived that the fallen leaves had disappeared, and that the young buds were shooting forth from the trees that shaded my window. It was a divine spring; and the season contributed greatly to my convalescence. I felt also sentiments of joy and affection revive in my bosom; my gloom disappeared, and in a short time I became as cheerful as before I was attacked by the fatal passion.

'Dearest Clerval,' exclaimed I, 'how kind, how very good you are to me. This whole winter, instead of being spent in study, as you promised yourself, has been consumed in my sick room. How shall I ever repay you? I feel the greatest remorse for the disappointment of which I have been the occasion; but you will forgive me.'

'You will repay me entirely, if you do not discompose yourself, but get well as fast as you can; and since you appear in such good spirits, I may speak to you on one subject, may I not?'

I trembled. One subject! what could it be? Could he allude to an object on whom I dared not even think?

'Compose yourself,' said Clerval, who observed my change of colour, 'I will not mention it, if it agitates you; but your father and cousin would be very happy if they received a letter from you in your own hand-writing. They hardly know how ill you have been, and are uneasy at your long silence.'

'Is that all, my dear Henry? How could you suppose that my first thought would not fly towards those dear, dear friends whom I love, and who are so deserving of my love.'

'If this is your present temper, my friend, you will perhaps be glad to see a letter that has been lying here some days for you: it is from your cousin, I believe.'

CHAPTER VI

CLERVAL then put the following letter into my hands. It was from my own Elizabeth:—

'My dearest Cousin,

'You have been ill, very ill, and even the constant letters of dear kind Henry are not sufficient to reassure me on your account. You are forbidden to write—to hold a pen; yet one word from you, dear Victor, is necessary to calm our apprehensions. For a long time I have thought that each post would bring this line, and my persuasions have restrained my uncle from undertaking a journey to Ingolstadt. I have prevented his encountering the inconveniences and perhaps dangers of so long a journey; yet how often have I regretted not being able to perform it myself! I figure to myself that the task of attending on your sick bed has devolved on some mercenary old nurse, who could never guess your wishes, nor minister to them with the care and affection of your poor cousin. Yet that is over now: Clerval writes that indeed you are getting better. I eagerly hope that you will confirm this intelligence soon in your own handwriting.

'Get well—and return to us. You will find a happy, cheerful home, and friends who love you dearly. Your father's health is vigorous, and he asks but to see you,—but to be assured that you are well; and not a care will ever cloud his benevolent countenance. How pleased you would be to remark the improvement of our Ernest! He is now sixteen, and full of activity and spirit. He is desirous to be a true Swiss, and to enter into foreign service; but we cannot part with him, at least until his elder brother return to us. My uncle is not pleased with the idea of a military career in a distant country; but Ernest never had your powers of application. He looks upon study as an odious fetter;—his time is spent in the open air, climbing the hills or rowing on the lake. I fear that he will become an idler, unless we yield the point, and permit him to enter on the profession which he has selected.

'Little alteration, except the growth of our dear children, has taken place since you left us. The blue lake, and snow-clad mountains, they never change;—and I think our placid home, and our contented hearts are regulated by the same immutable laws. My trifling occupations take up my time and amuse me, and I am rewarded for any exertions by seeing none but happy, kind faces around me. Since you left us, but one change has taken place in our little household. Do you remember on what occasion Justine Moritz entered our family? Probably you do not; I will relate her history, therefore, in a few words. Madame Moritz, her mother, was a widow with four children, of whom Justine was the third. This girl had always been the favourite of her father; but, through a strange perversity, her mother could not endure her, and, after the death of M. Moritz, treated her very ill. My aunt observed this; and, when Justine was twelve years of age, prevailed on her mother to allow her to live at our house. The republican institutions of our country have produced simpler and happier manners than those which prevail in the great monarchies that surround it. Hence there is less distinction between the several classes of its inhabitants; and the lower orders, being neither so poor nor so despised, their manners are more refined and moral. A servant in Geneva does not mean the same thing as a servant in France and England. Justine, thus received in our family, learned the duties of a servant; a condition which, in our fortunate country, does not include the idea of ignorance, and a sacrifice of the dignity of a human being.

'Justine, you may remember, was a great favourite of yours; and I recollect you once remarked, that if you were in an ill-humour, one glance from Justine could dissipate it, for the same reason that Ariosto gives concerning the beauty of Angelica—she looked so frank-hearted and happy. My aunt conceived a great attachment for her, by which she was induced to give her an education superior to that which she had at first intended. This benefit was fully repaid; Justine was the most grateful little creature in the world: I do not mean that she made any professions; I never heard one pass her lips; but you could see by her eyes that she almost adored her protectress. Although her disposition was gay, and in many respects inconsiderate, yet she paid the greatest attention to every gesture of my aunt. She thought her the model of all excellence, and endeavoured to imitate her phraseology and manners, so that even now she often reminds me of her.

'When my dearest aunt died, every one was too much occupied in their own grief to notice poor Justine, who had attended her during her illness with the most anxious affection. Poor Justine was very ill; but other trials were reserved for her.

'One by one, her brothers and sister died; and her mother, with the exception of her neglected daughter, was left childless. The conscience of the woman was troubled; she began to think that the deaths of her favourites was a judgment from heaven to chastise her partiality. She was a Roman Catholic; and I believe her confessor confirmed the idea which she had conceived. Accordingly, a few months after your departure for Ingolstadt, Justine was called home by her repentant mother. Poor girl! she wept when she quitted our house; she was much altered since the death of my aunt; grief had given softness and a winning mildness to her manners, which had before been remarkable for vivacity. Nor was her residence at her mother's house of a nature to restore her gaiety. The poor woman was very vacillating in her repentance. She sometimes begged Justine to forgive her unkindness, but much oftener accused her of having caused the deaths of her brothers and sister. Perpetual fretting at length threw Madame Moritz into a decline, which at first increased her irritability, but she is now at peace for ever. She died on the first approach of cold weather, at the beginning of this last winter. Justine has returned to us; and I assure you I love her tenderly. She is very clever and gentle, and extremely pretty; as I mentioned before, her mien and her expressions continually remind me of my dear aunt.

'I must say also a few words to you, my dear cousin, of little darling William. I wish you could see him; he is very tall of his age, with sweet laughing blue eyes, dark eyelashes, and curling hair. When he smiles, two little dimples appear on each cheek, which are rosy with health. He has already had one or two little *wives*, but Louisa Biron is his favourite, a pretty little girl of five years of age.

'Now, dear Victor, I dare say you wish to be indulged in a little gossip concerning the good people of Geneva. The pretty Miss Mansfield has already received the congratulatory visits on her approaching marriage with a young Englishman, John Melbourne, Esq. Her ugly sister, Manon, married M. Duvillard, the rich banker, last autumn. Your favourite school-fellow, Louis Manoir, has suffered several misfortunes since the departure of Clerval from Geneva. But he has already recovered his spirits, and is reported to be on the point of marrying a very lively pretty Frenchwoman, Madame Tavernier. She is a widow, and much older than Manoir; but she is very much admired, and a favourite with everybody.

'I have written myself into better spirits, dear cousin; but my anxiety returns upon me as I conclude. Write, dearest Victor,—one line—one word will be a blessing to us. Ten thousand thanks to Henry for his kindness, his affection, and his many letters: we are sincerely grateful. Adieu! my cousin; take care of your self; and, I entreat you, write!

'ELIZABETH LAVENZA.

'Geneva, March 18th, 17—.'

'Dear, dear Elizabeth!' I exclaimed, when I had read her letter: 'I will write instantly, and relieve them from the anxiety they must feel.' I wrote, and this exertion greatly fatigued me; but my convalescence had commenced, and proceeded regularly. In another fortnight I was able to leave my chamber.

One of my first duties on my recovery was to introduce Clerval to the several professors of the university. In doing this, I underwent a kind of rough usage, ill befitting the wounds that my mind had sustained. Ever since the fatal night, the end of my labours, and the beginning of my misfortunes, I had conceived a violent antipathy even to the name of natural philosophy. When I was otherwise quite restored to health, the sight of a chemical instrument would renew all the agony of my nervous symptoms. Henry saw this, and had removed all my apparatus from my view. He had also changed my apartment; for he perceived that I had acquired a dislike for the room which had previously been my laboratory. But these cares of Clerval were made of no avail when I visited the professors. M. Waldman inflicted torture when he praised, with kindness and warmth, the astonishing progress I had made in the sciences. He soon perceived that I disliked the subject; but not guessing the real cause, he attributed my feelings to modesty, and changed the subject from my improvement, to the science itself, with a desire, as I evidently saw, of drawing me out. What could I do? He meant to please, and he tormented me. I felt as if he had placed carefully, one by one, in my view those instruments which were to be afterwards used in putting me to a slow and cruel death. I writhed under his words, yet dared not exhibit the pain I felt. Clerval, whose eyes and feelings were always quick in discerning the sensations of others, declined the subject, alleging, in excuse, his total ignorance; and the conversation took a more general turn. I thanked my friend from my heart, but I did not speak. I saw plainly that he was surprised, but he never attempted to draw my secret from me; and although I loved him with a mixture of affection and reverence that knew no bounds, yet I could never persuade myself to confide to him that event which was so often present to my recollection, but which I feared the detail to another would only impress more deeply.

M. Krempe was not equally docile; and in my condition at that time, of almost insupportable sensitiveness, his harsh blunt encomiums gave me even more pain than the benevolent approbation of M. Waldman. 'D—n the fellow!' cried he; 'why, M. Clerval, I assure you he has outstript us all. Ay, stare if you please; but it is nevertheless true. A youngster who, but a few years ago, believed in Cornelius Agrippa as firmly as in the gospel, has now set himself at the head of the university; and if he is not soon pulled down, we shall all be out of countenance.—Ay, ay,' continued he, observing my face expressive of suffering, 'M. Frankenstein is modest; an excellent quality in a young man. Young men should be diffident of themselves, you know, M. Clerval: I was myself when young; but that wears out in a very short time.'

M. Krempe had now commenced an eulogy on himself, which happily turned the conversation from a subject that was so annoying to me.

Clerval had never sympathized in my tastes for natural science; and his literary pursuits differed wholly from those which had occupied me. He came to the university with the design of making himself complete master of the oriental languages, as thus he should open a field for the plan of life he had marked out for himself. Resolved to pursue no inglorious career, he turned his eyes toward the East, as affording scope for his spirit of enterprise. The Persian, Arabic, and Sanscrit languages engaged his attention, and I was easily induced to enter on the same studies. Idleness had ever been irksome to me, and now that I wished to fly from reflection, and hated my former studies, I felt great relief in being the fellow-pupil with my friend, and found not only instruction but consolation in the works of the orientalists. I did not, like him, attempt a critical knowledge of their dialects, for I did not contemplate making any other use of them than temporary amusement. I read merely to understand their meaning, and they well repaid my labours. Their melancholy is soothing, and their joy elevating, to a degree I never experienced in studying the authors of any other country. When you read their writings, life appears to consist in a warm sun and a garden of roses,—in the smiles and frowns of a fair enemy, and the fire that consumes your own heart. How different from the manly and heroical poetry of Greece and Rome!

Summer passed away in these occupations, and my return to Geneva was fixed for the latter end of autumn; but being delayed by several accidents, winter and snow arrived, the roads were deemed impassable, and my journey was retarded until the ensuing spring. I felt this delay very bitterly; for I longed to see my native town and my beloved friends. My return had only been delayed so long, from an unwillingness to leave Clerval in a strange place, before he had become acquainted with any of its inhabitants. The winter, however, was spent cheerfully; and although the spring was uncommonly late, when it came its beauty compensated for its dilatoriness.

The month of May had already commenced, and I expected the letter daily which was to fix the date of my departure, when Henry proposed a pedestrian tour in the environs of Ingolstadt, that I might bid a personal farewell to the country I had so long inhabited. I acceded with pleasure to this proposition: I was fond of exercise, and Clerval had always been my favourite companion in the rambles of this nature that I had taken among the scenes of my native country.

We passed a fortnight in these perambulations: my health and spirits had long been restored, and they gained additional strength from the salubrious air I breathed, the natural incidents of our progress, and the conversation of my friend. Study had before secluded me from the intercourse of my fellow-creatures, and rendered me unsocial; but Clerval called forth the better feelings of my heart; he again taught me to love the aspect of nature, and the cheerful faces of children. Excellent friend! how sincerely did you love me, and endeavour to elevate my mind until it was on a level with your own! A selfish pursuit had cramped and narrowed me, until your gentleness and affection warmed and opened my senses; I became the same happy creature who, a few years ago, loved and beloved by all, had no sorrow or care. When happy, inanimate nature had the power of bestowing on me the most delightful sensations. A serene sky and verdant fields filled me with ecstasy. The present season was indeed divine; the flowers of spring bloomed in the hedges, while those of summer were already in bud. I was undisturbed by thoughts which during the preceding year had pressed upon me, notwithstanding my endeavours to throw them off, with an invincible burden.

Henry rejoiced in my gaiety, and sincerely sympathised in my feelings: he exerted himself to amuse me, while he expressed the sensations that filled his soul. The resources of his mind on this occasion were truly astonishing: his conversation was full of imagination; and very often, in imitation of the Persian and Arabic writers, he invented tales of wonderful fancy and passion. At other times he repeated my favourite poems, or drew me out into arguments, which he supported with great ingenuity.

We returned to our college on a Sunday afternoon: the peasants were dancing, and every one we met appeared gay and happy. My own spirits were high, and I bounded along with feelings of unbridled joy and hilarity.

CHAPTER VII

ON my return, I found the following letter from my father:—

'My dear Victor,

'You have probably waited impatiently for a letter to fix the date of your return to us; and I was at first tempted to write only a few lines, merely mentioning the day on which I should expect you. But that would be a cruel kindness, and I dare not do it. What would be your surprise, my son, when you expected a happy and glad welcome, to behold, on the contrary, tears and wretchedness? And how, Victor, can I relate our misfortune? Absence cannot have rendered you callous to our joys and griefs; and how shall I inflict pain on my long absent son? I wish to prepare you for the woful news, but I know it is impossible; even now your eye skims over the page, to seek the words which are to convey to you the horrible tidings.

'William is dead!—that sweet child, whose smiles delighted and warmed my heart, who was so gentle, yet so gay! Victor, he is murdered!

'I will not attempt to console you; but will simply relate the circumstances of the transaction.

'Last Thursday (May 7th), I, my niece, and your two brothers, went to walk in Plainpalais. The evening was warm and serene, and we prolonged our walk farther than usual. It was already dusk before we thought of returning; and then we discovered that William and Ernest, who had gone on before, were not to be found. We accordingly rested on a seat until they should return. Presently Ernest came, and enquired if we had seen his brother: he said, that he had been playing with him, that William had run away to hide himself, and that he vainly sought for him, and afterwards waited for him a long time, but that he did not return.

'This account rather alarmed us, and we continued to search for him until night fell, when Elizabeth conjectured that he might have returned to the house. He was not there. We returned again, with torches; for I could not rest, when I thought that my sweet boy had lost himself, and was exposed to all the damps and dews of night; Elizabeth also suffered extreme anguish. About five in the morning I discovered my lovely boy, whom the night before I had seen blooming and active in health, stretched on the grass livid and motionless: the print of the murderer's finger was on his neck.

'He was conveyed home, and the anguish that was visible in my countenance betrayed the secret to Elizabeth. She was very earnest to see the corpse. At first I attempted to prevent her; but she persisted, and entering the room where it lay, hastily examined the neck of the victim, and clasping her hands exclaimed, "O God! I have murdered my darling child!"

'She fainted, and was restored with extreme difficulty. When she again lived, it was only to weep and sigh. She told me, that that same evening William had teased her to let him wear a very valuable miniature that she possessed of your mother. This picture is gone, and was doubtless the temptation which urged the murderer to the deed. We have no trace of him at present, although our exertions to discover him are unremitted; but they will not restore my beloved William!

'Come, dearest Victor; you alone can console Elizabeth. She weeps continually, and accuses herself unjustly as the cause of his death; her words pierce my heart. We are all unhappy; but will not that be an additional motive for you, my son, to return and be our comforter? Your dear mother! Alas, Victor! I now say, Thank God she did not live to witness the cruel, miserable death of her youngest darling!

'Come, Victor; not brooding thoughts of vengeance against the assassin, but with feelings of peace and gentleness, that will heal, instead of festering, the wounds of our minds. Enter the house of mourning, my friend, but with kindness and affection for those who love you, and not with hatred for your enemies.

'Your affectionate and afflicted father,
'ALPHONSE FRANKENSTEIN.

'Geneva, May 12th, 17—.'

Clerval, who had watched my countenance as I read this letter, was surprised to observe the despair that succeeded to the joy I at first expressed on receiving news from my friends. I threw the letter on the table, and covered my face with my hands.

'My dear Frankenstein,' exclaimed Henry, when he perceived me weep with bitterness, 'are you always to be unhappy? My dear friend, what has happened?'

I motioned to him to take up the letter, while I walked up and down the room in the extremest agitation. Tears also gushed from the eyes of Clerval, as he read the account of my misfortune.

'I can offer you no consolation, my friend,' said he; 'your disaster is irreparable. What do you intend to do?'

'To go instantly to Geneva: come with me, Henry, to order the horses.'

During our walk, Clerval endeavoured to say a few words of consolation; he could only express his heartfelt sympathy. 'Poor William!' said he, 'dear lovely child, he now sleeps with his angel mother! Who that had seen him bright and joyous in his young beauty, but must weep over his untimely loss! To die so miserably; to feel the murderer's grasp! How much more a murderer, that could destroy such radiant innocence! Poor little fellow! one only consolation have we; his friends mourn and weep, but he is at rest. The pang is over, his sufferings are at an end for ever. A sod covers his gentle form, and he knows no pain. He can no longer be a subject for pity; we must reserve that for his miserable survivors.'

Clerval spoke thus as we hurried through the streets; the words impressed themselves on my mind, and I remembered them afterwards in solitude. But now, as soon as the horses arrived, I hurried into a cabriolet, and bade farewell to my friend.

My journey was very melancholy. At first I wished to hurry on, for I longed to console and sympathise with my loved and sorrowing friends; but when I drew near my native town, I slackened my progress. I could hardly sustain the multitude of feelings that crowded into my mind. I passed through scenes familiar to my youth, but which I had not seen for nearly six years. How altered every thing might be during that time! One sudden and desolating change had taken place; but a thousand little circumstances might have by degrees worked other alterations, which, although they were done more tranquilly, might not be the less decisive. Fear overcame me; I dared not advance, dreading a thousand nameless evils that made me tremble, although I was unable to define them.

I remained two days at Lausanne, in this painful state of mind. I contemplated the lake: the waters were placid; all around was calm; and the snowy mountains, 'the palaces of nature,' were not changed. By degrees the calm and heavenly scene restored me, and I continued my journey towards Geneva.

The road ran by the side of the lake, which became narrower as I approached my native town. I discovered more distinctly the black sides of Jura, and the bright summit of Mont Blanc. I wept like a child. 'Dear mountains! my own beautiful lake! how do you welcome your wanderer? Your summits are clear; the sky and lake are blue and placid. Is this to prognosticate peace, or to mock at my unhappiness?'

I fear, my friend, that I shall render myself tedious by dwelling on these preliminary circumstances; but they were days of comparative happiness, and I think of them with pleasure. My country, my beloved country! who but a native can tell the delight I took in again beholding thy streams, thy mountains, and, more than all, thy lovely lake!

Yet, as I drew nearer home, grief and fear again overcame me. Night also closed around; and when I could hardly see the dark mountains, I felt still more gloomily. The picture appeared a vast and dim scene of evil, and I foresaw obscurely that I was destined to become the most wretched of human beings. Alas! I prophesied truly, and failed only in one single circumstances, that in all the misery I imagined and dreaded, I did not conceive the hundredth part of the anguish I was destined to endure.

It was completely dark when I arrived in the environs of Geneva; the gates of the town were already shut; and I was obliged to pass the night at Secheron, a village at the distance of half a league from the city. The sky was serene; and, as I was unable to rest, I resolved to visit the spot where my poor William had been murdered. As I could not pass through the town, I was obliged to cross the lake in a boat to arrive at Plainpalais. During this short voyage I saw the lightnings playing on the summit of Mont Blanc in the most beautiful figures. The storm appeared to approach rapidly; and, on landing, I ascended a low hill, that I might observe its progress. It advanced; the heavens were clouded, and I soon felt the rain coming slowly in large drops, but its violence quickly increased.

I quitted my seat, and walked on, although the darkness and storm increased every minute, and the thunder burst with a terrific crash over my head. It was echoed from Salêve, the Juras, and the Alps of Savoy; vivid flashes of lightning dazzled my eyes, illuminating the lake, making it appear like a vast sheet of fire; then for an instant every thing seemed of a pitchy darkness, until the eye recovered itself from the preceding flash. The storm, as is often the case in Switzerland, appeared at once in various parts of the heavens. The most violent storm hung exactly north of the town, over that part of the lake which lies between the promontory of Belrive and the village of Copêt. Another storm enlightened Jura with faint flashes; and another darkened and sometimes disclosed the Môle, a peaked mountain to the east of the lake.

While I watched the tempest, so beautiful yet terrific, I wandered on with a hasty step. This noble war in the sky elevated my spirits; I clasped my hands, and exclaimed aloud, 'William, dear angel! this is thy funeral, this thy dirge!' As I said these words, I perceived in the gloom a figure which stole from behind a clump of trees near me; I stood fixed, gazing intently: I could not be mistaken. A flash of lightning illuminated the object, and discovered its shape plainly to me; its gigantic stature, and the deformity of its aspect, more hideous than belongs to humanity, instantly informed me that it was the wretch, the filthy dæmon, to whom I had given life. What did he there? Could he be (I shuddered at the conception) the murderer of my brother? No sooner did that idea cross my imagination, than I became convinced of its truth; my teeth chattered, and I was forced to lean against a tree for support. The figure passed me quickly, and I lost it in the gloom. Nothing in human shape could have destroyed that fair child. *He* was the murderer! I could not doubt it. The mere presence of the idea was an irresistible proof of the fact. I thought of pursuing the devil; but it would have been in vain, for another flash discovered him to me hanging among the rocks of the nearly perpendicular ascent of Mont Salêve, a hill that bounds Plainpalais on the south. He soon reached the summit, and disappeared.

I remained motionless. The thunder ceased; but the rain still continued, and the scene was enveloped in an impenetrable darkness. I revolved in my mind the events which I had until now sought to forget: the whole train of my progress towards the creation; the appearance of the work of my own hands alive at my bedside; its departure. Two years had now nearly elapsed since the night on which he first received life; and was this his first crime? Alas! I had turned loose into the world a depraved wretch, whose delight was in carnage and misery; had he not murdered my brother?

No one can conceive the anguish I suffered during the remainder of the night, which I spent, cold and wet, in the open air. But I did not feel the inconvenience of the weather; my imagination was busy in scenes of evil and despair. I considered the being whom I had cast among mankind, and endowed with the will and power to effect purposes of horror, such as the deed which he had now done, nearly in the light of my own vampire, my own spirit let loose from the grave, and forced to destroy all that was dear to me.

Day dawned; and I directed my steps towards the town. The gates were open, and I hastened to my father's house. My first thought was to discover what I knew of the murderer, and cause instant pursuit to be made. But I paused when I reflected on the story that I had to tell. A being whom I myself had formed, and endued with life, had met me at midnight among the precipices of an inaccessible mountain. I remembered also the nervous fever with which I had been seized just at the time that I dated my creation, and which would give an air of delirium to a tale otherwise so utterly improbable. I well knew that if any other had communicated such a relation to me, I should have looked upon it as the ravings of insanity. Besides, the strange nature of the animal would elude all pursuit, even if I were so far credited as to persuade my relatives to commence it. And then of what use would be pursuit? Who could arrest a creature capable of scaling the overhanging sides of Mont Salêve? These reflections determined me, and I resolved to remain silent.

It was about five in the morning when I entered my father's house. I told the servants not to disturb the family, and went into the library to attend their usual hour of rising.

Six years had elapsed, passed as a dream but for one indelible trace, and I stood in the same place where I had last embraced my father before my departure for Ingolstadt. Beloved and venerable parent! He still remained to me. I gazed on the picture of my mother, which stood over the mantel-piece. It was an historical subject, painted at my father's desire, and represented Caroline Beaufort in an agony of despair, kneeling by the coffin of her dead father. Her garb was rustic, and her cheek pale; but there was an air of dignity and beauty, that hardly permitted the sentiment of pity. Below this picture was a miniature of William; and my tears flowed when I looked upon it. While I was thus engaged, Ernest entered: he had heard me arrive, and hastened to welcome me. He expressed a sorrowful delight to see me: 'Welcome, my dearest Victor,' said he. 'Ah! I wish you had come three months ago, and then you would have found us all joyous and delighted. You come to us now to share a misery which nothing can alleviate; yet your presence will, I hope, revive our father, who seems sinking under his misfortune; and your persuasions will induce poor Elizabeth to cease her vain and tormenting self-accusations.—Poor William! he was our darling and our pride!'

Tears, unrestrained, fell from my brother's eyes; a sense of mortal agony crept over my frame. Before, I had only imagined the wretchedness of my desolated home; the reality came on me as a new, and a not less terrible, disaster. I tried to calm Ernest; I enquired more minutely concerning my father, and her I named my cousin.

'She most of all,' said Ernest, 'requires consolation; she accused herself of having caused the death of my brother, and that made her very wretched. But since the murderer has been discovered—'

'The murderer discovered! Good God! how can that be? who could attempt to pursue him? It is impossible; one might as well try to overtake the winds, or confine a mountain-stream with a straw. I saw him too; he was free last night!'

'I do not know what you mean,' replied my brother, in accents of wonder, 'but to us the discovery we have made completes our misery. No one would believe it at first; and even now Elizabeth will not be convinced, notwithstanding all the evidence. Indeed, who would credit that Justine Moritz, who was so amiable, and fond of all the family, could suddenly become capable of so frightful, so appalling a crime?'

'Justine Moritz! Poor, poor girl, is she the accused? But it is wrongfully; every one knows that; no one believes it, surely, Ernest?'

'No one did at first; but several circumstances came out, that have almost forced conviction upon us; and her own behaviour has been so confused, as to add to the evidence of facts a weight that, I fear, leaves no hope for doubt. But she will be tried to-day, and you will then hear all.'

He related that, the morning on which the murder of poor William had been discovered, Justine had been taken ill, and confined to her bed for several days. During this interval, one of the servants, happening to examine the apparel she had worn on the night of the murder, had discovered in her pocket the picture of my mother, which had been judged to be the temptation of the murderer. The servant instantly showed it to one of the others, who, without saying a word to any of the family, went to a magistrate; and, upon their deposition, Justine was apprehended. On being charged with the fact, the poor girl confirmed the suspicion in a great measure by her extreme confusion of manner.

This was a strange tale, but it did not shake my faith; and I replied earnestly, 'You are all mistaken; I know the murderer. Justine, poor, good Justine, is innocent.'

At that instant my father entered. I saw unhappiness deeply impressed on his countenance, but he endeavoured to welcome me cheerfully; and, after we had exchanged our mournful greeting, would have introduced some other topic than that of our disaster, had not Ernest exclaimed, 'Good God, papa! Victor says that he knows who was the murderer of poor William.'

'We do also, unfortunately,' replied my father; 'for indeed I had rather have been for ever ignorant than have discovered so much depravity and ingratitude in one I valued so highly.'

'My dear father, you are mistaken; Justine is innocent.'

'If she is, God forbid that she should suffer as guilty. She is to be tried to-day, and I hope, I sincerely hope, that she will be acquitted.'

This speech calmed me. I was firmly convinced in my own mind that Justine, and indeed every human being, was guiltless of this murder. I had no fear, therefore, that any circumstantial evidence could be brought forward strong enough to convict her. My tale was not one to announce publicly; its astounding horror would be looked upon as madness by the vulgar. Did any one indeed exist, except I, the creator, who would believe, unless his senses convinced him, in the existence of the living monument of presumption and rash ignorance which I had let loose upon the world?

We were soon joined by Elizabeth. Time had altered her since I last beheld her; it had endowed her with loveliness surpassing the beauty of her childish years. There was the same candour, the same vivacity, but it was allied to an expression more full of sensibility and intellect. She welcomed me with the greatest affection. 'Your arrival, my dear cousin,' said she, 'fills me with hope. You perhaps will find some means to justify my poor guiltless Justine. Alas! who is safe, if she be convicted of crime? I rely on her innocence as certainly as I do upon my own. Our misfortune is doubly hard to us; we have not only lost that lovely darling boy, but this poor girl, whom I sincerely love, is to be torn away by even a worse fate. If she is condemned, I never shall know joy more. But she will not, I am sure she will not; and then I shall be happy again, even after the sad death of my little William.'

'She is innocent, my Elizabeth,' said I, 'and that shall be proved; fear nothing, but let your spirits be cheered by the assurance of her acquittal.'

'How kind and generous you are! every one else believes in her guilt, and that made me wretched, for I knew that it was impossible: and to see every one else prejudiced in so deadly a manner rendered me hopeless and despairing.' She wept.

'Dearest niece,' said my father, 'dry your tears. If she is, as you believe, innocent, rely on the justice of our laws, and the activity with which I shall prevent the slightest shadow of partiality.'

CHAPTER VIII

WE passed a few sad hours, until eleven o'clock, when the trial was to commence. My father and the rest of the family being obliged to attend as witnesses, I accompanied them to the court. During the whole of this wretched mockery of justice I suffered living torture. It was to be decided, whether the result of my curiosity and lawless devices would cause the death of two of my fellow-beings: one a smiling babe, full of innocence and joy; the other far more dreadfully murdered, with every aggravation of infamy that could make the murder memorable in horror. Justine also was a girl of merit, and possessed qualities which promised to render her life happy: now all was to be obliterated in an ignominious grave; and I the cause! A thousand times rather would I have confessed myself guilty of the crime ascribed to Justine; but I was absent when it was committed, and such a declaration would have been considered as the ravings of a madman, and would not have exculpated her who suffered through me.

The appearance of Justine was calm. She was dressed in mourning; and her countenance, always engaging, was rendered, by the solemnity of her feelings, exquisitely beautiful. Yet she appeared confident in innocence, and did not tremble, although gazed on and execrated by thousands; for all the kindness which her beauty might otherwise have excited, was obliterated in the minds of the spectators by the imagination of the enormity she was supposed to have committed. She was tranquil, yet her tranquillity was evidently constrained; and as her confusion had before been adduced as a proof of her guilt, she worked up her mind to an appearance of courage. When she entered the court, she threw her eyes round it, and quickly discovered where we were seated. A tear seemed to dim her eye when she saw us; but she quickly recovered herself, and a look of sorrowful affection seemed to attest her utter guiltlessness.

The trial began; and, after the advocate against her had stated the charge, several witnesses were called. Several strange facts combined against her, which might have staggered any one who had not such proof of her innocence as I had. She had been out the whole of the night on which the murder had been committed, and towards morning had been perceived by a market-woman not far from the spot where the body of the murdered child had been afterwards found. The woman asked her what she did there; but she looked very strangely, and only returned a confused and unintelligible answer. She returned to the house about eight o'clock; and, when one enquired where she had passed the night, she replied that she had been looking for the child, and demanded earnestly if any thing had been heard concerning him. When shown the body, she fell into violent hysterics, and kept her bed for several days. The picture was then produced, which the servant had found in her pocket; and when Elizabeth, in a faltering voice, proved that it was the same which, an hour before the child had been missed, she had placed round his neck, a murmur of horror and indignation filled the court.

Justine was called on for her defence. As the trial had proceeded, her countenance had altered. Surprise, horror, and misery were strongly expressed. Sometimes she struggled with her tears; but, when she was desired to plead, she collected her powers, and spoke, in an audible although variable voice.

'God knows,' she said, 'how entirely I am innocent. But I do not pretend that my protestations should acquit me: I rest my innocence on a plain and simple explanation of the facts which have been adduced against me; and I hope the character I have always borne will incline my judges to a favourable interpretation, where any circumstance appears doubtful or suspicious.'

She then related that, by the permission of Elizabeth, she had passed the evening of the night on which the murder had been committed at the house of an aunt at Chêne, a village situated at about a league from Geneva. On her return, at about nine o'clock, she met a man, who asked her if she had seen any thing of the child who was lost. She was alarmed by this account, and passed several hours in looking for him, when the gates of Geneva were shut, and she was forced to remain several hours of the night in a barn belonging to a cottage, being unwilling to call up the inhabitants, to whom she was well known. Most of the night she spent here watching; towards morning she believed that she slept for a few minutes; some steps disturbed her, and she awoke. It was dawn, and she quitted her asylum, that she might again endeavour to find my brother. If she had gone near the spot where his body lay, it was without her knowledge. That she had been bewildered when questioned by the market-woman was not surprising, since she had passed a sleepless night, and the fate of poor William was yet uncertain. Concerning the picture she could give no account.

'I know,' continued the unhappy victim, 'how heavily and fatally this one circumstance weighs against me, but I have no power of explaining it; and when I have expressed my utter ignorance, I am only left to conjecture concerning the probabilities by which it might have been placed in my pocket. But here also I am checked. I believe that I have no enemy on earth, and none surely would have been so wicked as to destroy me wantonly. Did the murderer place it there? I know of no opportunity afforded him for so doing; or, if I had, why should he have stolen the jewel, to part with it again so soon?

'I commit my cause to the justice of my judges, yet I see no room for hope. I beg permission to have a few witnesses examined concerning my character; and if their testimony shall not overweigh my supposed guilt, I must be condemned, although I would pledge my salvation on my innocence.'

Several witnesses were called, who had known her for many years, and they spoke well of her; but fear, and hatred of the crime of which they supposed her guilty, rendered them timorous, and unwilling to come forward. Elizabeth saw even this last resource, her excellent dispositions and irreproachable conduct, about to fail the accused, when, although violently agitated, she desired permission to address the court.

'I am,' said she, 'the cousin of the unhappy child who was murdered, or rather his sister, for I was educated by and have lived with his parents ever since and even long before his birth. It may therefore be judged indecent in me to come forward on this occasion; but when I see a fellow-creature about to perish through the cowardice of her pretended friends, I wish to be allowed to speak, that I may say what I know of her character. I am well acquainted with the accused. I have lived in the same house with her, at one time for five, and at another for nearly two years. During all that period she appeared to me the most amiable and benevolent of human creatures. She nursed Madame Frankenstein, my aunt, in her last illness, with the greatest affection and care; and afterwards attended her own mother during a tedious illness, in a manner that excited the admiration of all who knew her; after which she again lived in my uncle's house, where she was beloved by all the family. She was warmly attached to the child who is now dead, and acted towards him like a most affectionate mother. For my own part, I do not hesitate to say, that, notwithstanding all the evidence produced against her, I believe and rely on her perfect innocence. She had no temptation for such an action: as to the bauble on which the chief proof rests, if she had earnestly desired it, I should have willingly given it to her; so much do I esteem and value her.'

A murmur of approbation followed Elizabeth's simple and powerful appeal; but it was excited by her generous interference, and not in favour of poor Justine, on whom the public indignation was turned with renewed violence, charging her with the blackest ingratitude. She herself wept as Elizabeth spoke, but she did not answer. My own agitation and anguish was extreme during the whole trial. I believed in her innocence; I knew it. Could the dæmon, who had (I did not for a minute doubt) murdered my brother, also in his hellish sport have betrayed the innocent to death and ignominy? I could not sustain the horror of my situation; and when I perceived that the popular voice, and the countenances of the judges, had already condemned my unhappy victim, I rushed out of the court in agony. The tortures of the accused did not equal mine; she was sustained by innocence, but the fangs of remorse tore my bosom, and would not forego their hold.

I passed a night of unmingled wretchedness. In the morning I went to the court; my lips and throat were parched. I dared not ask the fatal question; but I was known, and the officer guessed the cause of my visit. The ballots had been thrown; they were all black, and Justine was condemned.

I cannot pretend to describe what I then felt. I had before experienced sensations of horror; and I have endeavoured to bestow upon them adequate expressions, but words cannot convey an idea of the heart-sickening despair that I then endured. The person to whom I addressed myself added, that Justine had already confessed her guilt. 'That evidence,' he observed, 'was hardly required in so glaring a case, but I am glad of it; and, indeed, none of our judges like to condemn a criminal upon circumstantial evidence, be it ever so decisive.'

This was strange and unexpected intelligence; what could it mean? Had my eyes deceived me? and was I really as mad as the whole world would believe me to be, if I disclosed the object of my suspicions? I hastened to return home, and Elizabeth eagerly demanded the result.

'My cousin,' replied I, 'it is decided as you may have expected; all judges had rather that ten innocent should suffer, than that one guilty should escape. But she has confessed.'

This was a dire blow to poor Elizabeth, who had relied with firmness upon Justine's innocence. 'Alas!' said she, 'how shall I ever again believe in human goodness? Justine, whom I loved and esteemed as my sister, how could she put on those smiles of innocence only to betray? her mild eyes seemed incapable of any severity or guile, and yet she has committed a murder.'

Soon after we heard that the poor victim had expressed a desire to see my cousin. My father wished her not to go; but said, that he left it to her own judgment and feelings to decide. 'Yes,' said Elizabeth, 'I will go, although she is guilty; and you, Victor, shall accompany me: I cannot go alone.' The idea of this visit was torture to me, yet I could not refuse.

We entered the gloomy prison-chamber, and beheld Justine sitting on some straw at the farther end; her hands were manacled, and her head rested on her knees. She rose on seeing us enter; and when we were left alone with her, she threw herself at the feet of Elizabeth, weeping bitterly. My cousin wept also.

'Oh, Justine!' said she, 'why did you rob me of my last consolation? I relied on your innocence; and although I was then very wretched, I was not so miserable as I am now.'

'And do you also believe that I am so very, very wicked? Do you also join with my enemies to crush me, to condemn me as a murderer?' Her voice was suffocated with sobs.

'Rise, my poor girl,' said Elizabeth, 'why do you kneel, if you are innocent? I am not one of your enemies; I believed you guiltless, notwithstanding every evidence, until I heard that you had yourself declared your guilt. That report, you say, is false; and be assured, dear Justine, that nothing can shake my confidence in you for a moment, but your own confession.'

'I did confess; but I confessed a lie. I confessed, that I might obtain absolution; but now that falsehood lies heavier at my heart than all my other sins. The God of heaven forgive me! Ever since I was condemned, my confessor has besieged me; he threatened and menaced, until I almost began to think that I was the monster that he said I was. He threatened excommunication and hell fire in my last moments, if I continued obdurate. Dear lady, I had none to support me; all looked on me as a wretch doomed to ignominy and perdition. What could I do? In an evil hour I subscribed to a lie; and now only am I truly miserable.'

She paused, weeping, and then continued—'I thought with horror, my sweet lady, that you should believe your Justine, whom your blessed aunt had so highly honoured, and whom you loved, was a creature capable of a crime which none but the devil himself could have perpetrated. Dear William! dearest blessed child! I soon shall see you again in heaven, where we shall all be happy; and that consoles me, going as I am to suffer ignominy and death.'

'Oh, Justine! forgive me for having for one moment distrusted you. Why did you confess? But do not mourn, dear girl. Do not fear. I will proclaim, I will prove your innocence. I will melt the stony hearts of your enemies by my tears and prayers. You shall not die!—You, my play-fellow, my companion, my sister, perish on the scaffold! No! no! I never could survive so horrible a misfortune.'

Justine shook her head mournfully. 'I do not fear to die,' she said; 'that pang is past. God raises my weakness, and gives me courage to endure the worst. I leave a sad and bitter world; and if you remember me, and think of me as of one unjustly condemned, I am resigned to the fate awaiting me. Learn from me, dear lady, to submit in patience to the will of Heaven!'

During this conversation I had retired to a corner of the prison-room, where I could conceal the horrid anguish that possessed me. Despair! Who dared talk of that? The poor victim, who on the morrow was to pass the awful boundary between life and death, felt not as I did, such deep and bitter agony. I gnashed my teeth, and ground them together, uttering a groan that came from my inmost soul. Justine started. When she saw who it was, she approached me, and said, 'Dear sir, you are very kind to visit me; you, I hope, do not believe that I am guilty?'

I could not answer. 'No, Justine,' said Elizabeth; 'he is more convinced of your innocence than I was; for even when he heard that you had confessed, he did not credit it.'

'I truly thank him. In these last moments I feel the sincerest gratitude towards those who think of me with kindness. How sweet is the affection of others to such a wretch as I am! It removes more than half my misfortune; and I feel as if I could die in peace, now that my innocence is acknowledged by you, dear lady, and your cousin.'

Thus the poor sufferer tried to comfort others and herself. She indeed gained the resignation she desired. But I, the true murderer, felt the never-dying worm alive in my bosom, which allowed of no hope or consolation. Elizabeth also wept, and was unhappy; but hers also was the misery of innocence, which, like a cloud that passes over the fair moon, for a while hides but cannot tarnish its brightness. Anguish and despair had penetrated into the core of my heart; I bore a hell within me, which nothing could extinguish. We stayed several hours with Justine; and it was with great difficulty that Elizabeth could tear herself away. 'I wish,' cried she, 'that I were to die with you; I cannot live in this world of misery.'

Justine assumed an air of cheerfulness, while she with difficulty repressed her bitter tears. She embraced Elizabeth, and said, in a voice of half-suppressed emotion, 'Farewell, sweet lady, dearest Elizabeth, my beloved and only friend; may Heaven, in its bounty, bless and preserve you; may this be the last misfortune that you will ever suffer! Live, and be happy, and make others so.'

And on the morrow Justine died. Elizabeth's heart-rending eloquence failed to move the judges from their settled conviction in the criminality of the saintly sufferer. My passionate and indignant appeals were lost upon them. And when I received their cold answers, and heard the harsh unfeeling reasoning of these men, my purposed avowal died away on my lips. Thus I might proclaim myself a madman, but not revoke the sentence passed upon my wretched victim. She perished on the scaffold as a murderess!

From the tortures of my own heart, I turned to contemplate the deep and voiceless grief of my Elizabeth. This also was my doing! And my father's woe, and the desolation of that late so smiling home—all was the work of my thrice-accursed hands! Ye weep, unhappy ones; but these are not your last tears! Again shall you raise the funeral wail, and the sound of your lamentations shall again and again be heard! Frankenstein, your son, your kinsman, your early, much-loved friend; he who would spend each vital drop of blood for your sakes—who has no thought nor sense of joy, except as it is mirrored also in your dear countenances—who would fill the air with blessings, and spend his life in serving you—he bids you weep—to shed countless tears; happy beyond his hopes, if thus inexorable fate be satisfied, and if the destruction pause before the peace of the grave have succeeded to your sad torments!

Thus spoke my prophetic soul, as, torn by remorse, horror, and despair, I beheld those I loved spend vain sorrow upon the graves of William and Justine, the first hapless victims to my unhallowed arts.

CHAPTER IX

NOTHING is more painful to the human mind, than, after the feelings have been worked up by a quick succession of events, the dead calmness of inaction and certainty which follows, and deprives the soul both of hope and fear. Justine died; she rested; and I was alive. The blood flowed freely in my veins, but a weight of despair and remorse pressed on my heart, which nothing could remove. Sleep fled from my eyes; I wandered like an evil spirit, for I had committed deeds of mischief beyond description horrible, and more, much more (I persuaded myself), was yet behind. Yet my heart overflowed with kindness, and the love of virtue. I had begun life with benevolent intentions, and thirsted for the moment when I should put them in practice, and make myself useful to my fellow-beings. Now all was blasted: instead of that serenity of conscience, which allowed me to look back upon the past with self-satisfaction, and from thence to gather promise of new hopes, I was seized by remorse and the sense of guilt, which hurried me away to a hell of intense tortures, such as no language can describe.

This state of mind preyed upon my health, which had perhaps never entirely recovered from the first shock it had sustained. I shunned the face of man; all sound of joy or complacency was torture to me; solitude was my only consolation—deep, dark, deathlike solitude.

My father observed with pain the alteration perceptible in my disposition and habits, and endeavoured by arguments deduced from the feelings of his serene conscience and guiltless life, to inspire me with fortitude, and awaken in me the courage to dispel the dark cloud which brooded over me. 'Do you think, Victor,' said he, 'that I do not suffer also? No one could love a child more than I loved your brother;' (tears came into his eyes as he spoke;) 'but is it not a duty to the survivors, that we should refrain from augmenting their unhappiness by an appearance of immoderate grief? It is also a duty owed to yourself; for excessive sorrow prevents improvement or enjoyment, or even the discharge of daily usefulness, without which no man is fit for society.'

This advice, although good, was totally inapplicable to my case; I should have been the first to hide my grief, and console my friends, if remorse had not mingled its bitterness, and terror its alarm with my other sensations. Now I could only answer my father with a look of despair, and endeavour to hide myself from his view.

About this time we retired to our house at Belrive. This change was particularly agreeable to me. The shutting of the gates regularly at ten o'clock, and the impossibility of remaining on the lake after that hour, had rendered our residence within the walls of Geneva very irksome to me. I was now free. Often, after the rest of the family had retired for the night, I took the boat, and passed many hours upon the water. Sometimes, with my sails set, I was carried by the wind; and sometimes, after rowing into the middle of the lake, I left the boat to pursue its own course, and gave way to my own miserable reflections. I was often tempted, when all was at peace around me, and I the only unquiet thing that wandered restless in a scene so beautiful and heavenly—if I except some bat, or the frogs, whose harsh and interrupted croaking was heard only when I approached the shore—often, I say, I was tempted to plunge into the silent lake, that the waters might close over me and my calamities for ever. But I was restrained, when I thought of the heroic and suffering Elizabeth, whom I tenderly loved, and whose existence was bound up in mine. I thought also of my father, and surviving brother: should I by my base desertion leave them exposed and unprotected to the malice of the fiend whom I had let loose among them?

At these moments I wept bitterly, and wished that peace would revisit my mind only that I might afford them consolation and happiness. But that could not be. Remorse extinguished every hope. I had been the author of unalterable evils; and I lived in daily fear, lest the monster whom I had created should perpetrate some new wickedness. I had an obscure feeling that all was not over, and that he would still commit some signal crime, which by its enormity should almost efface the recollection of the past. There was always scope for fear, so long as any thing I loved remained behind. My abhorrence of this fiend cannot be conceived. When I thought of him, I gnashed my teeth, my eyes became inflamed, and I ardently wished to extinguish that life which I had so thoughtlessly bestowed. When I reflected on his crimes and malice, my hatred and revenge burst all bounds of moderation. I would have made a pilgrimage to the highest peak of the Andes, could I, when there, have precipitated him to their base. I wished to see him again, that I might wreak the utmost extent of abhorrence on his head, and avenge the deaths of William and Justine.

Our house was the house of mourning. My father's health was deeply shaken by the horror of the recent events. Elizabeth was sad and desponding; she no longer took delight in her ordinary occupations; all pleasure seemed to her sacrilege toward the dead; eternal woe and tears she then thought was the just tribute she should pay to innocence so blasted and destroyed. She was no longer that happy creature, who in earlier youth wandered with me on the banks of the lake, and talked with ecstasy of our future prospects. The first of those sorrows which are sent to wean us from the earth, had visited her, and its dimming influence quenched her dearest smiles.

'When I reflect, my dear cousin,' said she, 'on the miserable death of Justine Moritz, I no longer see the world and its works as they before appeared to me. Before, I looked upon the accounts of vice and injustice, that I read in books or heard from others, as tales of ancient days, or imaginary evils; at least they were remote, and more familiar to reason than to the imagination; but now misery has come home, and men appear to me as monsters thirsting for each other's blood. Yet I am certainly unjust. Every body believed that poor girl to be guilty; and if she could have committed the crime for which she suffered, assuredly she would have been the most depraved of human creatures. For the same of a few jewels, to have murdered the son of her benefactor and friend, a child whom she had nursed from its birth, and appeared to love as if it had been her own! I could not consent to the death of any human being; but certainly I should have though such a creature unfit to remain in the society of men. But she was innocent. I know, I feel she was innocent; you are of the same opinion, and that confirms me. Alas! Victor, when falsehood can look so like the truth, who can assure themselves of certain happiness? I feel as if I were walking on the edge of a precipice, towards which thousands are crowding, and endeavouring to plunge me into the abyss. William and Justine were assassinated, and the murderer escapes; he walks about the world free, and perhaps respected. But even if I were condemned to suffer on the scaffold for the same crimes, I would not change places with such a wretch.'

I listened to this discourse with the extremest agony. I, not in deed, but in effect, was the true murderer. Elizabeth read my anguish in my countenance, and kindly taking my hand, said, 'My dearest friend, you must calm yourself. These events have affected me, God knows how deeply; but I am not so wretched as you are. There is an expression of despair, and sometimes of revenge, in your countenance, that makes me tremble. Dear Victor, banish these dark passions. Remember the friends around you, who centre all their hopes in you. Have we lost the power of rendering you happy? Ah! while we love—while we are true to each other, here in this land of peace and beauty, your native country, we may reap every tranquil blessing,—what can disturb our peace?'

And could not such words from her whom I fondly prized before every other gift of fortune, suffice to chase away the fiend that lurked in my heart? Even as she spoke I drew near to her, as if in terror; lest at that very moment the destroyer had been near to rob me of her.

Thus not the tenderness of friendship, nor the beauty of earth, nor of heaven, could redeem my soul from woe: the very accents of love were ineffectual. I was encompassed by a cloud which no beneficial influence could penetrate. The wounded deer dragging its fainting limbs to some untrodden brake, there to gaze upon the arrow which had pierced it, and to die—was but a type of me.

Sometimes I could cope with the sullen despair that overwhelmed me: but sometimes the whirlwind passions of my soul drove me to seek, by bodily exercise and by change of place, some relief from my intolerable sensations. It was during an access of this kind that I suddenly left my home, and bending my steps towards the near Alpine valleys, sought in the magnificence, the eternity of such scenes, to forget myself and my ephemeral, because human, sorrows. My wanderings were directed towards the valley of Chamounix. I had visited it frequently during my boyhood. Six years had passed since then: *I* was a wreck—but nought had changed in those savage and enduring scenes.

I performed the first part of my journey on horseback. I afterwards hired a mule, as the more sure-footed, and least liable to receive injury on these rugged roads. The weather was fine: it was about the middle of the month of August, nearly two months after the death of Justine; that miserable epoch from which I dated all my woe. The weight upon my spirit was sensibly lightened as I plunged yet deeper in the ravine of Arve. The immense mountains and precipices that overhung me on every side—the sound of the river raging among the rocks, and the dashing of the waterfalls around, spoke of a power mighty as Omnipotence—and I ceased to fear, or to bend before any being less almighty than that which had created and ruled the elements, here displayed in their most terrific guise. Still, as I ascended higher, the valley assumed a more magnificent and astonishing character. Ruined castles hanging on the precipices of piny mountains; the impetuous Arve, and cottages every here and there peeping forth from among the trees, formed a scene of singular beauty. But it was augmented and rendered sublime by the mighty Alps, whose white and shining pyramids and domes towered above all, as belonging to another earth, the habitations of another race of beings.

I passed the bridge of Pélissier, where the ravine, which the river forms, opened before me, and I began to ascend the mountain that overhangs it. Soon after I entered the valley of Chamounix. This valley is more wonderful and sublime, but not so beautiful and picturesque, as that of Servox, through which I had just passed. The high and snowy mountains were its immediate boundaries; but I saw no more ruined castles and fertile fields. Immense glaciers approached the road; I heard the rumbling thunder of the falling avalanche, and marked the smoke of its passage. Mont Blanc, the supreme and magnificent Mont Blanc, raised itself from the surrounding *aiguilles*, and its tremendous *dôme* overlooked the valley.

A tingling long-lost sense of pleasure often came across me during this journey. Some turn in the road, some new object suddenly perceived and recognized, reminded me of days gone by, and were associated with the light-hearted gaiety of boyhood. The very winds whispered in soothing accents, and maternal nature bade me weep no more. Then again the kindly influence ceased to act—I found myself fettered again to grief, and indulging in all the misery of reflection. Then I spurred on my animal, striving so to forget the world, my fears, and, more than all, myself—or, in a more desperate fashion, I alighted, and threw myself on the grass, weighed down by horror and despair.

At length I arrived at the village of Chamounix. Exhaustion succeeded to the extreme fatigue both of body and of mind which I had endured. For a short space of time I remained at the window, watching the pallid lightnings that played above Mont Blanc, and listening to the rushing of the Arve, which pursued its noisy way beneath. The same lulling sounds acted as a lullaby to my too keen sensations: when I placed my head upon my pillow, sleep crept over me; I felt it as it came, and blest the giver of oblivion.

CHAPTER X

I SPENT the following day roaming through the valley. I stood beside the sources of the Arveiron, which take their rise in a glacier, that with slow pace is advancing down from the summit of the hills, to barricade the valley. The abrupt sides of vast mountains were before me; the icy wall of the glacier overhung me; a few shattered pines were scattered around; and the solemn silence of this glorious presence-chamber of imperial Nature was broken only by the brawling waves, or the fall of some vast fragment, the thunder sound of the avalanche, or the cracking, reverberated along the mountains, of the accumulated ice, which, through the silent working of immutable laws, was ever and anon rent and torn, as if it had been but a plaything in their hands. These sublime and magnificent scenes afforded me the greatest consolation that I was capable of receiving. They elevated me from all littleness of feeling; and although they did not remove my grief, they subdued and tranquillised it. In some degree, also, they diverted my mind from the thoughts over which it had brooded for the last month. I retired to rest at night; my slumbers, as it were, waited on and ministered to by the assemblance of grand shapes which I had contemplated during the day. They congregated round me; the unstained snowy mountain-top, the glittering pinnacle, the pine woods, and ragged bare ravine; the eagle, soaring amidst the clouds—they all gathered round me, and bade me be at peace.

Where had they fled when the next morning I awoke? All of soul-inspiriting fled with sleep, and dark melancholy clouded every thought. The rain was pouring in torrents, and thick mists hid the summits of the mountains, so that I even saw not the faces of those mighty friends. Still I would penetrate their misty veil, and seek them in their cloudy retreats. What were rain and storm to me? My mule was brought to the door, and I resolved to ascend to the summit of Montanvert. I remembered the effect that the view of the tremendous and ever-moving glacier had produced upon my mind when I first saw it. It had then filled me with a sublime ecstasy, that gave wings to the soul, and allowed it to soar from the obscure world to light and joy. The sight of the awful and majestic in nature had indeed always the effect of solemnising my mind, and causing me to forget the passing cares of life. I determined to go without a guide, for I was well acquainted with the path, and the presence of another would destroy the solitary grandeur of the scene.

The ascent is precipitous, but the path is cut into continual and short windings, which enable you to surmount the perpendicularity of the mountain. It is a scene terrifically desolate. In a thousand spots the traces of the winter avalanche may be perceived, where trees lie broken and strewed on the ground; some entirely destroyed, others bent, leaning upon the jutting rocks of the mountain, or transversely upon other trees. The path, as you ascend higher, is intersected by ravines of snow, down which stones continually roll from above; one of them is particularly dangerous, as the slightest sound, such as even speaking in a loud voice, produces a concussion of air sufficient to draw destruction upon the head of the speaker. The pines are not tall or luxuriant, but they are sombre, and add an air of severity to the scene. I looked on the valley beneath; vast mists were rising from the rivers which ran through it, and curling in thick wreaths around the opposite mountains, whose summits were hid in the uniform clouds, while rain poured from the dark sky, and added to the melancholy impression I received from the objects around me. Alas! why does man boast of sensibilities superior to those apparent in the brute; it only renders them more necessary beings. If our impulses were confined to hunger, thirst, and desire, we might be nearly free; but now we are moved by every wind that blows, and a chance word or scene that that word may convey to us.

> We rest; a dream has power to poison sleep.
>   We rise; one wand'ring thought pollutes the day.
> We feel, conceive, or reason; laugh or weep,
>   Embrace fond woe, or cast our cares away;
> It is the same: for, be it joy or sorrow,
>   The path of its departure still is free.
> Man's yesterday may ne'er be like his morrow;
>   Nought may endure but mutability!

It was nearly noon when I arrived at the top of the ascent. For some time I sat upon the rock that overlooks the sea of ice. A mist covered both that and the surrounding mountains. Presently a breeze dissipated the cloud, and I descended upon the glacier. The surface is very uneven, rising like the waves of a troubled sea, descending low, and interspersed by rifts that sink deep. The field of ice is almost a league in width, but I spent nearly two hours in crossing it. The opposite mountain is a bare perpendicular rock. From the side where I now stood Montanvert was exactly opposite, at the distance of a league; and above it rose Mont Blanc, in awful majesty. I remained in a recess of the rock, gazing on this wonderful and stupendous scene. The sea, or rather the vast river of ice, wound among its dependent mountains, whose aerial summits hung over its recesses. Their icy and glittering peaks shone in the sunlight over the clouds. My heart, which was before sorrowful, now swelled with something like joy; I exclaimed—'Wandering spirits, if indeed ye wander, and do not rest in your narrow beds, allow me this faint happiness, or take me, as your companion, away from the joys of life.'

As I said this, I suddenly beheld the figure of a man, at some distance, advancing towards me with superhuman speed. He bounded over the crevices in the ice, among which I had walked with caution; his stature, also, as he approached, seemed to exceed that of man. I was troubled: a mist came over my eyes, and I felt a faintness seize me; but I was quickly restored by the cold gale of the mountains. I perceived, as the shape came nearer (sight tremendous and abhorred?) that it was the wretch whom I had created. I trembled with rage and horror, resolving to wait his approach, and then close with him in mortal combat. He approached; his countenance bespoke bitter anguish, combined with disdain and malignity, while its unearthly ugliness rendered it almost too horrible for human eyes. But I scarcely observed this; rage and hatred had at first deprived me of utterance, and I recovered only to overwhelm him with words expressive of furious detestation and contempt.

'Devil,' I exclaimed, 'do you dare approach me? and do not you fear the fierce vengeance of my arm wreaked on your miserable head? Begone, vile insect! or rather, stay, that I may trample you to dust! and, oh! that I could, with the extinction of your miserable existence, restore those victims whom you have so diabolically murdered!'

'I expected this reception,' said the dæmon. 'All men hate the wretched; how, then, must I be hated, who am miserable beyond all living things! Yet you, my creator, detest and spurn me, thy creature, to whom thou art bound by ties only dissoluble by the annihilation of one of us. You purpose to kill me. How dare you sport thus with life? Do your duty towards me, and I will do mine towards you and the rest of mankind. If you will comply with my conditions, I will leave them and you at peace; but if you refuse, I will glut the maw of death, until it be satiated with the blood of your remaining friends.'

'Abhorred monster! fiend that thou art! the tortures of hell are too mild a vengeance for they crimes. Wretched devil! you reproach me with your creation; come on, then, that I may extinguish the spark which I so negligently bestowed.'

My rage was without bounds; I sprang on him, impelled by all the feelings which can arm one being against the existence of another.

He easily eluded me, and said—

'Be calm! I entreat you to hear me, before you give vent to your hatred on my devoted head. Have I not suffered enough, that you seek to increase my misery? Life, although it may only be an accumulation of anguish, is dear to me, and I will defend it. Remember, thou hast made me more powerful than thyself; my height is superior to thine; my joints more supple. But I will not be tempted to set myself in opposition to thee. I am thy creature, and I will be even mild and docile to my natural lord and king, if thou wilt also perform thy part, the which thou owest me. Oh, Frankenstein, be not equitable to every other, and trample upon me alone, to whom thy justice, and even thy clemency and affection, is most due. Remember, that I am thy creature; I ought to be thy Adam; but I am rather the fallen angel, whom thou drivest from joy for no misdeed. Every where I see bliss, from which I alone am irrevocably excluded. I was benevolent and good; misery made me a fiend. Make me happy, and I shall again be virtuous.'

'Begone! I will not hear you. There can be no community between you and me; we are enemies. Begone, or let us try our strength in a fight, in which one must fall.'

'How can I move thee? Will no entreaties cause thee to turn a favourable eye upon thy creature, who implores they goodness and compassion? Believe me, Frankenstein: I was benevolent; my soul glowed with love and humanity: but am I not alone, miserably alone? You, my creator, abhor me; what hope can I gather from your fellow-creatures, who owe me nothing? they spurn and hate me. The desert mountains and dreary glaciers are my refuge. I have wandered here many days; the caves of ice, which I only do not fear, are a dwelling to me, and the only one which man does not grudge. These bleak skies I hail, for they are kinder to me than your fellow-beings. If the multitude of mankind knew of my existence, they would do as you do, and arm themselves for my destruction. Shall I not then hate them who abhor me? I will keep no terms with my enemies. I am miserable, and they shall share my wretchedness. Yet it is in your power to recompense me, and deliver them from an evil which it only remains for you to make so great, that not only you and your family, but thousands of others, shall be swallowed up in the whirlwinds of its rage. Let your compassion be moved, and do not disdain me. Listen to my tale: when you have heard that, abandon or commiserate me, as you shall judge that I deserve. But hear me. The guilty are allowed, by human laws, bloody as they are, to speak in their own defence before they are condemned. Listen to me, Frankenstein. You accuse me of murder; and yet you would, with a satisfied conscience, destroy your own creature. Oh, praise the eternal justice of man! Yet I ask you not to spare me: listen to me; and then, if you can, and if you will, destroy the work of your hands.'

'Why do you call to my remembrance,' I rejoined, 'circumstances, of which I shudder to reflect, that I have been the miserable origin and author? Cursed be the day, abhorred devil, in which you first saw light! Cursed (although I curse myself) be the hands that formed you! You have made me wretched beyond expression. You have left me no power to consider whether I am just to you, or not. Begone! relieve me from the sight of your detested form.'

'Thus I relieve thee, my creator,' he said, and placed his hated hands before my eyes, which I flung from me with violence; 'thus I take from thee a sight which you abhor. Still thou canst listen to me, and grant me thy compassion. By the virtues that I once possessed, I demand this from you. Hear my tale; it is long and strange, and the temperature of this place is not fitting to your fine sensations; come to the hut upon the mountain. The sun is yet high in the heavens; before it descends to hide itself behind yon snowy precipices, and illuminate another world, you will have heard my story, and can decide. On you it rests, whether I quit for ever the neighbourhood of man, and lead a harmless life, or become the scourge of your fellow-creatures, and the author of your own speedy ruin.'

As he said this, he led the way across the ice: I followed. My heart was full, and I did not answer him; but, as I proceeded, I weighed the various arguments that he had used, and determined at least to listen to his tale. I was partly urged by curiosity, and compassion confirmed my resolution. I had hitherto supposed him to be the murderer of my brother, and I eagerly sought a confirmation or denial of this opinion. For the first time, also, I felt what the duties of a creator towards his creature were, and that I ought to render him happy before I complained of his wickedness. These motives urged me to comply with his demand. We crossed the ice, therefore, and ascended the opposite rock. The air was cold, and the rain again began to descend: we entered the hut, the fiend with an air of exultation, I with a heavy heart, and depressed spirits. But I consented to listen; and, seating myself by the fire which my odious companion had lighted, he thus began his tale.

CHAPTER XI

'IT is with considerable difficulty that I remember the original era of my being: all the events of that period appear confused and indistinct. A strange multiplicity of sensations seized me, and I saw, felt, heard, and smelt, at the same time; and it was, indeed, a long time before I learned to distinguish between the operations of my various senses. By degrees, I remember, a stronger light pressed upon my nerves, so that I was obliged to shut my eyes. Darkness then came over me, and troubled me; but hardly had I felt this, when, by opening my eyes, as I now suppose, the light poured in upon me again. I walked, and, I believe, descended; but I presently found a great alteration in my sensations. Before, dark and opaque bodies had surrounded me, impervious to my touch or sight; but I now found that I could wander on at liberty, with no obstacles which I could not either surmount or avoid. The light became more and more oppressive to me; and, the heat wearying me as I walked, I sought a place where I could receive shade. This was the forest near Ingolstadt; and here I lay by the side of a brook resting from my fatigue, until I felt tormented by hunger and thirst. This roused me from my nearly dormant state, and I ate some berries which I found hanging on the trees, or lying on the ground. I slaked my thirst at the brook; and then lying down, was overcome by sleep.

'It was dark when I awoke; I felt cold also, and half-frightened, as it were instinctively, finding myself so desolate. Before I had quitted your apartment, on a sensation of cold, I had covered myself with some clothes; but these were insufficient to secure me from the dews of night. I was a poor, helpless, miserable wretch; I knew, and could distinguish, nothing; but feeling pain invade me on all sides, I sat down and wept.

'Soon a gentle light stole over the heavens, and gave me a sensation of pleasure. I started up, and beheld a radiant form rise from among the trees.* I gazed with a kind of wonder. It moved slowly, but it enlightened my path; and I again went out in search of berries. I was still cold, when under one of the trees I found a huge cloak, with which I covered myself, and sat down upon the ground. No distinct ideas occupied my mind; all was confused. I felt light, and hunger, and thirst, and darkness; innumerable sounds rung in my ears, and on all sides various scents saluted me: the only object that I could distinguish was the bright moon, and I fixed my eyes on that with pleasure.

'Several changes of day and night passed, and the orb of night had greatly lessened, when I began to distinguish my sensations from each other. I gradually saw plainly the clear stream that supplied me with drink, and the trees that shaded me with their foliage. I was delighted when I first discovered that a pleasant sound, which often saluted my ears, proceeded from the throats of the little winged animals who had often intercepted the light from my eyes. I began also to observe, with greater accuracy, the forms that surrounded me, and to perceive the boundaries of the radiant roof of light which canopied me. Sometimes I tried to imitate the pleasant songs of the birds, but was unable. Sometimes I wished to express my sensations in

* The moon

my own mode, but the uncouth and inarticulate sounds which broke from me frightened me into silence again.

'The moon had disappeared from the night, and again, with a lessened form, showed itself, while I still remained in the forest. My sensations had, by this time, become distinct, and my mind received every day additional ideas. My eyes became accustomed to the light, and to perceive objects in their right forms; I distinguished the insect from the herb, and, by degrees, one herb from another. I found that the sparrow uttered none but harsh notes, whilst those of the blackbird and thrush were sweet and enticing.

'One day, when I was oppressed by cold, I found a fire which had been left by some wandering beggars, and was overcome with delight at the warmth I experienced from it. In my joy I thrust my hand into the live embers, but quickly drew it out again with a cry of pain. How strange, I thought, that the same cause should produce such opposite effects! I examined the materials of the fire, and to my joy found it to be composed of wood. I quickly collected some branches; but they were wet, and would not burn. I was pained at this, and sat still watching the operation of the fire. The wet wood which I had placed near the heat dried, and itself became inflamed. I reflected on this; and, by touching the various branches, I discovered the cause, and busied myself in collecting a great quantity of wood, that I might dry it, and have a plentiful supply of fire. When night came on, and brought sleep with it, I was in the greatest fear lest my fire should be extinguished. I covered it carefully with dry wood and leaves, and placed wet branches upon it; and then, spreading my cloak, I lay on the ground, and sunk into sleep.

'It was morning when I awoke, and my first care was to visit the fire. I uncovered it, and a gentle breeze quickly fanned it into a flame. I observed this also, and contrived a fan of branches, which roused the embers when they were nearly extinguished. When night came again, I found, with pleasure, that the fire gave light as well as heat; and that the discovery of this element was useful to me in my food; for I found some of the offals that the travellers had left had been roasted, and tasted much more savoury than the berries I gathered from the trees. I tried, therefore, to dress my food in the same manner, placing it on the live embers. I found that the berries were spoiled by this operation, and the nuts and roots much improved.

'Food, however, became scarce; and I often spent the whole day searching in vain for a few acorns to assuage the pangs of hunger. When I found this, I resolved to quit the place that I had hitherto inhabited, to seek for one where the few wants I experienced would be more easily satisfied. In this emigration, I exceedingly lamented the loss of the fire which I had obtained through accident, and knew not how to reproduce it. I gave several hours to the serious consideration of this difficulty; but I was obliged to relinquish all attempt to supply it; and, wrapping myself up in my cloak, I struck across the wood towards the setting sun. I passed three days in these rambles, and at length discovered the open country. A great fall of snow had taken place the night before, and the fields were of one uniform white; the appearance was disconsolate, and I found my feet chilled by the cold damp substance that covered the ground.

'It was about seven in the morning, and I longed to obtain food and shelter; at length I perceived a small hut, on a rising ground, which had doubtless been built for the convenience of some shepherd. This was a new sight to me; and I examined the structure with great curiosity. Finding the door open, I entered. An old man sat in it, near a fire, over which he was preparing his breakfast. He turned on hearing a noise; and, perceiving me, shrieked loudly, and, quitting the hut, ran across the fields with a speed of which his debilitated form hardly appeared capable. His appearance, different from any I had ever before seen, and his flight, somewhat surprised me. But I was enchanted by the appearance of the hut: here the snow and rain could not penetrate; the ground was dry; and it presented to me then as exquisite and divine a retreat as Pandæmonium appeared to the dæmons of hell after their sufferings in the lake of fire. I greedily devoured the remnants of the shepherd's breakfast, which consisted of bread, cheese, milk, and wine; the latter, however, I did not like. Then, overcome by fatigue, I lay down among some straw, and fell asleep.

'It was noon when I awoke; and, allured by the warmth of the sun, which shone brightly on the white ground, I determined to recommence my travels; and, depositing the remains of the peasant's breakfast in a wallet I found, I proceeded across the fields for several hours, until at sunset I arrived at a village. How miraculous did this appear! the huts, the neater cottages, and stately houses, engaged my admiration by turns. The vegetables in the gardens, the milk and cheese that I saw placed at the windows of some of the cottages, allured my appetite. One of the best of these I entered; but I had hardly placed my foot within the door, before the children shrieked, and one of the women fainted. The whole village was roused; some fled, some attacked me, until, grievously bruised by stones and many other kinds of missile weapons, I escaped to the open country, and fearfully took refuge in a low hovel, quite bare, and making a wretched appearance after the palaces I had beheld in the village. This hovel, however, joined a cottage of a neat and pleasant appearance; but, after my late dearly bought experience, I dared not enter it. My place of refuge was constructed of wood, but so low, that I could with difficulty sit upright in it. No wood, however, was placed on the earth, which formed the floor, but it was dry; and although the wind entered it by innumerable chinks, I found it an agreeable asylum from the snow and rain.

'Here then I retreated, and lay down happy to have found a shelter, however miserable, from the inclemency of the season, and still more from the barbarity of man.

'As soon as morning dawned, I crept from my kennel, that I might view the adjacent cottage, and discover if I could remain in the habitation I had found. It was situated against the back of the cottage, and surrounded on the sides which were exposed by a pig-sty and a clear pool of water. One part was open, and by that I had crept in; but now I covered every crevice by which I might be perceived with stones and wood, yet in such a manner that I might move them on occasion to pass out: all the light I enjoyed came through the sty, and that was sufficient for me.

'Having thus arranged my dwelling, and carpeted it with clean straw, I retired; for I saw the figure of a man at a distance, and I remembered too well my treatment the night before, to trust myself in his power. I had first, however, provided for my sustenance for that day, by a loaf of coarse bread, which I purloined, and a cup with which I could drink, more conveniently than from my hand, of the pure water which flowed by my retreat. The floor was a little raised, so that it was kept perfectly dry, and by its vicinity to the chimney of the cottage it was tolerably warm.

'Being thus provided, I resolved to reside in this hovel, until something should occur which might alter my determination. It was indeed a paradise, compared to the bleak forest, my former residence, the rain-dropping branches, and dank earth. I ate my breakfast with pleasure, and was about to remove a plank to procure myself a little water, when I heard a step, and looking through a small chink, I beheld a young creature, with a pail on her head, passing before my hovel. The girl was young, and of gentle demeanour, unlike what I have since found cottagers and farm-house servants to be. Yet she was meanly dressed, a coarse blue petticoat and a linen jacket being her only garb; her fair hair was plaited, but not adorned: she looked patient, yet sad. I lost sight of her; and in about a quarter of an hour she returned, bearing the pail, which was now partly filled with milk. As she walked along, seemingly incommoded by the burden, a young man met her, whose countenance expressed a deeper despondence. Uttering a few sounds with an air of melancholy, he took the pail from her head, and bore it to the cottage himself. She followed, and they disappeared. Presently I saw the young man again, with some tools in his hand, cross the field behind the cottage; and the girl was also busied, sometimes in the house, and sometimes in the yard.

'On examining my dwelling, I found that one of the windows of the cottage had formerly occupied a part of it, but the panes had been filled up with wood. In one of these was a small and almost imperceptible chink, through which the eye could just penetrate. Through this crevice a small room was visible, whitewashed and clean, but very bare of furniture. In one corner, near a small fire, sat an old man, leaning his head on his hands in a disconsolate attitude. The young girl was occupied in arranging the cottage; but presently she took something out of a drawer, which employed her hands, and she sat down beside the old man, who, taking up an instrument, began to play, and to produce sounds sweeter than the voice of the thrush or the nightingale. It was a lovely sight, even to me, poor wretch! who had never beheld aught beautiful before. The silver hair and benevolent countenance of the aged cottager won my reverence, while the gentle manners of the girl enticed my love. He played a sweet mournful air, which I perceived drew tears from the eyes of his amiable companion, of which the old man took no notice, until she sobbed audibly; he then pronounced a few sounds, and the fair creature, leaving her work, knelt at his feet. He raised her, and smiled with such kindness and affection, that I felt sensations of a peculiar and overpowering nature: they were a mixture of pain and pleasure, such as I had never before experienced, either from hunger or cold, warmth or food; and I withdrew from the window, unable to bear these emotions.

'Soon after this the young man returned, bearing on his shoulders a load of wood. The girl met him at the door, helped to relieve him of his burden, and, taking some of the fuel into the cottage, placed it on the fire; then she and the youth went apart into a nook of the cottage, and he showed her a large loaf and a piece of cheese. She seemed pleased, and went into the garden for some roots and plants, which she placed in water, and then upon the fire. She afterwards continued her work, whilst the young man went into the garden, and appeared busily employed in digging and pulling up roots. After he had been employed thus about an hour, the young woman joined him, and they entered the cottage together.

'The old man had, in the mean time, been pensive; but, on the appearance of his companions, he assumed a more cheerful air, and they sat down to eat. The meal was quickly despatched. The young woman was again occupied in arranging the cottage; the old man walked before the cottage in the sun for a few minutes, leaning on the arm of the youth. Nothing could exceed in beauty the contrast between these two excellent creatures. One was old, with silver hairs and a countenance beaming with benevolence and love: the younger was slight and graceful in his figure, and his features were moulded with the finest symmetry; yet his eyes and attitude expressed the utmost sadness and despondency. The old man returned to the cottage; and the youth, with tools different from those he had used in the morning, directed his steps across the fields.

'Night quickly shut in; but, to my extreme wonder, I found that the cottagers had a means of prolonging light by the use of tapers, and was delighted to find that the setting of the sun did not put an end to the pleasure I experienced in watching my human neighbours. In the evening, the young girl and her companion were employed in various occupations which I did not understand; and the old man again took up the instrument which produced the divine sounds that had enchanted me in the morning.

So soon as he had finished, the youth began, not to play, but to utter sounds that were monotonous, and neither resembling the harmony of the old man's instrument nor the songs of the birds: I since found that he read aloud, but at that time I knew nothing of the science of words or letters.

'The family, after having been thus occupied for a short time, extinguished their lights, and retired, as I conjectured, to rest.

CHAPTER XII

'I LAY on my straw, but I could not sleep. I thought of the occurrences of the day. What chiefly struck me was the gentle manners of these people; and I longed to join them, but dared not. I remembered too well the treatment I had suffered the night before from the barbarous villagers, and resolved, whatever course of conduct I might hereafter think it right to pursue, that for the present I would remain quietly in my hovel, watching, and endeavouring to discover the motives which influenced their actions.

'The cottagers arose the next morning before the sun. The young woman arranged the cottage, and prepared the food; and the youth departed after the first meal.

'This day was passed in the same routine as that which preceded it. The young man was constantly employed out of doors, and the girl in various laborious occupations within. The old man, whom I soon perceived to be blind, employed his leisure hours on his instrument or in contemplation. Nothing could exceed the love and respect which the younger cottagers exhibited towards their venerable companion. They performed towards him every little office of affection and duty with gentleness; and he rewarded them by his benevolent smiles.

'They were not entirely happy. The young man and his companion often went apart, and appeared to weep. I saw no cause for their unhappiness; but I was deeply affected by it. If such lovely creatures were miserable, it was less strange that I, an imperfect and solitary being, should be wretched. Yet why were these gentle beings unhappy? They possessed a delightful house (for such it was in my eyes) and every luxury; they had a fire to warm them when chill, and delicious viands when hungry; they were dressed in excellent clothes; and, still more, they enjoyed one another's company and speech, interchanging each day looks of affection and kindness. What did their tears imply? Did they really express pain? I was at first unable to solve these questions; but perpetual attention and time explained to me many appearances which were at first enigmatic.

'A considerable period elapsed before I discovered one of the causes of the uneasiness of this amiable family: it was poverty; and they suffered that evil in a very distressing degree. Their nourishment consisted entirely of the vegetables of their garden, and the milk of one cow, which gave very little during the winter, when its masters could scarcely procure food to support it. They often, I believe, suffered the pangs of hunger very poignantly, especially the two younger cottagers; for several times they placed food before the old man, when they reserved none for themselves.

'This trait of kindness moved me sensibly. I had been accustomed, during the night, to steal a part of their store for my own consumption; but when I found that in doing this I inflicted pain on the cottagers, I abstained, and satisfied myself with berries, nuts, and roots, which I gathered from a neighbouring wood.

'I discovered also another means through which I was enabled to assist their labours. I found that the youth spent a great part of each day in collecting wood for the family fire; and, during the night, I often took his tools, the use of which I quickly discovered, and brought home firing sufficient for the consumption of several days.

'I remember, the first time that I did this, the young woman, when she opened the door in the morning, appeared greatly astonished on seeing a great pile of wood on the outside. She uttered some words in a loud voice, and the youth joined her, who also expressed surprise. I observed, with pleasure, that he did not go to the forest that day, but spent it in repairing the cottage, and cultivating the garden.

'By degrees I made a discovery of still greater moment. I found that these people possessed a method of communicating their experience and feelings to one another by articulate sounds. I perceived that the words they spoke sometimes, produced pleasure or pain, smiles or sadness, in the minds and countenances of the hearers. This was indeed a godlike science, and I ardently desired to become acquainted with it. But I was baffled in every attempt I made for this purpose. Their pronunciation was quick; and the words they uttered, not having any apparent connection with visible objects, I was unable to discover any clue by which I could unravel the mystery of their reference. By great application, however, and after having remained during the space of several revolutions of the moon in my hovel, I discovered the names that were given to some of the most familiar objects of discourse; I learned and applied the words, *fire*, *milk*, *bread*, and *wood*. I learned also the names of the cottagers themselves. The youth and his companion had each of them several names, but the old man had only one, which was *father*. The girl was called *sister*, or *Agatha*; and the youth *Felix*, *brother*, or *son*. I cannot describe the delight I felt when I learned the ideas appropriated to each of these sounds, and was able to pronounce them. I distinguished several other words, without being able as yet to understand or apply them; such as *good*, *dearest*, *unhappy*.

'I spent the winter in this manner. The gentle manners and beauty of the cottagers greatly endeared them to me: when they were unhappy, I felt depressed; when they rejoiced, I sympathised in their joys. I saw few human beings beside them; and if any other happened to enter the cottage, their harsh manners and rude gait only enhanced to me the superior accomplishments of my friends. The old man, I could perceive, often endeavoured to encourage his children, as sometimes I found that he called them, to cast off their melancholy. He would talk in a cheerful accent, with an expression of goodness that bestowed pleasure even upon me. Agatha listened with respect, her eyes sometimes filled with tears, which she endeavoured to wipe away unperceived; but I generally found that her countenance and tone were more cheerful after having listened to the exhortations of her father. It was not thus with Felix. He was always the saddest of the group; and, even to my unpractised senses, he appeared to have suffered more deeply than his friends. But if his countenance was more sorrowful, his voice was more cheerful than that of his sister, especially when he addressed the old man.

'I could mention innumerable instances, which, although slight, marked the dispositions of these amiable cottagers. In the midst of poverty and want, Felix carried with pleasure to his sister the first little white flower that peeped out from beneath the snowy ground. Early in the morning, before she had risen, he cleared away the snow that obstructed her path to the milk-house, drew water from the well, and brought the wood from the out-house, where, to his perpetual astonishment, he found his store always replenished by an invisible hand. In the day, I believe, he worked sometimes for a neighbouring farmer, because he often went forth, and did not return until dinner, yet brought no wood with him. At other times he worked in the garden; but, as there was little to do in the frosty season, he read to the old man and Agatha.

'This reading had puzzled me extremely at first; but, by degrees, I discovered that he uttered many of the same sounds when he read, as when he talked. I conjectured, therefore, that he found on the paper signs for speech which he understood, and I ardently longed to comprehend these also; but how was that possible, when I did not even understand the sounds for which they stood as signs? I improved, however, sensibly in this science, but not sufficiently to follow up any kind of conversation, although I applied my whole mind to the endeavour: for I easily perceived that, although I eagerly longed to discover myself to the cottagers, I ought not to make the attempt until I had first become master of their language; which knowledge might enable me to make them overlook the deformity of my figure; for with this also the contrast perpetually presented to my eyes had made me acquainted.

'I had admired the perfect forms of my cottagers—their grace, beauty, and delicate complexions: but how was I terrified, when I viewed myself in a transparent pool! At first I started back, unable to believe that it was indeed I who was reflected in the mirror; and when I became fully convinced that I was in reality the monster that I am, I was filled with the bitterest sensations of despondence and mortification. Alas! I did not yet entirely know the fatal effects of this miserable deformity.

'As the sun became warmer, and the light of day longer, the snow vanished, and I beheld the bare trees and the black earth. From this time Felix was more employed; and the heart-moving indications of impending famine disappeared. Their food, as I afterwards found, was coarse, but it was wholesome; and they procured a sufficiency of it. Several new kinds of plants sprung up in the garden, which they dressed; and these signs of comfort increased daily as the season advanced.

'The old man, leaning on his son, walked each day at noon, when it did not rain, as I found it was called when the heavens poured forth its waters. This frequently took place; but a high wind quickly dried the earth, and the season became far more pleasant than it had been.

'My mode of life in my hovel was uniform. During the morning, I attended the motions of the cottagers; and when they were dispersed in various occupations, I slept: the remainder of the day was spent in observing my friends. When they had retired to rest, if there was any moon, or the night was star-light, I went into the woods, and collected my own food and fuel for the cottage. When I returned, as often as it was necessary, I cleared their path from the snow, and performed those offices that I had seen done by Felix. I afterwards found that these labours, performed by an invisible hand, greatly astonished them; and once or twice I heard them, on these occasions, utter the words *good spirit*, *wonderful*; but I did not then understand the signification of these terms.

'My thoughts now became more active, and I longed to discover the motives and feelings of these lovely creatures; I was inquisitive to know why Felix appeared so miserable, and Agatha so sad. I thought (foolish wretch!) that it might be in my power to restore happiness to these deserving people. When I slept, or was absent, the forms of the venerable blind father, the gentle Agatha, and the excellent Felix, flitted before me. I looked upon them as superior beings, who would be the arbiters of my future destiny. I formed in my imagination a thousand pictures of presenting myself to them, and their reception of me. I imagined that they would be disgusted, until, by my gentle demeanour and conciliating words, I should first win their favour, and afterwards their love.

'These thoughts exhilarated me, and led me to apply with fresh ardour to the acquiring the art of language. My organs were indeed harsh, but supple; and although my voice was very unlike the soft music of their tones, yet I pronounced such words as I understood with tolerable ease. It was as the ass and the lap-dog; yet surely the gentle ass whose intentions were affectionate, although his manners were rude, deserved better treatment than blows and execration.

'The pleasant showers and genial warmth of spring greatly altered the aspect of the earth. Men, who before this change seemed to have been hid in caves, dispersed themselves, and were employed in various arts of cultivation. The birds sang in more cheerful notes, and the leaves began to bud forth on the trees. Happy, happy earth! fit habitation for gods, which, so short a time before, was bleak, damp, and unwholesome. My spirits were elevated by the enchanting appearance of nature; the past was blotted from my memory, the present was tranquil, and the future gilded by bright rays of hope, and anticipations of joy.

CHAPTER XIII

'I NOW hasten to the more moving part of my story. I shall relate events, that impressed me with feelings which, from what I had been, have made me what I am.

'Spring advanced rapidly; the weather became fine, and the skies cloudless. It surprised me, that what before was desert and gloomy should now bloom with the most beautiful flowers and verdure. My senses were gratified and refreshed by a thousand scents of delight, and a thousand sights of beauty.

'It was on one of these days, when my cottagers periodically rested from labour—the old man played on his guitar, and the children listened to him—that I observed the countenance of Felix was melancholy beyond expression; he sighed frequently; and once his father paused in his music, and I conjectured by his manner that he enquired the cause of his son's sorrow. Felix replied in a cheerful accent, and the old man was recommencing his music, when some one tapped at the door.

'It was a lady on horseback, accompanied by a countryman as a guide. The lady was dressed in a dark suit, and covered with a thick black veil. Agatha asked a question; to which the stranger only replied by pronouncing, in a sweet accent, the name of Felix. Her voice was musical, but unlike that of either of my friends. On hearing this word, Felix came up hastily to the lady; who, when she saw him, threw up her veil, and I beheld a countenance of angelic beauty and expression. Her hair of a shining raven black, and curiously braided; her eyes were dark, but gentle, although animated; her features of a regular proportion, and her complexion wondrously fair, each cheek tinged with a lovely pink.

'Felix seemed ravished with delight when he saw her, every trait of sorrow vanished from his face, and it instantly expressed a degree of ecstatic joy, of which I could hardly have believed it capable; his eyes sparkled, as his cheek flushed with pleasure; and at that moment I thought him as beautiful as the stranger. She appeared affected by different feelings; wiping a few tears from her lovely eyes, she held out her hand to Felix, who kissed it rapturously, and called her, as well as I could distinguish, his sweet Arabian. She did not appear to understand him, but smiled. He assisted her to dismount, and dismissing her guide, conducted her into the cottage. Some conversation took place between him and his father; and the young stranger knelt at the old man's feet, and would have kissed his hand, but he raised her, and embraced her affectionately.

'I soon perceived, that although the stranger uttered articulate sounds, and appeared to have a language of her own, she was neither understood by, nor herself understood, the cottagers. They made many signs which I did not comprehend; but I saw that her presence diffused gladness through the cottage, dispelling their sorrow as the sun dissipates the morning mists. Felix seemed peculiarly happy, and with smiles of delight welcomed his Arabian. Agatha, the ever-gentle Agatha, kissed the hands of the lovely stranger; and, pointing to her brother, made signs which appeared to me to mean that he had been sorrowful until she came. Some hours passed thus, while they, by their countenances, expressed joy, the cause of which I did not comprehend. Presently I found, by the frequent recurrence of some sound which the stranger repeated after them, that she was endeavouring to learn their language; and the idea instantly occurred to me, that I should make use of the same instructions to the same end. The stranger learned about twenty words at the first lesson, most of them, indeed, were those which I had before understood, but I profited by the others.

'As night came on, Agatha and the Arabian retired early. When they separated, Felix kissed the hand of the stranger, and said, "Good night, sweet Safie." He sat up much longer, conversing with his father; and, by the frequent repetition of her name, I conjectured that their lovely guest was the subject of their conversation. I ardently desired to understand them, and bent every faculty towards that purpose, but found it utterly impossible.

'The next morning Felix went out to his work; and, after the usual occupations of Agatha were finished, the Arabian sat at the feet of the old man, and, taking his guitar, played some airs so entrancingly beautiful, that they at once drew tears of sorrow and delight from my eyes. She sang, and her voice flowed in a rich cadence, swelling or dying away, like a nightingale of the woods.

'When she had finished, she gave the guitar to Agatha, who at first declined it. She played a simple air, and her voice accompanied it in sweet accents, but unlike the wondrous strain of the stranger. The old man appeared enraptured, and said some words, which Agatha endeavoured to explain to Safie, and by which he appeared to wish to express that she bestowed on him the greatest delight by her music.

'The days now passed as peaceably as before, with the sole alteration, that joy had taken place of sadness in the countenances of my friends. Safie was always gay and happy; she and I improved rapidly in the knowledge of language, so that in two months I began to comprehend most of the words uttered by my protectors.

'In the meanwhile also the black ground was covered with herbage, and the green banks interspersed with innumerable flowers, sweet to the scent and the eyes, stars of pale radiance among the moonlight woods; the sun became warmer, the nights clear and balmy; and my nocturnal rambles were an extreme pleasure to me, although they were considerably shortened by the late setting and early rising of the sun; for I never ventured abroad during daylight, fearful of meeting with the same treatment I had formerly endured in the first village which I entered.

'My days were spent in close attention, that I might more speedily master the language; and I may boast that I improved more rapidly than the Arabian, who understood very little, and conversed in broken accents, whilst I comprehended and could imitate almost every word that was spoken.

'While I improved in speech, I also learned the science of letters, as it was taught to the stranger; and this opened before me a wide field for wonder and delight.

'The book from which Felix instructed Safie was Volney's "Ruins of Empires." I should not have understood the purport of this book, had not Felix, in reading it, given very minute explanations. He had chosen this work, he said, because the declamatory style was framed in imitation of the eastern authors. Through this work I obtained a cursory knowledge of history, and a view of the several empires at present existing in the world; it gave me an insight into the manners, governments, and religions of the different nations of the earth. I heard of the slothful Asiatics; of the stupendous genius and mental activity of the Grecians; of the wars and wonderful virtue of the early Romans—of their subsequent degenerating— of the decline of that mighty empire; of chivalry, Christianity, and kings. I heard of the discovery of the American hemisphere, and wept with Safie over the hapless fate of its original inhabitants.

'These wonderful narrations inspired me with strange feelings. Was man, indeed, at once so powerful, so virtuous, and magnificent, yet so vicious and base? He appeared at one time a mere scion of the evil principle, and at another, as all that can be conceived of noble and godlike. To be a great and virtuous man appeared the highest honour that can befall a sensitive being; to be base and vicious, as many on record have been, appeared the lowest degradation, a condition more abject than that of the blind mole or harmless worm. For a long time I could not conceive how one man could go forth to murder his fellow, or even why there were laws and governments; but when I heard details of vice and bloodshed, my wonder ceased, and I turned away with disgust and loathing.

'Every conversation of the cottagers now opened new wonders to me. While I listened to the instructions which Felix bestowed upon the Arabian, the strange system of human society was explained to me. I heard of the division of property, of immense wealth and squalid poverty; of rank, descent, and noble blood.

'The words induced me to turn towards myself. I learned that the possessions most esteemed by your fellow-creatures were, high and unsullied descent united with riches. A man might be respected with only one of these advantages; but, without either, he was considered, except in very rare instances, as a vagabond and a slave, doomed to waste his powers for the profits of the chosen few! And what was I? Of my creation and creator I was absolutely ignorant; but I knew that I possessed no money, no friends, no kind of property. I was, besides, endued with a figure hideously deformed and loathsome; I was not even of the same nature as man. I was more agile than they, and could subsist upon coarser diet; I bore the extremes of heat and cold with less injury to my frame; my stature far exceeded theirs. When I looked around, I saw and heard of none like me. Was I then a monster, a blot upon the earth, from which all men fled, and whom all men disowned?

'I cannot describe to you the agony that these reflections inflicted upon me: I tried to dispel them, but sorrow only increased with knowledge. Oh, that I had for ever remained in my native wood, nor known nor felt beyond the sensations of hunger, thirst, and heat!

'Of what a strange nature is knowledge! It clings to the mind, when it has once seized on it, like a lichen on the rock. I wished sometimes to shake off all thought and feeling; but I learned that there was but one means to overcome the sensation of pain, and that was death—a state which I feared yet did not understand. I admired virtue and good feelings, and loved the gentle manners and amiable qualities of my cottagers; but I was shut out from intercourse with them, except through means which I obtained by stealth, when I was unseen and unknown, and which rather increased than satisfied the desire I had of becoming one among my fellows. The gentle words of Agatha, and the animated smiles of the charming Arabian, were not for me. The mild exhortations of the old man, and the lively conversation of the loved Felix, were not for me. Miserable, unhappy wretch!

'Other lessons were impressed upon me even more deeply. I heard of the difference of sexes; and the birth and growth of children; how the father doated on the smiles of the infant, and the lively sallies of the older child; how all the life and cares of the mother were wrapped up in the precious charge; how the mind of youth expanded and gained knowledge; of brother, sister, and all the various relationships which bind one human being to another in mutual bonds.

'But where were my friends and relations? No father had watched my infant days, no mother had blessed me with smiles and caresses; or if they had, all my past life was now a blot, a blind vacancy in which I distinguished nothing. From my earliest remembrance I had been as I then was in height and proportion. I had never yet seen a being resembling me, or who claimed any intercourse with me. What was I? The question again recurred, to be answered only with groans.

'I will soon explain to what these feelings tended; but allow me now to return to the cottagers, whose story excited in me such various feelings of indignation, delight, and wonder, but which all terminated in additional love and reverence for my protectors (for so I loved, in an innocent, half painful self-deceit, to call them).

CHAPTER XIV

'SOME time elapsed before I learned the history of my friends. It was one which could not fail to impress itself deeply on my mind, unfolding as it did a number of circumstances, each interesting and wonderful to one so utterly inexperienced as I was.

'The name of the old man was De Lacey. He was descended from a good family in France, where he had lived for many years in affluence, respected by his superiors, and beloved by his equals. His son was bred in the service of his country; and Agatha had ranked with ladies of the highest distinction. A few months before my arrival, they had lived in a large and luxurious city, called Paris, surrounded by friends, and possessed of every enjoyment which virtue, refinement of intellect, or taste, accompanied by a moderate fortune, could afford.

'The father of Safie had been the cause of their ruin. He was a Turkish merchant, and had inhabited Paris for many years, when, for some reason which I could not learn, he became obnoxious to the government. He was seized and cast into prison the very day that Safie arrived from Constantinople to join him. He was tried, and condemned to death. The injustice of his sentence was very flagrant; all Paris was indignant; and it was judged that his religion and wealth, rather than the crime alleged against him, had been the cause of his condemnation.

'Felix had accidentally been present at the trial; his horror and indignation were uncontrollable, when he heard the decision of the court. He made, at that moment, a solemn vow to deliver him, and then looked around for the means. After many fruitless attempts to gain admittance to the prison, he found a strongly grated window in an unguarded part of the building, which lighted the dungeon of the unfortunate Mahometan; who, loaded with chains, waited in despair the execution of the barbarous sentence. Felix visited the grate at night, and made known to the prisoner his intentions in his favour. The Turk, amazed and delighted, endeavoured to kindle the zeal of his deliverer by promises of reward and wealth. Felix rejected his offers with contempt; yet when he saw the lovely Safie, who was allowed to visit her father, and who, by her gestures, expressed her lively gratitude, the youth could not help owning to his own mind, that the captive possessed a treasure which would fully reward his toil and hazard.

'The Turk quickly perceived the impression that his daughter had made on the heart of Felix, and endeavoured to secure him more entirely in his interests by the promise of her hand in marriage, so soon as he should be conveyed to a place of safety. Felix was too delicate to accept this offer; yet he looked forward to the probability of the event as to the consummation of his happiness.

'During the ensuing days, while the preparations were going forward for the escape of the merchant, the zeal of Felix was warmed by several letters that he received from this lovely girl, who found means to express her thoughts in the language of her lover by the aid of an old man, a servant of her father, who understood French. She thanked him in the most ardent terms for his intended services towards her parent; and at the same time she gently deplored her own fate.

'I have copies of these letters; for I found means, during my residence in the hovel, to procure the implements of writing; and the letters were often in the hands of Felix or Agatha. Before I depart, I will give them to you, they will prove the truth of my tale; but at present, as the sun is already far declined, I shall only have time to repeat the substance of them to you.

'Safie related, that her mother was a Christian Arab, seized and made a slave by the Turks; recommended by her beauty, she had won the heart of the father of Safie, who married her. The young girl spoke in high and enthusiastic terms of her mother, who, born in freedom, spurned the bondage to which she was now reduced. She instructed her daughter in the tenets of her religion, and taught her to aspire to higher powers of intellect, and an independence of spirit, forbidden to the female followers of Mahomet. This lady died; but her lessons were indelibly impressed on the mind of Safie, who sickened at the prospect of again returning to Asia, and being immured within the walls of a haram, allowed only to occupy herself with infantile amusements, ill suited to the temper of her soul, now accustomed to grand ideas and a noble emulation for virtue. The prospect of marrying a Christian, and remaining in a country where women were allowed to take a rank in society, was enchanting to her.

'The day for the execution of the Turk was fixed; but, on the night previous to it, he quitted his prison, and before morning was distant many leagues from Paris. Felix had procured passports in the name of his father, sister, and himself. He had previously communicated his plan to the former, who aided the deceit by quitting his house, under the pretence of a journey, and concealed himself, with his daughter, in an obscure part of Paris.

'Felix conducted the fugitives through France to Lyons, and across Mont Cenis to Leghorn, where the merchant had decided to wait a favourable opportunity of passing into some part of the Turkish dominions.

'Safie resolved to remain with her father until the moment of his departure, before which time the Turk renewed his promise that she should be united to his deliverer; and Felix remained with them in expectation of that event; and in the mean time he enjoyed the society of the Arabian, who exhibited towards him the simplest and tenderest affection. They conversed with one another through the means of an interpreter, and sometimes with the interpretation of looks; and Safie sang to him the divine airs of her native country.

'The Turk allowed this intimacy to take place, and encouraged the hopes of the youthful lovers, while in his heart he had formed far other plans. He loathed the idea that his daughter should be united to a Christian; but he feared the resentment of Felix, if he should appear lukewarm; for he knew that he was still in the power of his deliverer, if he should choose to betray him to the Italian state which they inhabited. He revolved a thousand plans by which he should be enabled to prolong the deceit until it might be no longer necessary, and secretly to take his daughter with him when he departed. His plans were facilitated by the news which arrived from Paris.

'The government of France were greatly enraged at the escape of their victim, and spared no pains to detect and punish his deliverer. The plot of Felix was quickly discovered, and De Lacey and Agatha were thrown into prison. The news reached Felix, and roused him from his dream of pleasure. His blind and aged father, and his gentle sister, lay in a noisome dungeon, while he enjoyed the free air, and the society of her whom he loved. This idea was torture to him. He quickly arranged with the Turk, that if the latter should find a favourable opportunity for escape before Felix could return to Italy, Safie should remain as a boarder at a convent at Leghorn; and then, quitting the lovely Arabian, he hastened to Paris, and delivered himself up to the vengeance of the law, hoping to free De Lacey and Agatha by this proceeding.

'He did not succeed. They remained confined for five months before the trial took place; the result of which deprived them of their fortune, and condemned them to a perpetual exile from their native country.

'They found a miserable asylum in the cottage in Germany, where I discovered them. Felix soon learned that the treacherous Turk, for whom he and his family endured such unheard-of oppression, on discovering that his deliverer was thus reduced to poverty and ruin, became a traitor to good feeling and honour, and had quitted Italy with his daughter, insultingly sending Felix a pittance of money, to aid him, as he said, in some plan of future maintenance.

'Such were the events that preyed on the heart of Felix, and rendered him, when I first saw him, the most miserable of his family. He could have endured poverty; and while this distress had been the meed of his virtue, he gloried in it: but the ingratitude of the Turk, and the loss of his beloved Safie, were misfortunes more bitter and irreparable. The arrival of the Arabian now infused new life into his soul.

'When the news reached Leghorn, that Felix was deprived of his wealth and rank, the merchant commanded his daughter to think no more of her lover, but to prepare to return to her native country. The generous nature of Safie was outraged by this command; she attempted to expostulate with her father, but he left her angrily, reiterating his tyrannical mandate.

'A few days after, the Turk entered his daughter's apartment, and told her hastily, that he had reason to believe that his residence at Leghorn had been divulged, and that he should speedily be delivered up to the French government; he had, consequently, hired a vessel to convey him to Constantinople, for which city he should sail in a few hours. He intended to leave his daughter under the care of a confidential servant, to follow at her leisure with the greater part of his property, which had not yet arrived at Leghorn.

'When alone, Safie resolved in her own mind the plan of conduct that it would become her to pursue in this emergency. A residence in Turkey was abhorrent to her; her religion and her feelings were alike adverse to it. By some papers of her father, which fell into her hands, she heard of the exile of her lover, and learnt the name of the spot where he then resided. She hesitated some time, but at length she formed her determination. Taking with her some jewels that belonged to her, and a sum of money, she quitted Italy with an attendant, a native of Leghorn, but who understood the common language of Turkey, and departed for Germany.

'She arrived in safety at a town about twenty leagues from the cottage of De Lacey, when her attendant fell dangerously ill. Safie nursed her with the most devoted affection; but the poor girl died, and the Arabian was left alone, unacquainted with the language of the country, and utterly ignorant of the customs of the world. She fell, however, into good hands. The Italian had mentioned the name of the spot for which they were bound; and, after her death, the woman of the house in which they had lived took care that Safie should arrive in safety at the cottage of her lover.

CHAPTER XV

'SUCH was the history of my beloved cottagers. It impressed me deeply. I learned, from the views of social life which it developed, to admire their virtues, and to deprecate the vices of mankind.

'As yet I looked upon crime as a distant evil; benevolence and generosity were ever present before me, inciting within me a desire to become an actor in the busy scene where so many admirable qualities were called forth and displayed. But, in giving an account of the progress of my intellect, I must not omit a circumstance which occurred in the beginning of the month of August of the same year.

'One night, during my accustomed visit to the neighbouring wood, where I collected my own food, and brought home firing for my protectors, I found on the ground a leathern portmanteau, containing several articles of dress and some books. I eagerly seized the prize, and returned with it to my hovel. Fortunately the books were written in the language, the elements of which I had acquired at the cottage; they consisted of "Paradise Lost," a volume of "Plutarch's Lives," and the "Sorrows of Werter." The possession of these treasures gave me extreme delight; I now continually studied and exercised my mind upon these histories, whilst my friends were employed in their ordinary occupations.

'I can hardly describe to you the effect of these books. They produced in me an infinity of new images and feelings, that sometimes raised me to ecstacy, but more frequently sunk me into the lowest dejection. In the "Sorrows of Werter," besides the interest of its simple and affecting story, so many opinions are canvassed, and so many lights thrown upon what had hitherto been to me obscure subjects, that I found in it a never-ending source of speculation and astonishment. The gentle and domestic manners it described, combined with lofty sentiments and feelings, which had for their object something out of self, accorded well with my experience among my protectors, and with the wants which were for ever alive in my own bosom. But I thought Werter himself a more divine being than I had ever beheld or imagined; his character contained no pretension, but it sunk deep. The disquisitions upon death and suicide were calculated to fill me with wonder. I did not pretend to enter into the merits of the case, yet I inclined towards the opinions of the hero, whose extinction I wept, without precisely understanding it.

'As I read, however, I applied much personally to my own feelings and condition. I found myself similar, yet at the same time strangely unlike to the beings concerning whom I read, and to whose conversation I was a listener. I sympathised with, and partly understood them, but I was unformed in mind; I was dependent on none, and related to none. "The path of my departure was free;" and there was none to lament my annihilation. My person was hideous, and my stature gigantic: what did this mean? Who was I? What was I? Whence did I come? What was my destination? These questions continually recurred, but I was unable to solve them.

'The volume of "Plutarch's Lives," which I possessed, contained the histories of the first founders of the ancient republics. This book had a far different effect upon me from the "Sorrows of Werter." I learned from Werter's imaginations despondency and gloom: but Plutarch taught me high thoughts; he elevated me above the wretched sphere of my own reflections, to admire and love the heroes of past ages. Many things I read surpassed my understanding and experience. I had a very confused knowledge of kingdoms, wide extents of country, mighty rivers, and boundless seas. But I was perfectly unacquainted with towns, and large assemblages of men. The cottage of my protectors had been the only school in which I had studied human nature; but this book developed new and mightier scenes of action. I read of men concerned in public affairs, governing or massacring their species. I felt the greatest ardour for virtue rise within me, and abhorrence for vice, as far as I understood the significance of those terms, relative as they were, as I applied them, to pleasure and pain alone. Induced by these feelings, I was of course led to admire peaceable lawgivers, Numa, Solon, and Lycurgus, in preference to Romulus and Theseus. The patriarchal lives of my protectors caused these impressions to take a firm hold on my mind; perhaps, if my first introduction to humanity had been made by a young soldier, burning for glory and slaughter, I should have been imbued with different sensations.

'But "Paradise Lost" excited different and far deeper emotions. I read it, as I had read the other volumes which had fallen into my hands, as a true history. It moved every feeling of wonder and awe, that the picture of an omnipotent God warring with his creatures was capable of exciting. I often referred the several situations, as their similarity struck me, to my own. Like Adam, I was apparently united by no link to any other being in existence; but his state was far different from mine in every other respect. He had come forth from the hands of God a perfect creature, happy and prosperous, guarded by the especial care of his Creator; he was allowed to converse with, and acquire knowledge from, beings of a superior nature: but I was wretched, helpless, and alone. Many times I considered Satan as the fitter emblem of my condition; for often, like him, when I viewed the bliss of my protectors, the bitter gall of envy rose within me.

'Another circumstance strengthened and confirmed these feelings. Soon after my arrival in the hovel, I discovered some papers in the pocket of the dress which I had taken from your laboratory. At first I had neglected them; but now that I was able to decipher the characters in which they were written, I began to study them with diligence. It was your journal of the four months that preceded my creation. You minutely described in these papers every step you took in the progress of your work; this history was mingled with accounts of domestic occurrences. You, doubtless, recollect these papers. Here they are. Every thing is related in them which bears reference to my accursed origin; the whole detail of that series of disgusting circumstances which produced it, is set in view; the minutest description of my odious and loathsome person is given, in language which painted your own horrors, and rendered mine indelible. I sickened as I read. "Hateful day when I received life!" I exclaimed in agony. "Accursed creator! Why did you form a monster so hideous that even *you* turned from me in disgust? God, in pity, made man beautiful and alluring, after his own image; but my form is a filthy type of yours, more horrid even from the very resemblance. Satan had his companions, fellow-devils, to admire and encourage him; but I am solitary and abhorred."

'These were the reflections of my hours of despondency and solitude; but when I contemplated the virtues of the cottagers, their amiable and benevolent dispositions, I persuaded myself that when they should become acquainted with my admiration of their virtues, they would compassionate me, and overlook my personal deformity. Could they turn from their door one, however monstrous, who solicited their compassion and friendship? I resolved, at least, not to despair, but in every way to fit myself for an interview with them which would decide my fate. I postponed this attempt for some months longer; for the importance attached to its success inspired me with a dread lest I should fail. Besides, I found that my understanding improved so much with every day's experience, that I was unwilling to commence this undertaking until a few more months should have added to my sagacity.

'Several changes, in the mean time, took place in the cottage. The presence of Safie diffused happiness among its inhabitants; and I also found that a greater degree of plenty reigned there. Felix and Agatha spent more time in amusement and conversation, and were assisted in their labours by servants. They did not appear rich, but they were contented and happy; their feelings were serene and peaceful, while mine became every day more tumultuous. Increase of knowledge only discovered to me more clearly what a wretched outcast I was. I cherished hope, it is true; but it vanished, when I beheld my person reflected in water, or my shadow in the moonshine, even as that frail image and that inconstant shade.

'I endeavoured to crush these fears, and to fortify myself for the trial which in a few months I resolved to undergo; and some times I allowed my thoughts, unchecked by reason, to ramble in the fields of Paradise, and dared to fancy amiable and lovely creatures sympathising with my feelings, and cheering my gloom; their angelic countenances breathed smiles of consolation. But it was all a dream; no Eve soothed my sorrows, nor shared my thoughts; I was alone. I remembered Adam's supplication to his Creator. But where was mine? He had abandoned me; and, in the bitterness of my heart, I cursed him.

'Autumn passed thus. I saw, with surprise and grief, the leaves decay and fall, and nature again assume the barren and bleak appearance it had worn when I first beheld the woods and the lovely moon. Yet I did not heed the bleakness of the weather; I was better fitted by my conformation for the endurance of cold than heat. But my chief delights were the sight of the flowers, the birds, and all the gay apparel of summer; when those deserted me, I turned with more attention towards the cottagers. Their happiness was not decreased by the absence of summer. They loved, and sympathised with one another; and their joys, depending on each other, were not interrupted by the casualties that took place around them. The more I saw of them, the greater became my desire to claim their protection and kindness; my heart yearned to be known and loved by these amiable creatures: to see their sweet looks directed towards me with affection, was the utmost limit of my ambition. I dared not think that they would turn them from me with disdain and horror. The poor that stopped at their door were never driven away. I asked, it is true, for greater treasures than a little food or rest: I required kindness and sympathy; but I did not believe myself utterly unworthy of it.

'The winter advanced, and an entire revolution of the seasons had taken place since I awoke into life. My attention, at this time, was solely directed towards my plan of introducing myself into the cottage of my protectors. I revolved many projects; but that on which I finally fixed was, to enter the dwelling when the blind old man should be alone. I had sagacity enough to discover, that the unnatural hideousness of my person was the chief object of horror with those who had formerly beheld me. My voice, although harsh, had nothing terrible in it; I thought, therefore, that if, in the absence of his children, I could gain the good-will and mediation of the old De Lacey, I might, by his means, be tolerated by my younger protectors.

'One day, when the sun shone on the red leaves that strewed the ground, and diffused cheerfulness, although it denied warmth, Safie, Agatha, and Felix departed on a long country walk, and the old man, at his own desire, was left alone in the cottage. When his children had departed, he took up his guitar, and played several mournful but sweet airs, more sweet and mournful than I had ever heard him play before. At first his countenance was illuminated with pleasure, but, as he continued, thoughtfulness and sadness succeeded; at length, laying aside the instrument, he sat absorbed in reflection.

'My heart beat quick; this was the hour and moment of trial, which would decide my hopes, or realise my fears. The servants were gone to a neighbouring fair. All was silent in and around the cottage: it was an excellent opportunity; yet, when I proceeded to execute my plan, my limbs failed me, and I sank to the ground. Again I rose; and, exerting all the firmness of which I was master, removed the planks which I had placed before my hovel to conceal my retreat. The fresh air revived me, and, with renewed determination, I approached the door of their cottage.

'I knocked. "Who is there?" said the old man—"Come in."

'I entered; "Pardon this intrusion," said I: "I am a traveller in want of a little rest; you would greatly oblige me, if you would allow me to remain a few minutes before the fire."

' "Enter," said De Lacey; "and I will try in what manner I can relieve your wants; but, unfortunately, my children are from home, and, as I am blind, I am afraid I shall find it difficult to procure food for you."

' "Do not trouble yourself, my kind host, I have food; it is warmth and rest only that I need."

'I sat down, and a silence ensued. I knew that every minute was precious to me, yet I remained irresolute in what manner to commence the interview; when the old man addressed me—

' "By your language, stranger, I suppose you are my countryman;—are you French?"

' "No; but I was educated by a French family, and understand that language only. I am now going to claim the protection of some friends, whom I sincerely love, and of whose favour I have some hopes."

' "Are they Germans?"

' "No, they are French. But let us change the subject. I am an unfortunate and deserted creature; I look around, and I have no relation or friend upon earth. These amiable people to whom I go have never seen me, and know little of me. I am full of fears; for if I fail there, I am an outcast in the world for ever."

' "Do not despair. To be friendless is indeed to be unfortunate; but the hearts of men, when unprejudiced by any obvious self-interest, are full of brotherly love and charity. Rely, therefore, on your hopes; and if these friends are good and amiable, do not despair."

' "They are kind—they are the most excellent creatures in the world; but, unfortunately, they are prejudiced against me. I have good dispositions; my life has been hitherto harmless, and in some degree beneficial; but a fatal prejudice clouds their eyes, and where they ought to see a feeling and kind friend, they behold only a detestable monster."

' "That is indeed unfortunate; but if you are really blameless, cannot you undeceive them?"

' "I am about to undertake that task; and it is on that account that I feel so many overwhelming terrors. I tenderly love these friends; I have, unknown to them, been for many months in the habits of daily kindness towards them; but they believe that I wish to injure them, and it is that prejudice which I wish to overcome."

' "Where do these friends reside?"

' "Near this spot."

'The old man paused, and then continued, "If you will unreservedly confide to me the particulars of your tale, I perhaps may be of use in undeceiving them. I am blind, and cannot judge of your countenance, but there is something in your words, which persuades me that you are sincere. I am poor, and an exile; but it will afford me true pleasure to be in any way serviceable to a human creature."

' "Excellent man! I thank you, and accept your generous offer. You raise me from the dust by this kindness; and I trust that, by your aid, I shall not be driven from the society and sympathy of your fellow-creatures."

' "Heaven forbid! even if you were really criminal; for that can only drive you to desperation, and not instigate you to virtue. I also am unfortunate; I and my family have been condemned, although innocent: judge, therefore, if I do not feel for your misfortunes."

' "How can I thank you, my best and only benefactor? From your lips first have I heard the voice of kindness directed towards me; I shall be for ever grateful; and your present humanity assures me of success with those friends whom I am on the point of meeting."

' "May I know the names and residence of those friends?"

'I paused. This, I thought, was the moment of decision, which was to rob me of, or bestow happiness on me for ever. I struggled vainly for firmness sufficient to answer him, but the effort destroyed all my remaining strength; I sank on the chair, and sobbed aloud. At that moment I heard the steps of my younger protectors. I had not a moment to lose; but, seizing the hand of the old man I cried, "Now is the time!—save and protect me! You and your family are the friends whom I seek. Do not you desert me in the hour of trial!"

' "Great God!" exclaimed the old man, "who are you?"

'At that instant the cottage door was opened, and Felix, Safie, and Agatha entered. Who can describe their horror and consternation on beholding me? Agatha fainted; and Safie, unable to attend to her friend, rushed out of the cottage. Felix darted forward, and with supernatural force tore me from his father, to whose knees I clung: in a transport of fury, he dashed me to the ground, and struck me violently with a stick. I could have torn him limb from limb, as the lion rends the antelope. But my heart sunk within me as with bitter sickness, and I refrained. I saw him on the point of repeating his blow, when, overcome by pain and anguish, I quitted the cottage, and in the general tumult escaped unperceived to my hovel.

CHAPTER XVI

'CURSED, cursed creator! Why did I live? Why, in that instant, did I not extinguish the spark of existence which you had so wantonly bestowed? I know not; despair had not yet taken possession of me; my feelings were those of rage and revenge. I could with pleasure have destroyed the cottage and its inhabitants, and have glutted myself with their shrieks and misery.

'When night came, I quitted my retreat, and wandered in the wood; and now, no longer restrained by the fear of discovery, I gave vent to my anguish in fearful howlings. I was like a wild beast that had broken the toils; destroying the objects that obstructed me, and ranging through the wood with a stag-like swiftness. O! what a miserable night I passed! the cold stars shone in mockery, and the bare trees waved their branches above me: now and then the sweet voice of a bird burst forth amidst the universal stillness. All, save I, were at rest or in enjoyment: I, like the arch-fiend, bore a hell within me; and, finding myself unsympathised with, wished to tear up the trees, spread havoc and destruction around me, and then to have sat down and enjoyed the ruin.

'But this was a luxury of sensation that could not endure; I became fatigued with excess of bodily exertion, and sank on the damp grass in the sick impotence of despair. There was none among the myriads of men that existed who would pity or assist me; and should I feel kindness towards my enemies? No: from that moment I declared everlasting war against the species, and, more than all, against him who had formed me, and sent me forth to this insupportable misery.

'The sun rose; I heard the voices of men, and knew that it was impossible to return to my retreat during that day. Accordingly I hid myself in some thick underwood, determining to devote the ensuing hours to reflection on my situation.

'The pleasant sunshine, and the pure air of day, restored me to some degree of tranquillity; and when I considered what had passed at the cottage, I could not help believing that I had been too hasty in my conclusions. I had certainly acted imprudently. It was apparent that my conversation had interested the father in my behalf, and I was a fool in having exposed my person to the horror of his children. I ought to have familiarised the old De Lacey to me, and by degrees to have discovered myself to the rest of his family, when they should have been prepared for my approach. But I did not believe my errors to be irretrievable; and, after much consideration, I resolved to return to the cottage, seek the old man, and by my representations win him to my party.

'These thoughts calmed me, and in the afternoon I sank into a profound sleep; but the fever of my blood did not allow me to be visited by peaceful dreams. The horrible scene of the preceding day was for ever acting before my eyes; the females were flying, and the enraged Felix tearing me from his father's feet. I awoke exhausted; and, finding that it was already night, I crept forth from my hiding-place, and went in search of food.

'When my hunger was appeased, I directed my steps towards the well-known path that conducted to the cottage. All there was at peace. I crept into my hovel, and remained in silent expectation of the accustomed hour when the family arose. That hour passed, the sun mounted high in the heavens, but the cottages did not appear. I trembled violently, apprehending some dreadful misfortune. The inside of the cottage was dark, and I heard no motion; I cannot describe the agony of this suspense.

'Presently two countrymen passed by; but, pausing near the cottage, they entered into conversation, using violent gesticulations; but I did not understand what they said, as they spoke the language of the country, which differed from that of my protectors. Soon after, however, Felix approached with another man: I was surprised, as I knew that he had not quitted the cottage that morning, and waited anxiously to discover, from his discourse, the meaning of these unusual appearances.

' "Do you consider," said his companion to him, "that you will be obliged to pay three months' rent, and to lose the produce of your garden? I do not wish to take any unfair advantage, and I beg therefore that you will take some days to consider of your determination."

' "It is utterly useless," replied Felix; "we can never again inhabit your cottage. The life of my father is in the greatest danger, owing to the dreadful circumstance that I have related. My wife and my sister will never recover their horror. I entreat you not to reason with me any more. Take possession of your tenement, and let me fly from this place."

'Felix trembled violently as he said this. He and his companion entered the cottage, in which they remained for a few minutes, and then departed. I never saw any of the family of De Lacey more.

'I continued for the remainder of the day in my hovel in a state of utter and stupid despair. My protectors had departed, and had broken the only link that held me to the world. For the first time the feelings of revenge and hatred filled my bosom, and I did not strive to control them; but, allowing myself to be borne away by the stream, I bent my mind towards injury and death. When I thought of my friends, of the mild voice of De Lacey, the gentle eyes of Agatha, and the exquisite beauty of the Arabian, these thoughts vanished, and a gush of tears somewhat soothed me. But again, when I reflected that they had spurned and deserted me, anger returned, a rage of anger; and, unable to injure any thing human, I turned my fury towards inanimate objects. As night advanced, I placed a variety of combustibles around the cottage; and, after having destroyed every vestige of cultivation in the garden, I waited with forced impatience until the moon had sunk to commence my operations.

'As the night advanced, a fierce wind arose from the woods, and quickly dispersed the clouds that had loitered in the heavens: the blast tore along like a mighty avalanche, and produced a kind of insanity in my spirits, that burst all bounds of reason and reflection. I lighted the dry branch of a tree, and danced with fury around the devoted cottage, my eyes still fixed on the western horizon, the edge of which the moon nearly touched. A part of its orb was at length hid, and I waved my brand; it sunk, and, with a loud scream, I fired the straw, and heath, and bushes, which I had collected. The wind fanned the fire, and the cottage was quickly enveloped by the flames, which clung to it, and licked it with their forked and destroying tongues.

'As soon as I was convinced that no assistance could save any part of the habitation, I quitted the scene, and sought for refuge in the woods.

'And now, with the world before me, whither should I bend my steps? I resolved to fly far from the scene of my misfortunes; but to me, hated and despised, every country must be equally horrible. At length the thought of you crossed my mind. I learned from your papers that you were my father, my creator; and to whom could I apply with more fitness than to him who had given me life? Among the lessons that Felix had bestowed upon Safie, geography had not been omitted: I had learned from these the relative situations of the different countries of the earth. You had mentioned Geneva as the name of your native town; and towards this place I resolved to proceed.

'But how was I to direct myself? I knew that I must travel in a south-westerly direction to reach my destination; but the sun was my only guide. I did not know the names of the towns that I was to pass through, nor could I ask information from a single human being; but I did not despair. From you only could I hope for succour, although towards you I felt no sentiment but that of hatred. Unfeeling, heartless creator! you had endowed me with perceptions and passions, and then cast me abroad an object for the scorn and horror of mankind. But on you only had I any claim for pity and redress, and from you I determined to seek that justice which I vainly attempted to gain from any other being that wore the human form.

'My travels were long, and the sufferings I endured intense. It was late in autumn when I quitted the district where I had so long resided. I travelled only at night, fearful of encountering the visage of a human being. Nature decayed around me, and the sun became heatless; rain and snow poured around me; mighty rivers were frozen; the surface of the earth was hard and chill, and bare, and I found no shelter. Oh, earth! how often did I imprecate curses on the cause of my being! The mildness of my nature had fled, and all within me was turned to gall and bitterness. The nearer I approached to your habitation, the more deeply did I feel the spirit of revenge enkindled in my heart. Snow fell, and the waters were hardened; but I rested not. A few incidents now and then directed me, and I possessed a map of the country; but I often wandered wide from my path. The agony of my feelings allowed me no respite: no incident occurred from which my rage and misery could not extract its food; but a circumstance that happened when I arrived on the confines of Switzerland, when the sun had recovered its warmth, and the earth again began to look green, confirmed in an especial manner the bitterness and horror of my feelings.

'I generally rested during the day, and travelled only when I was secured by night from the view of man. One morning, however, finding that my path lay through a deep wood, I ventured to continue my journey after the sun had risen; the day, which was one of the first of spring, cheered even me by the loveliness of its sunshine and the balminess of the air. I felt emotions of gentleness and pleasure, that had long appeared dead, revive within me. Half surprised by the novelty of these sensations, I allowed myself to be borne away by them; and, forgetting my solitude and deformity, dared to be happy. Soft tears again bedewed my cheeks, and I even raised my humid eyes with thankfulness towards the blessed sun which bestowed such joy upon me.

'I continued to wind among the paths of the wood, until I came to its boundary, which was skirted by a deep and rapid river, into which many of the trees bent their branches, now budding with the fresh spring. Here I paused, not exactly knowing what path to pursue, when I heard the sound of voices, that induced me to conceal myself under the shade of a cypress. I was scarcely hid, when a young girl came running towards the spot where I was concealed, laughing, as if she ran from some one in sport. She continued her course along the precipitous sides of the river, when suddenly her foot slipt, and she fell into the rapid stream. I rushed from my hiding-place; and, with extreme labour from the force of the current, saved her, and dragged her to shore. She was senseless; and I endeavoured, by every means in my power, to restore animation, when I was suddenly interrupted by the approach of a rustic, who was probably the person from whom she had playfully fled. On seeing me, he darted towards me, and tearing the girl from my arms, hastened towards the deeper parts of the wood. I followed speedily, I hardly knew why; but when the man saw me draw near, he aimed a gun, which he carried, at my body, and fired. I sunk to the ground, and my injurer, with increased swiftness, escaped into the wood.

'This was then the reward of my benevolence! I had saved a human being from destruction, and, as a recompense, I now writhed under the miserable pain of a wound, which shattered the flesh and bone. The feelings of kindness and gentleness, which I had entertained but a few moments before, gave place to hellish rage and gnashing of teeth. Inflamed by pain, I vowed eternal hatred and vengeance to all mankind. But the agony of my wound overcame me; my pulses paused, and I fainted.

'For some weeks I led a miserable life in the woods, endeavouring to cure the wound which I had received. The ball had entered my shoulder, and I knew not whether it had remained there or passed through; at any rate I had no means of extracting it. My sufferings were augmented also by the oppressive sense of the injustice and ingratitude of their infliction. My daily vows rose for revenge—a deep and deadly revenge, such as would alone compensate for the outrages and anguish I had endured.

'After some weeks my wound healed, and I continued my journey. The labours I endured were no longer to be alleviated by the bright sun or gentle breezes of spring; all joy was but a mockery, which insulted my desolate state, and made me feel more painfully that I was not made for the enjoyment of pleasure.

'But my toils now drew near a close; and, in two months from this time, I reached the environs of Geneva.

'It was evening when I arrived, and I retired to a hiding-place among the fields that surround it, to meditate in what manner I should apply to you. I was oppressed by fatigue and hunger, and far too unhappy to enjoy the gentle breezes of evening, or the prospect of the sun setting behind the stupendous mountains of Jura.

'At this time a slight sleep relieved me from the pain of reflection, which was disturbed by the approach of a beautiful child, who came running into the recess I had chosen, with all the sportiveness of infancy. Suddenly, as I gazed on him, an idea seized me, that this little creature was unprejudiced, and had lived too short a time to have imbibed a horror of deformity. If, therefore, I could seize him, and educate him as my companion and friend, I should not be so desolate in this peopled earth.

'Urged by this impulse, I seized on the boy as he passed, and drew him towards me. As soon as he beheld my form, he placed his hands before his eyes, and uttered a shrill scream: I drew his hand forcibly from his face, and said, "Child, what is the meaning of this? I do not intend to hurt you; listen to me."

'He struggled violently. "Let me go," he cried; "monster! ugly wretch! you wish to eat me, and tear me to pieces—You are an ogre—Let me go, or I will tell my papa."

' "Boy, you will never see your father again; you must come with me."

' "Hideous monster! let me go. My papa is a Syndic—he is M. Frankenstein—he will punish you. You dare not keep me."

' "Frankenstein! you belong then to my enemy—to him towards whom I have sworn eternal revenge; you shall be my first victim."

'The child still struggled, and loaded me with epithets which carried despair to my heart; I grasped his throat to silence him, and in a moment he lay dead at my feet.

'I gazed on my victim, and my heart swelled with exultation and hellish triumph: clapping my hands, I exclaimed, "I, too, can create desolation; my enemy is not invulnerable; this death will carry despair to him, and a thousand other miseries shall torment and destroy him."

'As I fixed my eyes on the child, I saw something glittering on his breast. I took it; it was a portrait of a most lovely woman. In spite of my malignity, it softened and attracted me. For a few moments I gazed with delight on her dark eyes, fringed by deep lashes, and her lovely lips; but presently my rage returned: I remembered that I was for ever deprived of the delights that such beautiful creatures could bestow; and that she whose resemblance I contemplated would, in regarding me, have changed that air of divine benignity to one expressive of disgust and affright.

'Can you wonder that such thoughts transported me with rage? I only wonder that at that moment, instead of venting my sensations in exclamations and agony, I did not rush among mankind, and perish in the attempt to destroy them.

'While I was overcome by these feelings, I left the spot where I had committed the murder, and seeking a more secluded hiding-place, I entered a barn which had appeared to me to be empty. A woman was sleeping on some straw; she was young: not indeed so beautiful as her whose portrait I held; but of an agreeable aspect, and blooming in the loveliness of youth and health. Here, I thought, is one of those whose joy-imparting smiles are bestowed on all but me. And then I bent over her, and whispered, "Awake, fairest, thy lover is near—he who would give his life but to obtain one look of affection from thine eyes: my beloved, awake!"

'The sleeper stirred; a thrill of terror ran through me. Should she indeed awake, and see me, and curse me, and denounce the murderer? Thus would she assuredly act, if her darkened eyes opened, and she beheld me. The thought was madness; it stirred the fiend within me—not I, but she shall suffer: the murder I have committed because I am for ever robbed of all that she could give me, she shall atone. The crime had its source in her: be hers the punishment! Thanks to the lessons of Felix and the sanguinary laws of man, I had learned now to work mischief. I bent over her, and placed the portrait securely in one of the folds of her dress. She moved again, and I fled.

'For some days I haunted the spot where these scenes had taken place; sometimes wishing to see you, sometimes resolved to quit the world and its miseries for ever. At length I wandered towards these mountains, and have ranged through their immense recesses, consumed by a burning passion which you alone can gratify. We may not part until you have promised to comply with my requisition. I am alone, and miserable; man will not associated with me; but one as deformed and horrible as myself would not deny herself to me. My companion must be of the same species, and have the same defects. This being you must create.'

CHAPTER XVII

THE being finished speaking, and fixed his looks upon me in expectation of a reply. But I was bewildered, perplexed, and unable to arrange my ideas sufficiently to understand the full extent of his proposition. He continued—

'You must create a female for me, with whom I can live in the interchange of those sympathies necessary for my being. This you alone can do; and I demand it of you as a right which you must not refuse to concede.'

The latter part of his tale had kindled anew in me the anger that had died away while he narrated his peaceful life among the cottagers, and, as he said this, I could no longer suppress the rage that burned within me.

'I do refuse it,' I replied; 'and no torture shall ever extort a consent from me. You may render me the most miserable of men, but you shall never make me base in my own eyes. Shall I create another like yourself, whose joint wickedness might desolate the world? Begone! I have answered you; you may torture me, but I will never consent.'

'You are in the wrong,' replied the fiend; 'and, instead of threatening, I am content to reason with you. I am malicious because I am miserable. Am I not shunned and hated by all mankind? You, my creator, would tear me to pieces, and triumph; remember that, and tell me why I should pity man more than he pities me? You would not call it murder, if you could precipitate me into one of those ice-rifts, and destroy my frame, the work of your own hands. Shall I respect man, when he contemns me? Let him live with me in the interchange of kindness; and, instead of injury, I would bestow every benefit upon him with tears of gratitude at his acceptance. But that cannot be; the human senses are insurmountable barriers to our union. Yet mine shall not be the submission of abject slavery. I will revenge my injuries: if I cannot inspire love, I will cause fear; and chiefly towards you my arch-enemy, because my creator, do I swear inextinguishable hatred. Have a care: I will work at your destruction, nor finish until I desolate your heart, so that you shall curse the hour of your birth.'

A fiendish rage animated him as he said this; his face was wrinkled into contortions too horrible for human eyes to behold; but presently he calmed himself and proceeded—

'I intended to reason. This passion is detrimental to me; for you do not reflect that *you* are the cause of its excess. If any being felt emotions of benevolence towards me, I should return them an hundred and an hundred fold; for that one creature's sake, I would make peace with the whole kind! But I now indulge in dreams of bliss that cannot be realised. What I ask of you is reasonable and moderate; I demand a creature of another sex, but as hideous as myself; the gratification is small, but it is all that I can receive, and it shall content me. It is true, we shall be monsters, cut off from all the world; but on that account we shall be more attached to one another. Our lives will not be happy, but they will be harmless, and free from the misery I now feel. Oh! my creator, make me happy; let me feel gratitude towards you for one benefit! Let me see that I excite the sympathy of some existing thing; do not deny me my request!'

I was moved. I shuddered when I thought of the possible consequences of my consent; but I felt that there was some justice in his argument. His tale, and the feelings he now expressed, proved him to be a creature of fine sensations; and did I not, as his maker, owe him all the portion of happiness that it was in my power to bestow? He saw my change of feeling, and continued—

'If you consent, neither you nor any other human being shall ever see us again: I will go to the vast vilds of South America. My food is not that of man; I do not destroy the lamb and the kid to glut my appetite; acorns and berries afford me sufficient nourishment. My companion will be of the same nature as myself, and will be content with the same fare. We shall make our bed of dried leaves; the sun will shine on us as on man, and will ripen our food. The picture I present to you is peaceful and human, and you must feel that you could deny it only in the wantonness of power and cruelty. Pitiless as you have been towards me, I now see compassion in your eyes; let me seize the favourable moment, and persuade you to promise what I so ardently desire.'

'You propose,' replied I, 'to fly from the habitations of man, to dwell in those wilds where the beasts of the field will be your only companions. How can you, who long for the love and sympathy of man, persevere in this exile? You will return, and again seek their kindness, and you will meet with their detestation; your evil passions will be renewed, and you will then have a companion to aid you in the task of destruction. This may not be: cease to argue the point, for I cannot consent.'

'How inconstant are your feelings! but a moment ago you were moved by my representations, and why do you again harden yourself to my complaints? I swear to you, by the earth which I inhabit, and by you that made me, that, with the companion you bestow, I will quit the neighbourhood of man, and dwell as it may chance, in the most savage of places. My evil passions will have fled, for I shall meet with sympathy! my life will flow quietly away, and, in my dying moments, I shall not curse my maker.'

His words had a strange effect upon me. I compassioned him, and sometimes felt a wish to console him; but when I looked upon him, when I saw the filthy mass that moved and talked, my heart sickened, and my feelings were altered to those of horror and hatred. I tried to stifle these sensations; I thought, that as I could not sympathise with him, I had no right to withhold from him the small portion of happiness which was yet in my power to bestow.

'You swear,' I said, 'to be harmless; but have you not already shown a degree of malice that should reasonably make me distrust you? May not even this be a feint that will increase your triumph by affording a wider scope for your revenge.'

'How is this? I must not be trifled with: and I demand an answer. If I have no ties and no affections, hatred and vice must be my portion; the love of another will destroy the cause of my crimes, and I shall become a thing, of whose existence every one will be ignorant. My vices are the children of a forced solitude that I abhor; and my virtues will necessarily arise when I live in communion with an equal. I shall feel the affections of a sensitive being, and become linked to the chain of existence and events, from which I am now excluded.'

I paused some time to reflect on all he had related, and the various arguments which he had employed. I thought of the promise of virtues which he had displayed on the opening of his existence, and the subsequent blight of all kindly feeling by the loathing and scorn which his protectors had manifested towards him. His power and threats were not omitted in my calculations: a creature who could exist in the ice-caves of the glaciers, and hide himself from pursuit among the ridges of inaccessible precipices, was a being possessing faculties it would be vain to cope with. After a long pause of reflection, I concluded that the justice due both to him and my fellow-creatures demanded of me that I should comply with his request. Turning to him, therefore, I said—

'I consent to your demand, on your solemn oath to quit Europe for ever, and every other place in the neighbourhood of man, as soon as I shall deliver into your hands a female who will accompany you in your exile.'

'I swear,' he cried, 'by the sun, and by the blue sky of Heaven, and by the fire of love that burns my heart, that if you grant my prayer, while they exist you shall never behold me again. Depart to your home, and commence your labours: I shall watch their progress with unutterable anxiety; and fear not but that when you are ready I shall appear.'

Saying this, he suddenly quitted me, fearful, perhaps, of any change in my sentiments. I saw him descend the mountain with greater speed than the flight of an eagle, and quickly lost him among the undulations of the sea of ice.

His tale had occupied the whole day; and the sun was upon the verge of the horizon when he departed. I knew that I ought to hasten my descent towards the valley, as I should soon be encompassed in darkness; but my heart was heavy, and my steps slow. The labour of winding among the little paths of the mountains, and fixing my feet firmly as I advanced, perplexed me, occupied as I was by the emotions which the occurrences of the day had produced. Night was far advanced, when I came to the half-way resting-place, and seated myself beside the fountain. The stars shone at intervals, as the clouds passed from over them; the dark pines rose before me, and every here and there a broken tree lay on the ground: it was a scene of wonderful solemnity, and stirred strange thoughts within me. I wept bitterly; and clasping my hands in agony, I exclaimed, 'Oh! stars and clouds, and winds, ye are all about to mock me: if ye really pity me, crush sensation and memory; let me become as nought; but if not, depart, depart, and leave me in darkness.'

These were wild and miserable thoughts; but I cannot describe to you how the eternal twinkling of the stars weighed upon me, and how I listened to every blast of wind, as if it were a dull ugly siroc on its way to consume me.

Morning dawned before I arrived at the village of Chamounix; I took no rest, but returned immediately to Geneva. Even in my own heart I could give no expression to my sensations—they weighed on me with a mountain's weight, and their excess destroyed my agony beneath them. Thus I returned home, and entering the house, presented myself to the family. My haggard and wild appearance awoke intense alarm; but I answered no question, scarcely did I speak. I felt as if I were placed under a ban—as if I had no right to claim their sympathies—as if never more might I enjoy companionship with them. Yet even thus I loved them to adoration; and to save them, I resolved to dedicate myself to my most abhorred task. The prospect of such an occupation made every other circumstance of existence pass before me like a dream; and that thought only had to me the reality of life.

CHAPTER XVIII

DAY after day, week after week, passed away on my return to Geneva; and I could not collect the courage to recommence my work. I feared the vengeance of the disappointed fiend, yet I was unable to overcome my repugnance to the task which was enjoined me. I found that I could not compose a female without again devoting several months to profound study and laborious disquisition. I had heard of some discoveries having been made by an English philosopher, the knowledge of which was material to my success, and I sometimes thought of obtaining my father's consent to visit England for this purpose; but I clung to every pretence of delay, and shrunk from taking the first step in an undertaking whose immediate necessity began to appear less absolute to me. A change indeed had taken place in me: my health, which had hitherto declined, was now much restored; and my spirits, when unchecked by the memory of my unhappy promise, rose proportionably. My father saw this change with pleasure, and he turned his thoughts towards the best method of eradicating the remains of my melancholy, which every now and then would return by fits, and with a devouring blackness overcast the approaching sunshine. At these moments I took refuge in the most perfect solitude. I passed whole days on the lake alone in a little boat, watching the clouds, and listening to the rippling of the waves, silent and listless. But the fresh air and bright sun seldom failed to restore me to some degree of composure; and, on my return, I met the salutations of my friends with a readier smile and a more cheerful heart.

It was after my return from one of these rambles, that my father, calling me aside, thus addressed me:—

'I am happy to remark, my dear son, that you have resumed your former pleasures, and seem to be returning to yourself. And yet you are still unhappy, and still avoid our society. For some time I was lost in conjecture as to the cause of this; but yesterday an idea struck me, and if it is well founded, I conjure you to avow it. Reserve on such a point would be not only useless, but draw down treble misery on us all.'

I trembled violently at his exordium, and my father continued—

'I confess, my son, that I have always looked forward to your marriage with our dear Elizabeth as the tie of our domestic comfort, and the stay of my declining years. You were attached to each other from your earliest infancy; you studied together, and appeared, in dispositions and tastes, entirely suited to one another. But so blind is the experience of man, that what I conceived to be the best assistants to my plan, may have entirely destroyed it. You, perhaps, regard her as your sister, without any wish that she might become your wife. Nay, you may have met with another whom you may love; and, considering yourself as bound in honour to Elizabeth, this struggle may occasion the poignant misery which you appear to feel.'

'My dear father, re-assure yourself. I love my cousin tenderly and sincerely. I never saw any woman who excited, as Elizabeth does, my warmest admiration and affection. My future hopes and prospects are entirely bound up in the expectation of our union.'

'The expression of your sentiments on this subject, my dear Victor, gives me more pleasure than I have for some time experienced. If you feel thus, we shall assuredly be happy, however present events may cast a gloom over us. But it is this gloom which appears to have taken so strong a hold of your mind, that I wish to dissipate. Tell me, therefore, whether you object to an immediate solemnisation of the marriage. We have been unfortunate, and recent events have drawn us from that every-day tranquillity befitting my years and infirmities. You are younger; yet I do not suppose, possessed as you are of a competent fortune, that an early marriage would at all interfere with any future plans of honour and utility that you may have formed. Do not suppose, however, that I wish to dictate happiness to you, or that a delay on your part would cause me any serious uneasiness. Interpret my words with candour, and answer me, I conjure you, with confidence and sincerity.'

I listened to my father in silence, and remained for some time incapable of offering any reply. I revolved rapidly in my mind a multitude of thoughts, and endeavoured to arrive at some conclusion. Alas! to me the idea of an immediate union with my Elizabeth was one of horror and dismay. I was bound by a solemn promise, which I had not yet fulfilled, and dared not break; or, if I did, what manifold miseries might not impend over me and my devoted family! Could I enter into a festival with this deadly weight yet hanging round my neck, and bowing me to the ground? I must perform my engagement, and let the monster depart with his mate, before I allowed myself to enjoy the delight of an union from which I expected peace.

I remembered also the necessity imposed upon me of either journeying to England, or entering into a long correspondence with those philosophers of that country, whose knowledge and discoveries were of indispensable use to me in my present undertaking. The latter method of obtaining the desired intelligence was dilatory and unsatisfactory: besides, I had an insurmountable aversion to the idea of engaging myself in my loathsome task in my father's house, while in habits of familiar intercourse with those I loved. I knew that a thousand fearful accidents might occur, the slightest of which would disclose a tale to thrill all connected with me with horror. I was aware also that I should often lose all self-command, all capacity of hiding the harrowing sensations that would possess me during the progress of my unearthly occupation. I must absent myself from all I loved while thus employed. Once commenced, it would quickly be achieved, and I might be restored to my family in peace and happiness. My promise fulfilled, the monster would depart for ever. Or (so my fond fancy imaged) some accident might meanwhile occur to destroy him, and put an end to my slavery for ever.

These feelings dictated my answer to my father. I expressed a wish to visit England; but, concealing the true reasons of this request, I clothed my desires under a guise which excited no suspicion, while I urged my desire with an earnestness that easily induced my father to comply. After so long a period of an absorbing melancholy, that resembled madness in its intensity and effects, he was glad to find that I was capable of taking pleasure in the idea of such a journey, and he hoped that change of scene and varied amusement would, before my return, have restored me entirely to myself.

The duration of my absence was left to my own choice; a few months, or at most a year, was the period contemplated. One paternal kind precaution he had taken to ensure my having a companion. Without previously communicating with me, he had, in concert with Elizabeth, arranged that Clerval should join me at Strasburgh. This interfered with the solitude I coveted for the prosecution of my task; yet at the commencement of my journey the presence of my friend could in no way be an impediment, and truly I rejoiced that thus I should be saved many hours of lonely, maddening reflection. Nay, Henry might stand between me and the intrusion of my foe. If I were alone, would he not at times force his abhorred presence on me, to remind me of my task, or to contemplate its progress?

To England, therefore, I was bound, and it was understood that my union with Elizabeth should take place immediately on my return. My father's age rendered him extremely averse to delay. For myself, there was one reward I promised myself from my detested toils—one consolation for my unparalleled sufferings; it was the prospect of that day when, enfranchised from my miserable slavery, I might claim Elizabeth, and forget the past in my union with her.

I now made arrangements for my journey; but one feeling haunted me, which filled me with fear and agitation. During my absence I should leave my friends unconscious of the existence of their enemy, and unprotected from his attacks, exasperated as he might be by my departure. But he had promised to follow me wherever I might go; and would he not accompany me to England? This imagination was dreadful in itself, but soothing, inasmuch as it supposed the safety of my friends. I was agonised with the idea of the possibility that the reverse of this might happen. But through the whole period during which I was the slave of my creature, I allowed myself to be governed by the impulses of the moment; and my present sensations strongly intimated that the fiend would follow me, and exempt my family from the danger of his machinations.

It was in the latter end of September that I again quitted my native country. My journey had been my own suggestion, and Elizabeth, therefore, acquiesced: but she was filled with disquiet at the idea of my suffering, away from her, the inroads of misery and grief. It had been her care which provided me a companion in Clerval—and yet a man is blind to a thousand minute circumstances, which call forth a woman's sedulous attention. She longed to bid me hasten my return,—a thousand conflicting emotions rendered her mute, as she bade me a tearful silent farewell.

I threw myself into the carriage that was to convey me away, hardly knowing whither I was going, and careless of what was passing around. I remembered only, and it was with a bitter anguish that I reflected on it, to order that my chemical instruments should be packed to go with me. Filled with dreary imaginations, I passed through many beautiful and majestic scenes; but my eyes were fixed and unobserving. I could only think of the bourne of my travels, and the work which was to occupy me whilst they endured.

After some days spent in listless indolence, during which I traversed many leagues, I arrived at Strasburgh, where I waited two days for Clerval. He came. Alas, how great was the contrast between us! He was alive to every new scene; joyful when he saw the beauties of the setting sun, and more happy when he beheld it rise, and recommence a new day. He pointed out to me the shifting colours of the landscape, and the appearances of the sky. 'This is what it is to live,' he cried, 'now I enjoy existence! But you, my dear Frankenstein, wherefore are you desponding and sorrowful?' In truth, I was occupied by gloomy thoughts, and neither saw the descent of the evening star, nor the golden sunrise reflected in the Rhine.—And you, my friend, would be far more amused with the journal of Clerval, who observed the scenery with an eye of feeling and delight, than in listening to my reflections. I, a miserable wretch, haunted by a curse that shut up every avenue to enjoyment.

We had agreed to descend the Rhine in a boat from Strasburgh to Rotterdam, whence we might take shipping for London. During this voyage, we passed many willowy islands, and saw several beautiful towns. We stayed a day at Manheim, and, on the fifth from our departure from Strasburgh, arrived at Mayence. The course of the Rhine below Mayence becomes much more picturesque. The river descends rapidly, and winds between hills, not high, but steep, and of beautiful forms. We saw many ruined castles standing on the edges of precipices, surrounded by black woods, high and inaccessible. This part of the Rhine, indeed, presents a singularly variegated landscape. In one spot you view rugged hills, ruined castles overlooking tremendous precipices, with the dark Rhine rushing beneath; and, on the sudden turn of a promontory, flourishing vineyards, with green sloping banks, and a meandering river, and populous towns occupy the scene.

We travelled at the time of the vintage, and heard the song of the labourers, as we glided down the stream. Even I, depressed in mind, and my spirits continually agitated by gloomy feelings, even I was pleased. I lay at the bottom of the boat, and, as I gazed on the cloudless blue sky, I seemed to drink in a tranquillity to which I had long been a stranger. And if these were my sensations, who can describe those of Henry? He felt as if he had been transported to Fairy-land, and enjoyed a happiness seldom tasted by man. 'I have seen,' he said, 'the most beautiful scenes of my own country; I have visited the lakes of Lucerne and Uri, where the snowy mountains descend almost perpendicularly to the water, casting black and impenetrable shades, which would cause a gloomy and mournful appearance, were it not for the most verdant islands that relieve the eye by their gay appearance; I have seen this lake agitated by a tempest, when the wind tore up whirlwinds of water, and gave you an idea of what the water-spout must be on the great ocean, and the waves dash with fury the base of the mountain, where the priest and his mistress were overwhelmed by an avalanche, and where their dying voices are still said to be heard amid the pauses of the nightly wind; I have seen the mountains of La Valais, and the Pays de Vaud: but this country, Victor, pleases me more than all those wonders. The mountains of Switzerland are more majestic and strange; but there is a charm in the banks of this divine river, that I never before saw equalled. Look at that castle which overhangs yon precipice; and that also on the island, almost concealed amongst the foliage of those lovely trees; and now that group of labourers coming from among their vines; and that village half hid in the recess of the mountain. Oh, surely, the spirit that inhabits and guards this place has a soul more in harmony with man, than those who pile the glacier, or retire to the inaccessible peaks of the mountains of our own country.'

Clerval! beloved friend! even now it delights me to record your words, and to dwell on the praise of which you are so eminently deserving. He was a being formed in the 'very poetry of nature.' His wild and enthusiastic imagination was chastened by the sensibility of his heart. His soul overflowed with ardent affections, and his friendship was of that devoted and wondrous nature that the worldly-minded teach us to look for only in the imagination. But even human sympathies were not sufficient to satisfy his eager mind. The scenery of external nature, which others regard only with admiration, he loved with ardour:—

> ————'The sounding cataract
> Haunted him like a passion: the tall rock,
> The mountain, and the deep and gloomy wood,
> Their colours and their forms, were then to him
> An appetite; a feeling, and a love,
> That had no need of a remoter charm,
> By thought supplied, or any interest
> Unborrow'd from the eye.'*

And where does he now exist? Is this gentle and lovely being lost for ever? Has this mind, so replete with ideas, imaginations fanciful and magnificent, which formed a world, whose existence depended on the life of its creator;— has this mind perished? Does it now only exist in my memory? No, it is not thus; your form so divinely wrought, and beaming with beauty, has decayed, but your spirit still visits and consoles your unhappy friend.

Pardon this gush of sorrow; these ineffectual words are but a slight tribute to the unexampled worth of Henry, but they soothe my heart, overflowing with the anguish which his remembrance creates. I will proceed with my tale.

Beyond Cologne we descended to the plains of Holland; and we resolved to post the remainder of our way; for the wind was contrary, and the stream of the river was too gentle to aid us.

* Wordsworth's 'Tintern Abbey'.

Our journey here lost the interest arising from beautiful scenery; but we arrived in a few days at Rotterdam, whence we proceeded by sea to England. It was on a clear morning, in the latter days of December, that I first saw the white cliffs of Britain. The banks of the Thames presented a new scene; they were flat, but fertile, and almost every town was marked by the remembrance of some story. We saw Tilbury Fort, and remembered the Spanish armada; Gravesend, Woolwich, and Greenwich, places which I had heard of even in my country.

At length we saw the numerous steeples of London, St Paul's towering above all, and the Tower famed in English history.

CHAPTER XIX

LONDON was our present point of rest; we determined to remain several months in this wonderful and celebrated city. Clerval desired the intercourse of the men of genius and talent who flourished at this time; but this was with me a secondary object; I was principally occupied with the means of obtaining the information necessary for the completion of my promise, and quickly availed myself of the letters of introduction that I had brought with me, addressed to the most distinguished natural philosophers.

If this journey had taken place during my days of study and happiness, it would have afforded me inexpressible pleasure. But a blight had come over my existence, and I only visited these people for the sake of the information they might give me on the subject in which my interest was so terribly profound. Company was irksome to me; when alone, I could fill my mind with the sights of heaven and earth; the voice of Henry soothed me, and I could thus cheat myself into a transitory peace. But busy uninteresting joyous faces brought back despair to my heart. I saw an insurmountable barrier placed between me and my fellow-men; this barrier was sealed with the blood of William and Justine; and to reflect on the events connected with those names filled my soul with anguish.

But in Clerval I saw the image of my former self; he was inquisitive, and anxious to gain experience and instruction. The difference of manners which he observed was to him an inexhaustible source of instruction and amusement. He was also pursuing an object he had long had in view. His design was to visit India, in the belief that he had in his knowledge of its various languages, and in the views he had taken of its society, the means of materially assisting the progress of European colonisation and trade. In Britain only could he further the execution of his plan. He was for ever busy; and the only check to his enjoyments was my sorrowful and dejected mind. I tried to conceal this as much as possible, that I might not debar him from the pleasures natural to one, who was entering on a new scene of life, undisturbed by any care or bitter recollection. I often refused to accompany him, alleging another engagement, that I might remain alone. I now also began to collect the materials necessary for my new creation, and this was to me like the torture of single drops of water continually falling on the head. Every thought that was devoted to it was an extreme anguish, and every word that I spoke in allusion to it caused my lips to quiver, and my heart to palpitate.

After passing some months in London, we received a letter from a person in Scotland, who had formerly been our visiter at Geneva. He mentioned the beauties of his native country, and asked us if those were not sufficient allurements to induce us to prolong our journey as far north as Perth, where he resided. Clerval eagerly desired to accept this invitation; and I, although I abhorred society, wished to view again mountains and streams, and all the wondrous works with which Nature adorns her chosen dwelling-places.

We had arrived in England at the beginning of October, and it was now February. We accordingly determined to commence our journey towards the north at the expiration of another month. In this expedition we did not intend to follow the great road to Edinburgh, but to visit Windsor, Oxford, Matlock, and the Cumberland lakes, resolving to arrive at the completion of this tour about the end of July. I packed up my chemical instruments, and the materials I had collected, resolving to finish my labours in some obscure nook in the northern highlands of Scotland.

We quitted London on the 27th of March, and remained a few days at Windsor, rambling in its beautiful forest. This was a new scene to us mountaineers; the majestic oaks, the quantity of game, and the herds of stately deer, were all novelties to us.

From thence we proceeded to Oxford. As we entered this city, our minds were filled with the remembrance of the events that had been transacted there more than a century and a half before. It was here that Charles I. had collected his forces. This city had remained faithful to him, after the whole nation had forsaken his cause to join the standard of parliament and liberty. The memory of that unfortunate king, and his companions, the amiable Falkland, the insolent Goring, his queen, and son, gave a peculiar interest to every part of the city, which they might be supposed to have inhabited. The spirit of elder days found a dwelling here, and we delighted to trace its footsteps. If these feelings had not found an imaginary gratification, the appearance of the city had yet in itself sufficient beauty to obtain our admiration. The colleges are ancient and picturesque; the streets are almost magnificent; and the lovely Isis, which flows beside it through meadows of exquisite verdure, is spread forth into a placid expanse of waters, which reflects its majestic assemblage of towers, and spires, and domes, embosomed among aged trees.

I enjoyed this scene; and yet my enjoyment was embittered both by the memory of the past, and the anticipation of the future. I was formed for peaceful happiness. During my youthful days discontent never visited my mind; and if I was ever overcome by *ennui*, the sight of what is beautiful in nature, or the study of what is excellent and sublime in the productions of man, could always interest my heart, and communicate elasticity to my spirits. But I am a blasted tree; the bolt has entered my soul; and I felt then that I should survive to exhibit, what I shall soon cease to be—a miserable spectacle of wrecked humanity, pitiable to others, and intolerable to myself.

We passed a considerable period at Oxford, rambling among its environs, and endeavouring to identity every spot which might relate to the most animating epoch of English history. Our little voyages of discovery were often prolonged by the successive objects that presented themselves. We visited the tomb of the illustrious Hampden, and the field on which that patriot fell. For a moment my soul was elevated from its debasing and miserable fears, to contemplate the divine ideas of liberty and self-sacrifice, of which these sights were the monuments and the remembrancers. For an instant I dared to shake off my chains, and look around me with a free and lofty spirit; but the iron had eaten into my flesh, and I sank again, trembling and hopeless, into my miserable self.

We left Oxford with regret, and proceeded to Matlock, which was our next place of rest. The country in the neighbourhood of this village resembled, to a greater degree, the scenery of Switzerland; but every thing is on a lower scale, and the green hills want the crown of distant white Alps, which always attend on the piny mountains of my native country. We visited the wondrous cave, and the little cabinets of natural history, where the curiosities are disposed in the same manner as in the collections at Servox and Chamounix. The latter name made me tremble, when pronounced by Henry; and I hastened to quit Matlock, with which that terrible scene was thus associated.

From Derby, still journeying northward, we passed two months in Cumberland and Westmorland. I could now almost fancy myself among the Swiss mountains. The little patches of snow which yet lingered on the northern sides of the mountains, the lakes, and the dashing of the rocky streams, were all familiar and dear sights to me. Here also we made some acquaintances, who almost contrived to cheat me into happiness. The delight of Clerval was proportionably greater than mine; his mind expanded in the company of men of talent, and he found in his own nature greater capacities and resources than he could have imagined himself to have possessed while he associated with his inferiors. 'I could pass my life here,' said he to me; 'and among these mountains I should scarcely regret Switzerland and the Rhine.'

But he found that a traveller's life is one that includes much pain amidst its enjoyments. His feelings are for ever on the stretch; and when he begins to sink into repose, he finds himself obliged to quit that on which he rests in pleasure for something new, which again engages his attention, and which also he forsakes for other novelties.

We had scarcely visited the various lakes of Cumberland and Westmorland, and conceived an affection for some of the inhabitants, when the period of our appointment with our Scotch friend approached, and we left them to travel on. For my own part I was not sorry. I had now neglected my promise for some time, and I feared the effects of the dæmon's disappointment. He might remain in Switzerland, and wreak his vengeance on my relatives. This idea pursued me, and tormented me at every moment from which I might otherwise have snatched repose and peace. I waited for my letters with feverish impatience: if they were delayed, I was miserable, and overcome by a thousand fears; and when they arrived, and I saw the superscription of Elizabeth or my father, I hardly dared to read and ascertain my fate. Sometimes I thought that the fiend followed me, and might expedite my remissness by murdering my companion. When these thoughts possessed me, I would not quite Henry for a moment, but followed him as his shadow, to protect him from the fancied rage of his destroyer. I felt as if I had committed some great crime, the consciousness of which haunted me. I was guiltless, but I had indeed drawn down a horrible curse upon my head, as mortal as that of crime.

I visited Edinburgh with languid eyes and mind; and yet that city might have interested the most unfortunate being. Clerval did not like it so well as Oxford: for the antiquity of the latter city was more pleasing to him. But the beauty and regularity of the new town of Edinburgh, its romantic castle, and its environs, the most delightful in the world, Arthur's Seat, St Bernard's Well, and the Pentland Hills, compensated him for the change, and filled him with cheerfulness and admiration. But I was impatient to arrive at the termination of my journey.

We left Edinburgh in a week, passing through Coupar, St Andrew's, and along the banks of the Tay, to Perth, where our friend expected us. But I was in no mood to laugh and talk with strangers, or enter into their feelings or plans with the good humour expected from a guest; and accordingly I told Clerval that I wished to make the tour of Scotland alone. 'Do you,' said I, 'enjoy yourself, and let this be our rendezvous. I may be absent a month or two; but do not interfere with my motions, I entreat you: leave me to peace and solitude for a short time; and when I return, I hope it will be with a lighter heart, more congenial to your own temper.'

Henry wished to dissuade me; but, seeing me bent on this plan, ceased to remonstrate. He entreated me to write often. 'I had rather be with you,' he said, 'in your solitary rambles, than with these Scotch people, whom I do not know: hasten then, my dear friend, to return, that I may again feel myself somewhat at home, which I cannot do in your absence.'

Having parted from my friend, I determined to visit some remote spot of Scotland, and finish my work in solitude. I did not doubt but that the monster followed me, and would discover himself to me when I should have finished, that he might receive his companion.

With this resolution I traversed the northern highlands, and fixed on one of the remotest of the Orkneys as the scene of my labours. It was a place fitted for such a work, being hardly more than a rock, whose high sides were continually beaten upon by the waves. The soil was barren, scarcely affording pasture for a few miserable cows, and oatmeal for its inhabitants, which consisted of five persons, whose gaunt and scraggy limbs gave tokens of their miserable fare. Vegetables and bread, when they indulged in such luxuries, and even fresh water, was to be procured from the main land, which was about five miles distant.

On the whole island there were but three miserable huts, and one of these was vacant when I arrived. This I hired. It contained but two rooms, and these exhibited all the squalidness of the most miserable penury. The thatch had fallen in, the walls were unplastered, and the door was off its hinges. I ordered it to be repaired, bought some furniture, and took possession; an incident which would, doubtless, have occasioned some surprise, had not all the senses of the cottagers been benumbed by want and squalid poverty. As it was, I lived ungazed at and unmolested, hardly thanked for the pittance of food and clothes which I gave; so much does suffering blunt even the coarsest sensations of men.

In this retreat I devoted the morning to labour; but in the evening, when the weather permitted, I walked on the stony beach of the sea, to listen to the waves as they roared and dashed at my feet. It was a monotonous yet everchanging scene. I thought of Switzerland; it was far different from this desolate and appalling landscape. Its hills are covered with vines, and its cottages are scattered thickly in the plains. Its fair lakes reflect a blue and gentle sky; and, when troubled by the winds, their tumult is but as the play of a lively infant, when compared to the roarings of the giant ocean.

In this manner I distributed my occupations when I first arrived; but, as I proceeded in my labour, it became every day more horrible and irksome to me. Sometimes I could not prevail on myself to enter my laboratory for several days; and at other times I toiled day and night in order to complete my work. It was, indeed, a filthy process in which I was engaged. During my first experiment, a kind of enthusiastic frenzy had blinded me to the horror of my employment; my mind was intently fixed on the consummation of my labour, and my eyes were shut to the horror of my proceedings. But now I went to it in cold blood, and my heart often sickened at the work of my hands.

Thus situated, employed in the most detestable occupation, immersed in a solitude where nothing could for an instant call my attention from the actual scene in which I was engaged, my spirits became unequal; I grew restless and nervous. Every moment I feared to meet my persecutor. Sometimes I sat with my eyes fixed on the ground, fearing to raise them, lest they should encounter the object which I so much dreaded to behold. I feared to wander from the sight of my fellow-creatures, lest when alone he should come to claim his companion.

In the mean time I worked on, and my labour was already considerably advanced. I looked towards its completion with a tremulous and eager hope, which I dared not trust myself to question, but which was intermixed with obscure forebodings of evil, that made my heart sicken in my bosom.

CHAPTER XX

I SAT one evening in my laboratory; the sun had set, and the moon was just rising from the sea; I had not sufficient light for my employment, and I remained idle, in a pause of consideration of whether I should leave my labour for the night, or hasten its conclusion by an unremitting attention to it. As I sat, a train of reflection occurred to me, which led me to consider the effects of what I was now doing. Three years before I was engaged in the same manner, and had created a fiend whose unparalleled barbarity had desolated my heart, and filled it for ever with the bitterest remorse. I was now about to form another being, of whose dispositions I was alike ignorant; she might become ten thousand times more malignant than her mate, and delight for its own sake, in murder and wretchedness. He had sworn to quit the neighbourhood of man, and hide himself in deserts; but she had not; and she, who in all probability was to become a thinking and reasoning animal, might refuse to comply with a compact made before her creation. They might even hate each other; the creature who already lived loathed his own deformity, and might he not conceive a greater abhorrence for it when it came before his eyes in the female form? She also might turn with disgust from him to the superior beauty of man; she might quit him, and he be again alone, exasperated by the fresh provocation of being deserted by one of his own species.

Even if they were to leave Europe, and inhabit the deserts of the new world, yet one of the first results of those sympathies for which the dæmon thirsted would be children, and a race of devils would be propagated upon the earth, who might make the very existence of the species of man a condition precarious and full of terror. Had I a right, for my own benefit, to inflict this curse upon everlasting generations? I had before been moved by the sophisms of the being I had created; I had been struck senseless by his fiendish threats: but now, for the first time, the wickedness of my promise burst upon me; I shuddered to think that future ages might curse me as their pest, whose selfishness had not hesitated to buy its own peace at the price, perhaps, of the existence of the whole human race.

I trembled, and my heart failed within me; when, on looking up, I saw, by the light of the moon, the dæmon at the casement. A ghastly grin wrinkled his lips as he gazed on me, where I sat fulfilling the task which he had allotted to me. Yes, he had followed me in my travels; he had loitered in forests, hid himself in caves, or taken refuge in wide and desert heaths; and he now came to mark my progress, and claim the fulfilment of my promise.

As I looked on him, his countenance expressed the utmost extent of malice and treachery. I thought with a sensation of madness on my promise of creating another like to him, and trembling with passion, tore to pieces the thing on which I was engaged. The wretch saw me destroy the creature on whose future existence he depended for happiness, and, with a howl of devilish despair and revenge, withdrew.

I left the room, and, locking the door, made a solemn vow in my own heart never to resume my labours; and then, with trembling steps, I sought my own apartment. I was alone; none were near me to dissipate the gloom, and relieve me from the sickening oppression of the most terrible reveries.

Several hours passed, and I remained near my window gazing on the sea; it was almost motionless, for the winds were hushed, and all nature reposed under the eye of the quiet moon. A few fishing vessels alone specked the water, and now and then the gentle breeze wafted the sound of voices, as the fishermen called to one another. I felt the silence, although I was hardly conscious of its extreme profundity, until my ear was suddenly arrested by the paddling of oars near the shore, and a person landed close to my house.

In a few minutes after, I heard the creaking of my door, as if some one endeavoured to open it softly. I trembled from head to foot; I felt a presentiment of who it was, and wished to rouse one of the peasants who dwelt in a cottage not far from mine; but I was overcome by the sensation of helplessness, so often felt in frightful dreams, when you in vain endeavour to fly from an impending danger, and was rooted to the spot.

Presently I heard the sound of footsteps along the passage; the door opened, and the wretch whom I dreaded appeared. Shutting the door, he approached me, and said, in a smothered voice—

'You have destroyed the work which you began; what is it that you intend? Do you dare to break your promise? I have endured toil and misery: I left Switzerland with you; I crept along the shores of the Rhine, among its willow islands, and over the summits of its hills. I have dwelt many months in the heaths of England, and among the deserts of Scotland. I have endured incalculable fatigue, and cold, and hunger; do you dare destroy my hopes?'

'Begone! I do break my promise; never will I create another like yourself, equal in deformity and wickedness.'

'Slave, I before reasoned with you, but you have proved yourself unworthy of my condescension. Remember that I have power; you believe yourself miserable, but I can make you so wretched that the light of day will be hateful to you. You are my creator, but I am your master;—obey!'

'The hour of my irresolution is past, and the period of your power is arrived. Your threats cannot move me to do an act of wickedness; but they confirm me in a determination of not creating you a companion in vice. Shall I, in cool blood, set loose upon the earth a dæmon, whose delight is in death and wretchedness? Begone! I am firm, and your words will only exasperate my rage.'

The monster saw my determination in my face, and gnashed his teeth in the impotence of anger. 'Shall each man,' cried he, 'find a wife for his bosom, and each beast have his mate, and I be alone? I had feelings of affection, and they were requited by detestation and scorn. Man! you may hate; but beware! your hours will pass in dread and misery, and soon the bolt will fall which must ravish from you your happiness for ever. Are you to be happy, while I grovel in the intensity of my wretchedness? You can blast my other passions; but revenge remains—revenge, henceforth dearer than light or food! I may die; but first you, my tyrant and tormentor, shall curse the sun that gazes on your misery. Beware; for I am fearless, and therefore powerful. I will watch with the wiliness of a snake, that I may sting with its venom. Man, you shall repent of the injuries you inflict.'

'Devil, cease; and do not poison the air with these sounds of malice. I have declared my resolution to you, and I am no coward to bend beneath words. Leave me; I am inexorable.'

'It is well. I go; but remember, I shall be with you on your wedding-night.'

I started forward, and exclaimed, 'Villain! before you sign my death-warrant, be sure that you are yourself safe.'

I would have seized him; but he eluded me, and quitted the house with precipitation. In a few moments I saw him in his boat, which shot across the waters with an arrowy swiftness, and was soon lost amidst the waves.

All was again silent; but his words rung in my ears. I burned with rage to pursue the murderer of my peace, and precipitate him into the ocean. I walked up and down my room hastily and perturbed, while my imagination conjured up a thousand images to torment and sting me. Why had I not followed him, and closed with him in mortal strife? But I had suffered him to depart, and he had directed his course towards the main land. I shuddered to think who might be the next victim sacrificed to his insatiate revenge. And then I thought again of his words—'*I will be with you on your wedding-night*.' That then was the period fixed for the fulfilment of my destiny. In that hour I should die, and at once satisfy and extinguish his malice. The prospect did not move me to fear; yet when I thought of my beloved Elizabeth,—of her tears and endless sorrow, when she should find her lover so barbarously snatched from her,—tears, the first I had shed for many months, streamed from my eyes, and I resolved not to fall before my enemy without a bitter struggle.

The night passed away, and the sun rose from the ocean; my feelings became calmer, if it may be called calmness, when the violence of rage sinks into the depths of despair. I left the house, the horrid scene of the last night's contention, and walked on the beach of the sea, which I almost regarded as an insuperable barrier between me and my fellow-creatures; nay, a wish that such should prove the fact stole across me. I desired that I might pass my life on that barren rock, wearily, it is true, but uninterrupted by any sudden shock of misery. If I returned, it was to be sacrificed, or to see those whom I most loved die under the grasp of a dæmon whom I had myself created.

I walked about the isle like a restless spectre, separated from all it loved, and miserable in the separation. When it became noon, and the sun rose higher, I lay down on the grass, and was overpowered by a deep sleep. I had been awake the whole of the preceding night, my nerves were agitated, and my eyes inflamed by watching and misery. The sleep into which I now sunk refreshed me; and when I awoke, I again felt as if I belonged to a race of human beings like myself, and I began to reflect upon what had passed with greater composure; yet still the words of the fiend rung in my ears like a death-knell, they appeared like a dream, yet distinct and oppressive as a reality.

The sun had far descended, and I still sat on the shore, satisfying my appetite, which had become ravenous, with an oaten cake, when I saw a fishing-boat land close to me, and one of the men brought me a packet; it contained letters from Geneva, and one from Clerval, entreating me to join him. He said that he was wearing away his time fruitlessly where he was; that letters from the friends he had formed in London desired his return to complete the negotiation they had entered into for his Indian enterprise. He could not any longer delay his departure; but as his journey to London might be followed, even sooner than he now conjectured, by his longer voyage, he entreated me to bestow as much of my society on him as I could spare. He besought me, therefore, to leave my solitary isle, and to meet him at Perth, that we might proceed southwards together. This letter in a degree recalled me to life, and I determined to quit my island at the expiration of two days.

Yet, before I departed, there was a task to perform, on which I shuddered to reflect: I must pack up my chemical instruments; and for that purpose I must enter the room which had been the scene of my odious work, and I must handle those utensils, the sight of which was sickening to me. The next morning, at daybreak, I summoned sufficient courage, and unlocked the door of my laboratory. The remains of the half-finished creature, whom I had destroyed, lay scattered on the floor, and I almost felt as if I had mangled the living flesh of a human being. I paused to collect myself, and then entered the chamber. With trembling hand I conveyed the instruments out of the room; but I reflected that I ought not to leave the relics of my work to excite the horror and suspicion of the peasants; and I accordingly put them into a basket, with a great quantity of stones, and, laying them up, determined to throw them into the sea that very night; and in the mean time I sat upon the beach, employed in cleaning and arranging my chemical apparatus.

Nothing could be more complete than the alteration that had taken place in my feelings since the night of the appearance of the dæmon. I had before regarded my promise with a gloomy despair, as a thing that, with whatever consequences, must be fulfilled; but I now felt as if a film had been taken from before my eyes, and that I, for the first time, saw clearly. The idea of renewing my labours did not for one instant occur to me; the threat I had heard weighed on my thoughts, but I did not reflect that a voluntary act of mine could avert it. I had resolved in my own mind, that to create another like the fiend I had first made would be an act of the basest and most atrocious selfishness; and I banished from my mind every thought that could lead to a different conclusion.

Between two and three in the morning the moon rose; and I then, putting my basket aboard a little skiff, sailed out about four miles from the shore. The scene was perfectly solitary: a few boats were returning towards land, but I sailed away from them. I felt as if I was about the commission of a dreadful crime, and avoided with shuddering anxiety any encounter with my fellow-creatures. At one time the moon, which had before been clear, was suddenly overspread by a thick cloud, and I took advantage of the moment of darkness, and cast my basket into the sea: I listened to the gurgling sound as it sunk, and then sailed away from the spot. The sky became clouded; but the air was pure, although chilled by the north-east breeze that was then rising. But it refreshed me, and filled me with such agreeable sensations, that I resolved to prolong my stay on the water; and, fixing the rudder in a direct position, stretched myself at the bottom of the boat. Clouds hid the moon, every thing was obscure, and I heard only the sound of the boat, as its keel cut through the waves; the murmur lulled me, and in a short time I slept soundly.

I do not know how long I remained in this situation, but when I awoke I found that the sun had already mounted considerably. The wind was high, and the waves continually threatened the safety of my little skiff. I found that the wind was north-east, and must have driven me far from the coast from which I had embarked. I endeavoured to change my course, but quickly found that, if I again made the attempt, the boat would be instantly filled with water. Thus situated, my only resource was to drive before the wind. I confess that I felt a few sensations of terror. I had no compass with me, and was so slenderly acquainted with the geography of this part of the world, that the sun was of little benefit to me. I might be driven into the wide Atlantic, and feel all the tortures of starvation, or be swallowed up in the immeasurable waters that roared and buffeted around me. I had already been out many hours, and felt the torment of a burning thirst, a prelude to my other sufferings. I looked on the heavens, which were covered by clouds that flew the wind, only to be replaced by others: I looked upon the sea, it was to be my grave. 'Fiend,' I exclaimed, 'your task is already fulfilled!' I thought of Elizabeth, of my father, and of Clerval; all left behind, on whom the monster might satisfy his sanguinary and merciless passions. This idea plunged me into a reverie, so despairing and frightful, that even now, when the scene is on the point of closing before me for ever, I shudder to reflect on it.

Some hours passed thus; but by degrees, as the sun declined towards the horizon, the wind died away into a gentle breeze, and the sea became free from breakers. But these gave place to a heavy swell: I felt sick, and hardly able to hold the rudder, when suddenly I saw a line of high land towards the south.

Almost spent, as I was, by fatigue, and the dreadful suspense I endured for several hours, this sudden certainty of life rushed like a flood of warm joy to my heart, and tears gushed from my eyes.

How mutable are our feelings, and how strange is that clinging love we have of life even in the excess of misery! I constructed another sail with a part of my dress, and eagerly steered my course towards the land. It had a wild and rocky appearance; but, as I approached nearer, I easily perceived the traces of cultivation. I saw vessels near the shore, and found myself suddenly transported back to the neighbourhood of civilised man. I carefully traced the windings of the land, and hailed a steeple which I at length saw issuing from behind a small promontory. As I was in a state of extreme debility, I resolved to sail directly towards the town, as a place where I could most easily procure nourishment. Fortunately I had money with me. As I turned the promontory, I perceived a small neat town and a good harbour, which I entered, my heart bounding with joy at my unexpected escape.

As I was occupied in fixing the boat and arranging the sails, several people crowded towards the spot. They seemed much surprised at my appearance; but, instead of offering me any assistance, whispered together with gestures that at any other time might have produced in me a slight sensation of alarm. As it was, I merely remarked that they spoke English; and I therefore addressed them in that language: 'My good friends,' said I, 'will you be so kind as to tell me the name of this town, and inform me where I am?'

'You will know that soon enough,' replied a man with a hoarse voice. 'May be you are come to a place that will not prove much to your taste; but you will not be consulted as to your quarters, I promise you.'

I was exceedingly surprised on receiving so rude an answer from a stranger; and I was also disconcerted on perceiving the frowning and angry countenances of his companions. 'Why do you answer me so roughly?' I replied; 'surely it is not the custom of Englishmen to receive strangers so inhospitably.'

'I do not know,' said the man, 'what the custom of the English may be; but it is the custom of the Irish to hate villains.'

While this strange dialogue continued, I perceived the crowd rapidly increase. Their faces expressed a mixture of curiosity and anger, which annoyed, and in some degree alarmed me. I enquired the way to the inn; but no one replied. I then moved forward, and a murmuring sound arose from the crowd as they followed and surrounded me; when an ill-looking man approached, tapped me on the shoulder, and said, 'Come, sir, you must follow me to Mr Kirwin's, to give an account of yourself.'

'Who is Mr Kirwin? Why am I to give an account of myself? Is not this a free country?'

'Ay, sir, free enough for honest folks. Mr Kirwin is a magistrate; and you are to give an account of the death of a gentleman who was found murdered here last night.'

This answer startled me; but I presently recovered myself. I was innocent; that could easily be proved: accordingly I followed my conductor in silence, and was led to one of the best houses in the town. I was ready to sink from fatigue and hunger; but, being surrounded by a crowd, I thought it politic to rouse all my strength, that no physical debility might be construed into apprehension or conscious guilt. Little did I then expect the calamity that was in a few moments to overwhelm me, and extinguish in horror and despair all fear of ignominy or death.

I must pause here; for it requires all my fortitude to recall the memory of the frightful events which I am about to relate, in proper detail, to my recollection.

CHAPTER XXI

I WAS soon introduced into the presence of the magistrate, an old benevolent man, with calm and mild manners. He looked upon me, however, with some degree of severity: and then, turning towards my conductors, he asked who appeared as witnesses on this occasion.

About half a dozen men came forward; and, one being selected by the magistrate, he deposed, that he had been out fishing the night before with his son and brother-in-law, Daniel Nugent, when, about ten o'clock, they observed a strong northerly blast rising, and they accordingly put in for port. It was a very dark night, as the moon had not yet risen; they did not land at the harbour, but, as they had been accustomed, at a creek about two miles below. He walked on first, carrying a part of the fishing tackle, and his companions followed him at some distance. As he was proceeding along the sands, he struck his foot against something, and fell at his length on the ground. His companions came up to assist him; and, by the light of their lantern, they found that he had fallen on the body of a man, who was to all appearance dead. Their first supposition was, that it was the corpse of some person who had been drowned, and was thrown on shore by the waves; but, on examination, they found that the clothes were not wet, and even that the body was not then cold. They instantly carried it to the cottage of an old woman near the spot, and endeavoured, but in vain, to restore it to life. It appeared to be a handsome young man, about five and twenty years of age. He had apparently been strangled; for there was no sign of any violence, except the black mark of fingers on his neck.

The first part of this deposition did not in the least interest me; but when the mark of the fingers was mentioned, I remembered the murder of my brother, and felt myself extremely agitated; my limbs trembled, and a mist came over my eyes, which obliged me to lean on a chair for support. The magistrate observed me with a keen eye, and of course drew an unfavourable augury from my manner.

The son confirmed his father's account: but when Daniel Nugent was called, he swore positively that, just before the fall of his companion, he saw a boat, with a single man in it, at a short distance from the shore; and, as far as he could judge by the light of a few stars, it was the same boat in which I had just landed.

A woman deposed, that she lived near the beach, and was standing at the door of her cottage, waiting for the return of the fishermen, about an hour before she heard of the discovery of the body, when she saw a boat, with only one man in it, push off from that part of the shore where the corpse was afterwards found.

Another woman confirmed the account of the fishermen having brought the body into her house; it was not cold. They put it into a bed, and rubbed it; and Daniel went to the town for an apothecary, but life was quite gone.

Several other men were examined concerning my landing; and they agreed, that, with the strong north wind that had arisen during the night, it was very probable that I had beaten about for many hours, and had been obliged to return nearly to the same spot from which I had departed. Besides, they observed that it appeared that I had brought the body from another place, and it was likely, that as I did not appear to know the shore, I might have put into the harbour ignorant of the distance of the town of *** from the place where I had deposited the corpse.

Mr Kirwin, on hearing this evidence, desired that I should be taken into the room where the body lay for interment, that it might be observed what effect the sight of it would produce upon me. This idea was probably suggested by the extreme agitation I had exhibited when the mode of the murder had been described. I was accordingly conducted, by the magistrate and several other persons, to the inn. I could not help being struck by the strange coincidences that had taken place during this eventful night; but, knowing that I had been conversing with several persons in the island I had inhabited about the time that the body had been found, I was perfectly tranquil as to the consequences of the affair.

I entered the room where the corpse lay, and was led up to the coffin. How can I describe my sensations on beholding it? I feel yet parched with horror, nor can I reflect on that terrible moment without shuddering and agony. The examination, the presence of the magistrate and witnesses, passed like a dream from my memory, when I saw the lifeless form of Henry Clerval stretched before me. I gasped for breath; and, throwing myself on the body, I exclaimed, 'Have my murderous machinations deprived you also, my dearest Henry, of life? Two I have already destroyed; other victims await their destiny: but you, Clerval, my friend, my benefactor——'

The human frame could no longer support the agonies that I endured, and I was carried out of the room in strong convulsions.

A fever succeeded to this. I lay for two months on the point of death: my ravings, as I afterwards heard, were frightful; I called myself the murderer of William, of Justine, and of Clerval. Sometimes I entreated my attendants to assist me in the destruction of the fiend by whom I was tormented; and at others, I felt the fingers of the monster already grasping my neck, and screamed aloud with agony and terror. Fortunately, as I spoke my native language, Mr Kirwin alone understood me; but my gestures and bitter cries were sufficient to affright the other witnesses.

Why did I not die? More miserable than man ever was before, why did I not sink into forgetfulness and rest? Death snatches away many blooming children, the only hopes of their doating parents: how many brides and youthful lovers have been one day in the bloom of health and hope, and the next a prey for worms and the decay of the tomb! Of what materials was I made, that I could thus resist so many shocks, which, like the turning of the wheel, continually renewed the torture?

But I was doomed to live; and, in two months, found myself as awaking from a dream, in a prison, stretched on a wretched bed, surrounded by gaolers, turnkeys, bolts, and all the miserable apparatus of a dungeon. It was morning, I remember, when I thus awoke to understanding: I had forgotten the particulars of what had happened, and only felt as if some great misfortune had suddenly overwhelmed me; but when I looked around, and saw the barred windows, and the squalidness of the room in which I was, all flashed across my memory, and I groaned bitterly.

This sound disturbed an old woman who was sleeping in a chair beside me. She was a hired nurse, the wife of one of the turnkeys, and her countenance expressed all those bad qualities which often characterise that class. The lines of her face were hard and rude, like that of persons accustomed to see without sympathising in sights of misery. Her tone expressed her entire indifference; she addressed me in English, and the voice struck me as one that I had heard during my sufferings:—

'Are you better now, sir?' said she.

I replied in the same language, with a feeble voice, 'I believe I am; but if it be all true, if indeed I did not dream, I am sorry that I am still alive to feel this misery and horror.'

'For that matter,' replied the old woman, 'if you mean about the gentleman you murdered, I believe that it were better for you if you were dead, for I fancy it will go hard with you! However, that's none of my business; I am sent to nurse you, and get you well; I do my duty with a safe conscience; it were well if every body did the same.'

I turned with loathing from the woman who could utter so unfeeling a speech to a person just saved, on the very edge of death; but I felt languid, and unable to reflect on all that had passed. The whole series of my life appeared to me as a dream; I sometimes doubted if indeed it were all true, for it never presented itself to my mind with the force of reality.

As the images that floated before me became more distinct, I grew feverish; a darkness pressed around me: no one was near me who soothed me with the gentle voice of love; no dear hand supported me. The physician came and prescribed medicines, and the old woman prepared them for me; but utter carelessness was visible in the first, and the expression of brutality was strongly marked in the visage of the second. Who could be interested in the fate of a murderer, but the hangman who would gain his fee?

These were my first reflections; but I soon learned that Mr Kirwin had shown me extreme kindness. He had caused the best room in the prison to be prepared for me (wretched indeed was the best); and it was he who had provided a physician and a nurse. It is true, he seldom came to see me; for, although he ardently desired to relieve the sufferings of every human creature, he did not wish to be present at the agonies and miserable ravings of a murderer. He came, therefore, sometimes, to see that I was not neglected; but his visits were short, and with long intervals.

One day, while I was gradually recovering, I was seated in a chair, my eyes half open, and my cheeks livid like those in death. I was overcome by gloom and misery, and often reflected I had better seek death than desire to remain in a world which to me was replete with wretchedness. At one time I considered whether I should not declare myself guilty, and suffer the penalty of the law, less innocent than poor Justine had been. Such were my thoughts, when the door of my apartment was opened, and Mr Kirwin entered. His countenance expressed sympathy and compassion; he drew a chair close to mine, and addressed me in French—

'I fear that this place is very shocking to you; can I do any thing to make you more comfortable?'

'I thank you; but all that you mention is nothing to me: on the whole earth there is no comfort which I am capable of receiving.'

'I know that the sympathy of a stranger can be but of little relief to one borne down as you are by so strange a misfortune. But you will, I hope, soon quit this melancholy abode; for, doubtless, evidence can easily be brought to free you from the criminal charge.'

'That is my least concern: I am, by a course of strange events, become the most miserable of mortals. Persecuted and tortured as I am and have been, can death be any evil to me?'

'Nothing indeed could be more unfortunate and agonising than the strange chances that have lately occurred. You were thrown, by some surprising accident, on this shore, renowned for its hospitality; seized immediately, and charged with murder. The first sight that was presented to your eyes was the body of your friend, murdered in so unaccountable a manner, and placed, as it were, by some fiend across your path.'

As Mr Kirwin said this, notwithstanding the agitation I endured on this retrospect of my sufferings, I also felt considerable surprise at the knowledge he seemed to possess concerning me. I suppose some astonishment was exhibited in my countenance; for Mr Kirwin hastened to say—

'Immediately upon your being taken ill, all the papers that were on your person were brought me, and I examined them that I might discover some trace by which I could send to your relations an account of your misfortune and illness. I found several letters, and, among others, one which I discovered from its commencement to be from your father. I instantly wrote to Geneva: nearly two months have elapsed since the departure of my letter.—But you are ill; even now you tremble: you are unfit for agitation of any kind.'

'This suspense is a thousand times worse than the most horrible event: tell me what new scene of death has been acted, and whose murder I am now to lament?'

'Your family is perfectly well,' said Mr Kirwin, with gentleness; 'and some one, a friend, is come to visit you.'

I know not by what chain of thought, the idea presented itself, but it instantly darted into my mind that the murderer had come to mock at my misery, and taunt me with the death of Clerval, as a new incitement for me to comply with his hellish desires. I put my hand before my eyes, and cried out in agony—

'Oh! take him away! I cannot see him; for God's sake, do not let him enter!'

Mr Kirwin regarded me with a troubled countenance. He could not help regarding my exclamation as a presumption of my guilt, and said, in rather a severe tone—

'I should have thought, young man, that the presence of your father would have been welcome, instead of inspiring such violent repugnance.'

'My father!' cried I, while every feature and every muscle was relaxed from anguish to pleasure: 'is my father indeed come? How kind, how very kind! But where is he, why does he not hasten to me?'

My change of manner surprised and pleased the magistrate; perhaps he thought that my former exclamation was a momentary return of delirium, and now he instantly resumed his former benevolence. He rose, and quitted the room with my nurse, and in a moment my father entered it.

Nothing, at this moment, could have given me greater pleasure than the arrival of my father. I stretched out my hand to him, and cried—

'Are you then safe—and Elizabeth—and Ernest?'

My father calmed me with assurances of their welfare, and endeavoured, by dwelling on these subjects so interesting to my heart, to raise my desponding spirits; but he soon felt that a prison cannot be the abode of cheerfulness. 'What a place is this that you inhabit, my son!' said he, looking mournfully at the barred windows, and wretched appearance of the room. 'You travelled to seek happiness, but a fatality seems to pursue you. And poor Clerval—'

The name of my unfortunate and murdered friend was an agitation too great to be endured in my weak state; I shed tears.

'Alas! yes, my father,' replied I; 'some destiny of the most horrible kind hangs over me, and I must live to fulfil it, or surely I should have died on the coffin of Henry.'

We were not allowed to converse for any length of time, for the precarious state of my health rendered every precaution necessary that could ensure tranquillity. Mr Kirwin came in, and insisted that my strength should not be exhausted by too much exertion. But the appearance of my father was to me like that of my good angel, and I gradually recovered my health.

As my sickness quitted me, I was absorbed by a gloomy and black melancholy, that nothing could dissipate. The image of Clerval was for ever before me, ghastly and murdered. More than once the agitation into which these reflections threw me made my friends dread a dangerous relapse. Alas! why did they preserve so miserable and detested a life? It was surely that I might fulfil my destiny, which is now drawing to a close. Soon, oh! very soon, will death extinguish these throbbings, and relieve me from the mighty weight of anguish that bears me to the dust; and, in executing the award of justice, I shall also sink to rest. Then the appearance of death was distant, although the wish was ever present to my thoughts; and I often sat for hours motionless and speechless, wishing for some mighty revolution that might bury me and my destroyer in its ruins.

The season of the assizes approached. I had already been three months in prison; and although I was still weak, and in continual danger of a relapse, I was obliged to travel nearly a hundred miles to the county-town, where the court was held. Mr Kirwin charged himself with every care of collecting witnesses, and arranging my defence. I was spared the disgrace of appearing publicly as a criminal, as the case was not brought before the court that decides on life and death. The grand jury rejected the bill, on its being proved that I was on the Orkney Islands at the hour the body of my friend was found; and a fortnight after my removal I was liberated from prison.

My father was enraptured on finding me freed from the vexations of a criminal charge, that I was again allowed to breathe the fresh atmosphere, and permitted to return to my native country. I did not participate in these feelings; for to me the walls of a dungeon or a palace were alike hateful. The cup of life was poisoned for ever; and although the sun shone upon me, as upon the happy and gay of heart, I saw around me nothing but a dense and frightful darkness, penetrated by no light but the glimmer of two eyes that glared upon me. Sometimes they were the expressive eyes of Henry, languishing in death, the dark orbs nearly covered by the lids, and the long black lashes that fringed them; sometimes it was the watery, clouded eyes of the monster, as I first saw them in my chamber at Ingolstadt.

My father tried to awaken in me the feelings of affection. He talked of Geneva, which I should soon visit—of Elizabeth and Ernest; but these words only drew deep groans from me. Sometimes, indeed, I felt a wish for happiness; and thought, with melancholy delight, of my beloved cousin; or longed, with a devouring *maladie du pays*, to see once more the blue lake and rapid Rhone, that had been so dear to me in early childhood: but my general state of feeling was a torpor, in which a prison was as welcome a residence as the divinest scene in nature; and these fits were seldom interrupted but by paroxysms of anguish and despair. At these moments I often endeavoured to put an end to the existence I loathed; and it required unceasing attendance and vigilance to restrain me from committing some dreadful act of violence.

Yet one duty remained to me, the recollection of which finally triumphed over my selfish despair. It was necessary that I should return without delay to Geneva, there to watch over the lives of those I so fondly loved; and to lie in wait for the murderer, that if any chance led me to the place of his concealment, or if he dared again to blast me by his presence, I might, with unfailing aim, put an end to the existence of the monstrous Image which I had endued with the mockery of a soul still more monstrous. My father still desired to delay our departure, fearful that I could not sustain the fatigues of a journey: for I was a shattered wreck,—the shadow of a human being. My strength was gone. I was a mere skeleton; and fever night and day preyed upon my wasted frame.

Still, as I urged our leaving Ireland with such inquietude and impatience, my father thought it best to yield. We took our passage on board a vessel bound for Havre-de-Grace, and sailed with a fair wind from the Irish shores. It was midnight. I lay on the deck, looking at the stars, and listening to the dashing of the waves. I hailed the darkness that shut Ireland from my sight; and my pulse beat with a feverish joy when I reflected that I should soon see Geneva. The past appeared to me in the light of a frightful dream; yet the vessel in which I was, the wind that blew me from the detested shore of Ireland, and the sea which surrounded me, told me too forcibly that I was deceived by no vision, and that Clerval, my friend and dearest companion, had fallen a victim to me and the monster of my creation. I repassed, in my memory, my whole life; my quiet happiness while residing with my family in Geneva, the death of my mother, and my departure for Ingolstadt. I remembered, shuddering, the mad enthusiasm that hurried me on to the creation of my hideous enemy, and I called to mind the night in which he first lived. I was unable to pursue the train of thought; a thousand feelings pressed upon me, and I wept bitterly.

Ever since my recovery from the fever, I had been in the custom of taking every night a small quantity of laudanum; for it was by means of this drug only that I was enabled to gain the rest necessary for the preservation of life. Oppressed by the recollection of my various misfortunes, I now swallowed double my usual quantity, and soon slept profoundly. But sleep did not afford me respite from thought and misery; my dreams presented a thousand objects that scared me. Towards morning I was possessed by a kind of night-mare; I felt the fiend's grasp in my neck, and could not free myself from it; groans and cries rung in my ears. My father, who was watching over me, perceiving my restlessness, awoke me; the dashing waves were around: the cloudy sky above; the fiend was not here: a sense of security, a feeling that a truce was established between the present hour and the irresistible, disastrous future, imparted to me a kind of calm forgetfulness, of which the human mind is by its structure peculiarly susceptible.

CHAPTER XXII

THE voyage came to an end. We landed, and proceeded to Paris. I soon found that I had overtaxed my strength, and that I must repose before I could continue my journey. My father's care and attentions were indefatigable; but he did not know the origin of my sufferings, and sought erroneous methods to remedy the incurable ill. He wished me to seek amusement in society. I abhorred the face of man. Oh, not abhorred! they were my brethren, my fellow beings, and I felt attracted even to the most repulsive among them, as to creatures of an angelic nature and celestial mechanism. But I felt that I had no right to share their intercourse. I had unchained an enemy among them, whose joy it was to shed their blood, and to revel in their groans. How they would, each and all, abhor me, and hunt me from the world, did they know my unhallowed acts, and the crimes which had their source in me!

My father yielded at length to my desire to avoid society, and strove by various arguments to banish my despair. Sometimes he thought that I felt deeply the degradation of being obliged to answer a charge of murder, and he endeavoured to prove to me the futility of pride.

'Alas! my father,' said I, 'how little do you know me. Human beings, their feelings and passions, would indeed be degraded if such a wretch as I felt pride. Justine, poor unhappy Justine, was as innocent as I, and she suffered the same charge, she died for it; and I am the cause of this—I murdered her. William, Justine, and Henry—they all died by my hands.'

My father had often, during my imprisonment, heard me make the same assertion; when I thus accused myself, he sometimes seemed to desire an explanation, and at others he appeared to consider it as the offspring of delirium, and that, during my illness, some idea of this kind had presented itself to my imagination, the remembrance of which I preserved in my convalescence. I avoided explanation, and maintained a continual silence concerning the wretch I had created. I had a persuasion that I should be supposed mad; and this in itself would for ever have chained my tongue. But, besides, I could not bring myself to disclose a secret which would fill my hearer with consternation, and make fear and unnatural horror the inmates of his breast. I checked, therefore, my impatient thirst for sympathy, and was silent when I would have given the world to have confided the fatal secret. Yet still words like those I have recorded, would burst uncontrollably from me. I could offer no explanation of them; but their truth in part relieved the burden of my mysterious woe.

Upon this occasion my father said, with an expression of unbounded wonder, 'My dearest Victor, what infatuation is this? My dear son, I entreat you never to make such an assertion again.'

'I am not mad,' I cried energetically; 'the sun and the heavens, who have viewed my operations, can bear witness of my truth. I am the assassin of those most innocent victims; they died by my machinations. A thousand times would I have shed my own blood, drop by drop, to have saved their lives; but I could not, my father, indeed I could not sacrifice the whole human race.'

The conclusion of this speech convinced my father that my ideas were deranged, and he instantly changed the subject of our conversation, and endeavoured to alter the course of my thoughts. He wished as much as possible to obliterate the memory of the scenes that had taken place in Ireland, and never alluded to them, or suffered me to speak of my misfortunes.

As time passed away I became more calm: misery had her dwelling in my heart, but I no longer talked in the same incoherent manner of my own crimes; sufficient for me was the consciousness of them. By the utmost self-violence, I curbed the imperious voice of wretchedness, which sometimes desired to declare itself to the whole world; and my manners were calmer and more composed than they had ever been since my journey to the sea of ice.

A few days before we left Paris on our way to Switzerland, I received the following letter from Elizabeth:—

'My dear Friend,

'It gave me the greatest pleasure to receive a letter from my uncle dated at Paris; you are no longer at a formidable distance, and I may hope to see you in less than a fortnight. My poor cousin, how much you must have suffered! I expect to see you looking even more ill than when you quitted Geneva. This winter has been passed most miserably, tortured as I have been by anxious suspense; yet I hope to see peace in your countenance, and to find that your heart is not totally void of comfort and tranquillity.

'Yet I fear that the same feelings now exist that made you so miserable a year ago, even perhaps augmented by time. I would not disturb you at this period, when so many misfortunes weigh upon you; but a conversation that I had with my uncle previous to his departure renders some explanation necessary before we meet.

'Explanation! you may possibly say; what can Elizabeth have to explain? If you really say this, my questions are answered, and all my doubts satisfied. But you are distant from me, and it is possible that you may dread, and yet be pleased with this explanation; and, in a probability of this being the case, I dare not any longer postpone writing what, during your absence, I have often wished to express to you, but have never had the courage to begin.

'You well know, Victor, that our union had been the favourite plan of your parents ever since our infancy. We were told this when young, and taught to look forward to it as an event that would certainly take place. We were affectionate playfellows during childhood, and, I believe, dear and valued friends to one another as we grew older. But as brother and sister often entertain a lively affection towards each other, without desiring a more intimate union, may not such also be our case? Tell me, dearest Victor. Answer me, I conjure you, by our mutual happiness, with simple truth—Do you not love another?

'You have travelled; you have spent several years of your life at Ingolstadt; and I confess to you, my friend, that when I saw you last autumn so unhappy, flying to solitude, from the society of every creature, I could not help supposing that you might regret our connection, and believe yourself bound in honour to fulfil the wishes of your parents, although they opposed themselves to your inclinations. But this is false reasoning. I confess to you, my friend, that I love you, and that in my airy dreams of futurity you have been my constant friend and companion. But it is your happiness I desire as well as my own, when I declare to you, that our marriage would render me eternally miserable, unless it were the dictate of your own free choice. Even now I weep to think, that, borne down as you are by the cruellest misfortunes, you may stifle, by the word *honour*, all hope of that love and happiness which would alone restore you to yourself. I, who have so disinterested an affection for you, may increase your miseries tenfold, by being an obstacle to your wishes. Ah! Victor, be assured that your cousin and playmate has too sincere a love for you not to be made miserable by this supposition. Be happy, my friend; and if you obey me in this one request, remain satisfied that nothing on earth will have the power to interrupt my tranquillity.

'Do not let this letter disturb you; do not answer tomorrow, or the next day, or even until you come, if it will give you pain. My uncle will send me news of your health; and if I see but one smile on your lips when we meet, occasioned by this or any other exertion of mine, I shall need no other happiness.

'ELIZABETH LAVENZA.

'Geneva, May 18th, 17—.'

This letter revived in my memory what I had before forgotten, the threat of the fiend—'*I will be with you on your wedding night!*' Such was my sentence, and on that night would the dæmon employ every art to destroy me, and tear me from the glimpse of happiness which promised partly to console my sufferings. On that night he had determined to consummate his crimes by my death. Well, be it so; a deadly struggle would then assuredly take place, in which if he were victorious I should be at peace, and his power over me be at an end. If he were vanquished, I should be a free man. Alas! what freedom? such as the peasant enjoys when his family have been massacred before his eyes, his cottage burnt, his lands laid waste, and he is turned adrift, homeless, penniless, and alone, but free. Such would be my liberty, except that in my Elizabeth I possessed a treasure; alas! balanced by those horrors of remorse and guilt, which would pursue me until death.

Sweet and beloved Elizabeth! I read and re-read her letter, and some softened feelings stole into my heart, and dared to whisper paradisiacal dreams of love and joy; but the apple was already eaten, and the angel's arm bared to drive me from all hope. Yet I would die to make her happy. If the monster executed his threat, death was inevitable; yet, again, I considered whether my marriage would hasten my fate. My destruction might indeed arrive a few months sooner; but if my torturer should suspect that I postponed it, influenced by his menaces, he would surely find other, and perhaps more dreadful means of revenge. He had vowed *to be with me on my wedding-night*, yet he did not consider that threat as binding him to peace in the mean time; for, as if to show me that he was not yet satiated with blood, he had murdered Clerval immediately after the enunciation of his threats. I resolved, therefore, that if my immediate union with my cousin would conduce either to hers or my father's happiness, my adversary's designs against my life should not retard it a single hour.

In this state of mind I wrote to Elizabeth. My letter was calm and affectionate. 'I fear, my beloved girl,' I said, 'little happiness remains for us on earth; yet all that I may one day enjoy is centred in you. Chase away your idle fears; to you alone do I consecrate my life, and my endeavours for contentment. I have one secret, Elizabeth, a dreadful one; when revealed to you, it will chill your frame with horror, and then, far from being surprised at my misery, you will only wonder that I survive what I have endured. I will confide this tale of misery and terror to you the day after our marriage shall take place; for, my sweet cousin, there must be perfect confidence between us. But until then, I conjure you, do not mention or allude to it. This I most earnestly entreat, and I know you will comply.'

In about a week after the arrival of Elizabeth's letter, we returned to Geneva. The sweet girl welcomed me with warm affection; yet tears were in her eyes, as she beheld my emaciated frame and feverish cheeks. I saw a change in her also. She was thinner, and had lost much of that heavenly vivacity that had before charmed me; but her gentleness, and soft looks of compassion, made her a more fit companion for one blasted and miserable as I was.

The tranquillity which I now enjoyed did not endure. Memory brought madness with it; and when I thought of what had passed, a real insanity possessed me; sometimes I was furious, and burnt with rage, sometimes low and despondent. I neither spoke, nor looked at any one, but sat motionless, bewildered by the multitude of miseries that overcame me.

Elizabeth alone had the power to draw me from these fits; her gentle voice would soothe me when transported by passion, and inspire me with human feelings when sunk in torpor. She wept with me, and for me. When reason returned, she would remonstrate, and endeavour to inspire me with resignation. Ah! it is well for the unfortunate to be resigned, but for the guilty there is no peace. The agonies of remorse poison the luxury there is otherwise sometimes found in indulging the excess of grief.

Soon after my arrival, my father spoke of my immediate marriage with Elizabeth. I remained silent.

'Have you, then, some other attachment?'

'None on earth. I love Elizabeth, and look forward to our union with delight. Let the day therefore be fixed; and on it I will consecrate myself, in life or death, to the happiness of my cousin.'

'My dear Victor, do not speak thus. Heavy misfortunes have befallen us; but let us only cling closer to what remains, and transfer our love for those whom we have lost, to those who yet live. Our circle will be small, but bound close by the ties of affection and mutual misfortune. And when time shall have softened your despair, new and dear objects of care will be born to replace those of whom we have been so cruelly deprived.'

Such were the lessons of my father. But to me the remembrance of the threat returned: nor can you wonder, that, omnipotent as the fiend had yet been in his deeds of blood, I should almost regard him as invincible; and that when he had pronounced the words, 'I shall be with you on your wedding-night,' I should regard the threatened fate as unavoidable. But death was no evil to me, if the loss of Elizabeth were balanced with it; and I therefore, with a contented and even cheerful countenance, agreed with my father, that if my cousin would consent, the ceremony should take place in ten days, and thus put, as I imagined, the seal to my fate.

Great God! if for one instant I had thought what might be the hellish intention of my fiendish adversary, I would rather have banished myself for ever from my native country, and wandered a friendless outcast over the earth, than have consented to this miserable marriage. But, as if possessed of magic powers, the monster had blinded me to his real intentions; and when I thought that I had prepared only my own death, I hastened that of a far dearer victim.

As the period fixed for our marriage drew nearer, whether from cowardice or a prophetic feeling, I felt my heart sink within me. But I concealed my feelings by an appearance of hilarity, that brought smiles and joy to the countenance of my father, but hardly deceived the ever-watchful and nicer eye of Elizabeth. She looked forward to our union with placid contentment, not unmingled with a little fear, which past misfortunes had impressed, that what now appeared certain and tangible happiness, might soon dissipate into an airy dream, and leave no trace but deep and everlasting regret.

Preparations were made for the event; congratulatory visits were received; and all wore a smiling appearance. I shut up, as well as I could, in my own heart the anxiety that preyed there, and entered with seeming earnestness into the plans of my father, although they might only serve as the decorations of my tragedy. Through my father's exertions, a part of the inheritance of Elizabeth had been restored to her by the Austrian government. A small possession on the shores of Como belonged to her. It was agreed that, immediately after our union, we should proceed to Villa Lavenza, and spend our first days of happiness beside the beautiful lake near which it stood.

In the mean time I took every precaution to defend my person, in case the fiend should openly attack me. I carried pistols and a dagger constantly about me, and was ever on the watch to prevent artifice; and by these means gained a greater degree of tranquillity. Indeed, as the period approached, the threat appeared more as a delusion, not to be regarded as worthy to disturb my peace, while the happiness I hoped for in my marriage wore a greater appearance of certainty, as the day fixed for its solemnisation drew nearer, and I heard it continually spoken of as an occurrence which no accident could possibly prevent.

Elizabeth seemed happy; my tranquil demeanour contributed greatly to calm her mind. But on the day that was to fulfil my wishes and my destiny, she was melancholy, and a presentiment of evil pervaded her; and perhaps also she thought of the dreadful secret which I had promised to reveal to her on the following day. My father was in the mean time overjoyed, and, in the bustle of preparation, only recognised in the melancholy of his niece the diffidence of a bride.

After the ceremony was performed, a large party assembled at my father's; but it was agreed that Elizabeth and I should commence our journey by water, sleeping that night at Evian, and continuing our voyage on the following day. The day was fair, the wind favourable, all smiled on our nuptial embarkation.

Those were the last moments of my life during which I enjoyed the feeling of happiness. We passed rapidly along: the sun was hot, but we were sheltered from its rays by a kind of canopy, while we enjoyed the beauty of the scene, sometimes on one side of the lake, where we saw Mont Salêve, the pleasant banks of Montalègre, and at a distance, surmounting all, the beautiful Mont Blanc, and the assemblage of snowy mountains that in vain endeavour to emulate her; sometimes coasting the opposite banks, we saw the mighty Jura opposing its dark side to the ambition that would quit its native country, and an almost insurmountable barrier to the invader who should wish to enslave it.

I took the hand of Elizabeth: 'You are sorrowful, my love. Ah! if you knew what I have suffered, and what I may yet endure, you would endeavour to let me taste the quiet and freedom from despair, that this one day at least permits me to enjoy.'

'Be happy, my dear Victor,' replied Elizabeth; 'there is, I hope, nothing to distress you; and be assured that if a lively joy is not painted in my face, my heart is contented. Something whispers to me not to depend too much on the prospect that is opened before us; but I will not listen to such a sinister voice. Observe how fast we move along, and how the clouds, which sometimes obscure and sometimes rise above the dome of Mont Blanc, render this scene of beauty still more interesting. Look also at the innumerable fish that are swimming in the clear waters, where we can distinguish every pebble that lies at the bottom. What a divine day! how happy and serene all nature appears!'

Thus Elizabeth endeavoured to divert her thoughts and mine from all reflection upon melancholy subjects. But her temper was fluctuating; joy for a few instants shone in her eyes, but it continually gave place to distraction and reverie.

The sun sunk lower in the heavens; we passed the river Drance, and observed its path through the chasms of the higher, and the glens of the lower hills. The Alps here come closer to the lake, and we approached the amphitheatre of mountains which forms its eastern boundary. The spire of Evian shone under the woods that surrounded it, and the range of mountain above mountain by which it was overhung.

The wind, which had hitherto carried us along with amazing rapidity, sunk at sunset to a light breeze; the soft air just ruffled the water, and caused a pleasant motion among the trees as we approached the shore, from which it wafted the most delightful scent of flowers and hay. The sun sunk beneath the horizon as we landed; and as I touched the shore, I felt those cares and fears revive, which soon were to clasp me, and cling to me for ever.

CHAPTER XXIII

IT was eight o'clock when we landed; we walked for a short time on the shore, enjoying the transitory light, and then retired to the inn, and contemplated the lovely scene of waters, woods, and mountains, obscured in darkness, yet still displaying their black outlines.

The wind, which had fallen in the south, now rose with great violence in the west. The moon had reached her summit in the heavens, and was beginning to descend; the clouds swept across it swifter than the flight of the vulture, and dimmed her rays, while the lake reflected the scene of the busy heavens, rendered still busier by the restless waves that were beginning to rise. Suddenly a heavy storm of rain descended.

I had been calm during the day; but so soon as night obscured the shapes of objects, a thousand fears arose in my mind. I was anxious and watchful, while my right hand grasped a pistol which was hidden in my bosom; every sound terrified me; but I resolved that I would sell my life dearly, and not shrink from the conflict until my own life, or that of my adversary, was extinguished.

Elizabeth observed my agitation for some time in timid and fearful silence; but there was something in my glance which communicated terror to her, and trembling she asked 'What is it that agitates you, my dear Victor? What is it you fear?'

'Oh! peace, peace, my love,' replied I; 'this night, and all will be safe: but this night is dreadful, very dreadful.'

I passed an hour in this state of mind, when suddenly I reflected how fearful the combat which I momentarily expected would be to my wife, and I earnestly entreated her to retire, resolving not to join her until I had obtained some knowledge as to the situation of my enemy.

She left me, and I continued some time walking up and down the passages of the house, and inspecting every corner that might afford a retreat to my adversary. But I discovered no trace of him, and was beginning to conjecture that some fortunate chance had intervened to prevent the execution of his menaces; when suddenly I heard a shrill and dreadful scream. It came from the room into which Elizabeth had retired. As I heard it, the whole truth rushed into my mind, my arms dropped, the motion of every muscle and fibre was suspended; I could feel the blood trickling in my veins, and tingling in the extremities of my limbs. This state lasted but for an instant; the scream was repeated, and I rushed into the room.

Great God! why did I not then expire! Why am I here to relate the destruction of the best hope, and the purest creature of earth? She was there, lifeless and inanimate, thrown across the bed, her head hanging down, and her pale and distorted features half covered by her hair. Every where I turn I see the same figure—her bloodless arms and relaxed form flung by the murderer on its bridal bier. Could I behold this, and live? Alas! life is obstinate, and clings closest where it is most hated. For a moment only did I lose recollection; I fell senseless on the ground.

When I recovered, I found myself surrounded by the people of the inn; their countenances expressed a breathless terror: but the horror of others appeared only as a mockery, a shadow of the feelings that oppressed me. I escaped from them to the room where lay the body of Elizabeth, my love, my wife, so lately living, so dear, so worthy. She had been moved from the posture in which I had first beheld her; and now, as she lay, her head upon her arm, and a handkerchief thrown across her face and neck, I might have supposed her asleep. I rushed towards her, and embraced her with ardour; but the deadly languor and coldness of the limbs told me, that what I now hel ' in my arms had ceased to be the Elizabeth whom I had loved and cherished. The murderous mark of the fiend's grasp was on her neck, and the breath had ceased to issue from her lips.

While I still hung over her in the agony of despair, I happened to look up. The windows of the room had before been darkened, and I felt a kind of panic on seeing the pale yellow light of the moon illuminate the chamber.

The shutters had been thrown back; and, with a sensation of horror not to be described, I saw at the open window a figure the most hideous and abhorred. A grin was on the face of the monster; he seemed to jeer, as with his fiendish finger he pointed towards the corpse of my wife. I rushed towards the window, and drawing a pistol from my bosom, fired; but he eluded me, leaped from his station, and, running with the swiftness of lightning, plunged into the lake.

The report of the pistol brought a crowd into the room. I pointed to the spot where he had disappeared, and we followed the track with boats; nets were cast, but in vain. After passing several hours, we returned hopeless, most of my companions believing it to have been a form conjured up by my fancy. After having landed, they proceeded to search the country, parties going in different directions among the woods and vines.

I attempted to accompany them, and proceeded a short distance from the house; but my head whirled round, my steps were like those of a drunken man, I fell at last in a state of utter exhaustion; a film covered my eyes, and my skin was parched with the heat of fever. In this state I was carried back, and placed on a bed, hardly conscious of what had happened; my eyes wandered round the room, as if to seek something that I had lost.

After an interval, I arose, and, as if by instinct, crawled into the room where the corpse of my beloved lay. There were women weeping around—I hung over it, and joined my sad tears to theirs—all this time no distinct idea presented itself to my mind; but my thoughts rambled to various subjects, reflecting confusedly on my misfortunes, and their cause. I was bewildered in a cloud of wonder and horror. The death of William, the execution of Justine, the murder of Clerval, and lastly of my wife: even at that moment I knew not that my only remaining friends were safe from the malignity of the fiend; my father even now might be writhing under his grasp, and Ernest might be dead at his feet. This idea made me shudder, and recalled me to action. I started up, and resolved to return to Geneva with all possible speed.

There were no horses to be procured, and I must return by the lake; but the wind was unfavourable, and the rain fell in torrents. However, it was hardly morning, and I might reasonably hope to arrive by night. I hired men to row, and took an oar myself; for I had always experienced relief from mental torment in bodily exercise. But the overflowing misery I now felt, and the excess of agitation that I endured, rendered me incapable of any exertion. I threw down the oar; and leaning my head upon my hands, gave way to every gloomy idea that arose. If I looked up, I saw the scenes which were familiar to me in my happier time, and which I had contemplated but the day before in the company of her who was now but a shadow and a recollection. Tears streamed from my eyes. The rain had ceased for a moment, and I saw the fish play in the waters as they had done a few hours before; they had then been observed by Elizabeth. Nothing is so painful to the human mind as a great and sudden change. The sun might shine, or the clouds might lower: but nothing could appear to me as it had done the day before. A fiend had snatched from me every hope of future happiness: no creature had ever been so miserable as I was; so frightful an event is single in the history of man.

But why should I dwell upon the incidents that followed this last overwhelming event? Mine has been a tale of horrors; I have reached their *acme*, and what I must now relate can but be tedious to you. Know that, one by one, my friends were snatched away; I was left desolate. My own strength is exhausted; and I must tell, in a few words, what remains of my hideous narration.

I arrived at Geneva. My father and Ernest yet lived; but the former sunk under the tidings that I bore. I see him now, excellent and venerable old man! his eyes wandered in vacancy, for they had lost their charm and their delight—his Elizabeth, his more than daughter, whom he doated on with all that affection which a man feels, who in the decline of life, having few affections, clings more earnestly to those that remain. Cursed, cursed be the fiend that brought misery on his grey hairs, and doomed him to waste in wretchedness! He could not live under the horrors that were accumulated around him; the springs of existence suddenly gave way: he was unable to rise from his bed, and in a few days he died in my arms.

What then became of me? I know not; I lost sensation, and chains and darkness were the only objects that pressed upon me. Sometimes, indeed, I dreamt that I wandered in flowery meadows and pleasant vales with the friends of my youth; but I awoke, and found myself in a dungeon. Melancholy followed, but by degrees I gained a clear conception of my miseries and situation, and was then released from my prison. For they had called me mad; and during many months, as I understood, a solitary cell had been my habitation.

Liberty, however, had been an useless gift to me, had I not, as I awakened to reason, at the same time awakened to revenge. As the memory of past misfortunes pressed upon me, I began to reflect on their cause—the monster whom I had created, the miserable dæmon whom I had sent abroad into the world for my destruction. I was possessed by a maddening rage when I thought of him, and desired and ardently prayed that I might have him within my grasp to wreak a great and signal revenge on his cursed head.

Nor did my hate long confine itself to useless wishes; I began to reflect on the best means of securing him; and for this purpose, about a month after my release, I repaired to a criminal judge in the town, and told him that I had an accusation to make; that I knew the destroyer of my family; and that I required him to exert his whole authority for the apprehension of the murderer.

The magistrate listened to me with attention and kindness:—'Be assured, sir,' said he, 'no pains or exertions on my part shall be spared to discover the villain.'

'I thank you,' replied I; 'listen, therefore, to the deposition that I have to make. It is indeed a tale so strange, that I should fear you would not credit it, were there not something in truth which, however wonderful, forces conviction. The story is too connected to be mistaken for a dream, and I have no motive for falsehood.' My manner, as I thus addressed him, was impressive, but calm; I had formed in my own heart a resolution to pursue my destroyer to death; and this purpose quieted my agony, and for an interval reconciled me to life. I now related my history, briefly, but with firmness and precision, marking the dates with accuracy, and never deviating into invective or exclamation.

The magistrate appeared at first perfectly incredulous, but as I continued he became more attentive and interested; I saw him sometimes shudder with horror, at others a lively surprise, unmingled with disbelief, was painted on his countenance.

When I had concluded my narration, I said, 'This is the being whom I accuse, and for whose seizure and punishment I call upon you to exert your whole power. It is your duty as a magistrate, and I believe and hope that your feelings as a man will not revolt from the execution of those functions on this occasion.'

This address caused a considerable change in the physiognomy of my own auditor. He had heard my story with that half kind of belief that is given to a tale of spirits and supernatural events; but when he was called upon to act officially in consequence, the whole tide of his incredulity returned. He, however, answered mildly, 'I would willingly afford you every aid in your pursuit; but the creature of whom you speak appears to have powers which would put all my exertions to defiance. Who can follow an animal which can traverse the sea of ice, and inhabit caves and dens where no man would venture to intrude? Besides, some months have elapsed since the commission of his crimes, and no one can conjecture to what place he has wandered, or what region he may now inhabit.'

'I do not doubt that he hovers near the spot which I inhabit; and if he has indeed taken refuge in the Alps, he may be hunted like the chamois, and destroyed as a beast of prey. But I perceive your thoughts: you do not credit my narrative, and do not intend to pursue my enemy with the punsihment which is his desert.'

As I spoke, rage sparkled in my eyes; the magistrate was intimidated:— 'You are mistaken,' said he, 'I will exert myself; and if it is in my power to seize the monster, be assured that he shall suffer punishment proportionate to his crimes. But I fear, from what you have yourself described to be his properties, that this will prove impracticable; and thus, while every proper measure is pursued, you should make up your mind to disappointment.'

'That cannot be; but all that I can say will be of little avail. My revenge is of no moment to you; yet, while I allow it to be a vice, I confess that it is the devouring and only passion of my soul. My rage is unspeakable, when I reflect that the murderer, whom I have turned loose upon society, still exists. You refuse my just demand: I have but one resource; and I devote myself, either in my life or death, to his destruction.'

I trembled with excess of agitation as I said this; there was a frenzy in my manner, and something, I doubt not, of that haughty fierceness which the martyrs of old are said to have possessed. But to a Genevan magistrate, whose mind was occupied by far other ideas than those of devotion and heroism, this elevation of mind had much the appearance of madness. He endeavoured to soothe me as a nurse does a child, and reverted to my tale as the effects of delirium.

'Man,' I cried, 'how ignorant art thou in thy pride of wisdom! Cease; you know not what it is you say.'

I broke from the house angry and disturbed, and retired to meditate on some other mode of action.

CHAPTER XXIV

MY present situation was one in which all voluntary thought was swallowed up and lost. I was hurried away by fury; revenge alone endowed me with strength and composure; it moulded my feelings, and allowed me to be calculating and calm, at periods when otherwise delirium or death would have been my portion.

My first resolution was to quit Geneva for ever; my country, which, when I was happy and beloved, was dear to me, now, in my adversity, became hateful. I provided myself with a sum of money, together with a few jewels which had belonged to my mother, and departed.

And now my wanderings began, which are to cease but with life. I have traversed a vast portion of the earth, and have endured all the hardships which travellers, in deserts and barbarous countries, are wont to meet. How I have lived I hardly know; many times have I stretched my failing limbs upon the sandy plain, and prayed for death. But revenge kept me alive; I dared not die, and leave my adversary in being.

When I quitted Geneva, my first labour was to gain some clue by which I might trace the steps of my fiendish enemy. But my plan was unsettled; and I wandered many hours round the confines of the town, uncertain what path I should pursue. As night approached, I found myself at the entrance of the cemetery where William, Elizabeth, and my father reposed. I entered it, and approached the tomb which marked their graves. Every thing was silent, except the leaves of the trees, which were gently agitated by the wind; the night was nearly dark; and the scene would have been solemn and affecting even to an uninterested observer. The spirits of the departed seemed to flit around, and to cast a shadow, which was felt but not seen, around the head of the mourner.

The deep grief which this scene had at first excited quickly gave way to rage and despair. They were dead, and I lived; their murderer also lived, and to destroy him I must drag out my weary existence. I knelt on the grass, and kissed the earth, and with quivering lips exclaimed, 'By the sacred earth on which I kneel, by the shades that wander near me, by the deep and eternal grief that I feel, I swear; and by thee, O Night, and the spirits that preside over thee, to pursue the dæmon, who caused this misery, until he or I shall perish in mortal conflict. For this purpose I will preserve my life: to execute this dear revenge, will I again behold the sun, and tread the green herbage of earth, which otherwise should vanish from my eyes for ever. And I call on you, spirits of the dead; and on you, wandering ministers of vengeance, to aid and conduct me in my work. Let the cursed and hellish monster drink deep of agony; let him feel the despair that now torments me.'

I had begun my adjuration with solemnity, and an awe which almost assured me that the shades of my murdered friends heard and approved my devotion; but the furies possessed me as I concluded, and rage choked my utterance.

I was answered through the stillness of night by a loud and fiendish laugh. It rung on my ears long and heavily; the mountains re-echoed it, and I felt as if all hell surrounded me with mockery and laughter. Surely in that moment I should have been possessed by frenzy, and have destroyed my miserable existence, but that my vow was heard, and that I was reserved for vengeance. The laughter died away; when a well-known and abhorred voice, apparently close to my ear, addressed me in an audible whisper—'I am satisfied: miserable wretch! you have determined to live, and I am satisfied.'

I darted towards the spot from which the sound proceeded; but the devil eluded my grasp. Suddenly the broad disk of the moon arose, and shone full upon his ghastly and distorted shape, as he fled with more than mortal speed.

I pursued him; and for many months this has been my task. Guided by a slight clue, I followed the windings of the Rhone, but vainly. The blue Mediterranean appeared; and, by a strange chance, I saw the fiend enter by night, and hide himself in a vessel bound for the Black Sea. I took my passage in the same ship; but he escaped, I know not how.

Amidst the wilds of Tartary and Russia, although he still evaded me, I have ever followed in his track. Sometimes the peasants, scared by this horrid apparition, informed me of his path; sometimes he himself, who feared that if I lost all trace of him, I should despair and die, left some mark to guide me. The snows descended on my head, and I saw the print of his huge step on the white plain. To you first entering on life, to whom care is new, and agony unknown, how can you understand what I have felt, and still feel? Cold, want, and fatigue, were the least pains which I was destined to endure; I was cursed by some devil, and carried about with me my eternal hell; yet still a spirit of good followed and directed my steps; and, when I most murmured, would suddenly extricate me from seemingly insurmountable difficulties. Sometimes, when nature, overcome by hunger, sunk under the exhaustion, a repast was prepared for me in the desert, that restored and inspirited me. The fare was, indeed, coarse, such as the peasants of the country ate; but I will not doubt that it was set there by the spirits that I had invoked to aid me. Often, when all was dry, the heavens cloudless, and I was parched by thirst, a slight cloud would bedim the sky, shed the few drops that revived me, and vanish.

I followed, when I could, the courses of the rivers; but the dæmon generally avoided these, as it was here that the population of the country chiefly collected. In other places human beings were seldom seen; and I generally subsisted on the wild animals that crossed my path. I had money with me, and gained the friendship of the villagers by distributing it; or I brought with me some food that I had killed, which, after taking a small part, I always presented to those who had provided me with fire and utensils for cooking.

My life, as it passed thus, was indeed hateful to me, and it was during sleep alone that I could taste joy. O blessed sleep! often, when most miserable, I sank to repose, and my dreams lulled me even to rapture. The spirits that guarded me had provided these moments, or rather hours, of happiness, that I might retain strength to fulfil my pilgrimage. Deprived of this respite, I should have sunk under my hardships. During the day I was sustained and inspirited by the hope of night: for in sleep I saw my friends, my wife, and my beloved country; again I saw the benevolent countenance of my father, heard the silver tones of my Elizabeth's voice, and beheld Clerval enjoying health and youth. Often, when wearied by a toilsome march, I persuaded myself that I was dreaming until night should come, and that I should then enjoy reality in the arms of my dearest friends. What agonising fondness did I feel for them! how did I cling to their dear forms, as sometimes they haunted even my waking hours, and persuade myself that they still lived! At such moments vengeance, that burned within me, died in my heart, and I pursued my path towards the destruction of the dæmon, more as a task enjoined by heaven, as the mechanical impulse of some power of which I was unconscious, than as the ardent desire of my soul.

What his feelings were whom I pursued I cannot know. Sometimes, indeed, he left marks in writing on the barks of the trees, or cut in stone, that guided me, and instigated my fury. 'My reign is not yet over,' (these words were legible in one of these inscriptions;) 'you live, and my power is complete. Follow me; I seek the everlasting ices of the north, where you will feel the misery of cold and frost, to which I am impassive. You will find near this place, if you follow not too tardily, a dead hare; eat, and be refreshed. Come on, my enemy; we have yet to wrestle for our lives; but many hard and miserable hours must you endure until that period shall arrive.'

Scoffing devil! Again do I vow vengeance; again do I devote thee, miserable fiend, to torture and death. Never will I give up my search, until he or I perish; and then with what ecstasy shall I join my Elizabeth, and my departed friends, who even now prepare for me the reward of my tedious toil and horrible pilgrimage!

As I still pursued my journey to the northward, the snows thickened, and the cold increased in a degree almost too severe to support. The peasants were shut up in their hovels, and only a few of the most hardy ventured forth to seize the animals whom starvation had forced from their hiding-places to seek for prey. The rivers were covered with ice, and no fish could be procured; and thus I was cut off from my chief article of maintenance.

The triumph of my enemy increased with the difficulty of my labours. One inscription that he left was in these words:—'Prepare! your toils only begin: wrap yourself in furs, and provide food; for we shall soon enter upon a journey where your sufferings will satisfy my everlasting hatred.'

My courage and perseverance were invigorated by these scoffing words; I resolved not to fail in my purpose; and, calling on Heaven to support me, I continued with unabated fervour to traverse immense deserts, until the ocean appeared at a distance, and formed the utmost boundary of the horizon. Oh! how unlike it was to the blue seas of the south! Covered with ice, it was only to be distinguished from land by its superior wildness and ruggedness. The Greeks wept for joy when they beheld the Mediterranean from the hills of Asia, and hailed with rapture the boundary of their toils. I did not weep; but I knelt down, and, with a full heart, thanked my guiding spirit for conducting me in safety to the place where I hoped, notwithstanding my adversary's gibe, to meet and grapple with him.

Some weeks before this period I had procured a sledge and dogs, and thus traversed the snows with inconceivable speed. I know not whether the fiend possessed the same advantages; but I found that, as before I had daily lost ground in the pursuit, I now gained on him: so much so, that when I first saw the ocean, he was but one day's journey in advance, and I hoped to intercept him before he should reach the beach. With new courage, therefore, I pressed on, and in two days arrived at a wretched hamlet on the sea-shore. I enquired of the inhabitants concerning the fiend, and gained accurate information. A gigantic monster, they said, had arrived the night before, armed with a gun and many pistols; putting to flight the inhabitants of a solitary cottage, through fear of his terrific appearance. He had carried off their store of winter food, and, placing it in a sledge, to draw which he had seized on a numerous drove of trained dogs, he had harnessed them, and the same night, to the joy of the horror-struck villagers, had pursued his journey across the sea in a direction that led to no land; and they conjectured that he must speedily be destroyed by the breaking of the ice, or frozen by the eternal frosts.

On hearing this information, I suffered a temporary access of despair. He had escaped me; and I must commence a destructive and almost endless journey across the mountainous ices of the ocean,—amidst cold that few of the inhabitants could long endure, and which I, the native of a genial and sunny climate, could not hope to survive. Yet at the idea that the fiend should live and be triumphant, my rage and vengeance returned, and, like a mighty tide, overwhelmed every other feeling. After a slight repose, during which the spirits of the dead hovered round, and instigated me to toil and revenge, I prepared for my journey.

I exchanged my land-sledge for one fashioned for the inequalities of the Frozen Ocean; and purchasing a plentiful stock of provisions, I departed from land.

I cannot guess how many days have passed since then; but I have endured misery, which nothing but the eternal sentiment of a just retribution burning within my heart could have enabled me to support. Immense and rugged mountains of ice often barred up my passage, and I often heard the thunder of the ground sea, which threatened my destruction. But again the frost came, and made the paths of the sea secure.

By the quantity of provision which I had consumed, I should guess that I had passed three weeks in this journey; and the continual protraction of hope, returning back upon the heart, often wrung bitter drops of despondency and grief from my eyes. Despair had indeed almost secured her prey, and I should soon have sunk beneath this misery. Once, after the poor animals that conveyed me had with incredible toil gained the summit of a sloping ice-mountain, and one, sinking under his fatigue, died, I viewed the expanse before me with anguish, when suddenly my eye caught a dark speck upon the dusky plain. I strained my sight to discover what it could be, and uttered a wild cry of ecstasy when I distinguished a sledge, and the distorted proportions of a well-known form within. Oh! with what a burning gush did hope revisit my heart! warm tears filled my eyes, which I hastily wiped away, that they might not intercept the view I had of the dæmon; but still my sight was dimmed by the burning drops, until, giving way to the emotions that oppressed me, I wept aloud.

But this was not the time for delay: I disencumbered the dogs of their dead companion, gave them a plentiful portion of food; and, after an hour's rest, which was absolutely necessary, and yet which was bitterly irksome to me, I continued my route. The sledge was still visible; nor did I again lose sight of it, except at the moments when for a short time some ice-rock concealed it with its intervening crags. I indeed perceptibly gained on it; and when, after nearly two days' journey, I beheld my enemy at no more than a mile distant, my heart bounded within me.

But now, when I appeared almost within grasp of my foe, my hopes were suddenly extinguished, and I lost all traces of him more utterly than I had ever done before. A ground sea was heard; the thunder of its progress, as the waters rolled and swelled beneath me, became every moment more ominous and terrific. I pressed on, but in vain. The wind arose; the sea roared; and, as with the mighty shock of an earthquake, it split, and cracked with a tremendous and overwhelming sound. The work was soon finished: in a few minutes a tumultuous sea rolled between me and my enemy, and I was left drifting on a scattered piece of ice, that was continually lessening, and thus preparing for me a hideous death.

In this manner many appalling hours passed; several of my dogs died; and I myself was about to sink under the accumulation of distress, when I saw your vessel riding at anchor, and holding forth to me hopes of succour and life. I had no conception that vessels ever came so far north, and was astounded at the sight. I quickly destroyed part of my sledge to construct oars; and by these means was enabled, with infinite fatigue, to move my ice-raft in the direction of your ship. I had determined, if you were going southward, still to trust myself to the mercy of the seas rather than abandon my purpose. I hoped to induce you to grant me a boat with which I could pursue my enemy. But your direction was northward. You took me on board when my vigour was exhausted, and I should soon have sunk under my multiplied hardships into a death which I still dread—for my task is unfulfilled.

Oh! when will my guiding spirit, in conducting me to the dæmon, allow me the rest I so much desire; or must I die, and he yet live? If I do, swear to me, Walton, that he shall not escape; that you will seek him, and satisfy my vengeance in his death. And do I dare to ask of you to undertake my pilgrimage, to endure the hardships that I have undergone? No; I am not so selfish. Yet, when I am dead, if he should appear; if the ministers of vengeance should conduct him to you, swear that he shall not live—swear that he shall not triumph over my accumulated woes, and survive to add to the list of his dark crimes. He is eloquent and persuasive; and once his words had even power over my heart: but trust him not. His soul is as hellish as his form, full of treachery and fiendlike malice. Hear him not; call on the manes of William, Justine, Clerval, Elizabeth, my father, and of the wretched Victor, and thrust your sword into his heart. I will hover near, and direct the steel aright.

WALTON, *in continuation.*

August 26th, 17——.

YOU have read this strange and terrific story, Margaret; and do you not feel your blood congeal with horror, like that which even now curdles mine? Sometimes, seized with sudden agony, he could not continue his tale; at others, his voice broken, yet piercing, uttered with difficulty the words so replete with anguish. His fine and lovely eyes were now lighted up with indignation, now subdued to downcast sorrow, and quenched in infinite wretchedness. Sometimes he commanded his countenance and tones, and related the most horrible incidents with a tranquil voice, suppressing every mark of agitation; then, like a volcano bursting forth, his face would suddenly change to an expression of the wildest rage, as he shieked out imprecations on his persecutor.

His tale is connected, and told with an appearance of the simplest truth; yet I own to you that the letters of Felix and Safie, which he showed me, and the apparition of the monster seen from our ship, brought to me a greater conviction of the truth of his narrative than his asseverations, however earnest and connected. Such a monster has then really existence! I cannot doubt it; yet I am lost in surprise and admiration. Sometimes I endeavoured to gain from Frankenstein the particulars of his creature's formation: but on this point he was impenetrable.

'Are you mad, my friend?' said he; 'or whither does your senseless curiosity lead you? Would you also create for yourself and the world a demoniacal enemy? Peace, peace! learn my miseries, and do not seek to increase your own.'

Frankenstein discovered that I made notes concerning his history: he asked to see them, and then himself corrected and augmented them in many places; but principally in giving the life and spirit to the conversations he held with his enemy. 'Since you have preserved my narration,' said he, 'I would not that a mutilated one should go down to posterity.'

Thus has a week passed away, while I have listened to the strangest tale that ever imagination formed. My thoughts, and every feeling of my soul, have been drunk up by the interest for my guest, which this tale, and his own elevated and gentle manners, have created. I wish to soothe him; yet can I counsel one so infinitely miserable, so destitute of every hope of consolation, to live? Oh, no! the only joy that he can now know will be when he composes his shattered spirit to peace and death. Yet he enjoys one comfort, the offspring of solitude and delirium: he believes, that, when in dreams he holds converse with his friends, and derives from that communion consolation for his miseries, or excitements to his vengeance, that they are not the creations of his fancy, but the beings themselves who visit him from the regions of a remote world. This faith gives a solemnity to his reveries that render them to me almost as imposing and interesting as truth.

Our conversations are not always confined to his own history and misfortunes. On every point of general literature he displays unbounded knowledge, and a quick and piercing apprehension. His eloquence is forcible and touching; nor can I hear him, when he relates a pathetic incident, or endeavours to move the passions of pity or love, without tears. What a glorious creature must he have been in the days of his prosperity, when he is thus noble and godlike in ruin! He seems to feel his own worth, and the greatness of his fall.

'When younger,' said he, 'I believed myself destined for some great enterprise. My feelings are profound; but I possessed a coolness of judgment that fitted me for illustrious achievements. This sentiment of the worth of my nature supported me, when others would have been oppressed; for I deemed it criminal to throw away in useless grief those talents that might be useful to my fellow-creatures. When I reflected on the work I had completed, no less a one than the creation of a sensitive and rational animal, I could not rank myself with the herd of common projectors. But this thought, which supported me in the commencement of my career, now serves only to plunge me lower in the dust. All my speculations and hopes are as nothing; and, like the archangel who aspired to omnipotence, I am chained in an eternal hell. My imagination was vivid, yet my powers of analysis and application were intense; by the union of these qualities I conceived the idea, and executed the creation of a man. Even now I cannot recollect, without passion, my reveries while the work was incomplete. I trod heaven in my thoughts, now exulting in my powers, now burning with the idea of their effects. From my infancy I was imbued with high hopes and a lofty ambition; but how am I sunk! Oh! my friend, if you had known me as I once was, you would not recognise me in this state of degradation. Despondency rarely visited my heart; a high destiny seemed to bear me on, until I fell, never, never again to rise.'

Must I then lose this admirable being? I have longed for a friend; I have sought one who would sympathise with and love me. Behold, on these desert seas I have found such a one; but, I fear, I have gained him only to know his value, and lose him. I would reconcile him to life, but he repulses the idea.

'I thank you, Walton,' he said, 'for your kind intentions towards so miserable a wretch; but when you speak of new ties, and fresh affections, think you that any can replace those who are gone? Can any man be to me as Clerval was; or any woman another Elizabeth? Even where the affections are not strongly moved by any superior excellence, the companions of our

childhood always possess a certain power over our minds, which hardly any
later friend can obtain. They know our infantine dispositions, which,
however they may be afterwards modified, are never eradicated; and they
can judge of our actions with more certain conclusions as to the integrity of
our motives. A sister or a brother can never, unless indeed such symptoms
have been shown early, suspect the other of fraud or false dealing, when
another friend, however strongly he may be attached, may, in spite of
himself, be contemplated with suspicion. But I enjoyed friends, dear not only
through habit and association, but from their own merits; and wherever I
am, the soothing voice of my Elizabeth, and the conversation of Clerval, will
be ever whispered in my ear. They are dead; and but one feeling in such a
solitude can persuade me to preserve my life. If I were engaged in any high
undertaking or design, fraught with extensive utility to my fellow-creatures,
then could I live to fulfil it. But such is not my destiny; I must pursue and
destroy the being to whom I gave existence; then my lot on earth will be
fulfilled, and I may die.'

                                                                    September 2d.

My beloved Sister,

  I write to you, encompassed by peril, and ignorant whether I am ever
doomed to see again dear England, and the dearer friends that inhabit it. I
am surrounded by mountains of ice, which admit of no escape, and threaten
every moment to crush my vessel. The brave fellows, whom I have
persuaded to be my companions, look towards me for aid; but I have none
to bestow. There is something terribly appalling in our situation, yet my
courage and hopes do not desert me. Yet it is terrible to reflect that the lives
of all these men are endangered through me. If we are lost, my mad schemes
are the cause.

  And what, Margaret, will be the state of your mind? You will not hear of
my destruction, and you will anxiously await my return. Years will pass, and
you will have visitings of despair, and yet be tortured by hope. Oh! my
beloved sister, the sickening failing of your heart-felt expectations is, in
prospect, more terrible to me than my own death. But you have a husband,
and lovely children; you may be happy: Heaven bless you, and make
you so!

  My unfortunate guest regards me with the tenderest compassion. He
endeavours to fill me with hope; and talks as if life were a possession which
he valued. He reminds me how often the same accidents have happened to
other navigators, who have attempted this sea, and, in spite of myself, he
fills me with cheerful auguries. Even the sailors feel the power of his
eloquence: when he speaks, they no longer despair; he rouses their energies,
and, while they hear his voice, they believe these vast mountains of ice are
mole-hills, which will vanish before the resolutions of man. These feelings

are transitory; each day of expectation delayed fills them with fear, and I almost dread a mutiny caused by this despair.

September 5th.

A scene has just passed of such uncommon interest, that although it is highly probable that these papers may never reach you, yet I cannot forbear recording it.

We are still surrounded by mountains of ice, still in imminent danger of being crushed in their conflict. The cold is excessive, and many of my unfortunate comrades have already found a grave amidst this scene of desolation. Frankenstein has daily declined in health: a feverish fire still glimmers in his eyes; but he is exhausted, and, when suddenly roused to any exertion, he speedily sinks again into apparent lifelessness.

I mentioned in my last letter the fears I entertained of a mutiny. This morning, as I sat watching the wan countenance of my friend—his eyes half closed, and his limbs hanging listlessly,—I was roused by half a dozen of the sailors, who demanded admission into the cabin. They entered, and their leader addressed me. He told me that he and his companions had been chosen by the other sailors to come in deputation to me, to make me a requisition, which, in justice, I could not refuse. We were immured in ice, and should probably never escape; but they feared that if, as was possible, the ice should dissipate, and a free passage be opened, I should be rash enough to continue my voyage, and lead them into fresh dangers, after they might happily have surmounted this. They insisted, therefore, that I should engage with a solemn promise, that if the vessel should be freed I would instantly direct my course southward.

This speech troubled me. I had not despaired; nor had I yet conceived the idea of returning, if set free. Yet could I, in justice, or even in possibility, refuse this demand? I hesitated before I answered; when Frankenstein, who had at first been silent, and, indeed, appeared hardly to have force enough to attend, now roused himself; his eyes sparkled, and his cheeks flushed with momentary vigour. Turning towards the men, he said—

'What do you mean? What do you demand of your captain? Are you then so easily turned from your design? Did you not call this a glorious expedition? And wherefore was it glorious? Not because the way was smooth and placid as a southern sea, but because it was full of dangers and terror; because, at every new incident, your fortitude was to be called forth, and your courage exhibited; because danger and death surrounded it, and these you were to brave and overcome. For this was it a glorious, for this was it an honourable undertaking. You were hereafter to be hailed as the benefactors of your species; your names adored, as belonging to brave men who encountered death for honour, and the benefit of mankind. And now, behold, with the first imagination of danger, or, if you will, the first mighty and terrific trial of your courage, you shrink away, and are content to be handed down as men who had not strength enough to endure cold and peril; and so, poor souls, they were chilly, and returned to their warm firesides. Why, that requires not this preparation; ye need not have come thus far, and dragged your captain to the shame of a defeat, merely to prove yourselves cowards. Oh! be men, or be more than men. Be steady to your purposes, and firm as a rock. This ice is not made of such stuff as your hearts may be; it is mutable, and cannot withstand you, if you say that it shall not. Do not return to your families with the stigma of disgrace marked on your brows. Return, as heroes who have fought and conquered, and who know not what it is to turn their backs on the foe.'

He spoke this with a voice so modulated to the different feelings expressed in his speech, with an eye so full of lofty design and heroism, that can you wonder that these men were moved? They looked at one another, and were unable to reply. I spoke; I told them to retire, and consider of what had been said: that I would not lead them farther north, if they strenuously desired the contrary; but that I hoped that, with reflection, their courage would return.

They retired, and I turned towards my friend; but he was sunk in languor, and almost deprived of life.

How all this will terminate, I know not; but I had rather die than return shamefully,—my purpose unfulfilled. Yet I fear such will be my fate; the men, unsupported by ideas of glory and honour, can never willingly continue to endure their present hardships.

September 7th.

The die is cast; I have consented to return, if we are not destroyed. Thus are my hopes blasted by cowardice and indecision; I come back ignorant and disappointed. It requires more philosophy than I possess, to bear this injustice with patience.

September 12th.

It is past; I am returning to England. I have lost my hopes of utility and glory;—I have lost my friend. But I will endeavour to detail these bitter circumstances to you, my dear sister; and, while I am wafted towards England, and towards you, I will not despond.

September 9th, the ice began to move, and roarings like thunder were heard at a distance, as the islands split and cracked in every direction. We were in the most imminent peril; but, as we could only remain passive, my chief attention was occupied by my unfortunate guest, whose illness increased in such a degree, that he was entirely confined to his bed. The ice cracked behind us, and was driven with force towards the north; a breeze sprung from the west, and on the 11th the passage towards the south became perfectly free. When the sailors saw this, and that their return to their native country was apparently assured, a shout of tumultuous joy broke from them, loud and long-continued. Frankenstein, who was dozing, awoke, and asked the cause of the tumult. 'They shout,' I said, 'because they will soon return to England.'

'Do you then really return?'

'Alas! yes; I cannot withstand their demands. I cannot lead them unwillingly to danger, and I must return.'

'Do so, if you will; but I will not. You may give up your purpose, but mine is assigned to me by Heaven, and I dare not. I am weak; but surely the spirits who assist my vengeance will endow me with sufficient strength.' Saying this, he endeavoured to spring from the bed, but the exertion was too great for him; he fell back, and fainted.

It was long before he was restored; and I often thought that life was entirely extinct. At length he opened his eyes; he breathed with difficulty, and was unable to speak. The surgeon gave him a composing draught, and ordered us to leave him undisturbed. In the mean time he told me, that my friend had certainly not many hours to live.

His sentence was pronounced; and I could only grieve, and be patient. I sat by his bed, watching him; his eyes were closed, and I thought he slept; but presently he called to me in a feeble voice, and, bidding me come near, said—'Alas! the strength I relied on is gone; I feel that I shall soon die, and he, my enemy and persecutor, may still be in being. Think not, Walton, that in the last moments of my existence I feel that burning hatred, and ardent desire of revenge, I once expressed; but I feel myself justified in desiring the death of my adversary. During these last days I have been occupied in examining my past conduct; nor do I find it blameable. In a fit of enthusiastic madness I created a rational creature, and was bound towards him, to assure, as far as was in my power, his happiness and well-being. This was my duty; but there was another still paramount to that. My duties towards the beings of my own species had greater claims to my attention, because they included a greater proportion of happiness or misery. Urged by this view, I refused, and I did right in refusing, to create a companion for the first creature. He showed unparalleled malignity and selfishness, in evil: he destroyed my friends; he devoted to destruction beings who possessed exquisite sensations, happiness, and wisdom; nor do I know where this thirst for vengeance may end. Miserable himself, that he may render no other wretched, he ought to die. The task of his destruction was mine, but I have failed. When actuated by selfishness and vicious motives, I asked you to undertake my unfinished work; and I renew this request now, when I am only induced by reason and virtue.

'Yet I cannot ask you to renounce your country and friends, to fulfil this task; and now, that you are returning to England, you will have little chance of meeting with him. But the consideration of these points, and the well

balancing of what you may esteem your duties, I leave to you; my judgment
and ideas are already disturbed by the near approach of death. I dare not
ask you to do what I think right, for I may still be misled by passion.

'That he should live to be an instrument of mischief disturbs me; in other
respects, this hour, when I momentarily expect my release, is the only happy
one which I have enjoyed for several years. The forms of the beloved dead
flit before me, and I hasten to their arms. Farewell, Walton! Seek happiness
in tranquillity, and avoid ambition, even if it be only the apparently
innocent one of distinguishing yourself in science and discoveries. Yet why
do I say this? I have myself been blasted in these hopes, yet another may
succeed.'

His voice became fainter as he spoke; and at length, exhausted by his effort,
he sunk into silence. About half an hour afterwards he attempted again to
speak, but was unable; he pressed my hand feebly, and his eyes closed for
ever, while the irradiation of a gentle smile passed away from his lips.

Margaret, what comment can I make on the untimely extinction of this
glorious spirit? What can I say, that will enable you to understand the depth
of my sorrow? All that I should express would be inadequate and feeble. My
tears flow; my mind is overshadowed by a cloud of disappointment. But I
journey towards England, and I may there find consolation.

I am interrupted. What do these sounds portend? It is midnight; the
breeze blows fairly, and the watch on deck scarcely stir. Again; there is a
sound as of a human voice, but hoarser; it comes from the cabin where the
remains of Frankenstein still lie. I must arise, and examine. Good night, my
sister.

Great God! what a scene has just taken place! I am yet dizzy with the
remembrance of it. I hardly know whether I shall have the power to detail
it; yet the tale which I have recorded would be incomplete without this final
and wonderful catastrophe.

I entered the cabin, where lay the remains of my ill-fated and admirable
friend. Over him hung a form which I cannot find words to describe;
gigantic in stature, yet uncouth and distorted in its proportions. As he hung
over the coffin, his face was concealed by long locks of ragged hair; but one
vast hand was extended, in colour and apparent texture like that of a
mummy. When he heard the sound of my approach, he ceased to utter
exclamations of grief and horror, and sprung towards the window. Never
did I behold a vision so horrible as his face, of such loathsome yet appalling
hideousness. I shut my eyes involuntarily, and endeavoured to recollect what
were my duties with regard to this destroyer. I called on him to stay.

He paused, looking on me with wonder; and, again turning towards the
lifeless form of his creator, he seemed to forget my presence, and every
feature and gesture seemed instigated by the wildest rage of some uncontrollable passion.

'That is also my victim!' he exclaimed: 'in his murder my crimes are consummated; the miserable series of my being is wound to its close! Oh, Frankenstein! generous and self-devoted being! what does it avail that I now ask thee to pardon me? I, who irretrievably destroyed thee by destroying all thou lovedst. Alas! he is cold, he cannot answer me.'

His voice seemed suffocated; and my first impulses, which had suggested to me the duty of obeying the dying request of my friend, in destroying his enemy, were now suspended by a mixture of curiosity and compassion. I approached this tremendous being; I dared not again raise my eyes to his face, there was something so scaring and unearthly in his ugliness. I attempted to speak, but the words died away on my lips. The monster continued to utter wild and incoherent self-reproaches. At length I gathered resolution to address him in a pause of the tempest of his passion: 'Your repentance,' I said, 'is now superfluous. If you had listened to the voice of conscience, and heeded the stings of remorse, before you had urged your diabolical vengeance to this extremity, Frankenstein would yet have lived.'

'And do you dream?' said the dæmon; 'do you think that I was then dead to agony and remorse?—He,' he continued, pointing to the corpse, 'he suffered not in the consummation of the deed—oh! not the ten-thousandth portion of the anguish that was mine during the lingering detail of its execution. A frightful selfishness hurried me on, while my heart was poisoned with remorse. Think you that the groans of Clerval were music to my ears? My heart was fashioned to be susceptible of love and sympathy; and, when wrenched by misery to vice and hatred, it did not endure the violence of the change, without torture such as you cannot even imagine.

'After the murder of Clerval, I returned to Switzerland, heart-broken and overcome. I pitied Frankenstein; my pity amounted to horror: I abhorred myself. But when I discovered that he, the author at once of my existence and of its unspeakable torments, dared to hope for happiness; that while he accumulated wretchedness and despair upon me, he sought his own enjoyment in feelings and passions from the indulgence of which I was for ever barred, then impotent envy and bitter indignation filled me with an insatiable thirst for vengeance. I recollected my threat, and resolved that it should be accomplished. I knew that I was preparing for myself a deadly torture; but I was the slave, not the master, of an impulse, which I detested, yet could not disobey. Yet when she died!—nay, then I was not miserable. I had cast off all feeling, subdued all anguish, to riot in the excess of my despair. Evil thenceforth became my good. Urged thus far, I had no choice but to adapt my nature to an element which I had willingly chosen. The completion of my demoniacal design became an insatiable passion. And now it is ended; there is my last victim!'

I was at first touched by the expressions of his misery; yet, when I called to mind what Frankenstein had said of his powers of eloquence and persuasion, and when I again cast my eyes on the lifeless form of my friend, indignation was rekindled within me. 'Wretch!' I said, 'it is well that you come here to whine over the desolation that you have made. You throw a torch into a pile of buildings; and, when they are consumed, you sit among the ruins, and lament the fall. Hypocritical fiend! if he whom you mourn still lived, still would he be the object, again would he become the prey, of your accursed vengeance. It is not pity that you feel; you lament only because the victim of your malignity is withdrawn from your power.'

'Oh, it is not thus—not thus,' interrupted the being; 'yet such must be the impression conveyed to you by what appears to be the purport of my actions. Yet I seek not a fellow-feeling in my misery. No sympathy may I ever find. When I first sought it, it was the love of virtue, the feelings of happiness and affection with which my whole being overflowed, that I wished to be participated. But now, that virtue has become to me a shadow, and that happiness and affection are turned into bitter and loathing despair, in what should I seek for sympathy? I am content to suffer alone, while my sufferings shall endure: when I die, I am well satisfied that abhorrence and opprobrium should load my memory. Once my fancy was soothed with dreams of virtue, of fame, and of enjoyment. Once I falsely hoped to meet with beings, who, pardoning my outward form, would love me for the excellent qualities which I was capable of unfolding. I was nourished with high thoughts of honour and devotion. But now crime has degraded me beneath the meanest animal. No guilt, no mischief, no malignity, no misery, can be found comparable to mine. When I run over the frightful catalogue of my sins, I cannot believe that I am the same creature whose thoughts were once filled with sublime and transcendent visions of the beauty and the majesty of goodness. But it is even so; the fallen angel becomes a malignant devil. Yet even that enemy of God and man had friends and associates in his desolation; I am alone.

'You, who call Frankenstein your friend, seem to have a knowledge of my crimes and his misfortunes. But, in the detail which he gave you of them, he could not sum up the hours and months of misery which I endured, wasting in impotent passions. For while I destroyed his hopes, I did not satisfy my own desires. They were for ever ardent and craving; still I desired love and fellowship, and I was still spurned. Was there no injustice in this? Am I to be thought the only criminal, when all human kind sinned against me. Why do you not hate Felix, who drove his friend from his door with contumely? Why do you not execrate the rustic who sought to destroy the saviour of his child? Nay, these are virtuous and immaculate beings! I, the miserable and the abandoned, am an abortion, to be spurned at, and kicked, and trampled on. Even now my blood boils at the recollection of this injustice.

'But it is true that I am a wretch. I have murdered the lovely and the helpless; I have strangled the innocent as they slept, and grasped to death his throat who never injured me or any other living thing. I have devoted my creator, the select specimen of all that is worthy of love and admiration among men, to misery; I have pursued him even to that irremediable ruin. There he lies, white and cold in death. You hate me; but your abhorrence cannot equal that with which I regard myself. I look on the hands which executed the deed; I think on the heart in which the imagination of it was conceived, and long for the moment when these hands will meet my eyes, when that imagination will haunt my thoughts no more.

'Fear not that I shall be the instrument of future mischief. My work is nearly complete. Neither yours nor any man's death is needed to consummate the series of my being, and accomplish that which must be done; but it requires my own. Do not think that I shall be slow to perform this sacrifice. I shall quit your vessel on the ice-raft which brought me thither, and shall seek the most northern extremity of the globe; I shall collect my funeral pile, and consume to ashes this miserable frame, that its remains may afford no light to any curious and unhallowed wretch, who would create such another as I have been. I shall die. I shall no longer feel the agonies which now consume me, or be the prey of feelings unsatisfied, yet unquenched. He is dead who called me into being; and when I shall be no more, the very remembrance of us both will speedily vanish. I shall no longer see the sun or stars, or feel the winds play on my cheeks. Light, feeling, and sense will pass away; and in this condition must I find my happiness. Some years ago, when the images which this world affords first opened upon me, when I felt the cheering warmth of summer, and heard the rustling of the leaves and the warbling of the birds, and these were all to me, I should have wept to die; now it is my only consolation. Polluted by crimes, and torn by the bitterest remorse, where can I find rest but in death?

'Farewell! I leave you, and in you the last of human kind whom these eyes will ever behold. Farewell, Frankenstein! If thou wert yet alive, and yet cherished a desire of revenge against me, it would be better satiated in my life than in my destruction. But it was not so; thou didst seek my extinction, that I might not cause greater wretchedness; and if yet, in some mode unknown to me, thou hadst not ceased to think and feel, thou wouldst not desire against me a vengeance greater than that which I feel. Blasted as thou wert, my agony was still superior to thine; for the bitter sting of remorse will not cease to rankle in my wounds until death shall close them for ever.

'But soon,' he cried, with sad and solemn enthusiasm, 'I shall die, and what I now feel be no longer felt. Soon these burning miseries will be extinct. I shall ascend my funeral pile triumphantly, and exult in the agony of the torturing flames. The light of that conflagration will fade away; my ashes will be swept into the sea by the winds. My spirit will sleep in peace; or if it thinks, it will not surely think thus. Farewell.'

He sprung from the cabin-window, as he said this, upon the ice-raft which lay close to the vessel. He was soon borne away by the waves, and lost in darkness and distance.